The Amber Brooch

The Celtic Brooch Series, Book 8

Katherine Lowry Logan

COPYRIGHT PAGE

All rights reserved. No part of this book may be used or reproduced in any manner whatsoever without written permission of the author, except in the case of brief quotations embedded in critical articles or reviews.

This is a work of fiction. Names, characters, places, and incidents are the product of the author's imagination, or are used fictitiously, and any resemblance to actual persons living or dead, business establishments, events, or locales is entirely coincidental.

An original work by Katherine Lowry Logan. *The Amber Brooch* copyright © 2018 by Katherine Lowry Logan
Print Edition

Website: www.katherinellogan.com

THE CELTIC BROOCH SERIES

The Ruby Brooch
The Last MacKlenna
The Sapphire Brooch
The Emerald Brooch
The Broken Brooch
The Three Brooches
The Diamond Brooch
Family Trees
katherinellogan.com/books/the-celtic-brooch-family-trees

DEDICATED TO THE FOLLOWING SISTERS

Mimi & Kathy
Lorie & Lynn
Julie & Jennie
Molly & McKenzie

CAST OF CHARACTERS

Alphabetical Order

1. Adams, John: Judge in Leadville, Colorado
2. DeRemer, James Richard: Engineer for the Denver & Rio Grande Railroad Company
3. Desmond, Pat: Deputy Sheriff of Pueblo County
4. Fraser, Elliott: Chairman of the Board of the MacKlenna Corporation, husband of Meredith Montgomery, father of James Cullen Fraser and Kevin Allen Fraser, former equine vet (appears in all *Brooch* books)
5. Fraser, Jenny "JL" Lynn O'Grady: former NYPD detective, VP of Development and Operations MacKlenna Corporation, wife of Kevin Allen Fraser, mother of Austin, sister of Connor, Patrick "Rick", Shane, and Jeff O'Grady, daughter of Retired Deputy Chief Lawrence "Pops" O'Grady (appears in *The Broken Brooch*, *The Three Brooches*, *The Diamond Brooch*)
6. Garland, Annette: landlady in Leadville
7. Grant, Daniel: father of Noah, widower, Pinkerton agent, former Union cavalry officer, member of President Lincoln's security detail during the Civil War
8. Grant, Noah: 10-year-old son of Daniel
9. Hall, Joshua: sheriff in Leadville, Colorado
10. Hendrix, Leonard: employee of Dr. Marsh
11. Hughes, Craig: Amber and Olivia's seven-times great-grandfather, owner of Hughes Store in Leadville, Colorado, husband of Lindsey
12. Hughes, Lindsey: Amber and Olivia's seven-times great-grandmother, daughter of James Thomas MacKlenna II; wife of Craig

13. Kelly, Amber: sister of Olivia, daughter of Matthew and Elizabeth Kelly, mining lawyer, amateur paleontologist, gourmet cook
14. Kelly, Elizabeth: mother of Amber and Olivia, lawyer, managing partner of *Hughes & Hughes* Law Firm
15. Kelly, Matthew: father of Amber and Olivia, lawyer, managing partner of *Hughes & Hughes* Law Firm
16. Kelly, Olivia Allison: older sister of Amber, daughter of Matthew and Elizabeth Kelly, Realtor, lawyer, love interest of Connor O'Grady (first mentioned in *The Diamond Brooch*)
17. Lakes, Arthur: geologist, paleontologist
18. Mallory, Charlotte: surgeon, wife of Braham McCabe and mother of Lincoln, Kitherina, and Amelia Rose, sister of Jack Mallory (appears in all *Brooch* books except *The Ruby Brooch*, *The Last MacKlenna*)
19. Mallory, Patrick: adopted son of Jack Mallory (appears in *The Diamond Brooch* as Patrick Wilson)
20. McBain, Alice: David's mother (appears in *The Last MacKlenna*, *The Emerald Brooch*, *The Broken Brooch*, *The Three Brooches*, *The Diamond Brooch*)
21. McBain, David: veteran, author, President of MacKlenna Corporation, husband of Kenzie McBain, father of Henry, Robbie, and Laurie Wallis (appears in all *Brooch* books except *The Ruby Brooch*)
22. McBain, Kenzie: veteran, West Point graduate, MacKlenna Corporation attorney, wife of David McBain, mother of Henry, Robbie, and Laurie Wallis (appears in *The Emerald Brooch*, *The Broken Brooch*, *The Three Brooches*, *The Diamond Brooch*)
23. McBain, Laurie Wallis: daughter of Kenzie and David McBain (born during *The Three Brooches*)
24. McBain, Henry and Robbie: twin sons of David and Kenzie (appear in *The Broken Brooch*, *The Three Brooches*, *The Diamond Brooch*)

25. McCabe, Braham: former Union cavalry officer, lawyer, senator, husband of Charlotte Mallory and father of Lincoln, Kitherina, and Amelia Rose, Jack Mallory's brother-in-law, Kit MacKlenna Montgomery's first cousin (appears in all *Brooch* books except *The Last MacKlenna*)
26. McCabe, Lincoln: son of Braham McCabe and Charlotte Mallory (appears in all *Brooch* books except *The Ruby Brooch* and *The Last MacKlenna*)
27. Montgomery, Meredith: owner of Montgomery Winery, wife of Elliott Fraser and mother of James Cullen Fraser, breast cancer survivor (appears in all *Brooch* books except *The Ruby Brooch*)
28. Murphy, Mrs.: Alec Robinson's housekeeper in Denver
29. O'Grady, Connor: former NYPD detective, Vice President of Global Security for MacKlenna Corporation, brother of JL, Shane, Rick, and Jeff O'Grady, son of Retired Deputy Chief Lawrence "Pops" O'Grady (appears in *The Broken Brooch*, *The Three Brooches*, *The Diamond Brooch*)
30. O'Grady, Patrick "Rick": Marine, former NYPD detective, brother of JL, Connor, Shane, and Jeff, Director of Global Security MacKlenna Corporation, son of Retired Deputy Chief Lawrence "Pops" O'Grady (appears in *The Broken Brooch*)
31. Palmer, William Jackson: General, President of the Denver & Rio Grande Railroad
32. Price, Henly R.: Pueblo County Sheriff
33. Robinson, Alec: Daniel's father-in-law, Noah's grandfather, banker
34. Tabor, Horace: owner of the Tabor Opera House in Leadville, Lt. Governor of Colorado
35. Thompson, Ben: gunman, gambler
36. Vilines, Bob: campground host at Turquoise Lake near Leadville
37. Waldron, John: Pueblo County District Attorney
38. Weitbrec, R.F.: Denver & Rio Grande treasurer, onsite commander of hired army during the Royal Gorge War

1

The Present, Hughes Cabin, Colorado—Amber

DAWN DIDN'T BREAK in the Rockies like it did in the East. Light just seemed to ooze from the eastern skyline until it was day. For Amber Kelly, early morning in the Colorado mountains was where she met Mother Nature face to face; where life was simpler and uncomplicated; where she fell into its rhythm as easily as riding her chestnut gelding.

She clucked to her horse. He obediently picked up the pace and cantered toward Hughes Hill, a ridge lined with fir, spruce, and yellow pine. The ridge fell several hundred feet short of the alpine timberline, the point where the elevation was too high, and usually too cold, for tree growth.

"Come on, Bud. We're almost home." The agile horse stretched his muscled legs and crested the hill.

Almost home…

Hughes Cabin wasn't really her home. That was on a tree-lined street in the historic district of Denver, but the cabin was her heart's home. The logs had been stacked and chinked in the 1870s by her seven-times great-grandparents, Craig and Lindsey Hughes, hardworking Scottish immigrants. The Hughes family left home to follow their dreams, and through their son, Adam, established a legal dynasty. In the twenty-first century, Amber was part of that dynasty.

And that was her biggest problem.

She had twenty-four hours to decide whether to leave Hughes and Hughes, her family's Denver law firm, to pursue her own dreams. If a clear answer didn't emerge by tomorrow, she'd flip a coin. Making decisions for clients came easily. This one, however, was the mother of all decisions and indecision was making her physically sick. If she left the firm, her departure could cause an uproar between her and the managing partners—her parents, Matthew and Elizabeth Kelly.

That was terrifying. But not being true to herself was even more so.

Besides being a lawyer, she was a gourmet cook. She had written a business plan to start an online enterprise selling freeze-dried meals using her self-directed 401(k). All she had left to do was exercise her option on the old Wells Fargo Building in Denver. It was the perfect facility, the perfect location, the perfect price. But…

Was she ready to cross the Rubicon?

She'd given up one dream already—to pursue a career in paleontology. The light on her childhood dream of finding a *Stegosaurus*, a dinosaur that had lived around one hundred fifty-five million years ago, had dimmed but not blown out completely. She'd never give up her partnership in the firm to hunt fossils, but could she give it up to open Amber's Kitchen?

A new geological map had arrived the day before. After studying the map key, she'd marked two sites to search for fossils. Her goal for the weekend was to use the solitude to make a career decision and find a bone or two.

The road narrowed as she crested the hill, and the air cooled. Bud trotted across the clearing where the log cabin sat nestled among the aspens. After tending to her horse, she gathered her gear and headed over to the cabin to settle in and eat an early lunch.

The twenty yards or so to the front door was a walk down memory lane. In her mind, the property was full of little yellow markers used at crime scenes, each marking a place she had dug as a kid. She'd never found a fossil there, but she had found an 1877 Proof Liberty Head Double Eagle. The coin was worth over two hundred thousand dollars.

When she reached the wraparound front porch, she scraped her boots on the saw blade sunken in the dirt. The ground around the blade was packed from long use and mixed with mud and muck. As far as she knew, in her thirty-two years, it had never been replaced.

After a quick stomp up the plank steps to shake off any remaining mud, she did what she always did—stopped to take in the view. The mountains were ever changing and the world around them changed too, day by day, sometimes hour by hour. Today, the blue of the sky was graying rapidly as a thunderstorm rolled in. If she was going to do any fossil hunting, she'd better hurry before it was too wet to work outside.

The door to the two-bedroom cabin wasn't locked. A locked door was an invitation to bust it down or break a window. Instead of trying to secure the cabin, the family left notes asking uninvited guests to treat the property kindly and clean up after themselves. In her lifetime, nothing had ever been broken.

Each time she opened the door, she held her breath, afraid of what she might find, knowing an emptied cabin was a possibility. She stepped in through the yawning doorway, unable to take a full breath until she satisfied herself all was well. The furniture stood upright. There was no odor of decaying animals. The lanterns were lined up side by side on the mantel where she'd left them. The huge two-hundred-year-old loom was...

Broken.

A piece had fallen off the breast beam and left a gaping hole. She knew instantly she had only herself to blame, and mentally kicked herself in the butt. During her last visit, she and her sister Olivia had tried to slide the loom back a few feet, closer to the window for better light. The pressure from pushing on the beam must have loosened the cap.

She picked up the piece and studied it. There were no rough edges on either end of the break and no ridges, so the piece hadn't come unscrewed. Maybe there was a connector piece. She shrugged out of her backpack and dropped it on the floor. Then she got down on hands and knees and crawled under the loom. But she didn't find anything else.

It was possible a piece had broken off and rolled inside the breast beam. The interior was too dark to see and sticking her hand in there violated her number one rule—never stick your head or hand into a dark hole where creepy, crawly things could live. She grabbed a flashlight from her backpack and shined the beam into the opening. Something was in there. A box of some kind, but it was too far to reach. There wasn't anything in her backpack or field kit that would work as a gripper. She needed a coat hanger, but there weren't any in the cabin.

The fire iron might work. She had to take her time, or she'd push the box back too far to reach. With the flashlight in one hand, the poker in the other, she threaded the fireplace tool into the hole. Then, using the hook at the end, she slowly tugged the box toward her, inch by inch, until it hung over the lip. Once there, she set the flashlight aside, and easily pulled the box out the rest of the way.

The box measured approximately six by four by two inches and was inlaid with dogwood and Cherrywood, creating elaborate geometric patterns. The smooth wood gleamed from years of polish. How long had it been inside the breast beam? The loom had come from Scotland in the late 1870s. Had it been there all this time? Did her parents know about it? When they returned from Africa, she'd be sure to ask them.

She turned the box upside down and sideways searching for the latch. The dang thing didn't seem to have one. She shook it, and it rattled. Her curiosity was now thoroughly engaged. It was like finding fossils and trying to figure out how to put them together to form a skeleton.

If the box didn't have a latch, it had to open another way. She'd seen puzzle boxes before and knew they opened by moving a piece at one end, then the other end, and then going back and forth until the lid slid open. Knowing how far to move each piece and in what order was by old-fashioned trial and error.

She was tempted to put the box aside to tackle it later that night when a book would be her only entertainment, but a continuous roll of thunder shoved the temptation aside. The storm wouldn't hold off much longer, and she didn't want to be outside with a steady icy sheet driving into her face.

If she was going to do this the right way, she had to do it methodically, and that included taking notes. She retrieved a notebook from the field kit and sketched the box, noting the location and number of sliders. There could be twenty, thirty, forty moves to open the box. It would be tedious and slow going, but if she had one defining characteristic, it was patience.

Another deep bass-note of thunder rumbled across the sky and seconds later a torrential downpour pounded the tin roof. She glanced up, checking for leaks. The roof, like the rest of the cabin, was solidly built and as far as she could remember had never leaked.

She returned her attention to the box. Fifteen minutes ticked by, then another and another. She kept at it, moving pieces here and there. The hour mark was approaching when she moved a slider and the lid opened. The thrill of the accomplishment was heightened by the shock of the contents—an exquisite brooch with a huge amber stone in the center. The distinctive pattern in the metalwork spoke to its age. It was old. Not as old as the fossils she hunted, but old enough.

To meet the humanities requirements for her undergraduate degree in geology, she had taken classes in the middle ages and early modern periods. Based on what she learned in those classes, she believed the brooch was a Celtic work of art. It belonged in a museum, displayed as a standout showpiece, not hidden in an old cabin in the Colorado Rockies.

She didn't touch the stone directly. Instead, she pulled a white cloth, small brush, and a dental pick from the field kit, and used the brush to remove flecks of velvet and dust from around the stone. Then, gently, using the dental pick, she lifted the brooch from the box and placed it on the white cloth in her hand. The brooch was as mysterious as it was exquisite. Using the dental pick, she clicked a tiny latch on the side of the stone. The brooch heated in her hand.

An inscription, written in an unfamiliar language, probably Gaelic, was etched around the circumference of the stone. She sounded out the words...

"Chan ann le tìm no àite a bhios sinn a' tomhais a' gaol ach 's ann le neart anama."

An earthy-scented fog rose from the floor and quickly engulfed her. Her heart pounded, and she couldn't breathe. The fog jerked her left, then right, then back again, and her world disappeared around her in shades of black and amber.

2

The Present, Denver, Colorado—Connor

THE WHITE ONYX and marble lobby of the iconic Brown Palace Hotel and Spa, a restored nineteenth-century hotel in Denver, was abuzz with preparations for the anniversary weekend celebration. The Brown Palace had catered to the needs of kings, presidents, and rock stars for over a century and still retained much of its nineteenth-century ambiance.

Connor O'Grady, vice president of global security for MacKlenna Corporation, sat on one of the plush sofas in the center of the atrium facing the front door and studied the dozen or so hotel employees dressed in period costumes. The elegant dresses on the women and the men's frock coats and trousers reminded him of the clothes the MacKlenna clan had worn when they traveled back to 1881 San Francisco, almost two years ago now.

The family's patience and endurance had been tested since then. Hearts had been broken and mended, and the family had expanded, as had his sister's waistline. Former hard-ass NYPD Detective JL O'Grady and her husband Kevin Fraser were expecting their first child, and he couldn't be happier for them.

Connor would need a plus-one for the christening, and he had someone in mind. He glanced toward the front door and then at his watch. He was a pro at watching and waiting patiently, but not today. He teased a stray thread in the fabric that wrapped the arm of the sofa. If he kept it up, he'd unravel the damn thing and put a hole in the upholstery.

This wasn't his first trip to Denver and it wouldn't be the last. Over the past year, he'd made a dozen trips to the city visiting area ranches for sale. The corporation intended to retrain retired Thoroughbred racehorses to give them a second career. As soon as he'd been given the assignment, he'd enlisted the help of Olivia Kelly, a Denver real estate broker. Yesterday, she had phoned with news that a ranch had just come on the market that would be a perfect fit for the company. After reviewing the listing online, Connor agreed and rearranged his schedule.

After another quick glance at the door, he checked the time again. Olivia was late. Odd, because she was always prompt. The only time she'd ever been late for an appointment, she had phoned ahead. He pulled his cell phone from his pocket and checked the call log. No calls.

He scrolled through the phone's photo collections, looking at pictures of ranches they had visited. While he had been impressed with each property, he had been more impressed with her. She was in almost every picture he had taken.

She was a thirty-something knockout brunette with the most beautiful hazel-brown eyes he'd ever seen. He'd been tempted to make a move on her, but Pops warned him not to blend business with pleasure. He'd never known his wise father to be wrong about anything. Better to keep it professional until the company closed a deal. He knew she wasn't married, but she'd given him the impression she had a boyfriend. That wouldn't deter Connor unless the guy moved from boyfriend status to fiancé.

He glanced up from his smartphone and smiled when he spotted Olivia walking through the revolving door into the atrium. He stood and pocketed his phone. The smile she gave him rocked his world. Gorgeous as usual, dressed in a sage green suit with a pencil skirt, buttoned jacket, and four-inch heels. In the flat shoes she wore when they toured barns, the top of her head fell short of his shoulders.

She held out a hand as she approached. "Good to see you, Connor. I'm sorry I'm late."

Her warm hand fit snugly into his and he didn't want to let it go. "No problem. I used the time to return emails and texts." He pressed his other hand over hers and gave it a gentle squeeze before letting go. "This property is perfect. I hope we can negotiate the price."

"There's some wiggle room. They're motivated sellers, but they don't want to give it away. They're intrigued with your plans to turn the ranch into a retraining facility for retired racehorses." Her cell phone rang, and she dug into her purse. "Sorry about that. Let me turn this off so we won't be disturbed." She glanced at the caller ID and let out a little gasp. "Do you mind if I take this call? I hope it's about my sister."

"Not at all," Connor said.

She clicked accept. "Hi Bob. Have you heard from Amber? You haven't? That's not like her. Did she tell you what time she expected to leave? Aha… Hmm… No… I'm tied up until early afternoon. As soon as I'm free, I'll drive down there… Right… Okay… See you later." Olivia disconnected the call and tapped the phone against her palm.

"Is there a problem?" Connor asked.

"That was the campground host at Turquoise Lake near Leadville. My sister Amber and I leave our trucks and horse trailers there when we go up to the family cabin. Amber left her truck and trailer there Saturday morning and told Bob she'd return Sunday night before dark. She's not back yet."

"Can the campground host check on her?"

Olivia's eyebrows drew together as she twisted an amber and pearl embellished pendant necklace, which dropped into the blank space created by her V-neck blouse. The necklace elongated her neck, and he couldn't take his eyes off the shimmer of her skin or her elegant fingers, as they gently twisted the hint of sparkle above her breasts. She wore the necklace often, and he knew the inscription by heart: *I love you, sis, to the moon and back.*

"Bob doesn't have a horse and you can't get to the property without one, unless you want to drive miles out of the way," she said.

"What about the sheriff?" he asked.

She bit her lower lip and glanced away. "I can't ask him."

"Why not?"

"He doesn't believe we should be in the mountains by ourselves," she said in such a quiet voice Connor had to lean in to hear her.

"And you think that's what? A chauvinistic view?"

"Don't you?"

He straightened. "No. I think it makes good sense."

She narrowed her eyes at him. "I thought you'd be more open-minded."

When she narrowed her eyes and stared at him, he knew he was in trouble. "I'm as open-minded as they come. I know three women who could handle the wilderness by themselves."

"See—"

"But that doesn't mean I want them out there, Olivia." He used the same pitch and reflection Pops used in similar situations. But sounding like the retired deputy chief was too harsh a tone to use with Olivia. Connor instantly regretted it.

The brown in her hazel eyes darkened. "Amber and I can handle it." Then she took a breath, and her intense expression cleared somewhat, and she said more calmly, "We grew up going to the cabin almost every weekend. It's like a second home."

He didn't have to be a mind reader to understand what was going on with Olivia. She wasn't annoyed or impatient. She was scared, and his job was to be the compassionate neighborhood cop and find a way to ease her mind.

"I guess there's no cell reception at the cabin," he said.

"No electricity. No plumbing."

"Sounds more like camping out."

"If I were marketing the property, I'd call it upscale camping. It has a great fireplace, sweet spring water, and a warm bed. That's all the available accoutrements."

"You mean there's no chocolate on the pillow?" he asked with a hint of a smile.

She returned his smile with one of her own. "Only if you put it there." She scrolled through her text messages. "Amber asked me to go to the cabin with her, but I had an event to attend Saturday night and couldn't cancel." Olivia dropped her phone into her purse. "Something's wrong. I feel it in my gut."

Connor wanted to hug her, but their relationship wasn't at the hugging stage. In lieu of a hug, it was time to play the role of the neighborhood cop and get the cat out of the tree. "Let's postpone the appointment. We can visit the ranch this afternoon. Would that give us enough time to go to the cabin and check on Amber?"

"If you don't see the ranch this morning, I'm afraid another buyer will sign a contract before you get there."

"Tell the property owner you have a cash buyer, but you have to postpone until later today. Then I'll go to Leadville with you to search for your sister."

She continued to worry her necklace, her long slim fingers shaking slightly. "I can't let you do that. I'll have another agent take you to the showing."

"I want to see it with you, not another agent. I was a detective for more than a decade. I learned to trust my instincts. You sense something is wrong. Let's go."

She let go of the necklace before she broke the chain, and her furrowed brows relaxed as some of the tension eased from her face.

Score one for the neighborhood cop.

"Are you sure?"

"Positive, but"—and here he faked bashfulness—"there's a problem. I don't have a horse or even a cowboy hat."

She glanced down his jean-covered legs to his boots. When she looked back up at him there was a twinkle in her eye. "But you have the boots."

He gave her the same once-over she gave him. "I can ride in what I'm wearing, but I'm not so sure you can."

She picked at her skirt. "This won't work, will it? Lucky for me, I have jeans and boots in my trunk. When I list a property, I want to see every inch of it. I'll change at the barn."

"This hotel doesn't have a parking lot. Are you telling me it has a barn for guests to park their horses?" he asked, tongue stuck solidly in his cheek.

She laughed. "My parents have a ranch southwest of Denver. I'll change there and saddle a couple of horses." Then she gave him a questioning glance. "You do ride, right?"

He would have told her he did, even if he'd never been on a horse, and suffer the consequences later. "I didn't grow up on a horse, but I do ride."

"Well then, let's go, cowboy."

Before leaving the hotel, he stopped at the front desk and arranged to keep his room for another night. After they found Amber and viewed the property, he intended to ask Olivia to have dinner with him. If she turned him down again, he wouldn't ask a third time.

Connor went through the revolving door after her. "Are you going to call your parents and let them know about your sister?"

"They're in Africa on a safari and can't be reached right now."

"I'm sure there's an emergency contact number? I've got a few connections. Do you want me to try?"

"The travel agency can probably locate them, but I'll wait until after we go to the cabin."

Olivia's white Mercedes-Benz GLC was parked at the curb. She tipped the attendant, who held her door while she climbed in. Connor sat in the passenger seat, and after buckling his seatbelt, sent the company's legal counsel, Kenzie McBain, a text: *The sister of the broker I'm working with has gone missing. Postponing visit to the ranch. Will know more in a couple of hours.*

Kenzie responded: *Yikes. How old? Keep in touch.*

He replied: *Early thirties.* Then he slipped his cell phone into his shirt pocket.

"I'm sorry. I shouldn't drag you away from the appointment,"

Olivia said. "If you lose this property—"

"You'll find us another one."

She lifted her perfectly arched brow. "Thanks for the confidence."

She turned onto 20th Street, and by the time they reached the exit to Highway 25, she was well into another one of her Colorado stories. This one was about Chief Ouray, leader of the Utes. "It's been said," Olivia opined, "that he was the greatest Indian of his time with pure instincts and keen perception. A friend to the white man and protector to the Indians. Dad can tell you all about him. If he could meet anyone in American history, Chief Ouray would be on his top-ten list."

Thirty minutes later, Olivia drove down a tree-lined private drive that led to a luxury log home. "Sweet," Connor said. "Is this for sale?"

"Maybe someday, but not right now. My parents built out here ten years ago. I've had a dozen clients make an offer, but they won't sell."

"I can see you taking a client through the house, pointing out its unique features, calling it a little slice of heaven."

"*Almost Heaven, West Virginia,*" she sang.

"*Country roads, take me home/to the place I belong,*" Connor joined her in a duet of the chorus of the John Denver song.

"And it is, too," she said. "Besides all the amenities the house offers, there's the thermal-controlled greenhouse, five-stall barn with grid-tied solar panels, a stocked trout pond, fruit trees, and a library. Dad's history collection is so expansive, he built a scaled-down version of the house to hold it all. When he's not lawyering or exploring the world, he's out there reading and writing journal articles."

"If your parents ever decide to sell, I'll make a full-price offer."

"Another MacKlenna property?" Olivia asked.

Connor stared longingly at the house. "No. An O'Grady one."

"You'd leave Kentucky for Colorado?"

"I left New York almost three years ago and have been on the road since."

"I wouldn't call staying in a Scottish castle, a winery in Napa or Tuscany, or a Thoroughbred farm in Kentucky being on the road."

"They're all beautiful properties, but none of them are mine."

"But you get to enjoy them without worrying about maintenance and taxes. That counts for a lot."

"Maybe," Connor said. "I'd still like a place of my own." A place of his own for sure. But more important, a place where he could raise a family.

Olivia parked in front of the barn next to a Land Rover and claimed an overnight bag from the trunk. "There's a restroom inside if you need to use it. I'll change in the manager's office."

Connor entered the barn and walked into a world of dust motes and hay, of soft whinnies and tails swishing, of racks of tack and oat bins.

He used the facilities and then while he waited for her, he wandered through to the far side. The beams were solid and the posts, though chewed in places, were sturdy. The stall doors were polished oak with bars at the top, so the horses could see and sniff whoever walked by. Connor spoke to each one and scratched between their ears and eyes. For a city boy, he'd turned into an acceptable equestrian. At least he didn't embarrass himself when he trotted alongside experienced riders. He'd never ride like former Union cavalry officer Braham McCabe, but no one else would either.

Olivia came out of the manager's office wearing jeans, a red plaid button-up shirt, boots, and a Patagonia jacket looped over one shoulder. She'd never worn anything other than business attire while with him, and while he loved her legs in short, fitted skirts, he much preferred the woman standing in front of him now. She appeared more accessible, more natural, and he couldn't take his eyes off her.

"Dad has a canvas ranch jacket on the hook over there that will fit you. I'd hate for you to ruin your leather jacket. Take the hat, too."

Connor glanced across the barn in the direction she was pointing. "There are six immutable laws concerning cowboy hats.

Number one: don't mess with a hat that doesn't belong to you. Thanks, but no thanks."

"Dad won't care. He's got a dozen hats and a dozen pairs of boots. Forget the hat law. It doesn't apply here."

Connor removed the backup phone battery from his pocket before dropping his leather jacket in the car's front seat. He slid the battery in the pocket of the ranch jacket before donning a black Stetson with a slightly darkened sweatband. After adjusting the hat on his head, he asked, "What can I do to help?" When she didn't reply, he turned and caught her staring at him. "What's wrong?"

She shook her head. "I've never seen you without a jacket. You're carrying a gun."

"Colorado permits retired policemen to carry a concealed weapon. Does it bother you?"

She shrugged. "Not really. It's just...well...you don't seem the type."

Now, he was curious. "I'm not sure what that means."

"You're always immaculately dressed, hair perfectly barbered, nails buffed. I don't see the rugged outdoorsman hunter type when I look at you."

"If I had three-day whiskers and a hat slung low on my forehead, would that help?"

"Hmm. Sorry. I can't picture it."

Now he knew why he'd never made a pass at her. He wasn't her type, and he had subconsciously picked up the vibe that she wasn't interested. "I may not be the outdoorsman type, but I know how to hitch a trailer. You want me to hitch the trailer to the Land Rover parked outside?"

She looked at him for a moment, as a not-so-sure expression crossed her face, then she reached into her pocket and tossed him a set of keys. "If you need help, yell."

City slicker. That's what she thinks of me.

He tried to shrug off his insecurities, but he couldn't. Her opinion of him was more important than he wanted to admit.

This wasn't his first rodeo with either hitching a trailer or desiring a disinterested woman. He could do a bang-up job with a trailer hitch, but he crashed and burned when a beautiful woman brushed him off. The male ego was a fragile thing, even for males raised by loving parents with the right mix of discipline and reassurance.

He slid into the Land Rover and started the engine. The vehicle's camera system helped him reverse into the correct position to the tow bar. Then he got out, secured the hitch, and had the electrical cable attached by the time Olivia exited the barn leading one of the horses.

"I'm going to get back in the vehicle and flash the lights. Will you tell me if they're working correctly?" he asked.

"Sure," she said, running an expert hand over the horse's withers.

He flipped on the turn signal and lights, and yelled out the window, "Everything okay?"

"Yes," she yelled back.

While she loaded the first horse onto the trailer, he returned to the barn for the second one. "Who takes care of the animals when your parents aren't here?"

"They travel so much now that they had to hire a full-time manager. He lives in an apartment over the barn. His truck's not here. He must be out running an errand. That's why the horses haven't been put out yet." She took the reins from him and led the horse into the trailer to join the other one. "This is Doc. He's a sweetheart."

"As in Doc Holliday, the Arizona gunfighter?"

"What can I say? I told you Dad was a history nut. Holliday was a dentist, gambler, gunslinger, and an icon of the American West. He played a big part in a Colorado railroad war in the late 1800s. Dad has written several articles about the legal battle. After reading his first article, I decided to follow in his footsteps and go to law school."

"You're a lawyer, too?"

"Was."

"Unless you're disbarred, I think you still are, and I doubt you were disbarred," Connor said.

"I couldn't handle being inside all day. I stuck it out for five years, then packed up my stuff and walked out."

"Must have been hard on your dad."

"My dad, my mom, and Amber. My parents met at the University of Chicago Law School. My mom intended to return to Denver to practice in her family's law firm. Her plans conflicted with his, but he finally gave in and moved to Denver with her. I don't think he's ever regretted the decision."

"Have you ever regretted yours?" Connor asked.

Olivia stepped out of the horse trailer, raised the ramp, and closed it up. "Not one bit."

"What's the other horse's name?"

"Cochise."

Connor laughed. "I take it your dad was a *Bonanza* fan."

"Yep. Little Joe, impulsive and quick tempered, was his favorite character."

"Who could resist his smile and pinto horse. He might not have been as ruggedly handsome as Adam, but the girls fell for his innocent good looks, brown curly hair, and green eyes. My brothers and I had fistfights over who got to play Little Joe when we had stage productions in our basement. Somehow Rick always drew the Little Joe card, and I played Cochise."

Olivia burst out laughing. "Did your mom take videos? I'd love to see them. I bet they're hysterical."

"Yep, she did. But they're locked in a safe to be used only for blackmail and bachelor parties. When my brother Jeff got married, he hid the key, so we couldn't show them. One of these days, they'll see the light of day again."

Olivia opened the driver's side door and climbed in. Before she started the engine, she scrolled through the messages on her phone. "This is so unlike Amber. She's supposed to be in court at two o'clock this afternoon."

"She won't make it unless she shows up soon," Connor said.

Olivia's shoulders slumped. "I didn't want to alarm anyone else, but I should probably call her assistant to get someone to cover for her." She hesitated only a moment before sending a text. "Amber will be pissed, but I had to notify someone. I told the office she's sick. They won't believe me, but I had to say something. Amber is never sick. She's had a few sore throats, but never bad enough to go to the doctor, and never bad enough to miss work."

Connor reached for her arm and squeezed it gently. "I know you're worried. The only reassurance I can offer is that I have a friend who can move mountains, and he can be here within a few hours."

"Move mountains, huh?"

He glanced in the direction of the Rockies and pointed. "See that highest point over there? Mark the point now, because if you need his help, that point will be five miles in the other direction when the job's done."

"He must be a superhero."

"Some say he is. I've never seen his cape or anything, but I've heard stories."

Olivia looked off toward the mountains, biting the corner of her bottom lip. After a moment, she glanced back at him. "Did I tell you that Amber and I are twins?"

"I knew you had a sister, but you've never mentioned her by name until this morning."

"We don't have the same birthday. We're considered Irish twins."

"So you were born ten, eleven months apart?"

"Eleven. I don't think my parents were happy."

He laughed. "I don't blame them. So who's older?"

"I am," she said. "We try to give each other space. Hang out with different crowds and stuff. But we talk and text several times a day." Olivia glanced at her phone. "I should have heard from her at least half a dozen times. I'm afraid something serious has happened."

Even though Olivia didn't say, "This time," Connor heard the words in her intonation, and he considered the entire statement—

something serious had happened to her *this time.*

"Do you want me to drive so you can check and send messages?" he asked.

"Are you comfortable pulling a trailer?"

"I won't get us killed, if that's what you're asking."

"Sorry. I didn't mean to insult you."

"You didn't. I've pulled trailers carrying the farm's multi-million-dollar stallions many times. Sit back, power down, conserve your energy. We might have a long day ahead."

"You're right." She scooted out of the driver's seat and climbed into the passenger seat. "In case I get caught on a call, I'll plug the address into the GPS, so you won't miss a turn."

While Olivia tapped in the address, Connor sent a text to Kenzie: *Doubt I'll get back to see the property today. Fax an offer to Olivia's agency. Let's get this done. It's the perfect ranch.*

Kenzie would discuss it with Elliott Fraser, Chairman of the Board of MacKlenna Corporation, before she made an offer.

Connor put his phone away and started to drive. "If an offer comes in and you're not there, what happens?"

"If I can't be reached, my manager has the authority to present the offer. It's only happened once. They'll make every effort to find me. Why?"

"Elliott might make an offer based on the video presentation."

"Really? I'll let my office know." A minute later she said, "All done. But I'd be more comfortable if someone from MacKlenna Corporation sees the ranch in person before extending an offer."

"If it doesn't work out, Elliott will sell it and look for something else. Now, don't worry about the ranch and concentrate on Amber."

"Thank you." Olivia's voice rose slightly. "It's like you're reading my mind."

He checked the side mirrors and made quick adjustments. "You'll have to meet my sister. Once I figured her out, the rest of the female population was a snap."

"If you can read my mind, I'll have to be more guarded with my thoughts."

"Please don't. I like knowing you think I'm devilishly handsome." He glanced in her direction and found her blushing. He'd only been teasing, but the color on her cheeks confirmed what he'd hoped was true.

He changed the subject. "Tell me about Amber. What kind of law does she practice? What does she like to do? And most important, what the hell does she do out in the wilderness by herself?"

Olivia settled back in her seat and put one of her booted feet up on the dash. The leg of her tight jeans accentuated her firm calf muscle. No wonder he liked her in short skirts. She had gorgeous legs, dancer's legs.

"The cabin is located on my seven-times great-grandparents' silver mining claim. The mine played out over a century ago, but the family believed there were still silver deposits and refused to sell it. When my grandparents were living, we'd go on weekend camping trips. Dad and Granddaddy would spend the day shoring up loose beams and replacing rotting timbers. Mom and Granny worked in the cabin and tended the garden."

"When was the cabin built?"

"In the 1870s. My ancestors made enough money on their claim to move to Leadville and open a dry goods store. The store made them richer. Their son, Adam, started a law practice in Denver, and after his son, Andrew, joined him, the name changed to Hughes and Hughes."

"You're not a Hughes."

"My mother was."

Connor passed a sign that noted it was twenty miles to Leadville, but the GPS said twenty-five miles to their destination. If he kept her talking about her family maybe she wouldn't worry so much about her sister.

"My siblings and I were fifth-generation New York City cops. I understand the pressure to follow in family footsteps."

"Did you have a choice?"

"After I left the Marines, I got a degree in criminal justice and considered law school, but Mom died, and everything changed."

"I'm sorry for your loss. To lose a parent is one of the hardest trials life puts us through, aside from losing a child. It nearly killed me when Granny died, not only because I loved her so much, but because of the pain Mom went through. I couldn't do anything to make life easier for her."

"I know that feeling. Losing Mom nearly killed Pops, but he's got a companion now. I'm happy for him."

"Where do they live?"

"Usually on MacKlenna Farm, but they spend a lot of time at the wineries in Napa and Tuscany."

"And your brothers, where are they?"

"My brother Jeff is a lawyer. He handles corporate matters for MacKlenna Corporation. My other brothers, Rick and Shane, are directors of global Security. We're all based at the farm, but we travel extensively. For the last year, Shane has spent more time in Australia than in the States."

"I'd like to meet them."

"No, you wouldn't. They're not as handsome as me."

She took her foot off the dashboard and turned in her seat to face him. "Now I'm even more intrigued. I'll have to check the MacKlenna Corporation website."

"None of our pictures are there. It's a security issue."

"I thought I saw your picture when I was searching the website."

He knew exactly where she'd seen his picture. It was at the dedication of the museum in California that housed the artifacts found with the Confederate gold. And that was one topic he didn't want to talk about. The discovery had made his entire family multi-millionaires and since they were former cops, their wealth put targets on their chests.

"I think you saw a newspaper article." He changed the subject, asking, "What did you and Amber do during the trips to the cabin?"

"Amber searched for dinosaur bones and I worked in the garden."

He took his hands off the wheel and seesawed them, as if balancing the two activities before reclaiming the wheel. "Searching for dinosaur bones and gardening. I'm sorry, but neither one sounds entertaining. Does Amber still hunt fossils?"

"She's an amateur paleontologist. Her idol is Sue Hendrickson."

Deadpanned, he said, "I may have seen a wanted poster for her."

Olivia backslapped his arm. "She discovered an intact skeleton of *Tyrannosaurus Rex* in South Dakota, which ended up in a protracted legal battle. She now lives on an island off the coast of Honduras."

"I hope Amber doesn't follow Sue there. The drug trafficking in Honduras has led to the highest homicide rates in the world."

"I don't think that'll happen. Amber's satisfied with roaming the Colorado mountains."

Connor turned off the highway and onto Harrison Avenue in Leadville. "Do you want to stop and grab sandwiches at the grocery store to take with us?"

Olivia thought for a minute. "Amber keeps freeze-dried food at the cabin. We should be okay."

He made a face, his stomach rumbling. "Sounds very…appetizing."

"Oh, don't laugh. Amber is a gourmet cook. She has a large stainless steel freeze-dryer at home. She freezes her meals then seals them in mylar bags. They'll last twenty-five years on the shelf."

"Hmm. My mouth is already watering."

"Just wait. After you taste her cooking, you'll be begging for more."

If he ever had to beg, freeze-dried food wouldn't be at the top of the list. He drove past the grocery store, remembering the MRE's he'd eaten in the Marines. If he could survive those rations, surely, he could survive Amber's freeze-dried concoctions. He had to get his mind off food.

"Where does one study paleontology?" he asked.

"Amber studied geology at Yale. Got her master's degree in paleontology from the University of Chicago."

"And then decided on law?"

"She was going to return to Yale for her PhD, but she succumbed to family pressure and went to law school instead. She's got an impressive mining law practice now."

"With such an exciting career, no wonder she freeze-dries her food."

"Would you stop it? She's an interesting person. You'll like her."

"I'm sure I will. Tell me about her personal life. Does she have a boyfriend? Maybe she's in a group of freeze-dried devotees."

Olivia laughed. "She's had a couple of relationships that lasted longer than six months, but once the arguing starts, she bails."

Without missing a beat, he asked, "What'd they argue over? Which package to open for dinner?"

Olivia glared at him, but the twitch in her eye gave her away. "I can see now that we should have stopped at the grocery store. There's another market up the street."

"I'm just teasing." He drove past the second market, ignoring his rumbling stomach.

"Amber has lots of close male friends. She enjoys their company, and although she hasn't said so, I think one of the guys, a lawyer in Denver, is a friend with benefits. If you know what I mean."

"Sounds like a lucky guy."

"Sounds like a coward who's afraid of commitment," Olivia said.

"Who? The guy or your sister?"

"Both."

They rode in silence for several miles until they reached Turquoise Lake. "I'm sure you got some blowback when you quit practicing law. How'd your parents take it?" Connor asked.

"Not well. We didn't speak for several weeks. They didn't understand why I couldn't continue to practice and find something else to be passionate about. I started selling real estate as a side venture, focusing on multi-million-dollar ranches. When I sold my first one and made more in commission than I made practicing law, I quit. I love having my own business, setting my own hours, taking time off—"

"To do what?"

"I travel a lot."

"Where?"

"I love the UK. I could make repeated visits to Scotland and Ireland. I love Italy, Spain, and Greece, too, but Tuscany owns a place in my heart. How about you?"

"In the last year, I've been around the world and back again. I'd enjoy sitting in my own yard watching weeds grow. But I don't see my travel schedule slowing down anytime soon. How often do you go to the cabin?"

"Maybe once a month, I'll go with Amber. But I won't go by myself."

"Because it's dangerous, right?"

She folded her arms, turned her head slowly to the side, and glared at him. "Are we backtracking?"

"I couldn't resist. You walked right into our previous discussion on girls in the wilderness."

"It's not like that." She laughed, but there was no humor in it. "It's not a safety issue. If I enjoyed fossil hunting as much as Amber, I'd go. But going up there just to piddle around isn't fun, especially when I could be out hustling up new business." Olivia pointed toward the right. "The campground is that way." Connor drove down the road, passing numbered plots. "Her truck is over there on the right."

"The blue Land Rover?"

"That's it."

Connor pulled in next to Amber's vehicle, turned off the engine, and stepped out. "Why don't you go talk to the campground host. I'll look around here."

The doors to Amber's Land Rover were locked. None of the windows had been broken. The dashboard appeared intact, and the glove box was closed. Magazines on geology and empty water bottles were scattered on mud-dried floor mats in both the front and back seats. The vehicle was messy but not vandalized.

Hoofprints led from the back of the trailer through a grassy area toward a trail about twenty yards away. He followed the hoofprints. Amber must have mounted the horse near the trailer, since there weren't any footprints. He had to admit though, his tracking skills weren't anything to brag about, unless he was tracking a perp with blood on his shoes running across a concrete parking lot.

"Connor." Olivia walked toward Amber's truck accompanied by a weathered man with *former military* stamped on his bearing—stiff back, square shoulders, cropped gray hair, and a heavy limp on the right side.

Connor jogged in her direction, reaching the truck shortly before her. He extended his hand to the vet. "Connor O'Grady."

"Bob Vilines. You a cop? You got that look."

"Retired," Connor said. "You a Marine? You got that look."

"Tet Offensive."

Connor was also a Marine but didn't mention his service. "My dad was there. He doesn't talk about it much."

Bob shrugged. "Not much to say. It sucked."

Olivia broke the awkward silence that followed. "When Bob spoke to Amber Saturday morning, she was in a good mood and excited to get to the cabin."

"Was there anyone around who seemed to take notice or have a special interest in her?"

Bob thought a minute. "Campers on both sides were regulars. She's thrown back a few beers with both families. I watch who comes and goes around here. Nothing unusual happened all weekend. There was no particular interest in her truck and trailer either."

"The ground is pretty soft from the rain. I didn't notice any footprints or other hoofprints at the entrance to the trail. Is there another way to get to the cabin from here?"

"You could make your own trail, I guess. Never seen anybody do it, and I've been camping here since long before the Sugar Loaf Dam was completed."

Connor's gut told him whatever happened to Amber didn't begin here. "If you had to guess, why do you think she's still up there?"

Bob balanced his elbow against an arm slung across his chest and scratched at his chin, which clearly hadn't seen a razor in at least a week. "I figure she finally found that cache of bones she's been searching for since she was a kid. Either that or she found evidence that old mine has more silver in it. Don't think she's come to any harm."

"If she found a cache of bones, it better be the find of the century," Olivia said. "If not, I'll kick her butt from here to Denver."

Connor handed Bob a business card. "Here's my contact information. If you'll give me your phone number, I'll call you as soon as we have news."

Bob slapped the card in his palm. "There's no reception up there."

"I have a sat sleeve on my iPhone. Reception shouldn't be a problem." Bob gave him a cell number and Connor plugged it into his contacts. "I do have a question you should be able to answer. If Amber is injured and we can't get her down off the mountain, how far away is a rescue team?"

"The air ambulance and SAR would come from Denver. They can land at 14,000 feet, which is higher than you're going. They could be at the Hughes mine within an hour," Bob said.

"Sounds like you've used them before."

"A few times. People mix stupidity with alcohol and drugs and think they're invincible," Bob said.

Olivia unlocked the back of the horse trailer and lowered the ramp. "I can assure you, Amber isn't at the cabin taking drugs. She won't take them when she's sick. Why would she take them for recreation?" Olivia brought Cochise out and went back in for Doc. "If we miss Amber on the trail, and she shows up here, ask her to call Connor's phone."

Connor raised the ramp and locked up the trailer. "If you don't hear from me within twenty-four hours," Connor said, "call the number on my business card and tell them to send the cavalry."

3

The Present, Hughes Cabin, Colorado—Connor

AFTER RIDING THROUGH the quiet backcountry, they veered onto a less traveled path and wound around the shoulder of a hill. The air seemed heavier compared to Denver, full of moisture and scented with spruce needles and cedar. Olivia turned in her saddle and waved to Connor. He was lagging a few yards behind her, enjoying the view and the scenery. He applied gentle pressure with his calves and the horse moved forward.

"It's beautiful," he said.

"Yes, it is. This is the only way to really see the mountains," she said.

He wasn't referring to the beauty of the mountains, which was undeniable. His attention had been mostly focused on her, watching the way she gently swayed in the saddle as her horse worked the hills.

"How much farther to the cabin?"

"Thirty minutes or so."

"If you can't drive up here, how do you get supplies? You're limited to how much you can carry with you."

"The same way it's been done for over a century. Pack mules, but I imagine MacKlenna Corporation would use a helicopter."

Connor laughed. "It crossed my mind when we were loading the horses that it would save time if we flew up here."

She lifted her hands toward the sky. "And miss all this beautiful scenery?"

"It's just as beautiful from the air."

"Maybe, but you can't smell the pine and fresh air, or hear the musical trickle of water rippling over stones in a cold, mountain stream, or get the sense of how high the mountains rise above the surrounding landscapes."

"But we could get to the cabin in under thirty minutes instead of two hours."

She turned in the saddle, gripped the edge of the cantle. "Then why didn't you suggest it?"

"For the same reason I never went into another police precinct and told them how to do their job. You're the expert here. It was possible there was no place for a helicopter to land. After what Bob said, I know a landing is possible. I'm sorry I didn't suggest using one."

Olivia glanced up and studied the sky. "A storm's coming. If Amber needs medical care, a helicopter would be grounded. With horses, if we need to get her down the mountain, we can. And besides, if we have to search for her, we'll be going places a helicopter can't go."

"Just to be clear… If I'd suggested a helicopter, you would have nixed the idea?"

"I would have considered it." She paused before adding, "and then I would have nixed it." Her mouth quirked up at one corner. "Agreeing to ride up to the cabin told me a lot about your priorities. To you, people come first. Your time comes second. I appreciate that."

The breeze lifted her hair like lover's hands, brushing it aside so her neck could be kissed. She turned up her jacket's collar and adjusted her hat back farther on her head to keep her hair from flying about.

He forced himself to stop fantasizing about kissing her neck. "Tell me about the mules. Do you rent them in town, or what?"

She snapped her reins lightly. "We buy most of our supplies in

Leadville. Then we rent a couple of mules for the weekend and haul up what we need. Amber has been bringing freeze-dried food up for the past few years. There's enough at the cabin to feed a large family for an entire winter. We use the mules to bring up feed for the animals, garden supplies, lanterns, candles. Supplies like that."

"Who chops the wood?"

"Amber and I both know how to split and stack firewood. But a man comes up from Leadville twice a month to cut more wood for the seasoning pile and do a few chores."

His cop mind could weave dozens of scenarios around a woman alone in the wilderness and a man from town with an ax—all of them bloody as hell. "Is it the same man each time?"

Olivia reined in her horse and a look of horror flashed across her face, then vanished as quickly. "I know where you're going with that, and you can forget it. Gus has been coming up here for thirty years. He's trustworthy and has never sent anyone else to do what he's hired to do. He mends fences, cuts wood, keeps the place clean and critter-free. He's a little slow, but he would never hurt anyone, especially Amber."

From Connor's experience, people acted out of character and committed acts of cruelty all the time. Even nice men like Gus. A crow made an ugly squawk, like something had jerked its leg. An omen? God, he hoped not.

"When's the last time you talked to old Gus?"

"I don't talk to him. Amber does. And she hasn't mentioned having any problems."

The higher they climbed the darker the clouds turned, and the more Connor worried that Handyman Gus might have lost his cool.

They rode out of the woods and stopped at the fringe of another clearing. Ahead, nestled at the tree line, stood a picturesque log cabin with a wraparound porch, a small barn, and an enclosed square-pole corral.

"Is that it?" Now he understood what upscale camping truly meant.

"Yes, and I told you it was quaint."

He laughed. "This ain't quaint. *Quaint* is a cabin in the Smokies with a hot tub."

She gave him an annoyed look. "There's no hot tub, and there's no smoke coming from the chimney either."

At the corral, a bay stamped restlessly, lifting his head, ears pricked. "Is that Amber's horse?"

"That's Bud, and he knows we're here. He and Doc have been together a long time." Olivia kneed her horse and clicked. "Let's go, boy."

Connor caught the reins. "Hold up. If someone is in there with Amber, we can't go charging in."

Olivia stared at the cabin and released a perturbed breath that puffed out through her teeth. "The way I see it, I rearranged my schedule and inconvenienced a client. If she's with someone, I intend to ruin her interlude as payback."

"Answer this question: If Amber met someone she wanted to spend alone time with, would she skip a court appearance to do it?"

Olivia shifted in the saddle. Doc snorted and swished his tail. Either he was keeping off flies or he was agitated that he couldn't go visit Bud.

"Amber takes her job seriously. She'd never do that."

"That's what I thought." Connor didn't let go of the reins while he considered their options. "Amber could be with someone..." He had to be careful here. He didn't want to scare Olivia, but he wanted her to be aware of the possible danger. "Someone not of her own choosing."

Olivia's face went chalky white. "You're overreacting. Nothing like that has ever happened around here." Although she said it, he could see doubt in her darkened eyes. She gazed out over the clearing and slumped in the saddle. "Okay. What do you want me to do?"

"Nothing. Other than stay right here." He let go of the reins and dismounted. "I'm going to circle around and approach from the back. How many windows are there?"

"Two in the front, two in the back, and one on each side."

"Are they curtained?" His horse's nose bumped his shoulder blade.

"Yes, but I doubt they're closed. The two in the back are in the bedrooms. The right side is the kitchen. A large loom fills the area next to the window on the left side."

Connor tied the reins to a dwarfed pine that couldn't decide whether it was a tree or a bramble. Its coarse needle-shaped leaves trembled in the breeze. The horse shifted his weight and settled down to probing the withered grass bundled around the pine.

Connor unholstered and chamber-checked his Glock.

"You're expecting trouble, aren't you?" she asked.

"I always expect trouble." He had a fully loaded magazine, one in the chamber, and an extra magazine in his pocket. "I need you to do exactly what I say." He unlocked his phone and handed it to her. "If something goes wrong, get the hell out of here. Call the Leadville sheriff and my brother Rick as soon as you are a safe distance away. His number is on the recent call list."

"What can he do? He's not even in Colorado."

"He can get here soon enough." It would probably be too late for Connor and Amber, but Rick wouldn't stop until he found the killer.

"Let me go with you."

He grasped her stirrup to keep her in the saddle. "You're my ace in the hole. If something is going down in there and I get caught, too, you'll be the only hope of rescue. Don't let your stubbornness compromise your sister's life."

She jutted out her jaw. She didn't like it, probably didn't like him either at the moment. That didn't matter. "If there's trouble, take Doc with you. I don't see another horse. If you're chased, they'll have to ride Bud, and saddling him will take time. You'll have a head start."

"I don't like this," she said testily.

"If you did, I'd wonder about you. Stay alert and be ready to ride."

He touched his hat, wheeled around, and headed into the aspens.

Whispers from the wind, coming off the mountains, made shushing noises through the trees. Every hunting skill McBain had taught him, Connor used now as he circled the perimeter of the clearing, walking lightly through the dead leaves and dried branches so he wouldn't startle the birds, or worse, announce his presence to someone hiding on the grounds or inside the cabin.

Within a few yards of where he'd left Olivia, he reached a stream of frothy water, roaring to be set free from its banks as it rushed by. There was no way around it. He'd have to test the advertisement that claimed his boots were waterproof. The icy water sprayed his legs. When he reached the opposite bank, he heard a branch snap. He ducked behind a tree, his gun secured in a two-handed grip. He studied the shadows. When he didn't see any movement, he continued toward the rear of the cabin, passing the corral and the barn, baled hay visible in the loft. There were no human footprints on the well-worn muddy path from the side of the cabin into the woods.

The two small windows on the back wall were closed, but thin cotton curtains were pushed to the sides, allowing strips of light to filter into each room. As soon as he moved close enough, he'd be able to see inside. The cabin was constructed of hand-hewed logs with square notches and thick chinking between them. Many of the logs had hewing marks from the broadax. There was no denying the age of the cabin, or the love it had been given over the last century to keep it in fine shape.

The joints in his knees popped when he crouched and snuck up close to the windows and listened. There were no creaking boards or murmured voices. No groans or squeaky bedsprings. He sniffed. No lingering stench of death and violence.

Slowly, he raised his head and peeked over the windowsill and into a small bedroom with twin brass beds, both neatly made. He checked the other rear window. The second bedroom had a double bed covered with a patchwork quilt. A washstand with a porcelain bowl, an armoire in the corner, and a faded hand-hooked rug were the only other furnishings. Both rooms were tidy and clean.

He moved to the window on the side, and although he stayed crouched and kept his outstretched gun hand secured in the palm of the other, his gut told him no one was inside.

The kitchen area had a sink with a pitcher-style pump, a long table with two benches, a pie safe, and a cast iron wood stove. The rest of the room was filled with assorted small tables, a leather sofa, two rockers facing a stone fireplace, a cedar chest, a tall cabinet with glass panes, and a large weaving loom with dark-colored yarn or thread. He wasn't interested in the yarn, but he was interested in a large round piece that had fallen off the end of the loom, exposing a gaping hole. The piece lay on the floor next to a small wooden box and a canvas-pocketed tool kit.

The room appeared to be otherwise in order and uninhabited, but until he checked the areas he couldn't see from the window, he wouldn't relax his defensive posture or signal an all-clear to Olivia.

His boots abraded the plank floor as he crossed the porch, scanning the surroundings as he inched forward. Using the edge of his boot, he pushed on the unbarred door, and it squawked as it scraped open across the floor.

He had made enough noise to announce himself to the next county.

Slowly, he entered, moving through the room, gun still in hand. None of the furniture was upturned. No broken glass littered the floor. No crooked pictures hung on the walls. There was a faint scent of peat in the air, which was odd since there was a stack of split pine and cedar outside and a smaller stack in a bucket sitting on the hearth. He searched both bedrooms and found them as undisturbed from the inside as they looked from the outside. There were no dirty dishes in the kitchen or trash in the container.

He holstered his gun, squatted, and put his hand over the ash residue in the hearth. Cold as winter. On the floor next to the loom, was the broken piece, an backpack, a small wooden box, a dental pick, a brush, tape measure, and a scrap of white cloth, along with a well-used canvas tool kit with chisels, brushes, rock hammers, markers, and plastic baggies.

When he got a good look at the box, his heart thumped hard against his ribs. It was identical to the one Elliott Fraser had on his desk at MacKlenna Farm.

Before he touched anything, he wanted to take pictures. He reached for his phone then remembered he had given it to Olivia. He eyeballed the width of the box and the open end of the beam. The hole was slightly larger. The box would fit in there easily.

At the sound of horses' hooves crossing the yard, Connor drew his gun, flattened against the wall, and peeked out the front window. Olivia was galloping toward the cabin, leading Doc behind her. "Connor, is she here?"

He stepped out on the porch, holstering his gun once again. "What the hell are you doing? I told you to wait."

"I was watching with binoculars. I knew it was safe. Where's Amber?"

"I don't know," he said. "She was here. The beds are made, and the fireplace is cold."

"Did you check the trash? We recycle. If Amber prepared any freeze-dried food, the bags would be in the trash. We could tell how many meals she fixed."

"There's nothing there. Maybe she ate outside or on the trail."

"Amber would have saved the trash and thrown it away when she returned." Olivia dismounted and looped both horses' reins around the porch rail. She handed Connor back his cell phone as she shouldered her way past him, pausing at the door, sniffing. "What's that smell?"

"Peat."

She peeled off her gloves. "Like grass? Why would Amber make a peat fire?"

"I don't know that she did. The hearth is cold." He pointed to the puzzle box on the floor. "Have you ever seen that box before?"

"No. She must have brought it with her."

The hairs on the back of his neck stood on end. While Olivia walked through the cabin, he took several pictures of the room and more than a dozen pics of the items on the floor, including the loom's broken piece and the gaping hole in the beam. Before he picked up the box, he took several close-up pictures of the green velvet interior. David McBain, president of MacKlenna Corporation and former head of security, needed to see the pictures ASAP.

Connor forwarded a dozen images to him along with the message: *Does this box look familiar? I believe it came out of the loom.*

David responded immediately: *Kenzie had an identical one. She gave it to Elliott. Is anyone missing?*

Connor answered: *Olivia Kelly's sister, Amber.*

David responded: *I'll get on it. Don't mention Elliott's box. Find out where the loom came from.*

"That's a beautiful loom," Connor said. "Do you know where it came from?"

Olivia looked at him as if he'd asked the dumbest question in the world. "Is it important right now?"

Although irritation crept into her tone, he gave her a pass. Her sister was missing, and he was asking what she perceived as an inane question. "Humor me," he said politely. "I'm an investigator." She gave him an exasperated sigh. "It came from Scotland. My seven-times great-grandmother, Lindsey Hughes, received it as a wedding gift from her parents. Her husband had it shipped here. I think I heard once that the cabin was built around it." Olivia stared out the window into the forest. A tear trickled down her face. "I'm not sure about that part of the story though." She swiped at her cheek. "Let's go down to the mine and look around. Amber could be there."

He texted the additional info to David. Then Connor asked, "Does she go to the mine regularly?"

"She's hunted fossils on every inch of the property. Although she doesn't believe she'll find any, she can't stay away. She'll sit on a rock at the highest point and stare at the mountains as though she's waiting for them to speak to her."

"You said no one has been in the mine for years. She wouldn't decide to check it out on her own, would she?"

Olivia shook her head. "Never."

"Not even if the weather turned bad while she was there?"

She stooped to pick up Amber's tools and repacked them. "She'd come back to the cabin. But wherever she went, she'd never leave her tools behind. Look at this mess. When it comes to her gear, she's pickier than I am about my shoes." Olivia zipped the backpack and hugged it to her chest. "Something is wrong with Amber." Olivia glanced up at Connor. "We've got to find her."

The clues—a box, a sudden disappearance, a peat smell—were leading him toward a conclusion that didn't require leaps in logic, that wasn't at all farfetched, and one that no member of the MacKlenna Clan wanted to hear right now.

"Let's go to the mine," he said. "How far away is it?"

"Did you see the log steps in the back?"

"Yeah. Do they lead down to the mine?"

"It's the most direct route, but if you have supplies to move from the mine to the cabin, you can take a mule along the path that winds its way down there. It's twice as long though."

"Why didn't they build the cabin closer to the mine?"

"There's a foundation for a one-room cabin. Either my ancestors originally lived there, or the miners did. But this is such a beautiful spot. It's easy to see why they built a larger cabin here." She stood and hung Amber's backpack on a pegboard near the door. "I need to tell the sheriff what's going on."

Bringing the sheriff in on this situation could be a disaster, much like what happened to Amy Spalding's boyfriend last year. But Connor couldn't tell Olivia not to call the sheriff when it would give her peace of mind, which was more than he could do.

"Let's go to the mine and search Amber's usual haunts," he said. "At least we can tell the sheriff we looked for her. It will take him a few hours to round up a search party and get here."

"I disagree. Waiting will only delay him. We need to notify him now. He could be up here with a search team by the time we look around the mine entrance and surrounding property."

"What's his name?"

"Sheriff Joshua Hall," she said.

Connor did a Google search for the sheriff's phone number and placed the call. The sheriff answered, and after introducing himself and explaining the situation, Connor put the call on speaker and asked, "Do you have a search team who can come up here?"

The sheriff was silent for a moment before asking, "How well do you know Amber?"

"I've never met her. I'm here with her sister Olivia."

"So Olivia didn't tell you her sister has disappeared before and always comes home?"

Connor scowled at Olivia. Then to the sheriff he said, "The past is not prologue, Sheriff."

"What the hell does that mean?"

"Just because Amber has disappeared in the past and returned home safely doesn't mean it will happen this time. The outcome could be quite different. This disappearance has to be treated as the first time."

"Detective O'Grady, once or maybe twice, I could go with your theory"—incredulity laced the sheriff's deep voice—"but Amber has a lifetime history of this."

Olivia glanced at the floor, hugging herself.

"I had ten people up there last year," the sheriff continued. "We searched hundreds of acres. Finally, she came home on her own. Two years before that, we searched for a day and a half before she came back. She's disappeared a dozen times that I know of. She comes home with a big bag of fossils and apologizes for upsetting her family." He paused a moment before continuing, and Connor shot an even darker glance at Olivia. "The weather forecast is calling for rain tomorrow and the next day. As soon as it lets up, I'll bring a search team up there."

Connor was livid. He'd never met a law enforcement officer who refused to help. The sheriff was dishing up a side of vindictiveness for all the times he'd come up to search for Amber, only to have her come back on her own.

Connor punched the disconnect button and counted to ten to control his anger at the sheriff, and another ten to control his anger at Olivia. When he was reasonably calm, he asked, "Why in the hell didn't you tell me Amber had a history of disappearing?"

"Because it doesn't matter," Olivia said sharply. "Just because she's never been in danger before doesn't mean she's not this time. Isn't that what you just told the sheriff?"

He sat on the edge of the couch and looked her in the eye. "You should have told me."

She squared off with him as a visible display of emotion tightened her face. It wasn't confined to a lift of an eyebrow or barely visible frown. This was a full-blown, teeth-baring explosion. "You insisted on coming up here. I didn't trick you. My sister is missing, and I'm worried as hell. If you don't believe she's in trouble, you can ride down that damn mountain and drive her truck back to Denver."

Connor bristled. He had never heard her cuss. Not even when she broke a fingernail, or got locked out of her car, or had a piece of property sold out from under her. He modulated the tone of his voice. "I can't do this job without all the facts. You stand to make over a million dollars in commission when the MacKlenna Corporation buys a ranch. Why lie to me and risk that? Be honest with me, Olivia."

"I find that insulting. Do you think I care about a commission when my sister's life might be in danger?"

"This isn't about a commission. This is about lying. And you lied to me."

"I didn't lie to you."

He iced her with a cool gaze. "Lies of omission are still lies. I've been in law enforcement most of my life. I take all disappearances seriously. What else aren't you telling me?"

"Nothing. If you want to help, you have to believe me." It was said softly, but there was an ultimatum in her statement. If he wasn't going to believe her, he needed to get the hell out. She looked down at her hands, which were turning red from all the twisting and rubbing she was doing.

His cell phone rang, and the display flashed David's name and number. "O'Grady." He elbowed his way through their anger, zinging in the air like charged molecules before a rainstorm, and hurried out to the porch to speak privately.

"I confirmed the box is identical to Kenzie's," David said. "I thought as much but wanted to compare yer picture to her puzzle box."

"What's your gut telling you?" Connor asked.

"Another brooch has shown up. Let's keep this between us for now. I need a few hours to dig into Amber's background. What's the situation there?"

"Amber has a history of wandering off. The sheriff has searched for her several times, but she always comes home on her own. He refuses to come up here today."

"It's his job. What's his excuse?" David asked.

"An approaching storm."

"That's even more reason to get up there and look for her."

"Are you playing devil's advocate?"

"He's a professional," David said. "The sheriff needs to do his job. But personally, I'd rather he stayed away. We don't need him up there looking for someone he'll never find." David was quiet for a moment. Then, "What does Amber tell her family when she comes home?"

"That she's been fossil hunting."

"Maybe she's been traveling for years. Did ye think of that?"

"I did, but she wouldn't have left the evidence on the floor. She would have put the box back and returned the cap to the breast beam. Olivia claims she's never seen the box. As close as the sisters are, they would have shared the secret."

"Maybe she did, and Olivia has always stayed behind to cover for Amber. Let me talk to Elliott. I'll call ye back."

Connor stood there for a few minutes, watching dark clouds chase away the sun. Was it possible Amber found a brooch years ago and this wasn't her first trip to the past? No. He shook his head as if answering someone else's question. His logical mind wouldn't let him believe Amber was an experienced time traveler. His gut told him she was whisked away unprepared.

Olivia joined him on the porch. "I have to put the horses up. If you're going back down the mountain, you should go now."

He turned her to face him and tipped her chin with his finger, so she couldn't avoid eye contact. "I know you're worried, but I don't appreciate being lied to. I'm here to help, so let's play from the same sheet of music. Where do you want to search first?"

"Are you sure?"

"Dammit." He took a step back and drew a deep breath. He had to control his voice and not use his detective's tone, meant to intimidate. "If I wasn't, I'd tell you. I don't play games, Olivia."

She burrowed her hands beneath the folds of her shirt to either keep from smacking or hugging him. He didn't know. And the intense look in her eyes didn't give any hint of what she was thinking. A beat or two passed between them before she took a step toward him, her hand raised slightly, to touch his arm in an expression of reconciliation.

"I'm sorry I lied. I should have been honest with you, but I was afraid you'd take the same position as the sheriff, and I really wanted you to come with me."

He couldn't keep from responding to her, and so he did what he probably shouldn't do and kissed her forehead, letting his lips linger there if only for a moment. To him, the kiss said it all; he wanted to be there, he wanted to help, he wanted to protect her, and he expected honesty.

"I'm here," he said softly against her skin. "Since I won't be riding down the mountain, we should put the horses up."

"Let's start with that, then see what the weather does. Black clouds are rolling in and thunder is rumbling in the distance. I don't mind the rain, but thunder and lightning scare my horse"—Olivia kicked at clods of dirt on the porch—"and me, too."

Until today, she'd seemed invincible to him—polished and professional. Now he knew the truth. Her Kryptonite was her sister and a little bit of thunder and lightning.

"Do storms bother Amber?"

"She and her horse are friendly herd mates during a storm. Not much scares her. You could pick her up and drop her anywhere and she'd acclimate seamlessly. I don't get how we could have been raised the same yet act so differently in situations. She could have lived happily in this cabin in the 1800s. Not me. I like my creature comforts."

"Why do you come up here then?"

"I love the solitude. I love the mountains. I love the fresh air. But after a couple of days, I get antsy. I don't like being isolated from the world."

"So you miss electricity."

"And hot showers." She headed back inside. "Let me grab ponchos so we won't get soaked." He followed her inside where she snatched two ponchos off the pegboard and handed one to him. "This is oilskin-treated waterproof cotton. You won't get wet."

"I don't mind rain, and thunder and lightning don't scare me."

"Good to know," she said.

He removed his hat and slipped on the poncho, then left the cabin, canting the cowboy hat back onto his head.

After the horses were happily munching their oats, Olivia and Connor began their descent down the mountain toward the mine. Each step of the staircase was made from the flat side of half a log. They were old and narrow, and the corners were time-worn, but they were sturdy, solidly built.

"I really am sorry I didn't tell you about Amber. I get so upset when she does this, and I sort of wig out. I can't help it. She's my little sister and my responsibility."

"How old is she?"

"Thirty-two."

"She's an adult and a successful lawyer. She's not your responsibility."

Olivia continued climbing down the steps. "Saying she's not doesn't change what I believe. When I was six, she wandered away for the first time—"

"So, going missing isn't an adult pattern of behavior? It's a lifetime pattern."

"But she's never missed work or an obligation before. This time is different."

"Where did she go the first time?"

"We were playing while Dad and Granddaddy were cutting wood to shore up the mine shaft. Amber vanished. I panicked and screamed. Dad found her minutes later. She was sitting on the floor of the mine stacking rocks. She was oblivious to the danger. I got reamed out. She got hugs and kisses. What does that tell you?"

"That the punishment and rewards should have been reversed. But I can see how that experience would make an impression on a six-year-old."

They reached the bottom step. Directly ahead loomed the towering A-shaped timbers of the main headframe. It was buttressed with a large beam. Painted on the beam were the words—PRIVATE PROPERTY KEEP OUT.

"That's it?" he asked, pointing. "A bunch of boards that say keep out? I don't see much to explore."

"In the 1870s there was a saw mill, cabin, office, quarters for the miners, and a kitchen of sorts. It was a big operation. You can see the foundations for some of the structures, but that's about it. Unlike other mine sites, the family cleaned this one up decades ago and properly disposed of old equipment and ore bins."

"I don't get why Amber would come down here," he said.

Olivia pointed off to the right. "See that boulder up there? That's where she likes to sit and look at the rugged foothills of the Rockies and sketch what she imagines the land looked like millions of years ago. The landscape we see today is largely the product of uplift and erosion over the last eighteen million years. She's got a notebook with sketches that illustrate the geologic evolution of Colorado."

"And dinosaur bones," he added.

"She's dug all over the state and continues to find fossils."

"Just Colorado."

"Her focus is only on Colorado now. When she was in college, she participated in digs all around the United States, Africa, Asia, and Europe."

Connor glanced around the mine site. "How does she get to the boulder?"

"It's pretty easy to reach. Come on. I'll show you."

They took a path through the forest, climbing up the other side of the mine property, through irregular tree growth and a waterfall, until the landscape leveled off. They walked out onto the top of a flat boulder where he leaned against a jagged finger of a rock, nearly twice his height. It stood sentinel at the ridgeline.

"This is it. Amber's perch," Olivia said.

"I can see why she comes up here. Even on an overcast day, the view is spectacular." He looked down, far down. "It's higher than it seemed."

"I don't have a fear of heights, but I don't like it up here. Amber was forbidden to come up, but when Dad and Granddaddy realized they couldn't stop her, they taught her how to do it safely. Let's go. It makes me nervous."

"Is there any other path to take, or any other place she'd go to from here?"

"She forges her own path."

"How come I'm not surprised?" Connor cupped his hands at the sides of his mouth and yelled, "Amber." Her name echoed, bouncing off the surrounding mountain ridge. "Amber." He wasn't sure what to expect, but the haunting silence wasn't among his expectations. After a long moment, they turned and walked back through the woods, to the patter of a light rain falling on the dead leaves in their path.

"Where else do you want to look?" he asked.

Olivia glanced at him, an expression of grim determination on her flushed cheeks, so unlike her usual warm, approachable smile. "There's a cave about a quarter mile from here. It's a bit of a hike, but since it's going to rain, we'll have to wait."

He was aware of her standing close. Not touching him in any way. Yet he felt her fingertips on his skin, imagined her lips against his. "I don't mind the rain."

"It's too dangerous. I recommend we go back to the cabin."

They climbed back up the steps. By the time they reached the top, the first large raindrops pattered into the dirt, spreading to the size of silver dollars, and sending up explosions of dust and yard debris. Within moments, the rain blew into the clearing in force, coming down in thick, cold sheets like a wide moving wet wall.

The poncho kept his upper body dry, but dampness crawled up his legs and soaked the heavy cotton that clung to his skin. Rivulets ran off his hat brim and mingled with the droplets that fell from the darkening sky, slapping his face and chilling the back of his neck.

As they reached the porch, a bolt of lightning crackled, electrifying the air and ripping apart the sky. The lightning was followed closely by a deep rumble of thunder. He shook the rain from his poncho and hat, then wiped sweat and wet from his face with a handkerchief.

She removed her poncho, shook off the rain, then entered the cabin, glancing around the room again. Letting out a frustrated sigh, she returned the poncho to the hook before peeling off her riding gloves one finger at a time.

"If you start a fire, I'll fix a late lunch." She glanced at him. "Look at you. You're soaked. I'm so sorry. We should be walking around a beautiful ranch right now. Instead, you're stuck in a hundred-year-old cabin." She slapped the soaked gloves down on a table near the door. Wet leather met wood, sounding like a hand smacking skin. "This isn't what you planned for the day."

He hung up his poncho and hat. "My days rarely proceed as planned." He reached for her shoulders, caressed them. "I'm used to a flexible schedule. Although being in a cabin in the Rockies—*with a beautiful woman*—is a bit unusual, but I'm glad I'm here with you."

She reached up and patted both of his hands, her fingers slightly chilled despite the gloves she'd worn. "I'm glad you're here, too."

Her parted lips made for a perfectly kissable mouth. He was like a damn teenager on a first date, unsure of what to do. Before he could commit to a kiss, her lips closed, she removed her hands, and he eased his grip in response. He had hoped she wanted to connect in the most human of needs, the simple touch of skin to skin. But he was wrong. Even her attempt at a half smile was gone now.

"There are some of Dad's sweatpants in the armoire in the bedroom unless they've been stolen since the last time I was here." She lit one of the lanterns and the comforting smell of lamp oil permeated the air. The lantern glowed, throwing a soft mellow light over the cabin and its furnishings.

How many times would he put himself out there before he got it through his thick skull that she wasn't interested in anything beyond… Business? Friendship? If he continued to play the role of a fool, then he deserved the coldest of shoulders.

He masked his frustration, giving her an excuse to walk away. "Go change while I start the fire."

"Are you sure?"

He waved her away, not looking in her direction to hide any hurt that might spark in his eyes. "Go, before you get chilled."

"There should be enough kindling in the bucket to get a fire going. I'll bring in more later."

Connor set two logs on top of the grate and tossed in a handful of kindling. Once the fire was burning evenly, he dropped in a handful of softwood kindling between the hardwood logs. He had a blazing fire going by the time Olivia returned wearing black, form-fitting yoga pants.

She moved to stand in front of the fire and rubbed her hands. "Nice going."

His gaze slid over her ass, down her hamstrings to her muscular calves, then his eyes cut away quickly. "Easy enough to do with this kind of wood. I'll bring in more while I'm still wet."

She left the warm spot in front of the fire and crossed the room to the kitchen sink. "I'll get the coffee going while you're out." The coffee grinder sat on the table, the beans in the pie safe. She dumped the beans in the grinder and began to grind vigorously. The smell of fresh ground coffee soon spread through the cabin.

Connor settled Olivia's father's damp hat on his head once again, thankful he hadn't turned down the offer to borrow it. "Do you think you could rustle up a classic Italian hero sandwich? I'm starving."

"I thought you were Irish."

"I am, but my friend, Pete Parrino, is Italian. He got me started on them: prosciutto, capicola, sopressata, marinated mushrooms and peppers, and fresh mozzarella." Connor kissed his fingers. "*Delizioso.*"

She laughed. "How about baked salmon with a parmesan herb crust, scalloped potatoes, and fresh asparagus?"

"Add strawberry shortcake to that menu and I'll have died and gone to heaven even without a hero sandwich. I'm so hungry, I'll eat whatever you've got."

"Lunch will be ready when you get back." She pointed to the corner near the fireplace. "There's a leather log carrier over there if you want to load it up."

"Sure."

He stepped down the porch steps into the now-saturated yard and sloshed over to the wood pile. While he was gathering firewood, he filled the log carrier twice, leaving one load on the covered porch. When he went back inside the cabin, the mouth-watering aroma made his stomach growl.

He poked at the fire and threw on another log, pleased with how well it was burning. He didn't grow up with a fireplace in his family home in New York, but the guest house on MacKlenna Farm had a large one, and he was becoming more adept at building fires.

"I put hot water in the pitcher on the wash stand. You can clean up in the bedroom."

He brushed the wood shavings from his hands, letting the debris fall into the fire. "Thanks. My mother, rest her soul, would disown me if I came to the dinner table this dirty."

The water was steamy, and the soap had a natural, woodsy scent. Next to the washbowl was a wash kit complete with a new toothbrush, toothpaste, dental floss, lotion, talcum powder, razor, deodorant, small bottle of shave oil, and medicated shampoo—everything needed for an overnight stay in the mountains, except for a half-dozen condoms.

Dream on, cowboy.

On the other side of the washbowl, the handles of a natural-bristled hairbrush and matching mirror gleamed in the lantern light. He picked up the brush and ran his fingers along the scalloped edge. The handles of the brush and mirror were whispered reminders of the two metals that brought miners to Leadville—gold discovered in the early 1860s was later overshadowed by the silver rush that followed, the rush that brought Olivia's ancestors to the mountains.

He stripped down to his boxer briefs and washed his face, letting the layer of splattered mud and sweat from the day slide away. He moved on to his arms and chest. Then, reasonably clean, he dressed in the cotton sweatpants and black T-shirt she'd left on the bed. Refreshed, he returned to the kitchen to find her glowing in candlelight, and the aromas from the plated food added to a delicious shudder of anticipation.

He held the chair for her then took a seat across the table. "If this came from a package that will keep for twenty-five years, I'm sold. The salmon smells like it's been cooked perfectly. My compliments to the chef."

"As soon as we find her, you can tell her yourself."

They finished eating in silence and afterward took their coffee to sit in the rockers in front of the fire. "Is there any other place you want to search for Amber besides the cave?"

"There are three sites that I can think of. She's dug in all three but keeps going back. They are farther than the cave. Assuming this squall doesn't last long, we'll barely have time to get to the cave and back before the sun sets."

Connor's phone rang. He excused himself and went into Olivia's parents' bedroom before he answered David's call.

"I enlarged yer pictures of the box. There's a faint outline of a brooch on the velvet lining. The measurements are identical to the other brooches. It's safe to assume Amber has been whisked off somewhere. I'm still feeding information into the computer, but do ye have any ideas?"

Connor lowered his voice. "The Jurassic Period—a hundred fifty million to two hundred million years ago."

There was silence on the other end. Then finally David said, "Any chance it's some time closer to the last Ice Age?"

"I don't know. She's a mining lawyer with a degree in geology and a passion for dinosaurs. I don't have any idea where she could have gone, and if I press Olivia, she'll want to know why. Can you hack into her computer at work?"

"At work and home, but it'll take a few hours. If ye can get any information from Olivia, let me know."

Connor stood in front of the window and watched the torrent of rain for several minutes. He had been critical of Olivia for lying to him. Wasn't he doing the same to her? She'd been afraid of his reaction if he knew Amber had a history of disappearing. He was equally afraid of Olivia's reaction if he told her Amber had disappeared again, but this time she'd gone too far for them to reach without a well-planned rescue.

Olivia had nodded off in the rocking chair, her head tilted to one side. She was beautifully silhouetted by the lantern's feeble glow. He picked up an afghan folded over a cedar chest and remained there a moment, beyond the reach of the lamplight, quietly studying her.

Sleep had relaxed the tightness in her face, but when she woke, it would return. Where could Amber have gone, and if Olivia was asked if she had any ideas, what would she say? He covered her with the blanket and gathered it close about her shoulders while he tried to puzzle out the answers. He didn't want to go on another adventure, but he would. And God, he hoped to hell it wasn't to the Jurassic Period.

He added more logs to the fire and idled there near the warmth for a few minutes, listening to the rain's steadying murmur and watching shadows and light from the lanterns leap up on the log walls of the cabin, as if they were trying to find chinks to crawl through and escape into the rainy night.

Olivia's hands dangled over the arms of the rocker. He sat in the other chair and took one of her warm hands in his. Her long, eloquent fingers with manicured nails fit handsomely in his palm.

She stirred when he lightly squeezed her fingers, but she didn't pull away.

For the tenth time at least, he checked his messages. Nothing from David in the last five minutes. Connor didn't like being out of the loop, but there was nothing he could do, except wait patiently.

While Olivia slept, Connor did a web search for Amber. Several images came up. Besides identical hazel-brown eyes, he could see the echoes of Olivia in the graceful swoop of Amber's eyebrows, balanced mouth, and no-nonsense nose. They were both extraordinarily beautiful and talented women. But it was Olivia's moderate anxiety disorder, exactly like his mother's anxiety over the O'Grady kids, that he found utterly irresistible. Olivia would be an awesome mother to some very lucky kids.

He let his thoughts go quiet, but his memories wouldn't be silenced. He saw his mom in the kitchen, her slender hands dancing through the air, weaving dreams for her children. Connor swallowed around the sudden lump in his throat and forced his memories to go quiet too. He closed the browser, pocketed his phone, and closed his eyes. Before he could take two easy breaths, he fell into a fitful sleep.

4

1878 Leadville, Colorado—Amber

WHEN THE CLAUSTROPHOBIC fog lifted, Amber was no longer on the floor of Hughes Cabin. She was squatting on a crate in a dirt-packed alley filled with a season's worth of animal excrement, empty boxes, and garbage. The stench made her gag. There was a buzzing in her ears, and her head throbbed. Where was she? Her bouncing gaze made her head ache even more—worse than a tequila hangover. And she should know. She'd footed the bill for more than one parade of Patrón shots.

The faint smell of new-hewn timber seeped from the adjoining buildings and tickled her nose. Hundreds of hooves, wheels, and boots churned up the dirt in a rutted thoroughfare that intersected with her muddy alley. Honky-tonk music blasted from a saloon and drowned out the thunder of boots as pedestrians hurried along crooked boardwalks. A swirl of newsboys banged out of a nearby emporium hawking the daily news.

A mean-looking man idled nearby, his sheepskin coat hung open and his thumbs hooked in a shell-belt sagging from a slim waist. Beneath the cowboy hat was a hard face shadowed by whiskers. A black cigar was clamped between his teeth. He looked like a character actor in a low-budget film. Matter of fact, the whole scene resembled a Spaghetti Western. Had she been called to audition for the role of damsel in distress or maybe Big Nose Kate—Doc

Holliday's sidekick? Amber could play Big Nose, but damsel in distress wasn't a good fit for her. All she had to do now was find the casting director and audition for the part.

As if having an out-of-body experience, she stepped up on the wooden boardwalk and stopped the first person who walked by. "Do you know where the casting director is?"

A pimple-faced teenager scratched his cheek. "Don't reckon I do."

"Good job with the dialect." She gave him a thumbs-up and kept walking, dodging actors dressed in period costumes. When she came upon a woman wearing a cute hat that came down to a point on her forehead, Amber stopped and asked, "Love your hat. Is that yours or did you get it from wardrobe?"

The woman's eyes roved over Amber's clothing, and an expression of disgust spread across her face. The woman untangled the veil wound up on her hat, pulled the netting down, and adjusted it smartly. "Hughes Store." She opened her parasol and shoved past Amber, crowding her toward the edge of the boardwalk.

"I'll stop by there. Thanks."

Amber was dazed by all that was happening around her. She glanced down the street toward the mountains and the recognizable rolling terrain of the western slope of the snow-capped Mosquito Range. Her mouth dropped. She knew exactly where she was.

"Say it ain't so, Joe."

The surrounding mountains held the city of Leadville in the palms of their hands: Mosquito Range in one, Sawatch Range in the other. But this wasn't the Leadville of her childhood, or her teenage years, or even the city in the twenty-first century. If a production company was filming a Western in Leadville, the set designer would win an Oscar.

Her legs turned to jelly. She needed to sit down before she collapsed in the thoroughfare and was run over by a freight wagon. A bench outside the batwing doors of a saloon stood vacant and looked reasonably clean. Maybe if she rested for a while, her out-of-control world would straighten upon its axis again. Or, maybe she'd wake-up from this weird dream and be back in Hughes Cabin.

The tinkling of piano keys and the smell of beer and cheap whiskey drifted out of the saloon. The skills of the pianist fell somewhere between beginner and never-played-before. The off-key rendition of "In the Evening By the Moonlight" brought a dose of reality to the surreal mix of fact and fantasy.

Her senses seemed to be working fine, down to the gnawing pain in her empty stomach. Whatever was going on with her didn't involve sleepwalking or dreaming. She wasn't ready to rule out the only other logical explanation—filming a movie. But as she glanced around, there were no cameras or crew members wearing normal clothes. No trailers for the actors. No refreshment tent with donuts and coffee. No costume designers. No makeup artists. If this wasn't a dream or audition, then she had fallen into a wormhole and gone back to a time before automobiles and electricity.

Hold up one dang minute...

Worms belonged in tequila bottles, not in outer space, where they captured unsuspecting humans and hurled them about like fast-pitched softballs.

Next to her, a handful of miners lurked outside the saloon entrance, their voices abuzz in a mixture of European accents. Their faces were gnarled and creased as pieces of petrified wood. Their clothes needed a good dunk in the river. Sad to say, but even with the services of a barber and the purchase of new clothes, the men could never make themselves presentable enough, even to a spinster's desperate father.

When one of the miners, a man with corn-silk hair and a longhorn mustache, mentioned finding a deep red stone mixed in with the silver in his mine, her head snapped up.

"Found it the other day," he said, smoothing the mustache curving around his mouth. "First, I threw it away, then changed my mind and snatched it back."

Another man, beset with a coughing fit, held out his hand. "Let me see it."

The miner hawked and spat off to the side before pulling a stone from his pocket. "Thought I'd give it to June over at the Silver Dollar. Matches her red hair."

Amber stood to get a look at the stone. Her knees nearly gave way and one of the men caught her elbow in a steadying grip. "May I see that?"

The miner extended his arm in her direction with the gemstone glinting in the palm of his leathery hand. Her fingers curled around the pear-shaped gem, red with a hint of pink.

"This is an exquisite piece of rare rhodochrosite. Fifteen, maybe sixteen carats. Where'd you say you found it?"

His face tightened, his eyes narrowed. "None of your business where." He grabbed it from her and shoved it back into his pocket.

"Hang on to it. One day it'll be very valuable," she said.

"It's valuable today. Give me two bits and you can keep it."

One of the other men laughed. "He's hopin' those two bits marry up and raise a litter of pennies, make him a millionaire like Mr. Tabor."

Horace Tabor? Leadville's silver king?

"If I had two bits, I'd give it to you." She patted her pockets. She didn't have a dollar. She didn't have a penny either. Neither did she have any rings or earrings. Then it all came back to her. The puzzle box. The broken loom. The odd words. The smelly fog. The disorienting twisting about. The brooch...

"Damn."

She shoved past the men and dashed back to the alley. *Where is it?* Frantically, she tossed the crate aside and raked her nails through the mud. *Where is it? Dammit.* Then she stopped and took a long breath. What was she doing? She knew better. This wasn't how you excavated anything. She needed to calm down, swallow her panic, and search methodically. Start at the beginning. That meant returning to her squatting position on the crate. Okay. That's where she was when she came out of the fog. So where was the brooch?

She looked at her hands. Right or left? Left. She was sure of that. She was also sure that when she came out of the fog, she had been leaning forward with her hands covering her face. If she dropped the brooch, it would have landed near her left foot. It wasn't there now. She must have stomped it into the mud.

What she needed was a shovel or a stick. With all the crates and garbage, surely there was something usable. She pilfered through several piles of garbage but didn't find anything sharp. How many times had she been on a dig without a specific tool in her field kit and had to improvise? Dozens.

She picked up a crate and threw it against the wall until it splintered. Then she stomped on the weakened sides until it broke apart. Using two of the thicker pieces, she squatted and dug where she believed the brooch had fallen out of her hand, probing the soft ground as if her last meal was buried in the muddy patch of alleyway.

The brooch had been in the breast beam for a century and a half and she'd lost it within a few hours. She was almost hyperventilating when the stick hit a hard surface. She stiffened. Was it the brooch or a rock? She tossed the sticks aside and used her hands, throwing her rules out with globs of mud.

Faster…faster…deeper…deeper.

She slung mud until she glimpsed the amber brooch. Relieved, she sagged against the wall, breathing heavily. When her heart rate returned to normal, she marched over to a horse trough and washed the brooch in icy water. To get mud out of the crevices, she needed her tools. The dental pick and brush must not have made it through the…whatever.

The brooch was her ticket home and she couldn't lose it again. She shoved it down deep into the pocket of her jeans. And for the first time thought of home. How was she going to get there? The brooch was cold now, icy as the water in the trough.

It had heated when she opened it earlier. The magic was gone. The wormhole, or whatever it was, had closed and she was stuck here. Or was she? Maybe all she had to do was open the stone and say the odd words. Why wonder about it? Just recite the words and go.

But…

Did she have to go yet? The man with the rare rhodochrosite

had offered the gemstone to her for only two bits. Just think of that. Two bits. Twenty-five cents. What a treasure for a rock hound like herself. But where was she going to get the money? She had nothing to sell, nothing but the clothes on her back. And as cold as it was, selling her clothes wasn't an option.

She returned to the sidewalk wondering about that quarter. Where could she get an afternoon job? She doubted anyone would want legal advice, but she could cook. What year was it, anyway? Did women work anywhere other than saloons and brothels?

Needing to catch her breath, she leaned against the side of a building and breathed in and out slowly. She'd grown up around Leadville, and the high altitude had never bothered her before today. Must be the wormhole's fault and would wear off soon enough.

The constant hammering all around her was driving her nuts, making it hard to think clearly. How could one town have so much building going on? And then it hit like a claw hammer to her pounding head. It had to be the early days of the silver boom, when the city mushroomed from a few hundred citizens to several thousand.

Massaging her forehead, she stepped to the top of a set of rickety stairs leading down to the next section of boardwalk and stretched, looking down the street toward the landmark Tabor Opera House—the finest theatre west of the Missouri—if you believed the old ads. And there it was on the corner of 2nd Street and Harrison Avenue, a three-story building constructed of stone, brick, and iron.

Her mind drifted back to the last performance she'd seen there. What was the date mentioned in the building's history printed on the first page of the playbill? Maybe in the late 1800s. But she was pretty sure that a few years prior to Horace Tabor building his opera house, bank, and hotel, the owners of Hughes Store built theirs. She glanced down the street in the opposite direction of the theatre and there it was…her seven-times great-grandparents' general store.

The claw hammer pounded her head again. The magic brooch had given her the chance to meet her ancestors. How could she go home without saying hello? She couldn't. Maybe she could work at their store, spend some quality time with Grandfather Craig and Grandmother Lindsey, and earn some money to buy the gemstone from the miner.

Then she remembered what else happened around this same time. It was as if the stone knew the precise moment to kick her out of the wormhole. Now she knew she couldn't leave yet.

If she stayed for a few days, she could be part of the discovery and naming of the first *Stegosaurus*. And, she could nosedive into the Royal Gorge War and possibly save her ancestors thousands of dollars. Okay, that would take more than a few days. More like several weeks, maybe months, but her head was swimming now with possibilities instead of throbbing with pain. But what about her family? Well, her parents were on a safari and wouldn't miss her for a while, but Olivia would be going berserk.

Would she really?

If it was the late nineteenth century, her immediate family wasn't even born yet. Amber could get into a debate over parallel universes, but frankly, that was a waste of time. She was here now, and Olivia was in the future. If Amber could keep that concept separate from what was transpiring here, she'd be fine and so would Olivia.

The thought of being in the thick of the early days of paleontology tickled every inch of her from eyebrows to toes. This was a once in a lifetime opportunity. Her hand slid into her pocket and fondled the brooch. It was still icy cold. Even if she wanted to go home, she doubted the portal would open. Maybe she was here for a cosmic reason. She let the symphony of Leadville's sights and sounds settle over her while she considered her situation further.

How about taking her analysis indoors before she froze to death? If she froze, whatever purpose she had for being here would be laid to rest in a pine box in Leadville Cemetery's free section known as pauper's field.

Before she could do anything, she had to line up food and lodging. The starving-street-person-thing wasn't a good fit for her. She needed a grubstake. Fortunately, she knew someone, or rather she knew of someone, with a reputation for grubstaking prospectors and entrepreneurs.

She didn't intend to prospect, although with her knowledge she could. That left entrepreneurship. She could put up a shingle and practice mining law, but she needed a license for that. Passing a bar exam in the nineteenth century wouldn't be hard, but would they give a woman a chance?

There was another problem she had to deal with. Although it didn't rank at the top with food and lodging, it was up there close. There was no hiding the fact that she was a woman dressed in men's clothing, especially with a braid trailing down her back, but jeans, flannel shirt, and canvas jacket weren't acceptable attire for a woman in the 1800s. She could get away with wearing trousers for a day, maybe two, but if she wanted to fit in and get along, she had to dress the part. Since she didn't particularly care what she wore, a plain cotton skirt to fit over her jeans would work fine.

There was one other thing she needed—a believable backstory. Who was she and where did she come from? The emerging city was a transient place that attracted nomadic adventurers daily. She was just one more. Her story didn't have to be elaborate. A simple, believable lie that wouldn't raise eyebrows would work, and it was likely no one would care enough to ask.

She could barely forge a path from one block to the next on the crowded walkway. Some pedestrians found it easier to get where they were going by walking in the disgusting street. The thick layer of mud, horse manure, and decaying vegetable matter kept her on the sidewalk. She checked out the windows of every store, looking for help wanted signs. It was a matter of matching her skills—cook, performer, lawyer—with the needs of a respectable business.

She wove her way down the boardwalk until she spotted a sign that brought her to a sudden stop, which caused a rear-end collision. Someone fell into her and pitched her forward. She hit the glass pane window of the Hughes Store, Purveyor of Fine Goods, Firearms, and General Merchandise. The glass rattled but didn't shatter. A man standing behind a long counter adjusted his wire-rim glasses and turned his full attention to her. She quickly regained her balance and pushed away from the window in a heat-rising panic. Was that Grandfather Craig? She'd never seen a picture of him or his wife Lindsey. If it was him, what would she say? "Hi, Gramps. I'm your granddaughter from the twenty-first century. Did you know there was a magical brooch hidden in your loom?"

Instead of going in to speak to him, she scampered away. Panicking was not in her nature. In her everyday life, she adjusted to situations. She had honed those character traits through years of working on digs around the world and meeting clients deep inside mines. Disagreements and misunderstandings were handled with aplomb. So why was she running away from a man she'd heard lovely stories about her entire life?

Because having a conversation with him would make this crazy adventure—real. It would make having no money, no home, no job—real. But it would also make the possibility of naming the first *Stegosaurus*, of meeting the famous Drs. Lakes, Marsh, or Cope—real. And it also meant the possibility of being involved in the Royal Gorge War litigation—real!

Those possibilities far outweighed having no money, no home, no job.

For a moment, hurrying along the weather-warped boards, jostled on all sides by passersby, she wasn't sure which direction to go. The oompahs and blats from a brass band competed with the constant hammering and jingling harnesses.

The boardwalk ended, and for the second time today, she was struck with indecision. She almost laughed. Wondering what to do about her job back in the twenty-first century was inconsequential now. Why had she given it so much power over her? She scratched her head, unable to answer. What should she do now? Go right, left, or straight ahead?

A man—tall and strikingly handsome—swept past her. "Excuse me," he said in a strong Scottish accent. He jumped over stacked crates and bounded into the street, dodging wagons, carriages, and pedestrians, running a five-second obstacle course in under two seconds. He leapt to the opposite boardwalk and in two strides entered Tabor's Bank of Leadville. Except for the lingering scent of sweet tobacco, she never would have known he passed by.

A large dog with a sandwich board sign attached to her—advertising an upcoming production at the Tabor Opera House—ran out into the street and startled a team of horses pulling a wagon. The spooked horses reared and jostled the members of the five-piece band riding in the back playing "Camptown Races." The jerking motion sent the drummer boy flying. He and his drum landed in the street, directly in the path of a freight wagon.

Fear clogged her throat. She couldn't wave. She couldn't move. She could barely breathe. Then she found her voice.

"Stop!"

She rocketed off the uneven boardwalk and sprinted toward the child. Her eyes darted between the boy and the approaching wagon.

"Stop!"

Could she get to him in time? Her arms pumped. Her lungs gasped. She ran full out. From the driver's viewpoint, he couldn't see the boy crawling toward the drum. From her viewpoint, she could see everything, even the clock ticking down the seconds...

Five—Her arms pumped faster than her legs.

Four—Every footfall landed in the thick spongy earth.

Three—Terror played out in vivid color—blood red.

Two—Her field of vision narrowed to only the boy in the street, his arms outstretched.

One—She ran with a single purpose. The wagons and the powerful beasts that pulled them no longer existed. She ran with her eyes and mind focused on one helpless child.

Mud from the horses' hooves splattered in her face as she reached down and grabbed the little drummer boy by the sleeve of his jacket and slung him backwards, mere moments before the freight wagon rumbled by.

"My drum!"

Amber pressed the boy's head against her shaking body, so he couldn't watch the wagon wheels smash his treasured instrument.

The pressure was so heavy in her chest, she thought the wheel had run over her too. It took a moment for the death-cheating scene to penetrate her numbed senses, and she struggled to catch her breath. The crack and splintering of the wood had the boy pushing away from her, but she held him tightly, afraid of what he might do, afraid he might try to collect the pieces of the smashed instrument—the head and shell and leather strap.

"My drum!" he cried, flailing his arms.

She shivered with a deep convulsive shudder. "I'm so sorry." She didn't let go of him, although her superwoman moment was fading, and she wouldn't be able to control him much longer. Never in her life had she tried to comfort a child. She was acting on memory alone, hearing her mom and her granny quieting her little girl cries.

"Shh. You're okay now," Amber said.

"No. I'm not." His shoulders slumped beneath her hands. "My drum's broken."

She kissed the boy's head, covered now in muddied blond curls. "But you're alive."

"I want my...drum."

"Noah!" a man yelled.

Amber's glance lifted to see a man bounding across the street. His long legs cut the distance to only a few strides. It was the same man who had passed her earlier smelling of sweet tobacco. His chiseled face was clenched tight in fear and mirrored the ghostly look of terror that spread and deepened around his dark blue eyes. His lowered to one knee and reached for the boy. She released her hold and Noah fell into his arms.

"Are ye hurt, lad?"

The shaking boy twisted around and pointed into the street. "No, but my drum's busted, Pa."

He rubbed Noah's head, arms, chest to confirm the truth of his son's statement. "Thankfully, ye're not." His gaze shifted to Amber. "Thank ye for what ye did."

"I was afraid..." Her breathing was still heavy and erratic, and the words puffed out with her breath. "I couldn't get to him."

"I saw him fall…" His voice broke. "But I couldn't get to him in time. He would have died—"

"He's safe now." She laid her hand on the man's muscular shoulder that trembled beneath his black duster. He held Noah tightly to his chest. She looked away, not wanting to intrude on the life-affirming moment. Calmness washed over her with every deep breath she took.

It took several minutes before Noah wiped his face, saying, "I'll miss my drum, Pa, but I can get on without it."

Noah's maturity surprised her. If she'd had any money, she would have taken him that very minute to the music store and bought every instrument he fancied. It was rare to see that level of maturity in adults. Coming from someone Noah's age said a lot about his character and even more about his parents. She wanted to give Noah a fierce hug and tell him everything would be all right.

"I'm sorry I couldn't save the drum." The mix of sadness and disappointment in her own voice rivalled the unnatural acceptance in Noah's.

Noah's father's eyes slowly came into focus. But something remained in the tightness of his jaw and the set of his shoulders that reflected deep sadness or regret. He touched two fingers to the corner of his cowboy hat, offering a brief salute.

"I'm Daniel Grant. Thank ye for what ye did."

His voice rolled over her, warm, almost sensual. She straightened, shaking off the spell of his voice, and mirrored his salute with two fingers together at the corner of her eyebrow like her cousin Trey had taught her.

"Amber Kelly."

There was more she wanted to say, but the pain in her chest was holding her breath hostage. Damn the altitude. Her feet came unstuck from the mud, and she splashed back a step to grab a hitching post for support and lowered herself to the raised boardwalk. Noah and his father joined her there, holding tightly to each other.

When she finally caught her breath she asked, "Did you see what happened?"

"I saw Noah fall. I didn't know the band was playing today, or I would have been there watching."

"It was only planned about an hour ago, Pa. I didn't have time to tell you."

Daniel kissed the top of Noah's head. "That's okay, lad."

"A dog wearing a sandwich board sign ran out into the street and scared the horses. The wagon jerked, and Noah was pitched out," Amber said.

"It was Mr. Tabor's dog, Ripley. I hope she's not hurt," Noah said.

The scene played out in Amber's mind again. She closed her eyes and reran the reel for the third time, searching for the dog. "She ran away," Amber said. "She wasn't hurt."

"I'm glad," Noah said, his breath hitching. "Ripley's my friend."

"Mr. Tabor should take better care of his dog. Matter of fact, since he's the owner, he's responsible for damages and should buy you a replacement drum."

"I doubt Mr. Tabor will do that since it was an accident."

To Amber those were fighting words. "Mr. Tabor can be held liable for injuries caused by his dog, whether the dog bites someone, causes personal injury, or damages property."

Daniel pushed to his feet—coming to his full height—and so did she, but he was a good foot taller. There was a hint of rawhide toughness in the broad, strong shoulders tapering to narrow hips and long powerful legs. He was dressed in a long black duster, black suit over a white shirt, and a gray vest.

"Mr. Tabor is a businessman, but I doubt he'll accept responsibility."

She brushed off what mud she could and flipped her braid back over her shoulder. "I know the law, Mr. Grant, and Mr. Tabor can be sued."

Noah moved to stand in front of his father, and the resemblance between the two, sans mud and beard, was striking. Noah was his father's mini-me. He had the same set to his jaw, high cheekbones, and strikingly blue, almost navy eyes, set apart by the bridge of a princely nose. If she had truly stepped onto a movie set, Noah's father, in his middle- to late-thirties, would be the sexy star of the film, regardless of whether it needed an astronaut for a space odyssey, a cowboy for a western, or a blood thirsty warrior for a Viking adventure. He had that timeless look.

"If he's sued," Daniel said, "no jury in this town will hold him legally responsible."

"Maybe not. But the law is on your side."

Daniel's handsome face took on a frown. "If I had a lawyer with yer conviction, I'd have a suit filed today."

"If I had a law license to practice here, I'd offer to do it for you."

Noah picked up his drumsticks and wiped them on his pants. Drumsticks and no drum was like a boy without a dog. Her mind replayed the sequence of events. Was there something she missed? If she had jumped off the sidewalk a second earlier or sprinted faster, could she have saved Noah and his drum? If she had kicked it, the drum would have been damaged but not busted.

On reflection, her ifs didn't match the evidence. She'd jumped off the sidewalk as soon as she identified the problem. She didn't delay, and she ran as fast as she was capable. And if she had kicked the drum, she would have lost the split second she needed to jerk Noah out of the way. She had taken the correct steps, but she would see the loss in Noah's beautiful blue eyes in her dreams.

Noah tugged on Amber's jacket sleeve. "You're a lawyer?"

"I am, yes."

"Lawyers get licenses from Judge Adams, and you could get yours from him. Then sue Mr. Tabor."

"Judge Adams isn't back from Denver," Daniel said.

"He's back, Pa. He was walking into the courthouse when the wagon rode by. He had an armload of books and nodded to me, but I couldn't wave back because I was playing"—Noah's lower lip quivered—"I was playing my drum."

Amber rubbed her hand through Noah's hair, making it stand up like the bushy quills on a porcupine. "I should clean up a bit and put on a dress before I see the judge. He might not take me seriously the way I look now."

"He's not like that. He cares what you think, not what you look like." Noah took her hand. "Come on. I'll explain that we have an emergency."

Amber glanced at Daniel, hoping he would intervene. He didn't. "I should make an appointment. It isn't proper to go to court in mud-splattered jeans. Practicing law is a serious matter. And it would be disrespectful to meet a judge looking like I do right now."

"Ma always said, 'Don't put off for tomorrow what you can do today.' You don't have to worry about the judge. He's very kind."

"Noah's right about Judge Adams."

Noah broke away from his father and ran down the sidewalk.

"Come back here," Daniel yelled.

"Where's he going?" she asked.

"I reckon he's gone to the courthouse. It's been hard on Noah since his ma died."

She quickly caught on to the subtext and didn't respond for a moment. "I didn't lose my mom, but I was very attached to my grandmother. I don't think the hole in my heart has ever filled up. It's filled in some, but it's still there."

Daniel squeezed the bridge of his nose and didn't say anything for a moment or two. Finally, he said, "My father sent the drum from Scotland. It was a family heirloom and had been played during the Uprising. It had great sentimental value."

"I guess learning to play the instrument helped Noah get over the worst of his grief." Like Noah, she had taught herself how to weave after her grandmother died, to get over the worst of it.

"Now that he's lost the drum, I'm not sure what he'll do."

She held Daniel with a hard stare. "Come on. Let's go get Noah." She didn't know how, but she was going to get Noah a new drum. There was money to be made in Leadville, and she intended to make some for herself. She needed funds to travel to Morrison and possibly to Cañon City. She just had to match her skills with the city's needs.

They reached the steps to the courthouse and glanced up. The cupola was topped with a statute of Lady Justice standing above all else in town. That gave her hope and inspiration that she could help Noah.

"Mr. Grant. I'm going to try to fix this."

"Do ye have a plan?" He looked at her, a bit perplexed.

She hurried up the steps. "I always have a plan."

He held the door and she entered the building. "Good."

She turned back, scratched a spot below her ear, and smiled. "Except this time, I don't. I'm going to wing it."

Daniel pressed his lips together so tightly that his mouth was barely visible in the depths of his luxuriant and well-tended clipped beard. He nodded for her to step over to the side, away from the dozen or so men transacting city business in the corridor. There was no sign of Noah.

"I don't know what wing it means, but if ye're going in unprepared, that's not wise."

She glanced at the office door with Judge Adams' name painted on the door. "Noah's been in there for over five minutes in an *ex parte* conference. He could already have prejudiced his case. I'll have to play it as I see it." She gave Daniel's arm a gentle squeeze before crossing the hall and knocking on the Judge's door.

A male voice said, "Come in."

Daniel opened the door, removed his hat, and stepped aside for Amber to precede him into the judge's chambers. The pungent scent of sweetness and spice unfurled from the bowl of the judge's pipe and reminded her of her grandfather. She glanced around the office, but Noah wasn't there. Daniel frowned, but then his face relaxed. He obviously knew something she didn't. If he wasn't going to ask about Noah, she wouldn't either.

The judge finished straightening a set of books in his bookcase and walked heavily for such a rail-thin man toward his desk. He flung himself into a wooden swivel chair, which squeaked as he rocked in it. "How can I help you, Daniel?"

While Amber debated how to handle the uncomfortable situation, Daniel took the lead and said, "John, this is Miss Kelly, a lawyer from…"

"Chicago," Amber said.

"Miss Kelly has agreed to represent me, but she doesn't have a license in Colorado."

The judge raised speculative eyebrows toward Daniel. "I don't hand out licenses to everyone who requests them. Candidates must stand for a bar examination. Is your lawyer prepared to do that?"

Amber gave a slight nod to Daniel, indicating she could take it from there. "I am, your honor."

The judge eyed her with a measured glance. "I assume you've read the law or you wouldn't be here. The last lawyer who stood before me for an exam now has a successful Leadville practice. He has an uncanny ability to guess which way the judge and jury will lean. You might want to visit him after you leave here. So, Miss Kelly, where'd you study the law?"

Why did he have to ask a question that forced her to lie right off the bat? She broke away from his gaze and stared out the window, noting the whitewash on the building next door. It seemed so close that if she reached out her hand, she could touch the painted boards. Whitewash. Coverup. Gloss over. How appropriate that her mind was drifting in that direction.

The judge's comment butted the line between statement and question, allowing her to respond with a simple yes, or an explanation—in this case, a bigger lie. Since Yale didn't allow women in the 1870s she had to come up with another school.

Whitewash…

She shifted her stance slightly and arranged her features into a semblance of calm confidence. Her knees didn't knock, but they came damn close. "I attended Smith College near Hartford."

Coverup…

"I also studied geology under Dr. Marsh of the Peabody Museum of Natural History at Yale…College. Unofficially, since they didn't admit women."

Gloss over...

"Then, following in the footsteps of Ada Kepley, I earned a Bachelor of Laws from the Union College of Law in Chicago."

The muscles in her neck and back tensed in expectation of a karate chop between her shoulder blades that would come quickly and expectantly when her lies were exposed.

Because lies always were...

The judge put his pipe between his teeth with a click and hooked a long bony finger around the stem to support the bowl while he puffed. Then he removed it, and she saw for the first time the odd notch in his stained teeth probably worn by years of smoking. He returned to the bookcase. As he perused the shelves of law books, she was treated to a view of the small bald spot on the back of his head.

"Ah, here it is." He pulled down a book, held his pipe between his teeth while he paged through it, then smoothed it out before returning to his desk. Using the pipe as a pointer to emphasize his words, he asked, "Your first question, Miss Kelly is, 'What is the nature of law in general?'"

Amber considered the question and how to frame her answer. This was much like the two-hour defense of her master's thesis. And like then, she knew the material inside out and upside down. If she took her time, thought through the questions, she'd answer them accurately.

"In its most general and comprehensive sense," she began, "the law signifies a rule of action; and is applied indiscriminately to all kinds of action, whether animate or inanimate, rational or irrational. And it is that rule of action, which is prescribed by some superior, and which the inferior is bound to obey."

He closed the book and set it to one side of the polished top of his walnut desk. "How is a rule distinguished from a compact or agreement?"

"A compact is a promise proceeding from us, law is a command directed to us. The language of a compact is, 'I will, or will not, do this.' A law, however, says, 'Thou shall or shalt not, do it.'" She continued, and for the next ninety minutes the judge peppered her with questions about the rights of persons, the rights of things, private wrongs, and public wrongs. She stood attentively in front of his desk, hands clasped behind her back, and answered each thought-provoking question. She recognized some of them as coming from Sir William Blackstone's *Commentaries on the Laws of England*, the most important legal treaties ever written in the English language. The rest were questions about applying the law in cases that had come before his court.

Finally, he sat back in his chair. His pipe had long since burned out. He turned the pipe over and knocked the dottle neatly out against the edge of the ashtray on his desk. "I've examined dozens of lawyers during my twenty years on the bench. You are the first woman, and surprisingly one of the most intelligent. I look forward to having you in my court, Miss Kelly. Now raise your right hand and repeat after me."

As instructed, she raised her hand and for the second time in her career repeated the attorney's oath: "I solemnly swear or affirm that I will support the Constitution of the United States and the Constitution of the State of Colorado, and that I will faithfully discharge the duties of an attorney and counselor of law to the best of my knowledge and ability."

The judge placed a blank sheet of paper on his desk, followed by a nib pen, before pulling an inkwell toward him. He tapped the uninked pen on the blotter, staring at her as if to reassure himself that what he was about to do was the right thing. Reaching a decision, he dipped the pen, once and then again, before writing several lines in a forward-slanting script. He then signed and dated the document. After sprinkling sand over the writing, he blew off the excess. When he was satisfied the ink was dry, he meticulously folded the paper into thirds and slid it into an envelope.

"Here's your license, madam. If I have an opportunity to recommend you, I will in all good conscience. Good luck."

5

1878 Leadville, Colorado—Amber

DURING THE BAR examination, Daniel had stood quietly at the rear of the room. His presence made her nervous. She'd considered asking him to step outside and wait. But after the judge asked his first question, she slid into a zone, and forgot about him being there.

Now it was over, and Amber was a member of the nineteenth-century and twenty-first century Colorado Bar. How many other lawyers could say that? Zip, zero. Just her. As a lawyer and lover of history, her dad would be so proud of her. The day she and Olivia were sworn in as members of the Colorado Bar, he had stood at the rear of the room and beamed with pride. Today, if he'd been present, his smile would be ear to ear.

Amber left the judge's chambers with Daniel and stood outside in the corridor, almost trembling with excitement. "Where's Noah? I want to tell him I have a license and can represent him."

Daniel's eyes blinked rapidly as if his brain was struggling to process what he had witnessed. He looked away, shaking his head. Then after a moment, he gazed at her again, his eyes no longer blinking. Either he now accepted what he had witnessed as true, or else he shoved his confusion into another portion of his brain to take out and dissect later.

"Noah was in the closet."

She pointed toward the judge's door. "In there? In the judge's office? In the closet?"

Daniel guided her toward the exit. "The closet door was slightly ajar. If ye noticed, it was next to where the judge was straightening his bookcase. The judge is meticulous. The books didn't need straightening."

If she had spent time around children she might understand Noah's behavior, but she was at a loss and couldn't even dig up a similar childhood experience to draw from. "I don't get it. Why did he hide?"

"I don't know what he was thinking, but after ten minutes, I know he was asking that same question. The lad has never been accused of having idle hands. From the time he wakes up until he falls asleep, he's earning money, keeping up with his studies, or helping our landlady, Mrs. Garland, around the house."

"How old is he? He's very mature, or at least I thought so until you told me that he hid in the closet."

Daniel's lips curled up into a smile, holding the look of a proud dad. "Ten."

She had just been outfoxed by a ten-year-old who tricked her into appearing before the judge and lying to him. She wasn't happy about that, but at least she was in a position now to get a replacement drum.

"Should we leave the building and let him escape the closet?"

"He probably went out the window as soon as we left the room and is sitting on the steps, pretending he's been there all along."

She shuddered at the thought of the little guy dangling from the window ledge before dropping to the ground. She could see herself perched on Amber's rock. Going up there as a kid had been a dumb stunt, too, but it didn't mean she had to condone Noah's behavior.

"I can't believe the judge allowed him to do that, especially after almost getting run over by a wagon."

Daniel shrugged. "It's just a wee window."

She gave a brief, shocked laugh.

Daniel clapped his hat on his head, and they exited the building.

He was right about Noah. The boy was sitting on the steps with the dog that had caused the accident. He was removing the sandwich board by untying the straps attached to the placards. Seeing his dad, Noah pulled stiffly to his feet.

Daniel looked at his son with a cautious eye.

"I heard you went to see the judge. Did you get a license?" Noah asked.

Noah's stiffness alarmed her. In the past two hours, he'd fallen out of a wagon, been jerked up and pushed aside, and then dropped out of a window. The muscles in his back and shoulders were probably strained.

"Is there a doctor in town?" she asked.

"I don't need a doctor," Noah said quickly. "What I need is a lawyer to sue Mr. Tabor, so I can buy a new drum."

"I'm going to do that," she said, "but first you should see a doctor. You fell out of the wagon and I jerked you out of the street. Your arm and shoulder must be sore."

Neither she nor Daniel mentioned climbing out of the window. They had no proof he'd been in the office and escaped, but when Noah glanced up toward the corner of the building where the judge's office was located, he confirmed what they suspected.

"The doctor's office is on the way to the theatre, lad. If the doc's in, we'll stop there first," Daniel said.

"He's not in his office, Pa. He just rode out of town. It's Mrs. Miller's time."

Amber gave an exaggerated sigh even as a smile formed on her lips. "Do you know everything that happens in Leadville?"

"Most of it," he said. "I earn pennies from folks who don't know as much. I could have gotten a penny for telling someone Doc left town, and another penny for saying where he went."

"So, I got two pennies' worth of information for free. Is that what you're telling me?"

"Golly, Miss Kelly. I won't ever charge you for information. You're my lawyer."

"Then you shouldn't charge me for any information you might

have about a boy climbing out of one of those decorative, arched windows, say in the last ten minutes."

Noah seemed to physically deflate. He looked up at his dad, shoulders square, and his gaze didn't flicker. If he was in trouble, he intended to take his punishment like a man. "I can't give away information about myself."

Amber rolled back on her heels, signaling with her body language that she was stepping back and letting Daniel handle it from here.

"Why'd ye do it, son? Why'd ye hide in the closet?"

"Judge Adams saw the accident and was relieved I wasn't hurt. He didn't know about the drum, and I didn't have time to tell him our plan before you knocked on the door. He sent me to the closet and told me to wait. If I'd known you'd take as long as you did, Miss Kelly, I would have gone out the window before you came in." Noah looked down at his feet and kicked a few clots of dirt then returned his gaze to her. "Judge wanted to meet you without me butting into the conversation. He didn't say that exactly, but I figured it out."

"Oh, I see." She put her arm around his slender shoulders and hugged him. He twitched slightly, and she released him. He probably had reddish-looking bruises forming all over his back. "I was worried about you. Your pa knew you were in the closet, but I didn't."

He merely blinked as if struggling to make sense of that. Then he asked, "Why were you worried?"

"I don't pull a ten-year-old from the jaws of death very often," she said. "I have a vested interest in you now. In your education, your future." How she was going to do that, she didn't know, only that she had to try. Maybe, before she returned to her time, she could leave him a list of investments to make and situations to avoid.

Daniel tugged on a gold chain, lifted his watch from his vest pocket, and checked the hour. A photograph of a woman was tucked into the case back. He closed the watch before Amber could study her face, and slipped the timepiece back into his pocket, patting it reassuringly.

"We've taken up enough of Miss Kelly's time today—"

Noah's feathery brows drew together in puzzlement. "No, Pa. We have to go see Mr. Tabor about the drum."

The dog—a retriever, dark brown in color—nudged Noah's hand. If the canine continued to run through Leadville unleashed, she wouldn't survive much longer.

"We can do that another day," Daniel said.

Amber didn't want to come between Noah and his dad, but Noah had his heart set on replacing his drum, and she couldn't walk away from him now. "If you want me to represent you in a lawsuit against Mr. Tabor, I'd like to approach him today while the incident is still fresh on our minds. Do you know where we can find him?"

"He has an office at the theatre. We could start there," Daniel said, "But only if ye're sure it's not an inconvenience."

"I have chores to do, but they can wait." As long as she had enough time before dark to arrange room and board for the night, she'd slay as many dragons as she could with what was left of the day.

As they walked down the crowded and uneven boardwalk, they didn't have an opportunity to discuss the case. When she saw the theatre, she pulled Daniel and Noah into an alley to discuss the case. "Tell me about the drum. You mentioned it belonged to Noah's grandfather and that it was a family heirloom. Can you put a value on it?"

"I saw a similar one at Hughes Store. They wanted five dollars for it," Noah said.

"Do they still have it?" If the store stocked one drum, she could use that as a negotiating tool.

"They sold it."

"That's a shame. We know how much a replacement drum should cost, but we need to determine the value of your drum. It was a family heirloom shipped from Scotland. That adds to its value. What would you say it was worth?"

"I doubt the value of a family heirloom adds much, but the

shipping costs would. Folks are used to paying more to get merchandise from Chicago, St. Louis, New York City." Daniel's gaze lifted as he calculated in his head. "I'd ask for ten dollars."

"Good. I'll ask for twenty. Now, we need to put a value on Noah's pain and suffering, both from the fall and the anguish he's experienced because his grandfather's irreplaceable drum was destroyed. I suggest seventy-five dollars for a total demand of one hundred."

"One hundred dollars?" Daniel asked. "Mr. Tabor will laugh us out of his office."

Noah's eyes grew wide. "A hundred dollars is a fortune."

She returned her attention to Noah. "It sounds like a lot of money, but how can you put a value on your life? That's the issue. The unsupervised dog almost caused your death and did destroy your drum. And as much as you're favoring your back right now, I'm not sure we can rule out an injury to your back, arm, or shoulder."

He grimaced slightly as he twisted to face her. "There's nothing wrong with me."

She would drop it for now, but later she would mention to Daniel that Noah had to see the doctor as soon as he returned to town, not only to be sure he was okay, but if the case went to trial, she would need medical records to present to the jury.

"Come on. Let's go press our case," she said.

During the walk along Harrison Avenue and through the crush of people, Amber kept a practiced eye on Daniel. Every man he passed either tipped his hat in recognition or stepped aside to allow Daniel the right-of-way. He didn't move for anyone. And it wasn't just his height, it was the way he carried himself with military precision. The Civil War ended thirteen years ago. He would have been old enough to have served.

"What kind of work do you do?" she asked.

"I work for the railroad."

"Rio Grande or Santa Fe?"

"Rio Grande."

"Did you serve under General Palmer during the..." She paused, trying to remember what the Civil War was called at the time. "War of Rebellion?"

"Aye, for a while."

Her next question was to ask Daniel if he worked directly for Palmer, the president of the railroad, but they arrived at the theatre, and she turned her focus to her client. If she got involved in a discussion of the Royal Gorge War, she might reveal the result of a ruling the court hadn't yet made. It was best if she stayed in her lane right now.

Noah pointed ahead. "That's Mr. Tabor's phaeton. Do you see it?" There were half a dozen wagons and carriages parked alongside the street. She couldn't tell one from the other. "It's the one with the two black horses," Noah said.

"Beautiful pair of horses." As wealthy as Mr. Tabor was reported to be, he could afford to replace a kid's drum. Knowing both her opponent's assets and the value of her case before negotiating began meant she rarely left money on the table. She hoped her skills transferred to the nineteenth century.

Noah mounted the steps of the three-story building and pushed open the door. The ground floor was divided into two store sections. One section was occupied by Sands, Pelton, and Co., a men's clothing store. A mocha brown frock coat in the window display caught Daniel's eye. Removing his hat, he looked at the coat curiously but didn't slow his pace. Across the corridor was the J.S. Miller Drug Store, and at the rear of Miller's was Phil Golding's saloon.

"Mr. Tabor's office is in the front section of the second floor," Noah said, heading toward the staircase. "Mr. Tabor uses the furnished rooms for his residence and office. On the third floor are sleeping rooms for visiting actors and a few offices. You could rent one and have your own law office."

She didn't plan to lock herself into a lease. There were too many places to go, too much to see to stay in one place very long. "So you've been to Mr. Tabor's office before?" she asked breathlessly, winded from the hike up to the second floor.

"I run errands for him." Noah led her down a red-carpeted hallway, the dog jogging along behind them. A set of double doors that opened onto the theatre stood ajar. Noah stopped in front of a nearby door. "This is Mr. Tabor's office."

Noah's hand was poised to knock when Amber pulled it back, needing time to catch her breath. "Why don't you and your father wait out here and let me handle this." She lifted her gaze to Daniel, and he frowned. "I've got this," she said. "I'm going to pour it on really thick, and I can do that better if I go in alone." She didn't want Noah or Daniel reacting to her negotiating tactics. "You probably should officially hire me before I go in."

"Would ye represent us in a potential lawsuit against Mr. Tabor?" Daniel asked.

"I'd be glad to represent you in this matter." She extended her arm and his large warm hand swallowed hers. She was embarrassed by the calluses on her fingertips from fretting guitar strings. She'd never given the roughness of her fingers much thought until now. She withdrew her hand and shoved both into her jacket pockets.

"I expect a full report." The demand robbed his voice of its smoothness, and she almost saluted him. If she'd had any doubt about his previous military experience, she didn't now.

Noah marched over to a bench in the hallway and sat, his hands in his lap. "Will you be very long?"

"Not as long as I was with the judge." She swept back wisps of hair around her temples, tucked in her shirt, and brushed the muck off her jeans. Satisfied she'd done the best she could with what she had to work with, she knocked.

"Come in," a man said gruffly.

She opened the door, causing it to swing inward with a creak of protest. The dog slipped in ahead of her and disappeared behind an ornate desk that sat square in the middle of the room. Before she closed the door, her eyes met Daniel's, and his narrowed ever so slightly, as if he could see beneath her jacket, beneath her flannel shirt, beneath her skin, all the way to her heart. She didn't understand the look or her reaction to it, but now wasn't the time to dissect either one.

Her eyes adjusted to the yellow light coming from a gas chandelier. She quickly assessed the room and the man behind the desk with his distinctive mustache that would do a walrus proud. Mr. Tabor was not only the owner of the theatre, the Matchless Mine, the Tabor Bank, and the Tabor Hotel, but he was also the current lieutenant governor of Colorado and a well-known philanderer. Amber had grown up around Leadville, and you couldn't spend time in the town without hearing Horace Tabor tales.

Heavy velvet drapes covered two windows. A gaudy Victorian sofa stood on one side of the room, with a sideboard, bookcase, and table on the other, while two leather chairs faced the desk. The furnishings were large, heavy, and dark. And the man, looking bemused, smoothed his mustache.

The scent of a cigar permeated the room. The aroma reminded her of rain-soaked earth, loamy soil, and lying face-down in a meadow. She liked his choice of cigars, but she was reserving her opinion of him until their negotiations were over.

Mr. Tabor glanced up, looked closely at Amber, and as his eyes trailed the length of her body asked, "Who are you?"

"Amber Kelly, and I represent Noah Grant."

Mr. Tabor took a satisfied draw on his cigar then rolled the ash into a crystal ashtray. "Fine boy. Runs errands, helps around the theatre during productions. What's his complaint?"

"Your dog ran out into the street and collided with a bandwagon, jostling the musicians. My client, the drummer, fell off the back into the path of a freight wagon. The wheels ran over his drum and barely missed crushing his head."

Mr. Tabor leaned back in his chair, blandly regarding her while his thumb hung from the armhole of his vest. He cocked his boots on the desk corner. "I'm sorry about the boy and the drum."

"I suppose you'd say the same if the boy's head had been squashed under the wagon wheel?"

"No, that would have been horrible."

Even though she hadn't been offered a seat, she took one in front of his desk and crossed her legs. She glanced around the office again and asked, "Has Gladys Robeson performed here?"

"She was supposed to open tomorrow night but cancelled. She'll never be invited back."

"I'm sorry to hear that. I'm sure she'd have been a sell-out. Do you have many of those?"

He stroked the extravagantly large mustache and grinned at her like a licentious fool, giving her the creeps. "Every act I book is a sell-out."

"After we transact our business, we'll talk about an act I know will be a smashing success and would be available tomorrow night. I can promise the newspapers will write glowing reviews. Patrons will flock from all over Colorado to see the show." Okay, she was exaggerating, but she had to get his attention.

"Who's the talent?"

"A variety entertainer in the vein of Gladys Robeson. Interested?"

"Might be." Although his face remained bland and disinterested, he couldn't hide the excitement in his voice.

"Let's get this business concerning Noah Grant out of the way, and we can talk about a collaboration."

"Noah's accident wasn't my fault."

"That's where we disagree, Mr. Tabor. The cute retriever behind your desk is your property, and if your property causes injury or damages to others, you can be held liable."

"Not in Colorado."

"Yes, even in Colorado and even in Leadville, and my client has asked me to sue you for damages. I would much rather talk about booking an act that's a guaranteed money maker for you, but my client's drum was crushed when he tumbled off the wagon. And I intend to honor my client's requests. So, on his behalf, I'll file a civil complaint in the morning claiming damages and personal injury in the amount of five hundred dollars. I'll also file a civil action on behalf of Mr. Grant for loss of consortium in the amount of two hundred dollars.

"Now," she continued, "if we can dispose of this matter, we can talk about scheduling the act I know will delight your patrons."

"What's the name of the act?"

"One matter at a time," she said.

His smile faded, and his face became sharp-planed. "I want the name and the talent before I'll consider your demand."

She opened the humidor on his desk and looked at him. "Do you mind?" He shook his head and she selected one of a dozen cigars in the Spanish cedar-wood humidor. She gently pinched the cigar between thumb and index finger, working the entire length inch by inch, searching for hard or soft spots. Satisfied there would be no draw problems, she passed the cigar beneath her nose, taking in the sweet aroma.

Mr. Tabor leaned forward and struck a match. She looked at him, smiling, while he lit the tip. Then she puffed, sending the rich tobacco's fragrance into the air between them.

As soon as it was lit she realized her mistake and ordered her body not to react. Coughing would destroy the effect she was going for.

"The talent," she said between puffs, "plays guitar and a little banjo and fiddle, and has a gritty voice the men in Leadville won't stop dreaming about. And that's all you're getting until we settle this other business."

Mr. Tabor shook out the match and dropped the stick into an ashtray on his desk. "And she can open tomorrow night for a five-night run?"

She played with her cigar, rolling it between her fingers instead of smoking it. "One show per night for a five-night run."

He leaned back in his chair, locked his hands behind his head, and watched her. "Three hundred dollars and a release of all claims."

"Noah is ten. His father doesn't know yet if he might have a long-term back injury—three seventy-five."

"Three-fifty. And that's my final offer."

She rolled the cigar between her fingers then flicked the gray ash into the ashtray in a quick tap of her finger. "I believe I can get Mr. Grant to sign off on that."

Mr. Tabor lifted his brow. "You going to smoke that, or just twirl it about?"

She looked at it. "It's not to my taste." And stamped it out in the ashtray.

"Then we have a deal," he said.

She paused a moment. There was something else. "I want the dog. If she stays with you, she'll be dead within six months."

Mr. Tabor waved his hand in her direction. "Take her. Ripley's an annoying mutt."

So far, she hadn't seen anything annoying about her that supervision and love wouldn't cure. "If you'll give me paper and a writing instrument, I'll pen the terms of our agreement. Then we can get on with scheduling the entertainment."

He turned a crystal inkwell stand toward her and placed two blank sheets of paper on the desk, along with a pen with a fresh nib. She picked up the gold nib pen and removed the inkwell's lid. The strong scent of solvent and finisher escaped and mingled with the smoke from her cigar. She carefully dipped the nib into the indigo blue ink, then put pen to paper. If not for the constant dipping into the well and the scratching across the paper, she would have finished drafting the terms of their agreement in half the time.

After inking the date at the top of the paper, she handed the document to Mr. Tabor. He nodded toward the sand shaker next to the inkwell. "Aren't you going to dry your words?"

"What?" She threw a puzzled glance at the shaker and remembered the judge had sprinkled sand over his signature after signing her law license. She picked up the shaker and sprinkled coarse sand over her carefully constructed sentences. Mr. Tabor held up a leather wastebasket and she tipped the sand off the document.

He looked at her oddly, but she just handed him the agreement. "If you agree this incorporates all the terms we discussed, please sign. Then Mr. Grant will sign, releasing all claims against you." She pointed over her shoulder. "He's waiting in the hallway."

Mr. Tabor dipped the pen in the faceted inkwell then bent over the document, the top of his head revealing thinning brown hair streaked with gray. Carefully, he scratched his name above the straight line she had drawn for his signature. His gaze, which had been intently focused on the document, returned to her.

"After you obtain Mr. Grant's signature, we can move on to our next matter."

A quick glance at the document, and she gave him a closed-mouth smile. His signature would do a first-grade teacher proud. The ink showed controlled pressure on the pen. The letters were well-shaped, and even the flourish at the end of the "R" appeared practiced until perfect. His signature stood out in stark contrast to her easy writing style.

She stood, surprised by the stiffness in her knee joints, probably caused by her non-warmup sprint across the street to reach Noah before the freight wagon. Slowly, she eased away from the desk. "I'll be right back." The click of the door echoed in the hallway, and Daniel, sitting on a bench next to a sleeping Noah, jumped to his feet.

She whispered, "I need your signature on an agreement."

"What am I agreeing to?" Daniel whispered in return, as he stepped over to her.

"You're releasing all claims against Mr. Tabor, and in exchange he's paying you three-fifty."

"Three dollars and fifty cents? That will almost buy a new drum."

She smiled. "Not three dollars. Three hundred and fifty."

He cocked his head processing what she'd just said. "What'd ye do? Put a gun to his head?"

"I made him a deal he couldn't refuse. Please don't go in there and undo my work. Sign the agreement, take your money, and leave."

"As long as ye didn't do anything illegal."

"Promise." She held up two fingers. "Scouts honor."

"I don't know what kind of honor that is, but as long as ye say ye did nothing illegal or unethical, I'll take ye at yer word."

Amber and Daniel entered the office, and she pointed to the vacant chair and the paper on the desk. "You can sit here, read the agreement, and sign on the line next to Mr. Tabor's signature."

Daniel pushed the ashtray with the slightly smoldering cigar aside and read the terms. He nodded his tacit agreement and signed above the line. His fingers were long with short nails, and the backs of his tanned hands had a splattering of light-colored hair. His hands had a strength about them, the kind of strength that made her shiver down to her bones. She pushed thoughts of his hands aside and read through the document one last time before returning the agreement to Mr. Tabor.

"If you'll release the funds, we can conclude our business as it relates to the Grant family," she said.

Mr. Tabor opened a drawer in his desk and removed a green lock box. He drew out a stack of bills and counted out the agreed-upon amount. Before he handed it over, he said, "I want a name."

Amber had about three seconds to come up with a name and she did it in one. "Amber Kelly."

Mr. Tabor's eyes widened. "You?"

"Me. I have a voice that melts sugar with an explosive range, and I play multiple instruments. I'll fill the house every night—guaranteed." Amber held out her hand for the settlement funds. "I know you haven't heard of me, but folks will be talking about my performance for years to come."

He handed over the payment and Amber gave the money to Daniel. Then to Mr. Tabor she said, "I'll expect a thousand dollars for a five-night run."

"That's outrageous. Four hundred," he said.

Amber looked at the unsmoked cigar, wishing she could puff on it before clamping it between her teeth at a jaunty angle for effect. "Seven-fifty."

"Five-fifty."

She sensed Daniel tensing, and while these negotiations didn't concern him, he was responding as her clients often did when she negotiated on their behalf. That same tension always lodged a pinch of dread in her throat, but she didn't flinch, and she remained steadily focused on her adversary.

"Seven hundred," she said. "Anything less and I'll cut songs from my act." Amber rarely failed to get the desired results with her final offer. Several of her clients had told her she should play poker. But what they completely missed was that she was the inveterate poker player in every high-stakes negotiation.

"Why would I agree to such an outrageous contract?" His tone of voice held a combination of calculation and common lechery, and it made her skin crawl.

"If I don't fill the house three out of five nights, you'll only have to pay me three hundred fifty dollars." The look in his eyes—the shine of victory—told her the answer. He was no longer seeing the full amount of the contract, only half of it.

"I'll expect you here tomorrow night by six o'clock. Your performance will begin at eight."

"Oh, one more thing," Amber said. "I'll need instruments, a guitar, banjo, or fiddle. Whatever you can get."

"I can get a fiddle. Maybe a banjo, but I have a saxophone, if you can play that. A man skipped out on his contract but left the instrument behind."

"I can't play the sax. So here's the deal: I'll perform five consecutive nights, beginning tomorrow night, for the agreed sum of seven hundred dollars. If I don't fill the house three of the contracted nights, I'll only receive three hundred fifty dollars."

He nodded. "That completes our negotiations."

Amber picked up the pen again, wrote out the terms and conditions, and handed the document to Mr. Tabor. "When you sign on the dotted line, *that* will complete our negotiations."

He huffed, signaling he was reaching the limit of his patience with her. "You're an exhausting woman."

After he signed, she signed. "If you don't mind. I'll hold on to this one." After blotting the paper, she folded it, and slipped it into the inside pocket of her jacket. Then she reached out to shake his hand, noticing for the first time the tell-tale ink stains on her middle finger.

"It's been a pleasure doing business with you." She picked up the cigar. "I might have to smoke this later. Come on, Ripley. Let's get out of here."

As soon as the door closed behind them. Daniel rolled his head back and laughed. "I've never seen anything like ye. I was impressed with yer legal mind, but it comes in second to yer negotiating skills. Ye got Noah a three hundred seventy-five-dollar settlement, a dog, and ye booked an act at Tabor Opera House."

She disposed of the cigar in the brass spittoon. "I love cigars, the smell and the taste. I learned early on that a woman who holds her head high, puffs deeply and smiles slyly, usually has the upper hand. I just couldn't handle one today. What a waste. It was pretty good."

"Aye. Ye had the upper hand in there. Ye've learned a lot pounding the boards." His face turned stony. "Were ye acting earlier then, when ye met with Judge Adams? Are ye not really a lawyer?"

"I don't joke about the law. That's serious stuff. I'm a lawyer. I also sing. I'm a heck of a cook, and I hunt fossils. That's why I'm going to Morrison next week."

He looked at her genuinely mystified. "And ye wear men's trousers."

Now, she laughed. "Only until I can get to the store and buy a dress. Come on. Let's get out of here." She looked around the hall. "Where's the Chessie?"

"The what?"

"The dog. Chesapeake Bay Retrievers are called Chessies. Where is she?" As though she knew her own breed, Ripley trotted to her side and nuzzled Amber's hand.

Daniel gently rubbed Noah's head. "Come on, lad. Time to go."

Noah stretched his shoulder and held the side of the bench as he pushed to his feet. "What happened, Pa?"

"I'll tell ye when we get outside."

They exited the theatre as the last of the sunlight faded from the horizon. Twilight was descending, and she didn't have dinner plans, or a bed arranged for the night. She'd considered asking Mr. Tabor if she could use one of the sleeping rooms for visiting actors. But after the vibes she'd picked up, there was no way she'd sleep anywhere near the man.

"Let's talk over there." She pointed to the corner of the building away from the sidewalk traffic. "Mr. Tabor agreed to pay you three hundred seventy-five dollars, and part of the agreement is that you get to keep Ripley."

"Ripley? Really?" Noah asked.

"Yes, but you have to be a responsible dog owner. Be sure to keep her on a leash so she won't run out into the street again."

Noah knelt on the ground and hugged the yellow-amber-eyed dog. "Did you hear that Ripley? You're going home with me."

"I'm not sure Mrs. Garland will let Ripley come inside," Daniel said.

"When she sees what a good dog she is, she'll let her in. You can pay her a few dollars more a week, Pa. Please. She can't stay out in the cold."

"Miss Kelly can take her home with her until we can make arrangements with Mrs. Garland."

"I'd be glad to, but I just arrived in town when Noah fell. I haven't had time to make arrangements for a place to stay."

"Mrs. Garland has room," Noah said. "You can stay there."

"I'm sure she charges more than I can afford right now. I'll find something else."

Daniel took a wad of bills from his pocket. "I believe it's customary for a lawyer to get a percentage of a settlement. Twenty percent sounds fair to me."

"That money is for Noah's drum and medical expenses. I represented him without any expectation of payment. I'll ask Mr. Tabor for an advance."

Daniel peeled off several bills. "Ye earned yer twenty percent. Ye can either take the cash, or I'll pay it directly to Mrs. Garland. At fifteen dollars a week that gets ye a month's room and board. I didn't think ye'd get a dime from Mr. Tabor. The fact that ye got this much confirms Judge Adams' opinion of ye." He handed her the money and forced her hand to close around it. "Ye have no place to sleep. Arguing is useless. But I'd like to know what ye intend to do with the money."

She smiled. "Add it to the rest of my millions."

6

1878 Leadville, Colorado—Amber

NOW THAT THE sun was going down, so was the temperature. Trying to avoid the cutting wind blowing down her neck, Amber pulled her collar up and buttoned the top of her jacket. Where was she going to stay warm tonight? A quick glance up to the third floor of the opera house had her reconsidering the rooms available for performers. Where would she be safer? Close to Mr. Tabor or close to Daniel? Mr. Tabor gave her the creeps. Daniel didn't. Enough said.

"We better get to the boarding house, Pa," Noah said. "Mrs. Garland gets worried when we're late for dinner. Come on, Ripley. See you there, Miss Kelly, and thank you."

Amber watched Noah and Ripley run down the crowded sidewalk, dodging pedestrians, then she glanced up at Daniel. "Thanks for the money."

"Ye earned it," he said. "If ye're ready to go, I'll escort ye to the boarding house."

"You go on. I need to stop by Hughes Store to purchase a few personal items, and I don't want you to be late for dinner. Give me the address and I'll find my way there."

Concern flickered over his face. "Ye might be wearing pants, ma'am, but that doesn't mean yer safe after dark. I'll walk ye to the store, then to the boarding house. I'll be able to speak privately with

Mr. Hughes about ordering a drum for the lad without him hearing the details. I'd like to surprise him."

"He's so happy about having a dog he might forget all about the drum."

"I thought about that," Daniel said, "but Noah needs to continue his music lessons. His ma would have liked that."

Daniel took her arm and guided her across Leadville's wide rutted street, dodging wagons and horses and scattered bits of manure. He smacked the rump of a slow-moving mule as they darted through a gap in the traffic. The only difference between Leadville before dark and Leadville after dark was the amount of light on the street. Hammering continued. Freight wagons still rolled by jingling their harnesses, and pianos could barely be heard over the din of drunken voices coming from the saloons.

Leadville was a nineteenth-century Vegas. It didn't sleep.

They reached Hughes Store, and she steeled herself for doing what she'd been unable to do earlier—meet her ancestors. In the past three hours, she'd barely escaped being run over, stood for a bar exam, and negotiated Noah's settlement along with a theatre gig for herself. To be nervous now seemed rather silly.

Daniel held the door as she entered her seven-times great-grandparents' store.

A bell mounted at the top of the doorframe tinkled as they entered. This was no leather-hinged establishment. It was a nineteenth-century Walmart. The pleasing aroma of strong coffee and spices scented the store. There were bolts of fabric, bins filled with flour, coffee, and oats, tins overflowing with penny candy, butter churns and washing boards stacked high in every conceivable space, along with racks of ready-made clothes. If an item wasn't on one of the dozen or so floor-to-ceiling shelves that lined the store, or stacked neatly in aisles, it wasn't needed. The shop catered to the middle layer of Leadville's citizenry.

The man she had seen earlier dressed in a white shirt, suspenders, and apron approached Daniel. "Good evening. What can I help ye with?"

Daniel clasped the man on the shoulder. "Did ye hear about Noah falling out of the wagon?"

The man shook his head, tssking. "Thank the Lord he wasn't hurt."

Daniel nodded toward her. "Thanks to Miss Kelly's quick action."

The man turned a studied gaze on Amber. "Ye're a girl. I saw ye earlier when ye banged on the window."

"That was an ungraceful faceplant. I'm glad I didn't break—"

"The glass? I am, too," he said.

"I was going to say my nose." She couldn't take her eyes off his. It was like looking at her grandfather again.

"Miss Kelly, this is Mr. Craig Hughes, proprietor of the store."

She struggled to peel her tongue off the roof of her mouth. How could she be tongue-tied? In her law practice, she'd argued cases before the United States Supreme Court and had clients who were CEOs of *Fortune* 500 companies. Through her charity work she'd met presidents, congressmen, governors and movie stars. Never had she been tongue-tied. But right now, she couldn't think of anything to say. She glanced up at the patterned tin ceiling, hoping for inspiration.

"The lad's drum was busted when he fell off the wagon," Daniel said. "He said ye had one in stock."

The man ran a forefinger along his wide mustache and glanced around the store. "Sold that five days ago. I can put an order in for another one, if ye're interested. Probably take"—he lifted his eyes in thought—"three weeks to get here from Kansas City."

"How much?" Daniel asked.

"The one I had sold for five dollars. I got a fine guitar off a prospector last week in trade for supplies. Interested in that?"

"Noah seems partial to the drum."

Amber finally found her inspiration. "I'm interested. How much do you want for it?"

"Oh...I could probably let it go for, say...fifteen dollars."

"Make it ten and I'll take it."

"I don't know," he said, shaking his head, but the wry twist of his lips said he would enjoy haggling. "Fourteen and a half is as low as I can go."

"What a shame." Amber walked away, sensing he wasn't done and only needed a little encouragement to seal the deal. "I couldn't go a penny over eleven and a quarter." She set her tone to sound only semi-interested.

To give him time to think, she moved around the store, picking up cakes of soap and sniffing each one before choosing an oatmeal bar advertised for face and bath. She also found a toothbrush and Colgate toothpaste in a jar.

"Let me see that Colt .45," Daniel said.

Grandfather Craig slipped behind the gun case and reached to retrieve an Army Model Colt wrapped in its holster and set it on the glass top. "Took this off a fellow who needed money for a stage ticket west. Guess he gave up trying to be the next silver king." Grandfather Craig leaned an elbow on the counter. "No rust at all. It's been well cared for. I can let it go for thirty dollars."

"Come on, Craig. I can get one for seven from mail order."

Amber continued to browse, waiting to hear Grandfather Craig's bottom number. On a shelf with pens and inkwells, she found a brown leather journal with a tree design on the front. She added the notebook to her purchases and would start journaling tonight. She didn't want to forget one moment of her time here.

"I'll take it for fifteen," Daniel said.

"I like ya, Daniel, but I'd lose money letting the gun go at that price."

Daniel chuckled. "I'll come back tomorrow then and look through the catalogue." He looked at her. "Maybe I should hire Miss Kelly to negotiate for me. She's the best I've ever seen."

"It'll be the same price," Craig said, "regardless of who does the haggling. If ye need the gun now, this is the best you'll do."

Always be prepared to walk away.

She took her items to the counter. Craig Hughes left his conversation with Daniel and opened a ledger book to record her purchases.

"If ye're still interested in the guitar, I could maybe let it go for twelve dollars."

"Maybe…" She scratched her chin, thinking, stalling to keep him guessing. "If you…I don't know…throw in a music book, I'll take the deal."

His head bobbed, and he smoothed his brown hair absently, running his hand over the top of his head as he turned his back to the counter and looked at the shelves. He took a coffin-style wooden guitar case down and handed it to her.

"Can ye play this?" he asked.

"I hope so," she said.

She opened the case and bit the inside of her cheek to control her excitement. The rosewood and ebony instrument had a neck made entirely of ivory. It was a museum-quality guitar. She'd seen a similar one at the Met in New York City. It was exquisite. Her hands shook slightly as she gently lifted the guitar from the case. "C.F. Martin/New York" was stamped on the back of the pegbox.

"This is a Martin—a Martin guitar." Her voice was a reverent whisper.

Grandfather Craig's brow quirked as he looked at her with unveiled curiosity. "Twelve dollars is as low as I can go."

"Where'd you say this came from?" She rubbed her hand along the body. It was a priceless and irreplaceable instrument. She slowed her breathing. Grandfather Craig needed to believe he was getting the best end of the deal.

"Prospector nearly cried when he traded it for gear."

She understood why. Martin guitars were as timeless as the music they played.

She dug into her pocket for a pick with her personal imprint, something she was never without, and strummed a few chords, getting a feel for the strings vibrating beneath her fingertips. The instrument was badly out of tune. She stepped aside to let other customers pay for their purchases while she tuned the guitar by ear.

Daniel leaned back, cupped the edge of the stained pine counter with his hands, and crossed his long legs at the ankles. At first, she had thought he was a man of few words, but it wasn't that. He was probably a great conversationalist. No, he was studying her like a firefly in a jar. She'd had plenty of first dates with men like him. They were never sure what to make of her unusual interests. In Daniel's case, though, it was probably her odd dress and aggressive personality that he found standoffish. She couldn't worry about him now.

Once the instrument was tuned, she strummed a few more chords, finding the guitar perfect in tone and warmly melodious. She played her own version of the legendary "Hotel California" solo by The Eagles, moving quickly around the fretboard with precision and dexterity, using string bending and vibrato. She lost herself in the music and the tone of the instrument and was unaware of her audience until she stopped and glanced up. The last sound echoed from within the instrument and faded from the room. And what she saw on Daniel's face was not an expression of pensive admiration, but a perplexed frown that knitted his brow.

"I've heard Mexicans play the guitar like that. Is that where ye learned to play?" he asked with a cool bite to his voice. Whether he intended her to hear it, or was unaware it was there, he failed to keep it leashed.

"I was influenced by Spanish music, but I'm mostly self-taught."

Customers who had stopped to listen stood nearby wearing rather bewildered looks. A short man with a haggard face and deep sorrel hair said, "Not sure what I heard, but ma'am, you can sure play that guitar."

"I couldn't stop watching yer fingers," Grandfather Craig said.

"The music probably sounded more complex than what you're used to hearing." She placed the guitar back into the box on the counter and returned the pick to her pocket. "I love it, and I hope the previous owner doesn't want to buy it back."

She caught Grandfather Craig's shifting gaze and how his mouth twisted beneath his well-groomed mustache. "Heard he was killed in a mining accident two days ago. He was a good man. Said he'd come back to reclaim it. Reckon it's all yers now."

She stroked the cover of the case, wondering about the man who had traveled cross-country to strike it rich in Colorado, and who had taken such extraordinary care of his guitar. "I'm sorry. I would have enjoyed hearing him play."

Daniel had remained statue-still through her verbal exchange with Grandfather Craig, listening, watching, his face growing more intense, his jaw tighter.

Amber counted out the bills to pay for her purchases and handed over the payment. She did a quick mental calculation to figure out how much she had left for room and board and a dress or two for her performances. Next week, after she got paid for her gig, she'd have enough money to take the stagecoach to Morrison to go fossil hunting.

"Will Mrs. Hughes be here tomorrow? I need to pick out a warm dress, stockings, gloves…" She put her hand to her head. "A hat, too, I think."

Grandfather Craig placed her purchases in a brown sack and rolled down the top. "I'll let her know to expect ye."

"I look forward to meeting her." Amber came from a family of huggers and wanted to give Grandfather Craig a hug, but she couldn't. He would think it was odd, as would Daniel, who was still glaring at her, suspicion and confusion warring in his cobalt-colored eyes.

He hustled her outside where the orange wash of the sun's last light was fading, and twilight was closing in. He pulled her aside, looming large over her, and the sharpness in his voice cut through the chilly air.

"I've traveled through Europe, spent time in New York and San Francisco, Denver and Santa Fe, Kansas City and St. Louis, and I've never met a woman with yer legal prowess or brashness. Who are ye, and where did ye come from?"

"You heard my curriculum vitae in the judge's chambers. I don't have anything to add," she said.

"Yes, ye do." He jerked his hands to his hips, spreading open his duster and revealing for the first time a Pinkerton Detective Agency badge. Below the watch chain attached to his waistcoat by a T-bar, was the heavy gleam of a gun belt with a Colt .45 riding on his right hip. He'd said he worked for the railroad. Not even in this alternate universe could she have imagined him as a Pinkerton man.

"Stories grow in this town, Miss Kelly. And folks will talk about what ye did for Noah. The story will change as it's told. It always does. By week's end, the story will be that ye shot the driver to keep him from running over the lad. Men will see a kid looking to make a name for himself. No one will believe ye're a lass with fast legs. They'll only hear ye're a kid with fast hands." His tone hardened. "Do ye want that reputation?"

"That's ridiculous. No one will believe that. I'm an innocent bystander who just arrived in town and I'm not buying whatever you're selling. I haven't done anything wrong, and I'm not wearing a gun."

"Then tell me who ye are and where ye're from?"

She clenched her hand into a fist to give herself a moment to think. Then, "Amber Kelly and I just arrived here. Do you harass every stranger who comes to town, or just women who save your son's life?" She was deflecting because she didn't have an answer for his question. Finally, she threw out the name of the first city she could think of south of Leadville. "I just arrived from Granite. Before that I was in Colorado Springs, Wichita, Kansas City, and St. Louis. I travel around. I do some lawyering when I feel like it and sing for my meals when I don't. Anything else you want to know? Like what size shoe I wear?"

He folded his arms across his chest, his silver cufflinks twinkling in the light from the store window, and he looked down his nose at her. "Whatever ye tell me, just remember, specious explanations don't hold water any better than a leaky pot."

"You're full of horsefeathers. Now, I'm hungry and tired. If you're not going to introduce me to your landlady, then I'm going back to Tabor Opera House and ask Mr. Tabor if I can rent a room on the third floor."

Daniel's deliberate gaze reminded her of an opposing attorney trying to sniff out a bluff. "I won't have ye over there warding off his oily advances."

"Thanks for protecting my virtue. Although you'll let rumors spread about my fast hands." She let out an exasperated sigh. "If you intend to keep harassing me, I'm going, and I don't need your approval."

Her contractual obligations required her to remain in town for the next few days. By then she'd have traveling money and could leave Leadville on the first stage to Denver and then on to Morrison. But in the meantime, she had to come up with a plausible life story that would satisfy a Pinkerton agent.

"You're not the only person who's traveled. I've been to all those cities, too. My travels, my experiences, and my family influenced my thinking. You're right. You probably haven't met a woman like me, but that doesn't mean women like me don't exist."

Daniel raised his eyebrows, tipped back his hat, and turned an impenetrable dark gaze at her. "I'm suspicious by nature."

"Great. Then you have the perfect job."

He took her arm and directed her off the boardwalk and around the corner to a hardscrabble footpath lined with single-story ramshackle buildings.

"Where are you taking me?" she asked.

Light from the windows cast wavering shadows over him, giving him a wrathful look, like an avenging angel who had come to capture her.

"To jail." The note of authority in his voice along with the statement came across pointed and dangerous. "I'm deputized in seven states"—he patted his breast pocket—"and I carry 'John Doe' warrants."

She halted and tried to wrench her arm free of his grasp. "For what? Acting strange?" She fought to keep a quaver from her voice. "I haven't done anything illegal. And I'm not going with you."

She stepped around his scowling presence. "I saved your son this afternoon. Why are you acting like a jerk?" She stomped away and dropped under the weight of her worry onto a bench along the boardwalk—her packages under her arm and the guitar case across her lap.

He didn't come after her. Maybe he was going to leave her alone, but she doubted it. His personality was defined by his dogged determination.

He'll come back and ask again where I came from.

The hour was on the fringe of evening now, and the lamplighters were beginning their nightly routine of lighting the gas streetlamps on Harrison Avenue. The incessant hammering continued, and the boardwalk was as crowded with a throng of miners at this hour as it had been when she first arrived.

It seemed like a year ago now. She glanced back toward Hughes Store. Like most of the shops on the street, it remained open. It must be true that during the silver boom, you could buy a pan or a mule anytime in Leadville from sun up to sun up.

A column of dust mixed with golden aspen leaves swirled through the street, pulling bits of trash in its wake. A wisp of unblemished mountain air—cool and crisp—tapped her chin, like the gentle touch of her late grandmother.

What are you trying to tell me, Granny? Not to be discouraged. Not to give up. To go after what I want.

But what did she want? She wanted to spend time with her grandparents, to fossil hunt in Morrison, then go home. The first two she could accomplish. The third depended on the fickleness of the amber brooch.

7

1878 Leadville, Colorado—Amber

AMBER SENSED DANIEL'S intense glare before he joined her on the wide pine bench on the boardwalk. The supports squeaked under his weight. Although he tried to appear relaxed, the position of his hand, within easy access of his holster was a neon sign, flashing—*Try me if you dare*. He was a large man, well-built and athletic, and he smelled of newly tanned leather. She found herself leaning toward the scent like a foraging bumblebee.

"Ye're full of sass."

A statement rather than a question. A new tactic?

She turned to face him and offered a polite smile. "Can we talk about this over dinner? I'm starving. I'm not a threat to you or anyone else. I get that you're suspicious, but I haven't done anything wrong, and you won't find a wanted poster with my picture on it. I'm an educated free spirit with more than a bit of sass. You're right. So lighten up, Agent Grant."

He flashed the impenetrable dark gaze again. "Lighten up?"

"I just meant you shouldn't worry so much."

"If ye'd been guilty of a crime, ye would have run farther than a few feet."

She tapped her fingers lightly on the guitar case. "I have nowhere to run. Now, if we're finished here, I need to make arrangements for tonight."

"I'll take ye to meet Mrs. Garland."

She glanced back toward the general store. Imposing on her grandparents' historical generosity seemed safer. Daniel's suspicious nature could complicate her already complicated situation.

"I don't want to impose."

"Noah's had time to get to the boardinghouse and tell Mrs. Garland. Knowing her, she's already preparing the room."

If she went to the boardinghouse for the night, then tomorrow she could look for other living arrangements. Although in a town as crowded as Leadville, there probably weren't many available rooms, except for the actors' rooms at Tabor Opera House.

"If you're sure," she said.

He reached for the guitar case. "I'll carry this. If it's inconvenient, Mrs. Garland will let me know, and tomorrow I'll help ye find another room."

Amber shoved the package of personal items into one of her jacket's drop-in pockets. "It'll only be for a week. I could pay extra, if necessary."

Daniel escorted her across Harrison Avenue. She stopped in the middle of a wagon rut for a moment. "Noah came so close—"

Daniel tugged on her arm. "If ye stand here, it'll be ye who gets run over today."

She ducked her head against a gust of wind and continued to cross the rutted street. They reached the boardwalk on the other side and Daniel glanced back at the path they had taken.

"I'll see Noah falling off that wagon for the rest of my life. If ye'd been a second slower, ye wouldn't have reached him in time."

His memory of that moment had to be much worse than her own. She knew she had a chance, but for Daniel watching from the bank, he knew he had none.

Why had she been at that corner at that moment? If she'd found the lost brooch sooner, she wouldn't have been there. She stared down the length of the street to where the mountain peaks lay shrouded in the dark, just as her life beyond the wormhole was shrouded and inaccessible to her. She considered the opportunities she would have missed in her life if she hadn't been in the right place at the right time. This was just one more in her history of coincidences or fate or serendipity or stars aligning.

Stars aligning? That seemed more apropos.

Daniel took her arm and guided her down the boardwalk. They turned left onto 4th Street and walked toward a jagged dark line of silhouetted houses where wavering lamplight flickered behind curtains of thin muslin and ragged lace. At the corner of Pine Street, he pushed open a wrought-iron gate and ushered her through.

"This is it," he said.

This was no slap-and-dash boomtown boardinghouse. A sidewalk led to a covered porch which sported an impressive spool and spindle porch frieze. Lamps were aglow in several windows on both floors, and smoke trailed from the chimney.

She gained the little porch, just a half pace behind him. Daniel paused and put one hand on the doorknob, forcing her to stop. "Mrs. Garland is from Virginia. She's a very proper lady."

Amber stood still for a moment, trying to slow her heart, still racing from the change in oxygen levels in the high altitude. "Are you trying to tell me she won't appreciate my trousers?"

"Her opinion will likely be influenced by yer appearance."

Amber gave him a big fake smile. "So I should try to win her over with my charming personality because I'm dressed inappropriately. You sound like my sister."

"Sounds like yer sister has good judgment. Ye could try emulating her. As far as Mrs. Garland is concerned, if ye show her the respect ye showed the judge, ye should get on fine."

"How well do you know her?"

Daniel continued blocking the door. He glanced away, his jaw clenching, then returned his gaze to her, letting a heavy silence settle over them for a moment. "Her husband was a Pinkerton agent. He left the agency and came out here to try his hand at mining. He did quite well until he was killed in an accident. When I got this new assignment, Mrs. Garland offered to take care of Noah when I traveled."

Most of Daniel was in shadow, but in stark contrast, his face was lit by interior lamplight pouring from the windows, highlighting the angle of his jaw, the sharpness of his cheeks, and the depths of his eyes. In the Caravaggio-style lighting, his intense gaze gave her that I-feel-guilty flutter in her stomach. In return, she gave him her best professional opaque look. A mask she'd perfected that gave opposing counsel little insight into what she was thinking—her poker face.

"Where'd ye leave yer traveling bags?"

So much for her practiced look. *Note to self: It doesn't work on Pinkerton agents.*

There was a gradual freezing in the air and she pulled her jacket a little tighter around her. "I don't have any. I sold everything I had."

He dropped his hand from the doorknob and casually leaned against the doorjamb. Then he gave her a look, the kind of look her clients gave her when she gave them advice they didn't quite believe.

"Why'd ye do that?" The lamplight chased the shadows away, revealing a look of concern etched into his face. And for a moment he looked more like a dad than a Pinkerton agent.

The cold seeped under her jacket and the vapor from their breath misted the air. She had to warm up and knowing food and heat were only steps away eroded her remaining patience. There was no humor in her tone of voice when she said, "To buy a stagecoach ticket."

"From where?"

"I told you already. I just arrived from Granite." It was only about eighteen miles away, so surely there was a stagecoach traveling between the two towns.

He tipped back his hat, raised his eyebrows, and another heavy silence followed before he asked his next question. "Why were ye there?"

"If you need my life history before you introduce me to Mrs. Garland, I'll tell you. Otherwise, can it *w…a…it?*" The word came out as an uncharacteristic whine. "My ribs are gnawing on each other." She breathed deeply through her nose. "Just smell those fresh baked biscuits."

Before Daniel had a chance to respond the door flew open. If he'd been leaning against it instead of the doorjamb, he would have fallen to the floor. "Did you bring Miss Kelly?"

"He did," she said, stepping out from behind Daniel to find a very concerned Noah, holding his arm close to his body. "How are you feeling? Is your arm bothering you?"

He gave her a one-shoulder shrug. "Not so much. Just a little sore." He backed out of the way, so they could come inside. "I told Mrs. Garland you were coming. She said you could stay the night."

Amber made her way into the foyer. An elaborately carved hall-stand with a long-beveled mirror, hooks, and a bench seat stood near the door. She caught a glimpse of her disheveled and muddy appearance and nearly groaned. Her mother and sister would have fits if they saw Amber now. Dressed as she was, she shouldn't be allowed through anyone's front door.

Daniel placed the guitar on the bench. "Can I help ye with yer coat?"

She lifted the package from the front drop-in pocket and set it next to the guitar before shrugging out of the jacket. From the outer edge of her vision, she caught Daniel eyeing the Patagonia label, and she silently groaned. Before he had time to study the label further, she took the jacket away from him and hung it on a hook.

Daniel shed his coat. Then, as if performing a dance he'd done hundreds of times before, he untied the thigh thong, unfastened the large belt buckle at his waist, coiled his cartridge belt around his holster, and set the gun rig on the shelf above the hall tree. After brushing off the top of his hat, he placed it upside down on the shelf alongside the gun rig.

Meticulous, methodical, and surprisingly sexy, and she had to look away before he removed anything else.

She turned her attention to Mrs. Garland's house. Having completed a remodel of her home in Denver, Amber appreciated the work of skilled carpenters. Whoever did the custom wainscoting and inlaid wood ceiling was more than skilled. He was an artist, and he'd built the Garland residence to showcase the owner's wealth and standing in the community. The cost of shipping brass and crystal light fixtures and even a stained-glass window would have been prohibitive for most citizens of Leadville.

A chill penetrated Amber's bones despite the heat from a stove at one end of the parlor and a fireplace at the other. She moved to the fireplace, standing to one side of the screen, and held out her hands, grateful for the increasing warmth that slowly removed the cold from her hands and face. It would take a little bit longer to reach her feet.

A woman of middle age with steel-rimmed spectacles perched atop iron-colored hair set in dramatic curls, paused at the doorway and eyed Amber with curiosity. After hesitating a moment, she entered the room dressed in a light gray ensemble that swished softly on the carpet with each small step.

"Noah said I might have a new boarder." Her mouth was set with the certainty of someone who knew the right and wrong of the world. When she pulled her glasses from the top of her head, it disturbed her elaborate coif and several strands stood on end. She placed her glasses on her nose and with a spectacle-enhanced stare said, "I'm Mrs. Garland."

"Excuse my appearance." Amber swallowed with some difficulty as she prepared to tell more lies. "I had to sell my possessions to buy a ticket on the stagecoach from Granite. The cheapest ticket was for a seat riding up top. I thought safety and warmth were more important than fashion."

"If you put safety and warmth ahead of society's constraints, you're a brave woman. Welcome to my home, Miss Kelly."

"Please, call me Amber." If she'd been on better terms with the landlady, Amber would have smoothed the woman's hair. She glanced around looking for the dog, but she didn't hear, see, or smell her, and was afraid the retriever had been relegated to the outdoors. "I hope Ripley hasn't caused a ruckus."

Mrs. Garland smiled at Noah. "I was heartbroken when I heard what happened to Noah's drum. I couldn't say no to the dog. We've discussed rules and as long as he abides by them we shouldn't have any trouble."

"Where is Ripley now?" Daniel asked.

"In the kitchen. I told her to stay there." Noah glanced up at his dad with a hopeful smile. "She's a fine dog."

Daniel gently cuffed Noah's chin. "A dog who almost got ye killed."

"She almost got killed, too, Pa."

"And so did Miss Kelly. It was a miracle ye all walked off unscathed."

"The smell of those biscuits has my mouth watering," Amber said. "Shall we conclude business before dinner?"

Mrs. Garland returned her spectacles to adorn the top of her head, but it only made the misplaced hairs look worse. If Amber was so concerned about Mrs. Garland's hair, what in the world did the landlady think of Amber's clothes?

"Will fifteen dollars a week for room and board suit you? Noah said you wouldn't be staying long."

"No more than a week," Amber said. "I have a five-night performance contract at Tabor Opera House starting tomorrow. Then I plan to go to Morrison." Although she spoke with certainty—serendipity and a nosy Pinkerton agent—could easily upset her plans.

"A performance? Are you singing?"

"And playing the guitar, and a banjo if Mr. Tabor can find one."

"I would enjoy the theatre." Mrs. Garland looked down at Noah. "Maybe you'll escort me to the performance."

Noah looked at his dad with such an odd expression that Amber had to turn away to keep from laughing.

"I'll take ye both," Daniel said. "I heard Miss Kelly play at Hughes Store. She's very talented."

Mrs. Garland looked at Amber as if sizing her up. "I have a dress I wore to a ball in New York City a few years back. I can remake the dress to fit you."

"Oh, you don't need to do that. I thought I'd go to Hughes Store tomorrow and see what they have."

"They have a few nice dresses, but you'll need a special gown."

Amber wasn't sure what to say. She didn't want to offend Mrs. Garland, but saying yes without seeing the gown was like agreeing to be a bridesmaid, knowing the dress would turn into a horror story. She used her best diplomatic approach. "Tomorrow, we'll see what we can do."

"I'm sure you'll enjoy wearing the dress as much as I did." Then to Daniel, Mrs. Garland said, "The sheriff stopped by. He asked if you'd come to the jail this evening."

Daniel pulled out his pocket watch, clicked open the gold-plated cover, and peered at it from arm's length. "I'll go there after dinner."

"You said you'd help with my arithmetic lesson tonight, Pa."

Amber fixed Daniel with a stare. Would he put work before his son, a son whose loss he could be mourning?

"Do the best ye can, and I'll go over yer assignments when I come back."

She had no doubt he would go through the wanted posters in the sheriff's office looking for one with her smiling face below the words—WANTED DEAD OR ALIVE. He was an investigator and naturally suspicious. He might as well satisfy his curiosity and get it over with, but he was doing it at Noah's expense. And that pissed her off. If Daniel was going to ignore his parental responsibilities, then for tonight, she'd pick up the slack.

"I can help you. Math and science are my favorite subjects."

A look of surprise blossomed on Noah's face. "They are?" He scratched his head. "I thought you were a lawyer?"

"I'm a mining lawyer. I have a background in math and science."

"Isn't that nice?" Mrs. Garland hugged him, and Amber was touched by the affection the woman clearly had for Noah. "You'll get the highest marks in your class."

Daniel's gaze swung from Noah to Amber. "Thank ye." He patted his waistcoat pocket where his watch was kept. There was more on Daniel's mind. Amber could see it in his eyes, but he didn't offer anything more than a silent nod.

"I'll show you to your room," Mrs. Garland said. "You can wash up before dinner." She left the parlor expecting Amber to follow, but Daniel held her back for a moment.

"Ye've been kind. I've been rude, but I know ye're hiding something, and I won't quit looking until I discover what it is."

"Flashing a badge and a gun was threatening and rude. But I suppose it goes with the job." She returned to the hall tree to pick up the guitar and her personal items. Avoiding Daniel, she swept out of the room, trailing her new landlady.

She caught up with Mrs. Garland, standing in front of the last door at the end of the hallway. She opened the door to a small room with a potbelly stove and a small bathtub. "This is the washroom. My husband surprised me with this. A water pump brings in cold water and the drain empties it. I put two kettles of water on the stove in the evenings to heat. Mr. Grant and Noah take baths at night. You're welcome to use the room, but you must refill the kettles to heat for the next person."

Mrs. Garland opened the door next to the bathing room and lit a coal oil lamp. Gas lighting was evidently not available on every street in Leadville. "I hope this will suit you," she said.

Moonlight crept through lace curtains over partially drawn roller shades. The room was large enough for a bed heaped with quilts, a hand-braided rug, a marble-top washstand with pitcher, basin, and mirror, and an oak clothespress with five drawers and panel doors. The room, scented with lemon oil polish, was warm and welcoming. The lack of frills suited her fine.

"It's lovely."

After Mrs. Garland left the bedroom, Amber filled the pitcher with hot water from the washroom. Then she took a few minutes to cleanup and brush her hair. Instead of braiding it again, she left it loose to hang down her back. When she returned to the kitchen, she found Noah sitting at a square table with only a few crumbs on an otherwise empty dinner plate, Ripley on the floor by his feet, and Noah's homework spread out in neat piles.

She took a seat next to him. "What kind of math are you doing?"

"Fractions, and I don't understand the assignment."

Amber pulled the book over to study the lesson. "'Mary had one half of a dollar, and her mother gave her one half of a dollar more. How much money had she then?' I like fractions." She picked up a pencil and a piece of paper. "Let me see if I can help you understand."

Mrs. Garland placed a plate of fried chicken and potatoes in front of her, and she ate while she worked through math problems with him. After an hour, he seemed to catch on. While he worked on his own, she drew a *Stegosaurus*. Every few minutes, he would look at what she was doing and ask questions about her sketch. Kids loved dinosaurs, and she'd learned years ago that she could entertain them with drawings and stories.

When he finally finished his assignments, he put down his pencil and studied her face. "You came to my rescue twice today. Thank you."

She picked up the loose papers scattered around her plate and stacked them together, lightly tapping the ends of the pages against the table. "You're a special young man. I'm glad I was here to help."

Daniel walked into the kitchen. "Did ye get yer work done, lad?"

"Yes, sir. Are you going out now?"

Daniel flashed a grin at his son. "No, I just got back."

"Back? What time is it?" Noah asked.

"Almost nine. I told ye I was leaving, but ye were so engrossed in what Miss Kelly was teaching ye that ye didn't hear me."

"It was easy to pay attention to Miss Kelly, Pa. She explains concepts so they're easy to understand."

Daniel picked up the small stack of papers and thumbed through them. "I can see the progression. Here," he said pointing at one of the pages, "all the figuring is in Miss Kelly's hand. These pages are in yers." He thumbed through a couple more. "What is this drawing?"

Amber looked at the paper he held up, tapping a pencil against her lips.

"That's a *Stegosaurus*, a dinosaur that lived around a hundred fifty-five million years ago during the Jurassic Period," Noah said. "Miss Kelly told me all about it. One was found near Morrison last year by a schoolteacher named Arthur Lakes."

"That's why I want to go to Morrison," Amber said. "There's a treasure trove of prehistoric fossils and tracks there."

He pointed to the two smaller dinosaurs in the picture. "And these are wee dinosaurs."

"Yes. And look at their tracks. Can you just imagine hearing the tiny feet splashing in a shallow river meandering through a flat, dry landscape?"

"Flat? Not in Colorado."

"The landscape was completely different during the Jurassic Period, Pa. That's what Miss Kelly said, but I find that to be a wild tale."

"Looking at the Rockies now makes it hard to believe. How'd ye learn this?"

"I picked up bits and pieces from Dr. Marsh. But I formed my own opinions using what I learned studying geology from as far back as the ancient Greeks of the fourth century."

Noah collected all the papers, pencils, and books and stacked them together. "Can I keep the picture?"

"Sure," she said. "Just don't show it around. This is my interpretation of what the *Stegosaurus* looks like. Drs. Marsh and Cope would disagree."

Noah examined the sketch closely before tucking it inside his text book.

"Off to bed, lad," Daniel said.

Amber stood and put her arm gently around Noah's shoulder. "Will you let your dad look at your back and shoulder before you go to bed to see if you have any bruises?"

He tucked the books and papers under his good arm and gathered up his pencils. "I'm fine."

"I'm sure you are," she said. "But I'd feel better if your dad looked you over." When Noah frowned, she said, "Indulge me, okay?"

He glanced up at his dad with big, expressive eyes. "I'm fine, Pa."

Daniel put his hand on Noah's head. "I'm sure ye are, lad. But Miss Kelly has been very helpful today. No sense worrying her more. Let's go have a look." With a slight smile, Daniel left the kitchen.

Amber tidied up her place at the table. "Thank you for dinner," she said to Mrs. Garland, who had been sitting in a nearby rocking chair knitting, her hair neatly in place. "Only true Southerners know how to fry chicken perfectly every time."

An expression came over Mrs. Garland's gently wrinkled face—a look of sorrow, regret, loss. "Are you from the South? I didn't detect it in your voice."

"No. I'm from…Chicago, but my cousin had a good friend from Virginia, and he told me all about sweet tea and fried chicken."

"I hope your cousin's friend recovered from the war."

To Amber, her frame of reference for *the war* was Afghanistan and Iraq. But she knew that for Mrs. Garland, it was the Civil War. "It took a while, I think," Amber said.

A few minutes later, Daniel returned to the kitchen. "Noah has a few bruises, but nothing that looks serious. He would like to tell ye good night. Do ye mind going up to see him?"

"Not at all," she said. She left the room with Daniel.

"I know ye're not telling me the truth about who ye are—"

At this, she stopped thinking about Noah and hissed under her breath. "Button it, Daniel." She headed down the hallway toward the washroom.

"Miss Kelly," Daniel said.

She waved an airy hand.

"Ye're going the wrong way." His voice was low and unamused. "Noah is upstairs. First door on the left."

She gave her head a single vigorous shake, spun on her heel, and followed Daniel up the stairs. The second-floor dimly lit hallway unrolled beneath her feet. To the left was a closed door. Daniel twisted the crystal doorknob and stepped aside for Amber to precede him into the bedroom.

She poked her head around the door. An aromatic sweet smell hit her, and she breathed in a big whiff of scented soap. Noah sat up in a twin-size bed nestled in the corner of the room, reading a paperback book with a black and white illustration on the front.

"What are you reading?" she asked.

He held up the book, so she could see the cover and title. "It's about a girl named Alice who fell through a rabbit hole into a fantasy world populated by peculiar creatures."

"Oh, I love *Alice's Adventures in Wonderland*."

"You've read it?" Noah asked.

Amber nodded. "One of my favorites. 'Begin at the beginning,' the King said, very gravely, 'and go on till you come to the end: then stop.'" She laughed.

So did Noah.

The room was twice the size of hers with a double bed, Noah's single bed, a wardrobe, a neat—almost to a fault—walnut desk, a swivel desk chair, and a comfy reading chair. A collection of pencils in a pewter cup and a sheaf of papers filled the center of the spotless blotter. The top sheet was lined with the elegant cursive writing of a nineteenth-century scrivener. A small lamp sat near the other side of the blotter. Once lit, it would easily provide ample light while working at the desk.

Amber scooted the swivel chair on its brass rollers across the floor to face the bed, then she sat and leaned toward Noah. "Are you sure your arm and shoulder are okay? I hurt my arm when I was your age. It hurt, but I was more scared of what my parents were going to do to me."

"Why would they be mad?"

"Because I was climbing a big rock, and I wasn't supposed to do that."

"Did you get into trouble?" he asked.

"Worse than trouble. They told me never to climb the rocks again and if I did, they'd never bring me back to my grandparents' cabin."

"So you never climbed the rocks after that?"

She put her finger to her lips. "It's a secret." She glanced at Daniel, then turned back to Noah and whispered, "I never stopped climbing. I was just more careful." She leaned back in the chair, and it squeaked as she rocked.

"Thank you for helping me today," he said. "I miss my drum, but not like Pa would miss me if you hadn't been there to pull me out of the street."

"It was fate that brought me to that corner at that moment." Amber set the book he'd been reading on the nearby table next to a small brass plate stand holding a two-by-four-inch *carte de visite*. The portrait was of a young serene-looking woman with large shining eyes. The whiteness of her skin and slightly flushed cheekbones gave her an ethereal glow. Amber picked up the small photograph and studied the woman's face.

"Is this your mother?" she asked softly.

Noah nodded. "That was taken two years before she died."

Amber smoothed his thick, tangled hair away from his face. Her hand lingered along his crimson cheek, then dropped away. "Your mom was a beautiful woman. You favor her."

He smiled. "That's what Pa says."

Amber looked up to find Daniel staring at her. He had the same look on his face she'd seen earlier when they were standing on the front porch—grief, regret. He took the picture from her.

"Her name was Lorna. She died shortly after giving birth to our daughter." He put the portrait back on the stand then stepped over to the window and looked out at the street below.

"My baby sister died, too," Noah said. "Pa named her Heather."

A knot formed in Amber's throat. Although Olivia was alive and well in another time, Amber might never see her again. "I'm so sorry for your loss." Her voice cracked, along with a little bit of her heart.

She crossed the bedroom toward the door. "Sleep well, Noah."

Daniel looked over his shoulder at her.

"If Noah can't settle down or wakes up in pain," she said, "give him a sip of whisky." And with that, she left the room, biting back tears that threatened to make hot tracks down her cheeks.

Daniel and Noah's loss spoke to her disquieted spirit, and for the first time since she arrived in the past, she was beginning to conceptualize what it would mean long term. Even though there were dinosaur bones to discover, the fossils meant nothing without her family.

As soon as she reached her room, she opened the stone. Maybe she was sent to the past to save Noah, and now that he was safe, she could go home. Although the brooch didn't heat in her hand, she sounded out the ancient words anyway and waited for the fog, but nothing happened.

She dropped onto the bed, knowing in her heart that she was truly, hopelessly stuck in the past.

8

The Present, MacKlenna Farm, Lexington, Kentucky—David

David McBain, president of MacKlenna Corporation, scanned the information he'd obtained from hacking into Amber's laptop and synced it with his dark web research. In the past year, he'd tweaked the computer program he'd written, and it was now a highly sophisticated tool. No longer did he have to pay others to do what he could do for himself, which relieved him of worrying about an associate going to jail for illegal activities. Kenzie didn't know the extent of his hacking capabilities, and he intended to keep it that way. As for Elliott, he had plausible deniability.

The door opened and JL strolled into the room. When she and Kevin had married, she decided to use her real name—Jenny or Jen—instead of JL, but nobody in the family was buying into the change. It was too late. They all knew her too well. She was JL O'Grady, now Fraser, former NYPD detective and former MacKlenna Corporation vice president of global security. For Kevin's sake, they would call her Fraser, but never Jen.

Seven and a half months pregnant, she didn't move as quickly now, and she often had trouble getting up out of a chair, but she still moved with the grace of the ballerina she once had been. As she walked past the large monitor, words scrolled across the screen: Colorado 1870s. She stopped, studied the alert, then eased into the chair next to David, rubbing her belly.

"Are you researching the property Connor is looking at?"

David continued typing on the keyboard. "When'd ye talk to him last?"

She pulled her smartphone from her jacket pocket and scrolled through her text messages. "He sent a text last night during the flight. I didn't know he was going back to Denver. He sent a link to a ranch for sale. I think it's perfect. Can't wait to see it." She returned the phone to her pocket and rubbed the small of her back. "What are you doing?"

David swiveled in his chair to face her. "Has Connor mentioned Olivia Kelly to ye?"

"She's the broker he's been working with. Are you asking if I know he's got a thing for her? Yes, I know. Although I don't think it's reciprocal."

David turned his attention back to his keyboard and tapped a few more keys. "That's the impression I got, too."

A map of Colorado flashed on the screen with green blinking stars next to Cañon City, Leadville, and Morrison. JL pointed to the map. "Does the ranch have three locations?"

"Locations? Aye. But not for the ranch."

She leaned forward to get a better look at his computer monitor. It mirrored the image on the large screen mounted on the wall. "You're being cryptic, McBain. What's going on?"

He pushed away from the desk, crossed the room to the refreshment center, and put a pod into the coffee maker. "Do you want a cup of decaf or bottle of water?"

"No, and you're stalling. What are you not telling me? Is it about the woman Connor's interested in? Don't tell me she's married."

The desk phone rang. JL glanced at it. "Elliott's calling, but he can wait." She stood and gave David her best cop pose and matching glare. "Spill it." The phone rang again. David took a step toward the phone, but she backed up to block him. "Come on, McBain. The longer you dick around with this, the more upset I'm getting, and stress isn't good for the baby."

He really didn't want to have this conversation with her, but she was like a hound dog with a large brown nose low to the ground following a scent. "This is confidential for now. Olivia's sister has gone missing."

JL's gaze flashed to the large screen. "From one of those places? Give me something to do." She scooted her chair to the next monitor and tapped the keyboard to log in. "Connor will need more help. What's her name? How old is she? A teenager? Where was she last seen?"

David gave her a stony silence instead of answers. His cell phone rang. JL snatched it off the desk. "It's Elliott. Does he know about the sister?"

"Not unless Kenzie told him."

"People can't keep secrets around here. If Kenzie knows, Elliott knows. If Elliott knows, Meredith knows. If I know, Kevin knows, or will know. But you should have told me."

"Oh yeah?" David took the cup of coffee back to his desk. "Where have ye been for the last few hours?"

"At the doctor and meeting with the decorator about the nursery." He took the phone from her. "Enough said." He punched accept and the phone stopped ringing. "McBain."

"What the hell is going on around here?" Elliott asked. "There's a disturbance in the Force."

Smiling, David sat back in his chair and raked his fingers through his hair. He had worn a military haircut since graduating from high school. At Kenzie's urging, he'd been growing it out. His hair now curled over his collar. He hadn't told her, but he'd made an appointment with Elliott's stylist. The hair was coming off. He hated it falling into his eyes and teasing his neck.

"That's crap, Yoda," David said. "Ye've talked to my bride."

"I just got back from a run. I haven't talked to a soul in over an hour. But something is wrong. I sense it. Have ye heard from Meredith?"

"I talked to her about fifteen minutes ago. It's bad out there. The fires are heading to Napa. She said Kit and Cullen are devastated. They lost their house once, and now the whole winery could go this time."

"I'll call her. The winds could change any minute and they could be cut off. I should have gone out with her. I didn't have any idea Northern California would be ravaged like this."

"Nobody did. At least the inventory is safe in the wine cave. We shouldn't lose any product, except what's left on the vines. Kevin is supervising the move of the business records, paintings, computers, and antiques to the cave."

"Should I go meet her in San Francisco?"

"No. They're staying until they get evacuation orders. I've got a helicopter standing by to take them to the Sacramento airport. Meredith promised they wouldn't delay."

"Delaying can prove lethal. I'd feel better if she left now, but I know she won't until she's done all she can do."

"I heard from Pops earlier. Jeff, Shane, and Pete dismantled the security operation and moved the equipment to the cave. Now they're loading up the horse vans."

"I hate imposing on McCann Ranch, but until we have a facility of our own in Colorado, we'll have to board the horses there. Let's get a contract signed on a ranch today."

"Where are ye now? I want to talk about Colorado."

"I need a shower. Meet me in my office in thirty minutes. One more thing... After everyone leaves the winery, how will we know if the fire damages the property?"

"There are websites and aerial satellite footage showing areas that have burned. We'll know."

"Damn. I should be out there."

"Yer doctor doesn't even want ye around cigars. And ye want to be in the thick of that wildfire smoke? It's made the Bay Area air quality its worst on record. Clouds of ash and smoke are spreading beyond the flames. Cullen shouldn't be out there either with his heart condition. I know ye don't like it, but ye can't go."

"Don't tell me what to do." Elliott abruptly disconnected the call.

David glared at the phone, as if the phone had dropped the call, not the caller. He turned his attention back to JL to find her reading the notes he had jotted down on a legal pad.

"What the hell is this?" She jabbed her finger on the pad. "A puzzle box? An outline of a brooch? Olivia's sister isn't just missing, is she? She's like...disappeared."

David nodded, knowing the news of another brooch would remind JL of the last adventure, and how horrible that had been for her and Kevin. It hadn't been a picnic for the rest of the travelers either.

"Crap. The family is dealing with so much right now. We don't need this."

He took her hand and squeezed it. "How about we keep Kevin out of the loop for now."

Relief poured off her in waves. "Thanks for understanding. If we lose the winery, it'll devastate everyone, but it will traumatize him."

"I think ye're wrong, lass. It will traumatize Meredith, Kit, and Cullen. Kevin will come out of this stronger. He'll see the potential in rebuilding, and Meredith will spend more time in Tuscany bugging the crap out of Gabe."

"That could be a disaster. He only agreed to manage the winery if she left him alone to do his job. But what about Kit and Cullen?"

"Cullen will research ways to protect the winery from fire. Then he'll go back to his time and put modern fire reduction procedures in place to protect the property. He'll encourage property owners abutting Montgomery Winery to do the same. Ye can't stop fires from occurring, but ye can mitigate the damages."

"I hope Connor understands we can't go after Olivia's sister right now. Everybody but my brother Patrick is consumed with the fire. And afterward, there'll be too much to do."

"I forgot about Rick. Where is he?" David asked.

"Patrick, you mean? I'm sorry, but I can't call him Rick."

"He's Rick now. The Marines shortened his name."

"Then how come he can change his, and I can't?"

David laughed. "Ye might have lost some of yer hard edge, but ye'll never lose enough to be called Jenny. Sorry, lass, but that's the truth of it."

"You go right ahead and call him Rick, but I'll still call him Patrick, and as for where he is, I guess he's still at the VA. He had a checkup this morning. He was planning to fly out to San Francisco later today."

"He doesn't need to go to California, but he could fly out to Reno and meet up with yer other brothers. He could help drive the horses to Colorado."

"That makes more sense. Why don't you suggest it? If it comes from me, he'll think I'm trying to mother him. And don't tell him about the brooch. He'll want to go on an adventure, and the timing is terrible. Not only for Patrick or Rick or whatever he's calling himself right now, but for everyone. Let's hope you're wrong about this and Miss Kelly hasn't gone *really* missing."

"The evidence can't be ignored."

"But let's leave Patrick out of the loop. Okay? He's only been back from Afghanistan a few weeks and most of that time has been spent in the hospital." She held onto the corner of the desk as she pulled to her feet. "I just came by to pick up my plant. The movers left it in the window."

"We'll miss ye over here."

"They have food in the corporate center. All you have here is whisky and chocolate, which is fine if you're not pregnant. In my condition, I prefer healthy snacks." She paused a moment and then said, "I know you were the one who came up with my new position. Thanks. I like it."

"VP of development and operations fits ye fine. Ye'll be working with Elliott more. Can ye handle that?"

"I'm married to his son, an Elliott mini-me. What do you think?"

She walked back to her former office and David returned to his computer. He sent several documents to the printer, then password protected the file. Members of MacKlenna Adventure Company could access the file but no one else. Not even someone with his depth of computer knowledge.

With everyone managing the fire, he couldn't send anyone back to rescue Amber Kelly, except maybe Braham? David considered him for a moment, but the 1870s was too close to the time Braham left the past, and with his connections to the railroad and soldiers who fought in the Union Army, he might be recognized. Considering the unavailability of his assets, David couldn't recommend anyone to go back for Amber—yet.

"Are you ready? If not, I'll go on over."

JL's voice pierced David's concentration, and he jumped to his feet. "Hell, ye can't carry that. It's bigger than ye are." He took the small tree out of her hands. "I'll carry this if ye'll get the copies off the printer and grab my laptop."

They walked next door to the corporate center, and JL knocked on Elliott's office door while David set the plant down on her desk.

"Come in," Elliott said.

"Only if you're out of the shower and decent," JL said.

"I'm decent." David followed JL into Elliott's office. The bathroom door was open, and Elliott stood at the sink combing his hair. David had a flashback of Elliott years earlier, limping out of the bathroom, carrying a glass of whisky, and yelling about some goddamn this or that.

Elliott walked over and kissed JL's cheek. "I thought ye were at the doctor. How's my grandson?"

"I was there this morning. Prenatal appointments don't take all day."

"Aye. The only experience I've had is with Meredith. Hers did take all day and usually included chemotherapy." He visibly shivered. "I'm glad ye're here. I guess David wants to talk about the Colorado ranch."

JL raised her hand in a stop gesture. "Wait. Why do you think this baby is a boy?"

Elliott shrugged. "Oh, I had a dream, but I'd love a wee lass, and so would Meredith."

"A dream?" JL asked. "You expect me to believe that? The OB/GYN department is moving into a new wing at the hospital. Did you make a large donation just to get confidential patient information?"

He gasped. "I wouldn't do that, and the hospital wouldn't indulge me anyway."

"Aha. So you tried."

Elliott threw a grin at her to show he was kidding, but David wouldn't put it past him to try. JL and Kevin didn't want to know the sex until the baby was born. Their decision was driving the family nuts, especially the women who wanted to buy newborn clothes.

David changed the subject. "Have ye seen Kenzie?"

"When I came in from running, her door was closed."

"Still is." David punched in his wife's number on his smartphone. "Hey. When will yer conference be done?"

"Just ended. Why?"

"Can ye meet with JL, Elliott, and me in Elliott's office?"

"Oh, McBain. I'll meet you anytime, anywhere, especially if sex is involved."

He smiled. "Can ye hold that thought for about an hour and come in here and talk about the Colorado project?"

"I'll try to hold it for an hour and if that doesn't work out, I'm calling you for phone sex."

He laughed. "That won't be necessary."

"You two are disgusting," JL said, getting comfortable on the sofa. "I didn't have to hear Kenzie to know what she was saying."

"Just because ye and Kevin are separated for a few days, don't take yer frustration out on me."

Kenzie entered the office carrying a tray holding a carafe, coffee cups, and bagels. "Who's frustrated?" She kissed David. "Besides me. Let's hurry this meeting along." She set the tray on the table in front of the sofa. "Coffee and bagels left over from my conference. Help yourself." Kenzie sat down next to JL and patted her leg gently. "You feeling okay? How was your appointment?"

"Back hurts," JL said, shrugging. "It's part of the deal, right?"

David called Connor from Elliott's desk phone and when he answered, David put the call on speaker. "Connor, I'm in Elliott's office with JL and Kenzie. Where are ye now?"

"We're still at the cabin. Olivia is napping in another room."

Rick sauntered into the office. "Is that Connor on the phone?" Rick poured a cup of coffee from the carafe on the table. "Tell him I need ten minutes when he can work me in."

"I thought you were at the VA," Connor said.

"Just got back. My arm and side are fine. Healed up well. Still sore, but that'll take a while. I'm released to start rehab with Elliott's trainer instead of going to the VA. What's going on with you? When are you coming back?" He hitched his hip on the edge of Elliott's desk and sipped from a green MacKlenna Farm mug.

"Not today. Something has come up. David already knows about this, so I'll fill the rest of you in. As you know, I've been working with Olivia Kelly to find a ranch in Colorado for the company to buy. The perfect property just came on the market, so I flew up last night to visit the ranch today. When Olivia came to the hotel to pick me up this morning, she received a call that her sister Amber was missing."

"Where does she live? In Colorado?" Elliott asked.

"She lives in Denver, too," Connor said. "Amber spent the weekend at their family's log cabin in the mountains close to Leadville. She was supposed to return to Denver last night. No one has seen or heard from her since early Saturday. At my urging, Olivia postponed the appointment to see the ranch, and we drove to the cabin to look for Amber. There's no sign of her here."

"Did you notify the sheriff?" Elliott asked.

"He wasn't helpful," Connor said. "As it turns out, Amber has a history of disappearing for days at a time."

David hooked his laptop to the AV system and handed out summaries of his research.

"And how old is she?" Elliott asked.

"Thirty-two," Connor said. "She's a mining lawyer and an amateur paleontologist. When she comes up here to the cabin, she goes rock and fossil hunting and loses track of time."

"Do ye think she's in danger?" Elliott asked.

"Yes," Connor said. "When we entered the cabin, I discovered three things. Amber's bags hadn't been unpacked, even though she had supposedly been here for forty-eight hours. A piece of a very old loom had broken off and left a gaping hole in the loom's breast beam, and there was a puzzle box on the floor."

David projected the pictures Connor had taken onto the wall screen above the small conference table.

Kenzie walked over to the screen and looked closely. "That looks exactly like my puzzle box." She turned toward David. "Another brooch?"

"I enlarged interior shots of the box," David said. "Ye can see here"—he pointed with a laser pointer—"and here, a faint outline of a brooch. The measurements match the brooches we have."

"How'd you get it open?" Kenzie asked. "Not that you couldn't figure it out, but those suckers aren't easy."

"It was already open when I found it on the floor—empty."

"Jesus Christ." Elliott dropped into his desk chair. "Fires are burning California off the map, and the family is still recovering from the last clusterfuck."

"Do you think she's gone to one of those cities you highlighted?" JL asked. "What were they? I remember Leadville, but not the other two."

"Morrison and Cañon City," David said. "My best guess is 1878 or '79."

JL shoved a pillow behind her back and sort of wiggled to get comfortable. David had watched Kenzie do the same thing during both pregnancies. He had never told her, but he thought she looked even more beautiful when she was pregnant and nursing than at any other time. She was done though. The twins and Laurie Wallis were enough for her. A dozen wasn't enough for him.

"Just as long as it's not the Jurassic Period," JL said. "Why do you think she's gone back to the late 1870s?"

"The Kelly girls and their father have always been intrigued by the Royal Gorge Railroad War. The case went all the way to the United States Supreme Court. The Hughes family was heavily invested in the Rio Grande Railroad. The settlement cost them a ton of money. I found mention of two interesting historical characters involved in the railroad war."

"Who?" Rick asked.

"Bat Masterson and Doc Holliday," David said.

"Doc Holliday?" Rick asked. "*The* Doc Holliday? I've read Westerns my entire life. I love everything about the Old West—range wars, Indian wars, railroad wars, saloons, dancehall girls…"

JL palmed her forehead and took a deep breath. "Terrific."

"Everybody is in California," Elliott said. "We can't put a rescue team together."

"I'm going," Connor said. "If I can get another volunteer—"

"Count me in. I wouldn't miss this," Rick said.

Kenzie looked up from the document she was reading and stared at David, color draining from her face. His heart caught in his throat. "What's wrong, lass?"

"Olivia and Amber are…" She stopped, finger combed her hair, and held her hand there as if holding her head to keep it from falling off. "The Kelly sisters are… They're my best friend, Trey Kelly's, first cousins."

"Are ye sure?"

"He never referred to them by name. They were always just *the sisters*. Every winter until he went to Afghanistan, he'd go to Colorado to ski with them."

"Connor," David said, "ask Olivia about her cousin."

"I will as soon as she wakes up," he said.

"Add my name to the team. I'm going with you, Connor," Kenzie said. "I have to help Amber."

David moved to stand in front of her and glared. "No, ye're not. Ye can't leave the twins and Laurie Wallis."

"If I use the diamond or the amethyst brooch, I'll be back before they even know I'm gone."

"Ye don't know that for sure."

Kenzie came belly to belly with him. So close he could smell her coconut shampoo. So close he could taste the bagel and cream cheese she'd just eaten. So close he could feel himself inside of her. That close, but emotionally they might as well be a mile apart. What she was suggesting wasn't within the realm of possibility.

"Listen, McBain... Trey Kelly sacrificed his life for me"—she poked David in the chest—"for the mother of *your* children. Even if I'm separated from them for a few weeks, we can suffer through it. Trey's family has suffered for years without him. And he's never coming back. I will. And I have to do this."

David put his hands on her shoulders. "I can't let ye go, Kenz. Last time ye time-traveled, yer life and Laurie Wallis' life were put in danger. I won't let ye do it again."

Her face flushed red with anger. "I graduated at the top of my class at West Point and I did two tours in Afghanistan. I'm a trained soldier—"

"And ye almost died there, too."

"We've been married for seven years and we've never argued like this." She glared at him. "We've never disagreed over anything major, but this could strain our marriage. I owe a debt to Trey Kelly that I can never repay. Rescuing his cousin will go a long way in doing that. You can't stop me."

She whirled around and stormed out of the room.

9

The Present, MacKlenna Farm, Lexington, Kentucky—Kenzie

ELLIOTT FOLLOWED KENZIE into her office across the hall and closed the door quietly. "What's going on here, lass?" His expression was easy to read, his tone merely confirmed it. If there was one thing Elliott detested, it was friction and strife within the family.

She crossed her office to the wall of windows behind her desk and gazed out over the white, wood-planked paddocks. There wasn't a window in the mansion, security office, or the corporate center that didn't have a view of the fenced enclosures. The horses on MacKlenna Farm were turned out daily unless the weather was too severe. Today, mares and their yearlings romped in the paddock closest to her window.

Moms and their children.

Kenzie, the twins, and Laurie Wallis owed their existence to Trey Kelly's sacrifice. A day never went by without acknowledging his act of courage and love. For the first time since he covered her body with his to shield her from a bomber, she had a chance to repay him, repay his family. As much as she loved David, he would not stand in her way.

The wind blew through the trees and leaves drifted down to vanish from sight beneath the windowsill, and something froze inside her—like a deer stuck in the headlights—she wasn't sure which way to turn. Her head started to throb, pounding in her skull.

She faced Elliott. "Go away. I don't want to talk." She picked up a remote on her desk and dimmed the overhead lights to stop the flashing in her eyes.

"Suit yerself, but I'm going to talk to ye."

She covered her ears and whispered, "Lower your voice. You don't have to yell."

His hard gaze dissected her, top to bottom, as if she were a specimen in his vet lab, and she sneered at him. Casually, he sat in one of the chairs fronting her desk and crossed one leg over the other, in that irritating manner he had.

"I get that ye think ye owe the Kelly family for the sacrifice Trey made. I even get that ye believe ye should go rescue his cousin. What I don't get is why ye're fighting with yer partner. If ye want to go, I'll support ye. But ye can't leave until ye and David have resolved yer differences. Ye'll need to negotiate this."

"Negotiate?" She was incensed. "Are you crazy? Why should I negotiate when I'm in the right?"

Elliott flicked at the knife-edge crease down the center of his khakis, almost absentmindedly, and she wanted to slap his hand. *Stop that.* He probably wasn't even aware of his habitual tinkering with the dry cleaner's precision.

"Marriage," he continued, "is a partnership, and ye and David have one of the strongest ones I've ever seen."

She snorted. "From what I hear, you would have been laughed out of this office if you had given anyone marital advice fifteen years ago."

"Don't sass me, Kenzie."

"I'm not in the mood for lectures, insights, words of wisdom, or even advice from Obi-Wan or Yoda, whichever one you're supposed to be. Save your breath."

"I never thought the one thing that pulled ye and David together would pull ye apart," Elliott continued as if she'd offered no protest. "Ye're both soldiers. Ye fight the world as a unit. Ye're stronger together. Ye think ye can go back for Amber, find her, help her fight the battles she's gone back to fight, and do it without David."

Kenzie sat in her desk chair, crossed her legs and arms. "If Amber has a fourth of Trey's intelligence, natural ability, and wherewithal, then yes, I can help her without David being there."

"I'm going to tell ye the same thing I'd tell David if he were sitting in front of me. Ye won't like what I have to say, but here it is. Ye've lost yer single edge. Ye're a double edge sword now, and yer survival depends on both sides. Ye either go together, or neither of ye will go."

"You can't stop me, Elliott. Don't even try."

He stared at her and there was something in his eyes, as if he saw her exactly as she saw herself—the deer in the headlights—and he needed to slam on the brakes. "I can stop ye, and I will."

She braced her hands down on the desktop, stood abruptly, and leaned forward on her hands, getting into his face. "Are you threatening me?"

"No, I just want ye to get out of the headlights. Ye have three children and it's not practical for ye to go on an adventure."

If she'd been hit over the head with the butt of a rifle, her head couldn't possibly hurt worse. It was about to explode. She pressed the heels of her palms to her temples, ran out of her office, and burst through the door of the restroom.

A deafening blast, loud enough to puncture her ear-drums had her ducking. The T-Man attacked from every direction. Bombs exploded all around her. Smoke billowed. Flying shrapnel sliced through her flesh. Her gaze darted from one side of the outpost to the other. There was nothing close by to shield her. She had to find cover. Blood dripped down her side. Shaking violently, she dropped to her knees. Another explosion rocked the ground. Something heavy fell on top of her. She tasted blood. Bombs blasted all around her. There was no escaping the conflagration. The dense smoke made her cough. Her army fatigues were soaked with blood. The pain was excruciating. She was going to die and there was nothing she could do.

Someone grabbed her from behind, wrapped arms around her, and she screamed. "Run." She fought hard, punched and kicked.

"Shh. Ye're safe, Kenz. No one's going to hurt ye. There are no bombs, no explosions. Ye're safe here with me."

She pushed against him, fought to get her arms free to defend herself, but she remained harnessed to arms of steel. "Go. You'll die if you stay. Go. Now."

"Stop fighting me."

She pushed against the restraints, tears pouring down her cheeks. "Please. Go."

"I'm not leaving ye. Shh. It'll be over soon."

"I can't move my arms. I can't breathe. The smoke is so thick. Go away. Bombs will kill you, too."

"The bombs are gone. Ye're home. Ye're safe. I've got ye."

She rocked against him, struggling to pull air into her lungs.

"Ye're safe. Take deep breaths. Ye're not injured. Ye're not bleeding. Ye're hyperventilating. Breathe in. That's right. Now breathe out slowly."

David's voice was calm and reassuring, and she wanted to believe him. He pulled her onto his lap, held her against his chest, rubbed her back, and he hummed. The melodious sound, along with his warm breath blowing gently on her face, calmed her as nothing else could. The beat of his heart against her cheek brought her slowly back to sanity, leaving the pain and trauma of the war behind. She came back to him. Back to the present.

She took a breath as if preparing to dive into cold water. "I have to go back for Amber. I have no choice."

"Yes, ye do."

She cringed. "If it was your best friend who died, you'd already be packing your bags. Your resistance is because I'm a woman."

"Ye're damn right. Ye're my woman, and I won't allow ye to go by yerself. But ye can go with me."

"How nice of you to allow me to do that."

"Stop it, Kenz." He turned her around to face him. "Use that Mensa brain of yers and stop thinking with yer heart. Ye have three children and it drives ye nuts when ye travel and they're not with ye. How can ye leave this century, knowing ye could be separated for weeks?"

Her shoulders dropped, deflated, and she rubbed her fists across her eyes. "I didn't say it'd be easy. I didn't say I wouldn't go nuts, but this is something I must do. Why can't you see that?"

He watched her steadily, as if he knew the directions her mind raced. "I can. That's why I said I'd go with ye. But here's the deal—"

She pulled herself upright and for a moment her breath stopped. Then, "No. Deal."

He held up his finger. "One condition and it's non-negotiable. We'll take Connor and Rick. As soon as we've located Amber and made contact, if she's not in danger, we're coming home."

"I'm not leaving her behind. Just because she might not be in danger while we're there doesn't mean she won't be in danger later."

"Connor and Rick can handle whatever comes up."

"You don't know that." She knew from personal experience the family's time traveling adventures often went in directions no one anticipated, and without the means to communicate with team members, they were hamstrung.

"Jesus, Kenzie. Listen to yerself. They're former cops. Former Marines. They're professionals. They can handle themselves in all sorts of situations. We have to trust them to do what's best."

"They're going back to the 1870s. They're not trappers. Camping out is not their thing."

"Colorado had hotels, trains, and even primitive telephones in the 1870s. They won't be roughing it along the Oregon Trail like Kit did."

"We'll reevaluate the situation after we locate her?" she said.

He pushed damp hair off her face, behind her ears. "We can evaluate, we can discuss, but I'm not changing my mind." His tone made it clear he brooked no arguments.

She pulled away, indignant. "What's the point of a discussion if your mind is already closed to a change of plans?"

"Ye're the lawyer. If it's necessary, ye'll find a way."

She rested her head on his chest and they sat together on the bathroom's cold marble floor. The warmth of his body took away the chill, and the strength in his arms removed the fear.

David's attitude wasn't because she was any less a soldier than he was. It was all about their family. And family had been their top priority from the day she discovered she was pregnant with the twins. They had both had rough years growing up and had committed to not repeating their parents' mistakes. She also knew her husband well. He always had a plan and built into his plan was flexibility.

"How'd you find me?"

"I thought ye were just mad," he said, pushing to his feet. "But Elliott recognized what was happening. He told me ye were having a flashback. I'm sorry I missed the signs. I led ye there then abandoned ye." He pulled her to a standing position. "Wash yer face. Ye'll feel better."

She stood in front of the sink and splashed water on her face. David handed her paper towels and she patted her skin dry. Her eyes were red and puffy. Everyone in the office would know she'd had a meltdown. But they were all family and would understand.

David put a basket of personal items she kept in the bathroom on top of the counter and handed her a makeup bag she used for touch ups. An hour earlier, she'd had shiny bronzed skin, dark-rimmed eyes and a muted color on her lips. It was all gone now. A quick touch up wouldn't help much. Only a full-blown redo would make her presentable again. She'd go home at lunchtime and fix her face. Looking at David in the mirror, his expression said he had the same idea, but fixing her face would come after they made love and showered together.

"I thought I locked the door. How'd you get in here?"

"Opening a locked door without a key is as easy as locking it." He picked up a hairbrush and brushed her hair.

Sighing, she allowed herself to relax under his ministrations. "Is Elliott upset with me?"

"No. He was worried. He spent years yelling at people when his demons attacked him."

She canted her head one way and then the other, so he could

brush her hair. "Are you saying his demons recognized mine?"

David's deep brown eyes creased briefly. "What happened to ye in the war is something ye'll never forget." He kissed her hard then returned to brushing her hair.

She dug through the make-up bag, searching for a shade of lipstick close to what she'd been wearing. "Where do we go from here? Feed my demon?"

"And hope he dies," David said. "Ye feel guilty because ye survived and Trey didn't. That's why ye continue to have flashbacks. If helping Amber lessens the guilt, I'm all for it. We'll go together. Now, put on yer lipstick and let's go back to the meeting. We have plans to make."

With her hair brushed and fresh lipstick on, she was ready to face Elliott again. "Okay. I'm ready."

"Hold up a minute." He pulled her into his arms and kissed her. It didn't take much for one kiss to slide into another; for his hands to glide over her breasts, down her sides, and lift her short skirt over her hips; for her hand to slide inside his khakis. He hissed when she touched him.

"How is it that you know me so well?" she asked.

"I pay attention, and I know I can kiss ye if I don't mess up yer lipstick."

"And I know I can delay you for any meeting, with a simple touch."

"I'll be glad to accept the challenge. Anytime. Anywhere. And there's nothing simple about the way ye touch me." He took her lips in a scorching kiss, and she melted against him.

She raked a hand through his long hair. "Lock the door, McBain. The demons can wait."

10

The Present, MacKlenna Farm, Lexington, Kentucky—David

KENZIE AND DAVID entered Elliott's office holding hands. A bottle of Macallan 25 Years Old sat on the desk and Elliott and Rick held empty Glencairn glasses. David picked up the bottle and poured drams for his bride and himself.

"Here's to whatever they're celebrating." He clinked his glass to hers and sipped the sweetness he expected from a sherry cask whisky. This was joined by a citrus aroma with a hint of cinnamon and the impression of an open wood fire. The finish was long with a fantastic lingering spice. Drinking the Macallan after sex was like having one more orgasm.

He smiled at Kenzie, and she tipped her glass to him, a silent acknowledgement of the special moments they'd just shared.

Elliott glanced at David, and David signaled, *Ye were right.*

"I'll call Connor back and we can restart this meeting." Elliott placed the call. When Connor answered, Elliott said, "We're back now. What are ye going to tell Olivia?"

"I've been thinking about that. I could tell her I have to go back to the farm for a couple of days, but I hate to leave her behind to deal with the sheriff by herself."

"The sheriff could be a problem when Amber doesn't come back as expected. I don't want another situation like what we had with Amy Spalding's boyfriend. Ye should stay," David said.

"Kenzie and I will go."

"That makes sense," Connor said. "With Olivia's sister gone and her parents out of the country, she's all alone. I mean...she has friends and all, but I think she trusts me."

Looking at David, Elliott asked, "Can ye two handle it?"

David sat on the edge of the desk, his arm around Kenzie's waist. "Aye, but we want to take Rick with us."

Rick smiled and offered a salute. "I'm your man."

"Rick's never been on an adventure before. Ye need someone with experience. How about Pete?" Elliott said.

"Pete's got other commitments right now," Kenzie said. "Rick is a few weeks out of a war zone. His instincts are as sharp as they'll ever be."

"I'm still surprised every morning when I wake up and discover I'm home," Rick said.

"I bet you're finding civilian life flat and purposeless after the intensity of Afghanistan," Kenzie said.

He nodded. "You nailed that one."

"I've been there," she said. "If you go with us, you'll be immersed in something less stressful but with a similar challenge. I think it will be a good adjustment for you."

"How long will we be gone?" Rick asked. "Not that I have anything else to do right now, but Pops will ask."

"If we're using the diamond and amethyst brooches," Kenzie said, "we'll be back within a minute of leaving. Although for us, we could be in the past for days or weeks. It depends on how far we have to travel to find Amber once we get there."

"Won't the stones take us to her?" Rick asked.

"In Amy's case," JL said, "the stones took us to New York City, but Amy had gone to Pittsburgh for the weekend. If Amber is in Leadville, and she decides to take a trip to Denver or Morrison with the intention of returning, you might arrive in Leadville and have the choice of waiting for her to return or going after her."

"When are you leaving?" Connor asked.

David looked at Kenzie. "Twenty-four hours?"

She nodded. "I can be ready."

"Is there any information you need from Olivia that might help find Amber?" Connor asked.

David didn't want to divulge the extent of his intrusive investigation into Amber's life, so he just said, "We have enough to find her, but if there's something specific ye hear that might help us, let me know."

"If she's looking for a job in Leadville or wherever she goes," Connor said, "she might consider singing in a saloon or a theatre. She plays several instruments and might use her talent to earn money for room and board."

David already knew she performed regularly at charity benefits but didn't mention it. Maybe one day they could perform together. The family still talked about the sing off at Kevin and JL's wedding, and the kids clamored for an encore every time they all got together. If more musicians or singers joined the clan, they could call themselves the von MacKlenna Family.

"Wherever we land, we'll check out the local entertainment," Kenzie said.

"Then the three of ye, it is," Elliott said. "Let's keep the news of Amber and her brooch within this circle until after we get through the fire and its aftermath. Meredith couldn't handle it. She'll be pissed when she hears of it later, but after she thinks about it, she'll understand why she was kept in the dark. At least I hope so."

"There's no way I'm telling Kevin," JL said.

"The lad could handle it now," Elliott said.

"Oh, I know he could handle news of another brooch, but he'll go nuts over the expense, especially in light of the winery's future losses."

"Jack Mallory isn't going on this trip. That cuts the budget in half. Mr. High Roller always insists on first-class accommodations. Three-star hotels suit me fine," David said.

"For McBain, hotels are cheap, but transportation costs always eat up the budget," Kenzie said. "Now, should we tell Jack what's going on?"

"I vote no," JL said. "We texted this morning. Amy made him put his manuscript aside for a few days to focus on wedding plans. They have meetings scheduled with the wedding planner, preacher, musicians, photographer, you name it. He doesn't need anything else to distract him right now."

"Is Amy turning into a bridezilla already?" Kenzie asked.

"I don't think she will. There's a calmness about Amy that I wish I had. It seems to have calmed Jack."

David laughed. "I assure ye, it's not Amy's calmness that's relaxed Jack." David winked at Kenzie, and her cheeks pinked.

Elliott's phone rang. He checked for the caller's name and number. "It's Meredith. They must have told her to bug out." He pushed accept and put it on speaker. "Hey, Mer. I'm here with David, Kenzie, JL, and Rick. What's the latest update?"

"We just got evacuation orders." There was steel to Meredith's normally velvet voice, and it reverberated through the phone's speaker. "We ran out of time and couldn't store the replaceable furniture, but the antiques, collectibles, and paintings are in the cave along with all the records, computers, and security equipment. The bulk of this year's crop was already picked. But the later ripeners like cabernet sauvignon, merlot, and syrah grapes are still hanging and susceptible to smoke taint. If that's the case, we'll take a loss there, but hopefully we can save the vineyards."

"What about the fermenting wines?" JL asked.

"They were left open to the smoke-tainted air. We'll lose the fermenting wines, too. Kevin has been calculating potential losses. I told him I didn't want to hear the numbers right now. I'll have to get somebody in here to work with the insurance companies. Preferably an attorney who's handled large conglomerates that have lost entire operations to a fire. I've got the names of two attorneys who come highly recommended. My first choice is out of the country right now."

"Should I be concerned you're not including me?" Kenzie asked.

"If I could take everything else off your plate, I would. That's not fair to the company. You and Jeff are working your asses off already. I can't expect you to drop everything and work on this exclusively. If we're going to get back up and running, it has to be a full-time commitment."

"I've heard the devastation to Napa and Sonoma communities is enormous—the lives lost, the homes destroyed—the potential effects on the wine industry itself are not as obvious yet," Kenzie said. "But if I need to drop everything, I will. Let me know."

"Thanks, sweetie." Meredith exhaled deeply over the phone. "The impact may not be seen on wine shelves for years. Vintners are reckoning with the future of their businesses. It's tragic." Meredith's report on Napa's unprecedented situation echoed loud and long.

"We'll get through it, Mer," Elliott said.

The silence in the room stretched several beats until David asked, "What about the horses?"

"Shane, Jeff, and Pete left about thirty minutes ago. We're all meeting in Reno. I want to be away from the smoke but close enough to get back in a hurry. They'll take the horses on to Colorado then decide what to do from there. What's the latest on buying a ranch?"

"We've found one, but it'll be a few weeks before we can move horses onto the property," Elliott said. "I'll come out tonight. Meet ye in Reno."

"If you want to, but you can't come to the winery. The air is too smoky. We're all wearing respirator masks. With Cullen's heart issues, I wish he'd go back to Kentucky, but he won't leave. He almost ran off with a firefighter unit."

"Meredith, ye need to go," David said. "The winds could change and ye'll be trapped."

"Let me know as soon as ye get on the helicopter," Elliott said.

"Kit, Cullen, Maria, and Pops are with me in the car."

"Where's Kevin?" JL asked.

"He's driving behind us. We didn't have room for the computer equipment and files he packed. We're almost to the heliport. All the employees are gone. There's nobody left to watch it burn. Talk to you soon. Love you, El."

The phone went dead, and those in the room, all glassy eyed, held up their glasses for a refill. David poured a wee dram into each, and JL clinked her juice bottle to their drinks.

"*Slainte*," they all said in unison, then put down their glasses and left Elliott's office.

David squeezed Kenzie's hand as they walked out of the building. The twins were in school and Granny Alice had taken Laurie Wallis to a play date. They would have two hours alone to finish what they'd started in the bathroom. They needed uninterrupted time together to absorb all that happened and prepare for what was to come.

As they drove off in a golf cart, Kenzie said, "Montgomery Winery isn't just a business in the family portfolio. Along with the farm, the winery is the backbone of this family. Its destruction will destroy a piece of us all."

11

The Present, Hughes Cabin, Colorado—Connor

CONNOR WOKE, SHIVERING. Except for the glowing embers in the fireplace and the dim light of the oil lamps, he was surrounded by darkness with only the soothing sound of rain on the tin roof to remind him he was in the mountains with Olivia.

He sang quietly: "*His love's like/Rain on a tin roof/Sweet song of the summertime storm/And oh the way that it moves you/It's a melody of passion raging on/And then it's gone.*" Humming the next verse, he scratched his balls—the thing men did when they woke. As a kid, his brothers told him guys did that to be sure the Pooka, considered to be a vicious Irish prankster, hadn't stolen them while they slept.

He cracked his knuckles and gazed longingly at the beautiful woman dozing in the chair beside him. Olivia had a slight smile on her lips. For her, a slight smile was a dazzling smile and one that could change a man's day if bestowed on him. It certainly had changed his. He'd hoped for a romantic dinner tonight at the Palace Arms Restaurant to celebrate signing a contract for the purchase of the ranch. Instead, the candlelight dinner would be a freeze-dried gourmet meal in a cabin in the Colorado mountains without electricity or a hot shower.

If he was complaining, he deserved a swift kick in the ass.

The fire needed attention. He set about bringing it to life again, throwing on a few logs and tossing in more kindling. Soon, he had it roaring, infusing heat into the room.

Olivia's eyes opened slowly. "Sounds like it's still raining. It'll probably continue throughout the night." She folded the blanket he'd tucked around her, laid the soft wool across her lap, and distractedly combed the fringe with her fingers. "We're stuck here, I'm afraid."

"I don't mind being stuck in a mountain cabin with a beautiful woman and no electricity, but I should have been a better Boy Scout and come prepared with a bottle of wine and a corkscrew."

She gave him a slow promising smile. "I was a Girl Scout. Come with me." She took his hand and tugged him along behind her. "I need help with the table. Grab one end and help me move it over toward the sink."

He shot a quick glance under the table. He didn't see a hiding place under there. "What are we doing?"

"You'll see."

He lifted the table a couple of inches off the floor. "What's this made of? Aspen logs and lead?"

"It might be. It's over a hundred years old and solidly built."

"You're right about that." They moved the six-foot table off the multi-colored rug and across the floor a few feet. With the table out of the way, he had a full view of the mountain-scene rug with a black bear in the center. "Was this made on the loom?"

"My grandmother made it. My mother made the one in front of the fireplace, and Amber made the ones in the bedrooms."

"Where's yours?"

"In a closet. I'm the worst weaver in the family." She knelt. "Help me roll this up."

He had a suspicion he'd find a trapdoor under the rug, but when it was rolled and pushed aside, exposing the floor, there were no flat hinges or cut edges. Olivia stomped on one of the boards with the heel of her boot, triggering an invisible latch, and a door approximately three by five soundlessly sprung open on oiled hinges.

"Help me lift it," she said.

The door was as solid as the table. "You'd be protected if a tornado came through here, but I don't guess Colorado has many of those."

"You'd be surprised," she said. "Weld County, Colorado, has more tornado segments than any other county in the nation."

"That's hard to believe."

"Severe weather is a daily reality in Colorado," she said. "April through August can be nerve-wracking to homeowners. The first question I get from potential buyers when I show property is, 'Have there been tornadoes around here?'"

"I didn't ask, and you didn't mention it."

"There hasn't been one, in my lifetime at least, anywhere near the property you want to buy. Thankfully, tornado activity over the past three years is in decline."

"Let's hope that trend continues." He snagged a lantern hanging from a nearby hook and swung it back and forth over the opening in the floor. "Is this a potato cellar?"

She perched on the top step of what appeared to be as solidly built as the cabin. "No potatoes. Down here we keep what we don't want stolen. I'll take the lantern and guide the way. Watch your head. There's a low ceiling warning sign for tall people."

Even reading the sign, he bumped his head. "Ah. Crap."

Olivia let out an easy laugh, full of genuine affection. "Dad's noggin has put a few dents in the headrail."

He didn't see stars, but he did see a few tiny dots. "Then my dent is right beside his."

"Sit down on the steps if you're dizzy."

"I'm okay."

She turned the light toward him. "You're bleeding." She snagged a tissue from her pocket and wiped the blood. "There's a medical box down here. I'll give you a smiley face Band-Aid for your boo-boo."

"I'll settle for a kiss." He smiled. "That's a sure-fire remedy. At least, that's what my mom always said. After a kiss, the cut, bump, bruise never hurt again."

"Let me see what I can do." She stood on tiptoes and kissed his forehead. "Is that better?"

"Much." The kiss lingered in his mind and on his skin, and only her warm body entwined with his would quell his hunger for her. She stared up at him provocatively from under fluttering eyelashes and ran her tongue along the seam of her lips, giving him a look that said, "If you want to kiss me, it's okay with me." But what if he was wrong and jumped the guardrails? What would they do, stuck in the cabin overnight, with Olivia upset because he'd made a move on her?

Before he could analyze the look further, her mouth drew up in a sober smile and she glided away from him. The possibility that he'd blown his only chance exploded in his mind. He redirected his thoughts, but somehow, they landed on his sister and her husband. When they first met, they were like rabbits having a weekend fling. But Connor wanted more. He wanted a forever romance. Moving on her when she had no escape route wasn't gentlemanly. It wasn't how the O'Grady men treated women. He ran his hand over his hair and redirected his thoughts again, this time to the cold cellar.

The wall on the left held neatly stacked skis, poles, and an assortment of shovels and rakes. The wall on the right held a half-dozen floor-to-ceiling shelves stocked with labeled jars of canned goods and packages of freeze-dried food. The back wall was fitted with cubbyholes holding hats, jeans, shirts, jackets, underwear, shoes. And in the center were racks filled with thirty to forty bottles of wine.

His eyebrows went up, but his gaze remained steady. "This isn't a basement. It certainly isn't a potato cellar. It's all about wine."

"My grandparents started the collection, then my parents continued it, and now Amber and I keep it stocked. There isn't much to do up here at night except drink wine and sing."

"Sounds like perfect entertainment to me." *Add sex, and you'd have a trifecta.*

He followed her about the room like the shadows she created. "You said you put items down here so they won't be stolen. Do you have many uninvited guests?" His voice boomed in the confines of the basement and seemed to echo off the ceiling and walls.

"Two or three every year. Funny thing is, they always leave a note with cash thanking us for the hospitality. We've compared the handwriting on the notes and we're convinced the same people come back year after year. As far as we know, no one has ever found the basement." She pointed to the cubbyholes. "Feel free to take a clean shirt, jeans, whatever you need."

"I might borrow a clean shirt." He searched through one of the cubbyholes and found a polo shirt that should fit him. Then he looked through the packages of freeze-dried food. "This block-text handwriting reminds me of my kindergarten teacher—perfectly written and easy to read."

"Amber does that for me. Now, what would you like for dinner?" She picked up a package. "How about veal?"

"Chops or scaloppine?

"Scaloppine."

He stepped over to the shelves of wine and scanned the inventory. "Medium-dry riesling and pinot gris pair best."

"You sound like a sommelier. I'm impressed."

"I work for a winery, remember?" With all that she had on her mind, he didn't tell her about the fires closing in on Montgomery Winery. He pulled out several bottles until he found two that he would recommend. "When I first went to work for MacKlenna Corporation, I was given notebooks to study and had quizzes every week on Thoroughbred breeding, racing, wines, and pairings. Elliott and Meredith wanted us to know as much as possible about horses and wine."

"From what I've seen the last few months, you certainly know your wine and horses. Grab two of those wine glasses and the bottle opener. I think we've got everything else we need."

"What about breakfast?"

"Good idea. Lunch, too. Any requests?"

"Surprise me," he said.

She picked up a wicker basket and filled it with freeze-dried packages. Then, with food and wine to see them through the next twenty-four hours, they climbed back up to the first floor.

After setting the rug and table to rights, Connor asked, "What kind of music do you like?"

"All kinds, but I don't have a radio. Up here, you have to make your own music."

"There's a guitar and fiddle hanging on the wall. Are they just decorations?"

"If you can play, have at it."

Olivia opened one of the packages and poured the contents into a pan. Even preparing freeze-dried food she looked sexy. Maybe it was the lamplight backlighting her. No, it wasn't the lighting or the setting, because she stimulated every circuit in his man brain, whether she stood in sunlight or shadow, rain or dusty road, freezing cold or summer heat. His brothers would roll on the floor laughing at him for being such a romantic fool. Instead of groaning with frustration, he chuckled. Olivia cocked her head, apparently pondering the reason for his laugh.

"I was just remembering my earlier comments about freeze-dried meals," he offered quickly. "I'm a convert now."

"Not all freeze-dried food tastes the same. I could make the scaloppine and freeze-dry it, but you wouldn't eat it. You have to start with expertly prepared meals like Amber's." Olivia picked up the wine bottle. "Will you do the honors?"

That was one thing he could do, even using a vintage, direct-pull corkscrew. He wiped out the glass before pouring a small amount into one, then handed it to her. His pulse, which had been jumping up and down, easily settled to a quick, light thump, discernible in his fingertips. And then he touched her hand—her warm skin—and his pulse quickened again.

"You can be the designated sniffer," he said.

She gave the glass a swirl before hovering her nose over the top, taking a few short whiffs before tasting. "Nice. It has a lingering fruity taste." He filled her glass and one for himself. "When do you want to eat? I just need to add water to rehydrate the food and voilà"—she kissed her fingers—"another Amber original creation."

He sipped from his glass. "Lunch was spectacular, and I'm sure dinner will be, too, but let's drink wine and enjoy some music. I'm no Jimi Hendrix or Eric Clapton—"

"Or Paul McCartney?"

"Not even Paul," he said.

He crossed the room and picked up the guitar, strummed a few chords then took the time to tune the instrument by ear. "I've always believed that lead guitarists gave rock its icons, but rhythm players gave it soul."

She reclaimed her rocker in front of the fire and watched him over the rim of her glass. "Really? That's interesting. Who do you think informed your musical style?"

The question made him rewind his mental tape to the first day he picked up a guitar. "My mom sang and danced on Broadway. After school, I'd go by the theatre and watch her rehearse. She was in this production that had a guitar solo. The way the guitarist's fingers manipulated the strings mesmerized me. On the way home, I told Mom I wanted to play the instrument. My first lesson was the next day. God knows why, but I told my teacher I wanted to play like Elvis."

Olivia laughed. "I've watched you ride a horse, watched your hips sway in the saddle. You could do a great impersonation, at least with the dance part, since I haven't heard you play yet."

He flushed a little, realizing what she'd said, that she'd watched him and liked the way he moved in the saddle. Now if he could impress her with his musical talent, he might have the confidence to kiss her the next time he had an opening. God, he was pitiful. You'd think he was sixteen. But when a man was hoping for a—forever— he had to take his time.

Of all the songs in his repertoire, "Hotel California" by the Eagles best exhibited his talent. He'd start with that and move on from there.

He strummed the last chord and as the sound vibrated through the room, her eyes widened along with her smile. "You *can* play. Would you believe that's one of Amber's favorites? When she performs at local charity events, she always opens with that song. It's the string bending and vibrato that she loves. There's a timeless quality in the music she creates. It's the same with you. You two could do a record-worthy duet. I can't wait to hear you jamming with her."

He didn't want to jam with Amber. He wanted to... Thinking about what he wanted to do with Olivia only frustrated him more. "What about you? Do you play an instrument?"

"The piano, but you can't take that talent to a campfire jamboree." She refreshed their drinks. "Your act belongs on the stage. Denver has several small theatres. I believe you'd have a sellout audience. If you and Amber worked up a few duets, gosh, you could play anywhere."

"Denver puts on fantastic shows. I was the only male in a performance of *Girls Only* at the Garner Galleria Theatre & Bar a few weeks ago."

"Really?"

"Maggy O'Grady always said, 'The subject matter should never keep you from going to the theatre.' I was in Denver with a free night and a ticket. So I went."

"You should have called me. I would have rescued you."

He put the guitar aside and gazed at her for a long moment. The night was planted so clearly in his memory. She had turned down his dinner invitation, and as a consolation he'd gone to the theatre by himself. There was an ache in his body and soul, then as well as now, that would only be satisfied by pulling her into his arms and kissing her. But he didn't. Instead, he said, "You probably had other plans."

Her gaze left him and traveled across the room to the far corner. Whatever she saw there in the empty space was visible only in her mind. The worry lines between her eyebrows that had softened while she listened to the music appeared once again, and this time they set deeper into the smooth skin of her face.

"Maybe not." She looked at him and was unable to hide the storm clouds in her hazel eyes. And then she cleared her throat. "Are you hungry now?"

"I could eat something." Her stare was like a physical pressure on the center of his chest, and he wanted to know why she'd turned him down that night, and why she was turning him down now. His intentions couldn't be any more obvious. He was like a character in one of his mom's plays, suffering from unrequited love. The truth, he feared, was that he was a former cop from New York City and simply not her type.

"It'll only take a couple of minutes to put dinner on the table. Do you want to open another bottle of wine?" She held up the empty bottle and her fingers played along the label as if picking out a random tune on the piano. "I can't believe you drank all this."

"Me? I think you refilled your glass more than I did."

She laughed. "Maybe, but I never admit to anything until all my ducks are in a row, all my questions answered, all my doubts assuaged."

The lamp cast wavering shadows on her as she walked toward the kitchen area to heat water in the oversized iron pot. He had one thought circling about his head...

That was a merry little waltz around the elephant in the room.

Dinner was exceptional, the wine paired perfectly, and his dinner companion had him so turned on that he fidgeted constantly. Maybe he should go chop some wood. When his phone rang, he welcomed the distraction. "It's Sheriff Hall."

"Have you heard from Amber?" the sheriff asked.

"Not yet, but with this rain, she's probably holed up somewhere," Connor said. "I'm hoping we'll find her in the morning, or she'll find us."

"I've got a team ready to come up day after tomorrow, but if you hear from her, let me know."

"Sure thing." The call ended abruptly, and Connor couldn't hide his irritation. He swung his hand, accidentally knocking over his glass, spilling wine on his lap in a cool amber splash. Olivia wiped up the spill while he dabbed at his sweatpants with his napkin. The mishap didn't improve his mood. If he had his druthers he'd rather the sheriff stay far away, but Olivia wanted him there.

"What'd he say?" she asked.

"It's not in his job description to pick and choose cases to investigate."

"So he's not coming?"

"He'll be here, but not until day after tomorrow."

A devastating look crossed her face and Connor felt like an absolute cad. David and Kenzie were leaving in the morning and would return almost instantly with Amber. Olivia would hear from her sister in a few hours. He recalled David telling him about lying to Kenzie when she went back to World War II. He said it was the biggest mistake he'd ever made. Connor wasn't lying to Olivia per se, he just wasn't telling her everything he knew. But as he'd learned as a teenager, when he intentionally misled his mom, lies of omission were still lies.

"If the sheriff isn't coming up here tomorrow," Olivia said, "we'll cover as much ground as we can until he gets here. We'll find her, and if she's injured, I'll do everything I can to see that Sheriff Hall loses the job he's held for twenty years."

Silence filled the cabin, interrupted only by the soothing sound of rain. But it did nothing to soothe Connor, whose heart tried to crawl up his throat. If Olivia would campaign against the sheriff for neglecting his duty, he had little doubt what her reaction would be when she discovered the part he'd played.

A slap in the face, for starters. And downhill from there.

God help him. He'd prefer to face New York City's number one crime boss than the hell-hath-no-fury temper of a woman deceived.

12

The Present, MacKlenna Farm, Lexington, Kentucky—Kenzie

KENZIE SAT NEXT to David in the command center at the farm, drinking her fourth or eighth or twelfth cup of coffee for the day. She'd lost count around five o'clock. Now as it neared midnight, yawning, she'd switched to juice.

"You look exhausted. Can't you take a break, and I don't know…" She made her eyebrows dance. "Come to bed for a while."

He leaned toward her, cupping his ear. "Are ye asking me to make love to ye again? Didn't I give ye all the attention and pleasure this afternoon that ye wanted?"

"Oh," she sighed. "I can never get enough McBain. It's like eating premium ice cream. A McBain has all the right ingredients—voice, eyes, a heart bigger than Scotland." Her eyes zeroed in on his crotch. "After seven years of marriage, you still turn me into a quivering puddle."

His eyes darkened and filled with mischief. His lips half parted as his little finger hooked a strand of her hair and tugged her to him for a kiss. "And I never tire of hearing the sounds of yer pleasure."

She kissed him back, then remembering the hour, said, "Let's get in our correct lanes and figure out what we need to do before we drop and roll right here under the desk." She squared her shoulders as if that would redirect her hormones. "Do you know anything more than you did this afternoon?"

He cleared his throat, swiveled his chair to face the keyboard and monitor. "There are three distinct prints on the puzzle box: Amber's, Olivia's, and Connor's. The rest are partials and don't show up in any database. One partial matches a partial on yer box."

"After all these years, you pulled off a partial print? That's amazing. But how'd Connor lift any prints? He doesn't have any equipment with him."

"A MacGyver trick using soot and tape."

"I should have known. But what about the envelope Charlotte's sapphire brooch came in or the wrapping paper Jack found at Amy's house?"

"I sent Charlotte a text asking her to send me the envelope and another text to Jack asking for the wrapping paper. It's possible those prints haven't degraded."

"I'm surprised you haven't compared the prints before now."

"I've never put much effort in finding Digby other than visiting his office once."

"I find it curious that you don't want to meet the solicitor."

"It's not that I don't want to meet him. I have dozens of questions to ask, but I don't believe he exists. What we already know about the stones is dangerous enough. More information compounds the danger and puts all our lives at risk."

She jerked as if pulled by a puppeteer's strings. "You really believe that?"

"Once we recover Amber and her brooch, we'll have six stones. If twelve are needed to open the mysterious door in the cave beneath the castle, we'll be halfway there. It's possible…" He paused, turned again to face her, taking her hands in his. "Think about it, Kenz. We can't be the only ones who know about the stones. If there's a dark force of some kind, it has to be sensing the growing power of the stones we have."

"Would you stop watching sci-fi movies. That's crazy talk. There's no dark force. There's only Mr. Digby. And I believe he sends the brooches out when owners die."

"Then how do ye explain Amber's brooch? It's been locked up for over a century," David said.

"We don't know how long it's been inside the loom. Maybe Amber's grandparents put it there."

"Why would they put a valuable treasure in a cabin when they could put it in a bank vault?"

"Then it arrived with the loom. Hell, I don't know. But the brooches are all finding their way to us, and if we need help, Mr. Digby lends a hand. We know they were disbursed throughout the MacKlenna Clan because every brooch we find has a direct connection to the family. Which brings us to the Kellys. Do you know yet how they're related?"

"I found the title to the Hughes Mine, which led me to Craig Hughes' will. He left everything to his son Adam with a life interest to his wife, Lindsey MacKlenna Hughes. Lindsey was one of James MacKlenna's four legitimate children."

"The remaining brooches could link to unknown illegitimate children. I'm sure Meredith has had her genealogy team searching for possibilities but what good does that do? Are we going to ask strangers if they have a brooch? Sounds like a waste of time." Thinking about it gave her a headache. "Let's just deal with this one right now. What else have you discovered about Amber? What's her plan?"

David clicked several keys on the keyboard. "I've added additional pieces of information. The program should give us a more exact time frame." He squeezed her hand. It wasn't an anxious squeeze but one of confident waiting. The pointer on the screen whirled in circles then it stopped, and a date flashed—Fall 1878.

"Brr," Kenzie said. "Colorado mountains at that time of the year wouldn't be like fall in Kentucky. I'll have to rethink my wardrobe."

"Based on all the information I have, I'd say the time of year is ninety-seven percent accurate. As for where she landed, I can give ye odds in favor of Leadville, Cañon City, and Morrison, but based on anecdotal experience, Amber should have landed close to where she disappeared—the cabin or Leadville."

"I wonder what she was wearing."

"I asked Connor to check with Olivia. She said probably jeans, flannel shirt, and a canvas jacket."

"No hat. No gloves. She wasn't dressed for cold weather."

"If she landed near the cabin or town, she'd have been around people who could provide food and shelter. Her seven-times great-grandparents were in Leadville then. As for her skills and expertise, she's a gourmet cook, lawyer, plays multiple instruments, and knowledgeable about mining. Her knowledge and experience might be questioned, but I don't think anyone would believe she was a spy."

"Thanks." Kenzie shivered. "I could have gone all evening without remembering the London Cage."

"If I had just told ye who I was, that could have been avoided."

She kissed him. "You might have been slightly off your game that trip, but you saved my life."

David opened the desk drawer and pulled out a bottle of whisky and two shot glasses. She put one glass back in the drawer. "I've got too much to do tonight, but you go right ahead."

David poured his drink and took a sip while typing with one hand. "If Amber isn't in Leadville, it's a tossup between Morrison and Cañon City. The first *Stegosaurus* was discovered in 1877, and the Bone Wars between two famous paleontologists, Dr. Marsh and Dr. Cope, were going on at that time. Based on her passion for fossils, I believe she'll go to one of those cities. Plus, Cañon City is a double draw for her. It was at the center of the Royal Gorge War between the Rio Grande and the Santa Fe railroads."

"Why would she care about a railroad war?"

"I'm not sure she would, but from articles I found, her father has spent years researching what happened in the gorge and has written several articles about the lawsuit filed by Santa Fe. The case went all the way to the Supreme Court, arguing over which company had the right-of-way through the gorge. It got mean and ugly. I'm sure his passion for the case rubbed off on his daughters."

David clicked more keys and a map appeared on the large screen on the wall. "Here's the other draw: Garden City is located a few miles from Cañon City. Right there"—he pointed with a laser pointer—"A *Stegosaurus* was discovered in 1937."

"So she knows where one *will be* discovered. If it was me, I'd be hard pressed not to find it first."

"That would be fifty years before its time, and she might embroil it in a controversy. Plus, she'd steal the thunder from its rightful discoverer."

"We can't let her do that," Kenzie said.

"I agree."

Kenzie yawned. "What do you want me to do?"

David picked up an expandable file folder. "Ye won't get much sleep tonight." He put the folder in her lap. "Railway Company v. Alling 99 U.S. 463 (1878). The attorney for the appellants was Amber's six-times great-grandfather. The litigation nearly bankrupted the Rio Grande, in which Amber's family was heavily invested."

Kenzie pulled the documents out of the folder and thumbed through several pages. "Did you put this together? It's a lot of work."

"If ye're willing to pay, ye can get anything ye want."

"I hope you're not racking up serious expenses, especially since we haven't told Kevin about Amber's disappearance. I'd hate to dump thousands of dollars in receipts on his desk and expect him to pay them."

"For once, Kevin might turn a blind eye at the expense report. He wants Connor to be happy. Getting Amber back safely might make a difference in his relationship with Olivia."

Kenzie perused the original complaint filed in the Colorado District Court. "If Amber gets involved in the litigation, her goal would be to get the case settled, which presents an interesting dilemma. If this case has been used as precedent in future litigation, it could screw up jurisprudence well into the twenty-first century. She would know that, but would she care enough to put that before her family's interest?"

"We've all experienced that dilemma, and none of us have been able to stand by and not interfere."

Kenzie put the file back in the folder. "I'll need a couple of days to get up to speed on this case."

"Ye only have tonight, lass. Do the best ye can. What ye don't finish, ye can take with ye. In the meantime, I'll be investigating the paleontology angle."

"How far have you gotten?"

David pointed to a stack of papers topped with a picture of a scary-looking creature with big teeth that resembled a friendly dinosaur in the twins' toy collection. "I started Paleontology 101 about an hour ago. All I've learned so far is that dinosaurs were originally thought to be cold-blooded reptiles. The belief now is that they were warm-blooded. If Amber runs into Marsh or Cope—"

"She could fast-forward the field of paleontology by a century or more."

"With the exception of Braham's attempt to save Abraham Lincoln, this adventure has the potential of having the biggest impact on history."

Kenzie finished the rest of David's drink. The smooth golden liquor settled with a glow in her stomach, and she sighed. "The way I see it, we have to stop her."

David hefted another expandable folder from a drawer and added it to her stack of folders. "Aye, we do. But first we have to find her."

13

The Present, Hughes Cabin, Colorado—Connor

THE NEXT MORNING, as the sky was lightening from impenetrable black to a darkling gray, the shapes of the mountains began to stand in proper relief against the sky. Another gloomy day. Another day full of lies and deceptions. Another day to fall farther into a trap Connor would likely never escape. When had he become such a pessimist? He could narrow it down to the last twenty-four hours.

He shook his head in disgust and hunkered down at the table reading *The New York Times* on his smartphone while enjoying a freeze-dried breakfast—scrambled eggs, bacon, cinnamon rolls, and blueberries. Olivia joined him in the kitchen. One look at her tousled hair, sleepy eyes, and practical flannel pajamas, and he had one thought that was impossible to scrub from his man brain.

"I'm a terrible hostess. You shouldn't have let me sleep so late. How long have you been up?"

"It's only eight o'clock here. I'm still on Eastern time." His eyes returned quickly to his phone. Looking at her was killing him. He had tossed all night, unable to get her out of his mind, knowing she was sleeping on the other side of the wall. "I've been up for a while." He shifted uncomfortably in the chair and ate his blueberries.

She reached for the coffee pot on the stove and poured a cup.

"Looks like you figured out how to make coffee and rehydrate food."

"I'm getting one of these hydrating food machines." He picked up the bag the berries came in and shook it for emphasis. "If I had cupboards filled with these, I wouldn't have to throw out food that spoiled while I was traveling."

She laughed, and it was deep and throaty, and he liked the sound of it, especially in the morning. "The machines don't cook the food, Amber does, and she's an awesome cook." Olivia's breath hitched, and her eyes seemed to darken at the mention of her sister.

Trying to draw Olivia back from her dark thoughts, he said, "I'm not a crazy foodie. Irish stew, colcannon, beef and Guinness pie aren't considered fine cuisine. But wait until you taste Maria Ricci's cooking."

"Who is she?"

"My dad's companion. Maria doesn't push the envelope with creativity like Amber, but she can cook Italian cuisine as well as any of the top chefs in Palermo or Modena or Florence."

"We'll have to get her and Amber together to swap recipes."

Connor rubbed the back of his neck, shaking his head. "I don't know. Maria is very secretive when it comes to her recipes. She and Elliott Fraser's longtime cook, Mrs. Collins, are still dancing around each other in the kitchen. It's funny to watch."

The mucky sound of hooves sloshing through mud drew Olivia to the window, and Connor to his feet, his gun drawn. "Stay back until I know who it is."

She flattened against the wall while Connor lifted an edge of the curtain to see without being seen.

"Who is it?" she asked.

"If it was the nineteenth century, I'd say it was a posse—a dozen men dressed in heavy dusters and cowboy hats. But I don't see any tin stars on their chests."

She lifted the other side of the curtain. "The man on the roan horse with the white markings is Sheriff Hall. Will you talk to him while I get dressed? I didn't think he was coming today."

Connor dropped the curtain and holstered his gun. "Probably didn't sit well with him that a former NYPD detective was doing his job."

He picked up the curtain again and studied the man before he went out to meet him. The face of the sheriff, who was a large, full-chested man with graying hair and a short-cropped beard, was settled into cool impassivity. Connor instantly disliked him. Men with that kind of apathy didn't need to be working for the public.

The sheriff rode in as though he'd been born on the horse's back and had never once dismounted. He neared the cabin, and when he was almost adjacent to the horse trough, he reined to a stop. Connor could have sworn he'd seen the same scene in a western movie.

Casually resting both hands on the saddle horn, the sheriff took in the layout of the yard and outbuildings before dismounting and loosening the cinch, so the roan could breathe easily.

Connor counted slowly to ten and then even slower to ten again. He didn't want to give the impression he was relieved the cavalry had arrived. Because he wasn't. He had hoped to get Amber home before the sheriff showed up.

After sufficient time had passed, Connor walked out to meet the sheriff, and a brief and almost hostile glance passed between them. While the others watered their horses, the sheriff stepped up on the porch, chewing a toothpick, which was kept in constant motion, up and down, side to side, end over end. Gum and toothpick chewers annoyed the hell out of Connor. If the assholes had unresolved oral needs, they should smoke a cigar like a real man.

Pops would expect his son to check his attitude and exchange it for a professional one. It wasn't easy, but for his dad, he did. Even as a grown man, Connor strove to live up to his dad's expectations. One day, he intended to instill that same respect in his own children.

"Morning, Sheriff. What brings you up here today?"

The sheriff tipped his head back to eye Connor from under the brim of his hat, and in a slow-drawling voice said, "I talked to the Chief of the Colorado State Patrol after I got off the phone with you last night. They're sending an investigative team up this morning."

Connor crossed his arms and hitched his hip against the porch rail. "You didn't sound that concerned when we spoke. I'm surprised you called them."

"I talked to my deputy. He said he could get a search party together ready to ride this morning. You and Olivia are welcome to go with us. Is she still here?"

The fact that the sheriff didn't answer his question didn't go unnoticed. "She'll be out in a minute. Where's the forensic team coming from? Denver?"

The sheriff flicked the toothpick out into the yard. "Don't think I mentioned a forensic team."

Olivia joined them on the porch. She had dressed in jeans and smelled of soap. Her shoulder-length hair was pulled back in a ponytail. "Morning, Sheriff. Glad you're here." She pulled on her gloves, flexing her fingers to cement the fit. "If you'll give me a few minutes to see to the horses, we'll go out with you and your team."

Another toothpick materialized, and he worked it furiously up and down. It occurred to Connor that the wooden picks were the sheriff's signature feature. Not the badge. Not the gun. Not the job title.

"I thought we'd ride down toward the cave," the sheriff said.

"We were going there yesterday but it was raining too hard," Olivia said.

"According to the sheriff," Connor said, "the Colorado State Patrol's coming up." Then he turned his gaze back to the sheriff. "Do you have a warrant to search the premises?" Connor didn't care if the sheriff had a warrant or not. He wasn't going to stop anyone from going inside. There had been no foul play and there was nothing to hide, but if the sheriff was going to act like an asshat, so would Connor.

Sorry, Dad.

If a glare had the force of a .45, Connor would be dead, a bullet hole in his chest. "They'll have a warrant."

No one moved while Olivia glanced at them. First at the sheriff, then at Connor. The stress and tension responsible for the dark circles beneath her eyes now held her neck and shoulders bowstring tight, and fear seemed to coalesce with her frustration.

"Why do they need a warrant?" she asked.

Connor positioned himself to catch, grab, or protect Olivia depending on her reaction. "To search a possible crime scene."

Her look was veiled at first, then she gasped in soundless horror. "In the cabin? Amber wasn't hurt inside. She's out there somewhere." Olivia swung her arm to encompass the yard and beyond. "They'll waste time looking here, and too much time has already been wasted."

Connor's fingers stiffened and curled in toward his palms instead of reaching out to comfort her. When Amber returned later today with David and Kenzie, Olivia would remember this moment and blame him for putting her through hell.

"Olivia," he said gently. "The State Patrol has to rule out the possibility that Amber was hurt inside the cabin."

She winced and dragged her hands down her face. "There was no blood, no evidence of a fight, no broken glass. If there had been an altercation, we would have seen evidence of it." Then her keen eyes challenged the sheriff and pointed toward the door. "Whatever happened to my sister didn't happen in there."

Connor drew in a long breath, let it out. Olivia was wrong. Whatever happened to Amber *had* occurred inside the cabin. The faint odor of peat confirmed that.

"Did you find any evidence that she spent much time in the cabin when she arrived Saturday. Did she rest? Eat? Unpack? Anything?" the sheriff asked.

"A piece of the loom had broken off and we believe she found a puzzle box inside the breast beam. Her backpack was open, and she had unrolled her field kit and removed a few tools. The beds were made and there weren't any dirty dishes."

The sheriff removed the toothpick and pointed it at her as if it were a tiny wooden sword. "Do you think she broke the loom?"

Olivia rubbed her forehead the way one does with a pounding headache. But Connor knew it wasn't a headache pounding her head. It was the pressure of uncertainty, fear, confusion. On reflection, he should have insisted on a family meeting for an up or down vote on whether to bring Olivia into the fold.

"A few weeks ago, we tried to move it closer to the window. We must have loosened the piece. She could have bumped it, or it could have just fallen off."

"Do you have any idea what could have been in the puzzle box?"

Olivia shrugged. "Maybe the forensic team can figure it out. Isn't that what they do?"

"Where is it now?"

Connor had decided not to close the box in case David needed additional pictures. Now he wished he had. Whose prints would they find, and what trace evidence would be discovered inside the box? He needed to talk to David. No one outside the family had come this close to a brooch before, except Lillian Russell and a half-dozen other people in 1909 New York City. But they'd only been interested in the brooch's large diamond.

"The box is on the mantel," she said.

Connor checked the time. "I assume you don't intend to leave before the State Patrol arrives." He tried to keep his dislike for the sheriff out of his voice, but doubted he succeeded.

The sheriff's glance swung directly on him. "We'll wait. I'm surprised they aren't already here."

"Your men can wait in the barn. Would they like coffee?" Olivia asked.

"Thanks for the offer. We have our own provisions." He gestured with his chin. "I'll be out there with my men." With no further comment, he stepped away, making a show of pointing to his men and giving them hand signals, which they acknowledged with nods and signals of their own.

Connor followed Olivia back inside. "I've got a few calls to make. Are you okay?"

She whipped around to face him, hands on her small waist, drawing attention to her hourglass figure. God, she was beautiful.

"I want to know your opinion. I've done research on you. I've read articles in the New York papers about cases you've worked on, and about your family. I trust you, Connor. Tell me right now, what do you think has happened to Amber?"

He already knew she'd Googled him but reading up on cases he'd worked during his tenure with the NYPD showed a deeper level of interest. He saw that as a positive, but what good would it do him after this was all over and the truth came out.

He rubbed his hand over his mouth, tugged on his chin, thinking or delaying, he wasn't sure. "I think she's in some trouble." Now he scratched his whiskers. Every word he said, she'd throw back at him later. "But she'll be okay, and if I had to bet…" He took a deep breath, this was the big one that would be thrown in his face along with a slap. "I'd bet she'll be home by tonight."

"How could you possibly know that?"

"Because she's always come home before, right?" He should just shut up because all he was doing was digging a hole and stepping deeper into it. "And that's my gut reaction. Let the State Patrol come in, do their thing, and we'll ride out with the sheriff. That's all we can do for now."

Something like hope flashed across Olivia's face before her expression settled into guardedness. Quietly, she moved to stand against the doorjamb and stared out into the yard. "If we're going to talk about our guts, I'll tell you what mine says. Amber is in trouble and what's gotten her out of trouble all her life isn't working for her now. And if she doesn't get help soon, I might never see her again."

"You're overreacting." As soon as the words popped out of Connor's mouth, he cringed. It was too late to reel them back in or to even hope she hadn't heard him.

Her face turned blood red. "Overreacting?" She curled her hands into fists. "I thought you were on my side."

He flung his arms in frustration, and for a moment he thought they had really come loose from his shoulders and were circling around, planning a direct attack to beat the crap out of himself.

"There aren't multiple sides here, Olivia. There's just one—

Amber."

She gave him *the look*. All men knew the look. It was the expression that said men were the stupidest of all God's creations, and for the second time in less than fifteen minutes, he was shot with an imaginary .45. This time to his man brain. He instinctively tugged on the hem of his shirt to cover his groin.

"You're all a bunch of pint-sized brains stuffed in big hats." She snagged a poncho off the hook. "I'm going to the barn to saddle the horses." She whirled around and marched out.

He paced the room, carving canals through his thick unruly waves. First one side, then the other, then both sides together. "Damn woman." He should have just said, *"Amber found a magical brooch in the puzzle box and time traveled back to the nineteenth century. But she'll be okay because my friends are using another magical brooch to go back and get her."*

He sat down in the rocker and put his head in his hands. How could anything get so screwed up? He'd been afraid to ask her out. Now, after this, he'd be afraid to even say hello.

He took a moment to analyze the situation. Was he blowing the craziness out of proportion? Was he the one overreacting? No matter which way he looked at it, he knew he was doing the right thing for the family, although maybe not the right thing for himself. He had a secret to protect at all cost, even if it meant Olivia would never speak to him again. As for the sheriff, he was just being an asshole, first saying he wasn't coming and then showing up with the State Patrol in tow. It screamed intimidation.

When Connor got his anger under control, he called David. "The sheriff and a search party just arrived. The State Patrol is on its way with a search warrant. I'm struggling with whether I should tell Olivia the truth. What do you think?"

"Don't. She won't believe ye and she'll tell the sheriff about yer dumbass idea."

He didn't like David's response, but on the org chart, David was his superior. After a decade as a police officer and his time in the Marines, Connor understood levels of command. If he didn't like his orders, he could appeal to Elliott, but today, that would be a mistake. Elliott had his wife and the winery to worry about. Olivia's problems ranked low on the company's list of priorities.

"Okay. So what's happening there? What's the latest from Napa?" Connor asked.

"Everyone safely evacuated late yesterday afternoon. We don't know the extent of the damage yet," David said.

"Where are my brothers and Pete?"

"They drove the horses to Reno last night. Today they're taking them to McCann Ranch there in Colorado. Are ye and Olivia going out with the sheriff to look for Amber this morning?"

"Olivia told the sheriff what we found when we arrived here. The State Patrol will dust the puzzle box for prints."

"They'll identify yours, Amber's, and Olivia's along with a few partials they can't identify. That's no problem."

"What about inside the box?" Connor asked.

"A few fibers maybe, but nothing significant. I'm not worried."

"Would you tell me if you were?"

"I'll always tell ye what ye need to know."

Connor's sigh was intentionally audible. David was the ultimate commander and he had just sidestepped Connor's question. David never sent troops into the field unless they were fully equipped and informed. Knowing that fact was answer enough for him. As for telling David about the emotional turmoil taking place on the mountain, he probably already knew or suspected.

"What's your plan?" Connor asked.

"Kenzie is doing last minute research, Rick is pulling our gear together, and I'm finishing Dinosaurs 101. The plan is to leave in an hour."

Connor checked the time again. Mornings generally flew by at a blazing speed, but this morning, time crawled on one knee. "You should be back with Amber before noon."

"If the brooches work for us the way they worked for Amy and Kevin, then yes, we should be. If that was a fluke, I don't know when we'll be back."

"I don't believe it was a fluke. Be sure to tell Amber how worried Olivia is, and please hurry home."

"That's what I intend to do."

"If Amber wants to go back later and spend more time there, Olivia and I will go with her. But for now, she needs to come home and get straight with the sheriff and her sister."

"I'll call ye as soon as we get back," David said.

"Be careful. Oh wait. I forgot to ask. Did Kenzie make an offer on the ranch?"

"Aye, and she pushed for an early closing date. Got the sellers to agree to three weeks. Tell Olivia thanks."

If the luck of the Irish was with him, and if Olivia was still speaking to him after she heard from her sister, then maybe he could celebrate Amber's return and the contract on the ranch with Olivia tonight. As he thought about his luck, he found it somewhat ironic that the phrase wasn't Irish at all. It started in America during the gold and silver rush of the second half of the nineteenth century when most of the miners were Irish. Regardless of its origin, he hoped some of it would rain down on him.

He poured another cup of coffee and finished off the berries. Olivia needed to come back and eat a bite before they left. As if reading his mind, boots clunked across the hardwood porch planks. She breezed into the room and slapped a piece of paper into his hand.

"I just got served."

He glanced out the window but didn't see any additional horses or men. "From the State Patrol? Where are they? I didn't hear any horses ride up."

"They went to the mine first and came up the stairs." Olivia unzipped her backpack. "What do you want for lunch?"

"Surprise me," he said.

She tossed several packages of food into her backpack while he read through the search warrant. It authorized the State Patrol to search a three-room cabin. There was no mention of the cellar, and he didn't intend to tell them about it. The room had been a closely-held family secret for over a hundred years and since Amber wasn't in danger, at least not in this century, he wasn't going to tell the State Patrol of its existence. If they found the room on their own, so be it.

"It seems to be in order. Let's get out of here." He tossed the warrant onto the kitchen table and together they left the cabin.

The sheriff and a group of five men wearing State Patrol jackets were gathered in a rough circle next to the barn. The State Patrol officers were studying a map while the sheriff, fishing another toothpick from his pocket in an absent-minded manner, spun his spur in a tiny furrow he had dug in the dirt.

"I'm Detective Connor O'Grady, retired, NYPD." He pulled business cards from his pocket and dropped them on the corner of the map. "This is a historical cabin with items over a hundred years old. The owners would appreciate it if you went in as librarians, not cowboys. If you have any questions, you have my number."

Olivia had tied their horses' reins to the top rail of the hitching post. Connor snapped up the reins like a gunfighter on a draw. Holding onto the saddle horn, he swung his leg over the saddle without using the stirrups. He hoped he'd made his point. He might be a former cop from New York City, but he could handle himself in Colorado.

"If you find a lead, I've got three brothers and a sister, all retired detectives. The O'Gradys will search every inch of this mountain until we locate Amber." He touched two fingers to the brim of his hat in salute. Then he and Olivia rode off the property without waiting for the sheriff.

Connor checked the time. It was nine. By eleven or twelve, David should be calling. If all went as planned, Olivia could finally talk to her sister. Connor hoped to hell they created a believable story before they made the call. Olivia wouldn't be the only person who'd want to know where Amber had been. At least a dozen cops would be demanding answers, too.

14

The Present, MacKlenna Farm, Lexington, Kentucky—David

DAVID DROPPED HIS saddlebags in the garage before entering MacKlenna Mansion to meet with Elliott. He first stopped in the kitchen to see what Mrs. Collins was fixing for lunch. When the O'Gradys and the Riccis weren't on the farm, Mrs. Collins cooked more fish and seafood. She had a dish of baked salmon cakes with vegetables in the oven warmer. Before he scooped a couple of cakes and vegetables onto a plate, he checked the calendar on the wall just to be sure she hadn't prepared the meal for a special event.

Kenzie entered the kitchen. "What are you doing?" She put her arms around his waist and looked over his shoulder. "Yum. I want some, too."

He spooned a salmon cake and vegetables onto a plate and handed it to her. "Where are the kids?"

Kenzie sat down on a barstool. "Alice is bringing them over. Are you ready to go?" She bit into the salmon and moaned. "The food on MacKlenna Farm is better than a five-star restaurant in any major city. Did Mrs. Collins make this?"

"Aye. Maria is in California, remember?"

"I know, but Isabella pops in and cooks sometimes."

"Not lately. She's spending more time at the sorority house this semester than at the farm."

"She's adjusted so well, it's amazing. Just a few months ago, she was attending Barnard College in 1909."

David fixed another plate for himself and stood at ease in front of the sink while he ate. "Where are yer bags?"

"In the golf cart? Where are yours?"

"In the garage. I didn't want the lads to see them, but they'll know something is up by the way ye're dressed. And," he added with a wink, "ye look sexy as hell." He swallowed a bite before he asked, "Where'd ye get that outfit?"

"In the closet. It's a riding habit JL had made for the reunion in 1881 with Kit and Cullen. I had to let out the buttons. The jacket is a little tight in the bust, but I'll survive. Hopefully, I won't have to wear it more than a couple of days. But look at you. You're very dashing in your frock coat and ascot. Is Rick wearing a suit, too?"

David finished the last of his salmon cake and wiped his mouth. "With his cowboy fixation, he'll show up dressed like Clint Eastwood in *High Plains Drifter*."

"God, I hope not. We'll be burying him in Boothill Graveyard."

"That's in Arizona."

"Whatever." She emptied her plate and put it in the sink. "Did you tell him we were ready to go?"

The front door of the mansion opened and slammed closed. "Kenz." Five-year-old Henry dropped his voice an octave and fell into a passable Scottish accent.

Kenzie's jaw dropped. "Henry has never called me Kenz. What's up with that?"

David shook his head. "I don't know. Ye'll have to ask him."

"Where are ye, lass?"

"I'm in the kitchen, Henry."

"It's not Henry, my sweetling. It's Robert James McBain." Henry's twin brother also adjusted his inflection to sound more Scottish.

Kenzie covered her mouth to keep from laughing out loud but giggled behind her hand. "Are they auditioning for a performance?"

Henry and Robbie bounded into the kitchen and skidded to a stop. "Where'd ye get that funny hat?" Robbie asked.

"It's all..." Henry moved his hands around his head in robotic motions. "…tilted wrong. Here, let me fix it."

Kenzie formed an X with her forearms. "Don't touch the hat. It took me an hour to get it on right."

"No wonder. Look at all that hair piled on top of your head." Robbie shot a cockeyed glance at his dad. "Take your bride to the barber. She needs a haircut."

David knelt on one knee, rested his arm on his opposite thigh, and looked at the boys, eye to eye. "Yer mother's name is Mommy or Mom. If she wants to wear a funny hat, don't criticize her selection. If ye can't say something nice, don't say anything at all. Be respectful."

Robbie leaned over and whispered. "It's a stupid hat. If I can't tell her, you do it."

David stood, barely containing a laugh, and chucked Robbie's chin. "I wouldn't dare."

"Hey, Dad. You're wearing funny clothes too. Are your khakis at the cleaners getting a knife-edge crease?" Henry brushed his hand down his pant legs. "Granny Alice puts knife-edge creases in my pants. Do you think they look like Uncle Elliott's?"

Kenzie put her arm around Henry. "I think your creases are perfect, darling." She patted his head. He had so much product on that his waves and spikes didn't move. "Is JC giving you styling advice?"

"Please, don't mess with my hair, Mom."

"Okay, I won't but, I need to tell you that we're going away overnight, and you have to listen to Granny Alice. Whatever she says, you do. Got it?"

Henry's eyes darted between his parents as his face paled. "You're both going?"

"Again?" Robbie's eyes narrowed. "But you don't travel at the same time. Remember? That's the rule."

"We're making an exception this time."

Robbie put his finger to his chin and tapped it there. "You made an exception last time."

David glanced away, put his fist to his mouth, and cleared his throat.

"Where's Laurie Wallis?" Kenzie asked. "You were supposed to be watching her."

"Granny Alice is pushing her in the stroller. She told us to go ahead."

Henry made a face. "She had a stinky diaper."

"Granny Alice?" David asked.

Robbie giggled. "No, Da. Laurie Wallis."

Henry grabbed Robbie's arm. "Come on. We got to go upstairs. JC's waiting for us. If we're late, he'll go play with somebody else."

Robbie gave Henry a quizzical look and threw up his arms. "Nobody else is here."

Henry shoved his brother. "James Cullen's got other friends, stupid."

"Hey, no hitting. No name calling," Kenzie said. "Come here and give me a hug and be nice to each other. Hitting your brother is like hitting yourself."

Robbie punched himself in the arm. "Does that hurt, Henry?"

"No, does this?" Henry punched his own arm.

"Stop! It hurts," Robbie screamed. "Mommy, make him stop."

Henry punched his own arm harder until Robbie stopped screaming, grabbed his belly, and laughed. When Henry realized he'd been tricked, he shoved Robbie.

"Stop it, right now." Kenzie said. "And give me a goodbye hug."

David struggled to keep from grinning like an idiot. They were his lads. God, he loved them and wanted a dozen more.

The boys hugged Kenzie around the waist then ran toward the back staircase. "Bye, Kenz," Henry said.

"Bye, McBain," Robbie said.

The twins giggled hysterically all the way up the stairs. "Good idea, Robbie, calling 'em by those names."

Kenzie rolled her eyes and flashed a look at David. "I was anxious about this trip, but not now. If we need to stay a couple of weeks, I'll be fine. If I start acting strange, remind me of this little vignette."

A lump rose in David's throat. He hadn't expected it to be such an emotional experience to leave his children behind. "I don't know where they come up with this stuff. In another year, Laurie Wallis will be smack in the middle."

"Oh God, I hope not."

"We need another wee lass."

"You're a Johnny-one-note, McBain. Forget it. Even if you get me drunk, it won't work. No. More. Babies."

He stood there in the middle of the kitchen and all he could think about was kissing his bride. He lifted her chin with his fingertip and his lips found hers, a touch at first, and then an explosion of need as his tongue made its way deep within her mouth. Her arms came around his neck and he pulled her hips close to his. It was an amazingly intimate moment until a throat clear brought them to their senses.

"I thought ye were getting ready to go," Elliott said.

David stepped back from Kenzie but kept an arm wrapped around her.

"If anything happens to us, you'll take care of my kids, right?" Kenzie asked.

Elliott put his coffee cup in the sink and rinsed it out. "Hell, ye'll be back before those monsters know ye're gone."

She smacked his arm. "I can call them monsters but no one else can."

"Did ye tell yer dad ye were going away?"

"No, he'd worry. I'll tell him when we get back," she said.

"Who will worry?"

They all turned to see Rick strutting into the kitchen, dressed exactly as David had predicted: brown cowboy hat, leather vest with a shearling lining, round-collar shirt with dense blue stripes, brown poncho, rich leather boots, spurs, a black cigar, and a Colt .45 long gun.

"Look what I found," he said, snuggling Laurie Wallis to his chest.

Kenzie reached to take her daughter, but Rick pulled back and wouldn't let go of the two-year-old. "No, you can't have her."

Laurie Wallis giggled.

"Ye look like a damn Spaghetti Western outlaw. Ye'll get us all shot. Nix the poncho," David said.

Kenzie tugged on the fringe bottom. "The poncho is the only part I like. I'll take it."

"Can't have my poncho," Rick said.

"What about the gold?" David asked.

"Weapons, money, gold. Check," Rick said.

"'Oney, eck," Laurie Wallis said, repeating Rick.

"Mon...ey," Kenzie said, emphasizing the M consonant sound. Laurie Wallis held out her arms and Kenzie hugged her baby, kissing her face and head with loud smooches. "Love my baby girl."

"JL packed the weapons to your specifications," Rick said. "Elliott took care of the gold, and I had my clothes overnighted from New York. It was a group effort."

David took Laurie Wallis from Kenzie and hugged her tight. "It always is, isn't it lass." He nuzzled her chin and she giggled then squirmed to get down.

"Obbie, Enry?" Laurie Wallis asked.

"They went upstairs to see James Cullen," Kenzie said.

"Aurie Allis go too." She darted toward the stairs, but Kenzie grabbed her.

"No, you don't. You wait for Granny Alice."

"I'm up here, Kenzie," Alice said from the top of the staircase. "Let her come up."

The toddler pushed away from Kenzie. "Anny Alice said me go."

Kenzie stood at the bottom and watched her daughter climb up. "Hold tight. Take your time." Kenzie had one foot on the floor the other on the step ready to race up and grab her child if she teetered. When the little girl reached the top step, Kenzie exhaled. "Bye, sweetie."

Laurie Wallis threw a kiss back then tottered down the hallway.

When Kenzie turned back to David, her eyes were glistening. He opened his arms and embraced her. "We won't be gone long."

Kenzie licked her lips and took a deep breath. "Sorry about the drama. Let's get out of here before I change my mind."

"What about horses?" Elliott asked.

"Three Morgans were delivered this morning. They're good stock, but they won't look out of place," Rick said. "All have old tack in excellent condition."

Kenzie hugged Elliott. "I love Dad, but I'd rather you and Meredith raise the kids if anything—"

"Don't worry, lass. Ye're with David," Elliott said.

"But if anything happens—"

"Nothing will happen."

David sighed heavily. He had never seen Kenzie this worried, but then she'd never left her children longer than overnight. He looked forward to having her to himself, without anyone else climbing into their bed in the middle of the night.

Elliott dug into his pocket and pulled out the diamond and amethyst brooches. "Take both, just in case."

Kenzie gave them to David and he put them in his vest pockets, then he gave Elliott a hug and a slap on the back. "See ye soon."

Elliott went out into the garage with them where David gathered his saddlebags. "Where's yer gear, Rick?"

"At the barn. I left a groom in charge of the gear and horses. He tried to take the poncho, too."

"Ye should have given it to him," Elliott said.

David, Kenzie, and Rick—the gentleman, his lady, and the high plains drifter—walked across the lawn toward the paddock and barn beyond.

"What happens if we get separated, like the group did when they landed in Central Park?" Rick asked.

"Go straight to the Western Union Office. If the rest of us don't show up within an hour, send telegrams to Cañon City, Morrison, and Denver, and don't leave town until ye get a response," David said.

"In case we get split up, you need some of this gold." Rick dug into his saddlebags and gave Kenzie and David each a bag of nuggets. "That should be enough to buy the town."

They arrived at the barn and found the groom tending to the horses. "They're ready to go, Mr. McBain. They're fine animals. Are we keeping them?"

"Probably," David said.

They stepped into their saddles, reined their horses in the direction of the lake, and lifted them into a trot. When they reached their destination, they dismounted.

"If we get separated in the mountains, call out, but don't waste time looking. Make yer way to the nearest town and wait for news of the others. There are maps and compasses in our saddlebags, along with MREs in case we're forced to spend the night on the trail."

"Okay. I'm ready. Let's do this," Kenzie said.

They held tightly to their reins and the horses pranced restlessly. After locking arms, David opened the diamond brooch. They focused on Amber while they recited the magic words.

"Chan ann le tìm no àite a bhios sinn a' tomhais a' gaol ach 's ann le neart anama."

An earthy-scented fog rose from the ground in thick tendrils, enveloping them, jerking them left, then right, then back again, tossing them all about like a ship in a tempest. Until finally it swept them away.

15

1878 Leadville, Colorado—Amber

Amber woke before dawn, freezing, even though she was burrowed under a heavy woolen blanket with her knees pulled to her chest. She stuck out her toes, testing the air. It was several degrees colder. Outside the frosted mullioned window next to her bed, lights from Mrs. Garland's neighbors flickered and reflected on the puddles in the street.

Staying in bed wasn't an option, no matter how cold she was.

She shimmied out from the covers, hoping to keep what heat she had generated from dissipating, and hurried over to the warming stove in the corner. Hughes Cabin had identical stoves in the bedrooms, so she had grown up scraping out the ashes to bring sleeping coals to life. She rubbed her cold hands together, anticipating the heat that would soon fill the room. As quickly as she'd rushed over to the stove, she returned to bed to wait for the temperature in the room to climb above freezing.

While she waited, she replayed the previous day in her mind, minute by minute. The people and events whirled about and created a dizzying storm in her brain. Her eyes felt as if sand had been ground into them, rocks and all. It wasn't from a lack of sleep, but from the worries, questions, and fears that plagued her.

The foremost being…could she ever go home? She squeezed the brooch in her palm. It was cold as ice. She wasn't going home this morning.

She rubbed her forehead to stop the spinning thoughts and tried to focus on what she needed to do now. A bath was at the top of the list, followed by organizing her play list for tonight's performance. Then, if she had time left, she'd start a travel itinerary for next week. She would need transportation and lining that up was a priority. She was one of those people who booked flights six months in advance, and travel was going to be trickier in 1878.

The stove warmed the room within minutes, and although she didn't want to get up again, she had to. Since she hadn't heard Mrs. Garland moving about, she might beat her landlady to the kitchen and get a head start on preparing breakfast for the household. It wasn't that she thought she was a better cook, she just wanted to be helpful.

She had hand-washed her underwear and spot cleaned her jeans before she went to bed. They were dry, but her socks were still damp. She moved them closer to the stove and rushed off for a quick bath. The washroom was a comfortable temperature and the water was hot. After a quick wash, she dressed, and padded to the kitchen barefoot while braiding her hair. The welcoming scent of fresh coffee and frying bacon reminded Amber of her granny and mornings at the cabin, and almost brought a tear to her eye.

She hesitated in the doorway. "I thought I could start breakfast, but you're already up. What can I do to help?"

Mrs. Garland nodded toward the table. "The dress I mentioned last night is on the chair. Hold it up and let me see."

Amber was reluctant to even look, but she didn't want to appear ungrateful after Mrs. Garland made such a generous offer. If the dress was hideous, she'd turn her act into a comedy. She shot a hopeful eye in the direction of the table, and for a moment her breath stopped.

A white and gold silk brocade dress in a floral and vine motif was folded over the back of a straight-back chair. The fabric, glittering in the light of the coal oil lamp, all but melted in her hands when she touched it and breathed in the ethereal scent of violets.

She held the heavy dress up with two-finger pinches and clasped it at her waist to check the length.

"What do you think?" she asked.

"It looks beautiful with the color of your hair," Mrs. Garland said.

Amber turned the dress around, letting the gold-colored satin train swirl about her feet. The top had a low, tight bodice. From the waist down, the skirt looped up to show a decorative underskirt. Three-quarter sleeves were trimmed with gold-colored satin and white satin piping with blond lace at the collar and cuffs.

"This is the most beautiful gown I've ever seen." It was soft, luxurious, and expensive. If she had to bet, she'd put money on the gown coming from a couture house in Paris. "Where'd it come from?"

"Paris," Mrs. Garland said. "I wore it to a gala in New York City two years ago. Mr. Garland and I danced all night. He said to me, 'Nettie,'—my given name is Annette, but he called me Nettie." She paused to wipe her eyes, then added, "He said, 'You look like a queen in that dress.'"

Eyeballing the gown, Amber guessed it was at least one size too big. "Thank you for the offer, but I couldn't accept. It's too beautiful to alter."

"Nonsense. I'll never wear it again. A few seams will have to be taken in, but with my new sewing machine, it won't take long."

"You have a sewing machine?

"I got it a few months ago." She beamed with pride.

"How do you plug it in?"

"Plug?"

"What's the power source? How do you make it work?"

Mrs. Garland wagged her hands up and down. "The foot pedals."

Amber smacked her forehead. "Oh, I knew that. The altitude sickness is getting to me. Not only is it affecting my breathing, but my thought process too." She cast a glance in Mrs. Garland's direction. "Are you sure you'll never wear it again? Maybe you can just pin the sides."

Mrs. Garland blotted her eyes with a corner of her apron. "Mr. Garland died shortly after we returned from that trip. There are too many memories associated with the dress."

Amber teared up, too. She reached for the woman's thickly veined hand. "My granny told me once, 'We are truly alive in those moments when our hearts recognize our treasures.' To you, this dress is a treasure. If I wear the gown, the night you and Mr. Garland danced at the gala will come alive again." Amber placed her free hand across the woman's shoulders and squeezed her gently. "In that case, I accept your offer, but only if you'll let me help with the cooking."

Mrs. Garland smiled through her tears. "Daniel and Noah are very particular about what they eat."

Daniel's boot heels announced his presence moments before he appeared in the doorway of the kitchen. "I heard that, and before Miss Kelly thinks poorly of us, Noah and I will eat whatever we're served."

"Except for turnips," Mrs. Garland said.

"Maybe there is an exception." He picked up the coffee pot, filled a cup, and sipped slowly as he eyed the dress folded over Amber's arm. "Is that the dress for yer performance tonight?"

"Mrs. Garland is insisting I wear it."

"Ye should. Ye'll look bonny in it." He stood there wordlessly after that, as if not believing what he had said to her.

Amber's face heated, and she quickly changed the subject. "Did you sleep well?"

"Well enough."

His glance moved from her face to her sockless feet. When his eyes widened, she knew exactly what he was responding to—blue nail polish.

She redirected his attention asking, "How about Noah? Did he sleep okay?"

"He woke up once whimpering. He must have rolled over on his sore arm, but he went right back to sleep, and is still sleeping."

"Good," Amber said. "That's what he needs to do right now."

"Sit down, Daniel, and I'll fix your breakfast," Mrs. Garland said.

"What can I do?" Amber asked again. "I'll be glad to make biscuits."

"Are you sure?" she asked.

"Biscuits are one of my specialties."

Mrs. Garland's kitchen was a step or two up from the one at the cabin, but Amber had learned to cook anywhere and adjust accordingly. Moving easily around the room, she gathered the ingredients, mixed them together, and rolled out a sheet of dough. Next was the fun part, stamping out the biscuits in neat and systematic holes with the cutter. Within minutes she had a batch ready to go into the stove.

Mrs. Garland watched, nodding with approval. Then she checked the time on her lapel watch. While Amber waited for the first batch to bake, she made another one.

After several minutes, Mrs. Garland said, "The biscuits should be done."

Armed with protective towels around her hand, Amber opened the maw of the iron stove, which belched with heat and the aroma of buttermilk biscuits. With her usual efficiency, she shoveled the finished biscuits onto a plate then put the next batch into the pan and popped it into the oven. She dusted flour from her hands and when she turned, she was surprised to find Daniel watching her.

She faced him, arms akimbo. "What? Are you afraid I'll poison you?"

He quickly glanced down at the contents of his cup as if trying to read the coffee grounds. His cheeks turned pink. "No. I'm sure they'll be quite tasty." His suspicion was now tempered with amusement.

She returned to the dough and made another batch, wishing she had eyes in the back of her head. Was he watching her? If so, how did she look from the rear in tight jeans? She needed an apron. "I'm getting flour all over myself. Do you have an apron I can use?"

Mrs. Garland was turning the bacon in the skillet. "On the hook by the door."

Amber grabbed the gingham pinner apron and wrapped it around her, covering as much of her butt as she could. If she did nothing else today, she had to buy a dress or a skirt to cover her jeans. While she stood in front of the window overlooking the yard, she looped back the dark blue hangings, allowing the first light of morning to seep in through the sheer lace. It was the first look she'd had of the adjoining houses and a small neatly penned henhouse in the backyard. Her granny had kept hens at the cabin during the summer when they were there for long stretches of time, but it had been years since Amber had collected fresh eggs from a coop.

"Noah is probably staying home from school today," Daniel said. "I'll drop off his completed assignments at the schoolhouse and pick up today's lessons."

"I can do that." Amber opened the imposing iron stove and using her apron for a pot holder, pulled out another pan of biscuits, golden brown and flaky.

"You need proper clothes to visit Noah's school." Mrs. Garland filled a platter with cooked bacon and placed it on the table in front of Daniel. "You can't go around town dressed as you are now. A woman in trousers isn't appropriate."

"Aren't there exceptions for eccentric women and suffragettes?"

Daniel forked a couple pieces of crispy bacon onto his plate. "Aye, but I don't think ye want the reputation that goes with it."

Mrs. Garland picked out a handful of large brown eggs from a basket and cracked them over the skillet. "If you're going to the general store to buy a dress, I'll pin up one of mine for you to wear shopping. It will cut down on stares and gossiping."

"That's not necessary—"

"I believe it is," Daniel interrupted. "Ye were new in town yesterday. News of ye will have spread by now. More attention will be paid to ye, and ye want to sell tickets to yer show tonight."

"I guess you're right. Okay then. My first stop will be Hughes Store to buy a dress. Then I need to go to the theatre and spend a few hours rehearsing. If you want me to go by the schoolhouse or to the doctor, I can do either or both."

"I can manage, but thank ye," Daniel said.

When the rest of the biscuits and eggs were done, Mrs. Garland and Amber joined Daniel at the table. He eyed the baked circles of dough as Mrs. Garland deposited two biscuits on his plate. He split one and covered it with jam before hesitantly biting into it. He smiled before taking another bite. "No offense, Mrs. Garland, but these are the best biscuits I've ever tasted."

"None taken." Mrs. Garland looked at Amber from under her fine dark brows. "I hope you'll share your recipe."

"I'll be glad to."

"They remind me of Mrs. Hughes' biscuits. She had a plate of them, warm from the oven, in the store recently. Your biscuits are very similar."

Daniel ate four in rapid succession. The last one he gobbled up without butter or jam. "I look forward to breakfast tomorrow. Now, I'm off. I'll be back at noon to check on Noah, and if there are any biscuits left over—"

"I'll save some for you," Mrs. Garland said.

He had a flake from his last biscuit on the side of his mouth and Amber had the strangest sensation to lick it off. She gulped back the desire and instead tapped the identical place on her face, indicating to him that he needed to wipe his mouth.

He wiped his face. "If that was a biscuit crumb, I'm surprised there was one left." He stood but didn't move away from his chair, as if he had something else to say. "The only woman I've ever heard of who painted her toenails was Cleopatra."

Amber glanced down at her feet. "Oh…" The coffee cup in her hand trembled as she struggled to find a logical explanation. The motion created waves on the surface of the coffee. *Black as hell, strong as death, and sweet as love.* She set down the cup on the polished mahogany table, and after a moment to consider the truth, she told a lie.

"I've been to Egypt and heard that story, too. Painting my toenails is fun. I like looking down and seeing spots of color."

One thing she had learned in her relationship madness was when telling a lie of omission, to always wrap a portion of it in a thin layer of the truth. The lie in this case was that she hadn't been to Egypt. She got sick and had to cancel the trip. As for painting her toenails, that habit started when she and Olivia were teenagers and took turns painting each other's toes. They still made time in their busy schedules for toe-painting nights, but now they coupled it with sushi and wine.

"Look at it from my perspective, Miss Kelly. Blue toenails outside of Egypt would only enhance that reputation ye don't want. My advice is to keep yer feet covered."

What would he say about the *Stegosaurus* tattoo on her hip? Nodding, she buttered a biscuit, and the warm scent, redolent of her grandmother's kitchen, wafted over her. But instead of reminiscing further about her granny, she thought about Daniel, and she was tempted to show him the tattoo, just to mess with his nineteenth-century man brain.

He left the kitchen, and within moments, his boots thudded on the stairs as he went up to check on Noah. Then they thudded back down again. Amber followed the sound with her gaze until the front door creaked opened and closed behind him.

When Amber looked back at Mrs. Garland, the woman was pushing a wisp of hair from her forehead, smiling. "Daniel's a handsome man, and a lonely one. The life of a Pinkerton's wife is difficult."

Amber refilled her coffee, spooned in a bit of sugar, and stirred it around with her thoughts equally awhirl. Despite the warmth of the room and the hot china cup, her fingertips momentarily went cold. She set down the cup and twitched her hands to speed circulation and forced her mind to return to the present.

"Are you speaking from experience?" she asked.

"I have no family, but I do have a circle of friends. They kept me company when my husband was on an assignment with the agency. Now I have Noah and Daniel to care for." Mrs. Garland finished her breakfast and set her plate aside. "It was different for Daniel's late wife. She had family in Denver, so she coped fairly well."

"When did she die?" Amber asked.

Daniel was on a long-term engagement when the baby came several weeks early. He rushed home and arrived shortly before she and his infant daughter passed. There were too many memories in Denver, so Daniel asked for a transfer and brought Noah with him to Leadville. He's never forgiven himself for his wife's death. He's convinced if he'd been there sooner, she wouldn't have died."

"What do you think?" Amber asked in a soft voice.

"She got the best care available. There wasn't anything he could have done to change the outcome."

"That's a heavy load of grief and guilt to carry. It had to have been horrible for him yesterday to watch his son almost get run over and not be able to stop it."

"Daniel would not have survived Noah's death." Mrs. Garland sipped her coffee before continuing, "Before Noah came home last night, my neighbor had already told me what happened. Your bravery will make folks even more curious about you. That's one reason you should dress appropriately when you go back to town. Don't give them a reason to distrust you."

"Thank you for the advice."

"I'm doing it for Daniel and Noah. They don't need any trouble after all they've been through. That's why I allowed you to stay. Noah wanted to help you after what you did for him."

Mrs. Garland was right. If Amber intended to fill the house every night during her run, she needed to be accepted, not ostracized. She pushed back from the table. "Now, let me wash the dishes. I'll set the leftovers aside for Noah to eat when he wakes up."

"I'll get my sewing basket and we can fit the dress for you to wear tonight and something else to wear this morning."

An hour later, the elegant dress was pinned for alterations and Mrs. Garland had tucked in, tucked up, and tucked away one of her everyday dresses so that it fit Amber nicely.

Before leaving the house, Amber checked in on Noah. He was

sore and had a slight fever but seemed to be resting comfortably. When she stopped by the store, she'd ask Grandmother Hughes if she had something to cut his fever. Growing up, Granny always had herbal remedies for whatever ailed Amber and Olivia. If the Hughes family biscuit recipe survived over a hundred years, surely their catalogue of herbal remedies had, too.

16

1878 Leadville, Colorado—Kenzie

WHEN THE TOPSY-TURVY ride ended abruptly, Kenzie found herself suffocating in gray soupy air. Her surroundings were shrouded in a heavy fog, making it impossible to discern the features of the landscape. As the fog slowly evaporated, the autumn chill cut right through the wool of her traveling suit and every joint seemed to freeze in place.

She glanced south, where the morning sun struggled to break through the clouds, and its heat briefly touched her cheek. "Where are we?" she asked, pinching her nose.

The minimal research she'd done on Leadville in the nineteenth century led her to believe it would smell, but this was worse than she'd imagined. Smoke from wood- and coal-burning stoves mixed with the yucky stench of sulfur from the smelters, and those odors mingled with the stink of mud, manure, and unwashed men.

Her stomach roiled, and she gagged.

"Are ye going to be sick?" David asked, squeezing her gloved hand.

"I hope not." The bottom of her riding corset pinched, reminding her not to slouch. When she straightened, it helped her posture but did nothing for her stomach.

"Lift yer skirts before ye drag them in the mud."

"Damn." She bunched her long broadcloth skirt in her hands

and lifted the hem above her stout boots to keep it from touching the muck.

"I don't know where we are." The cold, moist air gave David's voice a hoarse sound, reminding her of his sexy early-morning voice when he nuzzled her ear and rubbed up against her. "Keep yer wee gun handy."

Her large muscles still resisted moving, and her body seemed twice as heavy as normal, but she patted her hip where she'd snugged a revolver into a secret pocket. "Don't expect a quick draw, but I can get to it soon enough." Freight wagons rolled down the street, splattering icy mud. "This street is as crowded as Times Square at Christmas. If we don't move, we'll get run over."

Rick gave Kenzie and David an odd look, as if he were coming out of some trance that had placed him somewhere else. "Christ. This is real."

"What'd ye expect? Disney World?" David asked.

"No, just the back lot at Paramount."

Her hand clenched the reins tighter, and she gagged a second time.

"Do I need to take ye home?"

"No, but next time I'm taking Dramamine. I'm getting too old for this."

She adjusted the loop of reins over her hand and following David, led her horse over to a fenced area next to Black Hawk Livery, where unsaddled horses were lined along the hitchrack.

The town looked substantial but crude. Two- and three-story brick buildings lined intersecting streets, and new construction seemed to be going on everywhere. The rapid building confirmed the explosion of silver mining in the vicinity. The buildings weren't hastily constructed clapboard buildings, but brick and mortar with more permanence in mind.

"This reminds me of Kit Montgomery's stories of landing in Independence, Missouri, in 1852," Kenzie said. "Kit said the town looked like a refugee camp with smoky fires and hundreds of tents and wagons with thousands of people milling about."

"You're giving refugee camps a bad name. This is worse." Rick removed his poncho and exchanged it for a dark-brown cotton duster rolled up behind his saddle. Then he unstrapped the holster from his flat hips and put it with the gun in his saddlebag.

"Ye going in unarmed?" David asked.

"I have a Colt in a shoulder holster. I just don't want to send the wrong message. I'll admit, I didn't take this seriously." He scratched the back of his neck. "My spidey senses are spiking off the chart. I can smell trouble."

"What yer smelling is the stench of manure and burnt coffee," David said.

"I know what that smells like. What I smell is something else, something unknown." Rick slipped the duster on over his jacket and rolled his shoulders, as if that could settle the tingling sensation on his neck.

Kenzie gave him a tense smile. "David and I still have some of that, but not as acutely as you do right now. Your instincts are why I wanted you to come along. The hairs on the back of my neck aren't lying flat, but they're not standing on end either."

David cocked a ruddy brow at her, and his mouth quirked up at one corner. "Mine are slightly aroused."

She rolled her eyes. "So what's new, McBain?"

"I figured ye out years ago, lass. Ye set me up and then roll yer beautiful eyes when I respond as ye hoped."

She gasped. "That's not true."

He laughed, brushing back a tendril of her hair that had blown loose of her bun. "The lady doth protest too much, methinks."

"If you're quoting Shakespeare, that means you and Cullen have been drinking too much whisky," Kenzie said.

Rick pointed. "If you want to take your act on the road, I see a sign for Tabor Opera House just ahead. I'm sure this nineteenth-century town would appreciate Kenzie's jokes and your sax, Dave."

"We've done that gig already," David said. "Once is plenty for this old Scotsman."

"We were quite successful, I think, don't you, McBain? As I

remember, your instant stardom distracted you from your mission, and I was kidnapped," she said in a strained voice.

David shot Rick one of his nastiest looks. "Thanks for the reminder, O'Grady. The lass has forgiven me, but she likes to torture me with the memory. Don't ye, Kenz?"

"It keeps you humble. But we learned a valuable lesson to never withhold information. The first person to see Amber, tell her we're here to help."

"We need to find out where we are first," David said.

"We're in Leadville," Rick said. "There's a mud-splattered sign over there that reads, CITY OF LEADVILLE INCORPORATED FEBRUARY 18, 1878."

"How can you see that far without a scope?" Kenzie asked.

"Practice," Rick said.

Kenzie's horse danced anxious steps. "That makes that mountain range the western slope of Mosquito Range. That's where Trey used to go skiing with Amber and Olivia."

"Then Amber should feel at home," David said.

"How anybody can feel at home in this thin air beats me. The view of those snow-covered high peaks is breathtaking and humbling, but if you can't breathe at ten thousand feet, why would you want to be here?" Rick asked.

"To make it rich in the silver mines. That's the draw." David secured the brooch to the inside of his vest pocket. "Let's go look for Amber and see if we can wrap this up in a couple of hours." He grabbed his saddle horn and tugged it to and fro before swinging onto his horse.

Kenzie put her foot in the stirrup and swung her leg over the saddle. "A lofty goal, McBain, but not very realistic."

"Wishing and hoping, babe. Ye ready?"

Rick swung into the saddle atop a red dun gelding with black points. "I'll follow a parallel street, cut back into this one up ahead, and meet you in three or four blocks."

"Look for Hughes Store," David said.

With a nudge from Rick's spurred heels, the dun trotted off.

Kenzie lost track of Rick when the horse headed into an alleyway. They were all wearing bullet- and stab-proof vests, but nothing came with a hundred percent guarantee. She could trust both Rick and David not to take any chances, and neither would she, but they were in a Wild West town with little law and less order.

She did a slow hundred-and-eighty-degree scope of the town—rough-looking men used to gunplay and knife fights hung out next to batwing doors. Lots under construction had building materials spilling from the boardwalks into the streets, forcing pedestrians to walk in traffic lanes. Everywhere, workmen barked orders and hammers clanged. If Amber was walking up and down this street, what was she doing for protection? Maybe she was trying to pass herself off as a boy. If she was, how was she hiding her long hair?

"We're not taking any chances here, right? We're from Chicago looking for business opportunities."

"Whatever my bride wants, my bride gets."

They rode slowly down Harrison Avenue, smiling and nodding at anyone who looked their way.

"There's the store," David said. "Up ahead on the left. We'll tie up out front. If we don't have any luck right away, we'll see if we can find rooms for the night."

The front of the general store was choked with wagons hauling bricks and other construction materials, and horses hitched to the rail. They squeezed their horses onto the hitching bar. "With all these people, I can't imagine there will be any rooms available."

David's brow furrowed. "Then I'll buy ye a house."

"You're my rock star, McBain."

"I figure without any kids crawling into our bed, I'll get lucky. I'll be damned if I'll share a room or a tent under the stars with anyone but ye, lass."

17

1878 Leadville, Colorado—Amber

IN LEADVILLE, THE last days of autumn were always cold, and once the sun slid behind the mountains, a bitter chill embraced the town, and that made even breathing painful. But the day hadn't progressed to that point yet. The strong sunlight was taking the early coolness from the air. For newbies, it would still feel cold as dead of winter, but thankfully, she wasn't a newbie.

Focusing on the worn path rutted in the dirt, she walked carefully toward the shops on Harrison Avenue. Everywhere she walked, there was a danger of twisting an ankle and ending up sprawled in the mud. That would really put a damper on her day.

Mrs. Garland had done a few quick alterations to a blue and white serge walking gown with a long bodice and a double row of buttons. Surprisingly, Amber loved how she looked in the dress and hoped she'd run into Daniel. Silver skirt-lifters hitched up the hem until it cleared the tops of her cowboy boots that didn't exactly go with the dress. But who would be looking at her feet? No one, unless they were bare. Using lifters was the only way to keep her skirt from sweeping up the mud and rotting offal collecting in the street.

If her sister could see her now, dressed appropriately for once, she wouldn't do her fake-faint complete with the back of the hand pressed to her forehead. Amber's style choices never lived up to

Olivia's expectations, but as she asked her sister frequently, "Why do I need a closet full of stilettos when I spend so much time in mines and fossil pits?"

Amber groaned, sidestepping another puddle on the path. The muck didn't bother her, but she didn't want to ruin the borrowed dress. She finally reached the relative safety of the weathered boards on Harrison.

Up ahead, leaning near the door of the general store, was a slender man sporting a three-day beard. He stood over six feet tall with full lips and a square jaw. A brown hat rode low on his head, intentionally hiding his eyes. He reminded her of the mean-looking guy she'd seen the day before. A quick sidestep, and she brushed past him and reached for the doorknob. His hand shot out and grabbed the knob first. She jerked hers back, as if his fingers had scalded hers.

He tipped his hat. Their eyes met and held. His were soft brown and engaging. Not what she'd expected. He wore familiarity like a warm cloak—the cock of his chin, the set of his eyes, cheekbones cut high and sharp. She knew him, but that was impossible.

She pulled her eyes away and placed her hand on the wood of the door, hoping it would push open. "Excuse me."

He didn't move his hand. Nor did he open the door. "Are you Amber Kelly?"

Thank goodness he had soft eyes, or she'd be beating on the door to be let in. Was he the kind of man Daniel had warned her about? No, not with eyes like that.

She couldn't keep an edgy tone from creeping into her voice when she said, "Yes, I am."

Standing closer to him, though, she was reminded of Daniel. Whoever this man was, he was also in law enforcement. She didn't know how she knew that, but she did. Now, the question was, had Daniel sent him, hoping to get more information from her? Good luck with that. She was tempted to flip open his duster to see if he wore a Pinkerton shield or maybe a sheriff's badge. He wasn't wearing a gun at his hip, but he could have one packed in a shoulder holster.

He pointed to an empty bench outside the general store. "Would you mind if we sat and talked?"

"I'm in a hurry," she said.

He shifted to one side, opening a clear path to the door, giving her a choice. "I won't take much of your time." He looked down, long lashes hiding his eyes, and hesitated for a moment before saying, "There's a serious matter I'd like to discuss. A legal matter," he said.

Her eyes roved up and down his frame. His clothes were clean, and the dark-brown leather of his boots looked new but muddy. The left boot had a gouge on the toe box that looked recent. The dark brown duster hadn't seen much wear either, nor the sable brushed cotton trousers that tightly wrapped muscular thighs. He spent hard-earned money on quality utilitarian clothing, and that said a lot about him.

"My specialty is mining law, and you don't look like a miner."

The floorboards creaked, and his duster rustled as he moved out of the wind, folded his arms, and tucked his gloved hands in his armpits. "I heard you handle other matters. I need a will."

She lifted her chin and looked him over one final time before deciding on whether to help him or not. "Are you about to freeze to death?"

He shivered. "I spent the last two years in Afghanistan—"

Her scalp tingled with alarm. That sounded as out of place as she felt.

"To me," he continued, "this is arctic air, freezing me from the inside out. Even winter days in New York aren't this cold."

She scratched the side of her head unsure of what was going on here, but the man wasn't giving off bad vibes, so the tingling settled down to only a mild annoyance. "Haven't you heard about Leadville's weather? The city has nine months of winter and three months of poor sledding."

He laughed at her joke, but she didn't. Instead, she remained guarded. "I can't think of any reason to go to Afghanistan unless you're working for Uncle Sam."

He rubbed his gloved hands. "I was in the Marines."

The Marines were as old as the country, but were they fighting in Afghanistan in the nineteenth century? She stepped out of the way of the customers entering and leaving the store.

"Do you want to go inside? There are chairs parked around a potbelly stove. We can talk there. I don't want you to freeze to death before I write your will."

He turned up his coat collar against a cold gust of air and shoved his hands into the deep pockets of his duster. He looked down the street with a grim expression. "Sure."

She didn't have much time and hurried to open the door. Ice scrunched beneath the *clink-ca-chink* of the spurs strapped to the heels of his boots as he stepped in line behind her. The door latch retracted with a click. Inside, he removed his hat and shoved his gloves into his pocket and hovered over her like a child afraid he'd get separated in a mall.

The first aisle was the least crowded, far enough away from women chatting as they fingered dry goods along the back counter. The scent of perfumes and toilet water wafted over her. Now she understood why the aisle didn't have as much foot traffic. She moved quickly to the next aisle, away from the distracting smells, and stopped when she eyed a woman rushing around a stack of crates wearing a perfectly tailored charcoal dress cinched at the waist. The Marine, following close behind, bumped into Amber, pitching her forward into bolts of fabric.

"Oh my God. I'm sorry. Are you okay?" He peered down from his considerable height and helped her regain her balance. "I was tailgating and not expecting you to slam on the brakes."

Amber adjusted the silly little hat Mrs. Garland had insisted she wear. "I think so." She glanced again at the woman. Grandfather Craig moved to stand next to her and lifted a box to clear her path. Was that Lindsey Hughes, her grandmother?

As if reading her mind, he asked, "Is that Lindsey Hughes?"

"Do you know her?"

"No, but she's the owner, right?" He idly threaded the brim of his hat through long, slender fingers.

There was something off about the man trailing her. He wasn't a scary stalker, but he was different from other men she'd met in the last twenty-four hours. He smelled clean and outdoorsy, and although he was unshaven, he wasn't scruffy. And his styled brown hair was thick and luscious, free of gels, waxes, or pomades, and he had a cute thing going on with his forelock.

Of the six rockers circling a potbelly stove, two stood empty. She moved toward them, but when her grandmother stepped out from behind the counter and headed in her direction, Amber stopped, and the cowboy bumped into her—again. This time he sent her into stacks of canned goods. Strong hands grasped her windmilling arms and yanked her hard, saving her from a nasty situation that could have injured her. The sudden yank, though, sent her flying into the muscular chest of her rescuer, where she instinctively gripped the lapels of his canvas duster.

"Why do people keep running into me? Yesterday, I face planted into a window." She pushed away from him, heaving a deep breath. "Christ. Who are you anyway?"

He gave her a deep-throated laugh. "Not him. That's for sure." His hat had been tossed aside when he'd grabbed her. He stooped, picked it up, and resettled it on his head.

All she heard for a moment, a snap-of-a-finger-moment, was his musical laughter. Then as quickly as the moment arrived, it was displaced by the squeak of chairs, a phlegmy cough, the clink of change as a customer paid their bill.

"Don't walk so fast and people won't run into you when you stop on a dime. You need stop-and-go signals, or maybe a warning light when you downshift."

Signals? Downshift? Styled hair? Was it possible he was from the future, too? She couldn't come right out and ask. Instead, she thrust her hands to her hips. "Who are you? Did Daniel Grant send you to harass me?"

"Don't know him."

"He's a Pinkerton agent. I thought you all hung out together, or something."

He laughed again. "You think I'm a Pinkerton man?"

"Aren't you? You look like one. You look like a cop."

"Nope. Just a Marine. Name's Rick O'Grady."

"O'Grady? Irish, huh? Why does that name sound familiar?"

Two ladies scrunched by, and Rick motioned for Amber to move toward the chairs and out of the path of shoppers. "You might have heard your sister mention the name. My brother, Connor, has been working with her real estate agency for about a year."

Amber was already having trouble breathing, but now she couldn't breathe at all. What the hell was going on here? She put her finger in her ear and twisted it, hoping that would help make sense of the craziness. She took several shallow breaths.

"You've got that blanched pasty look going on. You better sit down," he said.

She lowered herself to a chair and Rick sat in the one beside her. "Put your head between your knees."

Amber bent double, folded her arms, and rested her head there. "I don't understand," she said. "You're a Marine, not a Pinkerton. You know my sister." Her voice wobbled. Then she abruptly sat up and glared at him. "Did you travel through a wormhole, too?"

He put a finger to his lips. Then he leaned forward, rested his forearms on his thighs, his slender fingers clasped together. Speaking softly, he said, "Wormhole is as good an explanation as any, I guess. I know of your sister from Connor, but I've never met her."

A woman, dressed in a green riding habit, stopped and hovered next to Rick's chair, wrapping her hand around the top rail. "I've never met you or Olivia, but I've heard so much about you both."

Amber searched the face of a gorgeous woman with luscious auburn hair and beautiful, ageless skin. "Mary, Mother of God. Who are you?"

The woman laughed. "Not her. I assure you."

Amber scrubbed her face with her hands. This was even crazier—if that was possible—than her arrival yesterday in nineteenth-century Leadville. She whispered, "Now that I know you're not Jesus and Mary, who are you?"

A man vacated a chair on the other side of Amber and the woman took the seat. "We're here to help you. I'm Kenzie McBain." She pointed to Rick. "You've already met him, and..." She stretched to look around the store and signaled to a movie-star handsome man who carried himself like a warrior. Not a soldier. A warrior. The man had nothing to prove to anyone, and he knew it.

He walked up behind Kenzie and in a strong Scottish accent said, "We're drawing attention. We need to leave." He smiled at Amber. "I'm David McBain. Kenzie's husband."

"I need a drink," Amber said. "A stiff one. No, make that two. To hell with two. Give me a whole bottle."

"I'd prefer coffee," Kenzie said. "Where's Starbucks when you need it?"

"There's a saloon next door," Rick said. "Those who want to imbibe can have a hot toddie. Those who want a warm, but less potent libation, can have coffee."

Kenzie glared at him, tight-lipped, with an expression that clearly said she thought he was nuts. "Imbibe? Potent libation?"

His eyes darted side to side, as if he were checking that no one else would hear what he was going to say. "I'm just trying to fit in."

"Trust me. Talking like that doesn't help," Kenzie said.

Rick shrugged before offering Amber his hand. "If you feel wobbly, lean on me."

She nudged his hand away. "I'm okay. I want to speak to Lindsey Hughes before I leave, but I don't see her in the store. Let me ask about her." Amber crossed the wide-planked flooring, aware of Rick's footfalls behind her. "I'm going to stop at the counter."

He cautiously shifted to her side. "Thanks for the heads-up."

"Good morning, Miss Kelly," Grandfather Craig said. "I told Mrs. Hughes about ye. We're both looking forward to yer concert tonight."

"If I have time to get flyers printed, can I post one in your window?"

"Certainly, and I'll keep one here on the counter for folks to read while they're settling their accounts."

"That's kind of you." Amber glanced down a hallway looking for her grandmother. "Is Mrs. Hughes here?"

"She went to the bank."

"I'm going to have coffee with my friends. I'll be back later to buy a few things."

"She didn't want to interrupt ye earlier. I'll let her know as soon as she returns."

Amber left the store with the McBains and Rick and followed them next door, where sawdust covered the floor in a futile attempt to keep mud from spreading to the upper levels. She shivered once, twice, as unease tiptoed up her spine and back again. Then with a shake of her head, she stepped into the smoky saloon where the pungent tinge of unwashed bodies, over-applied perfume, and alcohol was an unwelcomed embrace.

18

1878 Leadville, Colorado—Amber

THE COOL TEMPERATURE of the autumn morning vanished in the steamy warmth of the saloon where men stood almost shoulder to shoulder drinking whisky at a marred oak bar. Almost every chair, every table was claimed by men playing at games of chance. Amber and the newcomers made their way through the haze and dim coal-oil lighting.

"Why aren't these men working?" Kenzie asked.

"There are so many people in Leadville, who knows. Maybe they don't have claims to work, yet," Amber said.

Rick snagged a table tucked into a corner at the front of the saloon from two miners who had no intentions of moving until he sneered at them. They quickly quit their claim and walked away from the table and six chairs.

"That was smooth, O'Grady. Do you have a habit of intimidating people like that?" Kenzie asked.

"Nah. They weren't even drinking. Paying customers should get the tables."

"I don't know why you want to be at the front of the saloon. It'd be better to sit in the back to see what's going on." Kenzie said.

"Not here," Rick said. "Most men entering a saloon survey what's in front of them. Few will notice us until they are well into the room and turn around. That gives us an advantage."

"I guess that's a Western saloon thing because it sure isn't logical to me."

"You need to catch up, Kenz. I'll give you a list of old movies to watch." Rick hooked a thumb at the busy bartender, whose garters resembled black slashes on the sleeves of his white shirt. "Four coffees," he called over.

"Make mine a whisky," Amber said.

Rick's mouth turned up in a sexy grin. He was the type of guy she enjoyed having as a close male friend. The kind she occasionally entrusted with benefits, but never a house key.

"Make that three coffees and a whisky for the lady." He pulled out a chair and held it while she sat. "This place does three kinds of business: gambling, prostitution, and alcohol. The working girls liquor up the miners, get a piece of their bankroll, and the gambling tables take the rest. It's the same blueprint in every cattle town, railhead, and mining encampment in this part of the country."

"You know all that from watching movies?" Kenzie asked. Amber's gaze swept the room, taking in the Western-style paintings, the scarred wide-plank floors, a defaced buffalo head mounted above the bar, and an upright piano tucked at the bottom of the stairs, probably terribly out of tune.

"Pops kept me supplied with Western novels while I was overseas. But I picked up the reading habit long before I was deployed. As a kid, that was my escape from three brothers and a bratty sister."

"I know a lot about the nineteenth century, but it's limited to a couple of topics. I don't know much about the culture." Amber put her elbows on a table in dire need of a good scrub. She was starting to unravel the puzzle that was now her life. "I know your names now, but that doesn't tell me who you are or how you found me." God, she was sounding exactly like Daniel.

"That's easy. David followed your cosmic footprints," Kenzie said.

Amber had a newborn's impatience right now. Getting information piecemeal wasn't improving her sense of humor or stopping her legs from bouncing. "Give it to me straight."

A waitress brought over three coffees and a shot of whisky. Before she walked away, she wiped the tabletop clean of spills. Amber's nose turned up at the overpowering smell of the woman's too-sweet perfume that attempted to mask other unpleasant odors.

Amber picked up the glass and studied the contents. Judging by the dark straw color, the alcohol appeared to be, if not a first-class whisky, not the house offering either. Before drinking, she inhaled the fumes, then tossed back the shot. A sensory blast that comes with high-proof liquors cleared her throat and a fiery burn relaxed into a warm, breathless hello.

"Of all the gin joints in all the towns in all the world…" she said.

"You walked into mine," Rick said.

"I thought you were just into Westerns," Kenzie said.

"I like the classics, and *Casablanca* is always on the top-ten list."

Amber set down the empty glass, wiggling it with her fingers, indicating to the waitress she wanted a refill. "How'd you know what gin joint I was in?"

"When you didn't come home from your weekend at the cabin," Kenzie began, "Rick's brother, Connor, went up there with your sister. He spotted the puzzle box right away and sent a picture to David. Connor wanted confirmation that the box was identical to the one I was sent a few years ago. There was an emerald brooch in my puzzle box. When I vanished, David figured out I was in London during the last year of World War II and went back to find me."

The waitress brought the refill, and Amber twisted the glass back and forth by quarter turns as she processed what Kenzie said. "World War II? God, that must have been horrible. At least there's no war in Leadville."

"It wasn't easy," Kenzie said. "I arrived during a bombing raid and quickly captured the attention of the British Secret Service. They had a few questions for me. None of which I could answer."

"Landing in a mining town is a piece of cake compared to what you went through, but it still doesn't answer the question of why you came after me."

"The brooches have a reputation for abandoning women in strange places. Mine took me to London. One of our cousins landed in the middle of a Civil War battle in 1864."

Amber gasped. "My God."

Kenzie continued, "Another one arrived on the Upper West Side in York City in 1909."

Wisely, Amber drank the second glass slowly, relieved that it amplified the benefits of the first. The aftertaste lingered in her mouth. "So you're telling me that I'm the fourth victim to be shot through this wormhole?"

Kenzie fiddled with her coffee cup, then took a sip. "Another cousin chose to go back to the Oregon Trail in 1852."

"Chose? Was she—?" Amber stopped and tamped down her surprise that anyone would choose to be dropped into another world. But then, the people sitting at the table with her had traveled by choice. "I was going to ask if your cousin was crazy, but I'd have to ask the same of you. Are you all a bit loony?"

"It runs in the family," Kenzie said.

"What? Being loony?"

"No, wanting adventure. It's part of being a MacKlenna. Your seven-times great-grandmother is Lindsey MacKlenna Hughes. Did you know that?"

Amber shook her head. "No. I didn't."

"I didn't think so, since Olivia never mentioned to Connor a possible connection to MacKlenna Farm."

Logic and science were subjects Amber knew or thought she did. Her world had been turned upside down in that damn wormhole, and she wasn't sure it would ever be right side up again.

"We can all trace our family lines back to the MacKlennas," Rick said.

Amber swished her hand to the side, clearing a mental whiteboard full of impossibilities and suppositions. "Sorry. It's not computing. I'll accept that I have a MacKlenna in my family tree. But that gets me nowhere. How did you know I was *here*? In Leadville?"

David jumped into the conversation. "I did a wee bit of research. Based on yer history and interests, I narrowed the possible locations down to Leadville, Cañon City, and Morrison. The only reason we needed to know where ye were, was to prepare for our trip to rescue ye. If ye went to Chicago in the 1920s, we wouldn't want to show up dressed like this. We also needed to know where to look for ye once we knew where we were going."

"Why those places? And how did you know the year?"

"David has a fancy computer program," Kenzie said. "He plugs in a person's interests and"—she snapped her finger—"the answer spits out."

"Sorry. Still don't get it. What's in my bio that would lead you to come here to 1878?" She had a pretty good idea why she was there, but she wanted to know how they figured it out.

David took a long drink of coffee then set the cup aside. He didn't speak right away, even though three sets of eyes were focused intently on him. Finally, he said, "Every case is different, Amber. In yers, I found four markers: the activities of Drs. Marsh and Cope in 1878 and 1879, the discovery of a *Stegosaurus* in Morrison, the presence of an undiscovered *Stegosaurus* near Cañon City that ye're fully aware of, and yer father's interest in the Royal Gorge War."

Amber whistled. "You really did your homework." She sat back and thought through what they had told her so far. Then she remembered what Kenzie had first said. Amber turned to her now. "You said, 'I've never met you or Olivia, but I've heard so much about both of you.' Did you hear about us from Connor or somewhere else?"

Kenzie glanced at David, and he covered her hand with his own. After a brief silent conversation between them, Kenzie turned her attention back to Amber. "My name was Kenzie Wallis-Manning. I went to West Point with your cousin, Trey. I was with him in Afghanistan."

Amber's shoulders slumped, and all the air seemed to leak from her body like a tire punctured by a round-head nail. "He saved your life. Is that why you came back for me? Because of Trey?"

"It's why David and I volunteered. There were others who would have come, but I wanted to do this for him."

"Connor wanted to come," Rick said. "But we decided he should stay with Olivia."

Amber perked up at the mention of her sister. "Does she know where I am?"

"We couldn't tell her," Kenzie said. "The sheriff's office and the State Patrol are out looking for you. You have to go back, so they'll call off the search."

Amber rotated her wrists and tugged on her fingers. "Olivia is going to be so pissed, but I can't leave yet. A little boy was in an accident yesterday, and I represented him to recover damages from Mr. Tabor. The settlement was sort of contingent upon my providing talent for a five-night performance." She stretched her fingers and popped the joints. "I signed a contract at the Tabor Opera House to sing and play the guitar. If I back out, it could cause a problem for him and his father. And besides, my brooch doesn't work."

"They never do right away," Kenzie said. "Mine didn't either. You're here for a reason."

Amber rubbed the large knuckles at the junction of her hand and fingers. "I saved his life. The little boy, I mean. That's reason enough, right?"

The question hovered in the air between them and another one of those odd looks passed between Kenzie and David, and in that look, a tome could have been written. "It could be," David said. "But I bet there's more to yer presence here than saving a wee lad."

Out of the corner of Amber's eye, she spotted Daniel on the sidewalk. He saw her and pivoted. "Oh crap. The man walking into the saloon is Daniel Grant. He's the boy's father. He's also a Pinkerton agent and highly suspicious of me. I guess he's Leadville's version of the British Secret Service. He'll be suspicious of you, too."

Daniel approached their table, his eyes solidly on David and Rick. "Miss Kelly." He tipped his hat, but other than that simple polished move, she doubted there was an at-ease muscle in his body.

Kenzie looked him up and down, but David and Rick didn't twitch a muscle at first. Then they slowly lifted their hands, placed them on the tabletop, and casually clasped their coffee cups. Daniel's body language shifted only slightly, but he dropped his hand that had been poised near the holster hidden beneath his coat.

Amber pulled out the chair next to her and patted the seat. Might as well invite him to join them. If not, he'd just stand there and draw more attention to their table. "Agent Grant, why don't you join us?"

Kenzie offered the first introduction. "I'm Mrs. David McBain, this is my husband, and my cousin, Rick O'Grady. And you already know my cousin, Amber Kelly."

The three men measured each other over brief handshakes, then Daniel took the proffered seat. "I could use a cup of coffee to warm up a bit." He nodded to the waitress. "Ellen, coffee please."

Amber watched the waitress sashay behind the bar and return with a steaming cup. Daniel jingled coins in his hand then casually dropped them in the pocket of her apron, smiling. Then sipping his coffee, he turned his attention to the men at the table.

"What brings ye to Leadville?" he asked.

"We're looking at business opportunities and ran into Amber in the general store. We didn't know she was here," Rick said.

"Are ye coming to her show tonight? I've heard her play the guitar. She's very talented."

"Amber mentioned a five-night performance contract, but we haven't heard the details yet," Kenzie said.

"Where'd ye find a guitar?" David asked.

"At Hughes Store. I bought a Martin for twelve dollars. Can you believe it? A miner traded the instrument for supplies. It's exquisite."

"A Martin? Here in Leadville?" David asked. "That's quite a find. And for only twelve dollars."

Amber read between the lines. McBain was wondering where she got the money. "I hope I'll be able to play it. My hands are so stiff today."

"I'll help you stretch them out. Then you can ice them for a while," Kenzie said. "That should help."

"Miss Kelly is also a gifted lawyer," Daniel said. "I was present yesterday afternoon when she stood for a bar examination before Judge Adams. She has an impressive grasp of the law."

Kenzie gave him a soft smile. "You don't have to tell us. We already know how talented she is."

"Her negotiation skills are equally impressive," Daniel continued. "She negotiated a settlement for my son. He even got a dog out of it as a bonus."

"That's a new twist. I bet you haven't done that before," Kenzie said.

"Not lately." Amber smiled at Daniel and his appreciative gaze raked over her. Her cousins threw furtive looks at each other, and it frustrated Amber that they knew something she didn't. Her clients did that occasionally and it drove her batty. In her gut, she knew they weren't telling her everything. If she was suspicious of them, no wonder Daniel was suspicious of her.

"I hope you got a percentage of the settlement," Rick said.

"I did. Although I had every intention of handling the case for free. I wanted Noah to have money to buy a replacement drum and pay doctor bills."

A concerned frown appeared on Kenzie's face. "Is he injured?"

"Just sore, I think," Amber said.

"What happened to his drum?" Rick asked.

"He was riding in the back of a wagon playing his drum. A dog ran out into the street and scared the horses. Noah fell off and the drum was smashed," Amber said.

Daniel cocked his head. "What Miss Kelly isn't telling ye is that she jerked Noah out of the way only moments before a freight wagon—" Daniel paused, his jaw tightened, and his steely gaze locked on something outside the window. Amber lightly touched his arm. He silently acknowledged her, and she withdrew her hand.

"It was *that* close?" Kenzie asked. "It had to have been terrifying."

A rush of cold settled in Amber's marrow and she turned her head slightly to see if the door had been left open. It wasn't, but her memory was fully exposed, along with the terror that had spurred her to action.

"It didn't seem so when I rushed into the street, but when the wagon wheels splattered us with mud and I held a shaking child, it became very real. Then I got mad, and I wanted to see justice served on the man responsible."

"Let me get this straight," Kenzie said. "Noah ended up with money for a new drum and the dog that caused the accident. And you got a five-night performance contract."

"When you're negotiating, sometimes you have to be creative," Amber said.

"I can see you and Kenzie on opposite sides of a legal argument. It would have to be a draw," Rick said.

"Ye're a lawyer, too?" Daniel asked.

"It runs in the family," Kenzie said, then changed the subject. "So that's how you got money to buy the guitar?"

"I used some for the guitar and some for room and board. It was very serendipitous."

"Speaking of room and board, we need to find a place to stay. Do you have a recommendation, Agent Grant?" Kenzie asked.

"I might. How long will ye be here?"

"Not more than a week," David said. "If we could get our business done, we'd leave tomorrow."

"What business is that?" Daniel asked.

"We're looking to buy a haberdashery or dry goods store. Our research leads us to believe you can make more money operating a business than mining silver," Kenzie said.

Rick pointed at David. "He wants to be the next Horace Tabor."

Daniel finished his coffee and set his cup aside. "If ye're reaching that high, go higher. Be rich like Joseph Glidden."

Amber glanced at Kenzie to see if she recognized the name. Kenzie deflected saying, "We'll start with a money-making venture and see how far we can go."

"I noticed the high cost of goods and services in Leadville. Is that because there's no railroad?" David asked.

"Transportation costs are set at extortionist levels. Once the railroad comes through town, that will change," Daniel said.

"The law suit between the Rio Grande and Santa Fe railroads will settle in a few months. This is the time to start a business," Amber said.

"The railroad owners aren't as convinced as ye are," Daniel said. "The fighting in the gorge is getting worse."

A foot pressed down hard on the top of Amber's boot. She was too far away from everyone except Kenzie. Her toes weren't accidentally being squashed. Kenzie was warning Amber to be careful. Discussing ongoing litigation when she knew the outcome was like falling head first down a slippery slope.

"If you need rooms, my landlady, Mrs. Garland, has one more available. I introduced Miss Kelly to her last night."

"You can stay with me, Kenzie," Amber offered. "David and Rick can share the other room."

Rick cleared his throat. "Thanks, but I'll find something..." He glanced up toward the second floor of the saloon. "A little less respectable."

Daniel pulled a pouch of tobacco from his pocket and tamped a load into a clay pipe. After lighting it he said, "Mrs. Garland has a room in the back so small it doesn't have an echo, but it does have a cot and an exterior door that will give ye a bit of freedom to come and go." He drew on the pipe, and the rich scent of tobacco wafted between them. "When ye visit the widow, ask about the room. Tell her I mentioned it to ye."

"No echo, huh," Rick said. "That might be a deal killer." Daniel clenched the pipe between his teeth, and Rick laughed. "Just kidding. That sounds perfect. I'll ask about it."

Daniel pushed back from the table. "I need to see the doctor about Noah. I might see ye at the boardinghouse later. If not, then at the theatre tonight." He stood and nodded slightly to Amber then Kenzie. "Ladies." He drew on the pipe and nodded to both David and Rick before exiting the saloon.

"He's an interesting man," Kenzie said.

Amber watched the batwing doors close behind him. "Meeting the three of you has only tangled his thoughts into more knots. He makes me nervous. And that rarely happens. He's suspicious of all of us now. That's why he wants you to stay at the boarding house. He doesn't want to lose track of anyone until he figures us out."

"I ken that," David said.

"He wouldn't believe our story if we told him." Kenzie finished her coffee and pushed the cup away. "We need to make plans. Olivia deserves to know you're safe."

An old man with tobacco-stained teeth and a longhorn mustache stopped at an adjoining table and spoke with the men sitting there about shares, assays, and yields per tonnage before moving on to their table. He approached Amber. "Are you Miss Kelly, the lawyer?"

She had no reason to deny her identity. "Yes, I am."

"Thought that was you. You can't throw a piece of silver across the street without hitting half a dozen solicitors. I heard you got a settlement out of Mr. Tabor. Anybody who can do that is the kind of lawyer I want, as long as you're cheap." He glanced at his feet then back up at her. "I mean 'fordable. I need a contract to sell my claim."

Amber turned in her chair and studied the miner. "How'd you hear about the settlement with Mr. Tabor?"

The man shrugged. "He was talking about it in the barbershop. Said he got the best end of the deal. I figured he was lying. So I went looking for you and found you here."

"Can it wait until tomorrow?" she asked.

"I need a contract today. Can you do it or not? I hate to pay good money for this. Friend of mine said all us miners were working for shysters in starched collars. No offense, ma'am."

"No offense taken." She considered how much time she needed to prepare for opening night. "I have a full day scheduled already. Are you clear on what you want, or do we need to hash out terms and conditions?"

"I know what I want. I just need someone to make it legal."

"Then meet me back here in an hour. I'll bring paper and pen and we can draft a purchase agreement."

The miner tugged out a silver pocket watch and flipped open the cover. After checking the time, he said, "One hour." Then he turned and left the saloon, whistling a jaunty tune.

Amber finished her whisky. "I have a question. If I go home to explain what happened to Olivia, can I come back?"

"There's no way to know," David said. "Ye should stay until whatever ye were sent to do is done."

"Don't you think I've already done it? I saved Noah's life."

"Having been in your position," Kenzie said, "you'll only know in hindsight."

Amber felt a prick of foolish tears. She never cried. To hold them back, she closed her eyes, and as her lashes drifted shut, she saw the same damn look pass between Kenzie and David. After a moment she opened her eyes again.

"Something else is going on here. I've seen you give each other odd looks." She nodded at Kenzie then David then Rick. "You're hiding something from me. Rick's a Marine, Kenzie's Army, and you"—she pointed at David—"were probably in some Scottish Secret Service unit. Not one of you will reveal any secrets until you're ready. I just need to know one thing. Is Olivia okay?"

"She's going nuts worrying about you," Kenzie said. "She believes you're injured, although I don't think she believes you're dead. She's physically fine, and Connor is taking care of her the best he can."

"Has she called our parents?"

"As of a couple hours ago, no."

"You're telling me—"

The waitress approached the table. "Can I get you more coffee or whisky?"

Amber handed over her glass. "Hit me again." The waitress walked away and Amber continued. "You're telling me that if I leave, I might not be able to return. But I shouldn't leave until I've done what I came to do, whatever that is, and I won't know until after I've done it. Do you know how crazy that sounds? Then on top of that, you're saying my sister is a basket case worrying about me."

The waitress brought the refill and set it down in front of Amber. She stared at it for a moment, then picked it up, and tossed back the fiery liquid. "Let's go home then, because Olivia and my parents are the most important people in my life."

David tapped his fingers on the tabletop. "There may be another way."

"Don't keep it to yourself. Tell us," Kenzie said.

"Amber can do a videotape to let Olivia know she's fine and will be home soon," David said."

"How do you plan to get it to her?" Kenzie asked.

"I'll email it once we get back home."

"If Amber's brooch is like the amethyst and diamond, she'll return around the time she left, so Olivia will never know she was gone. But if her brooch is like the ruby, sapphire, or emerald, she could be gone for days, weeks, or months. I think the video is a smart idea," Kenzie said.

There was a prickling on Amber's neck, a sensation she often had during trials and negotiations. She rubbed her hand across her nape to settle the sensation. It didn't help.

"I don't know if that will satisfy Olivia, and besides, I don't have my phone. Olivia will know the video didn't come from me. And what would I tell her? 'Hi sis, I'm in 1878 and not ready to come home.'"

"Tell her you're shacking up with a guy you met in the mountains and you're not ready to come up for air," Rick said.

Amber rubbed deep into her thumb, stretched and tugged on it. "Olivia would never believe it."

"Tell her the guy is a rock hound, too. Would she believe that?"

Amber stared at Rick. "I don't know."

"You'll have to convince her," Kenzie said.

Amber worked on her other hand, stretching that thumb, too.

"If Olivia saw me with a guy, she might believe it."

"Are you volunteering to be the guy, Rick?" Kenzie asked.

His eyes darkened as he considered the question. "It would have to be arms and legs, maybe no shirt. No head shot. I don't want to piss Connor off."

"Why would Connor care?" Kenzie asked.

"Trust me. It's a brother thing."

Amber rested her forehead in her hand, and shook her head gently, considering the deception. Was it worth it? There were no guarantees if she went home that she could come back. She glanced at Rick again. At first, he looked unruffled, but then she noticed a tic in his jaw as he clenched his teeth.

"How long have you been back from Afghanistan?" she asked.

He didn't respond right away, but his Adam's apple jumped slightly. "A few weeks."

Amber looked at David. "Can we give this twenty-four hours? It's asking a lot of Rick after what he's been through."

"Twenty-four hours won't change anything for me," Rick said. "I'll stay with you. I'll pose for a video, I'll even go fossil hunting. But I need a commitment from you that you'll never run off. I'll go wherever you want to go, but don't leave me out." He pointed at David. "This guy will beat the ever-loving shit out of me if I lose you. If we can reach a deal on that, I'm your man."

Amber's heart tightened a bit, but she wasn't going to second guess her decision. This was a once in a lifetime opportunity, and she couldn't pass it up. "You got a deal, O'Grady."

Kenzie slapped her hands together as if wiping them clean. "Then David and I will go home tomorrow. I want to hear your concert tonight."

Amber raised her hand in a stop gesture. "Wait. My brooch doesn't work. Remember? How will we get home?"

"We have the diamond and amethyst brooches with us," David said. "We'll leave the amethyst with Rick." His impervious dark gaze bore into her." Ye understand, don't ye, lass, that ye're now part of an elite group of people who have the power to change the world."

For a moment, she was struck dumb. Then, "What?" She was hardly aware of speaking aloud. "You can't be serious."

"Very serious, lass. Ye know the future. Ye know when events will happen. And ye can't tell anyone."

Kenzie's hazel eyes softened a bit when she asked, "What stone do you have in your brooch?"

"Amber. I'm a Taurus. It's my birthstone."

"Do ye remember the words written on the stone?" David asked.

"It's written in a strange language." She furrowed her brow, trying to remember the words. "Does it matter?"

"Probably not." David said.

Rick pushed to his feet and dropped coins on the table to cover their tab and a tip for Ellen. "Let's go make arrangements for tonight. I'd like to wander around town a bit this afternoon unless I'm needed to… I don't know… Pose nude or something."

Kenzie pointed at Rick, then at Amber. "This is strictly business, you two. There'll be no friends with benefits on this adventure. Got it?"

Rick snapped his fingers. "Aw, shucks—"

"Aw, shucks—" Amber said even as he did, snapping her fingers, too. Why Kenzie would care what she and Rick did in private puzzled Amber, but she let it go unanswered for now. She'd ask Rick later.

"Do you have plans after you meet with your client?" Kenzie asked.

"Darn. I forgot about him. I need to purchase a few supplies first. After I solve his problem, I need to go to the theatre and rehearse."

David checked the time. "Ye have just enough time to go shopping. Give us the address of the boarding house, and Kenzie and I will go see the landlady. We only need a room for tonight. Afterward, we'll meet ye at the theatre."

"Will you bring my guitar? I'll also need the music book in my room. It will save time if I don't have to go back to the boardinghouse. Mrs. Garland will want me to try on the dress she's altering for me to wear tonight. It'll have to wait until later."

"I'll take the client appointment if you want to spend more time rehearsing," Kenzie said.

"That's tempting, but I need to earn money. And if I do a decent job for him, he might come to my show and bring his friends. Thanks anyway."

"If you need help with the show," Kenzie said, "David plays a mean sax and Rick has a beautiful tenor voice."

"How do you know?" Rick asked.

"Because all the O'Gradys sang at JL's wedding—that you missed—and I heard you have the best voice in the family."

"I was deployed, that's why I wasn't there. I've watched videos from the entire weekend, and my name was never mentioned."

"I found Pops crying because you weren't there, and your nephew told me about your voice. So there."

Amber looked from David to Rick. "If you're serious, Mr. Tabor said there's a sax at the theatre, and I would love to sing a few duets if we can find songs that complement our voices. I was silently panicking, wondering how I was going to do a one-woman show."

"Don't panic. We've got this under control," Kenzie said. "We'll see you at the theatre in two hours."

David and Kenzie left the saloon, leaving Amber and Rick behind. "You don't have to babysit me," she said.

"I'll hang with you until you meet your client." He offered his elbow and he gripped her hand tight with the crook of his arm. "Come on. Let's go back to the store. Your grandmother is probably there by now."

"Oh my gosh. I forgot about her, too. Thank goodness there's muscle memory in my fingers, or I might forget every song I know." As they exited the saloon, she asked, "What's your favorite song to sing?"

He rubbed a knuckle across his lower lip, thinking. "I'm rather partial to Irish songs. But don't ask me to sing 'Danny Boy.' I cry every time."

"That's okay. I do, too."

19

1878 Leadville, Colorado—Amber

AT QUARTER TO eight that night, Amber was pacing in a dressing room below the stage at the Tabor Opera House, massaging the stiff joints in her hands. The carpeted, gas-lit room was lavishly furnished with a fainting couch, beveled glass mirrors, and a French upholstered-style dressing screen. But even with all the elegance and comfort surrounding her, she was stressed out. She worried about her voice, her stamina, and the audience's reaction to their first set. If they didn't get booed off the stage, the second and third sets should bring down the house.

During a break in the afternoon rehearsal, she and Rick had videotaped a message to Olivia using David's phone. They had staged a sexually suggestive scene on a red velvet sofa they found in the prop room. Rick had unbuttoned his shirt and Amber had bared her shoulders. With Rick's head out of the frame, she confessed to her sister she had met a sexy rock hound and wouldn't be home for a few days. The details were vague, but according to Kenzie who watched the video, very convincing.

As soon as David and Kenzie arrived back home, he'd send the video to Olivia from Amber's email address. She gave him her log in information, but she sensed he could access her email even without her password. He gave her the impression he would cross the moral/ethical lines for two reasons: to protect his family and to protect the brooches. A large gray zone surrounded both reasons. For someone who had never ventured into that zone, her lies had not only pushed her in there, but they had kicked her out on the other side.

Amber turned the page in the songbook and hummed the tune of the first duet on the evening's program. Kenzie had been spot-on about Rick's vocals. His high notes were steady, his tone was smooth, and his voice overall had a haunted smokiness. She knew she had a showstopper with Rick, and then she'd heard David on the sax. He played strong, cutting-edge solos, but the way he relaxed into his ballads and let the instrument sing to the crowd was simply magical. Watching Kenzie's pulse beat in her throat, Amber knew Kenzie had fallen in love with David the moment she'd heard the first note from his saxophone.

A loud knock on her door cut short further musings. "Come in."

The door opened a crack, and Noah timidly craned his neck around the frame. She dropped the songbook on a nearby chair and opened the door wider. "Noah." The gold-colored satin train attached to her dress puddled about her feet as she swirled to welcome him with a warm hug.

"I'm so glad to see you, sweetie."

He thrust a nosegay to within inches of her nose. "I bought flowers. Pa said it's the proper thing to do for stage performers on opening night."

She slipped the bouquet, made from a variety of flowers, from his hand and sniffed. "Your pa is a smart man." Her dressing room already smelled like a gift shop with bouquets from the McBains and Rick and a tin of gingerbread cookies from Mrs. Garland. "These are lovely. Thank you." She glanced over Noah's head and down the hallway. "Where's your pa?"

"He's with Mr. and Mrs. McBain. They're talking about the Highlands."

"Are they finding people they know in common?" she asked.

"Mr. McBain said he's spent most of his life in America. He doesn't know many people from there."

"If I met someone from Chicago, we probably wouldn't know the same people either." The McBains were experienced time travelers. Daniel wouldn't trip them up, but knowing they were having a conversation didn't help Amber's pre-performance jitters.

Two men slapping backs and laughing drew her attention to the hallway again. David and Daniel were on their way to her dressing room. They could almost pass for brothers—same coloring, height, weight, bone structure, similar voices, and dressed in identical black tailcoat tuxedos, dress shirts with stand-up collars, black cravats, and silver-gold brocade threads in their waistcoats. They must have shopped at the same gentlemen's emporium. The most powerful similarity, though, was that unnamed quality both men possessed. She couldn't describe it or identify it. She only knew it was there.

"Hi, Pa. I gave Miss Kelly the flowers."

Daniel stepped into the dressing room, and the space immediately steamed up. She was surprised the flowers didn't wilt. He tilted his head to one side, eyes narrowing. "Miss Kelly, ye look beautiful."

The way he said her name, the way he looked at her now with soft eyes that held a hint of desire, made her cheeks heat. Her face probably resembled her childhood Raggedy Ann doll with large red patches on either side of her nose. The gold and white satin Paris creation was cut low, showing a bit of cleavage, and his gaze lowered over her. She reached for her fan and snapped it open, fluttering it beneath her chin.

"Thank you. It's fancier than what I would normally wear, but it works for the stage."

Noah tugged on Daniel's cuff. "Come on, Pa. We need to find our seats."

"Where are you sitting?" she asked.

"We have one of the two proscenium boxes on the left side of the house," Daniel said. "We're sitting with Mrs. McBain, Mrs. Garland, and Mr. and Mrs. Hughes."

"Those are excellent seats. You'll enjoy the show from there." While taking a break during rehearsal, Amber had wandered through the auditorium and the horseshoe-shaped balcony. She'd also relaxed in one of the ornately carved wooden chairs with soft upholstery in the proscenium box closest to the stage.

David leaned against the door frame, arms crossed, grinning down at her, eyes crinkling into triangles at the corners. Rick pushed past David and entered the room. At her request, he had shaved his whiskers. Of the three men, he might be the best looking, only because he had that bad boy concoction of safe danger and unavailability that women found sexy. She had chased a bad boy once. Never again. Chasing one was a perpetually unobtainable goal, although it had been an exhilarating ride and some of the best sex she'd ever had.

"We need to get into place. Are you ready?" Rick asked.

Daniel swiveled, "O'Grady, right? I heard ye're singing with Miss Kelly."

"I can't say no to her smile. Can you?"

Daniel and Rick seemed to circle each other like two peacocks, shaking their brilliantly-hued, long tail feathers. David looked at her from behind Daniel's back, one eyebrow raised in question or perhaps amusement.

David's faint smile faded away and he gestured to Rick with his chin. "Bring the song book. I want to look at the music one more time." He grabbed Rick by the nape as though he were a disagreeable cat.

"See you in the wings, sweetheart," Rick said as he was forcibly removed from her dressing room.

They punched each other in the arms, speaking in low voices as they hurried away. Their footsteps retreated down the hallway until they were washed out by the sounds of Daniel shuffling his feet about the carpet, looking like he had something on his mind. He lifted his hand from the back of a walnut chair and proceeded to straighten and smooth his cravat.

Noah piped in. "Pa made dinner reservations in the dining room at the Clarendon Hotel. You'll be there, won't you, Miss Kelly?"

"I don't know, sweetie." She lifted her eyes to Daniel. "I haven't been invited."

Noah moved to stand between Amber and his dad. "I'm asking you. And besides, your cousins and Mrs. Garland are coming, too."

Daniel's shoulders lifted slightly, and he had the look of a silver miner uneasy in his Sunday suit. She had a sneaky suspicion he hadn't been on a date since his wife died. If he was on the rebound and needed a rebound girl, she wouldn't mind stepping into the role, so long as their time together wasn't part of a Pinkerton investigation. But how would she know? The scent of him lingered in the room now—the castile soap he favored, the faint citrus of hair oil, a whiff of pipe tobacco, and whisky.

A stagehand came to the door, interrupting them. "Miss Kelly, places. The show is about to start."

She glanced around the dressing room, slowly panicking. "Have you seen my guitar?"

"It's in the wings," the stagehand said.

"Thanks." She glanced at Daniel, trying to breathe deeply. "I guess I better go."

His gaze lingered on her as if he were reluctant to go, as if he wanted to imprint her face in his memory, as if he had something yet to say. "I hope ye'll join us for dinner. That is…unless ye have another invitation."

"I don't, and I'd love to join you. But would you mind including Mr. and Mrs. Hughes? He was so helpful picking out songs theatre patrons would enjoy. I'd like to thank them. I'll pay for their meals."

"David said he wanted to treat everyone to a celebratory dinner."

"Oh, that's nice." When she returned home, she'd plan a gathering and cook a special meal for her new cousins and introduce them to Olivia. If her sister was still speaking to her.

She followed Daniel and Noah out of the dressing room. They took the side door that led to the proscenium boxes, and she hurried in the opposite direction, humming the first few bars of "Ten Thousand Miles Away." It was an 1870s song that Grandfather Craig promised would be received with wild applause. She had never worried about a performance being well-received, but tonight she had a host of insecurities.

The eight-hundred-seat theatre was said to be the finest between St. Louis and San Francisco. After spending the afternoon rehearsing on the thirty-five by fifty-five-foot stage, she believed it. The main curtain was a hand-painted scene of the Royal Gorge and was backed by eight drop curtains, ready to lend the proper background for any scene the entertainment demanded.

David and Rick had convinced her that performing from the apron, the area in front of the proscenium arch, provided a more intimate setting. And since there was no sound system, it would be easier for those sitting in the back of the house and in the balcony to hear the performance.

The theatre was heated by a massive coal furnace, and the lighting was supplied by seventy-two gas jets. It was a beautiful performance space decorated around a red, gold, white, and sky-blue color scheme. The seats were red plush made by Anderson, a manufacturer of patented opera chairs. She knew that because Mr. Tabor had listened to part of the rehearsal, and during a break, he had reminded her that she needed to fill every one of the plush red chairs.

They would open the show with Grandfather Craig's song to set the tone. Then they would do a mix of songs from the late eighteen hundreds to the twenty-first century and judge the audience's reception to unfamiliar tunes.

When she and Rick were in the prop room, she'd also found a red, plush armless chair that would look nice on stage. She intended to sit while she played since she didn't have a strap for the guitar. Even if she'd had one, she wouldn't have used it. Moving around while trying to manage the dress's long train would have been too much of a distraction.

The stage manager had positioned a wooden music stand next to the chair on the apron. At exactly eight o'clock, Mr. Tabor walked out on stage.

"Good evening, ladies and gentlemen. Please welcome to the stage tenor sensation Mr. Patrick O'Grady, guitarist Miss Amber

Kelly, and one of the most influential saxophonists of the century, Mr. David McBain." Mr. Tabor glanced down at the introductions Amber had written for him, and continued, "You're going to be hearing the sax played tonight, not in a supporting role, but as a lead instrument. Mr. McBain has forged entirely new sounds for your listening pleasure. Now, sit back and enjoy the show."

Mr. Tabor passed her in the wings and bowed over her hand. "You filled the house, Miss Kelly. Four more to go."

If citizens of Leadville showed up to hear three unknowns, they must be desperate for entertainment. She wondered how many of her client's friends were in the audience. The miner had been pleased with her work and had promised to spread the word.

Rick and David walked out to a lukewarm reception. Matter of fact, if Kenzie and Noah hadn't been applauding there wouldn't have been much of a reception at all. Then Amber entered with a touch of nervous attitude, looked down at the audience with a taste of queenly majesty, and nodded when she spotted her client on the front row clapping enthusiastically.

David held her chair while she sat, then handed her the guitar. As soon as she was settled, he left the stage since he wasn't singing or playing in the first set. She strummed a few chords then she and Rick jumped right into "Ten Thousand Miles Away."

Oh for a brave and a gallant ship/ And a fair an' a fav'rin' breeze/ With a bully crew an' a captain to/ To carry me o'er the seas/ To carry me o'er the seas, me boys/ To me true love far away/ For I'm takin' a trip on a government ship/ Ten thousand miles away.

They had the audience on their feet, stomping and hollering. Grandfather Craig had been right. To watch her grandparents enjoying the show balanced out her sister's distress.

Then, O ye winds I ho!/ A rovin' I will go/ I'll stay no more on Erin's shore/ To hear the fiddlers play/ I'm off on the bounded Maine/ And I won't be back again/ For I'm on the move to my own true love/ Ten thousand miles away.

The noise and sheer energy threatened to shout down the plaster walls of the theatre. They followed "Ten Thousand Miles Away" with several more sea shanties, and the Irish miners—including her client—sang right along with them. After several songs, Amber announced, "We're going to slow this down a bit. Mr. McBain is coming back on stage to play a new tune for you. So catch your breath and enjoy his performance."

Rick took her guitar and escorted her off the stage to thunderous applause.

When they had discussed David's list of songs at the afternoon rehearsal, they decided the audience might be initially stunned, but since the songs he suggested were both soulful and universal they believed they should be warmly received. He intended to open with "Summertime."

David put the mouthpiece between his lips and Amber held her breath. The first note was even purer than it had been during rehearsal. Kenzie was right. David was a high-wire act of musical textures, and both the sound and the man were purely erotic. If the women in the audience didn't swoon, they had to be cold-hearted.

Slow, liquid notes rippled like gently rolling lake water.

When the last echo of "Summertime" faded, you could hear only the rapidly beating hearts of the women in the audience. Amber forgot to breathe. After a few seconds, a single clap resounded, and then a sharp whistle, and then another clap until the entire house was on its collective feet.

"Encore! Encore!"

Rick patted her back. "You can breathe now."

She blew out a breath. "I was scared to death."

David finished his set list then left the stage to a demand for another encore. "I'm done," he said. "Ye two have to carry the show for the next four nights, so get out there and knock 'em dead."

Amber and Rick nailed the rest of the show singing "Finnegan's Wake," "The Parting Glass," and "Star of the County Down," alternating between light-hearted ditties and soulful ballads.

The performance was flawless.

When they reached the end of the set, David brought out a banjo Mr. Tabor had found late that afternoon, and she and Rick sang a rousing rendition of "Paddy on the Railway." They were going to close with Rick singing "Danny Boy," but the audience was so fired up after "Paddy on the Railway" that by unspoken agreement, they finished with a bow and left the stage.

After thirty seconds of listening to "Encore, encore," they returned to a shower of coins and bills raining down on the apron. The audience demanded "Paddy on the Railway" again. They sang it, and the audience still wanted more. As they finished the song a second time, two men at the back of the house walked out. One of them was the man—the scary character actor—she'd seen on the boardwalk the day before. Good riddance.

Amber smiled up at Daniel sitting in the proscenium box. His bright eyes smiled back in return. "Folks, my picking fingers are tired. Come back tomorrow night and Mr. O'Grady and I will play your favorite tunes and more." She smiled down at her client, and he grinned as men beside him and behind him patted his shoulders.

Backstage, Amber hugged and kissed both David and Rick. "Thank you. I couldn't have done it without you." She glanced back out on the stage. "Look at all that money."

"We'll gather it for you, Miss Kelly. We won't keep any of it," the stagehand said.

Rick gave her a lopsided smile, sweat streaming down his face. "My mother pulled me into a few of her shows, but I've never enjoyed performing as much as I did tonight. Thanks for asking me." He then surprised Amber by kissing her on the mouth. If it hadn't happened so quickly, she could easily have fallen into it and kissed him back.

David smacked Rick on the arm. They shared a silent look while she held her breath, wondering what was going on.

Then David turned on his heel and stomped toward the side door. He yelled over his shoulder, "Don't screw around, O'Grady. We'll meet ye in the dining room."

The door slammed like a clap of thunder, and Amber blew out her breath. After the echo died away, she asked, "What's wrong with him?"

"Guess he didn't like me kissing you."

"It was just a congratulatory thing. I didn't mind."

"Yeah, but this is business. He doesn't want us to get caught up in the moment. If you know what I mean."

She knew exactly what he meant, and it was a reminder for her as well. "He doesn't want us to believe the lie we expect Olivia to believe."

"It's dangerous enough without us…you know…complicating the situation."

"Got it. Now tell me about your mother. She was on Broadway? No wonder you can sing. What shows? I've seen most of them."

"Name a musical, and I bet she was in the chorus. Let's get out of here." Rick kissed her again, but on the cheek instead of her mouth. "Your Pinkerton man is here," he whispered.

She turned, Rick's arm still around her. "Daniel." She stepped away from Rick. "Did you enjoy the show?"

Rick grabbed a hat off the shelf near the stage entrance, clapped it atop his head, and cut a hasty path toward the back door. "See you in the dining room, sweetheart."

Daniel glared at Rick's disappearing frame. "I thought I'd walk ye to the hotel, unless yer cousin intends to escort ye." The late fall wind whipped around the door as Rick exited, slamming it behind him. "I guess not."

"Rick thoroughly enjoyed himself tonight," she said with a flip of her wrist. "His exuberance is carrying him away."

"I've seen stage performances in London, Paris, New York City, Chicago, San Francisco, and ye and yer cousins could perform in any of those cities to a sellout crowd. Ye're immensely talented. Why are ye here when ye could be in Paris?"

"Because tonight this is where I want to be." She'd never wanted to sing or play professionally. She enjoyed what she did and wasn't looking for more.

The shadowed light from the gas lantern threw Daniel's profile into sharp relief, much as it had the night before, and once again she was struck by an even stranger flutter in her belly.

He turned his full attention to her, away from the echo of the slamming door, his dark blue eyes sober. "And tomorrow night...where will ye want to be?"

"Right here." A heated flush climbed up her neck to her cheeks, and she turned toward her dressing room. "I need to change." She could banter with Rick, let him kiss her on the mouth, but her belly didn't flutter. Why did she have to be attracted to a man from the nineteenth century? A relationship with Daniel would lead straight to the heartbreak hotel. She couldn't do that to herself, to Daniel, and certainly not to Noah, who desperately wanted a mother. Mrs. Garland was trying to fill that void for him, but because of his love for his dad, the void could never be filled for Noah until new love healed Daniel's heart.

"I'll wait out here," he said.

Which was where he should have stayed, but instead she invited him in. Daniel closed the dressing room door, and she disappeared behind the changing screen. "Tell me the truth. Did you enjoy the show?"

"As I said, ye're immensely talented, and as ye haven't answered, I'll ask again." And he did, in a dangerously soft voice. "Why are ye here when ye could be on a stage anywhere in the world?"

She walked out from behind the screen and turned her back to him. "Can you take your Pinkerton hat off and put your theatre critic hat on instead? I want to know what you thought of the show, and I'd also like help with the buttons."

"I'll help ye if ye'll answer my questions."

"Unbutton me and I'll tell you." His warm fingers brushed across her skin as he unbuttoned the satin buttons. If goose bumps had a color, there wouldn't be a square inch of flesh tone visible on her shoulders or neck. She slipped behind the screen again. "I hunt fossils. That's what I love. I play the guitar and sing. That's what I enjoy doing when I'm not digging up bones or representing ten-year-old boys who've lost their drums."

"Ye entertained hundreds of patrons tonight who spent most of the performance on their feet singing with ye and throwing money on the stage."

"Men were on their feet because Rick's extraordinary voice lifted them with songs that reminded them of home. Women were on their feet because David's passionate saxophone whispered in their ear like a lover's caress. If it had been just me—"

"I would have spent the entire evening on mine."

She sank into herself. The pain and longing in his voice was heart-wrenching. She wrapped her arms around herself, afraid if she didn't, she would rush from behind the screen and embrace him and his wounded heart.

"I don't think Kenzie ever sat down." Amber cringed, hoping she wasn't making light of his feelings. She hung Mrs. Garland's dress on a wall hook. Then she slipped on a dark wine-colored silk brocade gown decorated with red glass beads that she'd purchased that afternoon at an emporium near the theatre. The gown was more appropriate for the evening, and the buttons were on the front. She didn't have to risk the brush of Daniel's warm fingers on her skin.

"I don't think Noah ever sat down either," she said.

"Did ye enjoy it?" Daniel asked.

She stepped out from behind the screen again and gathered up her cape, fan, and gloves. "I enjoyed it. I always do, but not enough to give up searching for dinosaurs. I know that doesn't make sense to you. I love to perform. Don't get me wrong. But it doesn't compare to my real passion."

His eyes moved over her in more than a friendly assessment. "Fossil hunting?"

"I'm going to Morrison as soon as I fulfill my contractual obligations to Mr. Tabor. That's where a *Stegosaurus* was found recently."

"Are ye coming back to Leadville?"

Her throat seemed to have gone dry, but she couldn't lie to him, not when telling him the truth would save them both heartache in the end. "Probably not."

His eyes flashed briefly before going dull. "I've got to go to Denver next week for the railroad. I'll take ye. I can stay three or four days in case ye change yer mind and want to come back."

"I should tell you that David and Kenzie are leaving tomorrow, and Rick is staying behind. They believe I need a bodyguard."

"I agree wholeheartedly," Daniel said. "And I told that to the McBains. Ye arrived in Leadville wearing men's trousers, no luggage, and not a penny to yer name. Ye need protection. However, I'd trust Mrs. McBain with yer care before I'd trust Mr. O'Grady."

Amber folded her arms across the bodice of the gown as she tried to corral her rising anger. The matching opera gloves dangled from one hand, the fan from the other. The silk of the bodice felt cool and smooth against her bare wrists, but the coolness didn't lower her temperature.

"If I'd been wearing something like this"—she spread her hands and gave a slight bow as if on stage—"I never would have made it across the street in time to save Noah. You should be glad I was wearing trousers." For the second time that evening, she snapped open her fan and waved it dramatically below her chin.

"Now, if you're through telling me what I should and shouldn't do, I'm going out to dinner. I'm famished." She whipped the velvet cape about her shoulders and whirled out of the room, making it almost to the exit before she stopped, turned around, and returned to the dressing room. "So much for dramatic exits. I almost forgot my guitar."

Daniel had lit his clay pipe and was drawing reflectively upon it now, following the smoke as it drifted up to the tin-paneled ceiling. "The stagehand returned the instrument to its case and left it next to the chair ye were using on stage. He also left this." Daniel put a small canvas bag in her hand. "Money from yer fans."

"How did you know that? About my guitar, I mean."

"I'm paid to notice, Miss Kelly. And ye left yer reticule on the table there." He pointed behind her. "When ye've gathered all yer belongings, I'll escort ye next door." From a vase of flowers on her dressing table, he broke off a yellow carnation and weaved the bud into her hair, his eyes fixed softly on her face. "I'm glad ye were wearing trousers, but ye're too beautiful to hide in men's clothing."

The spicy peppery scent of the flower mingled with the sweet tobacco in his pipe and the combined scents had a hallucinatory effect on her. She could see him in her kitchen back home, leaning against the counter, his ankles crossed, a glass of wine in his hand. She saw spots and put her hand to her forehead as the room began to spin.

"I'm going to faint…"

When she opened her eyes again, she was reclining on the sofa with Daniel's hand clasped around hers. "What happened?"

"Ye fainted."

She made a move to sit, but he pressed down on her shoulder. "Don't get up yet, lass."

"I've never fainted."

"Ye have now."

"What's that smell? Vinegar? Smelling salts?"

He held up a small, silver hinged box. "This trinket is a vinaigrette. Have ye never seen one?"

"No."

"It masks foul odors, assists fainting women…"

"Sort of like a Swiss army knife. It does everything," she said.

He slid a sideways glance at her, and the gas sconces caught the silver-gold brocade threads in his waistcoat and gleamed off the penny-colored highlights in his carefully styled blond hair. "I haven't heard of that."

"It's like your trinket. It comes with a tag line: When you've painted yourself into a corner, improvise. Now, help me up. We need to go, or McBain will send the cavalry. And I don't want anyone else to know I fainted."

"Why?" His tone was as intimate as a caress, a brush of his hand across her cheek.

"Because they'll postpone their departure and they need to go. So…" She put her finger to her lips. "Don't tell them." He helped her stand but didn't let go of her arm. "My footing is solid. You can let go now."

"Are ye sure?"

No, she wasn't sure about anything, especially about Daniel. "I fainted because I'm hungry. As soon as I get something to eat, I'll be good as new."

"Then I won't let go until ye get food in yer stomach."

His impenetrable gaze fixed on her, ambling there for a moment. If he kept looking at her like she was his next meal, she'd become overheated in the small room, and probably would faint again. The episode alarmed her only because her recent breathing issues seemed to be getting worse. Only Rick seemed to notice when her breath gave out during the performance. Each time she became winded, he picked up the slack and sang louder or moved about the stage to draw attention away from her. What a great partner.

When she returned home, she'd make an appointment with her internist for the checkup she'd rescheduled three times in the past month. Until then, she'd stay hydrated and out of small rooms with sexy Pinkerton agents.

20

1878 Leadville, Colorado—Kenzie

FOLLOWING THE SHOW, David and Kenzie entered the lobby of the Clarendon Hotel next door to the Tabor Opera House. She flipped back the hood of her cloak, freeing her face of the soft anonymous folds and looped her hand into the crook of David's elbow. Subdued light rippled across the lobby's spacious interior with its carved columns, globed chandeliers, and arched doors. The room was all abuzz with theatre patrons dressed in evening finery.

"Oh, Mr. McBain," a woman's shrill voice called out as she made her way across the lobby, her playbill flapping in the air like the angling wings of a seabird.

David zigzagged to avoid her. "Keep walking." He slid his hand to Kenzie's back, encouraging her toward the dining room at a faster pace.

"Not even you, McBain, can stand off a passel of petticoats. You might as well surrender," Kenzie said, laughing.

The woman rounded a marble column and intercepted David before he reached the dining room. "Mr. McBain, will you autograph these playbills? I intend to tell all my friends they have to come to your next show." A small pencil was produced from a beaded handbag. "I never knew a saxophone could produce the sound you played tonight."

"What'd you like best about the show?" Kenzie asked.

The woman drew Kenzie's arm into hers, as if they were the best of friends. "I never knew the saxophone could sound so...so emotive. I was moved to tears."

Kenzie disentangled herself from the woman and said nonchalantly, "The sound is pure sex on the airwaves."

There was no mistaking the sudden jump of the woman's eyebrows, although the rest of her face remained composed. David made a sound deep in his throat. Unfazed, the woman continued, "Mr. O'Grady's voice was simply divine, and Miss Kelly's talent is extraordinary. The entire performance was better than any I've seen in New York or Chicago." The woman shifted to see around the column. "I've been waiting for Miss Kelly and Mr. O'Grady, too. Do you know if they're on their way?"

"Mr. O'Grady might already be here." Kenzie craned her neck to get a better view of the lobby. "I don't see him. He might be in the restaurant. Miss Kelly is protected by a Pinkerton escort, so she'll be detained until the agent is sure she'll be safe."

The woman's face no longer remained composed, and her gloved fingers touched her parted lips. "I didn't know she was *that* famous. Now I know why. Not only is she talented and beautiful, but her voice is evocative and flawless."

"You sound like a music critic," Kenzie said.

The woman fanned herself with one of the signed playbills. "My husband is the music critic for *The Reveille*. I often give him my opinion."

Kenzie leaned in, as if conveying a secret. "Miss Kelly is a sellout at every performance." Kenzie wasn't one for dissembling, but she couldn't pass up the opportunity to promote Amber's show. "Mr. Tabor was fortunate she was in town on a personal matter and had an opening in her calendar. She's booked a year in advance."

The woman clenched her autographed playbills to her breast. "I'm sending my husband to the theatre early tomorrow to purchase tickets for the next show."

If Kenzie didn't know David so well, she would have missed the slight shift of his shoulders. Enough with the fan interaction. He was ready to hit the bar. "Please excuse us," she said. "Maybe we'll see you at the next performance."

As the woman scurried away in a rustle of skirts, he glanced around as if concerned someone would overhear what he was about to say. Then to Kenzie, he said bluntly, "There won't be another performance and if ye tell anyone what just happened, ye won't like what I do."

She waved jazz hands. "Ooh. I'm so scared."

"Ye should be. I saw ye squirming in yer chair while I was on stage. If ye want me to scratch that itch tonight, ye'll keep quiet." The tone vibrating beneath his thinly veiled innuendo lowered seductively.

She removed one of her opera gloves, tugging purposefully on each finger. "Are you threatening me?"

He gave her a look that answered her question. "It's up to ye."

Occasionally, when dealing with McBain, she had to backpedal and come at him from another direction. This was important, but why? And pulling the true reason out of him would be like deconstructing a jigsaw puzzle one piece at a time—a layered process—instead of simply dumping the whole thing on the floor.

She pulled the glove off her other hand. "I get that this is important to you, but I don't understand why?"

He looked off for a moment and then returned his gaze to her. "The family doesn't see me as an entertainer. They know I'm a soldier." He rubbed his hands up and down her arms, sending erotic chills through her. "This crowd sees me as a performer."

She placed her hands over his to stop his roving fingers from distracting her. "Just to zoom out on this so I understand. Why do you care? We're leaving here. If it upsets you so much, why'd you agree to perform?"

"I didn't know it would. Turns out I was wrong."

"Wrong? You?" She shook her head. "I don't buy it. There's something else."

He shrugged. "Let it go. I need a drink."

Stalling, she brushed the skirt of her narrow, pale green velvet dress with the back of her hand, letting the warm fabric soothe her skin, but it didn't have the same effect on her mind. David was being evasive. Why? The diamond in her ring caught on a section of the fringe and she shook her hand to release the hold. While the diamond maintained its grip on the fringe, her brain sorted through the inconsistencies until the proverbial light bulb flashed in a tiny explosion of insight.

"It's Daniel, isn't it? His opinion matters to you. If you think he'll only see you as a performer, that's crazy. So what's really going on?"

David pulled a silver cigar case from his pocket, selected one, then closed the case with a click. "Ye're the puzzle solver." He pinched the cigar between his thumb and index finger, working the entire length. Then he passed the cigar beneath his nose, taking in the aroma. A match flared, and he puffed until the end of the cigar flared with fire and began to burn. The process was an erotic dance Kenzie had watched him perform hundreds of times.

"Let's see what I know," she said. "You believe Amber will bring Daniel to the future."

David hiked his foot against the lower rail of an untended lobby bar. "Go on."

"If Daniel comes to the twenty-first century, he won't understand at first why a saxophone player is the quasi-leader of the family. But all he'll have to do is attend one meeting and he'll see that everyone defers to you."

David drew a short draw, then removed the cigar from his mouth and studied it while smoke curled out into the room. He was trying for an impression of indifference, but she clearly saw through the smoke rings.

"This doesn't have anything to do with you performing tonight."

She watched his body language closely. His relaxed stance conflicted with the intensity in his eyes. When he was solving a problem, he needed a gut check to be sure his analyses and decisions were leading him in the right direction, and in the last few years, he had come to depend on her to do that. They were, as Elliott had said, a double-edged sword. But first, she had to identify the corner and flat-sided pieces of the puzzle.

"It's not because he's a Scotsman, either. Braham and Cullen are Scotsmen. They've never been a threat to you."

David rolled the tip of the cigar along the edge of an ashtray on the bar. His face now had an unreadable expression like a serious player in a high-stakes game of chance, and she knew intuitively that she was wrong about Braham and Cullen. One or both had been a threat to David, but when?

She grabbed him by the sleeve, dragging him away from the welter of excited prattle and flutter of swishing skirts gathering near them. "If you've got issues with Braham or Cullen, there's a story there you've never shared with me. Spill it."

"There's nothing to spill."

"You're pulling this out like taffy. I can see it in your eyes."

"If ye're so sure there's a story, tell me what it is."

"You're driving me nuts, McBain."

Sometimes in her role as gut-checker-in-chief, she had to make giant leaps, like putting the puzzle back together without using the flat-sided pieces. Daniel was a Scotsman like Braham and Cullen. But what else did they have in common? Cullen, Braham, and David all had the Civil War adventure in common. Daniel was old enough to have fought in the war. So what connected them? A woman? No, that couldn't be it. Daniel's wife was dead, and Braham would have died if not for...

Charlotte.

Goosebumps rose on the back of her exposed neck. "Does this have anything to do with Charlotte and your feelings for her? I know you were in love with her once."

The unflappable David McBain choked on cigar smoke and stared at her, frozen. "I wasn't—"

She placed a finger against his lips. "I know it was unrequited. I also know you still love her. Not like you love me, but you'll always have feelings for her. And before you ask, I'm not threatened by that. I know what happened in Washington. I've heard it from you,

Charlotte, Jack, and Cullen. The facts are always the same, but there is an undercurrent in all the stories. What happened in the past before we met doesn't matter now. If it did, I'd never be able to step foot in Scotland out of fear of running into one of your girlfriends, and I'd never be friends with Charlotte."

"If ye suspected, why didn't ye say something?"

"I've been waiting for you."

"Ye're the queen of confrontation, why wait?"

"Whoa. You should have told me. Throwing it back on me because I never asked isn't fair."

"Fair? Ye of all people know nothing's fair in love and war. And why the hell are we having an argument in the middle of a goddamn lobby in Leadville, Colorado?"

"We aren't arguing. We're having a discussion, and I agree. It should be in private, not promenading around the lobby of a fancy hotel, but this is where we are, and we're not going anywhere until this is settled. You're deflecting, and I want to know why Daniel is a perceived threat and Braham and Cullen aren't."

David shook his head. "I knew when I first heard yer name that ye'd always be one step ahead of me."

She paced in a small circle, putting her thoughts together, then stopped in front of him, wishing she had a podium with notes to stay on point while arguing her case.

"Besides politics," she began. "Braham has always had two passions: horses and wine. Those skills were transferable to the twenty-first century, and he and Charlotte have made a good life for themselves at Mallory Plantation. Cullen, on the other hand, is from the nineteenth century and intends to return."

Her mind was clicking, but she didn't have the important pieces yet. She proceeded slowly. "If Daniel goes to live in the future, he'll need work that challenges him. He's in law enforcement now, but to do that with a mainstream agency would be too big a challenge. I don't think even you could come up with a workaround for that, which means he'll want to join you."

Kenzie tilted her head, considering the pieces of the puzzle she had in hand, but there was still a four-sided, fully interlocking piece missing. What was it? David stroked his chin, playing with an invisible goatee. As far as she knew, the only information he had about Daniel was what he'd gleaned since they met earlier in the day. Oh no. There was more. Before the show, while she'd been talking to Noah, David had been asking Daniel about his family in Scotland.

The missing piece slipped into place and she had a moment of immense satisfaction, or as David often called her moments of insight—an orgasm. "I got it."

A smile etched lines at the corners of his eyes. "I love watching yer mind at work." He cupped her cheek and kissed her. "It's like having sex in public. So what is it?"

"There's only one thing that could threaten you that much. Daniel must be a MacKlenna."

David studied the cigar, rolling between thumb and forefinger. "If I use this stogie as a measure of time, I've smoked away five minutes, maybe six. Yer ability to solve puzzles is phenomenal, but ye're wrong. He's not a MacKlenna."

She stared at him. "He's not." If Daniel wasn't a MacKlenna, then what could possibly threaten David? She had another light bulb moment and the final piece popped into place. "Then he's a Fraser." Surprised, she stifled a desire to laugh out loud. The twists and turns of brooch adventures never failed to amaze her.

"Not exactly, but close enough," he said.

"So does he or doesn't he sprout from the Fraser family tree?"

"He's an offshoot." David's face went a little slack, as if a light within had winked out at the flip of a switch. "Daniel's sister is married to Blane Fraser."

"Blane is Elliott's middle name."

"And his father's and his grandfather's, all the way back for several generations."

She compressed her lips, and in her mind, constructed a Fraser family tree. She had seen it often enough, and as far as she could remember, there weren't any offshoots: no aunts, uncles, or cousins noted on the branches.

"What does that make Daniel? A great-uncle?"

David glanced up at the ceiling, as if processing information. "Several greats, I think. Four or five."

"That's a distant connection…"

"Hell, everyone in the family has a distant connection."

"That's true, but they're all direct lines. Daniel's isn't."

"It doesn't need to be," David said. "If he marries Amber, they'll have a double connection."

"We don't even know if they belong together, and if they do, what century they'll choose to live in. Let's not go marrying them off quite yet. And I still don't see how Daniel's position on the family tree threatens you. You're like a son to Elliott. The two of you even have a secret language. Elliott will welcome Daniel, but you'll always be his first born."

"We'll see." David removed his hat, ran a hand through his light brown hair. The light highlighted the few strands of gray at his temples. He appeared tired and somewhat disconcerted.

Since becoming part of the clan, Kenzie couldn't remember starting a day without overhearing a conversation between her husband and Elliott. She often wondered what Elliott had done during David's deployment, because surely, Elliott hadn't called David in Afghanistan to ask whether he should buy a stallion or sell shares of stock.

"Here's something to think about," she said. "Since Kevin's paternity became common knowledge, has anything changed between you and Elliott?" She waved her hand as if swatting away the question. "Never mind. Don't waste your time thinking about it, because the answer is no. And if anyone could threaten your position, it would be Kevin. My advice is to chill."

"Chill?" David stubbed out the cigar and pushed away the ashtray. "That's yer advice?"

"Right now, that's all I've got."

"I hope Elliott gets better legal advice than to chill and spill."

The rustle of skirts closed in on them and Kenzie prepared to tell the next autograph hound to come back tomorrow, but it wasn't a fan. The intruder was Mrs. Garland.

"There you are," she said breathlessly. "Daniel isn't here and Noah's worried. Have you seen him?"

"He's escorting Amber," Kenzie said. "I'm sure they'll be here any minute. David and I have been talking and lost track of time. Did we miss you coming through the front door?"

Mrs. Garland held a white lace handkerchief to her flushed cheek. Kenzie almost laughed thinking how many times three kids and a job had left her breathless, especially dealing with the twins—stubborn Scotsmen like their dad.

"No. We came across the walkway from the theatre," Mrs. Garland said. "The evening has exhausted Noah. He won't admit it, but I can tell. I should take him home, but he refuses to go."

"Where is he now?" Kenzie asked.

"Sitting at our table waiting for his father and Amber. I don't have the heart to insist he leave before he sees them. I'll go back and tell him it won't be much longer."

"Where are Mr. and Mrs. Hughes?" David asked. "I thought they were joining us."

Mrs. Garland pulled a piece of paper from her reticule and handed it to David. "The maître d' said Mr. Hughes stopped by after the show and cancelled. He left this note for you."

Kenzie glanced over David's shoulder to read the sweet thank-you note. "Amber will be disappointed. She was looking forward to getting to know them better."

Mrs. Garland pulled the strings of her bag taut, settled it neatly on her wrist, and smiled. "They're known to retire early. I wouldn't take offense."

"None taken." Kenzie realized for the first time why she was so drawn to the woman. Mrs. Garland's Virginia accent and the way she carried herself reminded Kenzie of Charlotte. Her cousin would always be an exemplary role model for how to handle yourself in stressful situations. A role model for not only the children to emulate, but adults as well—herself included.

"I'll see you at the table," Mrs. Garland said, as she gracefully strolled away.

Kenzie took as deep a breath as her stays would allow. "We haven't finished our conversation, McBain."

"Don't fret about it. We'll handle the new dynamics after we get home. A new Scotsman may be the least of our worries."

"You're thinking about the winery, aren't you?"

"If it all goes up in smoke, the repercussions will go far beyond the financial hit."

"This is the worst possible time to be away. We can't stay here. Even though time might not pass in the future, we need to be mentally fresh to deal with the aftermath of the fire. I've only been here a few hours and I'm exhausted."

"If ye're not used to the altitude, fatigue can be a problem in the Cloud City." He pulled her behind a column, and she tipped her head back until his lips came down and met hers with a passion that promised his life, his body, his love. "I want ye naked in my arms."

In a whispered breath against his lips she asked, "Does this mean you're taking back your threat?"

He raised an eyebrow at her.

For a moment time stood still and then she laughed. "Come on, McBain. Let's go talk to Noah." She corralled her petticoats, the hooked-up hem of her evening dress, and the yards of cloak. Then clasped her hand with his, and he tightened his grip on her fingers. Their clasp was a haven from the never-ending clatter of her subconscious as it worked through all they had discussed.

"Ye don't think less of me now, do ye?" he asked as they wended their way into the dining room, following closely behind Mrs. Garland.

"Because you exposed your insecurities? God, no. Have you forgotten I was hiding under a sink? And besides, I know you better than anyone. More than Granny Alice. More than Elliott. Maybe not as much as Meredith, but she knows everyone's insecurities."

21

1878 Leadville, Colorado—Kenzie

THE MAÎTRE D' at the Clarendon Hotel restaurant led Kenzie, David, and Mrs. Garland to their table, where Noah sat alone with his head down on his folded arms. Kenzie had spent the last two hours sitting next to him in the theatre, and she had fallen in love with his big blue eyes, his laughter, and his devotion to his dad.

Kenzie gently stroked his head. "Are you tired?"

He'd run his hand through his thick curls so many times that the pomade he'd used earlier to tame the unruly waves had failed and his hair now stuck out in all directions. The faint furrow of a straight part was visible on one side. Slowly, he sat back in his chair. One glance at his pink cheeks and tired eyes, and Kenzie wanted to sink to her knees right there on the polished wood floor and pull him close.

"Have you seen my pa?" he asked.

"He's escorting Amber from the theatre. She had to change clothes, and I bet she had a reporter or two who wanted an interview."

"Oh," he said. "I was worried. The streets are dangerous."

"They'll probably come across the walkway like you did. They'll be here shortly, but Mrs. Garland and I think you should go home and get some rest. You're probably still sore from your fall yesterday. The best thing you can do is get plenty of rest, drink lots of fluid, and ice your arm. Where I come from, it's recommended."

David signaled a waiter. After consulting with Mrs. Garland, two meals were ordered, along with cocktails for David and Kenzie. While they waited, Kenzie engaged Noah in a review of the show.

"Pa said Miss Kelly is the best guitar player he's ever heard. I couldn't take my eyes off her hands."

"What'd you think of Mr. O'Grady?" Kenzie asked.

Noah blushed. "Don't tell Miss Kelly, but Mr. O'Grady was my favorite." Then he looked abashedly at David. "No offense, Mr. McBain, but I knew almost every song Mr. O'Grady sang tonight, and it was fun to sing along with him."

They continued talking about the show for several minutes until the waiter returned with a basket of food. "The maître d' arranged transportation at your request," he said to David. "I'll carry the basket to the front door. A hack should be waiting there."

"Thank ye," David said.

Kenzie tousled Noah's hair and immediately had a heart pang, thinking of the twins and how they would have screamed if she'd messed with their hair. "Sleep well, big guy."

"I'll escort Mrs. Garland and Noah to the front door and get them settled in the hack. I'll be right back."

Noah didn't try to repair the hair damage the way her kids did. "Mrs. Garland said you and Mr. McBain are leaving tomorrow. Is that true?"

"That's the plan," she said. "We have twin boys and a little girl waiting for us to come home."

"If you were my ma, I'd never let you go away."

Seeing the loneliness in Noah's eyes, Kenzie was struck by how fortunate her children were to have two full-time parents, grandparents, cousins, aunts, and uncles. Although the family complained about the boys' precociousness—her description, not theirs—they all loved the three little McBains dearly.

Kenzie opened her arms. "Give me a hug, sweetie." Noah wrapped his arms around her, and his little body heaved a deep, heart-wrenching sigh. Over the top of his head, she gazed into

David's misting eyes. He was thinking of their children, too.

"We'll see you at breakfast."

He kissed her cheek and stepped out of her embrace. "Good night, Mrs. McBain."

She raised her right hand until the tip of her finger touched the outside edge of her right eyebrow, and she smartly saluted him.

"You're not a soldier," he said, grinning, but gave her a salute in return.

I was a soldier, and I'm here now because of what happened then.

She straightened his fingers and put his little hand in the correct position. "There you go." He tried again, and she smiled. The twins would fall in love with Noah in a heartbeat, and the other kids would gladly welcome him into their tight-knit club.

David took Noah's hand, winked at Kenzie, and escorted Noah and Mrs. Garland from the dining room.

While Kenzie watched them leave, she found herself pulled right back into the middle of her conversation with David, running a mental finger down the list of topics they had discussed. His non-denial denial that he'd been in love with Charlotte had stung, but what stung wasn't that he hadn't told her or that he'd once cared for Charlotte, but that his heart had been broken. For such a strong man, he had such a tender heart, and when he loved, he loved well and truly.

David returned to the dining room a few minutes later with Amber and Daniel. Every head turned to watch as they strolled across the waxed and polished wood floor covered with an Axminster carpet. Amber dazzled the diners in a dark wine-colored gown. Decorative red glass beads glimmered in the gaslight. An odd buzz of energy quieted to a low murmur. No one could take their eyes off her. And if they did, her two escorts dressed handsomely in tailcoat tuxedoes would simply blind them. The two men moved with panther-like grace and confidence to command the room.

A lump formed in Kenzie's throat. God, she loved her husband.

When they reached the table, and she could speak past the lump she asked, "Did you see Noah?"

"David said he'd just put them in a hack. I'll have a drink with ye, then go home to put him to bed." Daniel pulled out a chair for Amber and watched over her until she settled her dress, then he scooted the chair to the table.

"He'll already be asleep," Kenzie said. "He was dead on his feet, bless his heart."

Amber glanced around the dining room. "Where's Rick?"

Daniel cocked his head and frowned a little, so small a grimace that if Kenzie hadn't been watching she would have missed it beneath his short-cropped beard. "Sitting in the back corner with three women and a bottle of Champagne."

"He is?" Amber asked. "He could have waved when we came in."

Kenzie was nonplussed. She glanced at David. "Did you know he was here?" When David didn't react, she knew instinctively that he not only knew Rick was in the room, but he could accurately describe Rick's three dinner guests.

The waiter brought a bottle of Camus Freres Fine Champagne to their table. "You ordered Champagne?" Kenzie asked, trying to recall the last time her husband ordered anything but whisky. "How nice."

"No," he said.

"I hope I wasn't presumptuous," Daniel said. "I ordered it to celebrate tonight's outstanding performance."

"Thank you. Then I hope you'll make the toast." Kenzie nodded in David's direction. "You'd think a writer would be a better toast maker than McBain is known to be. But he just holds the glass aloft and says, *Slainte*."

Daniel laughed and laid his napkin carefully across his lap. "That's exactly what I intended to say." The waiter popped the cork and filled their glasses. Then holding his glass aloft, Daniel said, "To Miss Kelly, a talented and extraordinary woman, and to Mr. McBain, a talented musician and author, I assume. Thank ye for allowing me to share this evening with ye. *Slainte*."

Their crystal fluted glasses clinked in harmony. Kenzie sipped and nodded her approval of Daniel's choice.

Daniel tasted the Champagne and nodded in return. "What do ye write?"

"History and suspense," David said, then quickly changed the subject. "Shall we order dinner? I'm starving."

They perused their menus and placed their orders. Before leaving the table, the waiter topped off their glasses and left the bottle in a silver bucket near Daniel's chair.

Amber turned toward David, wagging her finger in a thoughtful way. "McBain? I've seen your book. About the Civil War, right? It's on display at my local bookstore. The placard said it's highly recommended by Denver book clubs—"

Kenzie swung the pointy-toe tip of her shoe smack into Amber's shin, and she jerked, color draining from her face. "What's wrong, sweetie?" Kenzie asked. "You're as pale as that white napkin."

Daniel jerked in his seat and turned quickly toward Amber, grabbing a small silver flask from his pocket. "Are ye going to faint again?"

"Again?" Kenzie asked.

Amber shot a scorching look at Daniel, and an even hotter look at Kenzie. "I was in my dressing room, which is small and hot, and I was dehydrated and hungry. The heat got to me. All I need is a thick, juicy steak and a good night's sleep, and I'll be good as new." Kenzie crossed her arms, and Amber held up a hand as if to forestall what she knew Kenzie would say next.

Kenzie ignored Amber and said, "If you're sick—"

"I'm not." Amber gave David a direct look. "There's no reason to change your plans."

"What are yer plans, exactly?" Daniel asked.

"Rick is staying here," Kenzie said. "At the end of Amber's contract, he'll escort her to Morrison for a few days to dig for fossils. Then she's returning to—"

"Chicago," Amber interjected quickly.

"I'm leaving Wednesday for Denver. I'll be there for several days and can extend my trip if necessary," Daniel said.

Amber took a sip of Champagne before saying, "It's not—"

"That would be appreciated," David said, talking over her.

Amber's eyes narrowed as she glared at David.

He pushed his Champagne glass aside, picked up his whisky glass, and swirled the contents before taking a long drink. Then he set it down hard. Kenzie had seen those moves before. Next, he would barrel ahead like a train on a straight track with no curves in sight.

"If ye're staying behind, lass, there'll be conditions." Although his voice was pitched low, those at the table could hear him plainly. "I may not be yer father, but I am yer protector, and ye will do what I tell ye."

Amber gave him a look that could have held back a weather front.

In response, he took another purposeful drink. The gauntlet had been thrown down. But when the waiter brought their entrées, Amber put her pique aside and tucked into her rare steak.

Kenzie had to bite the insides of her cheeks to keep from laughing. She knew David would gladly toss Amber over his shoulder and haul her ass back to the twenty-first century, but he couldn't interfere with the stone's purpose for her. Neither could he stay and babysit while she hunted fossils—not when the winery was burning to the ground.

Now that Kenzie had met Amber and been introduced to Daniel, she was convinced Amber would be safe under Rick's and Daniel's protection, and she and David could return home.

"I'd be pleased to make Miss Kelly's travel arrangements to the capital and arrange accommodations in the city," Daniel said. "The Denver, South Park, and Pacific Railroad has a passenger train to Morrison. It's a small quarry town about sixteen miles southwest of Denver. I wouldn't advise staying there, but a visit during the day with a professional bodyguard would be safe enough."

"Thank ye," David said. "Kenzie and I will stay until Wednesday morning. Once we see ye safely on the stagecoach, we'll make our own departure arrangements."

"But I thought—" Kenzie said.

"That we were leaving?" David interrupted. "I believe we should stay a few more days. There are more business opportunities we should investigate while we're here."

She pointed the tip of her shoe in his direction and jammed it into his shin. Not to shut him up as she had done to Amber, but as a thank you for not consulting her.

"Does that mean you'll play your sax again?" Amber asked.

David smiled. "That's one of the reasons I'm changing our plans."

Kenzie didn't believe that was one of the reasons at all. What was going on with him? She almost hated to ask his other reason, but she did. "And the other?"

He gave her a sly wink. "I intend to enjoy yer company." He picked up his glass of whisky. "Here's to time alone with my bride."

Later that night, she and David retreated from the world into a place of their own. And afterward, buried under handmade quilts, her cheek upon his muscular chest, and his arm looped around her, she willed the moon to stay its course. But this was a quirky time. And for some reason, she believed their fourth child had just been conceived in a brass bed with squeaky springs in Leadville, Colorado.

22

1878 Leadville, Colorado—Kenzie

After four days of long talks with Amber about practicing law and their complicated lives in the twenty-first century, it was time for Kenzie and David to say goodbye. The night before, she and Amber had decided to enjoy a private breakfast at the Tontine Restaurant on Harrison Avenue, one last chance for a cherished chat before they parted.

Prior to leaving Mrs. Garland's boardinghouse, David held her back a moment, letting Amber cross the porch to the steps ahead of Kenzie. "Be careful, lass," he whispered. "Amber's smart, and she knows we haven't told her everything about brooch lore and our experiences."

"Neither have you, McBain. You're still holding on to a few secrets." She and David had tried to pick up the threads of their conversation following the opening night performance, but interruptions during the day and their love fest at night allowed little time for talking. The absence of kids had turned frenzied quickies into slow erotic all-nighters.

David circled behind her and settled her coat on her shoulders. She slid her arms through the sleeves and fastened the silver cloak clasp. He kissed her neck. His warm breath tickled her, and she shivered.

"There's a glow about ye I haven't seen in some time."

She tied on a bonnet that covered most of her red hair and adjusted the bow to sit jauntily below her right ear. Then grabbing a pair of gloves, she paused to inspect herself in the mirror above the hall tree, and she winked at his reflection. "I wonder why," she mouthed.

Daniel came down the stairs carrying a valise and set it aside as he reached for the waistcoat he'd slung over the hall tree the night before. "Where are ye going?"

"Amber and I are eating breakfast in town."

"Why spend good money eating awful food? Mrs. Garland has the best breakfast in town." He shrugged into the waistcoat and topped it with a brown herringbone frock coat.

"You're a pragmatic Scotsman just like my husband. He asked the same question, and the answer is… Amber and I want some girl time." Kenzie straightened the bow then decided she didn't like the look at all. She removed the bonnet and exchanged it for a silly little hat that she secured with a hatpin. On the way out the door, she gave them a toodle-oo wave and hurried from the house to join Amber on the other side of the wrought-iron fence.

Daniel moved to stand in the doorway and hollered, "The stage leaves in ninety minutes. Don't be late."

Amber acknowledged Daniel's comment with a smile and a wave, then she took Kenzie's gloved hand and squeezed it. Together they steadied each other as they crossed the slippery street in boots that were never meant for slogging through the indescribable sludge.

"You need a good pair of sturdy walking boots," Kenzie said.

"The boots I wore here will work fine. They're not the best for fossil hunting, but they're better than anything else they're selling right now."

Kenzie pulled the collar of her coat tight to keep the cold from seeping down the back of her neck. "Be careful when you get to Morrison. You won't have clothes and equipment for fossil hunting like you're used to."

"I'll improvise, and I don't intend to gallivant around dressed as a woman, either. That'll make it harder to dig."

"I'm not thrilled about leaving you behind, especially with the weather changing." Kenzie shoved her free hand into her pocket. "I don't know how you're going to dig now anyway. It's too blasted cold."

"There'll be a couple more weeks of warm-enough weather. After that, there's no point in sticking around."

Surprisingly, Amber hadn't mentioned the Royal Gorge War. After reading the documents in David's file, Kenzie was now well-versed on the issues before the court, but she wasn't going to bring up the litigation. If Amber jumped into the dispute it could extend her stay by several months.

"Here we are," Amber said, pushing open the door of the Tontine Restaurant.

The steamy heat of the packed room vanquished the chill that had settled in Kenzie's bones during the brisk walk from the boardinghouse, and the aroma pulled the trigger on her appetite. She gave a cool nod to the mostly male patrons—some smiled, some eyes widened in recognition of Amber, and others glanced up but showed no interest at all.

Kenzie pointed toward an empty table. "Let's grab it quick."

They removed their coats, adjusted their hats, and tweaked their sleeves before settling themselves on opposite sides of a small table covered with a white tablecloth. The seating for two was positioned next to a grandfather clock that kept a persistent beat.

Kenzie signaled a harried-looking waiter—a young man wearing a stained white apron—who was rushing through the restaurant dispensing hot biscuits. He stopped at their table, smoothing his hands over the apron's smudges, as if he could magically make them disappear.

"What can I get ya', ladies?" he asked.

Amber smiled at the toothy young man. "Coffee, ham, sunny-side-up eggs, and biscuits, please."

Kenzie perused the blackboard. "I'll have the same." Sunlight from a side window reflected off the table tops straight into her eyes. She shifted in her chair to avoid the glare.

Amber glanced around the restaurant. "They say this place is equal to any restaurant in America and is the highest-priced grub joint in the world."

Kenzie laughed. "Don't worry. McBain's paying for breakfast."

The waiter returned with two cups of coffee that came with their own little cloud of steam above the rim. He set them hurriedly on the table, rattling the cups and spilling coffee into the saucers. "Sorry," he said, before dashing off to attend to another table.

Kenzie refrained from smirking at the waiter's back as he dashed off with his thumbs tucked into his apron band. She poured the overflow back into the cup.

"Tell me about the brooches again," Amber said, keeping her voice low, but loud enough for Kenzie to hear over the subdued laughter and clink of cutlery on fine china.

"I want to know why the brooch brought me here. Was it to hunt fossils? Save Noah? Meet Daniel? Meet my grandparents? Are there hoops I need to jump through before I can go home? Is there a checklist of tasks I need to accomplish? How will I know when it's time to go? You've said before you didn't know, but I need your best guess."

As Kenzie considered Amber's question, she settled carefully into the ladder-back chair. "Stick close to the party line," David had said. And that's what she intended to do. She crossed her legs, but her squirming caused the rails and spindles to make annoying creaking sounds. She considered moving to another chair as a stalling tactic, but the exasperated sighs coming from the other side of the table nixed that idea.

Kenzie slid the linen napkin from under the cutlery. "I don't know." A statement she would never make to a client. Then, "Only you will be able to answer that question." Something else she'd never say to a client.

Amber tapped her fingers on the tabletop, matching the metronome-like beat of the clock. "You said the same thing the first time I asked, the second, and the third. You've got to give me something before you leave. Anything that'll help me understand what's going on here."

Kenzie took a sip of coffee, appreciating the rich dark flavor, then set the cup and saucer aside. "When the emerald brooch took me back, I had no idea why I was in a war zone without the benefit of backup or even a weapon to defend myself." She paused, swamped by the memories. She twirled the absent West Point ring she always wore on her right hand, but couldn't wear in the nineteenth century.

"There's a tradition that all a West Point graduate has to do is knock his or her ring on the table and all Pointers present are obliged to rally to his or her side. I had my ring, but no one would have believed it was mine, or come to my rescue. I was a trained soldier and couldn't tell anyone."

"That had to have been horrible," Amber said.

"Dealing with Trey's death was the hardest thing I'd ever done. Dropped in the middle of World War II London was the second. Fortunately, I befriended Molly Bradford Hamilton who helped me get a job with Alan Turing at Bletchley Park."

"She's such a sweetheart. But tell me about Turing. The man fascinates me." Then Amber waved her hand. "But not now. Go on."

"One afternoon," Kenzie continued. "I met my grandfather at the canteen at Bletchley. He was an American GI on escort duty and just happened to be there."

Amber covered her mouth, gasping. "My God. Did he know you? Oh, that's silly. He wouldn't know anything about you. What'd you do? You didn't tell him, did you."

"No. It wouldn't have made sense to him." Kenzie took another sip of coffee before continuing. "My grandfather's story is, or rather was, a sad one. Right before D-Day, he was killed outside of London. He was posthumously labeled a spy and traitor and stripped of all his benefits. My grandmother received nothing."

"That's awful. At least you got to meet him."

The waiter delivered their plates and Kenzie picked at the eggs and ham. "Not only did I meet him, but I changed his future."

"I thought you said—"

"Avoid changing the future at all costs? Yes, I did, but I justified it. I believed the change would only affect my family."

"But you had no way of knowing what the ripple effect might be."

"Exactly. But I had to take a chance. My father grew up under the stigma of having a traitor for a father. It turned him into a jaded person and alienated him from his family. We didn't get along at all. When I interfered in my grandfather's life, I changed his legacy, which ultimately changed my Dad's life. When I got home, I didn't recognize him. He looked the same, but he had become a loving and caring man. It took me a while to trust that version of him."

"You changed what happened to your grandfather, which changed your father's life, but it didn't change yours. Is that what you're saying? I don't understand how that's possible."

"There's so much about the brooches we don't understand. But I can tell you this. If you screw with your family history while you're in the past, when you return to the future, what you remember might be completely different from the rest of your family's reality."

Amber glanced off, her expression one of deep thought. "That's scary."

"Yeah, it is. Go hunt dinosaurs for a few days, then hurry home. As a dear friend of mine was fond of saying, 'Round home, collect your two hundred bucks, and get the hell out of there.'"

Amber gave her a bittersweet smile. "That was Trey's favorite saying." She sighed deeply. "A day doesn't go by that I don't think of him."

Kenzie reached out and squeezed Amber's hand. "He's constantly on my mind. More so now that I've met you. And, I'm struggling with what he'd want me to do. Would he tell me it's safe to leave you behind? Or would he tell me to stay and ensure your safety? I don't know, and the uncertainty is"—Kenzie swallowed against the knot in her throat—"tugging on my heart."

Amber put her hand over Kenzie's, stacking it between her own. "I can only guess, but I believe he'd approve of what you're doing.

You're leaving me with adequate resources and a private bodyguard. You've got three babies waiting for you at home. It's time for you and David to go. You've done all you can do here."

Amber's reassurance lessened some of Kenzie's guilt, but not all of it. "I won't breathe easy until I see you again. Promise me you won't take any risks."

"I promise…" The word trailed off, ending in a small shrug.

Amber tried to release Kenzie's hand, but Kenzie held on. "Your hands are swollen. Is that from digging up fossils?"

Amber pulled back her hand and rubbed her fingers over the joints. "My joints are stiff, too, and the altitude has bothered me more than usual. I guess for those reasons alone, I won't be sticking around here very long."

"Good. Then I hope your knees, elbows, and ankles bother you, too. That way you won't stay more than a couple of days."

Amber laughed. "My knees are bothering me, so you might get your wish."

"Then why stay? Come home with us."

"Becaaaause…." Amber said, stretching out the word while leaning forward. "It's an amazing opportunity."

It was Kenzie's turn to laugh. "Okay, I get it. No more pressure from me."

"Good. Let's talk about something else. Tell me about the moment you knew you were in love with David."

Kenzie had to backtrack to catch up with Amber's new direction. She settled more comfortably in her wobbly chair. "Probably when I heard him play the sax at Bletchley. I told a fan the other night that the sound he creates with that instrument is like sex on the airwaves. Man, he turns me on when he plays." Kenzie did a little shoulder shimmy. "He turns me on with just a look, too, but we can't always drop and roll."

Amber's cheeks turned red. "Your room is right above mine. The rhythmic squeak-thump kept me awake for the last five nights."

Kenzie patted her face. "I'm blushing."

"Because you were caught, or because you're remembering?"

"Remembering," Kenzie said.

Amber set down her coffee cup, overly careful, and put her hand to her throat, pursing her breaths.

"You okay?" Kenzie asked.

"This altitude is killing me. It will be better in Denver. I'm okay now." Amber waved her hand. "Back to squeaky springs." She lifted her eyebrows. "I was almost driven to find someone to share mine."

"Anyone in particular?"

"Daniel has starred in a few of my fantasies."

Kenzie buttered a biscuit and took a bite watching Amber's pursed lip breathing closely. Her shortness of breath was more acute today, which could be a result of a longer performance last night followed by a late dinner with lots of Champagne. Kenzie had struggled the first couple of days walking the Leadville hills, but her heart and lungs had finally acclimated, and the higher altitude no longer bothered her. For some reason, Amber continued to struggle. Maybe it wasn't the altitude at all, but a medical condition that needed attention.

"I was tempted to go knock on his door and have casual sex with him."

The words casual sex interrupted Kenzie's musing about Amber's health. "What did you say? You're going to have casual sex with Daniel?"

Amber laughed. "I was checking to see if you were listening. Your mind was a million miles away."

"Sorry. I'm concerned about your breathing."

"Don't be. As soon as I drop down a few thousand feet, I'll be much better. And in answer to your question, no. I would never have casual sex with Daniel. You don't mess with a man like him unless you want a forever kind of guy."

"I can see that, so what about Rick? He's hot."

"That sums him up. But there are a few other descriptions that vie for consideration, like sexy, awesome sense of humor, talented. He'd make a horrible boyfriend. He's not interested in settling down, but he's a wonderful friend."

"Is he a friend-with-benefits kind of friend?" Kenzie asked.

"Benefits but no housekey." Amber laughed. "I think it's a perfect arrangement, but my sister Olivia is the complete opposite. When she jumps, she jumps with both feet. She had a bad break-up about eight months ago. The guy turned out to be a real jerk. He lied to her and broke her heart."

"What'd he lie about?"

"He was married. He'd been separated for months but ended up going back to his wife. Olivia can handle almost anything, but she has zero tolerance for liars. Now she's overly cautious."

"What has she said about Connor?"

"I think she's got it bad for him. I told her if she didn't make a move on him, or let him know she's interested, he'll walk away. But she's reluctant to get involved with someone, especially a guy who lives in another state. Now that I know Rick, when we get back, we can put some joint pressure on them."

"Distance isn't a problem for anyone working at MacKlenna Corporation. The company's jets are always available. Connor's a good guy. He's grounded and ready to settle down. Maybe it'll work out between them."

Amber held up her coffee cup, signaling the waiter for a refill. "Speaking of Rick, was he wounded during his deployment? I noticed the scars on his left side."

"I don't feel comfortable discussing his medical history. You'll have to ask him, but if you want a tidbit, David said some bureaucratic ineptitude is holding up his Medal of Honor. That should tell you everything you need to know about his character."

Amber pushed her cup toward the edge of the table for the waiter's convenience. Once filled, she scooted it back. "Medal of Honor? That's impressive. Do you know what happened?"

"He was protecting a fellow Marine from an enemy hand grenade. He was lucky. It was like what happened to Trey, but Rick's body armor absorbed most of the blast. He walked away."

They hit the pause button on their conversation while they finished eating, listening to the chatter and cutlery clanging against china dishes. After a few minutes, Kenzie said, "I've got a secret I'm dying to share, but you have to promise not to say anything."

"A secret?" Amber's fork hovered at chin level, eyes bright. "I love secrets." She put down the fork and made a cross over her heart. "Spill it."

Kenzie took a drink of coffee first. "After I was wounded, I was in the hospital for a long time, and I got a blood clot. Everything is fine now, but I can't take birth control pills. We tried condoms for a while and ended up with twins. My contraception of choice now is an IUD."

"I've never used one of those. Do they work okay?"

"Yes, unless the damn thing falls out." Kenzie paused and let a long silence ensue, waiting for Amber to jump to the right conclusion.

Amber pointed at her. "Yours fell out? You're kidding." She slapped her mouth. "Uh-oh."

Kenzie put her finger to her lips. "Don't say anything."

"Is this a bad time of the month?"

"For me, yes. For McBain, no. He wants his own rugby team. I can't tell him yet. He'll drive me nuts until I take a pregnancy test."

Amber clapped. "I'm so happy for—" Then she stopped and looked closer at Kenzie. "You're not happy."

"I didn't want any more children. Once you meet the twins, you'll understand why, but it'll make David so happy. His mother is with us full time now. She's wonderful, and the kids adore her."

"I can't wait to meet them. Robbie and Henry, right? And your daughter is Laurie Wallis." Amber grabbed Kenzie's arm, shaking it. "This is so exciting. I was with you when it happened. Well...not with you, exactly, but in Leadville with you. And after making me suffer through five nights of listening to you and David and those squeaky springs, it's right that you told me first."

Kenzie set her fork on the plate, tines down, and pushed it away. "I'm sorry we kept you awake."

"Don't be. It'll make this adventure more fun to tell." Amber finished off her eggs and buttered her last biscuit. "You said you knew you were in love with David when you heard him play. Did you guys hit the sheets while you were in the past? If you did, it's a wonder you got out of bed long enough to go home."

"We came close, but it wasn't until we were back in the present. We stayed in a beautiful boutique hotel in Bayeux."

"It wasn't the Villa Lara, was it?"

Kenzie nodded. "Have you been there?"

"My parents took us to Normandy when we were in high school. We met Trey and all his crew there, too. It was an amazing trip. Olivia and I went back after Trey died. It seemed like a place to connect with him, and we stayed at the Villa Lara."

Kenzie checked the time on her watch pin. "Oh gosh. Look at the time. We better go." She left coins on the table to cover the tab and bundled up again.

"Was everything smooth sailing between you two once you returned?" Amber asked, buttoning her coat. "Or did you have to adapt to being back in the future?"

Kenzie held the door and once outside braced herself against the mild gust that wrapped her skirts around her legs. "It was good until I discovered all the lies and how much he had invaded my privacy. But by then, I was hopelessly in love and forgave him, but not right away."

"Why'd he lie to you?"

"That's a long story, but we all learned a lesson. That's why we told you immediately who we were. David didn't tell me, and because he didn't, I almost got killed—twice."

"Ouch," Amber said. "I guess after three kids he's more than made up for it. Did he know you before? Is that why he went back to rescue you?"

"We'd never met, but he knew my half-brother. When I went missing, he asked David to find me."

"So your paths would have crossed at some point even if you hadn't time traveled."

That was a slippery slope question that Kenzie wasn't prepared to answer truthfully. "Elliott's tentacles spread around the globe. If my brother Jim hadn't mentioned me, Elliott would have figured it out, and David and I would have met eventually."

"Small world."

"Yep, it sure is."

Amber looped her arm around Kenzie's elbow and directed her across the street. "While I'm thinking about it, will you take my guitar home with you? I won't need it again, and I'd hate for anything to happen to it."

"I'll take care of it. Just leave it in your room and I'll get it."

"Thanks. Now do you have any advice you'd like to pass along before we temporarily part company? I generally take well-intended advice, so sock it to me."

Kenzie took a deep breath of mountain air, so cold it chilled her lungs. "Stay warm, don't get sick, and take care of those pesky joints. That's my first piece of advice or clump of advice. Second, don't lead Daniel on. If you get involved with him, be sure it's for the right reasons."

"Don't worry," Amber said. "Daniel's only interest in me is figuring out who I am. He hasn't said so, but I bet he's looked at all the sheriff's wanted posters for my picture, and he's probably sent telegrams to all Pinkerton offices with my description."

"I wouldn't worry about it unless you have an outlaw in your family tree."

"None that I know of."

"Then forget it, and don't act suspicious."

"If I did get involved with him, it would be dumber than dumb. What would I do with a nineteenth-century boyfriend? Talk about a long-distance relationship. I have no intention of spending the rest of my life without hot showers and twenty-first century medicine, although I never go to the doctor. But still..."

"Then don't have sex with him. It'll mess up your mind." As they turned the corner toward Mrs. Garland's white-painted boardinghouse bristling with architectural bric-a-brac, Kenzie said, "I have a third piece of advice, too. Noah is attaching himself to you. When you return to the future, it will break his heart. Whatever you do, don't over promise."

"That shouldn't be a problem since I'm leaving, and I doubt I'll ever see him again. But that's good advice. If he asks when I'll be back, I'll have to tell him I won't be returning to Leadville."

Kenzie pushed open the wrought-iron gate leading to the front porch of the boardinghouse. "Bless Mrs. Garland's heart. She'll have to deal with the heartache."

The door flew open and Noah bounded out carrying a suitcase. "Pa said I could go, too. He's already sent a telegram to my grandpa in Denver that I'm accepting his invitation to visit."

Amber whispered, "What's your advice now?"

Kenzie groaned. "To quote a friend who often speaks in baseball metaphors. 'Spahn and Sain and pray for rain.'"

"What does that mean?"

"Appeal to the heavens for rain to save you from having to face...whatever."

"In that case, I better start collecting animals two by two."

Kenzie burst out laughing. "Just so long as they aren't *Stegosauruses*."

23

1878 Leadville, Colorado—David

DAVID STEPPED OUT of the Spotswood and McClelland Stage Line Passenger and Express Company office on Harrison Avenue, pocketing the tickets he'd purchased for the stagecoach to Denver. The sun had slipped away, and dark clouds blanketed the peaks. The muted gray reminded him of Scotland. And that thought led him to consider Daniel and a future role in the clan for him.

After spending time with the Pinkerton agent, David had become rather fond of him. It was hard not to. He was sincere, honorable, intelligent, and a staunch Robert Burns fan. As for Daniel's suspicion of Amber, David was confident he had put that to rest after multiple conversations with him about Kenzie and Amber, their similarities and oddities. The ball was now in Amber's proverbial court to settle any remaining concerns.

Daniel had offered to make transportation arrangements, but David had declined the offer, and instead gone to the stage office and reserved all nine seats on the stagecoach to Denver. Kenzie had teased him about playing matchmaker. That was the brooch's job, not his. He was only a facilitator. If Rick rode atop with the driver, Amber and Daniel would have more than nineteen hours alone on a private stagecoach. The plan might have dissolved when Noah announced he was going, too. How that would play out on the long ride was anyone's guess.

Amber was a loving and nurturing woman and Noah appeared enamored with her. The lad, though, stood a chance of being deeply hurt if the brooch didn't bring Amber and Daniel together.

But that was way beyond David's sphere of control.

He stood next to the stage office door and searched the lot for his bride. A swirl of newsboys banged out of the saloon next door. They drew his attention as they ran toward him, chanting, "*The Herald!* Get your newspapers from us."

"Latest news from around Colorado." Another newsie thrust a paper under the eagle-like nose of a bespectacled man deep in conversation with one of the drivers. Dust from the stagecoach was still on the driver's coat sleeves.

David bought two papers, tipped both boys a penny, and carried his newspapers across the muddy yard, spotted with frosty grass. The smell of newly hewn lumber, used in the construction of an addition to the stage office, tickled his nose, and he sneezed. The lumber smell mixed with the odor of mud and manure churned up in the dust.

A line of coaches was parked in the yard, rutted by hooves and wheels, but only one was hitched and ready to depart. Spotting Kenzie and Amber sitting on a bench in a passenger-designated area, he made his way toward them. Amber's narrow hat, decorated with feather plumes, blocked Kenzie's face, but the rise and fall of her shoulders told him she was crying. Her pain caused his heart to drop a few beats. He could be shot without wincing, but when his bride hurt, her pain cut him into irregular-shaped pieces.

The two women had bonded instantly over their shared interest: the law and their love for Trey, and Kenzie had been unusually relaxed. As he reflected on their talks and intimate encounters, he had to admit their time in Leadville had been some of the happiest days of their marriage. For that reason alone, he wasn't ready to leave. He had to be honest with himself, though. Kenzie's state of mind was in large part due to her friendship with Amber. With her new friend gone, Kenzie's stress would rise to the top again, and she'd be in a hurry to return home to the wee ones, to work demands, to Elliott's beck-and-call privileges.

He laughed out loud. God, he loved her. The scent of her was on his skin, in his mind, lodged deeply in his heart.

The women had pulled apart by the time he reached them, tears straggling down their faces. "Sorry I wasn't at the boardinghouse to escort ye. Did ye have any trouble?"

"No," Kenzie said with a slight wobble in her voice, as she wiped her face. "Daniel arranged for a hack to bring us here. Did you get the tickets?"

He handed them to Amber. "Ye have the entire coach."

"That's excessive, isn't it?" she asked.

"Mayhap, but for me, it's a safety issue. Having the entire coach will give ye room to stretch out and sleep. Plus, ye won't have sick people coughing and spreading germs. Regardless of what ye say, I don't believe ye're feeling yer best."

"I'm blaming it all on the brooch. I've grown up in this altitude. It shouldn't bother me, but it does. Thank you for being so thoughtful."

David folded the newspapers and slipped them into his pocket. "Where's Noah?"

Kenzie pointed toward the stagecoach. "He's already claimed his seat."

"And Ripley's seat, too," Amber added.

David shook his head. "I'm surprised Daniel allowed the dog to come along."

"He doesn't know about Ripley. She followed us here. As soon as Noah saw her, he opened the door and Ripley jumped in, mud and all," Kenzie said. "If you hadn't bought all the seats, there wouldn't have been extra room."

"Are ye blaming the additional passengers on me, lass?"

Kenzie laughed. "I'm not, but Daniel might."

"Mrs. Garland told me Daniel still feels guilty over his wife's death and being with his father-in-law exacerbates those feelings. That's why he's avoided going back to Denver," Amber said.

Kenzie's expression telegraphed her thoughts and David knew

what was coming. "That's not fair to Noah to be cut off from his mother's family. Daniel needs to man up."

"I think he—" Amber began.

"Don't go anywhere," David said. The women were traipsing down a Daniel-bashing-trail and he wasn't going to participate. He maneuvered past them and navigated a path through the rutted yard to inspect the coach and the matched dapple-gray six-horse team.

The horses' joints showed no sign of heat, swelling, or pain in the lower legs. His limited soundness check showed no abnormalities or cause for concern. The leather harnesses were cleaned and oiled and the brass fittings were polished. The eight-ply leather belts that insulated the coach from the constant pounding of the wheels over makeshift roads were tight without signs of deterioration. The front brakes were oiled, the wheels solidly constructed, the hubs well-greased, and the whip was as pliable as a snake in the sun.

"Are you going to kick the tires, too, McBain?"

"Are ye sassing me?" he asked.

"Kenzie might think you're paranoid," Amber said, "but I appreciate your attention to detail. Does it look safe enough?"

"Aye, the trek over the mountains and then nineteen hours from Fairplay to Denver riding in a stagecoach sounds unbearable to me. Are ye sure this is what ye want?"

"I've ridden that long across the desert in a jeep with worn-out shocks. It's not so bad," Amber said.

"It's not too late to change yer mind and go home with us."

"I know how long the trip will take, the conditions of the road, and the dangers ahead. Call me crazy, but I still really want to go to Morrison. At lunch the other day, Grandfather Hughes gave me an exhaustive mile-by-mile, blow-by-blow of what I can expect to find on the road. Once we get past the Weston Pass to Fairplay, it won't be so bad."

The stagecoach driver came around the coach, smoothing one end of a long drooping mustache covering compressed lips. His eyebrows, bleached nearly white by constant sun exposure, were furrowed in a frown. He tipped back his wide-brimmed hat and pulled up the neckerchief that protected mouth and nose from the elements. Under his arm, he carried a U.S. Mail pouch. After nodding to a man polishing one of the parked stagecoaches, he climbed up into the driver's box and settled in.

He glanced around the yard and nodded toward David. "All aboard. Departing in five minutes."

"We're waiting on two more passengers," David said.

"Just one." David, Kenzie, and Amber whirled to find Daniel at the rear of the stagecoach tying a horse's reins to a boot support. "Do ye have anything to go back here?"

"My bags are already stowed," Amber said.

A street urchin with curly blond hair tufting from under a faded red cap ran up to Daniel. "Mr. Hood over at Western Union sent me to give you this telegram, sir." Daniel flipped the lad a coin, which the boy pocketed before running down an alleyway.

Daniel stuck his finger under the seal of the sharp-cornered envelope and removed a slip of paper, but prior to reading the telegram his eyes fixed upon Amber, and he smiled. The attraction between them was indeed mutual. An unexpected wave of protectiveness rose in David, and he wanted to stop a relationship from developing before Amber risked more than she could afford to lose.

He made a sound deep in his throat. Kenzie squinted a question at him. He twitched his finger. He had taught her only a couple of the signs he and Elliott used to secretly communicate. *Wait*, the sign said to her. A beat passed between them, and she returned her attention to Daniel with a slight lift of her chin. *Understood*, her nod said in return.

Daniel read the telegram then shoved the paper into his jacket pocket. His eyes turned dark. "Wait for me," he shouted to the driver, then withdrew to the mouth of the alley.

"Hurry up," the driver said. "We have to get through the mountains before dark."

Daniel pivoted and, throwing out a Gaelic curse, "*Faigh muin*," followed the street urchin down the alleyway.

"What'd he say—?" Amber asked.

"Why so secretive?" Kenzie asked.

David tilted his head down and gazed at her, as if looking over a pair of glasses, a not so subtle look.

"Oh," Kenzie said, glancing at Amber. "It's none of our business."

Amber opened her mouth to say something, but no words came out. Then her concerned expression softened. "I hope he won't be in a dark mood during the trip. That won't be much fun."

"He's a professional. He'll manage," Kenzie said.

"Ye best get aboard," David said to Amber.

Her eyes glistened as she hugged Kenzie again. "I have something for you." She dug into her reticule and placed a coin in Kenzie's hand.

"I don't need twenty dollars. You keep it."

"It's a Proof Liberty Head double eagle worth at least two hundred thousand dollars, in our time. It's from the money thrown on stage that David, Rick, and I divided. Take it to a coin collector. If I'm right, it'll pay for your children's college education."

"You found it," Kenzie said, trying to press it back into Amber's hand. "You keep it."

Amber braced her hands behind her back. "I have one in a lock box in a Denver bank. A collector would be suspicious if I showed up with two. Hold on to it."

"We'll talk about it when you come back," Kenzie said.

David kissed Amber's cheeks. "Remember, lass, ye promised not to take any chances with yer health and safety. I know the altitude is bothering ye. Now I know about yer joints. If yer condition gets worse, I expect ye to come home. Don't make me regret leaving ye behind."

"I'm fine, but maybe you should say the same thing to Rick. Where is he, by the way?"

Kenzie scratched a place behind her ear, ducking her head slightly. "Ah, I believe his fan club was demanding another, shall we say, curtain call."

David glared, and irritation crept into his voice. "Why didn't ye tell me?"

She imitated him, looking down her nose. And for a brief second, he thought they were discussing Jack Mallory, not Rick O'Grady. The men were nothing alike. Rick was a warrior, and Jack was a pain in the ass.

Kenzie checked the time on her watch pin then glanced in the direction of the alleyway. "Here he comes. Right on time."

Rick waved, a cigar perched between two fingers. His saddle bags tossed casually over one shoulder, and his horse trailed behind him.

"Five more minutes and ye'd been left behind."

"Come on, McBain. Do you see all Americans as lesser mortals, or is it just me?" He cinched down the bedroll tucked under his arm to the D ring on the saddle.

"It's not just you, Rick," Kenzie said.

"Aren't you riding inside the coach?" Amber asked.

He put his arm around her shoulder. "Are you saying you'd miss me, sweetheart?"

She patted his chest. "Not as much as the members of your fan club."

"Aw shucks, ma'am." He tied his horse to the rear of the stagecoach. "Where's Daniel?"

"A street urchin brought him a telegram and he hustled off, cursing," Amber said.

"Sounds encouraging." Rick opened the stagecoach door. "Hello little guy. I didn't know you were coming with us."

"Yes sir, Mr. O'Grady. My grandpa in Denver asked me to come for a visit. Can we sing during the trip?"

"Sure. We'll have a first-class hootenanny."

"What's that?"

"A gathering of entertainers performing for their own enjoyment."

"It's a shame Mr. McBain isn't coming with us. He could play the sax."

David hooked his hand over the lip of the window, its leather side curtain rolled to the top. "Maybe next time, lad. Ye take care of Miss Amber for me. Will ye do that?"

"I sure will, sir."

"There's no heat in there, so snuggle up with her and stay warm in that brown bear coat David bought." Kenzie said. "And if you're still cold, the bear rug should cover all four laps if you sit close together."

"Wasn't the point of renting the entire coach to give us room to stretch out?" Rick asked.

Amber laughed. "Five days ago, you were freezing just standing out on the boardwalk. You'll be cozying up to me before we get out of Leadville."

Rick winked at her. "Babe, save me a seat on the other side of you."

Kenzie pulled him in for a hug. "Your sister will kick my ass for leaving you here, so don't go Rambo on me and get yourself hurt again."

"I've already assured David, I'll take care of Amber and get us both home safely in a couple of weeks. You don't have to worry, and neither does JL. Keep her calm, will you?"

Kenzie squeezed him again in a tighter hug. "I'll still worry, and so will she."

"There's Daniel," David said, nodding toward the alleyway. "From the way he's stomping through the mud, he doesn't seem any happier than when he left."

Daniel handed Amber an envelope. "I got this at the telegraph office. It's for ye."

"Who's sending me a telegram?"

"Open it and ye'll find out," David said.

Amber slipped a piece of paper from the envelope. "It's from Mr. and Mrs. Adam Hughes. They're picking Rick and me up at the train station and have invited us to stay with them while we're in town."

"Isn't that lovely," Kenzie said. "I'll be sure to stop by the store and tell Mrs. Hughes you received an invitation from her son."

"Oh, will you do that? Thanks. Tell her I'll write from Denver." A wistful expression crossed Amber's face. "When you see Olivia, tell her I love her."

Kenzie stepped closer to David's side, and he put his arm around her waist. "We will. Please be safe."

"I can't wait to see you again and share news," Amber said.

From the expressions on their faces, David knew the women shared secrets. Kenzie never divulged anything told her in confidence, so he'd never hear Amber's news. But his bride would eventually tell him hers. This time, though, he already knew.

Daniel shook David's hand. "I hope to see ye again. Have a safe trip west."

David pressed his other hand on top of Daniel's, and what passed between them in that instant said more than any conversation ever could. Kenzie had already accused him of starting a bromance with Daniel, and he had laughed it off. But the friendship they had developed could, aside from Kenzie, be David's longest-lasting affair.

"We'll meet again," David assured him.

Daniel boarded behind Rick. "What's this?"

"She jumped in, Pa. I couldn't send her back."

"What if yer grandpa doesn't want her?"

"How could he not, Pa?"

Daniel pounded the side of the stagecoach. "I don't know, lad, but we'll soon find out."

The driver slapped reins on the horses' haunches and they took off at a trot with the coach's wheels slogging through the red mud of Leadville.

David and Kenzie stood in the stage lot watching the stagecoach long after it had disappeared. Sniffling, she said, "I hope we're doing the right thing."

He hugged her tighter. "I hope so, too, lass. Now let's go home. If we don't see Rick and Amber in a few days, we'll have to come back after them."

"The way the brooches work, they could already be there."

David and Kenzie turned toward the street that would take them back to the boardinghouse to pick up their personal items and Amber's guitar. After a tearful goodbye with Mrs. Garland, they stopped by Hughes Store for another goodbye with Mr. and Mrs. Hughes.

"I wish we all could have stayed here longer," Kenzie said as she and David walked down the boardwalk toward the livery where the horses were boarded.

"Now I know what it takes to get ye away from the twins and Laurie Wallis."

"Oh yeah. What's that?"

"A girlfriend."

"Are you jealous?"

"Me? The man who's had more sex in five days than I've had in the last five months?"

Kenzie stopped and glared at him. "Months? Think again, McBain. Two weeks, maybe. But I've never neglected you. Not even when I was pregnant."

He rolled back his head and laughed. "Aye. Ye're right, lass." Then he pulled a handkerchief from his pocket and unfolded it.

Kenzie glanced at the small object nestled in the handkerchief, her mouth wide open. "Where'd you find that?"

"In the bed. Do ye want to explain what this means?"

She groaned. "You know damn good and well what it means."

He counted forward nine months, smiling. "What are the odds ye'll have twins again? Maybe two wee lassies this time."

She covered her face with her gloved hands and shook her head. "Geez, McBain. Don't put me through that."

"What I don't get is how yer wee thing came out?"

"Expulsions happen in three percent of cases. This isn't the first time I've been a statistic, and if my luck holds, we'll have another set of twins."

"Did ye know?"

"I couldn't feel the strings, so I thought I might have lost it in the privy. I'm glad you found it and not Mrs. Garland."

He pulled her aside, out of the path of foot traffic. "I don't know much about this, but should we wait a few days, ye know, to give the bairns time to settle in yer womb before we go through the time tunnel again?"

His wife had the decency to bite her cheek instead of laughing outright. "They'll be fine, but if something happens, I'll give you another chance."

He kissed her right there on Harrison Avenue, and he didn't give a damn who was looking their way. His heart took off like a balloon full of helium. "I love ye."

They continued their stroll to the livery, holding hands as if time didn't matter. In a way, it didn't. He collected their horses, paid the boarding bill, and watched over his bride as she mounted up.

"Let's go home," he said.

He directed them toward the wide road leading down Third Street, out of town until traffic thinned, listening to the animals' rhythmic pounding of their hoofs in the mud-covered macadam. For a moment, David relaxed into the motion, letting go of worries and concerns.

Another bairn, possibly two. He couldn't be happier, and then worry slipped in as he remembered the dangerous circumstances of Kenzie's last pregnancy. As soon as he got to a phone, he'd call her OB/GYN and ask if it was safe for her to go through it again. No matter how many kids he wanted, he would never put his bride's life at risk.

He reined his horse over to a scrim of trees, dismounted, and helped Kenzie to the ground.

"Don't lose me in the wormhole," she said.

"I won't." With both sets of reins wrapped around his hand, he hugged Kenzie to his side, and pulled the diamond brooch from his pocket. "Are ye ready?"

She nodded and closed her eyes. "There's no place like home. There's no place like home. There's no place like home."

Laughing, David kissed her again. "Don't forget to click yer heels." Then he spoke the magic words that would take them to the future.

24

The Present, MacKlenna Farm, Lexington, Kentucky—David

WHEN THE FOG lifted on a crisp, sunny day full of autumn aromas, Kenzie and David were standing on the bank of MacKlenna Farm's lake, the water reflecting a rich shade of teal. Gold, red, and orange leaves of the woodland pasture provided a dramatic backdrop for the stallions lazing in their white painted-fenced paddocks.

Kenzie tilted back her head, closed her eyes, and smiled with the warmth of the sun on her face. "Time to break out the tweeds and enjoy a warm cup of burgoo."

David took advantage of her canted head and pursed lips, and he kissed her. The kiss was only a touch at first, then a burst of hunger as his tongue caressed her lips. They'd made love before she'd gone out for breakfast with Amber, but he wanted her again. And wanted her now. If the grounds around the lake weren't covered by video surveillance, he'd take her here. The eagerness with which her breasts and hips pressed against him, was all the reassurance he needed that she wanted him as well.

He nibbled lightly on her bottom lip. "Welcome home, lass."

She reached down and rubbed his erection. "Hmm. Is this patch of ground surveilled?"

"Afraid so," he groaned. "Can we freeze this moment for about an hour and meet in the shower?"

"We could try. But I think it will thaw before either of us can clear our calendars of what's waiting for us."

"I thought ye did that before we left."

"Nope. I assumed we'd only be gone a few minutes, and I could pick up where I left off."

He kissed her once more. "Let's see how long we've been gone." He dug into the bottom of his saddlebag where his mobile phone was hidden in a leather pouch, and he turned it on. "Same day, five minutes later."

"Five days in the past, five minutes in the present." She held on to his arm and dunked her booted feet, one by one, into the lake to rinse off the top layer of mud. "I don't understand how that's possible, but I'm glad it is."

He pulled up his recent call list and clicked on Elliott's name.

Kenzie dragged her feet in the thick grass to dry her boots. "Who are you calling, Connor?"

"Not yet. I want to talk to Elliott before I email the video, and I want to email the video before I call Connor. I'm just checking messages."

"Wait a minute," Kenzie said. "You gave Rick the amethyst brooch. So why aren't they here? They should be. Right?"

David rubbed the base of his neck, thinking. "If they're traveling with the amber stone, they could arrive today, tomorrow, next week, next month. We don't know that stone's properties."

"But wouldn't Rick use the amethyst since he knows how that stone works?"

"I would," David said. "Maybe the amber is more powerful. Until we understand the inscription on the stone, we won't know for sure. That's why we made the video—to explain Amber's absence."

"It sure will be easier when we get all the keys to the cave door in the castle and can just walk in and out without worrying about which brooch we're carrying and when it will bring us home."

"God, I hope that day comes long after I'm dead. I don't want the responsibility of guarding *that* door."

There was a quaver in Kenzie's voice when she said, "Which

leaves us with the responsibility of ensuring all the kids have a clear understanding of what's at stake."

"If we fail, hopefully reading the log will instill that responsibility. It has all the adventures, lessons learned, and mistakes made."

She removed her gloves and folded them over the waistband of her riding skirt, then took his hands and caressed his palms with her thumbs. The sensation shot straight to his groin. "Why don't you go talk to Elliott and take my horse to the barn. I want to shower before I see the kids, and if I go in that direction they'll see me. I can go through the tree line and only be seen by your eye-in-the-sky security force."

"They've already seen ye. I'll have to delete the video before anyone studies it too closely and realizes we just appeared out of a lakeside fog." His phone rang, and he looked at the face. "It's Elliott. He already knows we're here." He put the call on speaker, so Kenzie could hear the conversation. "McBain."

"Are ye leaving or are ye back?" Elliott asked.

"We're at the lake. Just got back."

"Did ye find Amber?"

"Yes, but we need to talk privately. Where's JL?" David's horse nudged him with his nose, pushing David closer to the lake. David slung the reins over the horses' necks to prevent them from dragging, leaving the horses to lap at the water.

"At home resting. Why?"

"I need to talk to ye first before I see her," David said.

"Why? Is something wrong with Rick?"

"Not exactly."

"What the hell does that mean?"

Kenzie turned her penetrating gaze on David, mouthing, "Just tell him."

David shook his head and used two fingers to point at his eyes. The conversation with Elliott had to take place in person. David had left a team member behind, and he had some explaining to do.

"Ye still there?"

"Aye, sorry." The horses moved away from the lake to graze in the field. "We need to talk in person and not around JL."

"Don't try to protect her," Elliott said. "Ye know it pisses her off. If it concerns her, she wants to know. Don't sugarcoat it. It'll come back to bite ye in the ass."

"She's pregnant. I don't want to upset her." He wanted to shout that Kenzie hopefully was too. Together they walked arm in arm toward the tree line and the stone path that cut through to their house. The lake was special to them, so they'd built the McBain residence on a knoll overlooking the water. He'd let the horses graze there for now. The entire farm was fenced. They couldn't get loose and roam Old Frankfort Pike. If they wandered too far away, he'd send a groom to collect them.

"Ye think that matters?" Elliott asked. "I can tell ye right now, it doesn't."

David gripped Kenzie's hand tighter with the crook of his arm. "All right. Call her. Let's meet in my office in fifteen minutes."

"Where's Kenzie?"

"I'm walking her to the house. She wants a shower before she sees the kids."

"Tell her to call me ASAP."

David took a deep breath and shrugged a bit, as though his jacket were too tight. Then said in a tone he hadn't used with Elliott in over a decade, "She'll get to ye when she has time."

Kenzie gasped.

"God, ye're in a shitty mood," Elliott said.

Maybe he was, but life had to change. Demands on his bride's time and attention had to change, and it might as well start today. "I'll see ye in fifteen minutes."

Kenzie stopped on the path and swirled to confront him, dropping their clasped arms. "Why are you mad at Elliott? Or..." She frowned at him. "You're mad at me and taking it out on him?"

David removed his black felt hat, ran his fingers through his hair, and counted to ten. "JL is seven and a half months pregnant, and he's not worried about upsetting her. Ye have three small children and a husband, and Elliott still believes he should come first. If ye're pregnant again, his beck-and-call privileges will be revoked." David slapped his hat back on his head. "Hell, they should be revoked even if ye're not."

"Hold on, cowboy. You're messing with my job and we agreed, you'd never pull rank on me."

"I'm not." He tugged her forward, and they crossed the final twenty feet in silence until they reached the fence that separated the path from their front yard. He punched in the code and the gate swung open.

"I'll never pull rank on ye, but I'll use my last breath to protect ye." He turned her to face him. "When I found ye, naked and beaten, on the floor of the Cage, it nearly killed me. When I found ye in the back of the truck with a head wound, I thought for a moment not only were ye dead, but I was, too. When we were in San Francisco, and ye were struggling through yer pregnancy, I knew then, if I lost ye, there would be no reason for me to go on." He pulled her into his arms, wishing he could keep her there, protected every hour of the day.

She leaned back and clasped his face between her hands. "I love you, McBain, and I can't imagine life without you, but neither can I imagine life without the freedom to do what I love doing. You've got to back off. If I'm pregnant, we'll compromise and find a workable solution." She took a deep breath and when she continued, her voice was steadier. "Until then, let me talk to Elliott about my workload. I've budgeted for two new attorneys, but he's afraid if there are more lawyers in the company, I won't know everything that's going on."

"He'll have to deal with it."

Her brows shot up and she glared at him. "David. Stop it." A breeze came through the trees in a gust that blew his hat back on his head, as if Kenzie had flicked it with her finger. "If I didn't know better," she continued, "I'd say you're acting like a jealous asshat."

He pulled her to him again, letting her cheek rest above his heart. "Ye're my life, Kenz, and above all, I want ye happy and safe. I remember how close we were to losing ye. It scares me knowing ye might go through another pregnancy and get sick again."

"You can't put me in a bubble, hon. If I am pregnant, my OB/GYN will monitor this pregnancy closely. We'll be fine. Relax. And let me handle Elliott."

Softly, he said, "Okay. I'll be waiting in the wings, yer knight in shining armor."

25

The Present, MacKlenna Farm, Lexington, Kentucky—David

THIRTY MINUTES LATER, after taking a hot shower with his bride, David sauntered into the security center to find Elliott and JL sitting on stools in front of the refreshment bar, deep in conversation. The monitors on the walls flashed views of the stallion barns, paddocks, the corporate center, the main entrance to the mansion, the lake, and various other locations throughout the three-thousand-acre farm. At this hour of the afternoon, only one guard monitored the computers. The rest were patrolling the grounds. With any luck, the guard's attention had been focused elsewhere when he and Kenzie came out of the fog.

"There he is." Elliott picked up a freshly brewed cup from the coffee maker's drip tray and handed it to David. "Dark roasted, dab of cream, no sugar, and ye're late—"

"Where's Rick?" JL asked.

David sipped, sighed at the welcoming taste of his favorite high-octane. "Come in my office and we'll talk."

With Elliott's assistance, JL climbed off the barstool carrying a bottle of juice and entered the corner office. David shut the door, and the latch fell with a sense of finality. Neither Elliott nor JL would leave the room happy. Hell, he wouldn't, either.

David stepped toward his desk but changed his mind. He didn't want the modern L-shaped furniture to be perceived as a barrier, so he took a seat on the sofa next to JL. She put her feet on top of the Thoroughbred racing magazines stacked on the coffee table, and Elliott sat across from them in an upholstered chair and crossed his legs. David glanced at JL's ankles. Not that he was checking her out, but after Kenzie's last pregnancy, he was more aware of problems that could occur, and wanted to be sure JL wasn't dealing with swelling issues. Even pregnant, her dancer's legs remained classical and elegant.

"Where's Rick?" JL asked again. "And if you don't tell me, I'm calling Pops. And you don't want to mess with him."

JL was right about that. The retired deputy chief had never been angry at David, but he'd seen it up close. Pops could intimidate the most stalwart members of the security force with just a look from his piercing light brown eyes.

"I'll tell ye everything ye want to know, but first I have two quick tasks." He didn't wait for an answer. Instead, he opened the laptop sitting on the table next to the sofa. Both JL and Elliott knew he couldn't be bullied or threatened, and while he tried to be accommodating, occasionally they just had to wait.

She cradled her juice bottle in one hand, picked at the label with the other. "Can you at least tell me where he is?"

"Denver," David said without glancing up.

He accessed the security log, found the video footage taken at the lake twenty-four hours a day, and deleted the last sixty minutes of tape. Next, he hacked into Amber's home network and sent an email to Olivia that included the video of Amber and Rick. Satisfied he hadn't left any footprints, he logged out and turned his attention to Elliott and JL.

She glared intently at him with her former-cop eyes. "You told me where, but not *when*. I'm out of patience. Spill it."

He threw one arm along the back of the sofa and turned toward her. "We weren't sure where we would land. Turns out it was Leadville. We split up to search the city, and Rick found Amber at her ancestors' general store. He was upfront with her and confessed right away that he was from the twenty-first century. They were having a friendly chat by the time Kenzie and I arrived several minutes later."

"How long had she been there?" Elliott asked.

"About twenty-four hours. Not long, but she'd been a busy lass. She'd rescued a Pinkerton agent's son from being run over by a freight wagon, obtained her law license, negotiated a settlement for the lad and a contract for a five-night performance at the Tabor Opera House for herself, purchased a guitar worth six figures in the twenty-first century, arranged housing in a respectable boardinghouse, and met her seven-times great-grandparents."

"Geez," JL said. "If she moves that fast, I wish she'd been with us in 1909 New York City."

"I heard she's a top-rated Colorado attorney. If she can do all that with only the clothes on her back and a razor-sharp mind, she's got my full attention and a job offer," Elliott said.

"Save your job offer for later," JL said. For just a second, something akin to rage flashed across her face before her expression settled into frustration. "I want to know why you're here and my brother isn't."

"Amber wasn't ready to come home. She wanted to go fossil hunting in Morrison."

"What? Are you serious?" JL asked. "Rick is in the nineteenth century babysitting a rock hound?"

David held up a placating hand. "Let me explain."

She jabbed at his extended hand as if it were a punching bag, leaving a stinging mark on his palm. "There's no explanation wide enough, deep enough, or long enough that'll satisfy me. I can't believe you left behind a soldier recovering from a battle wound, who's only been stateside a few weeks, and has never time traveled. Does that make sense to you?"

"Look," he said, rubbing his hand. "Rick came back moody and unfocused. I wasn't sold on Kenzie's recommendation to take him along, but as soon as he dressed in what we jokingly called his Clint Eastwood costume, he changed."

"How? He probably became more unfocused."

"No. He became the old Rick again. He performed five nights at the Tabor Opera House, singing to a standing room only crowd. He dined with beautiful women, flirted with Amber, joked with Daniel's son, and charmed the owner of the boardinghouse. That's not the Rick we've seen lately. Going back was good for him."

JL crossed her arms and chewed on her bottom lip, as if not sure of something. Then she looked David in the eye. "Wasn't five days enough?"

"He's a grown man, and ye're not his mother." David tried to say it with compassion, but from JL's wide-eyed expression she didn't receive it that way.

"You don't have to be mean."

Silence fell over the room and they sat there as still as statues in a tableau.

Elliott finally broke the silence. "Ye mentioned a man named Daniel and his son. Is he the Pinkerton agent?"

"Aye, Daniel Grant and his ten-year-old son, Noah. But we're getting ahead of the story. Let me back up. When we told Amber we had come to take her home, she said she couldn't leave yet because she'd signed a performance contract that she couldn't break."

"What difference did that make? She was going to leave the century."

"Her contract was tied to the settlement she'd negotiated for Noah. She was afraid Mr. Tabor might sue the boy's father for bad faith. She didn't want to cause problems for them, so she had to fulfill her contract."

"Didn't she care that her sister was going bat-shit crazy with worry?"

"Aye, and that the sheriff was looking for her. We told her. That's when we came up with the idea of taping a video message that Kenzie and I could bring back, hoping that would call off the sheriff and relieve Olivia's worry."

"While Amber and Rick went fossil hunting?" JL asked.

"We didn't see a downside. There was no war, no bad cops, no Oregon Trail. It seemed safe enough. Plus, Daniel agreed to escort

Amber and Rick to Denver. From there they could take day trips to Morrison."

"Do ye think Daniel Grant is her soul mate?" Elliott asked.

"I hope so," David said. "He's an honorable Scotsman. And his sister married Blane Fraser."

Elliott scratched his chin in thought. "That would be my four-times great-grandfather."

"Fourth or fifth. We'll have to look at yer family tree."

"That's interesting. That would make him an uncle several times removed," Elliott said. "So the fossil dig was an excuse for Amber to spend more time with Daniel, and yer early departure was to bring the video back so Olivia would know her sister was alive and well and falling in love."

"Something like that."

"Okay, smart guy," JL said. "So why aren't they back yet? The way the brooches work, you've only been gone a few minutes. They should be here, or in Denver. Have you heard from Rick? I haven't." She huffed, held out her hand. "Let me see the video."

David opened his camera app and clicked on the video. JL watched it, shaking her head. "Looks like you might be confused about Amber's soul mate. If you ask me, she has the hots for Rick."

"Who said it was Rick?"

"Who else would it be?" She handed Elliott the phone, and she fell silent, her eyes seeming to look inward. "During Rick's first year on the force, a perp sliced him with a knife right below his nipple," she finally said. "I recognize the scar. Connor will, too. He won't like it. My brothers have a strict dating code and messing with Connor's girlfriend's sister is a violation."

"Was he sending ye a message?" Elliott asked.

"Knowing Rick, yeah," JL said. "Look at the video. Amber's head could easily have covered the left nipple instead of the right. He wanted us to know it was him and that he was okay. But what I don't get is why Amber and Rick aren't here. What brooch do they have?"

"Rick has the amethyst, and Amber has hers, which is an amber.

Kenzie and I traveled with the diamond."

JL put her feet on the floor and took a long cleansing breath. "We know the amethyst brooch returns you to within minutes of the time you left. So I ask again. Why aren't they here?"

"The stones didn't come with a list of rules," David said. "We're figuring this out as we go along. The amber brooch could be more powerful than the amethyst." He threw up his hands. "I don't have an answer."

"I do," JL said. "Something has happened. You said they were going to Denver. Had they left before you abandoned them? How were they getting there? By train?"

David tried suppressing his growing irritation. It didn't work. "I didn't abandon them. We divided forces. And they were traveling on a private stagecoach. There was no train in Leadville yet."

"I've heard about stagecoach travel. They were held up, horses broke down, and they crashed. To get to Denver, they probably had to go through the mountains. What time of year was it there?"

"Late fall."

"They could have run into snow and icy roads. Rick will be freezing his ass off after spending two years in the desert. You've got to go back, David. You don't have a choice. Take Connor, or even Shane. He's in Reno."

"I'm not ready to buy into a stagecoach accident," David said.

"Look," JL said. "They should be home and they're not. There are only two conclusions you can draw—they're hurt, or they lost the brooches."

"When Kit left, she was gone for months," Elliott said. "I knew she'd gone back to discover her identity. Waiting all that time…not knowing if she was dead or alive nearly killed me. There's no reason to be left in limbo the way I was. Ye've got to go back, David."

"None of us should ever go through that kind of worry." David's voice thickened, and he fell silent. Then he roused himself. "JL, send Connor a text. Tell him ye need to talk privately and to call as soon as he's free. Don't mention me. He'll want answers ye can't give him yet."

JL sent the text and thirty seconds later, her phone rang. "It's Connor," she said to David and Elliott. "I've got to talk to him."

David nodded.

"Hi, Con." She put the call on speaker. "Are you free to talk?"

"Not really. Where's David?"

David gathered his thoughts. He couldn't leave Connor in the dark. He had to talk to him. "I'm here. Where are ye now?"

"About a mile from the campground where we parked the truck and horse trailer. We're with the sheriff, his deputies, and a search team from the State Patrol. We're spread out working a search grid."

"Then listen to what I have to say without reacting, and text any questions ye have. There's an email in Olivia's inbox from Amber with a video explaining her disappearance. Ye need to get Olivia to check her email. Can ye do that discreetly?"

"Sure."

"Call back when ye can talk without being overheard."

JL disconnected the call, pulled to her feet, and crossed over to the window that overlooked the paddocks and a five-furlong training track. After a moment, she whirled back to face him. If her eyes were any indication, her blood was boiling darker than the coffee in his cup.

"I've never questioned your judgment, but you left them behind. You shouldn't have done that. If anything happens to my brother, I'll never forgive you."

"I know ye're upset JL," David said.

"Upset?" Her voice rose, along with the heat in her eyes.

"Let's talk to Connor and figure out our next steps," David said.

"I'm not waiting." She headed toward the door. "I'm going to Colorado. Kevin's in Reno. Maybe he can meet me in Denver."

Elliott rose to block her path, reaching out to hold her still. "The lad's got plenty on his mind right now. He doesn't need more to worry about, and neither does Meredith. I'll go with ye to Denver, but we don't need to tell the others what's going on. Look," he said, hugging her. "We've gone through hell with the stones—torture, assault, heart attack, stroke, head injury, stabbing—but we've always come through, and we will this time, too. Mayhap the amber and amethyst stones are in conflict and will sort themselves out given time."

"Rick doesn't have time to wait," she said, sniffing. "I've got to tell Kevin. If I don't, he'll be furious."

While Elliott comforted JL, David tapped his fingers against his forehead and visualized the stagecoach. The parts and equipment had been in good working order and the horses sound, but the weather could have caused a stagecoach accident in the mountains. Elliott might be right. The stones could be in conflict. He didn't see how that was possible, but with each new stone they acquired, they gained more knowledge about their properties.

He pushed to his feet. "Kenzie and I are going, too. We'll figure this out when we get to Denver. I'll call and have the plane readied."

There was a light knock on the door, and David drew it back to find Kenzie standing there, an impatient look on her face. "The kids are on play dates. What's going on here?" Her eyes narrowed then roved the room taking in the three occupants. "What's wrong? Have you talked to Connor?"

"Aye." David grabbed his laptop and headed out the door. "We're going to Denver. Pack a bag."

She spun on her heel, following. "Okay, but what era clothes should I bring?"

"What ye're wearing will do. If anybody goes back, it won't be ye."

She jumped ahead of him, and the ghost of a smile flitted across her face. "Nothing's changed. Trey's cousin is still missing. We'll see about who goes and who stays. Won't we, McBain?"

26

The Present, Near Leadville, Colorado—Connor

CONNOR, OLIVIA, AND the search teams rode down the mountain near Leadville and reached the campground about mid-afternoon. The weather, although brisk and overcast, had remained dry throughout the day. Autumn had booted summer aside with a swift kick and a patented gust of cool air. For Connor, it had been a long three days, and he was tired and saddle sore. But he'd spent time with Olivia and even under the circumstances, he was glad to be there.

They approached the end of the well-worn trail that led to the parking lot. This would be a good time to stop and charge his batteries. With a light touch of his heels, Connor directed his horse toward the toothpick-chewing sheriff. The mud was worse on that part of the trail and it sloshed with each plodding step, splattering Connor's jeans. He reined in the horse, and the gelding lifted his head with a snort.

"I need to stop at the truck and charge my batteries. What's your plan for the rest of the day?"

The sheriff reined in his horse, too, and crossed his wrists over the pommel. "We'll look at the map and figure out where we're going next. How long do you need?"

Connor scratched his whiskered cheek as he estimated how long it would take to give both batteries a full charge. "A couple of hours, but I'll settle for one."

"We don't have much daylight left. Thirty minutes is all I can give you," the sheriff said.

Connor fell back into line with Olivia, wondering why the sheriff even bothered to ask. They rode side by side, and occasionally her leg brushed his, sending an electrical charge up his leg.

"The sheriff intends to stop at the campgrounds and study the map. I need to charge my batteries. Do you want to check email? Call your office? Return phone calls?"

"All of the above," she said.

There were dark circles under her eyes from a lack of sleep and worry. Her jeans were muddy and ripped, and her slumped shoulders gave her a defeated look so out of character as to be almost cartoonish. Her bedraggled appearance sent a throb of affection through him so sharp it was painful.

"I've been out of touch long enough. I need to find out what's happening at the office."

"What do you want to do about tonight? Ride back up to the cabin?" It was the last place he wanted to go, but he would, if that was what she wanted. "Or maybe stay in Leadville, and go up the first thing in the morning?"

"It's too late to go to the cabin. It'll be dusk in a couple of hours. If we stay in Leadville, we'll have to board the horses. We're close enough to bunk at the ranch. Let's save some money and go home."

He liked the sound of that.

"I want a hot shower and clean clothes," she said. "I'm sure you do, too."

"I should drive to Denver. I'm still paying for a room at the hotel, and my gear's there."

"After all you've done for me, I'll pay for the hotel, and that includes an empty room for one more night. I know from personal experience, once you get to the ranch, the last thing you'll want to do is pass up a hot shower and drive all the way to Denver. We can go up there tomorrow."

"You have mud on your face." He rubbed the spot, smiling, hoping to lift her spirits. "Let's stop on the way to the ranch and pick up a couple of steaks and a bottle of wine. I'll feed you tonight."

"Dad keeps a freezer full of steaks and a cellar full of wine, but you can do the honors. I'll sit back and watch."

He stroked her face again, pretending there was more mud to wipe away, but he was too drawn to her to remove his fingers. She took his hand and squeezed it. He leaned over and kissed the spot where his fingers had been.

"We'll find her. I promise," he said.

But when they found Amber, his part in the cover-up—while it might eventually be forgiven—would never be forgotten.

They rode in silence along with the deputies who'd kept a stern professional demeanor during the ride, rarely speaking except in undertones to another deputy. There was little professional courtesy extended to Connor. When he and Olivia reached the truck, they dismounted.

"There's a tie-up point at the rear of the trailer," she said. "We can leave the horses there until we talk to the sheriff. Let's eat, check messages, then conference with him."

They tied up, lifted the saddle flaps, and loosened the girths by a hole or two to allow the horses to relax a while. Connor wished his tight back and thigh muscles could be loosened as easily. He needed a hot shower and a deep tissue massage. The odds of getting a massage today weren't great, but at least he could get a shower.

"How about I drive to Leadville and grab us some lunch?"

Olivia dug into her saddlebag and pulled out her phone and packages of dehydrated food. "As soon as I check messages, I'll ask Bob for a cup of hot water and hydrate some chicken and vegetables. Does that work for you?"

"Any chance for a Coors?"

"I'll ask him."

"That's okay. I'll be driving or riding after lunch. I'll wait." He still had the key fob, so when he approached the door it unlocked automatically. After plugging his phone into the charger, he checked his messages, finding one from JL saying she was on her way to Denver. No explanation. No follow-up text messages. He was in the process of sending a message to JL when Olivia gasped. "What's wrong?"

She yanked out a Bluetooth headset and slapped her phone into his palm, anger radiating off her like flames rising out of an open fire pit. "A message from my sister."

He watched the video and listened to Amber's spiel. He didn't believe a word she said, but from Olivia's reaction, the one person who mattered believed every word.

"I've been agonizing for days, worried sick about her, and she's shacked up with a rock hound she met while fossil hunting. The guy is as thoughtless as she is. I've had it. I'm done with her. Let's get out of here."

Connor replayed the video. There was something familiar about the man whose face was hidden from view. He played it for a third time, studying the man closely, and noticed the fine line of an old scar beneath his nipple.

Rick?

What the hell was his brother doing? He handed the phone back to Olivia. "You need to show that to the sheriff."

She shook her head, her eyes glistening. "I can't. I'm too embarrassed. Do you mind?"

"Can't say as I blame you."

He climbed out of the truck and headed toward the sheriff, but before he reached the group of law enforcement officers huddled around several vehicles with attached trailers, he stopped and watched the video again. If David was back from the nineteenth century, why send a video? Wasn't Amber back, too? And if she hadn't returned with David, she should have returned shortly thereafter. David sent the video to satisfy Olivia and the sheriff. But why not just produce Amber?

Because that wasn't possible, which lead him to ask the question: Why not? The only logical answer was because Rick and Amber had a dysfunctional brooch and were stuck in the past.

Connor approached the sheriff and his deputies and said without fanfare, "Olivia received an email from Amber. A video was included."

If the sheriff's kill-the-messenger look had been a cocked gun, Connor would be on the ground with a bullet in his head.

The sheriff snapped out a rough-looking hand, scarred on the palm and missing the tip of his middle finger. Connor hadn't noticed that before. His Sherlock Holmes-like observation skills and ability to quickly read situations was slacking a little bit.

"Give it to me." The sheriff watched it. His face turned red, his eyes bulged, and his lips pressed so tightly together there was hardly any daylight between the top lip and the bottom. After forwarding the video to his own phone, he returned the device to Connor. "Tell Amber to call me. The sheriff's department will expect her assistance—again—during our spring fundraiser."

Connor's first reaction was to chuckle, but he didn't. "Is that sufficient repayment?"

"Between you and me, detective, she'll never be able to repay the department for the inconvenience, wear and tear on our animals, and my deputies' frustration. But it's our job, and if she goes missing again, we'll go look for her. I just hope to God, she goes missing in someone else's county."

"I think this will be the last time." Connor tried for a tone of conviction but didn't think he pulled it off. He shook hands with the sheriff. "Thanks, and thanks to your deputies. I'll pass along your message when I see her."

He returned to the vehicle and handed Olivia her phone. "The sheriff wants to talk to Amber when she returns. The department needs help with its spring fundraiser."

"It won't be the first time she's done community service. He should come up with something disgusting for her to do."

"Like muck barns?"

"No, that doesn't bother her. He should make her work in a daycare. She can't relate to kids unless she draws pictures of dinosaurs or sings songs they don't understand. But that wears off quickly. Then she's stuck. For such a smart person, she can be so damn clueless."

Olivia clicked on the video again. "I wonder who the man is?"

"You'll have to wait until you talk to your sister. If we could see his face, we could run facial recognition software and find out."

"I guess that's why he didn't show himself."

The mixture of anger and betrayal flashing in her eyes was heartbreaking. Seeing his brother in a compromising position with Amber made Connor feel like an even bigger asshole for putting Olivia through three days of hell.

"Let's load the horses and get out of here," she said.

Twenty minutes later, they waved goodbye to the sheriff and drove toward the campground's exit. "Do you think your handyman will go to the cabin and check on Amber's horse?"

"I'll text him now and ask him to board the horse in town. He'll also need to clean the cabin. I thought we'd go back there later today."

"The dishes were washed, the beds were made, the log holder restocked. There's not much to do."

"Dispose of the garbage. That's about it. But he'll check the stoves and the fireplace to be sure there are no live embers. I'd hate the place to burn down on my watch."

Olivia tapped on her phone. "I can't believe Amber did this to me and inconvenienced you. I'm sorry, and I'm so embarrassed. If you want another agent in my office to handle the purchase of the ranch, I'll be glad to step aside and let someone competent handle the transaction."

Connor pulled over to the side of the road, shoved the gear into park, and turned to face her. "Listen, because I'm only going to say this once. What Amber did is not your fault. You're not responsible for her. Your concern and worry were legitimate, but it's no reflection on you. If anything, it shows how loving and compassionate you are and what lengths you'll go to protect those you care for. I don't want another broker. I want you."

After months of frustration, he pulled her into his arms and lowered his mouth, pausing for only an instant to inhale her before his lips touched hers. He almost moaned as the rush of desire flooded his body with heat. Maybe he did, because as her body melded to his, she gave an answering groan.

It was everything he thought it would be. She responded with the same urgency as he cradled the back of her head and threaded his fingers underneath her hair, holding her there, as he slid his tongue between her lips. Realization oozed through him like honey purling through veins—Olivia was finally warming to him. And all he knew was the heat and textures of her mouth—soft and sensual and eager.

Their lips parted. "I've wanted to do that for the longest time," he said.

A slight flush of amusement momentarily relieved the wan paleness of her skin. "And I've wanted you to, but I also wanted to keep it professional. I guess I failed."

"Trust me. You haven't failed at anything. I never picked up a clue." He tossed her hat onto the back seat and kissed her again, then pulled away with a grin. "Can we continue this later?" He scratched his face. "I want to shave. My stubble is scraping your skin. I don't want to give you a bad whisker burn, and I definitely don't want to stop kissing you."

"Sure, but first I want to do something I've wanted to do for months."

She tossed his hat onto the back seat, landing on top of hers, and she kissed him with a flirtatious invitation to misbehave. And he did. He tugged her close, consuming her mouth. No kiss had ever made him go so hot and shaky. It was possessive and carnal and dominating to a degree that alarmed him. He had visions of dragging her down onto the seat and pounding into her until her screams echoed like a canyon's cry, and his release erupted like a…like a what? Herd of mustangs? God help him, because he was too weak to help himself.

A knocking on the window brought them back to their present

reality, his heart thudding in his ears. He rolled down the window. "What do you want, Sheriff?"

"I forgot to ask. Do you have any idea who the man is with Amber?"

Irritated that God had found a way to help him, Connor shot back, "Some lucky son of a bitch who doesn't have a cop beating on his window. Goodbye, Sheriff." Connor put the truck in gear and drove away from the campground.

Olivia exploded in hysterical laughter. Not that the situation was that funny, but for her, it was a release from days of worry and stress.

"He's got to think the Kelly girls have gone to hell in handbaskets."

"If that's where you're going, sweetheart, so am I."

"I guess that means you're spending the night at the ranch."

He pulled out onto the highway, giving her a sideways glance. "We're finishing what we started before either of us takes another call or responds to a text. Scoot over here next to me. I want to touch you while I drive."

She moved to the middle seat and buckled herself in. Connor slung his arm over her shoulder and stroked down her cheek, running his fingers over the smoothness of her skin to her neck, past the collar of her T-shirt, and farther down to the swell of her breasts, and the more he teased her, the harder it was to focus on the road. Olivia rested her head on his shoulder, her hand over his thudding heart, and they drove back to the ranch in silence, contemplating an evening in each other's arms.

27

The Present, Kelly Ranch, Colorado—Connor

THE SUN WAS slowly disappearing behind the serrated peaks of the Rockies by the time Connor and Olivia arrived back at the Kelly Ranch. They left the horses in the care of the farm manager and made their way across sandstone pavers toward the main house, fingers woven together. The residence, constructed of spilt cedar and native Colorado red rock, sat at the highest point of a private valley. Other than their footfalls, the nearby splash in the trout pond was the only other sound to break the evening's stillness.

"This must be what heaven is like." Connor inhaled the cool air scented with spruce needles and spice, cedar and sandalwood.

"I haven't been to MacKlenna Farm or Fraser Castle or Montgomery Winery, but Colorado is the stairway to heaven."

"Then we're on the top step, and I intend to kiss an angel." He pulled her into his embrace, holding her firmly against his chest, grazing his hands down her hips. The kiss was hot, spicy, and erotic, and she drew a deep, staggered breath in response to the same wave of heat flushing through his veins. "I want to kiss every inch of you, and it'll take all night and most of the morning before I finish and start all over again."

A sensuous private embrace wrapped around him when her voice lowered, and she whispered suggestively, "The front door's the shortest distance to the shower. I'll race you."

At the front porch, they fumbled, laughing as they tried to yank off their boots. "Let me help," he said. She held onto his shoulders, bracing herself as he stooped and pulled off one boot then the other. She made a move to help him. "I can do it. Open the door." He hopped around on one foot as he pulled and tugged, finally getting them off. Then he meticulously lined up his boots—toes to the wall—and put hers there, too, while she punched in the security code on the keypad that unlocked the front door.

Looking down at their boots lined up in a neat row, she laughed. "That has to be a first."

"Growing up, we had to. With five kids, you'd never find your shoes if you didn't put them in a certain spot. I live with two of my brothers now, and we still line up our shoes at night."

She laughed again. "You'd have heart failure if you saw my closet at home."

He gave her a quick kiss. "I'll have heart failure if I don't see you naked in the next thirty seconds."

The door swung open and she invited him inside with a welcoming sweep of her arm. Before he could cross the threshold, she grabbed his hand and pulled him close, moving in a slow-waltzing step through the grand foyer.

"Do you need to punch in a code?" he asked.

"Oh, gosh." She broke their hold. "You distracted me."

"I'll be sure to tell the police that when they rush out here to respond to the silent alarm."

She punched in a code on the security panel next to the door and flipped a light switch to turn on the chandelier. The lights dimmed after a slight adjustment to the slider. His arms snaked around her and their bodies made contact. A jolt passed through him; her proximity was electric. From the sudden widening of her eyes, she thought so, too. He whipped off her wide-brimmed hat and tossed it onto a curved branch of the coat rack. It spun for a moment, then settled there.

She laughed. "Impressive."

He flipped his own hat, but this time he failed to land the toss, and the hat dropped to the floor.

She laughed again.

"Win some, lose some," he said.

His phone rang but he ignored it, letting the call go to voicemail. Olivia led the way into the main living area with high ceilings, enhanced with rich alder, birch walls, and crown moldings. The interior was as beautiful as he'd imagined. Right now, though, his thoughts weren't on a Colorado ranch house, but on the rancher's daughter.

He pulled her into his arms again, dipped his head, and rubbed his lips against hers, their hungry mouths fused. She slid her arms around his waist, her hands meeting at his spine, holding him to her, just as he held her to him. They shifted the angle of their heads several times but didn't break the kiss until he pulled away and pressed his lips against her neck just beneath her ear.

"Which way to the shower?"

"There are guest rooms at the top of the steps on the right and left."

He took her hand and led her toward the staircase that seemed to magically rise from the floor without support. As soon as his foot landed on the first step, his phone rang again.

"Whoever it is, they're persistent."

"And they can wait," he said in a tone that reflected his annoyance.

They made it to the top of the stairs where he once again pulled her in for a kiss. His phone rang for a third time.

She ran her fingers through his hair, studying his features in the light drifting up from the foyer. "You better take the call. They're not going to give up."

"Neither am I," he said against her lips. He wanted to tell her that she was the most beautiful woman he'd ever seen, and that he couldn't think of anything except how much he wanted her. But the damn intrusion was too persistent and couldn't be ignored. "I'll return the call after we shower." The call went to voicemail, then immediately rang again.

Her gaze gleamed up at him, liquid with desire, her lips full and reddened from his kisses. "Take the call. It must be important."

The next kiss was hot, long, and reciprocal. "Nothing is more important than you, this moment, and us."

"Take the call." She murmured his name as his lips trailed one kiss after another along the side of her neck, the tip of his tongue around the shell of her ear.

He reached into his pocket, checked the face of the phone, then let out a frustrated sigh. "It's Elliott. If it was anyone else, I'd let it go, but I can't keep ignoring him." He clicked accept and said, "O'Grady."

"Where the hell are ye?" Elliott asked.

"At Olivia's parents' ranch."

"The jet just landed in Denver. We're staying in the guest house at the ranch we're buying. David's rented a helicopter, and we'll be there within the hour. How long will it take ye to get to the new property? We need to talk."

"That ranch is about thirty minutes south of the Kelly Ranch."

Olivia, overhearing the conversation, said, "We have a heliport."

He cupped the side of her face, nodding. She understood as well as he did what leaving the ranch would mean for them, for their plans, for their first night in the same bed. If he could get Elliott and David to stop at the Kelly Ranch first, then Connor wouldn't have to leave, and he and Olivia could salvage some of their evening.

"The Kelly Ranch has a heliport. Stop here on your way."

"Who's there with ye?"

"Just Olivia."

There was silence on the other end. Elliott must have muted the phone. Then after a moment, he said, "Send the address, and if ye have them, the GPS coordinates."

Connor tilted Olivia's head to his chest, relief swimming over him. "What's your ETA?"

"Soon. Turn on the lights," Elliott said.

Connor ended the call, but before he pocketed the device he handed it to Olivia. "Will you text the address, landing instructions,

GPS coordinates? Whatever you have."

"I have all three. Business associates fly in on helicopters all the time. It's the trendy way to get here." She flipped on the hall light and texted the information.

Connor returned the phone to his pocket and enfolded her in his arms. "As much as I want to take a shower with you, I won't start something else we can't finish right now. It's not fair to you. You deserve more than a quick shower."

"I can't believe you're saying that."

"Why?"

A devilish spark rallied in her eyes, and she gazed up at him, smiling. Dimples he hadn't seen lately came out in full force and he kissed them both. "You're more concerned about my feelings than your own needs. From the men I've known, that's rare."

"Mom taught me more than how to line up my boots."

If he'd been so concerned about her feelings he wouldn't have kept the truth from her. He'd hoped they would have time to cement their relationship before she learned the full story, but Elliott's visit would more than likely destroy that hope.

Damn, I should have told her the truth.

This was his last chance to gather her close and hold her against the coming revelations. If he could weather it for her, he would. When it was all said and done, she would find him as contemptible as other men more concerned with their needs than her feelings.

"Your mom must have been an amazing woman."

"She was." The knot under his heart grew a bit. The O'Grady kids and Pops had yet to fully recover from her death. They were a strong Irish Catholic family and depended on their church, their community, and each other.

"I'll go turn on the landing lights. It'll be dark by the time the helicopter lands. Then I'll hop in the shower. I've never met Elliott and want to look presentable."

"He won't care."

"Maybe not, but I do."

She stepped away, but he pulled her back and kissed her again, hard and thoroughly, his tongue firmly inside her mouth. The kiss lasted no more than a few seconds before it ended, his chest inflating around a deep breath that he then expelled in a gust.

"We'll pick up from here later," he said, although he doubted that would happen.

"I'll hold you to it." They clasped hands and walked down the hallway before stopping in front of a closed door. The doorknob pressed against his right hip as she wrapped her arms around his neck, rubbing against him seductively. "Use this room. It's next to mine. I'll grab a pair of jeans and a T-shirt from Dad's closet."

He couldn't think straight. "Keep rubbing against me like that, sweetheart, and I'll take you right here, right now, and to hell with the landing pad lights."

"I knew if I ever…you know…let my guard down, we'd be like this."

He kissed the tip of her nose. "I'm glad you did." He placed his hands on her shoulders and turned her away from him. "Go, while I still have my wits about me." He opened the door and flipped the light switch. Light from table lamps on each side of a queen-size bed and from a comfy nook next to a wall of windows filled the room. "I'll see you in a few minutes."

She put her hands behind her back and leaned against the door frame, so her body pitched slightly forward in a teasing manner. "If you're like me, you'll want to stand in the shower until the water runs cold. Don't. Dad installed tankless water heaters. The hot water never runs out and you'll… I don't know." She gave him a teasing smile that rocked his world. "Shrivel up."

"We wouldn't want that"—his grin widened—"would we?" He let the innuendo hang there for a beat as she swiveled, chuckling, and disappeared behind the door of her bedroom.

Twenty minutes later, Connor padded down to the great room, wearing more of Mr. Kelly's clothes—jeans and a cream-colored cashmere sweater. Olivia had included a pair of boxers, but he'd passed on those and gone commando. If they ended up in bed later that night, he didn't want her to laugh at the white baggy boxers.

The view from the front of the house was deceptive. The Kelly Ranch was an expansive mountain estate, nestled in a private valley and surrounded by towering pines and aspens. From what he'd seen of the house so far, it had to be over ten thousand square feet. If there was a full basement, it could be closer to fifteen. Fireplaces with built-in cabinetry, granite countertops, and stained-glass windows depicting scenes of the ranch bookended the great room, tastefully furnished with brushed leather furniture and native print area rugs.

The rooms were authentic, elegant, yet understated with a soft color palette. Not that he was an interior design expert, but after viewing more than three dozen ranches, taking copious notes, and listening to Olivia's descriptions, he'd trained his eye to notice quality, even in the cozy-up spots. Meredith had wanted first impressions, along with details about the ranches he visited. If he'd reported back that a room had leather chairs and tan walls, she would have given the job of finding a Colorado ranch to someone else, a job he'd grumbled about when first given the assignment. Sure, he could handle the security end, but picking a ranch that would satisfy her was way above his pay grade.

That all changed when he met Olivia, and the project became a dream job.

The most important feature of the Kelly Ranch was the breathtaking view of the lake and the mountains beyond, which could be enjoyed from multi-level decks and the large windows along the backside of the house. He stood there transfixed by the view. Olivia had told him once, "You can remodel a house, but there's nothing you can do to enhance a view if you don't have anything to work with."

He moved across the room to the wet bar and poured whisky into a Glencairn glass. Sipping, he walked back to the windows, where he sat in an oversized chair. The lights from the landing pad were about a hundred yards from the house. He would easily hear the rotor blades long before the helicopter was close enough to land. When it did, he'd walk down to meet Elliott.

Looking out over the peaceful landscape, Connor was as far removed from the turmoil of the last few days as he could be while remaining on the planet.

Olivia came up behind his chair, leaned over, and kissed his cheek. "Did you find everything you needed?" She tried to straighten, but he tugged on her arm to keep her close, and he kissed her, lingering for a moment to inhale the scent of her hair and body lotion. She smelled fresh and light, with lemon and bergamot orange, sensual and soft with base notes of vanilla and incense. Wine tasting had introduced him to the delightful aromas of wine and women. To him, vanilla was an aphrodisiac.

"The bathroom was well stocked. I even threw my clothes in the washing machine."

"Aren't you handy to have around? If I had known you were doing a load, I would have given you mine." She glanced up, listening. "The helicopter's coming."

"You must have super-human hearing like Radar O'Reilly. I don't hear anything." Seconds later, he heard the faint noise of the rotor blades. "Just for the record, I'm not happy about this. I've been dreaming of having you to myself, and Elliott shows up now, just as we're getting better"—Connor winked—"acquainted."

"Come on. We have a golf cart in the garage. Let's drive down to meet him then send him on his way."

"Okay, but I need my boots."

"Looking at the size of your feet, I think Dad's loafers will fit. He's got big feet, too."

The tender look she gave him filled his heart. He cleared his throat, ridding it of the knot that had moved there. "I wore your dad's hat and jacket. Now I'm wearing his jeans and sweater. I'm going to put my foot down and wear my own boots. I'll meet you in the garage."

Instead, he met her in the driveway, hopped onboard, and kissed her neck and ear while she piloted the electric cart along a concrete path toward the heliport. They reached a well-lit yellow line and she stopped the cart, waiting beyond the site perimeter until the helicopter was cold. He intended to meet with Elliott and David, introduce them to Olivia, and quickly send them on their way. That idea went south, as did his hope for the evening, when he saw that Elliott and David weren't the only ones exiting the helicopter.

Connor gripped the cart's roof support and swung out of the vehicle. "Damn."

"Who are the others?" Olivia asked.

"The pilot is David McBain. The woman behind him is his wife Kenzie, and the pregnant woman is my sister JL Fraser." Connor was more interested in who wasn't on the helicopter than who was. Something was screwy.

He walked toward the group. "I didn't know you were all coming."

"It was a last-minute thing," Kenzie said.

Elliott extended his hand. "Ye must be Olivia. I'm Elliott Fraser. Glad to finally meet ye."

"You too, Mr. Fraser."

"Mr. Fraser was my father. I'm Elliott."

Connor introduced her to David, Kenzie, and JL. He'd wanted Olivia to meet his family on his own terms, not like this. He'd just have to make the best of it.

"Did you have any trouble finding the heliport?" Olivia asked.

"Not a bit," David said.

"My parents have lots of clients and friends who fly up for weekends." Then to Connor she said, "Since there's not room for everyone, I'll take Kenzie and JL up to the house in the cart. You guys can take your time. The whisky will be ready to pour when you get there, or wine, if you prefer."

"Diet Coke," David said. "I'm driving tonight."

"Thankfully, I'm not," Elliott said.

JL put her hands to her lower back and stretched side to side. "I need to walk, but that hill looks daunting. I'll gladly take a seat in your chariot. From the size of your house, Amber, I could walk laps around the first floor."

Connor caught JL's slip immediately, but Olivia wasn't bothered by it. She and Amber must be called by each other's names frequently.

"There's a yoga studio next to the exercise room, if you want to do a mini session."

"I had a two-hour session this morning. Elliott's trainer and master yoga instructor are both sadists. Wait until you meet them. You'll think Ted is especially charming, but don't let his beguiling smile suck you in. He's a killer."

"Maybe you should change trainers."

JL gasped. "That's blasphemy. Ted and his partner are fixtures in the organization. He keeps us all in running shape, and when I say running, I mean *running*. Someone is always training for a big race. Kevin and Meredith are competing in a spring triathlon. God bless them."

"I'd love to do one of those. My excuse is finding time to commit to training right now."

"Are you a runner?" Kenzie asked.

"A little bit. My sport *du jour* is mountain biking. A few years ago, I got in the lottery and did the Leadville Trail 100 MTB, under the sub-twelve-hour cut-off by only ten minutes. I'll never do that race again. It's a challenge to even catch your breath."

"Bikers have the coolest clothes, too." JL climbed into the seat Connor had vacated. "Sounds like you're an intense competitor. You'll fit right in with the MacKlenna Clan."

Connor smiled, not realizing how important it was that his sister liked the woman he was falling in—He dug his boot heels firmly into the ground and stopped that thought from forming. It was too risky right now. As if rebelling, his mind flashed back to the image of their side-by-side boots. He sighed, letting that one go, too.

The lights of the cart dimmed as it moved farther away from the landing pad. When they were out of earshot, Connor asked, "What's going on? Has the situation deteriorated in Napa? And where the hell are Rick and Amber?"

"We don't know the full extent of the damage," Elliott said. "The mandatory evacuation order is still in place. We'll know more tomorrow. Everyone's in Reno tonight. They wanted to get far enough away from the smoke, but stay close enough to go back as soon as they were allowed in."

"As for Rick and Amber, we're not sure," David said.

"What?" Connor's insides curled. If there was one person you could always count on to be sure of anything, it was David. "What the hell do you mean, you're not sure?"

"Amber wanted to stay for two more weeks to go fossil hunting in Morrison. Rick agreed to stay with her."

"And you left them behind? What the hell were you thinking? And what the hell was he thinking? Screwing around with her—"

"There's nothing going on between them," David said. "They made the video to stop the sheriff from looking for her."

"It didn't look that way to me."

Elliott put his hand on Connor's shoulder. "We're doing the best we can."

Connor shrugged off Elliott's hand, then immediately regretted showing such disrespect. "Sorry." He walked ahead of Elliott and David while he considered what they'd told him. But it wasn't making sense. Even if they stayed behind, they should be home by now. He turned and asked, "Which brooch do they have?"

"Rick has the O'Grady brooch, and Amber has hers."

Connor glanced up at the house as the women reached the landing leading to the porch, their shapes, especially JL's swollen belly, silhouetted by soft lights glowing beyond the arc of the windows.

He turned his mind back to his brother. "If Rick has the amethyst, he should already be home. So why isn't he?"

"We don't know. That's why I'm going back tonight."

"You think they're in trouble, don't you?" Connor reached out and pinned David against the trunk of a tree with a solid hold on his shirt. "You left my brother in the nineteenth century without backup." Connor raised his fist to punch David, but Elliott clamped down on his arm.

"Don't beat him up. He's got to go back and fix this mess," Elliott said.

Connor released his grip on David's shirt and stepped away.

"Look," David said, straightening his clothes. "If ye want to hit me, go ahead. I'd react the same way. But here's the deal. Kenzie and I were on the ground and saw no downside to leaving them there. Amber wanted more time to hunt fossils. Rick agreed to be her bodyguard or babysitter, whichever way ye want to look at it. Plus, she had the attention of a Pinkerton agent, who Kenzie and I believe is her soul mate."

"But something's gone wrong, or they'd be here," Connor said.

"We left them in the stagecoach lot in Leadville. Amber and Rick, along with the Pinkerton agent and his ten-year-old son were taking the stage to Denver. Amber even had an invitation from her six-times great-grandfather to stay at his house while she was in the city. There wasn't a war, and no one was stalking them. With two soldiers protecting her we believed she was safe."

"What time of year was it?"

"First of November."

Connor walked away from David, pacing in frustration as he thought about his brother. The memory of Rick being MIA for a terrifying twenty-four hours hit Connor hard and fast. The brothers had been minutes away from boarding the MacKlenna Corporation jet to go search for him, when news came that Rick had been found shot and bleeding out. The fear that had engulfed Connor at that time, struck again. If he was going to help Rick, he had to be calm and focused.

"If the stagecoach was traveling through the mountains to Denver, they could have run into snow and icy roads. The coach could have crashed, gone down a mountainside." He stopped pacing and looked hard at David. "If they were lost or injured, they would have used a brooch and come home. As I see it, the only possibilities are—incapacitation or…" Connor's heart dropped, and an involuntary chill swept through him, threatening to make his teeth chatter. He didn't have the courage to finish the thought.

"There's another possibility," David said. "The brooches don't work, and they're stuck in the past."

"They have two brooches," Connor said. "I could understand Amber's not working because that fits with what we know of the stones, but there's no reason the amethyst shouldn't work."

"Unless the amber brooch is more powerful and has properties like the ruby, sapphire, and emerald. It could be two weeks or six months before they come home."

"How could the amber be more powerful than the amethyst if it doesn't return travelers to the moment of sendoff? That's what makes the diamond and amethyst our most powerful stones."

"On the plane to Denver," David said, "I was looking at pictures of the door in the cave beneath the castle. There is an A at the top and a faint turned A at the bottom of the door. I don't know the purpose, or even if there is one. But we now have two brooches with stones that start with the letter A." David thumbed through pictures on his phone, clicked one open and showed it to Connor. "It looks like this."

Connor studied the picture. "I agree it looks like an upside-down A, but what's the significance?"

"It's a universal qualifier. To quote Wikipedia, 'It's a logical constant interpreted as—for all.' And don't ask me what that has to do with the stones, because I don't know. It's possible the amber brooch won't fully function until all the stones have been recovered, and until then it can act as an interceptor."

"You're saying it'll override the powers of other brooches. That's bullshit. You wouldn't have been able to use the diamond brooch to come home, if that was the case."

"I didn't say I had all the answers," David said.

"Sounds like you don't have any."

"Here's something else to stick in yer craw, detective," David said. "What shape do ye have if ye put one turned A end-to-end with another A?"

Connor thought for a moment, trying to figure out where David was going with the idea of two As, one inverted. No bulb went off immediately. "A diamond, but I don't see—" The light bulb flashed like a photographer's flash powder as understanding burst from the darkness. "You suspect the diamond brooch is the super nova of brooches. That's why it worked for you and Kenzie."

David shrugged. "It's a working theory."

They reached the bottom of the steps to the tiered porch and paused there a moment. "I'm going back tonight," David said. "I'm leaving in a couple of hours. This is, as Elliott said, my mess to clean up."

"I'm going too. I'm not sure what I'll tell Olivia."

"I was hoping ye would volunteer before I drafted ye. Tell her good night and by morning, ye'll be back."

Connor hadn't planned to tell her good night at all. Only good morning. "What about Kenzie? She'll want to go, too."

"I don't want to take her, but she says nothing's changed, and her original position remains the same—she's got to help Trey's cousin."

"I called the owners of the ranch we're buying," Elliott said. "They agreed to rent us the guest house and use of the barns until the closing. Shane and Pete will take the horses there. They have an airfield, plus a heliport. For now, we can operate from that location."

"The timing sucks." With any luck, Connor could bring Amber home before Olivia discovered his deception. Hearing the story directly from her sister might lessen the anger Olivia would direct at him. And if he thought that was likely to happen, there was a bridge in Brooklyn he could buy.

"I agree," Elliott said. "But the stones have never asked our opinion."

"They just expect us to respond." Connor's voice was abnormally loud, and he lowered it a decibel. "The damn stones have amped up the pressure and have more control over us than we have over them. I don't like that."

They crossed the porch and before entering the house through a set of French doors, Connor removed his boots. They found the women sitting at the kitchen bar nibbling on raw vegetables. JL was drinking from a juice bottle, and Olivia and Kenzie were drinking red wine—a Montgomery Winery's Pinot Noir.

Elliott picked up the bottle and studied the label. "The 2012 was a good year. I wonder how long it will take for the vines to recover from the fire."

"The grapevines will be fine in a couple of years," JL said. "Fire doesn't kill them. It'll burn them back and they won't have a crop next year, but they'll recover. At least that's what Kevin told me."

"Let's hope he's right, lass." Then to Olivia he said, "Which way to the bathroom?"

She pointed. "Down the hall to the right."

David sat on a barstool next to Kenzie and glanced at the bottle Elliott had picked up. "I saw a bottle of Balvenie at the wet bar," she said. "That should make you happy."

He shook his head. "I'm not drinking tonight. Remember, I'm driving."

"Driving? Really? Your ulcer is acting up, isn't it?" Kenzie asked. "I should have known you were in pain." She kissed him. "You always deflect, trying to mask it. Now I understand what was really going on the other night."

David kissed her back. "We'll talk about it later."

"I can almost bet he's not taking his medication, Kenz. And on top of his ulcer acting up, he's turning forty. That's the real source of his stress," JL said.

David growled at her. "Are ye spying on me?"

"I'm a detective," JL said. "It didn't take me long to figure out your moods. You've been grumpy and avoiding Maria's spicy food. Ergo—your ulcer is acting up. Your brawn will never cure the painful sores in your stomach lining, but medication will."

Olivia pointed from David to JL and back again. "You two aren't brother and sister, but you sure act like it."

"JL talks to everybody like that," Kenzie said.

Olivia laughed. "I'll have to remember not to take it personally. Now," she said, putting down her wine glass. "I promised Connor I'd grill him a steak. You guys hungry?"

Kenzie refilled both wine glasses and munched on a carrot.

"That's like asking if they're Scotsmen. They're always hungry."

"I'm Irish," Connor said.

JL finished her juice and tossed the bottle into the recycle bin. "I need to pee, and I'd love a juicy, rare steak."

"Elliott's in the powder room," Olivia said.

"He's been in there a long time. Hmm. Has he said anything about his recent PSA?" JL asked.

"He's still stage one and his doctor continues to recommend active surveillance," David said.

"Isn't that sort of personal?" Olivia asked.

"Nah, everybody knows about his prostate cancer and mini stroke. He's in there talking to Meredith or Kevin," JL said. "He can't go thirty minutes without talking to one of them."

Olivia opened the freezer and took out six steaks. "If you can't wait, there's a bathroom at the top of the stairs."

"I need to put my clothes in the dryer," Connor said. "I'll show you where it is." He hovered over JL as she hopped off the stool.

"My brother is taking me to the potty. Good God, what's become of me?"

He put his arm around her waist. "Come on, sis. I don't want you to have an accident." He winked at Olivia on his way out of the room.

"Ha. Ha. I'm not an invalid. I'm pregnant. And I pity your wife, if you ever have one. You'll drive her nuts."

That wasn't the impression he wanted to leave with Olivia, but after the news he had to share with her shortly—that he had to leave tonight with Kenzie and David—he wasn't sure it mattered.

28

The Present, Kelly Ranch, Colorado—Olivia

OLIVIA STOOD IN front of the microwave thawing steaks while Kenzie flipped through packages of freeze-dried meals in the cabinet. There was a familiarity about her that Olivia could neither explain nor deny. They'd had a couple of telephone conversations in the last few months, but they had been short and business-like. Olivia had never picked up on the closeness she experienced now. It was sisterly. That thought made her wonder what Amber would think of Kenzie. Would they be a natural fit, too? Yes, they would. Her sister would appreciate Kenzie's sense of humor and effortless way she had of interacting with those in her orbit.

Kenzie pulled out two packages and closed the cabinet door. "What do you think of Connor?"

It took a beat or two for Olivia to switch gears and return to the moment. She replayed Kenzie's question and giggled, like a teenager infatuated with a boy in her class.

She turned her back to David and whispered, "We were racing to the house, and when we got to the door, we had to take off our boots. They were too muddy to wear inside. We were in such a hurry we nearly fell on our asses trying to pull them off."

"And…why were you in such a hurry?" Kenzie teased.

Olivia gave a little flick of her head and said with a bit of sassy humor, "Oh, I don't know. It must have been the weather."

"Okay, I've got to hear this, but hold up a minute." Kenzie turned to David who was sitting at the counter, scrolling through his phone, pretending to ignore them. "Hey, David. Would you mind getting my sweater from the helicopter?"

He stood immediately, as if rocketed from the barstool. "Did ye leave anything else ye might need?"

"I don't think so."

"Where's yer purse?"

She shrugged. "I didn't bring one?"

He cocked his head, examining her in such a way that made Kenzie blush. "Where'd ye put yer wee lipstick?"

She reached into her jeans pocket and pulled out a tube of Bobbie Brown lip color.

Olivia laughed. "How long have you two been married?"

"Seven years," David said. "And tomorrow I'll love her more than I do right now."

"Well, you act like newlyweds."

Kenzie leaned into him. "We've had a good week. Haven't we, McBain?"

"One of our best." He pulled her into his arms and kissed her. "And the week's not over."

Olivia stepped around the kissing couple. "While you two heat up the kitchen enough to thaw the steaks, I'll go get you a sweater. Although the way that man is holding you, like you're part china, part Tupperware, I don't think you'll need one."

Kenzie broke the kiss and glanced over her shoulder at Olivia. "China and Tupperware? I don't get it."

"Look at his hands. He holds you like you're a china doll, but kisses you like you're indestructible and can handle his intensity. You must both be warriors, because not just any woman could handle him."

Kenzie turned back to David and kissed him again. "She's right, you know?"

They both moaned a reply, and Olivia left the kitchen, stroking her bottom lip, still a little swollen from Connor's last kiss. She jogged up the steps, her nipples tingling just thinking about him. She wandered down the hall, lost in her thoughts and passed the door to the bedroom Connor had used. The door was slightly ajar, and voices were coming from within.

"What'd you think when you saw Rick with Amber in that video?" JL asked.

"I wanted to bust his balls. What about you?"

"As soon as I realized it was our brother, I wanted to smack him. Then David explained the purpose of the video was to satisfy the sheriff and calm Olivia. Knowing Rick, he was just having fun with it," JL said.

Fun. What the hell?

Olivia edged closer to the door. Connor and JL knew the man in the video, and it wasn't just any man. It was their brother. Anger boiled up inside Olivia as the siblings' conversation continued.

"Elliott hasn't said anything, but I know he's worried Amber will fall for Daniel and want to live in the past with him," JL said.

"That would kill Olivia," Connor said. "She and Amber aren't only sisters, they're best friends. I don't see Amber giving up her life and family to live permanently in the nineteenth century."

"Kit did."

"But she was misplaced as an infant. She belongs there."

What the hell? The conversation was straight out of the *Twilight Zone*.

"Kenzie's crazy about Amber. She said they had a blast shopping and having tea with Lindsey Hughes."

The dryer door closed, the spinner dial clicked, and the clothes began to tumble. "Who's Lindsey Hughes?" Connor asked.

"You've got that turned to the wrong heat," JL said, ignoring his question.

"No, I don't."

"Yes, you do."

"Leave me alone. They're my clothes."

"As much as you pay for your jeans, you need to dry them on a low heat," JL said.

"All right," Connor said. "I give up. You set the temperature. Now answer my question. Who's Lindsey Hughes?"

"Olivia and Amber's seven-times great-grandmother. Her son, Adam, slid easily into Yale and subsequently started a prestigious family law firm that Amber is a member of today."

"Did they tell Lindsey Hughes they were from the future?"

"No," JL said. "Amber wanted to ask Lindsey where the brooch came from, but Kenzie wouldn't let her. What about you? How'd you keep from telling Olivia the truth?"

"It was the hardest thing I've ever done. But what could I tell her? I didn't know where Amber was, when she'd return, or even if she was safe. And if I'd told her Amber was in a space-time vortex, what good would that do?"

Space-time vortex? Olivia couldn't be any more confused if she'd walked into a movie theatre in the middle of a sci-fi film.

"You could have told her the story of the brooches and a bit about all the adventures."

"I didn't know how she'd react. What if she'd repeated the story to the sheriff? Then we would have had one hell of a mess. And David said not to tell her."

"Kevin's going to be pissed when he finds out what's going on here, and that I kept him in the dark. It's hell when we try to protect people," JL said. "And it inevitably comes back to bite us in the ass."

A sense of betrayal swept through Olivia. Her body shook, and acid churned in her stomach. She was going to be sick. She took several deep breaths as a thunderous rage began to build inside her, a rage fueled by lies and liars. The sickening moment passed, but not the anger going full steam through her mind, her heart. She swiped the back of her hand across her lips, as if that could wipe away every kiss Connor had given her. How could any man stoop to such a level of deception?

The crunching sound she heard was her heart breaking into tiny pieces. She leaned against the wall, her knees buckling, and a rock the size of a fist stuck in her throat. If she could, she'd truss Connor up and pitch him out the window, and the others, too. All of them.

People she'd welcomed into her home. People who'd lied to her.

She threw her arm against the door, slinging it open. It banged against the doorstop on the baseboard and bounced back, almost smacking her in the head. She caught the knob and gripped it with a sweaty palm. "What the hell is going on here?" Connor stared at her as if his world had just imploded. Good. She hoped it had. Pointing at him, her hand shaking, she asked, "Where is my sister?"

JL patted her brother's back. "Good luck." Her mouth was drawn in a sober smile as she ducked between Olivia and the door. "I'm going downstairs. If you need me…" JL left the sentence unfinished and closed the door behind her.

Tears clouded Olivia's vision as she stared at the man she was—until a few moments ago—falling in love with. That tie that binds had been snapped, severed, ripped in half. Now she could barely look at him without being sick.

"You knew… All this time. You knew…"

"Olivia, this situation is complicated," he said.

"Honesty is never complicated." Her muscles quivered, her heartbeat pounded, sending pains across her chest. Her anger was so intense, it scared the hell out of her. He made a move forward, and she stepped backward in an angry choreographed dance.

"Let's go downstairs," he said. "Bring Elliott and David into the conversation." His words sounded distant, like she was hearing an echo and the source was miles away. "I know you're hurt," he continued, "and mad as hell, but I had a reason for not telling you what I knew."

"A reason? Are you kidding? There's no reason that could justify putting me through three days of anguish. Then you had the gall to kiss me like there was no tomorrow. I guess you knew there wouldn't be one after I learned the truth."

Olivia's words flew at him as if they were rocks, pounding him with all her pain. She slapped him, and they both froze, staring at each other. He didn't look away or touch his face. It was as if the slap had no effect on him at all. And then his expression changed, and he looked at her, almost sympathetically, as if he completely understood why she was throwing words at him so fiercely. And that pissed her off even more.

She wanted him to hurt, to feel pain as deeply as she did at that moment. Hurting him was her only thought when she picked up a porcelain vase. But he moved too fast and stopped her from hurling it at him. There was a short tussle, and the vase, forced from her hands, hit the floor and shattered like her dreams.

"Look what you did." She jerked away, searching for another target. On the bed, a stack of washed and folded summer clothes awaited to be shelved. She scooped them up and pitched them across the room, creating a swirling path of Amber's tops and shorts and bathing suits she kept at the house for quick changes.

"Would you really have gone to bed with me, knowing my trust would be destroyed?" She stared stonily at the heap of shorts and shirts scattered in a muddled mess, just like her feelings for him. "I've lived in fear for days that Amber was possibly dead, and you knew what happened to her. I'll never forgive you for not telling me."

Connor's eyes shimmered, and he moved slowly toward the door as if he'd aged years in the last few minutes. "Is there anything I can say?"

"No. Just go." He left, and she slammed the door behind him. What were her options? Drive back to Denver or stay put and lock herself in her room until they left. In her state of mind, driving back to Denver wasn't really an option. She fell onto the bed. The light in her life had gone out as surely as if someone had thrown a blanket over her head, extinguishing all sight and sound.

It was in times like this that her grandmother had poured out hugs and words of wisdom. What would she say now? Probably something like, "You'll never lose at anything, Olivia. You'll either win or learn a valuable lesson."

She hadn't won this time so what was the lesson? Not to trust a sexy, lying Irishman. She rolled over on her back and hugged a pillow to her chest. A friendship had just ended with a smackdown and a romance ended like a crash at Indy. But Amber was safe, and

Olivia had learned another life lesson.

A knock on the door had her throwing the pillow aside. "Go away. Leave me alone." She rolled off the bed and sat on the floor.

The latch clicked, and the door opened. "Olivia, I need to talk to you."

"I don't want to talk. Just go away."

The bed dipped as Kenzie sat then slid to the floor beside her.

"Please leave me alone," Olivia said.

"I can't, sweetie. It's not my nature," Kenzie said.

"Then act out of character for once."

"I'm a storyteller, although they're usually just one-liners, but I need to tell you something and you need to listen."

"I'm not in the mood."

"You know," Kenzie sighed. "I don't care. I'm going to tell you anyway."

Olivia clasped her knees to her chest and rested her head there. "Make it quick."

"Okay. This part is just for context, so bear with me. Several years ago, I was living in London while working on a joint-degree program between Harvard and Cambridge. My thesis was on the settlement of international disputes, with an emphasis on Winston Churchill. I was knee-deep in World War II research."

Olivia bristled. "I don't care."

"One day," Kenzie continued, ignoring Olivia's protest, "I received a package in the mail. I didn't recognize the return address, but I opened it and found a puzzle box. I was intrigued. It took me about an hour to open it, and inside was a Celtic emerald brooch."

Exasperated, Olivia said, "Please leave me alone. Maybe some other day, I'll listen to your story."

"The inside of the stone," Kenzie continued, "was engraved with a Gaelic inscription. When I spoke the words, a fog swept over me and carried me back in time to 1944. I arrived in London the night of a bombing, and I was scared shitless. I recited the words again, but the brooch wouldn't take me home. Fortunately, David came to my rescue, but it wasn't an easy journey."

"Kenzie, go away."

"Sorry, Olivia. I can't. You see, Amber found a brooch like mine in the puzzle box she left on the floor at the cabin. The brooch carried her away to Leadville in the year 1878."

Olivia looked up. "You're insane. You're all insane. Take your crazy story and leave me alone." She jumped to her feet and collapsed on the nearby window seat where she twisted a throw pillow viciously, as if she were strangling it.

Kenzie stood. "I want to show you something. She unzipped her jeans and lowered them on one side, exposing her left hip. "See this web of scars, Olivia? Do you want to know how I got them?"

"I'm sorry you were injured, Kenzie. I really am—"

Tears filled Kenzie's eyes. "Trey Kelly saved my life in Afghanistan."

Olivia gasped. "You're… You're that…Kenzie."

She zipped her jeans. "I owe Trey my life. He was my best friend." She sat down next to Olivia. "I met him the first day of classes at West Point. We were inseparable. We deployed together. And because of him, I have three beautiful children. Because of him, Amber's disappearance is a top priority in my life, in David's life, in Connor's life, in Elliott's life. Because of Trey, we're here for you and for Amber. Work with us. Don't fight us."

Olivia tossed the pillow aside, snagged a tissue from a box, and blew her nose. "Trey talked about you all the time. I thought the two of you would get married. Then when he died, and you didn't come to the funeral, I asked about you. Trey's grandfather, Cav Cavanaugh, told me you almost died in the blast too, but Trey protected you. I'm sorry I didn't recognize your name."

"You wouldn't have known my married name. Would you believe I met Cav the first night I was in London during the war? He was a young man, and so handsome. I met his friend Molly, too. She got me a job at Bletchley Park."

"How's that possible?"

"That's what I'm trying to explain. When I heard Amber had disappeared," Kenzie continued, "under familiar-sounding circumstances, I knew I had to help her. David and I, along with Connor's brother, went back for her. David and I just came home after spending five days in Leadville in the year 1878."

"If what you're telling me is true, where's Amber now?"

"She wanted to go fossil hunting in Morrison. It was something she'd dreamed of doing, and she couldn't pass up the opportunity. We told her it wasn't fair to you, and she struggled with that.

"We don't have a Celtic brooch rulebook," Kenzie continued, "but we do know that the diamond and amethyst brooches return travelers to within minutes of their departure. We left MacKlenna Farm this morning, spent five days in Leadville, then returned to the farm, and only a few minutes had passed since we left. We don't know the properties of Amber's brooch, so we don't know when it will bring her home. When Rick agreed to stay an additional two weeks and protect her while she searched for fossils, David came up with the idea of taping a video to explain her absence."

"Then she'll be home in two weeks?"

Kenzie pushed to her feet and paced the room, picking up clothes along the way. "We're not sure, so we're going back tonight to get her. I know this seems crazy and otherworld-ish, but it's real."

Olivia threw her wadded-up tissue in the trashcan and snagged a fresh one. "The only thing real to me is that Connor didn't trust me enough to tell me about Amber."

Kenzie sat on the bed and folded clothes. "David told him not to tell you. And those orders came from Elliott."

"Is Elliott Fraser the godfather? Does he wield influence by fiat, without question? 'Do this because I say so?'"

"You wouldn't have believed Elliott or Connor." Kenzie matched up a bathing suit top to its bottom and folded them neatly together. "You're not even convinced of it now. And telling you the truth could have complicated the situation. His lie was one of omission." She stopped folding, letting her hands and the bathing suit drop to her lap, and she looked at Olivia with penetrating green eyes. "He never meant to hurt you."

"You know, don't you, that lies of omission are still lies."

"The family is painfully aware of what lies of omission are. It's a heartbreaking reality of being part of the Celtic brooch clan." Kenzie picked up a T-shirt and folded it into a perfect square. "We have secrets we can't share with others, and we dodge the truth to protect the stones. None of us volunteered for this. It was hoisted on our shoulders and we're doing the best we can." She folded another T-shirt. "Look, I'm sorry you were lied to, but it was necessary, and the truth is, we'd all do it again."

"You don't know how much it hurts."

"Give me a break, Olivia. I do know. I was so mad at David for lying to me, and it took a while to get over it, but eventually I forgave him. I had to. I loved him." Kenzie put the folded T-shirts aside and returned to the window seat. "Don't let your anger drop roadblocks in your path that'll keep you focused on problems instead of solutions."

"I feel like I'm skiing down a steep mountain on a cloudy night. The moon peeks through. I see a familiar landmark and have a glimmer of hope that I'll get home safely. Then it goes dark again, and I want to stop and wait for daylight, when everything will be clearer."

"Let's go talk to David. He has pictures of Amber. They'll help you see the situation clearer."

Olivia shredded the tissue in her hand. "Pictures? Why would I believe any pictures you have? They could be altered to show anything you wanted to prove. I need my sister back. And I need you to tell me where she is."

Kenzie took the shredded tissue, threw it in the trash, and handed Olivia a fresh one. "The last time I saw Amber, which was late this morning, she was getting on a stagecoach to Denver with Rick O'Grady, Pinkerton Agent Daniel Grant, and Daniel's ten-year-old son, Noah. That's where she is or should be."

Olivia didn't want to cry, but she couldn't stop the sudden rush of emotion. She drew a ragged breath. "Okay, let me see the pictures."

Kenzie took her hand, tugged on it. "Come on. Let's go find

David."

"I don't want to see Connor. Will David come up here?"

"No, because he's hungry. He banished Connor to the deck to grill steaks."

"He'll overcook them." She had no evidence to support that, but right now, Connor couldn't do anything to please her.

"No, he won't. Connor can't hard-boil an egg, but he could have his own grilling show on cable. It's his forte. Grilling won't do much for a bad piece of meat, but a good cut in his hands is a foodie's orgasm."

Olivia squeezed her eyes shut in frustration and heartache, then opened them. "I might be able to forgive him, but I'll never forget what he did. He let me worry needlessly, put me through hell. I'll never be able to trust him again."

"That's a shame," Kenzie said, "because he's a trustworthy person. And I know he's agonized over this, but he did what he was asked to do. He did what was best for the mission, for the family, and although you don't believe it, for you."

"I don't want to talk to Elliott either."

"Elliott can take care of himself and he's big enough to handle your anger. He runs a billion-dollar business and makes decisions that affect our lives. When it comes to the brooches, he listens to our opinions, but ultimately the decisions are his as Keeper and chief of the clan. He has our respect, our devotion, and our trust."

"Keeper? Of what?"

"From what we've learned, the brooches are ancient. At one time, the Keeper had control over all of them. We don't know how many, a dozen or more. Hundreds of years ago, they were scattered among the clan for safekeeping. Now, they're finding their way back to the Keeper."

"How many does he have?"

"Five: a ruby, sapphire, emerald, amethyst, and diamond."

"What stone does Amber have?" Olivia asked.

"An amber."

"That's her birth stone. She would have seen the irony in that."

Olivia pulled herself up with effort, like someone drawing the scattered pieces of a puzzle into one disjointed pile. "I need to wash my face."

Kenzie followed Olivia to the bathroom. "Connor wanted to go back for Amber, but he stayed to help you deal with the sheriff, knowing he'd have to lie to you. He's a good Irish-Catholic boy, and he'll spend the next year going to weekly confession. He could have left you to deal with Amber's disappearance on your own, but he refused to abandon you."

Olivia turned on the water and splashed her face, patted it dry, and rubbed on a bit of lotion. "You make him sound honorable when I don't see him that way at all."

How did she see him? She glanced around the bathroom. The towel he'd used was neatly folded over the handle of the shower's glass door. The bathmat was hanging on the towel heater to dry, the toilet seat was down, and the toothbrush, toothpaste, and razor he'd used were lined up on a dry washcloth. The room was as neat and orderly as it had been before he used it. His clothes were gently tumbling in the dryer, set to low heat. How could you complain about a man who put the toilet seat down without being asked?

"Come on," Kenzie said. "Let's go see David's pictures."

Olivia stood at the bathroom door and stared back into the room. "I don't think I've ever met such a fastidious man who showed no sign of the trait. He's been out in the mud and rain for days and never once complained."

"He's not fastidious. He's just well-trained. With six children in the house, they all had to toe the line."

Olivia turned out the bathroom light. "I thought there were five kids."

"JL had a teenage pregnancy and her son was raised as their brother. It's a long story. He's a neat kid. He's the starting forward at the University of Kentucky."

"Connor never mentioned it. In fact, he's never really talked about his family much."

"The O'Grady family is the most loving group of people I've

ever been around. They would give you the shirt off their backs."

Kenzie took her hand and led her from the room. Olivia closed the door, wanting to forget everything that happened in and around the room since they'd walked through the front door an hour or so ago.

At the bottom of the stairs Kenzie hugged her. "Listen to Elliott with an open mind. He's an amazing man. He can smooth ruffled feathers, and I love him dearly. Once you are part of his inner circle, your back will always be protected. Amber is in the inner circle by circumstance. You, if you want it, can be in the circle by choice. And I don't think anyone, other than his wife Meredith, has ever been given that option before."

29

The Present, Kelly Ranch, Colorado—Olivia

KENZIE AND OLIVIA entered the kitchen at Kelly Ranch to find Elliott, JL, and David huddled in a serious conversation. Their heads popped up and their eyes darted from Kenzie to Olivia. They seemed to know without asking what had occurred upstairs. David filled a wine glass, and Elliott pulled out a stool.

"Sit down, lass."

Elliott set his calloused hands gently on her shoulders. They were large, warm, and strong. Olivia knew he had spent years working as a large-animal veterinarian. She wondered how many skittish colts his hands had gentled and how many had kicked him in the shins, which was exactly what she wanted to do.

"We know ye're upset with how this went down," Elliott said.

"Upset?" she asked. "That's a—"

Elliott held a finger close to her lips and looked at her straight on. "This is the time for listening." There was more than a trace of his heavy burr in his voice. His eyes went hard, his face stern. "Connor did exactly what I told him to do. He was to stay with ye, protect ye from the sheriff. Ye see, when a lass named Amy Spalding disappeared with the diamond brooch, her boyfriend was charged with her murder, even though there wasn't a body. We didn't want that to happen to ye."

Olivia sat straight, incensed. "*No one* would ever suspect me—"

Elliott held a finger to her lips again. "We know from experience innocent people are arrested. What we did, we did for yer protection. I know it doesn't seem like it now, but that's the truth of it."

There was a slight shift in Elliott's posture and he stepped aside, making room for David, as if they were a well-trained tag team. "We've never had anyone in the circle who didn't know the story of the stones from personal experience," David said. "We'd hoped we could keep it from ye until Amber returned and told ye the story herself, thinking ye'd be more receptive to her telling than ours. We're sorry ye found out before ye were ready to hear it." David stopped and seemed to breathe heavier. "We believe there's a problem with the stones Rick and Amber have with them. We're going back tonight to bring them home."

"Where are you going?" Olivia struggled for a less confrontational tone.

David pulled pieces of paper from his jacket pocket and handed one piece to Olivia. She opened the broadsheet. "Read the masthead," he said.

"*The Reveille*. That's Leadville's first newspaper."

"What's the date?" David asked.

"November 1, 1878."

"That's the date I bought this paper from a newsboy in Leadville." He handed her his cell phone. "Click on the camera app and scroll through the pictures."

She put the broadsheet aside and scrolled through the photos, pausing at the video of Amber. A pressure band threaded itself around her head. It was an anger band, tightening inch by maddening inch. She gripped the phone, surprised it didn't crush in her hand as it mirrored the ever-tightening band.

Her finger shook as she swiped to the next picture. "Where was this taken?"

"That's an interior shot of Hughes Store on Harrison Avenue," he said. "The man in the apron is yer seven-times great-grandfather. The woman beside him is his wife, Lindsey MacKlenna Hughes."

They had a genuine look about them, not one created by a

makeup artist or Photoshopped. She could see traces of her grandfather—something in his eyes. She shook her head as if coming out of a trance and swiped to the next picture.

"This guy looks like Connor. Is this Rick?" she asked.

"Aye. They performed five nights at the Tabor Opera House to a standing room only crowd," David told her. "Mr. Tabor wanted to add matinees. Even offered to double the contract price, but Amber and Kenzie had every afternoon planned, and she didn't want to give that up."

"To do what?" Olivia asked.

"Shop, sightsee, have lunch with Mr. Hughes, or afternoon tea with Mrs. Hughes," Kenzie said.

Olivia glanced up, and gave Kenzie a look that said, *I don't believe you.*

Kenzie nodded. "Really."

"Amber hates to shop, and to stop whatever she's doing long enough for afternoon tea is unthinkable. How'd you talk her into it?"

Kenzie smiled. "I didn't. She planned every outing. Told me at breakfast what we were going to do. We laughed nonstop."

"Amber? Are we talking about the same person?" A single tear ran down Olivia's cheek, and she patted it away. "She's been unhappy for a long time. She's wanted out of the law practice for over a year but didn't want to hurt our parents like I did when I quit." Olivia scrolled to the next picture, wondering what else she was going to discover about her sister.

"The woman in that picture"—Kenzie pointed—"is Mrs. Garland, the owner of the boardinghouse where we stayed in Leadville. She's the sweetest lady. She had afternoon tea with us, too."

The next picture was of Amber standing next to a stagecoach. Olivia's imagination was fully engaged by the image, by Amber's split-skirt traveling suit, a cute little hat that a gust of wind would carry off, and what looked like a bear coat slung over her shoulders. "I guess this is before she left Leadville for Denver."

"That's right before we parted," Kenzie said. "She was so excited."

Olivia scrolled to the next picture. "Who's this man?" She enlarged the picture for a better look. "I've seen him before."

"Someone who resembles him. Is that what you mean?' Kenzie asked.

Olivia tapped his face. "No, him. You're going to think this is strange, but I saw him outside the old Wells Fargo Building in Denver. Amber has an option…" Olivia sighed. "*Had* an option to buy. It's expired now. But I met the owner there to negotiate the terms. The vision was only a flash, but I know it was him."

"What do ye mean, it was only a flash?" Elliott asked.

"I see someone, a flashbulb goes off, and an image is preserved in my brain. Like a snapshot. I saw Connor in the lobby of the Brown Palace Hotel years ago, long before I met him there."

Elliott looked at her curiously, his head tipped to the side. "How often does this happened to ye?"

"Sometimes daily. Sometimes I'll go weeks without having one." She tapped the screen again. "So who is he?"

"Pinkerton Agent Daniel Grant," Elliott said.

Olivia shot JL a look. "That's who you and Connor were talking about." Then she swung her gaze to Elliott. "JL said you were afraid Amber would stay in the past with him. She wouldn't do that."

Elliott's brow, etched with worry, smoothed out and his concern visibly slipped away. "It always nags at me when brooches carry family members to the past. I worry they won't come home."

"What was Daniel wearing in the vision?" David asked.

Olivia thought a minute. "A long black duster, black suit over a white shirt, and a gray vest. He was crushing a piece of paper in his hand. I was about ten feet from him. He wasn't happy."

"Besides the Wells Fargo Building, what else did ye see?" David asked.

"Horses, wagons. That's all I remember." She continued staring at the picture. Then she put down the phone and picked up her wine glass. Something didn't feel right, and she couldn't put her thumb on it.

Kenzie sat on a barstool next to her. "Your visions are of people you'll meet in the future. Right? Daniel doesn't live in the twenty-first century. How could you have a vision of him if it's impossible to meet him?"

The door to the back porch swung open and Connor entered the kitchen carrying a tray of grilled steaks. "Who's hungry?"

Olivia's eyes locked onto his and for the briefest of moments she forgot everything but the feel of his lips against hers. Then sadly, the moment passed, and all she remembered were the lies. She looked away, ignoring him, and picked up the phone again.

Kenzie broke the awkward silence, holding up two freeze-dried packages: grilled red potatoes and oven-roasted asparagus. "If I understand this process correctly, all I have to do is add hot water and we'll have gourmet dishes." She grimaced at one package and then other. "I'm going in with an open mind, but I can't imagine these tasting like anything other than cardboard."

"You'll be pleasantly surprised," Connor said.

Kenzie's eyebrow arched. "So you've tasted one of these?"

"Salmon, fruit, eggs, bacon. Each one was delicious," Connor said, glancing at Olivia.

"Let's eat in the dining room," Olivia said. "I'll set the table." She scooted off the stool and escaped from the room. As soon as dinner was over, she'd see them all to the heliport and then she'd never have to lay eyes on any of them again.

She gave a white damask tablecloth a snapping shake and was spreading it over the table when Connor walked in. One corner was flipped up and he smoothed it down.

"Can we talk?"

"We don't have anything to say to each other." She grabbed a handful of silverware from a drawer in the credenza and with her hands shaking, slowly set the table.

"Have you forgotten you lied to me about Amber's disappearances?" Connor asked.

Olivia moved from place setting to place setting without looking up at him. "If you'd told me the truth, I wouldn't have had to cover for Amber."

"So it's okay if you lie to protect someone, but no one can do that for you?"

She stiffened, folded her arms, and held her elbows, struggling to keep herself together. Finally, she looked up at him. "I agonized for days over my sister and you knew she was safe, but you didn't tell me. I can't get over that."

"The secret wasn't mine to tell."

"How did you think I would feel? Or did you even bother to think?" She swung open the china cabinet doors and decided to use her great-grandmother's china and crystal instead of her mother's. Her hands shook so badly that the plates rattled against each other. Before she broke one, she set them down on the corner of the table.

"I'm leaving in a couple of hours to go back for Amber and Rick." Connor picked up the plates and set one down at each place setting. He then collected matching salad bowls from the cabinet and placed them around the table, too. When he finished with the plates and bowls, he found napkins in a partially open drawer of the credenza. While he disbursed the napkins, she set crystal glasses on the corner of the table, staggering them to make room for six. If he wanted to place the glasses, too, she'd let him. She didn't trust herself to hold them.

When he finished with the glasses, he stood on the other side of the table and held onto the back of a chair. In a voice filled with regret but carrying an undercurrent of hope, he said, "I'd like you to go with us."

"Go where? On some fantasy adventure? No thank you."

He released his grip on the chair and moved toward the door. She took a step to follow him, because she wasn't through talking, but her shoe caught on the chair leg and jolted the table, rattling the glassware.

Connor froze.

Olivia froze, so did her breath. When nothing crashed to the floor, her breath seeped out. "Do you think if I go that I'll forgive you?"

His gaze switched from the table to her. "Tick through this situation, Olivia, and you'll see it has little to do with me. I can almost bet some jerk lied to you and hurt you deeply. So now all lies are unforgivable, even those meant to protect you.

"Here's the deal," he continued. "If you don't go with us there will always be a barrier between you and Amber that can never be breached. What she'll remember as a life-changing experience, you'll remember as one full of lies. She'll be alone with her excitement, and you'll be stuck in your anger. Is that what you want?" In an instant his eyes flickered and changed from dark and intimate to dark and somber. "It's not what I want for you."

"You're dead wrong. I can enjoy Amber's adventures without experiencing them firsthand. I've done that all my life."

"See, that's part of the problem. Your sister's not afraid to fully live, to take risks, to climb to the top of the rock."

"I've taken plenty of risks in my life. I gave up a high six-figure income to sell real estate."

"That wasn't much of a risk. You had a safety net, Olivia. You could have gone back to the law firm."

He gazed over her shoulder, and she knew exactly what caught his eye. Hanging on the wall behind her was a picture of twelve-year-old Amber standing on her rock with her arms outstretched and Olivia on the ground gazing up at her. If he moved closer to the photograph, he'd be able to see Band-Aids on Amber's knees and elbows. If he moved even closer, he could see Olivia's spotless shorts and matching top.

His gaze drew back to her. "Someday the risk of remaining where you are will be scarier than taking a risk without a net."

"Dinner's ready," Kenzie called from the kitchen. "Grab your plates from the dining room and let's eat."

"I'm done here. You have an hour to decide. What's it going to be?" Defeat and loss were thinly veiled in Connor's eyes. She tried to straighten her spine but failed, and instead, she dropped into the closest chair. He nodded, almost like making a final bow, and left the room. Footsteps retreated down the hallway until they were washed out by the opening and closing of the porch door.

Her anger and fear had mixed a powerful cocktail that flowed through her bloodstream and was making her physically sick. She gripped her belly. *What should I do, Granny?*

Forgiveness isn't easy, Olivia. It often feels more painful than the hurt. But if you want to find peace, you must forgive. It won't change what happened in the past, but it will change the future.

Olivia picked up a dinner plate and held it against her breasts, feeling as fragile as the china and wanting desperately to be as resilient as Tupperware.

30

1878 Colorado—Daniel

SUNLIGHT GLINTED OFF the turbulent water of Bear Creek on the far side of the railroad tracks. The ageless sound of raging water, cold and swirling, as it tumbled over rocks and tangled debris moved Daniel to a rare state of peace. He tipped his head back against the leather stagecoach seat, feeling the strength of the fall sun upon his face. The cantering horses pulled the swaying stagecoach through the valley and into the small foothills toward the settlement of Morrison.

It was from there they would catch the train to Denver. It had been his intention to do further investigation at the Pinkerton Agency into the identities of Amber, Kenzie and David McBain, and Rick O'Grady. Now he wouldn't have time. While in Leadville, though, he'd sent inquiries to the office in Chicago, which held the country's largest criminal database and collection of mug shots, inquiring of the *cousins* but nothing was found. Nor was a record found of Amber having attended Smith College, much less graduating from Union College of Law in Chicago. She could have used a *nom de plume*. But why?

It was as if they'd all materialized out of a fog.

Amber and Kenzie McBain, especially, were enigmas to him. Although neither woman had mentioned being part of the vanguard of the national reform movement, they were both highly educated and progressive in their views and opinions on women's rights, particularly their right to vote, so he assumed they were. While both were well-read, he found the lapses in their knowledge surprising. It was as if they'd slept through entire decades and had only been given summaries of the years' events. If it had been only Kenzie or only Amber who had never heard of Joseph Glidden, who had patented barbed wire and was one of the richest men in America, it wouldn't have seemed so unusual, but for both, it appeared highly suspect.

And so was the powerful attachment he had developed to Amber. No amount of deliberating could erase what had become an illogical passion. Her smile had snatched his heart in an instant.

The stage lurched, and the sudden jolt brought him back to the confines of the stagecoach where Noah—with Ripley's head in his lap—and Rick slept quietly on the rear-facing leather seat. Amber was also asleep, her head resting on Daniel's shoulder. Her head had cushioned his cheek while he'd dozed off and on, and the rose scent of the soap she'd used in her hair had filled his nostrils and tantalized his imagination, locking him in his own dreamscape.

A stupor seemed to surround him now, as if he'd taken a few stiff drinks.

She opened her hazel eyes and smiled up at him, cheeks faintly flushed with pink. "Good morning, or is it afternoon?" Her languid smile, fresh from sleep, had him imagining her head on a pillow next to his.

"Mid-afternoon," he said.

While the clacking stage rocked back and forth, a metronome in motion, she rolled her shoulders and stretched. "Thank you for being my pillow. Your arm must be numb by now."

His arm had gone numb some time ago, but he hadn't wanted her to move. "Aye, but I didn't want to wake ye."

She poured water from a canteen onto a handkerchief and washed sleep from her eyes. "You should have. I would have gone right back to sleep. I didn't get much sleep at the Meyer Ranch stopover."

After setting the handkerchief aside to dry, she separated the sections of her long golden-brown braid and ran her fingers from her scalp to the slightly curled ends. It had been five years since he'd watched a woman perform her morning ablutions, and he didn't realize how much he'd missed those special moments. Amber washed her face and dressed her hair unabashedly, as if she always performed for an audience of one. An unaccustomed shot of jealousy sprang from his heart, stinging like nettles.

He was astute enough to recognize the unusual familiarity she had with Rick, but after watching them interact during late-night dinners and while performing on stage, Daniel was convinced their relationship wasn't of a romantic nature. There was more expectation between them than sweet anticipation. But what cinched it for him was that Kenzie had the same familiarity with him. Yet she and her husband cared deeply for each other. Or so the moans and squeaky bedsprings coming from their bedroom late at night led him to believe.

Amber weaved her hair again, and he found the dance of her deft fingers highly erotic. He wanted to quiet her hands and do the task himself. But if he ever twirled his fingers around a handful of her un-brushed, glossy hair and kissed her full on the mouth with the passion he'd tamped down for years, he wouldn't re-braid her hair. Instead, he'd cast the unwoven, rose-scented strands about her shoulders, letting them drift over her breasts, down her belly...

She paused, three sections of her hair wrapping her fingers. "Are we almost to Morrison?" She regarded him with a contemplative eye as if reading his mind.

He guiltily cleared his throat. "Almost."

She continued braiding. "What time does the train leave for Denver?"

"We shouldn't have to wait long." Daniel turned in his seat and studied her. He'd been waiting for the right moment to tell her about his new assignment. He should do it now before Noah woke up. In a quiet voice he said, "The agency has ordered me to Cañon City on railroad business. I need to leave Denver tomorrow."

She made a surprise O with her mouth, then her expression

quickly changed to one of obvious disappointment. "How long will you be gone?"

He volleyed back a similar expression. "I'm afraid a few weeks." His tone merely confirmed his dismay.

Her eyes went wide for a moment, emphasizing the dark circles beneath her eyelashes. Then they narrowed in calculation. "That means I won't see you again after today. I'll only be in Denver a couple of weeks. I was hoping… Oh well…" She finished her braid, rolled, and pinned it at her nape.

He let his breath out slowly, unsure of his intentions. He didn't want her to leave, but if he asked her to stay, what could he offer her? He had a good salary, but he didn't have a home to give her. And what about Noah? His son needed a mother. He wanted a wife.

He wanted her.

"Ye'd mentioned that ye might be going to Cañon City. Is that a possibility now?" His heart was thumping faster, as though he'd run flat-out for miles. He had to find a way to see her again without pledging himself to her, which he wasn't ready to do.

"I'd like to go, but Rick only signed up for two weeks and he promised he'd take me home."

"Why Cañon City?" Rick asked, yawning.

"I didn't know you were awake," she said. "Daniel has to leave shortly after we arrive in Denver for a lengthy assignment there. If we're only staying two weeks, we won't see him again after today."

"What's going on there?" Rick asked.

"A railroad war." She paused and chewed her bottom lip. Then she continued, "According to the newspapers, the United States Circuit Court for the District of Colorado found in favor of the Atchison, Topeka and Santa Fe Railroad to lay tracks through the Royal Gorge. The Court said the Denver & Rio Grande could use Santa Fe's line through the gorge where it was too narrow to build their own. But the Rio Grande believes it has a prior right to the gorge, so it appealed the Circuit Court's decision to the Supreme Court."

"Why can't they lay their own track? Two railroads occupy the same valley all the time," Rick observed.

"Because west of Cañon City is a formidable ten-mile-long canyon that in some places is over a thousand feet deep with sheer granite walls plunging into the tumbling Arkansas River. At its narrowest point, the canyon is only thirty feet wide. You can't get two tracks through there, and to get even one track will be an engineering feat."

"I still don't understand why the Rio Grande is fighting if they have a right to use the track."

"Money," Amber said. "Both railroads want the right-of-way through the gorge to the rich mining fields in Leadville. The Rio Grande believes they have a previous right. Santa Fe has the opinion of the District Court, claiming its right. If you control the track, you control ingress and egress to Leadville. How many Rio Grande trains will get through if Santa Fe controls the switches?"

"Why don't they just build a bridge?"

"That's an engineering feat, too. But it's going in the wrong direction. You don't want to go across. You want to go through."

"Oh," he said thoughtfully. "So…" He shrugged. "What's the solution?"

"I want to hear this, too," Daniel said.

The coach pitched forward. Daniel grabbed her arm to keep her from sliding off the seat. Then the coach jerked back sharply. The driver whistled and snapped his whip.

She broke into a relieved smile. "Thanks for catching me. I would have landed on the floor."

"What's the solution?" Rick asked again.

"Simple. Wait for the Supreme Court's decision," she said.

"That could be months," Daniel said.

"In my opinion," she said, "the lower court erred in not recognizing that an 1872 Act of Congress granted the Rio Grande the right to use the entire fifty-mile stretch. The Rio Grande's bondholders and board of directors need to sit tight and wait on the Court."

"And while they're waiting on the Court," Daniel picked up her line of thought saying, "Santa Fe has crews grading for a rail line west of Cañon City at the mouth of the gorge. A couple months ago, Rio Grande's graders and track-laying crews tried to leap-frog ahead of Santa Fe. That's when crews started sabotaging the other company's tracks, blocking encroachments, and keeping crews bottled up."

"Is that where the Pinkerton Agency is sending you?" Rick asked.

"We're needed elsewhere. Santa Fe hired the sheriff of Ford County, Kansas, to bring in recruits to take control of Rio Grande's stations from Denver to Cañon City."

"Wait a minute." Rick dropped his feet to the floor of the coach with a loud thud, and Noah flailed his arms, startled in his sleep. Ripley raised her head, looked around, then returned to her protective position. "The sheriff of Ford County, Kansas, is…" Rick's voice stammered into momentary silence. Then he continued, "…Bat Masterson. He'll bring his buddies Doc Holliday and Ben Thompson and probably other gunfighters like 'Dirty' Dave Rudabaugh and Josh Webb. You don't want to mess with those guys."

Amber's eyes traveled to some indeterminate spot above Rick's head and grew distant, as if she were looking into the past, or maybe even into the future. Daniel followed her gaze to see where she was looking. Other than the leather upholstery and leather walls and ceiling, there was nothing notable about the interior that would require such a look of concentration.

"What do ye see?" he asked. Then followed the question with a thin smile and a faint unease. "I've watched ye gaze off before and wondered what ye see that no one else can."

"I'm sorry. I know it's distracting. Bad habit. When I was a kid, I'd find pieces of bones and would have to imagine what the missing pieces looked like. In answer to your question, I was thinking about Rick meeting Bat Masterson and going all fanboy on me."

A wry smile teased the corners of her lips. She knew he didn't understand the connotation and she had no intention of disabusing him of whatever untoward notion he arrived at on his own. He fell into a silent study of her. She enjoyed being provocative. And quite frankly, he enjoyed the stimulating mental challenge she sparked. She was like an onion. Removing each layer just exposed another one.

"That's not beyond the realm of possibility." Rick rested his forearms on his thighs and cracked his knuckles.

Daniel had no idea what a fanboy was, but if Rick and Amber were implying some unnatural act between two men—between Rick and Bat Masterson—then Daniel was turning a deaf ear and a blind eye to the realm of possibility. Both Amber and Rick seemed to have vast knowledge on a variety of topics, but on this matter, he couldn't imagine any woman even knowing such unnatural acts took place.

Even Amber.

He turned his mind back to the gorge, back to a topic that could politely be discussed in mixed company. But he didn't like where his mind was going with that either. He'd had numerous conversations with other agents and railroad men about the situation in the gorge, but none were as knowledgeable of the legal maneuverings as Amber.

At first blush, it appeared to him that Amber had confidential information that could only be gleaned from the inside. But which side. Was she a spy? And if so, who was she working for? She wasn't with the Pinkerton Agency or he would know.

He thought back to her bar examination in front of Judge Adams. Her legal knowledge was extraordinary. Yes, there were brilliant legal minds in the country, but they were encased in the brains of men educated at Oxford and Cambridge in England and Harvard, Yale, Princeton in America.

A brilliant female legal mind supposedly educated at Smith College and Union College of Law in Chicago, if in fact she attended classes there, was unimaginable. Even for a suffragette.

"What's your job there?" Amber asked in an apparent attempt to change the subject.

His assignment would be obvious to anyone familiar with the situation in the gorge and around Cañon City, so telling her wouldn't divulge confidential information. "To retake control of Rio Grande's stations. Santa Fe is holding a key defensive position at Rio Grande's roundhouse in Pueblo." That was the first objective. He wouldn't mention the second, which was to establish a fort in the gorge and hold that position while waiting on the Court's ruling.

"Masterson's not a U.S. Marshal and has no authority to defend property in Colorado," Rick said, cracking his knuckles again. "Someone must be trying to use influence to obtain an appointment for him. But it won't work," he added.

"How do ye know? Do ye have a crystal ball?" Daniel asked.

A look of surprise appeared on Rick's face. Quickly concealed. "Ah..." he shot a glance at Amber.

"He's just guessing. He has a bromance with all Western heroes," she said.

"A what?" This time Daniel couldn't restrain his curiosity. He was stunned, his mind almost refusing to accept this fresh revelation. Rick's attraction wasn't limited to Masterson but extended to all Western heroes, whoever they were. No wonder David wasn't threatened by his wife's familiarity with Rick. But if he wasn't interested in women, then why did he entertain so many in Leadville? Once again Daniel turned his mind back to the gorge, back to the topic that could politely be discussed.

"The Rio Grande is losing money. That's not news to anyone. The management wants a solution that doesn't bankrupt the railroad or get people killed. Ye're well versed in the goings-on. What do ye suggest?"

"The same thing I said earlier," she said. "The District Court erred, and the bondholders and the board of directors need to wait on the Supreme Court. If they think leasing its track to Santa Fe will solve their problem, they're mistaken, and that decision will come back to bite them in the...pocketbook."

"When ye meet Noah's grandfather, maybe ye can persuade him to sit tight. He's a bondholder."

"I don't know that I'll meet him, but if I do—"

"I hope ye do, because I have a favor to ask."

"Sure. What is it?"

He looked closely at Noah to be sure he was still asleep. Satisfied that he was, Daniel said, "I don't trust him. That's the reason I've rarely brought Noah back to Denver. When I agreed to the visit, I didn't know I'd be called away. Now, I'm afraid of what he might do while I'm gone."

She raised her eyebrows. "Like what?"

"He has business interests in other parts of the country, and he travels extensively. I'm concerned that while I'm away on assignment, he'll leave town and Noah will be left in the care of the housekeeper."

"He would do that?" she asked.

"He always puts his interests above others, and aye, he would. That's why I haven't brought Noah to see him for a while."

"I'll do what I can, but unless Noah contacts me, I won't know what's going on."

"That's why I'd like ye to stay at the Robinson residence."

She shook her head. "No. I can't impose on a man I don't know."

"Ye don't know the Hughes family either."

"That's different. They're—" A subtle shadow crossed her face, and she looked away, as if searching for words to complete her thought. "They're not total strangers," she continued. "I know Mr. and Mrs. Hughes in Leadville, but I don't know Mr. Robinson at all."

"Ye know Noah and ye know me. Besides, it will please Noah. He doesn't know his grandfather well, and he'll feel more comfortable if ye and Rick are with him, especially if his grandfather up and leaves town. He'll be frightened."

"You're using your son to get what you want. That's not right."

He wanted to be sure she heard his answer over the creaks of the coach, the squeaks of horse tracings, and the clatter of hooves, so he leaned closer. "I'll use whatever, whoever I can to protect my son."

"We've already confirmed our stay with Mr. and Mrs. Hughes,

and Noah's grandfather hasn't invited us."

"True, but I'll send Mr. Robinson a telegram from the Morrison train station and inform him that I'm traveling with acquaintances in need of accommodations in Denver. He has a mansion on the corner of 19th Avenue and Sherman Street and there's room for additional guests."

"Maybe." Her voice was muffled, lower than a whisper, more like a vibration that he sensed rather than heard.

"Will ye do it for the lad?" Daniel asked in the same whispery tone.

The teams' rhythmic canter slowed, and the sudden drag of a brake indicated the stage was coming to a stop. The snort of the horses and jingle of the traces punctuated the sudden silence. There was a dip and rise from the driver's box as he jumped to the ground. Moments later, the door swung open… "Welcome to Morrison."

Daniel and Amber seemed poised on either side of bank scales nearly equal in weight, tipping slightly one way, then the other.

Amber bit her lip and then finally said, "I'll do it for Noah. Send the telegram."

31

The Present, Kelly Ranch, Colorado—Olivia

THE DINING ROOM at the Kelly Ranch sparkled under the glow of the chandelier and candelabras, and the china, crystal, and silverware glistened on a tablecloth of pristine white. But the conversation was somewhat subdued. Elliott sat at the head of the table with Connor and David on either side of him. Olivia sat at the opposite end with JL and Kenzie on either side of her, giving the impression of opposing generals and their advisors.

The McBains did most of the talking, reliving their adventures in Leadville. The couple struck Olivia as logical and intelligent. But so did some of the crazies who claimed they were abducted by space aliens. Unlike abductees, the McBains had supposedly unaltered pictures and a video of Amber. Who was Olivia supposed to believe? These intelligent people, or her rational mind, which screamed time travel was impossible.

There was, however, one disturbing thought she couldn't dispel no matter how she twisted, stretched, or tried to cover it up. She'd seen Daniel Grant before. And in her mental picture of him, he wore nineteenth-century clothing, and horses and carriages appeared in the background. If that picture existed in her mind, it meant she would see him there one day. To get through dinner, she shelved the sobering thought.

Kenzie and Olivia washed the dishes while the guys disappeared to talk logistics. Whatever that meant. JL's indigestion earned her an excuse from KP duty and within minutes she was asleep on the small sofa in front of the large kitchen window.

"She's the cutest pregnant woman I've ever seen," Olivia said. "She moves like a ballerina but talks like a cop."

"I heard that," JL groaned.

"I thought you were asleep," Kenzie said.

"With all that pot rattling, are you kidding? But thanks for the compliment. I feel fat and ugly most of the time."

"Trust me," Olivia said. "There isn't an ounce of fat on you. You're fit and beautiful."

JL rolled over and covered her head with a pillow. "Just remember, if Elliott ever offers his trainer to loosen you up, tell him no thanks."

Kenzie chuckled. "She's right, although none of us would be in the shape we're in, if not for Ted and his team. We all complain but rarely miss a session."

"That's because nobody wants to miss their post-workout massage from Anne's healing hands," JL said.

Kenzie folded the towel she'd used to dry the crystal, rotating her neck side to side. "That's true, too, and boy could I use a massage right now. The bed at Mrs. Garland's boardinghouse didn't have much support."

"I bet it had squeaky springs, though," JL said with a howl. "How much do you want to bet you'll end up pregnant again? Time travel messes with your cycle. Just ask Kit and Charlotte."

"The bed did have squeaky springs and Amber teased me about it."

JL tossed the pillow aside and sat up. "Say it ain't so. You said absolutely no more babies and now you're trying to get pregnant. Are you crazy?"

"I didn't say I was trying to get pregnant."

"You might not have come right out with it, but you certainly insinuated it. And you can't be pregnant for Amy's wedding. I had to beg her to wait until I had my baby. And now you'll be pregnant and miss all the girl fun."

"I'm not in Amy's wedding party, so it doesn't matter if I'm pregnant."

JL snorted then curled back into a ball and covered her head again with the pillow. "In a few weeks, David's going to be sick every morning."

"You mean Kenzie?" Olivia asked.

JL peeked out from under the pillow. "Kenzie doesn't get morning sickness. David does. Why he wants more kids is beyond me."

"How many do you have?" Olivia asked Kenzie.

"Five-year-old twin boys and a two-year-old daughter."

Olivia topped off their wine glasses and disposed of the wine bottle. "That's a handful."

"It is, but I have lots of help," Kenzie said. "The family complains about the twins, but there isn't a soul who wouldn't drop everything to help out, if needed."

"I guess with all that help you can vanish for a few days."

Kenzie sat on the barstool and sipped her wine. "I haven't seen them in days, but for them, they saw me this morning. After forty-eight hours, if the twins haven't seen one of us, they'll show up at the security center and demand to see McBain. It cracks the staff up. They play along, telling the boys that David and I are on a secret mission, that the twins don't have security clearance to know what we're doing, and that they'll have to come back when they turn six."

"And they're okay with that?" Olivia asked.

Kenzie laughed. "They think it's cool."

"So what happens when they turn six?"

"We haven't thought that far ahead. But now it's become such a big deal that we'll have to come up with something creative. They're already counting the days until they can go through the fog again."

Olivia put soap in the dishwasher and pushed the start button. "What's the fog?"

"Stinky is what it is," JL said. "Here's the deal. You open a brooch, say the magic words, and a fog that smells like peat covers you up and whisks you away on a roller-coaster ride through space."

Olivia shivered as she had a flashback to the moment she'd entered the cabin and was hit with that earthy scent. She had an acute sense of smell and Connor had remarked on the lingering scent as well. Her stomach dropped to her feet and an undercurrent seemed to sweep her away. There were now two signs: the mental picture of Daniel and the scent of peat. One more, and she wouldn't be able to deny the truth of what they were telling her.

"Is it weird? The fog, I mean?" Olivia's tone was light but hesitant. "It must not be scary, if the boys want to go again."

"All the kids have gone back and forth, but all they really remember is the fog. Because of their ages, they don't understand that they traveled to a different time. The older kids do, but the little ones only remember that they went on an adventure."

"The trip isn't scary," Kenzie said. "But arriving unprepared is insane. Arriving in the middle of a war is hell."

"It must have been horrible for you and Amber," Olivia said.

"From what Amber said, I don't think she was scared. She knew she wasn't in danger, and she was familiar with where she was and the city's history. Compared to Kit, Charlotte, Amy, and me, Amber's adventure has been rather tame. That's what concerns me."

Olivia sat down next to Kenzie. "What does?"

Kenzie leaned back in the swivel barstool and crossed her arms. "The brooches put you in situations that challenge you and often put you at risk."

"But you said Amber wasn't in danger," Olivia said, "and if she's just going to dig fossils around the Morrison Formation, I don't see any danger in that."

"Amber's adventure could be different," JL said. "Maybe it'll be smooth sailing for her, but I doubt it."

Kenzie pointed her thumb over her shoulder toward JL. "Don't pay attention to her. She's a glass half-empty kind of person."

JL huffed out an unladylike noise. "You try working on the streets of New York City. The litmus test for your worldview will be half-empty, too, missy."

Olivia's cell phone pinged with a text message. One of her

agents got a contract on a Kelly Agency listing for a multi-million-dollar mansion in Denver. She sent a congratulatory text then scanned her calendar. The next three days were clear. She'd left them open to spend time with her parents, who were expected home from their travels abroad. She had looked forward to their return. Not anymore. How could she possibly explain Amber's absence?

Olivia stepped over to the bar and grabbed a bottle of the pinot noir, glancing into the great room as she closed the door to the wine fridge. David and Elliott were asleep at opposite ends of the sofa. Connor was asleep in the easy chair, his feet propped up on the ottoman, hands resting on his flat abdomen, long lashes casting half-moon shadows on his windburned cheeks. His full lips slightly parted as he breathed softly in deep sleep.

So that's how the men discussed logistics.

Connor could sleep there all night. Her heart was too close to the edge of the cliff on Heartbreak Ridge than she cared to admit. And right now, she didn't want to even hear his voice. But that wasn't what her body wanted. It wanted to relive every moment from the first kiss in the car to the interruption phone call. Her finger traced the outline of her bottom lip. Memories could be hell.

She opened the bottle of wine and refilled her glass. Kenzie covered hers with her hand. "No more for me. I need to at least be able to follow David's instructions when we land in Denver. Another glass and I would be a hindrance in an emergency."

"How long do you think you'll be gone this time?" Olivia asked.

"We'll be back tonight, but I don't know how long we'll be in the past. A day, a week, a month. If I had to guess, I'd say a day or two. Why?"

"Just wondering. Where will you stay?"

"Amber has an invitation to stay at the home of Adam and Christine Hughes, your ancestors. I don't know if we'll stay with her—"

"What?" Olivia asked. "She's going to stay in my house?"

"Your house?" Kenzie asked. "I don't know where you live, or where Adam Hughes lived when he was alive."

"I do," Olivia said. "It's 5431 California Street in Curtis Park. A red brick, two-story, side-bay, Italianate-style home, featuring a transom window over the front door. It's one of twenty-five residences built in the 1870s still standing today."

She dropped to the barstool and put her head in her hands. "I can't believe this. The house came on the market three months ago, and I snapped it up on day one. A few days ago, I found a contractor to restore it to its original condition. I've searched the historical society, library, and old newspapers looking for pictures. And Amber's going to stay there? You've got to be kidding me."

The picture, the smell of peat, her house. One, two, three.

David entered the kitchen and strode toward them, yawning. "*Kemosabe*, we need to get ready to leave."

"What about horses? Aren't we taking any this time?" she asked.

"We didn't need them in Leadville. If we need horses in Denver, we'll rent them from a livery."

"What if we're… I don't know. Stuck on the trail somewhere?"

"That's not likely to happen unless Amber is stuck there, too."

Kenzie nodded, saying nothing for a moment, frowning a little so that a line formed between her ruddy brows. She was thinking hard and blinking harder. "If the stagecoach crashed and they're stuck, we'll need a rescue litter, SAR Pak, ropes, pulleys, rigging, cold-weather gear."

"It's all on the plane."

"Why didn't you tell me?"

"Ye asked if I'd packed the gear and I said yes. Look, we're going back to check on Amber and Rick. If everything's copacetic, we'll hop back into the fog and come home."

"Copacetic and *kemosabe*. Where'd you come up with those?"

"I just talked to the boys."

"Aha. So they learned two new words today."

"I won't repeat the Gaelic cuss words."

"Would you please explain to their Gaelic instructor that although the Scots have a rich and vivid language, I don't want my children cussing, especially in a language I don't understand. And that goes for their French instructor, too."

"I've spoken to her, and she assured—"

Olivia formed a T with her hands. "Time out. Can we talk about Amber? If I understand this, you're going into the fog tonight to find her. If she's in Morrison fossil hunting, then you'll come right back."

"No, we're staying until she finishes her work," David said.

"Then how long will you be gone?"

"Regardless of how long we stay in the past, ye'll see us soon after we leave," he said.

"That doesn't make any sense." Olivia's mind veered off the road in a direction she didn't want it to go, and it created a staccato pounding of her heart. She lifted her wine glass, drained it, then set it down so hard it cracked on the granite countertop.

"I'm going too," she blurted out.

"Are ye sure?" David asked.

She tossed the broken glass into the recycle bin. "I don't want to think about my decision. I just want to go." She blew out several hard breaths, as if starting the next rep of barbell curls. "What do I need to take with me?"

"That's the wrong question," David said. "Ye should ask, 'What do I need to do before I go?' Ye and Connor have to put yer differences aside. Adventures are dangerous enough without having team members so angry they can't look at each other. It puts us all at risk."

A prick of foolish tears forced Olivia to close her eyes, holding them back so nobody would see them fall. But even as her lashes drifted shut, she saw David watching her. Could she forgive Connor? If the answer was yes, then she had to do it now. Restoring the lost trust wouldn't be easy, but she could let go of the anger.

She patted her chest to settle her heart. "I can do that."

Kenzie broke into a relieved smile. "Then grab your hat and boots and you'll be ready. David has money. If there's anything we need, we'll buy it there. If you have a Swiss army knife, I'd pack that, but otherwise—"

"We should take the helicopter over to the new ranch," Elliott said, sauntering into the kitchen. He headed straight to the coffee pot, selected a pod, and placed it in the coffee machine.

"If we're only going for a few minutes, why not leave from here?" Kenzie said. "JL's asleep. We could be back and celebrating by the time she wakes up."

The aroma of dark roast coffee filled the room. "I don't mind staying here so long as Olivia's parents don't show up and have us arrested." Elliott spooned in sugar and stirred the dark brew.

"They'll be in London for the next few days. You'll have the house to yourself. The farm manager knows I have company. He won't bother you. But if anybody shows up, tell them I'm in the bathtub. It's a family joke. I could spend hours in there soaking and reading."

"Is Connor still asleep?" David asked.

"He went to the helicopter," Elliott said.

David crossed the kitchen to the coffee maker while placing a call on his cell phone. "Olivia's going. We'll leave from here." He put in a pod and pressed start. Then turned to those standing around the kitchen and said, "Connor's bringing up our gear. I want to take a shower, then we'll leave."

Olivia waved her hand in the direction of the staircase. "There are six showers upstairs. Take your pick."

David winked at Kenzie. "Do ye want to freshen up before we leave?"

She pushed off the barstool. "*Kemosabe*, I thought you'd never ask."

Connor entered the kitchen carrying saddlebags over both shoulders and handed them to David. "I don't suppose you brought me a change of clothes and a dopp kit."

"Sorry, buddy. I figured ye had what ye needed."

"Take whatever you want from the bathroom," Olivia said. "There should be shave bags in the cabinet to carry toiletries. If you need another pair of jeans or jacket…"

"I'll take your dad's hat and jacket, if you don't think he'd mind."

"Help yourself," she said.

Kenzie, David, and Connor went upstairs, leaving Olivia and Elliott at the kitchen counter.

His eyebrows drew together in a frown and he narrowed his eyes at her. "I have a piece of advice for ye, lass."

She glared, unsure if she wanted any advice from him. If he gave her some, would she even take the time to consider it?

"Ye're going back to a time when women had few rights. It's not at all what ye're used to. Ye'll need protection, and the lad will protect ye whether ye want it or not. But it'll go easier on ye both if ye put yer anger aside."

"I can put my anger aside, Elliott," she said testily. "It's the broken trust that can't be put back together so easily." She was going to tell him she couldn't put her broken heart back together, either, but her voice quavered, and she stopped.

"Then that's my second piece of advice. Ye don't have to trust him with yer heart, but ye absolutely must trust him with yer life." Elliott's pupils were so dark they were indistinguishable from the irises, and the spark glinting in those chocolate pools was anything but sympathetic. She didn't want his sympathy anyway. Matter of fact, she didn't want anything from him, including his advice.

Needing something to do, she stepped over to the coffee machine and made a cup for herself and slowly sipped the brew while reading flyers her mother had posted on the refrigerator door.

A few minutes later, Connor reentered the kitchen wearing his clean clothes. He walked across the wooden floor, his footsteps echoing loud in the room. He went straight to the wet bar and grabbed a bottle of water. "What have you heard from Meredith?" he asked Elliott.

"She said Pops had an early dinner and retired for the evening. Shane and Pete boarded the horses overnight and have checked into the hotel. Kit and Cullen were having cocktails with Kevin. They're waiting to hear when they can return to the winery."

The weight of Connor's stare was painful. She raised her chin to meet it with her own. "Elliott asked me to put my anger aside. I'm willing to do that, as long as you'll forget—"

"Forget what? Forget that I kissed you? That you kissed me back? Sorry." Connor's unwavering gaze bore down on her. "Can't do that. Can you?" He sounded calm, as if he were asking nothing more than if she wanted sugar in her coffee or ice in her tea.

She gave him a frosty smile, burying the expectancy that pulled against her ribs, the same feeling she'd had when he first lowered his head to kiss her. She pushed it away, snapping her shaky fingers. "Yes, just like that," she said, amazed at the steadiness in her voice.

"Don't worry, Olivia. You're safe from my advances." Doubt in his voice, though, shouted out, loud and clear. The fine lines at the corners of his eyes shivered like the surface of the water when a pebble is thrown into the stillness. Turning away from her, he took his drink and left the room.

Elliott's expression said he didn't approve of her treatment of Connor.

She gripped the edge of the counter to hold herself upright, and with a pang, she followed Connor with her eyes. He sank down into the chair where he'd slept earlier, his head resting on a cushion, eyes closed. If she thought she could temporarily blow off her intense feelings for him as easily as snuffing out a candle flame, she was wrong. She glanced at Elliott's profile, set in an obstinate frown.

Being a good hostess, she said, "I need to get ready to go. Do you need anything?"

"Aye, but ye're going to flat-out deny me. Go on. Do what ye need to do."

"Deny you? Do we all have to play by your rules? Your rules tilt the table, and everything slides to your side."

She'd meant her words as a barely concealed jibe. A little parry and thrust in response to him but it spilled out with more bitterness than she'd intended. She smoothed her eyebrows, attempting to smooth out the mess splattering all over her life. Care needed to be taken when dealing with men like Elliott. When pricked, they instinctively stung their tormentors.

"Okay. I give," she said. "What am I going to deny you?"

"I don't like dissension. It doesn't bode well for an adventure. If ye don't fix it now"—he tapped his chest with his thumb—"here, where the hurt sits like a lead ball, it'll only fester. Then when trouble comes ye'll put the weight of yer pain first, instead of what yer mind tells ye is the right thing to do."

She assembled a reasonable tone and said, "I've put my anger aside. What else do you want me to say? To do? What?"

The lines around Elliott's eyes made him look older than the streaks of silver in his brown hair would indicate. "If ye have to ask, then I'm not sure what the lad sees in ye." He took his cup and walked out on the porch, pulling his cell phone from his pocket.

Olivia put down her cup and raced up to her room to pack. She'd seen disappointment in clients' faces both when she practiced law and when they missed out on buying the home of their dreams, but she'd never seen disappointment in someone's eyes because she failed to do something.

She couldn't think about it now.

After rummaging through her closet, she found an old pair of jeans, two shirts, underwear, and socks. Amber would crack up. Olivia never traveled without multiple outfits for each day, along with matching shoes, jewelry, and handbags. Was this the beginning of a change? She shrugged. Time would tell.

An old tapestry bag hung from a hook at the back of the closet. She opened it and neatly packed her belongings. Before she went back downstairs, she took a few minutes to pen a letter to her parents to explain her absence. Then realizing how absurd the explanation sounded, she tore it up. How could she possibly explain what she didn't fully understand?

When David and Kenzie left the room next door laughing, Olivia rushed out to meet them, slinging her bag over her shoulder. "Love the outfit. I didn't know you were dressing in period-style clothing." She pressed her hands down her jeans-clad legs. "I'll look out of place. Is that a problem?"

"Keep your hat on and people will think you're a boy," Kenzie said.

David's mouth twisted with a suppressed smile. "Come on, Kenz. A man would have to be blind to mistake Olivia for a boy."

Kenzie tucked her hand into the crook of Olivia's arm. "Don't pay any attention to him. You'll be fine. I wore this home today. It really needs to be washed but I can get away with wearing it again. If we stay longer than a day, we'll have to go shopping."

They descended the stairs. "Do you have questions about what's going to happen?" Kenzie asked.

"No. Let's just do it." She grabbed her jacket and hat from the coat tree. She tried not to think about earlier when she and Connor had rushed into the house with only one thing on their minds—taking the shortest route to the shower. That seemed like a lifetime ago.

The hat Connor had worn was still on the floor from his missed toss. She picked it up, grabbed his jacket, and headed off to find him.

Elliott had returned to the kitchen, drinking from a full mug. Connor was leaning forward on the counter, elbows propping him up. The two men were having a quiet conversation. Connor's head shot up when Olivia entered the room, and the pain in his eyes sliced her heart into itty-bitty pieces.

"If ye're ready, Connor, let's get out of here," David said.

Olivia handed him the coat and hat. "Thanks," Connor said. "I'll be sure to have both professionally cleaned when I come back."

Elliott hugged Kenzie, David, and Connor, and gave Olivia a quick kiss on the cheek. "Be safe. Don't take any chances and come right back home. I'll be sitting here drinking coffee until I see ye again."

"Let's go outside," David said.

On the way to the lighted porch, Connor said to Elliott, "Give JL a hug."

"Give it to her yerself when ye get yer ass back here." Elliott remained in the kitchen, calmly sipping coffee and scrolling through messages on his phone as if Olivia and the others had just stepped outside to take in the evening air.

David, Kenzie, and Connor didn't seem as calm as Elliott. But she sensed no fear from them, only anxious anticipation. David and Kenzie linked arms, and he waved his other elbow at Olivia. "Come here, lass, and hook up."

She would have preferred to hook up between David and Kenzie, but they were laced tighter than a Kim Kardashian corset. Connor took her arm.

"What happens if the bond breaks?" she asked. "Will we be scattered like pick-up sticks?"

"That happened when we went back for Amy Spalding." Connor sounded impatient and uneasy. "We were scattered all around Central Park. But there was a purpose to the stone's madness, although frightening and frustrating for us."

"What happens if we get separated now?" Olivia asked.

"We were fine when we landed in Leadville," Kenzie said. "But sometimes the stones have something special in mind for a particular traveler. Don't get scared. Just go to the meeting place."

"Have ye picked a location?" David asked.

"Let's meet at Olivia's house," Kenzie asked.

"The address is 5431 California Street," Olivia said. "But how does the stone know where to go?"

"Focus on Amber. Picture her in your mind and say her name over and over," Kenzie said.

Connor softly hummed "Hotel California." For a moment she thought of nothing except the warmth of his breath against her cheek, and the comfort his presence had given her the last few days.

David opened a large diamond brooch and spoke in an odd language. As soon as he finished speaking, a fog formed at their feet and quickly enveloped their legs. She leaned into Connor as the fog reached her shoulders. Her heart pounded, adrenaline pulsed through her veins, and an intense pressure squeezed her chest. She watched David as she often watched flight attendants. If anything went wrong with their flight, he would know.

The fog slapped her face like an open hand and the scent of peat filled her nostrils, swept into her lungs. The fog was like being dunked in a whisky barrel filled with only the distinctive aroma. She licked her lips, hoping for just a drop to coat her mouth, dry from fear.

And I was thinking to myself/ 'This could be heaven or this could be hell'/ …/ Welcome to Hotel California.

"There's nothing to be afraid of." Connor hugged her arm to his side. "Relax and enjoy the ride."

On a dark desert highway, cool wind in my hair…

Conversation ceased as the porch floorboards creaked beneath her feet. A whirling motion jolted her right, left, and back again like Dorothy in the tornado. And that was the last she knew…

32

1878 Denver, Colorado—Amber

Upon their arrival at the Denver, South Park & Pacific Railroad station at Sixth and Walnut Streets, Daniel took the baggage and went in search of a carriage for hire while Noah took Ripley for a short walk. Amber and Rick stayed inside the station instead of waiting on the breezy uncovered wooden platform. To the near side of the platform stood a water tower and coal shed to fuel the trains, and to the far side a telegraph pole slung wire to a shack where the station master dozed on a stool.

A tide of people poured out of the station toward the street in one direction, new arrivals pushed through the front door in the other. The station's noise rang in Amber's ears—the sighs and clanks of a squat locomotive with a coffee-grinder stack coupled to a car and started up the grade toward town. Inside the depot, carts loaded with baggage rumbled this way and that across the sawdust-strewn plank floorboards.

"Did you know railroads have served Denver since the end of the Civil War, but no consolidated station existed until the completion of the Union Depot in 1881?" Amber asked.

Rick looked pointedly at her, shaking his head. "I didn't know that. And that piece of information certainly made my day."

She'd been around him long enough now to figure out when he was teasing, when he thought she was acting odd, and when he wanted to grab her in a bear hug and squeeze her last breath out of her. Right now, it was a combination of the first two. She'd thought, over time, he would drive her nuts, but just the opposite had occurred. He was attentive, funny as heck, and resourceful.

Occasionally, though, his black moods cancelled out the funny ones, and his temperament turned toward the dark side at least once a day, with no rhyme or reason to what set him off. He didn't talk about the war, but she knew when the darkness came, he'd slipped into a quagmire of despair. The first few times, she'd snapped back at him, but that only played into some perverse game, so now when his mood flipped, she sang spicy sea shanties. The upbeat energy of the music flipped his brain back to normal and by the second verse, his eyes would be bright again. She couldn't imagine what he'd been through, or what Trey had been through before his life ended.

"I'm glad it made your day. The only reason I know stuff like that is because Olivia is a Denver history aficionado. Did I tell you that already?"

He grinned around an unlit black cigar clenched between his teeth. "If you did, I must not have been listening."

"I don't believe it. You always pay attention, especially when you pretend to be asleep."

He made a face as if he'd heard wrong. "You knew I was awake in the stagecoach? God, I thought I was better than that."

She laughed. "I didn't know. You had me fooled."

"I was just watching out for you, sweetheart. I didn't want Daniel to take advantage of you while you were sleeping. You never know about those Scotsmen."

"Thank you for watching out for me."

"It's my job." He looked at her, one eyebrow slightly raised. "Now, what were you saying about your sister being a Denver history buff?"

"So now you want to hear? Well, every time a client asks a question about Denver that Olivia can't answer, she researches the topic until she drives the family crazy with a bunch of unrelated tidbits. That's how I know about the railroad."

He removed his cigar, looked at the teeth marks, grimaced, then put it in his pocket for later. "I bet you don't overwhelm your family with details when you learn something new about dinosaurs."

"You think you know me so well, huh." She shrugged. "You're right. The family is sick of hearing about the creatures."

"Would you like a piece of advice?" he asked.

His non-sequitur threw her off a bit. "Not particularly. But tell me anyway."

He cleared his throat as if preparing to make a major announcement. "You should stay clear of Daniel unless you're just interested in a hookup."

"Why'd you bring that up?"

"Because if you two get anywhere near something combustible, the sparks you generate will ignite and burn the town down."

One side of his mouth curled up, and that set her back on her heels a little. Whatever she thought she was keeping from him—about her feelings for Daniel—she wasn't. The advice was like a giant hand pushing down on her chest.

"You're exaggerating. It's not *that* bad."

Rick pushed his hat back, scratching his head distractedly. "You've got color in your cheeks now and a sharpness in your eyes. How come? You didn't get that much sleep on the trip here."

"The altitude. I can breathe easier."

"That's your story, huh? Whatever... Look, you're beautiful, intelligent, and a natural with Noah. A man would have to be blind not to see that. And trust me, Daniel would qualify for sharpshooter school. Guys live for the maybe. And the look in his eyes when you're in the room is one of hope. You should have seen him grinning when you were sleeping on his shoulder."

"O'Grady, you're sick. Just because your mind is on sex twenty-four/seven doesn't mean all men are like that."

"What rock have you been living under?"

"Did you really say that?" she asked.

"Yeah, I did, but I wasn't thinking about you being a rock hound. Look, I want you to be happy, but screwing a nineteenth-century Pinkerton man will be moving you backward not forward. You'll be Benjamin Buttoning, and no telling where you'd end up. Maybe the Jurassic Period, but you'd like that."

"Benjamin Button? Where do you come up with this stuff?"

"I watched a ton of movies during my deployment."

"I thought you only watched Westerns."

"I watched whatever I could to escape boredom, the horrors of war, and loneliness." He took a deep, shivery breath, then another. "But we're not talking about me."

"Don't worry about me and further complications with Daniel. He's leaving tomorrow." The thought of him going away made her belly ache. But what could she do? Short of hog-tying him, nothing.

She moved to stand in front of one of the station's street-facing windows, one gloved hand gripping the edge of the sill for balance. After riding in a stagecoach and train for twenty-four hours, she had yet to regain her land legs. The air was only slightly warmer here, and not as thin as in Leadville. That eased her breathing somewhat. When had her breathing issues started? A few weeks ago? That couldn't be right, but as she thought back, she'd been having problems even before she rode up to the cabin that Saturday morning.

A train departed with another load of passengers, and the station quieted. She checked the time on her yellow gold lapel watch decorated with tiny seed pearls that Kenzie had insisted Amber purchase before leaving Leadville.

The door swung open, and she turned quickly, hoping it was Daniel. It wasn't, and her face drooped with disappointment. A gust of cool air, carrying the hint of rain and the stink of sewage, blew in with a man, almost obscured under a bundle of packages. Behind him a porter pushed a cart loaded with crates marked PROPERTY OF YALE UNIVERSITY FRAGILE.

The man set the packages down on top of the cart and she got a decent look at him—Van Dyke beard, a great mane of obsessively groomed black hair fiercely tamed with a copious amount of grease, a worsted sack coat, and a badly tied two-in-four knot. He didn't look like a rock hound, so what could he be shipping from Denver to Yale in crates marked FRAGILE? Only one thing—fossils. That could only mean someone was digging in Morrison.

She nudged Rick. "See the man over there with the Van Dyke beard, snapping his pocket watch open and shut repeatedly? He's shipping crates to Yale University marked FRAGILE."

"So?"

"He's shipping fossils."

"How do you know?"

The porter pushing the cart spit and hit a spittoon with remarkable accuracy. Amber scrunched up her nose. "Short of looking inside the crates, I don't, but historically, it fits. If he's shipping fossils, that means a dig is going on in Morrison. Tomorrow we'll look around."

"Great. I can't wait." Rick snapped a sarcastic salute, then slowly dropped his hand and adjusted his kerchief, revealing a small spy camera attached to the bandanna. He turned his body at an angle and snapped pictures of the man and crates.

"I didn't know you had a camera."

"David asked me to take pictures of people and places."

"Did you get pics in Leadville, too?"

"He did. Then he switched out the memory card, so he could transfer pictures to his phone. You know, in case he needed evidence to show your sister." Rick turned to get shots from another angle. "I'll give you another piece of advice, if you're open to hearing it."

She sighed. "Okay, one more. And then we have to go. Daniel is standing outside with the carriage."

"If you're sure where you want to end up, let that guide the decisions you make while you're here."

"That's philosophical, Mr. Samwise." She swept through the sawdust on the way to the door, her hat box swinging at her side. "You better be careful, or this story we're in will put you, like Sam, in your greatest moments of peril."

"Ha! I've heard of Sam, I know he's Frodo's loyal sidekick, but

I'm not a big *Lord of the Rings* fan. I guess you're my Frodo then, and I'm taking my bodyguard job seriously." He opened the door and held it for her. "That includes guarding your heart, too."

She paused and looked up at him. "That's more than you signed up for. Just get me back in one piece. My heart can take care of itself." She leaned against him as they walked toward the street, feeling the solidness of Rick's arm tight against her side.

A second carriage squeaked to a stop next to where Daniel stood waiting, its harnesses jingling. She was surprised to find the street crowded with carriages, buckboards, and horses. Whatever had detained him, it wasn't searching for a carriage.

The driver hopped off his perch and pulled open the door. Daniel took her hat box and gave her a hand up into the carriage, the touch tingled her fingers. It was an electrifying effect she tried to ignore but couldn't. How could she, with her hand trembling ever so slightly? He returned the hat box to her, smiling as if he knew exactly what he was doing to her.

"Sorry I took so long. I bumped into another agent and I couldn't break away."

"Anything you can share?" she asked, settling into the seat.

"As soon as I get ye settled at the Robinson residence, I need to leave for a meeting."

"Will you be back before dinner?"

He stood aside and allowed Rick to enter behind her. "Meetings typically run long." Daniel closed the door and stepped out of the way. "Noah and I will ride in the other carriage."

The carriage wheels churned the mud as the pair of horses strained forward and pulled away from the curb. "Does it bother you that we're staying with Daniel's late wife's family?" Rick shifted in the seat and his knees briefly brushed hers.

Her fingers still tingled from the touch of Daniel's hand, but when Rick brushed her knee there was nothing more than awareness.

"I couldn't say no when Daniel asked me to stay there to watch over Noah. If he settles in quickly and doesn't need us there, we can leave and go stay in a hotel."

Rick smiled. "I'm with you, babe."

"I'm glad I've got you to hold my hand."

He grinned even bigger. "And I got you to kiss good night."

"In your dreams, O'Grady."

He put his arm around her shoulders, pulled her to him, and kissed the top of her head. "After this is over, if you ever need me for anything—a drinking buddy, a confidant, someone to give you a hug, and if you insist, a one-night stand—you can count on me for more than great sex."

Amber's smile turned quickly into a laugh that vibrated up through the soles of her dainty shoes. "Are there really four more just like you?"

"Jeff's married, but Connor's got the itch. He wants to settle down, have kids, the whole nine yards. Shane and I will have to carry on by ourselves."

"Olivia has that itch, too. Maybe we'll be related someday."

He turned to face her and took her hand. "Let's make a pledge. If Connor and Olivia get married, you'll be maid of honor and I'll be best man, and we can hook up if there's no one else in our life. What do you think?"

"If that happens, O'Grady..." She paused, did a little mental shimmy, thinking about being naked with him, then finally said, "As long as there's nobody else for either one of us on the horizon, then you've got a deal."

He did a fist pump. "Yes."

"You're something else." She squeezed his hand. "Thanks for hanging out with me."

"I'm at your service, sweetheart."

As they crossed the Larimer Street Bridge, he gazed out the window and she studied his profile. He was a hot, sexy guy, but he wasn't long-term relationship material for her or anyone.

She turned her attention away from him and focused on the scenery. During the ride she saw little that resembled the twenty-first century city she knew. Tiny buildings and structures were sprinkled along a grid of platted streets. Small trees courageously guarded the main boulevard.

He turned his head side to side, looking out the windows of the carriage. "Do you know where we are?"

"Without street signs I'd be completely lost. The city is a step up, though, from the frontier towns we stopped in to change horses on the way to Morrison."

"There's a boom coming, right? When does it hit?"

"It's already started. The city is growing, not as fast as Leadville, but it'll catch up. After the fire of 1863, flammable building materials were prohibited downtown. All shops were rebuilt with stone or brick. That's why you don't see any wooden structures in the business district."

"Is that more of Olivia's trivia?" he asked.

"She can tell you everything about the city since it was founded in 1858 at the confluence of Cherry Creek and the South Platte River. It was only a collection of tents and flimsy wooden structures."

He spread his hands wide. "And look at it now. Who would have thought it would grow into this?"

She laughed. "Come back in ten years, it'll look completely different. You'll see structures still standing in the twenty-first century. But right now, there are only about twenty houses standing that will be here in our time. Olivia just bought the house that Adam and Christine Hughes live in now."

"It's still standing?"

"It needs work. She wants to restore it to its original condition. We'll have to get inside so you can take pictures to show her what it looked like when it was new."

He lowered his voice, conspirator to conspirator. "Stick with me, baby doll. I'll get you in."

Amber laughed. "We won't have to break in. We can stop by for a visit."

They traveled through the business district, crossed Cherry Creek, and traveled up 19th Avenue to Sherman Street, along a quiet dirt road. It was far enough removed from the bustle of downtown to be considered a fashionable area.

"Is the Robinson house still standing?"

"Homes around here will come down in the early 1900s for the downtown expansion. But in this decade, houses on this street are showplaces." The carriage lurched to a stop in front of a stern, massive, almost medieval mansion with a pillared, arched entryway constructed of sandstone and surrounded by a low retaining wall topped with decorative iron scrollwork. Rick opened the door and helped her down, and they waited there, at the edge of the dirt road, until Daniel, Noah, and Ripley alighted from their carriage.

"It's an impressive house."

"Scary. Out here all by itself. I just hope Mr. Robinson isn't as scary."

Daniel walked up to her. "I'm a mess," she said. "My riding skirt is dusty, creased, and stained, and my hair is a wreck. We should have stopped and bathed before we came here." She glanced up at the mansion. If she hoped to have any influence over the Rio Grande's situation in the gorge, and limit her ancestors' financial exposure, first impressions were important.

"Alec knows we've been traveling for two days. You'll have time to bathe before you see him. Don't fret."

"I thought he'd be here to meet Noah."

A vertical line appeared between Daniel's eyebrows, and he chuckled at that, but it was a raw broken sound. He tucked her gloved hand under his arm and escorted her to the house. "Few things matter more than his bank."

Daniel was wrong. Noah's grandfather was home and waiting in the foyer, dressed in a coat of fine wool. He was fiddling with his shirt cuffs, adjusting them to protrude a proper half-inch beyond his coat sleeves. He was an attractive man of medium height. His beard and mustache were neatly trimmed, and his graying brown hair gleamed with Macassar oil.

Noah ran to him, and Mr. Robinson stooped to hug him. Amber got a whiff of bay rum and lavender, a complex and masculine aroma.

Noah stepped out of the older man's embrace and moved to stand next to his dad and Ripley. Daniel gave his son a reminder pat on his back. "What'd ye say, lad?"

Noah yanked his cap off his head, held it close to his chest. "Thank you, sir, for inviting me. This is my dog, Ripley. She's a…" Noah looked up at Amber. "What kind of dog is she?"

"Chesapeake Bay Retriever, or Chessie for short," she said.

"She looks like a mighty fine dog," Alec Robinson said.

Daniel clapped his former father-in-law on the back with one hand and gave him a hearty shake with the other. "Good to see ye."

Alec smoothed his mustache and his shoulders eased a bit, tension flowing out of his stance. He'd been as anxious about the visit as Daniel had been. Now she wondered if Daniel's comments fearing his father-in-law would leave town were just a ruse to manipulate her into staying here.

"It's been a long time, Dan."

"These are my traveling companions I mentioned in my wire. Miss Kelly and her cousin, Mr. O'Grady."

She'd prepared for a mutual inclination of their heads and polite greeting, but Alec bowed low over her hand. Between his warm fingers lightly squeezing hers and his unreadable eyes drooping at the corners, she found herself momentarily tongue-tied.

"Looks like the Irish have invaded my home."

She untied her tongue and said quick-wittedly with a wink, "You've got the luck of the Irish with you now."

He laughed and squeezed her hand again. "My son-in-law says you have a rare interest not only in fossils, but in finding a resolution to the volatile situation in the gorge. You are an uncanny woman, Miss Kelly."

A middle-aged woman, primly dressed in black, appeared in the foyer, a chatelaine dangling from her waist. The suspended chains with thimbles, keys, and scissors clinked against each other as she strode across the foyer. "Mr. Robinson, we have rooms prepared for Miss Kelly, Mr. O'Grady, and Noah. If Miss Kelly and Noah will come this way, we'll get them settled in."

Mr. Robinson released Amber's hand to his housekeeper, who patted it gingerly. His attention seemed to be wavering, drifting away from them, disappearing into indifference. Not overtly, but she sensed it.

"Pa," Noah said. "I want to stay with you and Rick."

"After yer bath, lad," Daniel said, "ye may join us in the library."

Noah perked up. "Thank you, sir." He gave his dad a hug and with Ripley trotting behind him, Noah marched toward the waiting butler, standing by the newel post at the bottom of the staircase.

Amber found being relegated to her room to nap while Noah was invited to the library insulting. For today, though, being insulted took second place behind exhaustion. Until she rested, her mind wouldn't be sharp enough for a serious intellectual conversation with Mr. Robinson or anyone else.

"I'd like to get my bag from the carriage," she said.

The housekeeper put her arm around Amber's waist and guided her toward the staircase with its hand-carved mahogany banister and railing. "The bags have already been taken to your rooms. Come along. A hot bath and a warm bed await you, along with a special concoction from the Robinson family doctor."

"If the concoction is a cup of tea with a shot of whisky, I'll have a double."

Alec laughed. "Now I know the Irish have arrived."

Amber glanced over her shoulder at Rick. "If you go out, let me know." Her voice sounded odd, miles away, as if someone she didn't know was speaking on her behalf. His eyebrows went up, but his gaze remained steadily on her, as if he were trying to determine what was really on her mind. She nodded, giving him a brave smile, although she didn't feel particularly brave at all. Lifting the hems of her skirts a modest inch, she set about to climb the stairs.

"Rest easy, lass," Daniel said.

She looked at him, even more confused. Her brain wasn't getting enough oxygen. She needed hours of uninterrupted sleep. Maybe a concoction didn't sound so bad after all. Were they trying to manipulate her? If so, why? Right now—so tired and dirty—she simply didn't care. Carefully, she placed her foot on the bottom tread and glanced up, wondering how in the world she'd ever make it to the top landing.

33

1878 Denver, Colorado—Amber

Amber reclined in an elegant four-poster bed in an opulent bedroom filled with Victorian black walnut furniture, intricate needlepoint pillows, and tapestries hanging on the wall. Dressed in a velvet and silk peignoir, she felt almost decadent. The décor wasn't her taste, but she couldn't complain about the luxurious surroundings, and the attention she'd received from Mr. Robinson's housekeeper, Mrs. Murphy, and from Millie, the family's brownish-black Siamese cat.

The room had a decidedly feminine touch. So much so that she'd originally thought the room had belonged to Mr. Robinson's wife. But Mrs. Murphy had informed her the late Mrs. Robinson predeceased her daughter and neither had ever lived in the Sherman Street house.

The fireplace on the opposite side of the room was decorated with a mahogany mantel and topped with polished brass candlesticks. The gas lamps with delicately etched chimneys created a warm, romantic glow, and cast enough light for her to write in her journal.

She'd been jotting down observations and drawings religiously since the second day of her adventure. None of her sketches would ever win an art award but they were enough of a likeness that she wouldn't forget what people and places looked like. Her drawing of the bedroom wasn't half bad. Although she didn't need so many drawings now that she knew Rick had a spy camera, but she doubted he'd take pictures of furniture and wallpaper.

Her travel skirt was draped over the top of the decorative room screen, a soiled and stained reminder of the exhausting stagecoach trip from Leadville.

"Oh," Amber said, remembering another note she wanted to make.

Millie had been asleep under the covers and peeked her head out. "Meow."

Amber rubbed her belly. "I wasn't talking to you. Go back to sleep." The cat meowed again. "I didn't want to forget to tell Olivia about the fringe, multi-colored tassels, lace, and stained glass." Satisfied she'd covered all the room's features, she slipped the pencil into its loop and closed the journal, patting the cover.

Olivia would love the mansion, nineteenth-century Denver, and especially Leadville. She'd be swishing her dresses with tucks and horizontal folds, pleats and flounces along the city streets, soaking it all in. If she'd gone to the cabin with her that Saturday morning, they could be sharing this adventure together.

Amber put her hand on her chest. The shortness of breath was worrying her. The thin air hadn't bothered David or Rick, and Kenzie had only been bothered the first day or two. Maybe Amber should cut her trip short. Go home, get better. She could try, but the brooch, pinned in its usual spot above her heart, beneath her gown, hadn't heated up since her trip there. It wasn't ready to take her home.

Since she was so familiar with the excavation sites in Morrison, she would only need two days, maybe three, to poke around. And if there was a dig going on, maybe she could interview a few bone diggers, find out exactly what they knew about the *Stegosaurus*, or what they suspected.

Maybe I can give them a little... I don't know... Insider information.

Would it be so wrong to speed up their understanding of paleontology? Maybe she could bring Cope and Marsh to the negotiating table, share information with both men and hope they might stop trash talking, stealing, and vandalizing each other's camps. She could really screw up history, though. Marsh's attempt to discredit Cope, and Cope's attempt to discredit Marsh led to the Bone Wars and intrigued the public. That intrigue brought more interest to the study of dinosaurs, and with interest came investors who sponsored more digs, more studies, more scientific articles.

Kenzie had changed history when she went back in time. Could Amber change it a little bit without consequences? Was it worth the gamble? She tapped her fingers on the journal. Bottom line—she couldn't answer either question.

With the dying fire, the air in the room was chilly now, but beneath the quilts, warm and cozy. The fire needed stoking once more before she turned down the lamps.

She'd slept through half the afternoon and most of the evening but did wake up when Mrs. Murphy brought in a dinner tray about eight o'clock. She had eaten most of the chicken fricassee served with rice, but only nibbled at the pound cake before promptly falling back to sleep. A couple bites of pound cake would taste good about now. But alas, glancing over at the marble-topped table set near the fireplace, the dinner tray was gone. And with it, the cake. But Mrs. Murphy had left behind a small silver tray with a crystal brandy decanter and matching snifters.

There was a vague memory of a visit from Robinson's physician—who wore the crumpled look and grumpy manner of an old world-weary doctor—and an even vaguer memory of her telling him to go away and leave her alone. She didn't like doctors and certainly didn't need to see one trained in nineteenth-century medicine. He'd probably want to do a blood-letting.

The time on her lapel watch pinned to her pillow read midnight, but when she put the timepiece to her ear, it wasn't ticking. She couldn't remember when she wound the dang thing. Kenzie had warned her, "Don't forget to wind your watch." Amber remembered to put her iWatch on the charger at night. Why couldn't she remember a task as simple as turning the crown a few times?

She climbed out of bed, stretching her stiff neck and shoulders, listening to the creaking of the house settling, the wind moaning around the corners, whispering through invisible cracks and crevices. There was something comforting about the symphony, but comfort reminded her of Olivia. At a time like this, they'd be texting each other. Amber sighed. She needed pound cake. Her sweet tooth needed a fix. And her melancholy needed a distraction.

It took a minute to locate her cotton and silk house slippers under the bed and another minute to find the velvet-sashed robe that Mrs. Murphy had folded over a nearby chair. The robe, with its tiers of lace cascading down the front and sleeves, was one of several items Kenzie had insisted she purchase during their Leadville shopping excursions.

Amber smiled, remembering David and Kenzie and how much in love they were. Kenzie should know by the time Amber returned home if she was pregnant. Amber rubbed her belly, wondering what it would be like to carry a child. Her parents were dying to be grandparents, but they'd have to wait a while longer. Hopefully, Olivia would have news of a budding relationship with Connor to share with their parents. At least the news would raise their mother's level of expectation above that of a pipe dream and take the pressure off Amber.

She slipped into the robe and searched the room for a clock and the missing pound cake. When she couldn't find either, she cracked open the door, palm flat against the wood panel and listened. Since she didn't hear the familiar tread of Mrs. Murphy's stout black shoes, she decided it was safe enough to go wondering around the house. How difficult could it be to find a clock and a piece of cake.

Subdued light filtered into a small landing area at the top of the grand staircase. Down the hallway, toward the room where she knew Noah was sleeping, a dimmer light flickered. She tiptoed, and when she approached the corner of the hallway that would take her to the grand staircase, she ran smack into the rock-hard chest of a man—*bong*.

She all but bounced off him.

She shrieked, grabbed her chest, invoking a primitive instinct to calm her racing heart. Inhaling deeply to control her breath, she picked up the scent of whisky and sweet tobacco and the wind-blown chill of the night. And like a bloodhound, she picked up the familiar scent of Daniel.

He grabbed her shoulders to keep her upright. "Are ye off to raid the kitchen?"

With his hands settled on her, the tension that had been mounting in her shoulder blades and into her neck melted under his soft touch. Assured of her balance and that she wasn't going to topple over and fall into his arms, she stepped away, carrying the warm imprint of his hands still on her.

She quivered in that odd prelude she experienced when she knew a man wanted to kiss her. "I'm looking for a clock," she said. "I wanted to know the time."

He teased a smile at her. "Where's yer wee watch?"

Guiltily she said, "I forgot to wind it."

"It's not useful then." He opened his coat, pulled out his pocket watch, and flipped the casing open, angling it toward the gas lamp for her to see the time. On the back of the cover was a picture, she now knew, of his late wife, looking slightly younger than the woman in the *carte de visite* she'd seen at Noah's bedside.

Daniel closed the watch. "Two-thirty."

She finger-combed her hair to one side and let it all drape over one shoulder, twirling the ends around her finger, something she did when deep in thought. Although right now, her thoughts weren't deep. It was that oxygen-to-the-brain-thing again.

She looked around the empty hallway and lowered her voice. "I don't suppose that's two-thirty in the afternoon."

He gave her a wide smile, all straight white teeth. "Are ye that anxious to go find yer fossils?"

"I guess that's a no."

She folded her arms, tapped her fingers against her biceps, wondering what she'd do until morning if she couldn't fall back asleep. He was so close to her that on her next breath, she deeply inhaled the scent of him again. He stood still, frozen with an expression of deep concern etched on his features, yet he somehow managed to look delicious and dangerous at the same time. What was it Rick had said to her?

If you're sure where you want to end up, let that guide the decisions you make while you're here.

She wanted to go home without longing for a man she could never have a relationship with. If she was thinking about a middle-of-the-night activity that involved a sexy Scotsman and a feather bed—she could just forget it.

"What are you doing walking about at this hour? Did your meeting just end?"

He was dressed in dinner clothes, neat, but not freshly pressed. His cravat was slightly askew, as if done in haste or undone and redone. His blond curls were beaten, but not entirely bowed, by some hair application or other.

"It ended a while ago," he said, without offering any explanation of where he'd been since. But he smiled, and there was something in his eyes. Something that caused her breath to catch.

"Good night, then." She made a slow about-face and returned to her room. But before she could close the door, Daniel was standing there, leaning against the doorjamb, holding onto the ornate brass knob.

"I'm leaving early in the morning. I'll try to come back in three or four days, but it depends on the situation I find in Cañon City." At the sound of a door closing somewhere in the house, he glanced down the hall then back at her. "I have a favor to ask."

She tugged on his arm, pulling him inside the room. "Get in here before someone sees you. Mr. Robinson probably wouldn't like me entertaining you in my room in the middle of the night. He'd kick me out, and I'd have to trod the boards every night to support myself."

"I'm sure most theatres in Denver have already heard of ye and would offer ye a contract."

That's what she was afraid of. If anyone did a deep dive into her background they'd come up empty, which was probably already frustrating Daniel. "You're asking for another favor? You want to know what I think of the last one? You made it all up. You said you were afraid of what Mr. Robinson might do in your absence. You tricked me, and I want to know why!"

There was a bite in her voice, but she didn't care. Let him feel the marks of her teeth. When her clients resisted her advice, when her parents interfered in her life, when her sister drove her insane about her wardrobe or boyfriends, she could stomp down her feelings and keep an emotional distance. But with Daniel it didn't work so well because of the lies standing sentry between them, lies she couldn't do a damn thing about.

She pushed the door closed and moved toward the scrap of remaining heat in the fireplace, her beribboned robe whispering softly over the floorboard. She bent to tend to the fire.

"Let me do it." He stepped in front of her, tossed two logs on the grate, and using the bellows, coaxed the dying embers to reluctant life. "I'm disappointed ye sent the doctor away. He saw Noah through a serious illness a couple of years ago. He's a good doctor. He might know why ye fainted."

"I was hot, dehydrated, and hungry." Her voice took another bite out of him. "That's…why I fainted." Her hands tightened into fists. Her family knew never to discuss her health. It was a non-starter for any conversation. "This isn't about me, Daniel. It's about you. Why make up a story about a nice man who appears to be fond of you?"

Doubt and suspicion lingered in his face for a moment, then cleared. He put down the bellows and stepped over to the window, his fingers furrowing his hair. Using the back of his hand, he lifted the velvet drape lining one side of the window, holding back the thick fabric while he gazed out onto the quiet street. "Alec can be controlling, especially when Noah's education and future are discussed." Daniel turned to face her, letting the drapery fall back into place. "The lad is his only heir, and he has certain expectations."

"But you're his father. Alec can't do anything without your permission." He poured two snifters of brandy from a decanter and offered one to her. She accepted the glass. "I don't have a dog in this fight. If Alec tries anything while you're gone, other than send you a telegram, there isn't much I can do."

He sipped from his glass. "Then I'll pay ye a retainer. Ye'll be able to represent my interest."

She held out her hand. "A nickel will take care of it." Daniel reached into his vest pocket and pulled out a Liberty half dollar, placing the near-mint condition coin in her palm. The silver, warmed by his body heat, now warmed her chilled hand. There was an envelope in her journal. The coin would go there to remember this moment, to remember him.

"Since I've retained ye and ye're now my legal representative, I'll tell ye what I heard tonight. There's a rumor Alec is moving to California."

"Why would he invite Noah here and then leave?"

He stared at her, face impassive, gaze steady. "A new business opportunity."

Light sprang from the flickering fire, wavering in bright swaths over the plaster walls, and the scent of smoke mixed with her curiosity and concern. "He wouldn't run off with Noah, would he?"

"I don't know."

She sank onto the settee. The furniture was broad and deep and richly upholstered with embroidery over the wool cushions, arms, and the tall curving back, and smothered in elaborately patterned antimacassars crisscrossing the back and sofa arms. She wormed the tip of her finger into a hole of the crochet lace doily spread over the sofa's arm.

"Nothing surprises me anymore," she said, "but I'm having trouble reconciling the man I met earlier with what you're telling me now."

"Up close," Daniel said, "it's hard to really see a man, particularly if ye don't know him well. Yer mind is free to imagine him any way ye wish."

Was her opinion of Alec based solely on his warm reception?

Yes, it was. And because of that, she could imagine him any way she wished. "I'll stay for a while and watch out for Noah, but I can't stay forever." Amber picked at the doily where she'd stretched the yarn. "Whatever you do, don't get killed on the job."

"Would ye miss me?" He still had that smooth tone to his voice. But there was also a note of uncertainty in it. He kept his gaze fastened on her.

Locked in his gaze, she couldn't move, her heart drumming so loudly she was certain he could hear it. "Noah would be devastated."

"I didn't ask about Noah. I asked about ye."

"Yes, I would miss you." She needed to redirect their conversation. What had they been talking about. Oh, about her staying for a while. "I need to tell Rick what's going on."

"I'd prefer ye keep this between us for now."

"I can't," she said. "If he's going to protect me, he has to know what's happening. I wonder where he is now?"

"He was at the Denver Press Club and then the carriage driver dropped him off at the Palace Saloon and Theatre on 15th and Blake Streets."

"He shouldn't get into much trouble there." She leaned forward, studying Daniel's strained posture.

"It has upscale burlesque shows." Daniel stooped and tossed another log on the fire. The firelight glowed on the handsome planes of his face. The wood snapped as the flames threw out unneeded heat. He straightened, rested his elbow on the mantel, and made more furrows in his thick hair.

"Spill it, Daniel. You can't shock me. What's going on?"

He poured another inch of brandy into her snifter and an equal measure into his own. He took his time, giving her the impression that he was gathering his thoughts before sharing what he was thinking. "I'm uncertain about Rick. Ye called him a fanboy. Said he had a bromance with Western heroes. I thought ye were implying—"

She covered her mouth to smother a laugh. "You think Rick is a homosexual?"

"What's that?"

The term must not have made it into the popular lexicon of the day.

"A man with a sexual preference for other men, or a woman who prefers women. But I assure you, Rick is as straight as the street in front of this house. He's not a sybarite either."

"He's not?"

She shook her head.

"Ye're sure?"

She nodded. "If Alec is entertaining Rick it's because he's good company. And besides, I have pretty accurate radar, and it didn't go off when I met Alec."

"I don't know that word either."

"It's when you sense something is wrong. It's your gut feeling that makes the hairs on the back of your neck stand up. That's why I don't think he'll try anything."

"Ye're not feeling well. Yer…radar…could be—"

"Malfunctioning?"

"I speak Gaelic, French, and Italian, but some of yer words are new to me."

"You can blame that on my…uncle. He's a wordsmith and enjoys making up words. I forget they're not part of the lexicon." She squinted at him. "Do you know that word?"

His broad shoulders straightened, and his chest seemed to expand. If he'd had feathers, surely, they would have ruffled. "I'm not illiterate."

"I didn't mean to imply…" She waved away the rest of her thought. "Look, let's drill down and come up with a plan."

"Okay, but first"—his navy-blue eyes zeroed in on hers—"I want ye to see the doctor tomorrow."

"Absolutely not."

Now, his eyes pinned her with a warning. "The circles under yer eyes are worse now than they were this morning, even though ye've slept more than half the day. I demand ye see him tomorrow."

"Demand? You're in no position to demand anything of me."

"Do ye distrust doctors that much?"

"My grandmother trusted her doctor. She adored him. But he

messed up, misdiagnosed her disease, and botched the surgery. She never left the hospital. I'll have to be on my deathbed to take a doctor's advice."

The shock on his face was immediately swallowed by confusion. "But ye insisted Noah go to the doctor."

"He had a physical injury a doctor could fix without screwing it up. I don't want to rid the world of physicians. I just don't need them."

"Ye can't blame the whole profession for the mistake of one."

"Oh, yeah? I can," she said pointing to herself. "I may not look it, but I feel much better. Another day of rest, and I'll be ready to go fossil hunting. Don't worry about me." She used a lighter tone to change the subject. "By the way, how'd the meeting go?"

He set his glass on the table across from her and picked up Millie, who had been curled up on the opposite side of the sofa. His long fingers disappeared into the cat's thick coat. He scratched her between her half-closed eyes.

Amber pointed toward the cushion the cat had vacated. "Have a seat."

Daniel lowered himself onto the sofa. The cat settled into his lap and her paws swatted at his pocket watch chain.

"We have a plan in place," he said, "men to carry it out, and a good chance I won't be needed more than a few days. I hope to be back sooner than I thought." He shifted to face her and rested one long arm along the back of the sofa. The tips of his fingers brushed her shoulder. "I worry about ye." His tone dropped, becoming as intimate as a lover's touch.

Millie butted his stilled hand, demanding Daniel resume petting her.

Amber, aware now that her hands were clenched, relaxed them and petted the cat, too. Her hand touched Daniel's as they both ran their fingers through the smooth and sleek top coat of fur.

"Please don't worry about me. You don't need the distraction."

The diffuse firelight accentuated the worry lines in his face, highlighted a golden streak in his blond hair, and emphasized the straightness of his nose. He toyed with a strand of her hair. "That's impossible." His eyes roved over her and his mouth twitched with the tiniest and briefest of smiles. "I find if I'm not worried about ye, I'm arguing with ye, or strategizing, or even humming along. Ye're a woman of many talents." He dropped a tendril of hair and picked up another one close to her ear, brushing her neck with the back of his hand.

She anchored her attention on him, careful not to move or blink or think beyond this moment. She was silent for a long time and so was he, seemingly content to listen to the crackling fire as sparks floated like fireflies into a darkened corner of the room. Millie wiggled on his lap and turned over to present a belly for him to rub. He obliged, and Amber thought how sweet it would be to have him rub her belly, and other places, too.

There was a powerful scent about him. If confidence in a two-thousand-dollar suit could be bottled, that's how he smelled. Yet there was something else. A coniferous scent of fir needles and cedar wood. But it wasn't the typical woodsy smell found in shaving lotions. This was the pure scent of manliness, and it tugged at her on a primal level. He was a man who made decisions and stuck by them; a man who defended those he loved; a man who fought for values and beliefs; a man with intellectual curiosity.

A shock of recognition blew through her. Those were the must-have boyfriend traits she'd listed in her first lock-and-key diary, long ago. In that moment, an uneasy possibility stole past her recognition and encamped in her mind; a possibility she couldn't dislodge.

Could she stay in the past to be with him?

His eyes were softer, his face flushed. The tip of his tongue escaped briefly to touch his bottom lip. Daniel's thumb slid over the line of her jaw, and he gazed at her, a visual caress. He nudged her chin up with his thumb.

Millie sensed something was about to happen and leapt off the sofa. Daniel gave Amber a moment to say the words that would stop him, or make a simple gesture that meant no, but she had no words, no signal. Her only coherent thought was how natural it seemed to slip into his arms and share a kiss.

His mouth came down slowly, tentative at first, then he kissed her full on the mouth. The first kiss slid easily into the next. His beard tickled her chin, and when their tongues touched, she tasted the fresh dried fruit and citrus zest of sweet brandy on his tongue that now moved against hers, tantalizing her mouth. His hands slid up her arms and cupped her nape, pulling her closer to him. She could hardly breathe from having him so close.

Then her breathing connected with her brain, alerting her with red-hot flares. It wasn't his proximity exacerbating her breathing problem. Gasping, she pulled away from him, terrified. "I can't breathe." Fear made the condition worse. She cupped her hands to her mouth and fought for her next breath and the next.

Daniel pushed to his feet and swept her into his arms, cradling her there, and carried her to the bed where he loosened the sash at her waist. "Take slow breaths. Breathe in. Breathe out." He put his head on her chest and listened to her heart.

She pushed him away. "Too heavy." Her heart palpitated. Nothing like this had ever happened to her before, and it scared her. Not enough to trust a nineteenth-century doctor, and barely enough to trust one from her own century. It was sickness from the high-altitude with lower oxygen levels, it had to be. With time and rest, she'd get better.

"I want ye to see the doctor."

"No. I have mountain sickness. It'll go away."

Daniel sat on the edge of the bed and placed his hand over hers, and then his entwined fingers tightened around her much smaller ones. "Yer heart is racing. Please…" There was more than concern in his voice. The tone bordered on fear, much like her own, but she refused to give into it.

She pressed her hand over his lips, and his breath warmed her skin. "I'll see a doctor as soon as I go home. That's the best I can do."

"That's not good enough." He snagged a towel from the bar at the side of the wash basin cabinet and wiped sweat from her forehead before adding a pillow beneath her head to prop it up higher.

"Maybe not, but it'll have to do. When you come back in a few days, I'll be better. You'll see." She squirmed to get comfortable, but her robe was wrapped around her legs, restricting her movements. She freed a shoulder and arm from one side of the confining garment.

"Wait. I'll do it." He gently lifted her shoulders and pulled off the soft velvet robe, revealing the thin silky gown that lay in soft folds along her curves. His eyes roved the length of her. He made an odd noise from the back of his throat and mumbled something in a language she didn't understand before jerking the covers up to her chin.

He stepped away from the bed, brushing cat hair from his lap, and revisited the decanter of brandy. Avoiding eye contact he said, "I'll stay until ye fall asleep."

"You need sleep, too."

"I'll leave shortly." His voice, pitched low, hummed with intensity and promise.

He poured another drink, clinking the mouth of the decanter against the glass, as if his hand was shaking. The silence stretched between them. She placed her hand on her chest, feeling the beat of her heart beneath her spread fingers. The beat was now close to her warm-up biking heart rate. Still high but easing down.

Before Daniel turned his attention back to her, he placed another log on the fire and stoked the embers beneath. Eventually, he rejoined her, sitting at the foot of the bed where he leaned against the bedpost.

"Go on to bed," she said. "I'll be fine now."

"Not yet. I want to be sure before I leave that ye're not in distress. It's my fault ye got overheated and couldn't breathe. I shouldn't have…"

Since he let the sentence drop, she asked, "Shouldn't have what? Kissed me?"

There was a whimsical twist at the corner of his mouth that

mixed a bit of shouldn't-have with glad-I-did. He had a kissable mouth, no bow in the top lip, but it was the whole package that made him sexy, and what marvelous antics he could do with those lips from smiling to kissing to…

"It was nice." Nice? Did she really say that? She sighed. It had been much more than nice. She rubbed her finger along her lower lip. "Your beard…hmm…tickled."

"Ye mean scratched."

His mouth quirked again, and he scraped his jaw, his fingernails making a rasping noise against his whiskers. His brows collided above his nose, as if he were deep in thought. About what? Whether he should shave before kissing her again? She liked his beard—the woodsy scent of it, the softness, even the ticklishness. And the whiskers gave him some of the bad boy look she found sexy. But most of all, his beard gave her the feeling that everything he set out to do would get done. And whatever he set out to accomplish, the feat would be epic.

A low knock startled them, and they looked sharply in the direction of the door. "Amber," a whispered voice said.

She glanced at Daniel. "Rick? At this hour?"

"Are you awake?" Rick's voice rose out of the whisper range, as if his hearing was impaired and he thought he was talking more softly than he was.

Amber threw back the covers without considering the appropriateness of what she was wearing. Daniel, sitting at the end of the bed, pressed down on her still-covered feet. "Don't get up."

"He's had too much to drink. He'll wake up the household. Better let him in."

Daniel's gaze flicked almost imperceptibly at her breasts—the rise and fall of them visible beneath the plunging neckline of the silky gown—as he flipped the quilt back up to her chin. "He won't like me being here."

But I like you here.

"He won't care. Just let him in."

Daniel opened the door enough to let Rick slip through, without throwing the door wide open for anyone else passing by to see inside the room.

"I saw light beneath the door and figured you were awake." Wobbling slightly, and in a serious state of dishabille with the ends of his cravat hanging loose, vest unbuttoned, tuxedo jacket hanging by two fingers over his shoulder, Rick threw a hard glance at Daniel. "What are you doing here?"

Before Daniel could answer, Rick's gaze landed on Amber. "I'll be damned. Well, you two do whatever you want. I'm going to bed."

"It's not what ye think," Daniel said. "Amber had a breathing attack."

From the dramatic lift of a singular eyebrow, Rick wasn't buying into the explanation.

"I woke up, ran into Daniel in the hallway, and we've been sitting here talking until I had a breathing episode," she said. "He carried me to bed, and then you knocked. All very innocent."

Rick gave a low murmur of assent. "If you say so."

Amber rearranged her pillows again, trying for a different position to ease the pain in her chest. "So how was the party?"

Rick flung his jacket onto a chair and slapped his palms then slid one hand down the other. "I got out of there as fast as a sprinter pushing off from the starting block."

"Liar."

He laughed. "No orgies. No drugs. No loud music. Just alcohol, scantily dressed women, and games of chance. I stayed for a while, then walked back here."

"Alcohol, prostitution, and gambling. Your run of the mill party, huh," she said.

He sat heavily on the opposite side of the bed and kicked off his shoes. "Unless I'm overstaying my welcome, I'll tell you what I found out." He fluffed a pillow and relaxed against the headboard. Millie jumped up on him, and Rick immediately cuddled the cat.

Daniel leaned against the bedpost, ankles crossed, looking as attentive as an audience witnessing a stage production.

"You smell like someone poured a bottle of cheap perfume all over you."

"Must not be too bad, the cat loves me. Listen to her purr." Rick raised his arm and sniffed his white shirt. "You're right, though. A few women might have rubbed up against me, and I might have kissed one or two, but—"

"O'Grady, stop." Daniel's mouth was tight with disapproval. "That's not a topic to discuss in front of a lady."

"Are you kidding? Amber doesn't care."

She wheezed out a laugh. "You're right, I don't, but skip the salacious details and just give us the scoop."

"Guess who's coming to town?"

"You're dragging this out, O'Grady."

"Benjamin Franklin Mudge, Dr. Othniel C. Marsh's trusted fossil collector, is coming to Denver to lecture and meet with investors."

Amber wheezed again. "How do you know?"

"I overheard Alec mention he was sponsoring Mr. Mudge's trip. I don't know any more details than that, but I figured you'd be interested in hearing a lecture by a fossil collector."

She rolled over, kissed his cheek, and petted the cat. "You're right. This news is better than anything I could have imagined. Mudge is a prestigious geologist, teacher, and avid collector. Marsh hired him to lead fossil hunting expeditions. He worked with Arthur Lakes in Morrison and Marshall Felch in Cañon City." She rubbed her hands together. "And he'll be in Denver. I can't wait to meet him and hear about his work with Dr. Marsh."

"Didn't ye study under Dr. Marsh?"

A chill settled over her, and she pulled the covers around her shoulders. How many lies ago was that? A sense of foreboding screamed at her. "Not exactly. I might have exaggerated my resume for the judge."

Daniel's fingers wrapped around the intricately carved bedpost, clenching it until his knuckles stood out like white stones. "I wonder how many other exaggerations I'll find"—his voice pierced her disclaimer—"when I, as ye say, drill down?" His mouth tightened, flattening into a grim line, and his smoldering gaze locked on her, held her immobile until he turned on his heel. Millie jumped off the bed and followed Daniel as he stormed from the room. The door closed with finality and a protesting creak.

"Oops," Amber said.

Rick caught her gaze and lifted his eyebrows as if to say he agreed. Then he laughed, and it was a warm, uncomplicated sound, refreshing after Daniel's abrupt departure. "Now we know who the cat loves." Rick brushed hair from his trousers. "You know, don't you. Daniel has a bad case of Amber-itis. And I know he kissed you."

"How do you know that?"

"When you gave me that peck on the cheek, his body shifted, and he almost reached for his pistol. He considered it again, when he caught you in a lie."

"You're observant. I didn't notice. But yeah, he did, and I kissed him back, and it was nice. But then I had trouble breathing and he carried me to bed. That was nice, too, except for the not-breathing part."

"Nice? You're a legal eagle, Am. Don't you have any synonyms for nice in that expansive vocabulary of yours? And don't give me cordial, ducky, fair, good, okay, swell. I'm sure those words don't describe Daniel's kiss. And if they do, you won't be dipping in for seconds."

She flipped through her mental thesaurus. "How about erotic and romantic?"

"That's still vanilla, but better than okay and swell. How about steamy and tangy, hungry and insatiable? Maybe even ripe and salty. Use your imagination."

"Okay, you made your point. But steamy and tangy? I doubt those words are used in Westerns. What else were you reading during your deployment? Romance novels?"

His smile was enough to entice any girl to start stripping off her clothes. Thank God, she was immune to him. He rolled off the bed and gathered his jacket.

"Here's the deal, Am. You're not leaving the house until the dark circles disappear. And covering them up with makeup won't work. So, go to sleep, and while you're sleeping in tomorrow, I'll go check around. See what I can find out about Dr. Mudge's visit."

With the pain she was in right now, she didn't object. "If you see Daniel before he leaves for Cañon City straighten him out, if you can. I don't want him leaving town thinking I lied to him."

"But you have."

"Not about anything important."

"Nothing important? Like you're from another century isn't important. Like you're not one of the country's top ten mining lawyers. Like you're not independently wealthy. What's more important than who you are?"

"My beliefs, values, and ideals that make up the essence of who I am."

"That's crap. It sounds like a Hallmark card."

"Come on, Rick. What I believe, what I value are more important than my status or wealth or what century I'm from. That's the person I want Daniel to see."

"And believe in," Rick said. "I get that. But when a guy catches a girl in one lie, he knows he's only scratched the surface."

She rolled over onto her side. "Thanks for the pep talk, O'Grady. Remind me not to initiate another relationship conversation with you. Turn out the lights on your way out?"

The light in the room dimmed lower and lower as he turned down each lamp until the only light remaining was the flickering fire. "Good night, sweetheart," he whispered. The door closed softly, and the latch clicked in the deafening silence.

34

1878 Denver, Colorado—Amber

AMBER ROLLED OVER in bed, searching for the warm hollow Daniel surely left behind. But there was no imprint in the bed, nor was there the scent of him on her sheets, her skin, in her hair. It was as if he'd never been there.

And that was the thing about lucid dreams.

Some hint at reality more than others. And this one did particularly. She couldn't ever remember having dream sex before, but man oh man, it was great. An erotic mix of fast and slow, rough and gentle, deliberate and imaginative; teasing, dirty talk, and lots of fingers and tongue.

She shivered—from her thoughts, not the temperature in the room—and squirrelled into the warmth of the thick covers, recalling every glorious moment of the dream. Would Daniel be the same lover in real life as he'd been in her make-believe world? She hoped so. He certainly had the makings of a first-class lover.

When she bumped into him last night, or more accurately early this morning, rocking a dinner jacket and stellar smile, she'd thought how handsome he looked. But even in his normal trousers and jacket, he was hotter than a Carolina reaper, perhaps the world's hottest chile pepper, and her go-to spice when she needed a hint of heat in her dishes.

Her dream world certainly knew now where to find its go-to

spice.

"Yum." She fanned her mouth, as if she'd nibbled on a hot pepper, or an even hotter earlobe, or a scorching bottom lip, or… Never mind. She'd gone far enough with imaginary nibbling.

The dream had convinced her of one indelible truth. She wasn't returning to the twenty-first century without having sex with Agent Dan. She had to know if he was it—the missing link in her life; the completeness she'd never found in random hookups or long-term lovers. Not that she had broad experience, but she wasn't a virgin either. But if he was—the one—how could she leave him?

What would Olivia say? What would Kenzie say? She already knew what Rick would say… "Don't do it."

A hookup wasn't going to happen today. Daniel had hopped on a train and headed south. And then she remembered what occurred that sent him fleeing her room—lies. But darn it. She just couldn't tell him the truth.

Daniel, you see, the reason I lied is because I'm from the twenty-first century.

If she told him that, he'd put her away. The imagined sound of a bolt sliding into a cell door lock rang in her ears.

Dwelling on it now wasn't productive. The situation could wait until she and Rick could talk privately. She stretched, moving a bit this way and that. Her breathing had eased somewhat. There was still a pile of bricks on her chest, but not like last night. The breathing attack had scared the crap out of her, and the fear in Daniel's eyes had alarmed her. But his quick action—calm and tender—had relieved her fear.

She'd never been involved with a take-charge kind of guy. Matter of fact, she avoided them religiously. Did she want a man who would pick her up and carry her away? Did she want a man with a plan? Sure. Just so long as the plan was hers.

She stretched a few more times and considered getting on the floor for a few yoga poses, but when she put her feet on the floorboards, she yanked them back. "Dang. It's cold." Forget the poses. Until she fully recovered from whatever was going on with her lungs, she'd take it easy and not exert herself too much, unless it involved a hot Scotsman and a feather mattress.

Next time, they'd have to start out kissing on the bed instead of scrunching up on the small sofa. Maybe when Daniel returned to Denver, Rick would help facilitate another late-night rendezvous. But somehow, she didn't think he'd be complicit in an activity that, in his opinion, wasn't good for her emotional well-being.

Finally, she got out of bed, crossed the room, and caressed the heavy velvet drapes as she gazed out at the leafless trees in the yard. Sunlight burst through a bank of clouds and streamed through the tall window. She shaded her eyes, closing them for a moment. "Man. What's that?" The sun had taken a holiday for over a week and she'd spent a majority of her time indoors, protecting her throat from the late fall dampness.

She tied back the drapes and opened the window. Not only was it sunny, but reasonably warm for the season. And she knew right then that being outside in fresh air was better for her lungs than remaining inside breathing fumes from oil lamps and cigar smoke. Before she gave the day more thought, a plan was hatched. She was going to Morrison.

Mrs. Murphy had hung Amber's clothes on pegs in the French-style armoire, standing tall upon clawed feet, its mirrored doors reflecting the sun's golden light in starburst patterns on the walls and floor.

She flipped through the skirts and gowns and walking suits and settled on a jacket and skirt of navy wool broadcloth, along with black leather riding boots. Drawers beneath the hanging clothes held various ribbons, lace cuffs, gloves, corsets, chemises, and other undergarments. She pulled a chair over to the wardrobe and stood on it so she could reach the hatboxes on the top shelf.

"No funky hat today," she said out loud. A black wool felt derby completed the ensemble.

When she stared at her reflection, she was surprised by the woman gazing back, not because of the nineteenth-century garb, but because of the wicked smile that reached her eyes. Her dream, stored for safe keeping, might not be playing on a conscious level, but her subconscious wouldn't stop hitting the replay button.

Was Daniel thinking of her the way she was thinking of him? Was he as distracted, imagining making love with her? Or were nineteenth-century men different? Somehow, after last night, she didn't think so. Although she wanted him to be thinking of her, she didn't want him distracted from the work he was sent to do in Cañon City. Instead of thinking of her, she'd settle for being remembered—in an erotic way—when he fell asleep at night.

She clattered down the stairs. If Rick had already gone out on his walkabout, she'd be marching back up to her room to change into a gown appropriate for convalescing, not by choice, but because Mrs. Murphy would harangue her until she did.

"Is Amber awake?" Rick asked.

Oh, good. He's still here.

"I'll send a breakfast tray up at ten, but I don't expect her to leave her room today." The rise and fall of an Irish voice was followed by the muted cling of dome lids against silver serving platters and bowls.

Oh, bad. So is Mrs. Murphy.

With a swish of skirts and briskly clicking heels, Amber followed the voices into the formal dining room. Mrs. Murphy, dressed in a dark skirt with gray shirtwaist tucked smartly into the waistband and armored with a spotless white pinner apron, stood at the sideboard inspecting the serving platters. The aroma of fried bacon and black coffee permeated the dining room, flooded with morning light from an east-facing window. A white linen tablecloth glittered, and crystal cut glassware, polished silverware, and fine china gleamed.

"Not only have I left my bedroom," Amber announced from the doorway, bestowing a good-natured smile on the housekeeper, "but I also intend to leave the house."

"Miss Kelly, please return to your room. You're simply not well enough to go out. Mr. Grant left specific instructions for your care."

Amber crossed over to the buffet and peeked under the domes covering the platters to find scrambled eggs, cheese, bacon, biscuits, sausage, porridge, and a bowl of apples. She scooped eggs onto a plate.

"The way I see it, if Mr. Grant was so concerned, he shouldn't have rushed off with an expectation that his orders would be followed. I feel much better this morning. The sun is shining, and I need fresh air. I'm not used to being cooped up inside. It's either go out or go insane. And that's not a pretty look for me."

The sound of a crystal glass clinking against china came from Rick's direction. His hand was probably shaking from a soundless, deep-belly laugh. She didn't turn his way to see if he was laughing. Instead, she chose to ignore him.

"I see," Mrs. Murphy said, her sharp nose twitching. She picked up empty platters and bustled from the room, the charms on her chain tinkling as her ample hips swung through the narrow servant's door.

Rick turned in his chair, twisting his mouth to hold in a laugh until Mrs. Murphy was out of the room. "Did you practice those lines? If so, you delivered them with chilling conviction."

"Good morning, detective. Or is it lieutenant?"

"*Sir* will do." He pulled out a chair for her to sit next to him. "You look better this morning. Daniel's kiss must have…I don't know…" He shrugged. "Relaxed you enough that you slept peacefully through the rest of the night."

She ignored him for a beat as she drummed her fingers on the table. "I slept well and woke up hungry."

He glanced at her full plate. "I can tell. And you probably had a dream or two that woke you with a smile."

"I had one." She held up her index finger. "It went on and on and on."

He laughed. "That's the only kind to have, and I hope it was in Dolby Vision."

She grinned, and then turned her attention to her plate.

"Now that you're up and feeling better, what do you plan to do with yourself today? Write in your journal? Sketch? Read?"

She prepared herself as best she could for the skirmish she was certain was coming as soon as she announced her intentions. "Go to

Morrison."

He turned his head sharply, giving her the stare to end all stares, and his raffish forelock, usually held in place by his hat or a hair product, fell over his right eye.

"You can't be serious!"

She unfolded the fluted napkin pleat by pleat. "Oh, but I am."

"After what happened to you last night, you're not going to Morrison. If you want to go for a carriage ride around Denver, I'll agree to that, but not a round-trip train ride, and whatever else you're thinking of doing."

"Calm down." She dug into her eggs and swept a generous serving into her mouth. "Look, the quicker I get my work done, the quicker we can go home."

"You don't have any work to do. You just plan to dig in the dirt. You're not up for it. I agreed to act as your bodyguard to keep you safe. That's what I intend to do."

"But—"

"If you try to go on your own, I'll catch you."

The implicit threat—*if you try, I'm taking you home*—was clear.

"Think hard before you make any plans on your own."

"What's the difference if I ride in a carriage or on a train?"

"The train is full of coal dust."

"It is not, and this is insane. You can't stop me from doing what I came here to do." But the bitter truth was with brute force, he could. She pushed a piece of sausage around the flower pattern on the china plate drawing designs in the congealing grease, considering how she could block or go around his power play. "I'll make a deal with you."

He folded his hands and crossed his legs. "I'm not making any deals."

She picked up a cup and saucer and rose to fill it from a carafe on the sideboard, inhaling the fragrant aroma of freshly ground coffee. "You have to negotiate, Rick. That's part of working together."

His mouth twisted into a wry grimace. "Who said we were working together?"

"Oh, stop it." She returned to the table with a cup of coffee. But approaching him from the side, she noticed a red mark on his neck. Teasingly, she flicked at the skin just below his jaw. "Looks like a hickey. I guess one of those scantily dressed women went vampire on you last night."

He drew his head away from her fingernail, blushing. "It's a razor burn."

"Liar. That's why you don't want to leave town today. You're planning on a little afternoon delight." She glanced at her watch pin and did quick mental calculations. "If we leave now and don't have any delays, we'll be back in plenty of time."

Except for a slight blush, there was nothing else to indicate what he was thinking. She thought she'd guessed wrong, and then he smiled. "You're as good as any detective I've worked with. Okay, I'll compromise. We'll leave as soon as we can and take the next train to Morrison. When we arrive, we'll have time to stretch our legs before getting back on the train for the return trip."

"I'd like to stop at the hardware and lumber store to get supplies for a field kit. I saw one directly across from the Morrison depot. They should have the picks, chisels, and brushes I need. I'd also like to check at the livery to be sure we can rent horses tomorrow."

"No, we're getting right back on the train."

"If you'll agree to walk around Morrison and make plans for the next trip, I'll agree to shorten our stay to, say…eight days."

"Three days."

"Forget it."

He stood, leaned on the table with his knuckles and shifted his head until it came close to hers, looking far too menacing. And for the first time since meeting him, she saw the warrior beneath his sexy exterior.

"I thought we were negotiating, sweetheart."

She could do menacing, too. Bending forward with her elbows placed squarely on the table, she came within inches of his face. So close, in fact, she could practically taste the apple butter seasoned with cinnamon he'd spread on his biscuit. "I'm trying to, but you're being unreasonable."

He leaned in even closer. "*Moi?*" Then he straightened and although he didn't have a mustache, he did the one-hand, finger-thumb smoothing thing men with facial hair often did. "Okay. Five days. Last offer."

"Seven."

"Five."

"Six and a half."

"Six," he said.

"Done."

"Damn, Amber. Do you always have to win?"

"I get paid to win." She popped up out of her seat. "Allow me to stand you a drink. Where's the whisky?"

"I don't want a drink. Finish your breakfast. You're as ornery as my sister. I'll go arrange transportation to the train station." He walked out of the room, but she called him back.

"What's her name?"

He smiled ruefully. "JL O'Grady Fraser."

"I'm not asking about your sister."

"I'm a discreet guy, sweetheart. I never kiss and tell. Besides, if you knew, you'd use her to finagle an extension when you run out of days."

"I wouldn't do that. I might be a hard-ass negotiator, but I always negotiate in good faith. I never go back on my word."

"If you say so. I'm going to the stables. I'll meet you in the foyer in fifteen minutes. Don't forget your bear coat. You might not need it now, but Morrison will be cold." He gave her an expectant look, as if he thought their business wasn't yet concluded. If he suspected she'd change their Morrison itinerary, he was probably right. But she'd wait until they arrived there, and she had more control over their schedule. When she didn't say anything out loud, he walked away, the thick rug in the back hallway muffling his footsteps.

Returning to her breakfast, she spread a dollop of apple butter on her own biscuit and considered how much time she had left and what she hoped to accomplish. The remaining hours would slip by like a rushing stream if she didn't find a way to dam the creek. She laid her knife on her plate crosswise, wondering if there was a way to do that.

While munching on the crusty bread, the front door slammed shut and footsteps approached the dining room, echoing through the house. Noah, with Ripley trotting behind him, plowed into the room.

He stopped and stared at her, a question in his sharp eyes. "You're dressed to go out, but Mrs. Murphy said you were resting today."

She put down the biscuit and wiped her fingers on the cloth napkin. "Rick and I are taking the train back to Morrison. I need to buy supplies for a field kit and arrange transportation for tomorrow."

"What's a field kit?"

"Tools of the trade when fossil hunting—hammers and chisels and things."

"Oh." He patted Ripley's head then snuck a piece of bacon from the buffet and slipped it to the dog. "Can Ripley and I go?"

She picked up her crystal water glass, taking her time before responding. She turned the glass right and left and watched sunlight flash from the facets and splinter into rainbows on the tablecloth. She didn't know who was supervising Noah's schedule in his father's absence and didn't want to assume she had any authority in that regard.

"Where's your grandfather?" she finally asked.

"He went to work." Noah hung his head, and although his body language said he was giving up, she knew he was marshalling his arguments and would march them out, one by one as needed. "Ripley and I don't have anything to do."

"I thought boys had dogs so they'd always have a friend to play with."

He sat next to her, one arm resting on the top rung of the ladder-back chair, mimicking Daniel's pose, the one she'd often seen at

Mrs. Garland's breakfast table. "I got tired of throwing sticks and Ripley got tired of chasing them. If I went with you, you could teach me more about dinosaurs. It would be a science lesson."

"That's an interesting argument," she said. "But tell me this. What would you be doing if you were in Leadville right now?"

"I'd be at school."

"Oh, that's right. You should be in school here, too."

Ripley sat next to her chair and whined for attention. She scratched the dog's head and fed her a few scraps from her plate.

"My grandfather's going to hire a tutor to teach me while I'm in Denver."

"Do you like that idea?"

Noah sucked in his upper lip, and she could tell he was mentally weighing the pros and cons. "I'd rather have a holiday."

"But a tutor can give you advanced instruction in math and science. You'll be ahead of your class when you return to school, and you'll be able to help other students who don't know as much as you."

"But that doesn't help me today, Amber. So can I go with you and Rick?"

"It's okay with me. Go ask Mrs. Murphy and tell her we'll be back by mid-afternoon. If she agrees, grab your hat and coat."

While Noah went to find Mrs. Murphy, Amber perused the front page of the *Denver Times* spread out in front of where Rick had been sitting. A quick read of a couple of newspapers always gave her a grasp of the town she was visiting and its leading citizens, regardless of the century.

An above-the-fold article reported on Senator Jerome B. Chaffee. He was retiring from the United States Senate and Nathaniel P. Hill was running to fill his seat. She turned the page and scanned the articles there, finding an interesting notice about Horace Tabor.

> *The Denver Times is involved in a nice libel suit. Mr. Tabor has sued it for libel and places damages at $30,000. He has employed able*

counsel and will push the suit energetically. If the suit should be successful we are sure the Times will not receive much sympathy, for its personal attacks on men of character have been unjustifiable in every way.

Employed an able counsel? Mr. Tabor should have hired her. But when the suit was filed, they hadn't met. She thumbed to the next page. The first headline grabbed her and wouldn't let go.

GIGANTIC AMERICAN REPTILES – Prof. O.C. Marsh, in the last number of the American Journal of Science, states that the Museum of Yale College has recently received the greater portion of the skeleton of a huge reptile, which proves to be one of the most remarkable animals yet discovered. It was found on the eastern flank of the Rocky Mountains, in beds which are regarded as corresponding nearly to the Wealden of Europe, and which may be classed as upper Jurassic. The remains are well preserved but are embedded in so hard a matrix that considerable time and labor will be required to prepare them for a full description. The characteristics already determined point to affinities with the Dinosaurs: Plesiosaurs, and more remotely with the Chebonians, and indicate a new order, which may be termed Stegosauria, from the typical genus here described.

In this specimen, some of the teeth preserved have compressed crowns, and are inserted in sockets. Others are cylindrical and were placed in rows, either in thin plates of imperfect bone, or in cartilage…

The present species was probably about thirty feet long and moved mainly by swimming. For its discovery, science is indebted to Prof. A. Lakes, and…

She closed the paper. At least they got the length right, but the swimming part was all wrong, but that wouldn't be proven for a while. She tapped her fingers on the table thinking how opinions concerning the *Stegosaurus* had changed through the decades, through the centuries. Early on, Marsh believed the dinosaur was bipedal due to its short forelimbs, but he'd changed his mind. When was that exactly? Around 1890, she thought.

The other big controversy that continued for years concerned the plates on the dinosaur's back. Dr. Marsh was convinced they'd been used as armor. But it was later decided, long after Marsh died, that the plates were too thin and too shallowly embedded in the skin to be a protective device. What would the good doctor think if he knew the prevalent idea was that the alternating plates were used as display structures to attract mates?

If Amber met him this week, could she—would she—tell him?

She folded the paper and set it aside just as Noah returned. The cadence of his boot heels sounded remarkably like his father's, and she expected to look up and see Daniel. But it was Noah, and his head hung even lower than before. She knew immediately Mrs. Murphy had said no.

"She said I couldn't go."

Her stomach—eggs and biscuit and all—did an uneasy lurch. "Why? Did she give you a reason?"

"My grandpa isn't working this afternoon, so he's taking me shopping."

"That's awesome."

"But I'd rather go with you and Rick."

She patted the seat of the chair next to her. "Sit down, young man." He plopped into the chair and Ripley laid her head in Noah's lap. "You were so excited to come here. He's your momma's dad, and he wants to love you like he loved her. Enjoy every moment you have with him, because one day he won't be here."

Noah teared up. "One day you won't be here either."

The sad tone of his voice, the look of disappointment on his face, the slump of his body like the weight of the world was too heavy to bear, had tears burning the backs of her eyes. She scooted in her chair until the slats of the ladder-back dug into her shoulder blades, giving her a different kind of pain. If she broke down, Noah would, too. He wanted hope, but she couldn't offer him a forever, and she couldn't lie to him either.

"You're right. One day I won't be here." She took hold of his hand, squeezed it lightly. "Wherever I go, you'll always be in my heart."

He pushed to his feet, knocking over his chair. "I don't want to be in your heart." He yanked his hand away. "I want you to be my ma. You like my pa. I know you do."

Amber sat in shocked silence. Before Noah, she rarely spent time with kids. The law firm hired high schoolers to run errands, and the associates in the office had babies and toddlers she smiled and cooed over, but not kids with problems she couldn't fix with a phone call or a diaper change. What would her granny do?

Amber warmed all over, remembering the hugs, the scent of fresh vegetables and roses from her granny's gardens, the tickling hair that fell from her bun and brushed across Amber's cheek, the softness of her shoulder. Her granny always stopped whatever she was doing and gave Amber her undivided attention, making her the most important person in the world at that moment in time.

That was what her granny would do.

"You can marry him," Noah continued in a pleading voice. "We can all live with Mrs. Garland in Leadville."

Holy Cinderella, Batman.

Marry Daniel? Live in Leadville? The train was leaving the station and her bags were still on the platform.

Holy nightmare.

All she wanted was to have sex with the guy. Noah wanted her to marry his dad and live in a boardinghouse.

Holy knit one, purl two.

Amber brought her feet under her and stood slowly, unsure of her next steps, or even if her legs would carry her there. The chair creaked in response. Or was that her bones creaking? Ripley paid her only a smidgeon of attention before lowering her head and closing her eyes. Oh, the life of a dog.

"Do you suppose we can talk about this without getting angry?" She bent to pick up Noah's overturned chair and set it right again. This situation was so far out of her element, she couldn't think of what else to do. Setting a chair upright was an action step. Did she have another?

Noah swiped at a tear dripping down his cheek. "I'll try."

Remembering her granny's hugs, Amber put her arm around Noah's shoulder. "It sounds like you want to have a grown-up conversation."

That's a good start.

"Let's go to the parlor where adults do that. Okay?" She needed time to think of a plan and changing rooms would give her a moment or two to come up with something. Or maybe Rick would intervene. He'd been a boy once. He'd lost his mother. He'd know what to say to Noah. That was an excellent idea. But where was he now? If they walked slowly, took baby steps, executed a few roundabouts, maybe Rick would rescue her—again.

She took Noah's hand—because that was what her granny would have done—and led him away with Ripley tagging along behind them. They reached the parlor entirely too soon, and she bought another minute by closing the large divider doors, first one side and then the other, instead of pulling them together at the same time.

The room smelled of lemon oil and fear. No. She had to lay claim to the fear smell. It was all hers. The morning sun beamed in through two floor-to-ceiling windows, and she thought of Star Trek and beaming up to Starfleet, and her amber brooch and spinning wildly out of control.

Stop it, Amber. Focus. Focus on the furniture. Focus on anything except marrying Daniel and becoming an instant mother.

The sun glistened off the tops of the polished mahogany furniture, and the pianoforte positioned in the corner with a music book opened on the stand.

Okay. That's a good start.

A modest fire crackled in the fireplace throwing off much-needed heat in the chilly room that bristled with decorum.

That works, too. Keep going.

Noah stood in front of a patterned, tufted parlor chair with embroidered piping, hands clasped behind his back.

Okay.

But when she realized he looked like a miniature of his dad, she thought of marriage and a life in a boardinghouse, and she started wigging out again.

Poke the fire. Do something.

She grabbed the fire iron, poked and poked and poked, but all she was doing was taking her confusion out on the damn log. She set the poker aside and brushed off her hands. Noah remained standing by his chair, waiting for her to sit first.

"Please, sit down." She took a seat opposite him on the floral velvet sofa, demurely crossed her legs at the ankles, and rested her clenched hands in her lap.

Relax. You're sending the wrong signals.

She released her fingers and worked up a nervous smile.

Noah sat, feet firmly planted on the oriental rug. Ripley sat attentively at the side of the chair, guarding her master. Noah looked up expectantly.

Amber cleared her voice. "Now, why exactly do you want a mother? And why do you want me to fill that role?"

"Well, Miss Amber," he said formally. "The reason I want you as my mother is because…well…because…you see…well… Since my ma died, my pa's been sad. I've heard him cry at night when he thinks I'm asleep. He tosses and turns in bed, and sometimes he gets up and goes downstairs. When he comes back, I smell whisky. I don't mind when he drinks whisky because he never gets mean or anything like that, but when he cries, that hurts me because I can't help him. Sometimes he looks at my ma's picture in his watch, and there's such longing in his face that I have to turn away."

Noah shuffled his feet, stared at his hands, then continued. "When I saw Pa look at you for the first time, I saw a look in his face I've never seen before. It wasn't that you had just saved me, it was…well… He wanted you to save him, too."

Amber's heart cracked and splintered. She opened her arms and pulled Noah in for a fierce hug. "Noah, you're such a caring soul. You're always thinking of other people." She sniffed. "Your dad is so lucky to have you." She dug into her pocket for a handkerchief and wiped her nose.

"I try to make Pa smile when he's sad, like I throw sticks for Ripley when she wants to play. Pa changed when he met you. He's not sad like he was. He smiles. When you were on stage singing, he was the happiest I've ever seen him. Even when my ma was alive." Noah ran his hands through Ripley's fur.

"You asked me why I wanted a ma, why I wanted you." He stopped petting his dog and looked up at her. "I don't need a ma, Amber. Pa gives me a mountain of love. And if you ask Pa, he'll say he doesn't need a wife. But, here's the truth…we both need you. You make us smile, and we laugh because you say funny things we don't understand. You give great hugs, you're a wonderful cook, and you have time for others. Digging in the dirt for fossils is something men do, but it doesn't stop you from doing it too. You're smart, and I've never asked you a question you couldn't answer. You know math and science better than my teacher. You're different, but Pa and I like that." He puffed out his little chest when he finished.

A stream of tears poured from her eyes, as if a faucet had been left open to run up a huge water bill. "You're amazing. You have the biggest heart, just like my granny."

"So you'll do it?" he asked.

"Do what exactly? Marry your dad and live with Mrs. Garland in Leadville?"

He nodded.

She laughed and ruffled his hair, realizing she'd missed so much in her life because kids weren't part of it.

"All I can promise is that I'll talk to your dad and tell him about our conversation."

Noah licked his lips, and his eyes told her that he had one more point to make. She held her breath, knowing this was the big one. The one he'd been building up to.

"My ma and pa were always hugging and kissing. Like the McBains. And at night when the lights were off, and they were in bed, they moaned a lot. The next day, they were always smiling. If you and Pa hugged and kissed—"

She placed a finger across his lips. This was one topic they weren't going to discuss. If he needed a birds and bees lesson, he'd have to get it from Rick. "As I said, I'll tell him about our conversation."

"You promise?"

"I promise. Now, go play. I've got some fossils to find."

Noah and Ripley ran out the front door, and she sat there motionless, gazing into the flames, seeking the soothing influence of the fire. What was she going to do? She knew in her heart she couldn't stay, so how could she prepare Noah and Daniel for another major loss in their lives?

Daniel, we'll have to do this together, and we better do it right, for all our sakes.

35

1878 Denver, Colorado—Olivia

THE ROLLER-COASTER RIDE through time happened quickly, confusing Olivia's brain with a dizzying array of visual images and both high and negative Gs. She'd had no time to prepare for the next twist or turn, and her internal organs had been tossed like a bag full of corn, especially her stomach, which was now probably lodged inside her brain.

She opened her eyes. Closed them. Opened them again. Rubbed them. Closed them. Took a few deep breaths and opened them again. Nothing changed.

The town spread out before her could have been heaven, it could have been hell, or could be a movie lot at Paramount Pictures. If her eyes didn't believe what she saw, then the stink of manure, unwashed bodies, and garbage certainly did. She had traveled through time and that reality ping-ponged from the logic side of her brain to the creative side and sent waves of shock zip lining down her spine.

Where was Connor? As soon as she found him, she'd apologize for all the horrible words she'd thrown at him. But where was he? She'd been gripping his steel-band arm during the twisting and turning. And now he was gone, and so were Kenzie and David.

If I stay in the shadow of this wagon, shaking like a fool, I'll never find them.

A train whistle sounded, she jerked, and the ground shuddered with the rhythmic vibration of a passing train.

Move. Step up on the walkway. Look for help.

Amber had come through the fog by herself and had managed. Olivia could manage as well. She could be afraid yet choose to act. Courage was not the absence of fear, but the triumph over it. Granny's advice always came in handy.

"On we go." Olivia took several deep breaths then hopped up on the walkway.

See, that's not so bad.

She gripped the railing and surveyed the scene.

One- and two-story clapboard and brick buildings lined both sides of a wide dirt boulevard. Across the street were, according to their signs, the Doll & Louis Upholsters, Hageloor Veterinary Surgeons, Haggert Tailors, St. Charles Hotel, Wholesale Grocer, Simonton Livery, Feed & Sale Stables, and the Rocky Mountain Herald Newspaper.

She didn't recognize the buildings or the businesses.

For someone well versed in Denver history, places, and physical features she was clueless as to where she was. She'd never been here before. Never seen this corner. Never seen these buildings. Was she even in Denver?

She was in some godforsaken place in a time not her own.

Kenzie had said if they became separated, she was to go to the meeting place—her house in the twenty-first century. She couldn't go there until she figured out where she was, assuming she was even in Denver. There was no Uber to call to request a lift to 5431 California Street. And if she could flag a taxi, if they even existed, she had no money to pay the driver.

So what was she to do now? She bit her lip too hard, then rubbed it with her knuckles. Her ability to roughly know where she was even in unfamiliar places was a well-developed homing instinct and had served her well in her business. But she didn't even have that at her disposal. She couldn't tell north and south from east and west.

Where are the mountains?

The skyline would give her two cardinal directions. The southern Rocky Mountains lay west, the High Plains lay east. Once she knew that, she could find her way around the city.

The door to the Patrick Frain Saloon swung open and the smell of whisky and beer and the scorched scent of burnt coffee spilled out along with off-key piano music. The boardwalk pulsed with pedestrians and she pushed her way through the crowd. When she reached the end of the block she eased out into the street and looked in the direction of the train whistle.

A slice of sun hovered over snow-capped Mount Rosalie, the highest summit of the Chicago Peaks in the front range of the Rocky Mountains. A shudder of relief went through her. Buildings could change, street names could change, but the mountains always stayed the same. Amber disagreed.

Don't tell your clients that. Extreme weather events constantly reshape the landscape. Just look at what happened during the historic rains in 2013.

And Amber would be right. But that didn't alter Olivia's spiel when she drove clients around the Mile High City and its environs.

Now, thanks to the identifiable mountain range, she knew east from west. As soon as she figured out what street she was on, she'd be on her way. But there was no street sign at the intersection. There had to be a sign somewhere. Then she spotted an address on the fascia above the Gothic arches of a two-story brick building—15TH & HOLLADAY STREETS—and let out a throaty laugh. How weird was that? This was her wheelhouse. From here, she could make her way through the city.

"Olivia!"

She spun in the direction of the voice. "Connor!" Vast relief settled over her.

He removed his hat and waved, smiling. A breeze lifted his light brown hair on one side, sending a strand across his forehead.

She waved back. "Stay there. I'm coming over."

The crinkle around his dark green eyes and the dimple that punctuated his smile warmed her heart. "No. You wait. It's too dangerous."

She waved him off. Dangerous? Who was he kidding? She even drove in New York City. What was a little traffic congestion?

Wagons, carriages, and riders on horseback went wherever they found an opening, and pedestrians dodged here and there among them. When she saw an opening, she took it, and ran the gauntlet to the other side.

Connor stood next to a hitching post anxiously awaiting her, his arms outstretched like a proud dad watching his child take its first steps. When she reached him, she grabbed his hand. Hers was icy with tension. His was warm with relief. He pulled her into his arms, and the warmth spread to her face and neck and down to her belly and beyond. It felt so right to be there, and then she remembered the pain of his lies and pulled back from his embrace.

"I'm so glad to find you," she said.

"Where were you?"

She pointed over her shoulder. "In the shadow of that wagon. You wouldn't have seen me. Why'd we get separated?"

He escorted her up the steps to the boardwalk. "I think the damn stones are becoming unstable. It's time to get out of this business."

It was hard to hear over the sound of a brass ensemble coming from a dance hall. "Let's cross the side street. It's too noisy here to talk." Crossing the next street wasn't nearly as dangerous. They stopped on the southwest corner of 15th and Holladay. "Where are Kenzie and David?"

"They could be on the other side of the city or down the block. Do you know where we are?"

"Yes." Not only had she found Connor, but she knew where they were. She pointed to the two-story brick building in front of them.

"You have that look about you." His gaze stayed fixed on her in a disbelieving sort of way. "You have a story, don't you?"

"This was originally called McGaa Street after William McGaa, who helped name the city's streets. But he turned into the town drunk. The city fathers voted to remove his name in favor of Benjamin Holladay, the stagecoach king. Holladay established his headquarters in this building." She pointed to redirect Connor's attention.

He laughed, and she smirked. "Go on," he said. "I'm listening."

She leaned in, looked around to be sure no one could hear her and said, "By the 1880s Denver was booming, and Holladay Street had become the center of the city's red-light—"

"Rick! What are ye doing here?"

Olivia and Connor turned to see a man exiting the Wells Fargo Building.

"Sorry. You've got the wrong O'Grady," Connor said.

Square jaw, chiseled face, dark blue eyes, neatly clipped beard. Olivia recognized him immediately. He was the man in her flash. The man in David's picture. She brazenly walked up to him. "You're Agent Grant, aren't you?"

He touched his hat. "Yes, ma'am." His eyes stayed on her, moving from the top of her head to the bottom of her boots. She pushed back her hat to see him better. A small, barely visible frown and a discreet shake of his head preceded a pissed-off look that had her stepping away from him.

"Who are ye?" he asked.

The sharpness in Daniel's tone took her aback, and for a moment she couldn't answer. When she found her voice, her words were delivered with cold deliberation. "Olivia Allison Kelly."

"Miss Kelly is looking for her sister," Connor said. "We were told Amber traveled with you from Leadville. Unless you abandoned her along the way, you should know where she is, along with my brother."

Daniel and Connor squared off, two men of equal height and body build, both in law enforcement, neither easily intimidated. Connor was armed. She assumed beneath the black duster, Daniel was as well.

"Who are ye?" he asked Connor.

"Connor O'Grady. I guess you know my brother Rick. If your

opinion of him isn't favorable, don't take it out on me." Connor went in for the laugh. He didn't get one, but at least the quip raised a slight smile on the agent's face.

Daniel scratched the back of his neck, shaking his head slightly. "Is that the same for ye, Miss Kelly? If my opinion of yer sister is unfavorable, I'm not to take it out on ye?"

On a scale of one to ten, she relaxed to an eight, but she'd been off the charts at about a fifteen, so that wasn't saying much. She gave him a sly smile. "Amber is such an agreeable soul, I can't imagine you having an unfavorable opinion of her."

This time amusement flitted across his face.

"Olivia! Connor!"

They all turned to see Kenzie on the opposite corner, hands cupped at her mouth, David beside her.

Daniel opened his mouth to speak but, at first, nothing came out. Then, "The McBains are here, too?"

The couple crossed the street and David extended his hand. "Good to see ye again."

Daniel shook it, then kissed Kenzie on both cheeks. "I'm surprised to see ye here. I thought ye were heading west."

"That was our intention, but after the stage left Leadville, we realized we'd made a mistake leaving Amber. We should have sent a telegram," David said.

Daniel's eyes narrowed. "That would have been wise. But now that ye're here, maybe ye can convince Amber to see a doctor to find out what's ailing her."

"I heard she was having breathing issues," Olivia said, "but telling her to go to the doctor has never worked. She hates them. If our mother can't get her to the doctor, no one can."

"Amber has never mentioned her parents. I assumed they were deceased," Daniel said.

Olivia gave Daniel a pointed look. "They're out of the country on vacation, but they're alive and well. And in fact—"

"Alive and well and anxious to get their daughters home," Kenzie interjected. "Where is Amber now?"

"She and Rick are with my son Noah at my father-in-law's residence on Sherman Street."

David took a step toward Daniel. "Why'd her plans change?" Tension etched David's face. "When we left ye at the stage in Leadville, she intended to stay at the Hughes residence. Why the switch?"

Daniel stood his ground, but he visibly bristled. With his eyebrows drawn down, he looked hard at David, then his gaze shifted to Connor to Kenzie to Olivia, sending each of them a silent message to back off. No one moved.

"The telegram I received before leaving Leadville was from the agency, informing me of new orders to report to Cañon City. I was concerned for Noah's welfare. He barely knows his grandfather Robinson. It wasn't until we reached Morrison that I had a chance to talk to Amber in private. I explained that having her with him would ease the lad's adjustment. She agreed."

Olivia jumped out of the path of a man—his hat pulled low over his brows—before he ran over her. Connor quickly moved to stand behind her, and his hands closed over her shoulders protectively. She was acutely aware of him, and the hypnotizing aromatic blend of cedar, smoke, and exotic spices on his hands and in his hair.

"How long will you be in Cañon City?" Kenzie asked.

Daniel held up the crushed paper in his hand. "The agency can't make up its mind whether to send me to Pueblo or Cañon City. I don't know how long I'll be out of town. It could be several weeks. There are two railroads trying to build up the canyon to Leadville, courts contradicting themselves, and owners hiring gangs of cutthroats to protect their rights."

"I'm familiar with the Royal Gorge War. Whose rights are you trying to protect?" Olivia asked.

"I'm hired out to the Rio Grande."

Olivia slipped on her gloves and straightened the seams, while considering the Royal Gorge War timeline. The lease would be the next step in the process. "If General Palmer is down there, tell him not to lease the tracks to Santa Fe. That will only complicate the litigation and cost the Rio Grande hundreds of thousands of dollars."

"Yer sister said the same thing. Ye should talk to the general, convince him, not me."

"I'll be glad to."

"In the meantime," Kenzie said, "if this conversation is to continue, is there a restaurant nearby where we can escape the press of men going in and out of the Wells Fargo office and get a cup of coffee?"

Olivia pointed. "The St. Charles Hotel is down the street. It should have a restaurant."

"We could get rooms there, change out of our traveling clothes, then call on Amber," Kenzie said.

"That's not necessary," Daniel said. "There's room at my father-in-law's. How long do ye intend to stay?"

"That depends on Amber," Olivia said. "But I'd like to leave as soon as possible. And I wouldn't want to impose on your family. A hotel will suit our needs."

Daniel's face creased with concern. "Maybe, but Amber would like ye close by. If she has another attack ye can convince her to see the doctor."

"What kind of attack did she have?" Olivia asked.

"She couldn't catch her breath. When she lay down, it eased somewhat, and then she fell asleep. When I left a while ago, I gave the housekeeper instructions that Amber wasn't to leave the house today," Daniel said.

Olivia glanced up at Connor. "We need to go by the house first and talk to her. Then decide what to do." She turned her gaze back to Daniel. "Where exactly is the house? What's the address?"

"If ye're not familiar with Denver, ye should take a hack. The residence is on the corner of 19th Street and Sherman. It's a two-story with a mansard roof."

Olivia knew the area, and the corner as well. General William Jackson Palmer was another early resident of Capitol Hill, but she wasn't sure his house was built yet.

"Is there a livery nearby?" David asked. "I'd prefer to rent a carriage or horses to get around the city."

"There's one down the street," Olivia said.

Kenzie gave her a questioning look. "Have you been scoping out the real estate already?"

Olivia smiled. "I'm always looking."

"If I had a carriage, I'd offer to take ye," Daniel said, "but I only have my horse. Did ye take a hack here? Ye're blocks from the railroad station."

"Yes, we did. Then David wanted to send a telegram. That's why we're here," Connor said.

"Ye could have sent yer telegram at the train station."

"He didn't think about it until after we left the station," Kenzie said.

Olivia looped arms with Kenzie. "Let's get off this corner and warm up. Shall we go?"

David extended his hand to Daniel again. "It was good to see ye. If ye can make it back for a visit while we're still here, I'd like to talk to ye about a job."

"For me or ye?" Daniel asked.

Before David could answer, Kenzie kissed Daniel's cheek. "It was good to see you. I'm sorry you're leaving. Hurry back, if you can."

Daniel glanced at Olivia. She saw something unreadable in his eyes, and she was struck by how beautiful they were, lined with dark, thick lashes. But it was the depth and warmth of them that pulled her in, and she would have willingly stayed there.

"Thank you for helping Amber. I hope we'll see you again," Olivia said.

Kenzie tugged on her arm. "Shall we go?"

"About the job…" Beneath the brim of Daniel's hat his apprehension was clearly visible.

"Come back and we'll talk," David said.

Kenzie and Olivia walked away, arm in arm. "I quit counting the lies we told him." She gave Kenzie a sour face. "Lies seem normal, and I'm becoming numb to the truth. Is that how it is with the brooches?"

"You have to stay as close to the truth as possible, or sidestep, or dance around without committing. Inevitably you'll get caught and you won't remember which lie you told and you'll end up telling a different story," Kenzie said.

"I hate lying."

"We all do, sweetie. But sometimes we have to lie to protect the brooches or—"

"Don't say it," Olivia answered swiftly, almost sharply.

"What?" Kenzie asked.

"Sometimes we have to lie to protect those we love. I've heard too much of that." Olivia swallowed an ache rising in her throat. "I'm glad Daniel's leaving. I'd hate to keep lying to him."

"Does that mean you're going to give Connor a break now that you've experienced our conundrum?"

Olivia had boxed herself into a corner. Connor had lied to her just as she had lied to Daniel. If Amber had gone home and was safely in the future, Olivia would have told him Amber caught the train to Chicago and wasn't coming back. There was no way she could tell him the truth. He simply wouldn't understand.

The irony wasn't lost on her.

36

1878 Denver, Colorado—Amber

THE TRIP TO Morrison was entirely too short. Amber and Rick disembarked, walked across the street to the hardware and lumber store for supplies, talked to the owner of the livery about renting horses, then caught the next train back to Denver.

She didn't gripe, argue, or mention her chest pain. If she was going to return the next day, she had to have his cooperation. Not that she couldn't do it all by herself, because she could—any other time. Today, though, her feet felt as though a trainer had affixed twenty-pound weights to the bottoms of her boots.

Stressing over her health was as worrisome as the sickness. Why did she have to get sick now? You'd think suffering through a series of sore throats would be enough. Maybe she had walking pneumonia. She wasn't sure what the symptoms were, but it sounded like a legitimate possibility. The cure, she figured, was rest and staying hydrated. But wasn't there a cough and fever involved? Where was Google when you really needed a search engine?

Now, as they rode in a carriage back to Alec's house, she hated to admit, even to herself, that she was afraid to be alone. If she had another attack and no one was there to help her...

"I'll escort you inside, then I'm taking off for a couple of hours."

Rick's statement intruded on her angst. "Where are you going?"

"I thought you knew."

"Oh, her. I forgot. How long will it…take you?"

He laughed. "I'm not going to see a woman. Although I'm flattered by the note of jealousy I detect in your voice."

She backhanded his arm. "You do not."

He laughed again. "Alec arranged a meeting with Chief Ouray, the tribal leader of the Utes. I've read he's a skilled negotiator and fluent in Ute, English, and Spanish. For me, meeting him is like you meeting Dr. Marsh or Dr. Cope."

"What I know of him is limited to my high school history class, which was years ago. If you meet him, you can't tell him about the White River Utes rampage and what happens to the Utes in Colorado," she said.

"Why not? Aren't you trying to change what happened in the gorge?"

"I'm just trying to save the railroad a few dollars. Interjecting yourself in the history of Native Americans is different. The timber, mining, and cattle interests in Denver tried for years to remove the Utes from the state. What if you stop the massacre at the White River Agency and something worse happens to them?"

"Worse? Right now, they have almost the entire western third of Colorado. What could be worse than losing all that, plus getting kicked out of the state?"

She pressed her palm against her pounding forehead, wondering how she was going to survive this trip. "What are we doing here?"

"I know why I'm here. I came to rescue you. But if it's any consolation, all time travelers have had this problem."

"My head is spinning. Is there something you're going to do with the information?"

"Write a blog post," he said, matter-of-factly.

"You have a blog?" Her surprise changed quickly to delight. "I can't wait to read it." She waited for the blush to creep up his neck, the way it did when she teased him about something, but he surprised her.

His eyes turned dark, and he was deadly serious when he said, "Don't you dare tell a soul. I don't use my real name."

"You have a *nom de plume*? What name are you using?" She just looked at him, one eyebrow slightly raised. She didn't think he would answer, but that didn't stop her from asking.

"I'm not telling you. There are already three writers in the clan and the competition among them is fierce. I do this for a hobby, not to make money, and I don't want to be part of their race to make the best-seller list."

"You have to write a book to make the list."

When he didn't respond, she gazed at him with her mouth falling open, and her heart swelling with excitement for him. "You've written a book?"

"Nobody knows, and if it gets out, you'll be the only one on the list of possible leakers. I'll get even—I swear."

"That's so awesome. At least tell me what it's about."

His voice held a sharp edge when he said, "A Western, and that's all I'm saying."

"That's it? We're not going to talk about your writing career?"

"There's nothing to talk about." His voice was deadpan, neutral. And, that meant, she would get nothing else from him.

After a few moments, as if they hadn't been talking about anything else, he asked, "Would you like to go out to dinner tonight? I've heard there are a couple of fine restaurants in the city. Or we could take in a show."

"Thanks for the invitation, but I'll stay in. I want to spend time with Noah and write a to-do list for tomorrow. We're still going back, right?" For Amber, this adventure held echoes of the childhood euphoria she'd had when finding her first fossils around Hughes Cabin. She couldn't wait to get her hands in the dirt and talk to other rock hounds. If it would make her feel better tomorrow, she'd even agree to drink whatever elixir the local quack had in mind to give her.

Rick scratched his beard-stubbled chin. "You know… You surprised me out there today. You always surprise me, but today you really did."

"Oh, yeah? How so?"

"I thought you'd complain. You didn't. I thought you'd demand we rent horses and go for a ride. You didn't. I thought you'd want to see more, do more, and bug the crap out of me, but you didn't. I'm not used to being so wrong. You were a real trooper. I'm looking forward to going back tomorrow."

She pinned him with a look. "Why?"

He shrugged, obviously not wanting to make a big deal of his confession. "I enjoyed listening to you talk to the clerk at the hardware store about the variegated clays and shales and beds of shaley sandstone weathering brown…"

She laughed. "How could you possibly remember that?"

He cupped the sides of his head. "I have phonographic ears."

She laughed again, touching his arm affectionately this time instead of smacking it, which she did often. "There's no such thing. And if I surprised you, you surprised me. Any man who would hang out while I hunted dinosaur bones is extraordinary." She winked. "I might have to reconsider a friends-with-benefits relationship with you."

He pulled her in for a breath-stealing side hug. "Just say the word, sweetheart."

The hug squeezed her chest and made her cough. "You're killing me, O'Grady." She scooted over before he hugged her again.

The carriage wheels rattled down the dirt road and came to a stop in front of Alec's residence. Smoke spiraled from the chimneys in the four corners of the mansion, and the early afternoon sun was slanting toward the parlor's large mullioned windows. The bare branches of the Rocky Mountain maples planted in the front yard pointed toward the sky, as if the arms of the leafless trees were raised in surrender.

The driver jumped down and opened the door. Rick preceded her out of the carriage, carrying a brown bag with the tools she'd purchased. He slung the sack, the tools clinking together, over his shoulder. "Come, my dear." He lifted her, setting her feet firmly on the ground. "You can't weigh a hundred pounds even in all those clothes."

"Thank goodness I do, or I'd blow away in the wind gusts that move in through the plains." She smiled and slid her hand around his proffered arm. The uneven mud and gravel created a hazard for a woman in a long skirt, or lead-weighted feet.

They passed through the gate and strolled up the walk to the porch. As they neared the front door, it flew open and Olivia barreled out, squealing, "Amber!"

Shocked, Amber fell back against Rick's chest, and he held her shoulders to keep her upright. "Oh my God. What are you doing here?"

Olivia grabbed her, and they locked in a tight embrace, giggling and crying as if they'd been separated for months instead of a week—and a century and a half—but no one was counting years.

"I can't believe you're here."

Their arms were all but padlocked around each other's waist. Nothing could separate them now. "I came with Kenzie and David and Connor. We were worried about you."

Olivia looked up at Rick. "Hi. I'm Olivia, and you look exactly like Connor."

He kissed her cheek. "And you look exactly like Amber."

They walked through the doorway, laughing. Amber tugged off her gloves, removed her hat, and handed both to the butler. "Where are Mr. and Mrs. McBain?"

"They're in the parlor, Miss Kelly."

"And Noah? Is he here?"

"He's with his grandfather downtown."

Olivia took Amber's hand and led her into the parlor where Kenzie and David sat on the sofa, their heads together in hushed conversation.

"I can't believe you came back," Amber said.

Kenzie climbed to her feet and hugged her. "It seems like months ago that we left you in Leadville."

"In some ways it feels like it."

Rick hugged a man standing near the window who could easily be his twin. "Hey, bro. Good to see ya. This is a surprise."

Amber extended her hand. "You must be Connor!"

He gave her hand a teasing swat. "Put that away and give me a hug. I've been waiting a long time to meet you." Connor's chest was broader than Rick's, but other than that, their hugs were identical. The same pull-you-in-and-squeeze-you-tight. The real kind of hug that gathers you in for seconds and thirds.

Amber coughed from having her lungs squashed flat. She looked around the group to see who she was missing. "David! I forgot to hug you."

"Kenzie always gets top billing. I'm just an afterthought." He kissed Amber's cheeks before hugging her but didn't try to squeeze the life out of her like the O'Grady men.

Amber took a seat in a rosewood framed, button-tufted parlor chair next to a matching sofa. "How'd you find us? Did you go by the Hugheses?"

David and Kenzie returned to the sofa, and Olivia took the other parlor chair while Rick lounged comfortably on the arm of Amber's chair. Millie ran into the room and pounced on Amber's lap. Her hands entwined with Rick's as they rubbed the cat's belly, which got raised eyebrows from David and Connor.

"Looks like ye have a friend," David said.

"She's taken to us, hasn't she, Rick?"

"Yeah, but she likes me better."

"I don't know about that. She slept with me, not you."

"Amber," Olivia said. "We don't care about the cat. We want to know about you. How are you feeling? Don't you think you need to go home and see a doctor?"

"Other than a little tired, I'm fine. So, did you go by the Hugheses or not?"

"We didn't have to. As soon as we arrived..." Olivia paused and looked around the room and said in a low voice, "We got separated in the..." She made circle motions with her hand. "Connor found me right away, and then we ran into Daniel Grant at the Wells Fargo office."

Amber wasn't surprised, she was bowled over. And not just

because Olivia had already met Daniel, but because he was still in town. "How on earth did you know who he was?"

Olivia laughed. "David had a picture, but I'd seen Daniel before."

Amber leaned in her sister's direction and whispered, "In a flash, you mean?"

"It's okay. I told them about the sightings."

"What sightings?" Rick asked.

"Olivia sees people."

"Dead people? Like in the movie *The Sixth Sense*?" He narrowed his eyes, and his gaze swept over Olivia like a mental frisking.

"No, Olivia sees living people." Amber turned her attention to her sister. "When did you see him?"

"I don't know. Probably around the time you asked me to find a building for your kitchen and retail store."

"Why didn't you tell me?"

"Tell you what? That I saw a man coming out of the building? Anyway, I wouldn't have known the significance without seeing David's picture of him."

"Did he recognize you?"

"He recognized Connor and called him Rick. Then he glanced at me and the color drained from his face. Bless his heart. He looked like he could use a stiff drink. He probably hit the closest saloon after we left him," Olivia said. "Nice guy, though. Gorgeous eyes."

"I felt sorry for him," Connor said. "Then when Kenzie and David showed up, he regained his equilibrium and seemed fine after that."

"So he told you about the change in plans."

"Yes, and why he wanted you here—even though I'm not sure I believed him," Kenzie said. "I think he just wanted to know where you were."

Millie bumped Amber's hand to keep stroking her. "Where is Daniel now?" Amber asked as she obeyed the cat.

"He was going to the train, but I believe he'll come back."

"I'm not so sure." Amber glanced behind her. Although she

didn't see any of the staff or hear the clack of their shoes on the hardwood floors, she had a prickly sensation—a pins and needles sort of feeling—on the back of her neck, like the warnings she'd get in the mountains when the weather threatened to turn bad or a wild animal crept too close.

She glanced up at Rick. "Would you mind closing the doors? Somebody might overhear."

He stepped across the oriental rug, closed the matching pair of doors with stained-glass inserts and identical window above the transom, and returned to his perch on the arm of Amber's chair. The cat meowed, and he picked her up off Amber's lap and cradled her in the crook of his arm.

"Daniel caught me in a couple of lies last night."

"Just one," Rick said. "And he suspects there are more. He's suspicious, probably of all of us, but he doesn't seem to trust Amber."

"Well, thanks," she said.

Millie jumped down and scratched at the door to be let out. Rick opened one side to find Mrs. Murphy standing there eavesdropping.

She recovered quickly, and using the end of her apron, wiped smudges from the woodwork. "Would you like refreshments?"

"Whisky, hot tea for the ladies, and cake, if you have any." Rick waited until she stepped away before he closed the door again. "I'd watch what you say around here. The walls have ears."

"Finish your story about Daniel," Kenzie said. "What'd he do when he caught you lying?"

"He stormed out, left early this morning. I'll be surprised if I see him again."

"Get ready then, because I have a feeling he'll be back tonight. Alec is having a dinner party and invited the Rio Grande board members and their attorney, Adam Hughes," Kenzie said.

"Isn't that exciting?" Olivia said. "I can't wait to meet Adam."

"You can't tell him who you are, but you can ask about his house," Kenzie said.

"I know. I'll have to lie to him, too." Olivia and Connor briefly exchanged glances before she looked away and directed a question to Amber. "So how was Morrison? Was it everything you thought it would be?"

"A clerk at the hardware store told me Arthur Lakes is still on the hogback but intends to leave shortly to spend a few months with Dr. Marsh at Yale. I hope I can track him down tomorrow."

"Dr. Lakes? That's awesome." Olivia raised her hand to give Amber a high-five and they slapped palms. "I know you're excited to meet one of your heroes."

Brisk footsteps sounded outside the door, along with the creak of a cart's wheels. Before Mrs. Murphy could knock, Rick opened the door. "I'll take that. Thank you." He pushed the cart into the room and closed the door again. "Who wants a drink?"

"I'll take one," Connor said.

Rick poured the drinks and handed a glass to Connor.

"You look tired," Olivia said. "Why don't we go upstairs? Catch up. Take a nap."

"Before you go…" Kenzie glanced at David and he squeezed the back of her neck and gave her a look that said his world orbited hers. "We came back because we were worried about Amber and Rick. Now that we know you're okay, unless you need something, we're going home. We're concerned about the crisis at the winery, and David is especially worried about Elliott. We feel confident Rick and Connor can handle everything here."

Amber almost hated to ask, but she did. "When?"

"Now," Kenzie said. "I haven't seen my kids in a week."

"I hate to see you go—again, but there's no reason for you to stay," Amber said. "I'll be done in Morrison in a couple of days, then we'll go home."

"Are you sure?" Kenzie asked. "There's not anything else to keep you here?"

"I could find plenty to do in Cañon City, but I'm not sure I could convince Rick to take me there."

"Isn't that where Daniel went?" Connor asked.

"He's guarding the stations along the line from Denver to Cañon

City. I don't know where exactly."

She caught the barest flicker of a glance between Kenzie and David, and his brows drew together, knotted in a frown of concentration. Kenzie tapped her fingers on her lap, and the room grew quiet, save for the murmur of the fire and the gentle creak of settling timber. A small, cold shudder of premonition flowed up Amber's back, making her scalp twitch. She shook her head to clear it, and looked up to find Rick's eyes on her, soft brown and full of speculation.

"What's going on?" she asked. "I feel like I'm the only one in the room who hasn't been let in on the secret."

"If there's a secret, I don't know it either." Olivia glanced at Kenzie. "Is there a secret? I don't like being left out in the cold. There have been too many omissions already. We don't need more."

Kenzie broke the silence. "I've told you both that the brooches have a purpose and we never know what it is until we debrief. It's possible Amber's already fulfilled that, but we don't know. Something important could come from the meeting with Dr. Lakes, whoever he is, in Morrison, or dinner with Adam Hughes and the board of directors, or even with Daniel. We don't know. I wish we did."

"Are we in danger?" Amber asked.

"If I thought you were in physical danger, I wouldn't leave," Kenzie said.

"We already know our moral code is in the process of shattering," Olivia said. "Our integrity is shot to hell. We're all a bunch of liars and trying to rationalize it is a waste of energy."

"What would you have us do?" Connor asked. "Give the stones to the government and be done with them? Sink them in the middle of the ocean? Bury them under the melting icecap? We didn't ask for this. Kenzie didn't ask to be dropped into the middle of an air raid or tortured by the British Secret Service. Charlotte didn't deserve to be threatened by General Sherman. We were singled out to bear this burden. And if our code of ethics is corrupted because of it, then so be it. I'm sorry I lied to you, Olivia. I'm sorry I *had* to lie to you." He finished his drink, refilled his glass, then moved to stand by the window and stared out into the darkening afternoon sky.

Amber knew her sister as well as she knew herself, maybe better, and the tension in the room wasn't from her or Kenzie or David or Rick. It rippled from Connor and Olivia. From the tears shining in her eyes, it was obvious to all of them that Olivia was in love with Connor, and he with her, and her sister was too damn scared to take a chance.

Amber leaned in to Rick, and he rubbed her neck. He said without words that he understood. Having him there for support helped push past the knot in her throat. Her sister deserved a good man, and if Connor was anything like his brother, then she knew he was exactly what Olivia wanted and needed, if only...

"Ye'll have two brooches with ye." David's statement disrupted the ripples and pulled everyone's attention away from the undercurrent. "Connor has the amethyst, and Amber has her brooch. If ye don't come back right away, we'll give ye a week before we come back again to bring ye home for good."

"This is turning into a revolving door mission. There's never been this much coming and going," Kenzie said.

"I don't want to come back, so don't piss around," David ordered. "Go to Morrison, get yer work done, and come home."

"If Amber has another breathing attack, I'm taking her home immediately," Rick said.

Olivia put her hand to her throat and worry wrinkled the bridge of her nose. "How many have you had?"

"I'm fine, and I'm not going to talk about my health," Amber said.

"You never want to talk about it." Olivia appraised her with eyes that held a combination of fear and worry and love. "You're the opposite of a hypochondriac. Instead of having a preoccupation with the belief that you have a disease, you ignore symptoms and warning signs. So far, you've lucked out, but that won't last forever."

"If I talk about it, it'll become a self-fulfilling prophecy, just like Granny."

"And what? You think you'll die because you're sick. God, Amber. You're not going to die. Not now anyway. When you're older, maybe, but that's different. You need to see a doctor."

"I will. As soon as I get home, I'll go see that specialist Mom wanted me to see. The internal guy."

Olivia pinned Amber with a look of almost manic intensity. "He's called an internist."

Amber scratched her nose, grinning. "I know. I've talked to him. I haven't seen him as a patient, but I've met him."

Olivia put her hands to the sides of her head and grabbed at her hair. "You're incorrigible." She dropped her hands and blew out a long breath. "All right, then, we won't talk about it. Just so long as Rick has it under control, I won't harp."

Kenzie pushed to her feet. "If her health issues continue, get Amber home immediately. And please be careful."

"That's not a request, ladies," David said. "That's an order."

Amber and Olivia gave him snappy salutes. "Aye-aye, cap'n."

David wrapped his arm around Kenzie's waist. "If yer ready, lass, let's go home."

"We should leave the room," Connor said. "We don't want to be sucked up in the vortex. Safe travels. See you soon."

After hugs all around, the Kellys and the O'Gradys left the parlor and stood guard at the door until the faint smell of peat wafted out into the foyer through the cracks.

Connor sniffed. "I think they're gone." He opened the doors to find the room empty. "It's just us now. Let's take care of each other and pray we all get home."

Amber tucked a strand of her hair behind her ear, feeling a deep longing well up in her chest, but she tried not to let it show. Losing Kenzie to the fog again saddened her. Due to Kenzie's past relationship with Trey, her leaving was also a reminder he was gone, and while the fog could bring Kenzie back, it would never bring him.

Olivia picked up on Amber's sudden melancholy. "Come on, sis. Let's go see what you've got in your closet. We'll need to dress for dinner, and Kenzie said you had a dress that might work for me."

"She doesn't know you well. If she did, she'd know you haven't set foot in my closet since I was twelve years old."

Olivia laced her arm with Amber's and they strolled through the foyer. "That's not true. I was in there a year ago."

"Oh right. I remember now. Not. Are you crazy? You haven't been in my closet in twenty years."

"It seems like a year ago. Besides, Kenzie said she picked out your wardrobe and I trust her judgment, even though I've only known her for a few hours."

Amber turned back to look at the guys, standing side by side, hands on their hips. "If you both go out"—she wagged her finger at Rick—"keep Connor away from that vampire who sucked the heck out of your neck."

Connor backhanded Rick in the chest. "What the hell?"

Rick ducked. "She's making it up. I cut myself shaving and she's convinced it's something else."

"Don't give me that crap. I'm the one who told you when you were a freshman in high school to tell Mom your hickey was a razor burn."

"Yeah, and I almost got away with it until she put alcohol on the spot. When it didn't sting, she knew the truth, and I got grounded."

"You're such a dumbass."

"Don't leave the house, Amber," Rick said. "Even if you hear a paleontologist is on the corner selling bones. I know you, you'll be out of here faster than light drains from a high desert sky at sunset."

"Coming from a man who's spent the last two years in the desert, you'd know how fast that is. But I'm not going out. I promise."

"That goes for me, too," Olivia said.

Amber and Olivia snickered all the way up the stairs. "What a pair." When they reached Amber's bedroom, they went in and she pushed the door closed, rotated the key, and the bolt scraped home. "I don't want anyone barging in while we sort through the last few days. What's going on with you and Connor? I know you're in love with him."

"Only if you tell me about Rick and Daniel. And I mean everything."

Amber stacked pillows and settled in on the bed, leaning against the headboard. "You go first."

Olivia joined her on the bed. "I was worried sick about you. I knew you weren't fossil hunting. I felt it in my gut that you were in danger. For three days, Connor knew the truth and didn't tell me. Then I found out where you were, and I've never felt so betrayed."

Amber rolled over and propped up on her elbow. "Would you have believed him?"

"No. But he could have tried. Instead, he let things heat up between us. We were moments from having sex when Kenzie, David, Connor's sister, and Elliott Fraser showed up at the ranch, and I learned the truth. I was furious."

"How do you feel about him now?"

Olivia fell back on the bed. "I'm crazy about him. But I'm still—"

"Stop it," Amber said. "Your excuses are as thin as *obleas*. Everything's changed now. You're part of the brooch lore, and you two are so cute together."

"What's the brooch lore?"

"I don't know. But every story Kenzie told me involved a love affair. She ended up with David. Charlotte ended up with Braham. Kit and Cullen got married, and Jack and Amy are getting married soon. This time it's you and Connor. It took my disappearance to bring you two together."

"But what about you and Rick?"

"I adore him. I trust him, but I don't get excited when he touches me or looks at me with those dreamy eyes. The feeling's just not there, and no amount of time will make it happen. He's a friend for life, but not any more than that."

"Do you tingle when Daniel touches you?"

For a moment, Amber didn't answer. "Yes, I do. But there's a problem. He lives in the nineteenth century and I live in the twenty-first. I don't plan to live here, and I doubt he'll live there. So nothing can come of it."

"You won't know for sure until you ask him."

"Ask him? How would I go about doing that?"

"I don't know. Get him in bed, and then right before he…you know… Oh, Amber. I can't advise you. I can't figure out my own life. Just do what feels right. It's not like we have reserved seats for the return trip and only four of us can go."

Olivia climbed off the bed and crossed the room to the wardrobe, where she swung open the doors and picked through the dresses hanging there on hooks. "I met Noah at lunch. He's precious and he adores you, which confused me because you've never been around kids. What'd you talk to him about? Math and science?"

"Yep. It was a two-player connection, vertically, horizontally, and diagonally."

"I bet you drew dinosaur pictures. That would have won him over."

Amber pulled a quilt folded at the end of the bed over her and snuggled down into its warmth. "It's scary how well you know me."

Olivia held up a dress. "Ooh. I love this. The gold silk all but melts in my hands."

"That was my performance dress, a gift from our landlady in Leadville. She insisted I keep it. Before I left, I hid money in her cookie jar."

"It's gorgeous. Are you going to wear it tonight?"

"No, you can." Daniel had seen her wear it so often, there was nothing special about it. He wouldn't be at dinner anyway, so it didn't matter. But Olivia would look gorgeous, and Connor wouldn't be able to resist her.

"Look at the way it glitters in the lamplight." Olivia clasped it at her waist to check the length. "The bodice looks low and tight. Did you spill out of it?"

"Not really. You'll look beautiful. If you intend to make up with Connor, it will set the stage for a conversation you two need to have."

"What are you going to wear?"

Amber yawned. "The emerald silk, I think."

Olivia hung the dress up and went back to the bed. "Is there an alarm clock? I know they don't have electricity, but do they have one you wind up?"

"There's no clock, but Mrs. Murphy will wake us up in time to dress."

Olivia pulled some of the quilt over on herself and snuggled with her sister. "I'm glad I found you. I was so scared."

Amber slung her arm over Olivia. "I'm glad you did, too. Now, let's go to sleep. I'm tired."

"Oh, I remember what I wanted to ask you," Olivia said. "Don't you think it's weird that Kenzie met Trey's grandfather when he was a young man in World War II. Then Kenzie became Trey's best friend. Then she came to rescue you. Like it was all planned out long before we were born?"

"I don't see how that's possible."

"Who would have thought time travel was possible?"

"Touché." A sinking sensation in the pit of Amber's stomach told her that she was missing something. *Dem bones, dem bones, dem dancing bones.* If the foot bone was connected to the leg bone and the leg bone was connected to the knee bone, then she was missing the leg bone—a huge gap of knowledge. There was much more to the brooch lore than she and Olivia had been told.

The threads of their lives had intertwined more than half a century ago. Now, would they weave a beautiful piece of fabric or would they just hang on to the fringe of each other's hearts?

37

1878 Denver, Colorado—Daniel

D ANIEL SPENT THE morning with General Palmer in Cañon City, discussing the litigation and possible showdown at the Santa Fe roundhouse in Pueblo, forty miles away.

"This is the center of our operations right now. We're badly in need of men we can trust. I'm counting on you," the general had said, before confirming that the board was considering leasing the tracks to Santa Fe. Daniel pressed Amber's concerns, and at the end of the discussion, the general requested Daniel return to Denver immediately and personally invite the woman lawyer to Cañon City to meet with him the next day.

As he rode to Alec's house from the train station, Daniel wasn't sure Amber would agree to the general's request. She'd seemed convinced of her position, but what evidence, if any, did she have that if the railroad followed her recommendation they would ultimately prevail? That was what the general wanted to know. So did Daniel. He also wanted to know how she'd become so entwined with his life, and not just his home life.

A line of graceful carriages stood waiting in front of the mansion. Alec hadn't mentioned a dinner party when they had spoken briefly that morning. He was a man of means and connections, and could easily plan a soiree with little notice, but what did that mean for Amber and her sister, the O'Gradys and McBains? Was the event in their honor?

"Evenin', Mr. Grant." The groom reached for the reins and ran an expert hand over the horse's withers. "I'll take Rambler up to the barn."

Daniel swung down from the leather as his horse pricked his ears and whickered. "Hope ye've got a good currycomb. He trotted through a wee bit of mud today, plus coal dust from two train trips." Daniel pulled his rifle from the saddle scabbard and held it by the stock, close to his thigh.

The groom clicked his tongue. "Yes, sir. I'll take care of him." Rambler heaved the equine equivalent of his owner's satisfied sigh, knowing he was coming home to a hot meal and a clean bed.

When Daniel entered the house, he handed over the rifle first, then his hat and gloves to the butler. Finally, he untied the thigh thong and unfastened the large belt buckle at his waist. "Who are the dinner guests?" he asked casually as he coiled his cartridge belt around his holster and set the gun rig on the shelf above the hall tree.

The butler placed the rifle and the hat turned upside down with the gloves inside on the shelf, alongside the gun rig. "The Rio Grande Board of Directors and local businessmen, sir."

"What about the Kelly sisters, the O'Gradys, and the McBains? Are they still here?"

"The McBains mysteriously departed this afternoon."

"Did they say where they were going?"

"I didn't see them leave. So I don't know." The butler assisted Daniel as he shed his canvas duster. "Dinner is over, and the guests have retired to the library for whisky and cigars. Shall I ask Mrs. Murphy to prepare a plate for you?"

"I'll pick at whatever is left on the sideboard." Daniel brushed his coat sleeves, straightened his cuffs, and ran a hand through his hair. When he passed the parlor and found it empty, he assumed Amber and Olivia had retired for the evening.

He entered the closely packed library. The open windows did little to relieve the stuffiness and the scent of whisky. He recognized

Colonel Greenwood, Colonel Dodge, former Governor Alexander Hunt, and Charles Lambord, another colonel in the 15th Pennsylvania Cavalry under Palmer. There were at least two dozen men in the smoke-filled room, and they all seemed focused on someone standing in front of the fireplace who was too short to be seen over the heads of the crowd.

"Don't you believe Drs. Marsh and Cope's feud is hurting their cause?" Governor Hunt asked.

"Their feud has turned into an outright war."

Amber's melodic voice, smooth and warm as a well-aged whisky, breezed from the direction of the fireplace. The realization that she was the focus of the crowd's attention poured shock through Daniel like a chilled waterfall on bare skin and temporarily froze the breath in his lungs.

"They seem determined to battle it out in the newspapers and scientific journals," she said. "But it's my opinion, their skullduggery has sparked interest in their collections that otherwise wouldn't be there."

Daniel bumped a man's shoulder with an unrepentant "Pardon me" before elbowing his way toward the fireplace, toward her.

Amber held court, surrounded by Denver's upper class. The taffeta beneath her emerald silk moiré skirt rustled when she moved in the figure-hugging gown, drawing the hungry eyes of the men in the room. Drawing his, as no woman ever had.

Alec captured his square lapels as if he were about to make a political speech and said, "Like the others, I'm more inclined to believe they would achieve more if they combined their skills and resources."

She fluttered a hand-painted fan delicately over her décolletage, and the lamplight glinted off its silver casing. "But aren't you more interested in dinosaurs and prehistoric life because of their intense rivalry and hatred for each other?"

"If there's an article in the paper that mentions either of the men," Colonel Greenwood conceded, "I read it first. You never know if one has shot the other."

There was a bark of laughter from Alec, and then a rumble of laughs ran among the other men. Except for Daniel. He wasn't even slightly amused. Not that the colonel's comment wasn't humorous. In fact, it was. But it hit too close to his own murderous thoughts. Although his victim wasn't one of the scientists. It was the beautiful woman who had every man lusting for her.

The ache in his gut was like the ache that had batted him about while he sat in the proscenium box at the Tabor Opera House. But it hadn't been a wrenching ache then. What was the difference?

It wasn't one thing. It was him. He was different. In Leadville, he had yet to kiss her, or hold her in his arms, or fall in love.

"There is a disadvantage," Amber continued. "They're digging up bones and announcing new species at a furious rate, and they have little regard that some of the species they're identifying have already been named."

"Are you saying Marsh and Cope have both given the same species different names?" Alec asked.

"Exactly," she said.

There was some general laughter at that.

Daniel watched her turn with an easy grace, alert to every nuance in the room, as alert as she'd been on stage. Although she had yet to notice him. He would know if she had. Her eyes would brighten, just as they had while she was on stage each time she glanced up at him.

She was playing to the audience now, and there wasn't a man in the room who wasn't enthralled by her charm. He didn't want other men ogling the creamy skin above her breasts or listening to the sensuous sound of her voice raised in logical and riveting arguments.

"The first person who discovers a species gets to name it," she said, "which is fair. But it has resulted in duplication of names. It'll take scientists a while to straighten it out and give credit where credit is due."

"What would you name a dinosaur?" Colonel Lambord asked.

"How about Amberosaurus or Kellyosaurus? Those are good names." Her eyes grew wide and bright, and her head bobbed playfully. "Right?" She gestured toward the crowd. "Don't you agree?"

"Certainly," Alec said. "I'll draft a letter and advise the doctors of those lofty suggestions."

A robust cheer followed, and a man offered, "I'll send a letter, too."

Amber pinked high on both cheeks and fanned herself vigorously before bestowing a benign smile on the attentive press of men.

When the room quieted, the colonel said, "I heard there was a problem in Morrison with both doctors fighting for control."

She stopped fanning and pulled the tassel through her fingers, as if counting beads on a rosary. Her eyes took on a deep-in-thought look, or maybe, a deep-into-the future look. It was the same expression she'd had in the stagecoach when she'd stared at the roof lost in thought. Then she blinked, leaving Daniel to wonder if she was scrying, or some such, gaining mystical insights from the patterns of thick cigar smoke rising toward the painted ceiling medallion.

"Dr. Lakes sent specimens to both Cope and Marsh. But Marsh acted first and sent his field collector Dr. Mudge to secure the spot and get Lakes on his payroll. So the bones coming out of the hogback in Morrison have gone to Yale."

"Which one do you think will survive history? Marsh or Cope?" Alec asked.

She ran her fingers through the fan's tassel once again. "Dr. Marsh will probably secure his position in history by naming more dinosaurs than any other paleontologist. But Cope will probably name more prehistoric animals," she added. "And paleontologists yet to be born will make outsized contributions to our knowledge of all these ancient beasts." Then with a rustle of skirts, she made a slight bow, and picked up her half-empty glass from a nearby table. "And that gentlemen, is my prediction."

Daniel was convinced now that she was scrying, but where was her crystal ball?

Applause erupted. Glasses clinked down on tabletops, chairs scraped across the hardwood floor, and animated voices rose in a murmur. Instead of the crowd disbanding, they formed a line to take her hand and tell her how much they enjoyed her presentation. Two, if Daniel heard correctly, asked her to dinner. One asked to escort her to the theatre, and another to a scientific meeting. He was torn between yanking her out of the room full of fawning men or leaving the room quietly.

Without waiting to hear her replies, Daniel abruptly left the room to find the nearest bottle of whisky. He was about to pour a healthy portion into a waiting glass when Rick entered the dining room unobtrusively through the servants' door.

"I didn't know you were coming back tonight," Rick said, joining Daniel at the sideboard. He poured himself a glass of Champagne. "Did you hear our girl? Not only can she sing, but she can make a scholarly presentation and equally woo a crowd."

"If those men had heard her sing, half would have proposed on the spot. The other half would have gone home to ask for a divorce." Daniel fought to keep his tone neutral, suspicion out, but failed at both.

Rick put a comradely hand on Daniel's shoulder. "Your jealousy is showing. I wouldn't let Amber see it."

"That room is full of millionaires. Powerful men, not only in Denver but in Colorado. I'm a Pinkerton agent with a ten-year-old son."

"Your self-pity is unbecoming. I wouldn't let Amber see that either."

With a scowl, Daniel filled his glass and took a large sip, holding the liquor in his mouth a moment before swallowing hard.

"Let me tell you something, Mr. Pinkerton Man. Amber doesn't care about money or position. What was she wearing when you met her? I heard it was jeans and a flannel shirt. She's happiest when she's digging in the dirt or cooking some of the best food—especially biscuits—that I've ever eaten. So ditch the self-pity and tone down the jealousy. It's you she's interested in. Not how much money you have in your pockets."

Rick drank his Champagne. "Here's something else for you to

think about." He tipped his glass toward Daniel. "You have something special that no one else in that room has."

"What's that?"

"Fearlessness. Not one of those men would know what to do with her. She'd intimidate the hell out of them. Not you, though. She's a challenge to your heart and your intellect. And if you spend the next sixty years together, she always will be."

"What made ye so smart, O'Grady?"

"A loving mother, a devoted father, brothers who always have my back, a sister who's taught me what women want, and hundreds of lonely desert nights. But there's a more important question you haven't asked. What makes me so dumb? That's harder to answer. But it has to do with ghosts of dead buddies. I can't get settled until they do."

Now it was Daniel's turn to give Rick a clap on the back. "I understand about ghosts. I was on President Lincoln's security detail and was with him the night he was assassinated. I'll never stop reliving the night and wondering what I could have done differently."

Rick's face paled, and he had the pained look of a man who'd been punched without apparent provocation.

"Take a deep breath. Take a drink."

Rick did both. Then after a brief pause, he switched to a different subject, as if the ghosts who haunted them both had temporarily left the room. "You should have heard Olivia's presentation."

"I didn't know she had an affinity for dinosaurs, too." Daniel said.

"She didn't talk about dinosaurs," Rick said in a quiet voice. "She wowed the audience with her legal expertise. She was charming, witty, and knowledgeable."

"Amber has considerable legal knowledge, too, especially about the situation in the gorge. Why didn't she participate?"

"She did. But after the guests discovered she had mining and engineering experience, they weren't interested in what she had to say about the railroad."

"General Palmer's interested. He wants to meet her. That's why I'm back."

"After the board members report to him, Palmer won't need to meet her. Between Olivia and Amber, there wasn't a question without an answer. The girls also cornered Adam Hughes, the board's attorney, and huddled for almost an hour."

"Palmer will study the reports, but he'll want to question the source."

A roar of laughter erupted from the foyer, and Daniel tossed back the entire contents of his glass. "Tell me this... Does Amber have a damn crystal ball?"

Rick cleared his throat. "If she does, I haven't seen it. All I know is that she's intelligent, forward thinking, and extremely perceptive with a creative imagination." He twirled his Champagne glass in a circle on the top of the sideboard. "There's this saying: 'If you can imagine it, you can create it. If you can dream it, you can become it.' That's Amber. Loaded to the gills with vision and chutzpah."

Daniel cut a slice of roast turkey from the leftovers on the server and ate it with a helping of dressing and potatoes. Between hungry bites he said, "She's lying to me. What else am I going to uncover?"

"If she's lying, it's not to cover up an illegal activity. She has secrets. We all do, and that includes you. When you can be honest with her, she'll be honest with you." Rick set down his glass and straightened a perfectly knotted four-in-hand necktie. "I'm going with Alec to his club."

"What about Connor?"

"He and Olivia are looking for a quiet place to have a private conversation. There's a misunderstanding that needs straightening. I have faith that my brother will confess his mortal sins, make an act of contrition, and receive absolution."

Daniel slanted a suspicious look at Rick. "What about ye and Amber?"

Rick's aloof smile thawed, and Daniel wondered what was behind it. "Oh, I have no mortal sins to confess."

"That's not what I meant."

"Don't worry. My brother might be ready to shackle himself to a beautiful woman, but not me. Bad timing. Don't let me stand in your way." He emptied his Champagne glass and set it down on the sideboard. "Don't wait too long to make your move."

The house emptied quickly, and Rick and Alec left for the Press Club. Daniel took his drink to the library, sat down in front of the fire, and closed his eyes.

Don't wait too long to make your move.

If Daniel let Amber go, leave Denver, would he find her again? He didn't think so. If he sold his stocks and bonds in the Rio Grande, he could buy a house and make a life with Amber. But if the company won the lawsuit and succeeded in getting the line to Leadville, the value might double.

When he returned to Cañon City, he'd talk to General Palmer and explain his situation. Knowing the general, he'd say sell, and that was what Daniel was inclined to do.

He closed his eyes and let his mind drift.

The house was still when he woke sometime later. The embers and dimmed gas lamps added to the eeriness of the room. He picked his glass up off the floor where he had dropped it when he fell asleep. There hadn't been enough liquid left to dampen the carpet. He set the empty glass on the table then stood, stretching his back and shoulders.

It was this kind of quiet stillness that always took him back to April 1865. He'd helped carry the slain president from Ford's Theatre to the house across the street, and there he sat vigil for nine hours until the end came. Everyone left with the president's body and Daniel was there alone, until the ghosts took up residence. He ran from the Petersen House with a keepsake and never looked back.

Wondering about the time, he flipped open his pocket watch: three o'clock. He tucked it back into his waistcoat pocket while making his way toward the staircase. His nap would probably keep him awake the rest of the night.

Amber's door had a sliver of light seeping beneath it. Was she still awake? He walked toward his room with Rick's haunting words once again echoing in his brain: *Don't wait too long.* Grass rarely grew under Daniel's feet. Why was he letting it grow now? He glanced down at the floor, half expecting to see green blades sprouting from the carpet.

How many nights had he and Amber bumped into each other in Mrs. Garland's kitchen, unable to sleep from the sound of squeaky springs coming from the McBain's bedroom—two, three. Then later, when the bedroom grew quiet and there was no other sound to keep him awake, he'd toss and turn, remembering the scent of roses in her hair, the swish of her night dress swirling at her ankles, a step so light he barely noticed the slapping of her feet on the wooden floor, or the peculiar color on her toes.

There would be no accidental meeting in Alec's house. If Daniel wanted to see her, he'd have to knock on her door. It wasn't at all proper, and Alec would be furious. He'd accuse Daniel of taking advantage of her, and he'd probably be right. It was too late to call on her, and he needed to see his son.

Inside the bedroom, a single lamp, turned down low, burned unsteadily. The clouds that had rolled in earlier, along with his train had cleared now, allowing a wash of moonlight to creep through the window and bathe a swatch of the room with yellow light. Noah was curled into a ball in his single bed, in the room they shared. Ripley, asleep at the foot, raised her head, glanced at Daniel, then rolled over onto her side. A satisfied hum slipped from Daniel's lips at the sight of the boy and his dog, and his chest heaved a heavy sigh.

He kissed his son's warm forehead. And as he did every night, he said a silent prayer for Noah's protection. He was humbled by the knowledge that his prayer had been answered. Amber had been sent to protect him.

Quietly, he crossed over to the washstand and gently touched the cabinet card with Lorna's image propped up on the shelf below the mirror. He traced the outline of her face and swallowed the thick knot that rose in his throat unbidden. He'd been a widower for five years. A few women had come into his life during his assignments, but none had touched his heart until now. The bed behind him was a lonely place. And if he didn't act, it would remain so.

The water he poured into the washbowl was tepid, but lukewarm was better than freezing, and God knew he'd washed up plenty of times in water too cold to drink. He stripped down to his trousers, washed up, and brushed his hair and teeth.

When his head hit the pillow, his mind wouldn't turn off. His senses were alive with the memory of Amber's scent and taste, the sound of her voice, the sway of her hips. If he could bury himself in her once, his obsession would be appeased. As soon as that thought formed, he swatted it away. Once would never be enough.

Without a purpose in mind, he tossed a clean shirt over his damp hair and left his bedroom. A drink would settle his mind. He ambled down a hallway lit by gaslights set in sconces and paused before a door leaking bright light from underneath.

A loud meow followed by a thump and Amber's hushed command, "Come here, Millie."

Fists clenched, he forced himself to keep moving. Alec and Rick could be returning soon, and he didn't want to compromise her.

The door opened, and Millie ran out, meowing. He picked her up. "Are ye off to chase some mice?"

Amber stuck her head out. Her paleness worried him, putting him in mind of his late wife lying under quilts, shivering despite the roaring fire. He mentally shook off the grim vision.

"I didn't know you were here."

He was alarmed by the breathless rasp to her voice. "It's late. Ye need to sleep."

"My brain won't shut off, and the cat abandoned me. Come in." She opened the door wide enough for him to pass through. "Have a snifter of brandy."

He glimpsed her silhouette in the light from a single gas lamp, casting wavering shadows about the room. The lace and silk bed jacket over a long matching gown clung to her curves, and the sight of her lusciousness caused an immediate stirring in his loins. Her unbound hair, pulled to one side, tumbled past her shoulder and draped over one breast.

He didn't expect the naked emotion, painted by the yellow gaslight with such intensity on her face. How many cloudy nights had he traveled that lonely road begging the moon to peek through, so he would see a landmark and know he was almost home.

However many there had been, he knew now he had seen his last.

38

1878 Denver, Colorado—Amber

From the moment Daniel had swept past Amber on the sidewalk in Leadville, to this minute, he had haunted her dreams. Had her dream summoned him tonight like a vision in a crystal ball? She rubbed her eyes, moistened her lips in a nervous gesture. After being so focused earlier in the evening, her brain was now a jumble of thoughts thrashing about in her mind, and she struggled to make sense of the tangle.

"Why did you come back? You're supposed to be in Cañon City." She swung a shawl around her shoulders and settled into the curve of the small sofa, tucking her legs beneath her.

"Ye're cold. I'll stoke the fire." He set the cat on the loveseat and picked up the poker. A fringe of flames sputtered over the bed of glowing embers. He tossed in a handful of kindling and topped it with logs. Light sprang up, dancing over the flowers in the wallpapered walls. "General Palmer sent me back with an invitation. He'd like ye to join him in Cañon City for lunch."

"Me? Whatever for?" Meeting General Palmer would be her dad's dream come true. She would gladly meet with the general for her dad's benefit, but right now she had to prioritize dreams, and meeting with Palmer would rank number three, behind exploring Morrison and kissing Daniel. And the order of those two fluctuated, hour by hour. "After tonight, I don't think that's necessary. Olivia gave the board of directors unsolicited legal advice. I'm sure they'll share the information with the general."

"Rick told me about the dinner conversation and that Olivia is as well versed as ye are. I heard some of yer question and answer session in the library."

Amber puffed her cheeks, slowly expelled air, disappointed that he hadn't shown himself. The evening had been delightful, but she had missed him terribly. "I'm sorry I didn't see you."

"Ye were busy." Daniel returned the poker to the wrought-iron stand and brushed detritus from his hands before furrowing his fingers through his damp hair. The muscles of his arms and shoulders shifted fluidly under his untucked shirt. "It reminded me of yer fans lining up after yer performances."

She smiled. "I don't think anyone has been so interested in what I had to say since I defended my—"

Slight frown lines appeared between his eyebrows. "Defended what?"

She rubbed her tired eyes, thinking how she could best explain defending her master's thesis. "When I finished my education, I met with several professors to review what I'd learned."

Daniel filled snifters with brandy and handed one to her. "Like what ye did in Judge Adams' office?"

"Very much like that." It wasn't until Daniel placed the glass in her hand that she realized she was shaking from worry and fatigue. She tossed down the brandy, sighing as the heat of the familiar sweet taste loosened the knot in her throat that formed every time she had to obfuscate.

"What about tomorrow? Will ye agree to go?"

The brandy burned a path to her stomach and out to her limbs, but it didn't stop the shaking. "If the general is serious about talking to me, Olivia should go. She's more informed, and I'm going to Morrison with Rick. Do you know where he is?"

"With Alec at his club."

"What about Olivia and Connor?"

"Rick told me earlier she and Connor were looking for a quiet place to talk."

"Then they're in the house somewhere." If they were in Connor's bedroom that opened all sorts of possibilities for her sister, but she didn't believe Olivia would pick up where she and Connor left off before they were interrupted at the ranch house. Without a guarantee of privacy, Olivia wouldn't take the risk of getting caught in a compromising position.

"She should be in her room at this hour."

"In Leadville, we met several times in the middle of the night."

A furtive look darted across his face. "Not in yer bedroom."

"If it will make you feel better"—she pointed toward her bed—"That's my bedroom. This is my sitting room."

"It does, but not by much." He finished his drink then set the empty glass on the table. "What do ye plan to do after ye finish in Morrison?"

"Go home. Unless Rick will take me to Garden Park."

"That's close to Cañon City."

"I know. The site has lots of fossils of Late Jurassic mammals, turtles, and even crocodiles, plus the rivalry between Marsh and Cope really plays out in Garden Park. I'd like to go. But"—she took a few shallow breaths against the pain in her chest—"I don't think he'll take me."

"Come with me to Cañon City. Then after ye meet with the general, I'll send an escort with ye to Garden Park. If I can get away, I'll join ye."

"Are we bargaining?" She prodded him gently, here and there, waiting to see what really had brought him to her room in the middle of the night.

"Yes, if that's how ye see it."

"You don't have the manpower to spare, and besides, Rick and I have an agreement that I can't rescind or amend. I promised him I would go home."

"Where is that?"

"Are you interrogating me again?"

"No. I know ye have bits of information ye don't want to tell me, but is the location of yer home too big a secret to share?"

"Big or little, a secret is a secret. Size doesn't matter."

There was a charged silence, save for the wind and the rustle of bare tree limbs against the window panes, and the fire, always the fire, crackling and popping and spitting sparks into the air.

"Why is the location a secret?" His blue eyes stayed steady on her face, as he stood there next to the sofa, one hand in his trouser pocket.

Stillness seemed to hold there in his expression, as if he was intentionally holding back the half-smile that easily toppled her heart so quickly it scarcely missed a beat, a heavy beat between being free and being conquered, between being truthful and not...

Exasperated, she said, "Chicago. It's in Chicago."

With a sweep of his gaze, he evaluated her anew, testing the weight of her words, and she sensed he weighed other things as well. "Is that where ye're going?" he asked.

She opened her mouth to lie once again but didn't. Instead, she petted the cat, thankful for the distraction. Finally, she asked, "What's on your mind, Daniel? This isn't about where I live or where I'm going."

The room was charged with an understood but unspoken potential, and he shifted slightly. As if trying to decide to go or stay. Decision made, he eased onto the sofa beside her. "I don't want ye to leave before I finish my assignment."

"Noah is fine. His grandfather hired a tutor. Noah just needs to meet boys his age. I recommend he go to school while he's here and work with the tutor in the afternoons."

"I'm not talking about Noah. I'm talking about ye. I want ye to stay. If Rick must leave, I'll escort ye wherever ye want to go."

Millie jumped to the floor and scooted under the couch, flicking the tip of her tail.

"What's she looking for?"

"She was chasing a ball of twine earlier. It must be wedged beneath the sofa."

Daniel stooped down to look, found the ball, and tossed it

across the room. Millie chased after it and swatted it under the bed.

"Are you hoping if I stay long enough, an agent will have time to uncover some criminal activity?"

"Ye're not a criminal. I don't know what ye're hiding, but I hope ye'll grow to trust me enough to tell me the truth."

"I haven't committed a crime. I'm not running from an abusive husband. I don't have a secret identity." She played with the fringe on her shawl, staring distractedly at the modest fire curling around the logs. "But there are some things I can't tell you right now."

"I know ye have secrets. I accept that."

"Not dangerous ones or hurtful ones."

Millie jumped back onto the settee and stretched long and deep before climbing onto Daniel's lap. "How do ye feel?"

"Are you asking Millie or me?"

He tilted his head, considering her question. "I know how Millie feels. I can hear her." He held the cat up to his ear. "I was right. She's pleased."

She's being held by you. How could she not be pleased?

He set the cat back on the floor. "Have ye had another breathing episode since last night?" He pulled one end of the ribbon tied in a bow at the end of her braid. Then slowly, erotically, unbraided her hair, smoothing the ripples in the thick strands.

I'm about to have one now.

"No." She lied, and the look he gave her said he knew the truth. Last night he'd stormed out when he recognized her lie, but tonight she knew instinctively he would let it go unchallenged. Something flitted through his expression and whatever it was, it worried her a great deal. He didn't move, didn't touch her at all. His presence alone warmed her in all the places his lips had heated the night before.

She closed her eyes, focusing on his voice, his touch as he traced the line of her jaw. His fingers teased her neck as they circled around to her nape and with the slightest pressure he gathered her to him, shaking, and his lips hovered a breath away from hers.

She set both hands on his chest, feeling the cadence of inhalation and exhalation along with the pulse of his heartbeat, so much stronger than her own. The warm scent of the soap he had used mixed with his natural musky scent and reminded her of tangled sheets, skin sliding on skin, and whispered words of urgency.

Everything narrowed down to what she could feel and hear. The certainty of his arms about her, the steadiness of his breathing.

"I need ye, lass. I need ye in my life. Don't leave yet."

She knew he ached to kiss her. A strange ripple, like a stone tossed into a creek, went through her, burning hot and wet, and the breath caught in her throat, in a dry sounding gasp. His mouth brushed slowly over hers before settling with gentle pressure. His beard rasped her chin and the tip of his tongue tasted her lips.

He broke away and stood. Then ever so gently, he swept her into his arms and carried her across the room where, in the light of the flickering fire and a single lamp, he lay her gently on the bed. The feather mattress shifted as he lowered himself to her side and touched her face with such tenderness, tears filled her eyes.

"Don't cry, lass."

He kissed her eyes, and when he kissed her on the mouth, she tasted her own salty tears. She thought she was prepared to explore the taste and textures and savor the smells and sounds that would follow. But as their lips brushed, she knew in her heart she wasn't prepared at all. His mouth was a feast, the apple-scented brandy, the whisky undertones. She could lose herself in the taste of him, and the low moans rumbling in his chest, and the clean, manly scent of his skin.

This was so different from what she was accustomed to. It wasn't a form of punctuation or hasty dash at the end of a conversation. This was urgent, wild, and fresh, and it eroded her balance.

This was her dream.

Her fingers curved over the hard planes of his shoulders and neck. He took a quick breath and reached down, his hand skimming over the silk of her gown, over her breasts.

"Take off your clothes," she said. "I want to touch you."

"No. Ye're not well. I won't risk hurting ye." He kissed her lightly and gazed into her eyes. "I have to know, though. Will I be yer first?"

"If I say no, will you be disappointed? If I say yes, will you leave?"

"If ye say no, I'll be jealous of the man who took ye first. If it's aye, then I'll wait."

"You're already waiting."

"I'll wait longer."

"You're not my first." But he would be her last. The thought took her by surprise. When those sorts of premonitions invaded her psyche, they scared her, and this one scared the hell out of her, and she didn't want to analyze what it could mean.

He combed his fingers through her hair, holding it away from her head. "Was it Rick?" He released the strands, letting them drift back over her shoulders.

A faint moan escaped her lips and all resistance fled, burned away by the heat of his touch. "Was what Rick?"

He directed inquiring eyes on her. "Yer first."

"No, but a man much like him." The bad boy who broke her heart really wasn't anything like Rick. He was selfish and insensitive, and Rick was neither. And it wasn't that Rick was afraid of commitment, either. It was just that he wasn't ready for a commitment now. Even if she waited five years for him, he would never be her soul mate.

"I still won't take ye. Not until ye're well."

She threaded her fingers into his damp hair, gazing into his deep blue eyes. "Are you hoping I'll want to make love so desperately that I'll go to the doctor?"

"If ye ever want me as desperately as ye *don't want* a doctor, I'd consider that the ultimate compliment." He trailed a finger down her neck, across the swell of her breasts, down to the juncture of her legs. "Ye're so beautiful. So precious."

She cupped the side of his face, steeped in need, immersed in sensation. "I want you naked against me, but I'm afraid I won't be able to breathe."

"Being inside of ye, Amber, I won't be able to breathe."

It was the first time she remembered him ever calling her by name, except in her dream. She threw her head back and arched against him. His mouth fitted over hers and he kissed her fully. There was promise in his power, held in check to protect her. Her mind and body were completely governed by sensual impulses. As a desperate ache cambered low in her body, she surrendered to the primal rhythms pulsing through her veins.

And she finally understood that knowing him, loving him, would leave her forever torn between the centuries.

39

1878 Denver, Colorado—Amber

AMBER ROLLED OVER in bed, yawning, and placed the back of her hand over her eyes, willing herself to slide back into the warm cocoon of the down coverlet and erotic dreams. Daniel stirred, and she flung one arm across him, and snuggled against his shoulder.

"Good morning to you too, sis."

Amber sat bolt upright like a woman stuck with her missing hatpin. "Where'd you come from?"

Laughing, Olivia rolled onto her side and propped her chin on her hand. "What you're really asking is, 'Where'd Daniel go?' He left when I snuck in, shortly before daybreak."

"Was I… Were we…"

"Appropriately covered? Dressed? Compromised? What?"

Amber fell back and pulled the coverlet over her head. "All the above," she groaned.

Olivia pulled down the decorative cover. "You were both sound asleep, snuggling. I hated to wake him. He had the most disgustingly delicious smile."

"That's an oxymoron."

"Okay," Olivia pursed her lips in thought. "Gorgeous smile, relaxed, and innocent."

"You certainly weren't looking at Agent Grant then. The smile, yes, but relaxed and innocent? Nah. How about tense and dangerous?"

"Nope. He looked like Noah—adorable and huggable."

"He must have been dreaming of catching me in more lies and slamming a jail cell door in my face."

"Oh, stop it. He doesn't believe you're a criminal. A prevaricator, maybe, but not someone who belongs behind bars. Besides if he locked you up, he couldn't sleep with you."

Amber manufactured a tone of denial. "He didn't sleep with me."

"Looked that way to me. I mean you were both in this bed, asleep."

"Sleep, yes, but we didn't…" Amber gave up, frustrated. "Nothing happened."

Olivia pinned her for a moment, a frog to a dissection pan. "Amber, something happened in this room last night."

"No. I mean it. We didn't—"

"I know you didn't have sex. Daniel was fully clothed and that mop of yours wasn't all in a tangle."

Amber pulled her hair into a ponytail, twisted it, and looped it all into a sloppy bun at the top of her head. "Leave my mop out of this. Not everyone is gifted with hair that looks as good coming out of bed as it does going in."

"It's time to cut it off. You're too old to have hair down to your butt."

"Why are you giving me such a hard time?"

"Because something happened in this room, in this bed. Body language doesn't lie. Daniel was a soldier. Now he's a cop or a secret agent or something, and he didn't hear me enter the room. When I shook him awake, he looked down at you first. He knew exactly where he was. He kissed your mouth, kissed my forehead, and left the room. And I swear…" Olivia crossed her heart. "I heard him whistle. The man's in love."

Amber pulled the covers back over her head, and when a rush of shivers tickled her spine, she did a shimmy-shake.

Olivia tugged the covers down again. "Stop hiding. Did you hear me? He's in love."

"Yes, I heard you, and I don't want to talk about it. But where were you all night? Did you and Connor do the horizontal happy dance? Or make the beast with two backs?"

Olivia climbed out of bed and crossed the room to the fireplace. "You know me. I wouldn't risk getting caught." She stirred the embers, tossed on some kindling, then stacked logs on the grate. "Besides, we had too much to talk about."

"You're lying. Your neck's all red. You guys were making out. I don't know why you're denying it. So what'd you talk about?"

Olivia poked at the logs until the fire began to blaze. "We're starting over. Not completely over, but we're resetting the relationship to right after the first kiss. We figured that's a good place to restart."

A muffled knock turned Olivia's attention from the fireplace. She set the poker aside and hurried to open the door. "Coffee? How marvelous. I'll take the cart. Thank you, Mrs. Murphy. You're so kind, so sweet."

Olivia's profuse praise caused Mrs. Murphy's cheeks to flush, a faint smile growing on her lined face. "I'll send up hot water for bathing."

Olivia closed the door and pushed the cart over to the table. "I could get used to this." She lifted one of two dome lids. "Scones. I could definitely get used to this." After slipping a wrapper on over her nightgown, she poured two cups of coffee. "Get your butt over here. I'm not serving you in bed."

Amber found her slippers on opposite sides of the room, with one missing a tassel. It was probably under the sofa, too. She threw open the curtains and draped them around the glass-knob tie backs. The sun poured in through the window. She stood there a minute to let her face soak in some vitamin D. After so many rainy days, a moment or two of sun exposure, sans hat and sunscreen, wouldn't kill her.

"We've got another pretty day." She sat, staring at the steam as it rose in gossamer curls from the dainty china cup. Then slowly, she raised the coffee to her lips and tested the temperature with a sip of the full-bodied brew. It was scalding. She waited a few seconds before taking another tentative taste. "If you're starting over with Connor, I guess that means you're not mad at him now."

The delicate high-pitched clink of Olivia's cup against the saucer preceded her answer. "I know why he lied. I don't like it, but I understand he had no choice. If I hadn't come on this trip, I never would have known, and I would have thrown away my future with him."

Amber smiled and gave her sister's hand a squeeze. "So you have a future?"

Olivia buttered a scone and laid the knife across the plate. "We're going to go home and see how it goes, but yes, I think so."

"Is he going to move to Colorado?"

"His base will be at the new ranch, but he'll still travel within the US. As soon as Rick gets settled, he and Shane will do all the foreign travel."

Amber spread apple butter on one half of a scone and grape jelly on the other, and did an eeny, meeny, miny, moe to decide which one to bite into first. "How many locations are there?" she asked, wiping jelly from her lips.

"Let's see." Olivia counted on her fingers: "Kentucky, California, Scotland, New York, Colorado, Italy, Australia, and they're looking at Spain and Germany, plus more locations in the US—New Mexico, Florida, and a couple others."

"Sounds right up your alley. Wouldn't it be fun to travel through Spain looking for a hacienda to buy? I'm so happy for you."

Olivia lifted another silver dome to find a bowl of sliced apples. She scooped a spoonful onto her plate. "But what about you and Daniel, and why didn't you have sex?"

"He's worried about my health."

Holding an apple slice an inch from her mouth, Olivia pegged Amber with a steely gaze. "Just so there's no misunderstanding, so am I." Olivia's taffeta dressing gown gleamed in the sunlight and the butterflies embroidered in purple metallic cord seemed to take flight, reminding Amber of her own travel through the fog.

"I promise…" Amber crossed her heart. "As soon as I get home, I'll go to the doctor and get a prescription that will fix me right up. And I promise to take all my pills."

"I couldn't ask for anything more than that." Olivia took another bite of the scone. "You know, that was honorable of Daniel not to make a move on you last night."

"He was too honorable," Amber said. "I didn't beg, but I came close. Now it might not ever happen."

"Don't say that."

"It's true. I can't ignore it. Our relationship is too complicated. I don't want to live here. God knows what I said last night that could affect the field of paleontology throughout the next century. And what we both know of the Royal Gorge War could screw up the case. We've got to be careful, and I've especially got to be careful around Daniel. I can't lead him on and then abandon him."

"You can take him with you."

"He's not Millie the cat."

"I didn't mean that," Olivia said. "I know you can't pick him up and abscond with him."

"If Daniel goes home with me, he'll have to go because it's best for Noah and for him. And how can he evaluate an unknown? I can list the advantages of living in the twenty-first century—better health care, longer life expectancy, access to unprecedented knowledge, ease of travel, the ability to communicate with anyone at any time, indoor plumbing—but to him, they would be science fiction terms and concepts." She put her elbows on the table, her chin in her palms, and tried to come up with possibilities. "I don't know what to do."

"Give it time. It'll work out."

"But that's just it. I don't have time."

Olivia sighed. "We can stay as long as you want. You don't have to rush."

Amber picked up her plate to scoop apples onto it and discovered a white envelope with a faint circle imprint from the raised bottom of the plate. Her name was written without flourishes in an elegant and easy to read script.

"Did you know this was here?"

Olivia nodded. "Mrs. Murphy pointed it out before she released the cart."

"Why didn't you tell me?"

"We needed to talk before you lost yourself in a love letter."

Amber slit the envelope open with an unused knife and extracted a single sheet with a few lines of decisive slanting script, dated and signed. And even though the letter was short, it used the entire page. "Ah…" Between the date and the signature, Daniel had written a message of love, and it brought her to tears.

I woke with the taste of ye on my lips. What I feel for ye has taken thorough possession of my wits and makes me almost unfit for anything else. Until we meet again, your devoted servant, Daniel

"Read it out loud," Olivia said.

All Amber could do was cry and dab at her eyes with a corner of the white cloth napkin with the grape jelly stain.

Olivia snatched it out of Amber's hand and read it. "'*I woke with the taste of ye on my lips.*' Oh my God. '*What I feel for ye has taken thorough possession of my wits.*' I think I'm going to faint. How romantic. '*And makes me almost unfit for anything else.*' Christ, Amber. This guy could write for Hallmark. '*Until we meet again, your devoted servant, Daniel.*' If you don't confess your undying love to him, you're nuts."

Amber gently tugged the paper from between Olivia's fingers. "Give me my letter." She folded it and slipped it back into the envelope and tapped it lightly against her palm. "This doesn't help."

Easing out of the chair, she opened a drawer in the armoire and gathered her journal. "I wrote down notes and descriptions of everywhere I've been since I came through the fog. I wanted to share this adventure with you." She slipped the letter into a pocket for mementoes. "Having you here now means everything to me."

Olivia stood and hugged Amber. "I'd give you the moon, if I could. I've worried over you my entire life, and I'll probably never stop. But if I hadn't come here, our relationship would never have been the same again. I'll treasure every note you've written, even the details of this room, which I think is gaudy, by the way." Olivia reclaimed her seat and wiped her eyes. "So what's the plan for today?"

Amber picked up her napkin and after finding another clean corner, wiped her damp cheeks. "Daniel asked me to go to Cañon City to meet with General Palmer about the railroad. I can't go. I want to go to Morrison. Will you go with him?"

"Only if it's because you'd rather dig for bones and not because you're too scared to face him."

"Why would I be scared?"

"Because he confessed his love for you, and you don't know what to do about it. So you'll fall back on your MO and run away."

"That's not my MO."

Olivia swatted the air with a flip of her hand. "Whatever…"

Pursing her breath, Amber walked over to the window with the journal holding Daniel's letter pressed against her breasts. "The mountains are calling my name, Liv. I need to go."

"You can't continue to put dinosaurs ahead of the living."

"It's not that. Not this time. I need thinking space. I have decisions to make. Bring Daniel back tonight, and I'll tell him the truth."

"I can't stand to see you so distressed." Olivia stepped over to the window and they put their arms around each other and pressed their heads together like conjoined twins. "You better tell me everything he knows about you, or I'll tell him something different, and he'll be so angry he won't listen to anything else you have to say."

"It won't matter. After I tell him I'm from the twenty-first century, the conversation will come to a screeching halt, a blunt quick jab to the heart."

At the knock on the door, they both turned as one to stare. "Come in," they said in unison, their voices melding into one command.

Mrs. Murphy entered with two housemaids carrying pails of hot water for the hip tub. "I have a message from Mr. Grant. He said the general requested his presence immediately and asked that Mr. Connor O'Grady and Miss Olivia join him in Cañon City at one o'clock. The other message is from Mr. Rick O'Grady. He requested Miss Amber be prepared to leave at nine."

"What time is it now?" Amber asked.

"Eight," Mrs. Murphy said.

"Please tell both men we'll be ready to leave at nine," Amber said.

"Shall I pour the water into the tub?" one of the housemaids asked.

"We can handle it," Olivia said. "Thank you."

Mrs. Murphy and the housemaids left the room and Olivia and Amber stood there looking at the pails of steaming water. "Did I say I could get used to this? I lied. You go first," Olivia said. "But how do you wash your hair?"

"With a good brushing and a little cologne water." Amber unstoppered a bottle of eau de cologne she'd purchased from Grandmother Hughes. "Smell."

Olivia inhaled. "Lavender, rosemary, and something else."

"Bergamot. It's a light citrus aroma. The oil eradicates body odor, tames frizzy hair, and gets rid of scalp build-up. Give it a try."

"Okay, but you know how I am about smells. If I hate it, I'll have to wash my hair."

"Just pretend you're at the cabin without modern conveniences. You survive there without a shower."

"But only for two nights, and while I'm there I wear jeans and go grubby. Here I'm dressing in yards of silk and lace."

Amber matched her sister's eye roll.

Eventually, Olivia took a hip bath and brushed cologne into her hair without complaint, while Amber settled for a thorough sponge bath, realizing her picky sister's toilette would otherwise make them late.

An hour later, they met Rick and Connor in the foyer, both men waiting patiently by the bronze and ironwork front door, arms clasped behind their backs, talking in quiet tones.

As soon as Connor laid eyes on Olivia, a smile split his face. He followed her progress until she neared the last step, then he walked forward, standing in a ray of sunlight beaming through the stained-glass window, his auburn hair glinting in the multi-colored light.

"You look beautiful."

Amber thought he did, too, and she was sure her sister, if she wasn't already hopelessly in love, had fallen *splat* at Cupid's feet.

Connor's arm circled protectively around Liv's waist, and then he kissed her lightly on the mouth. Her cheeks pinked to her ears.

As Amber's gaze lingered on Rick, he shook his head smiling. She handed him a rucksack with her extra clothes, field kit, and journal. "Hold this, please." She crossed the foyer to the overburdened coat rack, the heels of shoes striking the floorboard in an annoying *clack, clack*. She pushed the forest of outerwear aside looking for her coat. "I wonder where it is."

"What? Your coat?" Rick held up his arm, and a small smile teased the corners of his eyes. "Would this be the one?"

"Who are you? Houdini?"

Rick settled the coat on her shoulders. "I've been called that before."

Why wasn't she surprised others thought of Rick as a master of illusion and an escape artist? Others might have pegged him as a bad boy, just as she had. But in the last few days, she'd seen the real Rick O'Grady, and she'd seen his heart. He wasn't a bad boy. He was a loyal friend who would do anything in the world for her.

Enough about Rick. Worrying about Daniel was a full-time job right now.

Her fingers moved like dancing feet up and down the edge of her coat, counting the five large buttons to be sure they were intact. She couldn't breathe in a corset today, so she'd left it off. As soon as she had a chance, she was changing into her jeans, flannel shirt, and canvas jacket. She couldn't work in all these layers. The clothes were simply too heavy.

"Where's Noah? Isn't he going?" Amber asked.

Rick slung her rucksack over his shoulder and gathered up his saddlebags. "He went to the kitchen to get a picnic basket. He'll be right back."

"Okay, we're off." Olivia gave Amber a peck on the cheek. "Have fun and be careful. And don't overdo. We'll see you tonight."

"Wait," Connor said. "Where is your brooch, Amber?"

She patted above her breast. "Pinned to my chemise, but it doesn't work."

"What stone do you have?" Connor asked Rick.

"The O'Grady stone," he said. "You take it." He dug into his vest pocket, withdrew the brooch, and handed it over.

Connor refused it. "No, you keep it in case of an emergency."

"If there's an emergency, Amber's stone will work," Rick said.

"How do you know?" Connor asked.

Before Rick could answer, Noah, with Ripley snapping at his heels, rushed into the foyer, a picnic basket swinging at his side and a canteen slung over his shoulder. "Sorry it took so long, but you can't have a picnic without fried chicken."

"Hmm," Amber said. "Better keep it away from me, or it'll all be gone by lunchtime."

Noah grinned. "That's what I told Mrs. Murphy, so the cook made a double batch."

She tugged on the brim of his cap. "How'd you get to be so thoughtful?"

"Pa says to always think about someone else's needs first. I don't always, but I try."

"And you do a darn good job. So are you ready to go on a dinosaur hunt?" Amber asked.

"Sure am. Pa gave me a notebook just like yours this morning, so I could draw pictures and make notes to write my school report."

She didn't know if she was more touched that Daniel bought his son a special notebook for their adventure, or worried that the identical notebook was an attempt to forge a stronger bond between

Noah and the woman Daniel might want to be his son's new mother.

Amber linked arms with her sister, and together they walked outside where two carriages stood waiting. One driver was tasked with taking Connor and Olivia to the Denver & Rio Grande Railroad station at 19th and Wynkoop Streets, and the other to take Amber, Rick, Noah, and Ripley to the Denver, South Park & Pacific Railroad station at Sixth and Walnut Streets.

As the carriage carrying Olivia and Conner took a different turn and disappeared, Amber had the strangest sensation that the roads she and her sister were traveling would take them not only to different destinations, but to different spiritual ones as well.

She tried to smooth the unwanted emotions from her mind and heart as she might smooth folds from a new geological survey, but they kept crinkling up again. She settled back in her seat, every breath a struggle. Today was one of the biggest days of her life—to be in Morrison when dinosaur bones were first discovered. The joy, however, seemed to be slipping away, moment by agonizing moment.

40

1878 Morrison, Colorado—Amber

THE LOCOMOTIVE STEAMED, hot breath coiling from the smokestacks, out of the Denver, South Park & Pacific Railroad Station at ten o'clock. The train was surprisingly noisy clattering down the tracks, hurtling through the morning. The drawing room style Pullman car Rick rented for the day smelled of new carpet and wood polish. Red velvet wallpaper covered the walls and a Persian carpet covered the floor. Tasseled silk blinds were discreetly lowered in the event they wanted privacy. Amber raised them to let in the sun. At the far end of the carriage, a washroom gleamed with polished brass.

They were riding in style.

Rick sat in one of the two large armchairs, legs crossed, reading one of several newspapers he'd bought at the station. Ripley slept close by on the carpeted floor. She and Noah sat side by side on the sofa across from Rick, journals in hand.

"This is beautiful," she said, "but why'd you spend so much money for a forty-five-minute train ride? This is more excessive than the private stagecoach."

"There was no room available in the semi-private car we traveled in yesterday, and I refused to allow you and Noah to ride in a rattling train with cinders and ashes sifting through windows. You would have coughed all the way to Morrison."

"Okay, but the cost is going on my tab, along with the private stagecoach, cabs, wardrobe, dining out, and incidentals."

"Good luck with that," Rick said.

"Where are we going when we get to Morrison?" Noah asked.

"I have a list of sections along the hogback, plus one non-dinosaur site called the Dakota Ridge Trail that I think we should visit, if we have enough time. The trail is a six-point-five-mile loop with incredible views of the red sandstone formations." Growing up, she'd biked the trail several times and wondered about its origin. Was it an old mining trail or Indian trail? So far, she hadn't found anyone who knew. After today, she'd have a better idea.

Noah looked up from his journal, clicking his pencil back and forth between his teeth. "Rick, did you fight for the Union or the Confederacy? I asked Pa, but he didn't know."

Rick made a show of folding the newspaper and tossing it on the side table, signaling to Noah that he had Rick's full attention. "I fought for my country, for the Marines, for my family, and for Lady Liberty. Does that answer your question?"

For an instant Noah look confused, then he asked, "But was that for the North or the South?"

When Rick didn't answer, Amber did. "He fought for the Union."

As Rick sat rigid in the chair, his jaw tightened, and he gritted his teeth. He was sliding into that dark place where he was tightly wound and easily angered. But today she didn't have the breath to sing to him, not even one short sea shanty. If she stayed calm, he would slowly drift out of it.

The train swayed around a bend and while Noah twiddled his pencil between his teeth, his journal slid off his lap. Ripley stood and sniffed the book.

"I know. I know." Noah snatched it up and patted the dog's head. He then thumbed through several pages to find his place again. He'd been copying Amber's sketch of the hogback, including fossils found at specific locations.

"I met with Chief Ouray yesterday," Rick said in a light tone, full of hesitation, as though he was searching for proper balance and was unable to find it.

"I'm sorry I forgot to ask. How was it?"

He stared out the window for a moment. "I have several pages of notes."

"I've heard of him," Noah said. "Pa says he's a good man."

"He is, Noah. I'm going to write about him. I want other people to know what we know." Rick picked up another newspaper from the stack and returned to the task of reading the daily news.

"Amber, how did the bones get into the rocks and turn to stone?"

She smiled, fondly remembering a similar query to her grandfather when she was a child. "That's the same question I asked when I found my first fossil. It led to years of questioning, digging, research, and reading. I've never stopped asking questions, but I do my research first. Then, when I can't find the answers, that's when I go to the experts."

"Is Dr. Lakes an expert?"

"He's an insatiably curious scientist, talented illustrator, and teacher. His discoveries last year set off the dinosaur bone rush in Colorado and throughout the West. Yes, he's an expert."

"That makes him pretty important. Will he take time to talk to you?"

"I hope so."

Noah's concentration on his sketch continued as he delicately erased and shaded the dinosaur's vertebrae. Using the flat edge of his hand, he brushed the eraser's rubber shavings off the page. "Amber?" He said her name as a question, as if he wasn't sure she was still beside him.

"Yes, Noah. I'm still here." She'd been staring out the window, watching the landscape as it spread and grew as they climbed higher, thinking about Daniel and wondering if she'd see him again.

Noah looked up at her, raising one eyebrow slightly in a move that she'd seen his father make dozens of times. "How did the bones get in the rocks on the hogback?"

She yawned, patted her hand against her mouth. "The short answer is that it took millions of years."

"That's a long time."

She flipped back a few pages in her journal to a sketch of North America. It showed the Cretaceous Interior Seaway with an arrow pointing to the western edge where Colorado was located today.

"Hundreds of millions of years ago, there was an interior seaway that split the continent of North America into two land masses." She lightly drew over the lines in the sketch, so he could see the area she was talking about. "The dinosaurs roamed along the western edge of the sea, where I've marked the location of Colorado. See?"

He nodded, chewing on his pencil meditatively.

"They died there."

There was a long pause in the conversation before he asked, "Why did they have to die?"

She felt the weight of his stare and raised her head to meet it, intuitively knowing that Noah wasn't only asking about dinosaurs but also about his mother and sister.

"Sometimes people we love are taken from us before their time. We don't understand why, and we beat ourselves up trying to find a reason. But we're not meant to understand. We can't see things clearly now. We're squinting in a fog, peering through a mist. But one day, the weather will clear, the sun will shine, and we'll see it all as clearly as God sees us. Then we'll fully understand. At least that's what my granny told me when my cousin Trey died." Amber put her arm around Noah's shoulders. "When you think of your mom and Heather, you can believe they see everything clearly."

"Can they see me?" he asked, a single tear sliding down his cheek.

"I believe so," she said.

He wiped the tear with the back of his hand. "That means they already know what happened to the dinosaurs."

"I guess so." She laughed and glanced over at Rick expecting to see his face buried in the paper, but he was watching her, his eyes glistening.

She put her fingers to her lips, puckered, and threw him a kiss. He smacked his face, smiled slightly, and returned to reading the paper.

"So Noah, until we can see clearly, the four leading theories of what happened to the dinosaurs are: One, a big meteorite crashed into Earth, changing the climatic conditions so dramatically that dinosaurs couldn't survive. Two, ash and gas spewing from volcanoes suffocated them…"

"Wait, stop please, so I can take notes."

She watched him write and when he finished, she continued. "Three, diseases wiped out entire populations. And, four, food chain imbalances led to starvation. And someday they'll figure it out."

"Maybe a geologist named"—He paused to square his shoulders—"Noah Grant will solve the mystery?"

She hugged him, smiling. "Maybe."

Her closest friend in the world was her sister, but Olivia had never been interested in geology or dinosaurs. She tolerated Amber's interests but could barely get through a conversation when it involved rocks and fossils. This precious child had somehow come into her life and stolen her heart, not only because his fascination with geology and paleontology equaled hers, but because of his compassion, intelligence, and humility. She swallowed the lump in her throat. She had fallen in love with a ten-year-old. Leaving him might be more painful than leaving his dad. No, they were a package deal, and would equally break her heart.

He finished writing and asked, "So the dinosaurs died. What happened next?"

"About sixty-five million years ago the sea drained, and a sudden uplift called the Laramide Orogeny formed huge mountains where the Rockies are today. The seabed tilted at a forty-five-degree angle." She stacked her hands on the side and tilted them to show him the angle.

"Then, about forty million years ago, the mountains began to erode, and the continent entered a volcanic period that buried the mountains under ash. A period of erosion followed and washed away the softer rock layers to reveal the much older and harder rocks that make up the Rockies today. The layers of the seabed came to the surface as a long chain of ridges or hogbacks."

"And brought the dinosaur bones to the surface?"

"Exactly, and that's why Dr. Lakes is working near Morrison." As much as she wanted to find him, she didn't think she'd have the energy to look. Fighting for her next breath was exhausting.

"But how did they turn into rocks?"

"You are full of good questions today."

He blushed.

"You're really thinking this through. When the dinosaurs died they were buried in the seabed mud. Over time more sediment covered the remains. Eventually they were encased…" She had to stop to catch her breath, and then she continued, "in this newly formed sediment and turned into fossils."

Noah drew a bone, covered it with sediment, and then made notes to describe the process, just as she had done with her drawings, matching notes to numbers and symbols.

When he finished writing his notes, she continued. "As the bones decayed, water infused with minerals—" She had to stop again.

Noah glanced up. "Take your time."

"Seeped into the bones," she continued, "and replaced the natural chemicals in the bones with rock-like minerals."

He tapped his pencil against his journal. "So water ran into the bones and changed the bone chemicals with rock chemicals."

"Yes, and that process created a heavy, rock-like copy of the original bones."

He wrote another note. "Is this a correct statement?" He pointed to the note.

"The fossil has the same shape as the original bone but is chemically more like a rock," Amber read. "Yes, that's correct." His ability to understand complex scientific concepts amazed her.

"I'm thinking about questions other students will ask when I give my report at school," he said. "They'll want to know if they find a fossil, how they can be sure it's not really a rock?"

She flipped a page in her journal and pointed to a broken fossil. "Fossils will preserve the internal bone structure. If there's a break, you should be able to see the different canals and webbed structure of the bone, like these," she said, pointing to the sketch and catching her breath. "But on the outside, fossils are smooth, and most rocks have a rougher texture."

"So if I find a rock and it's smooth, I'll know it's a dinosaur bone."

"Not exactly. If you dig up a rock in your grandfather's yard, it's unlikely to be a fossil, but if you dig up a rock on the hogback, then there's a good chance you could have a fossil." It was becoming more and more difficult to carry on a conversation for the breaks she had to take.

"So, it's about location."

"It's always about location," she said.

He gave her a quizzical look.

"That's a joke and one of Olivia's favorite lines."

"If…" He lowered his voice. "If something happened to Ripley and we buried her. Would she become a fossil?"

"Most animals don't fossilize. They simply decay and disappear from the fossil record. Only a small percentage of the dinosaur genera have been or will be found as fossils."

"How do you know?" he asked. "Maybe I'll find some when I grow up."

"That's certainly possible." She did a quick mental calculation. Dr. Lake closed his quarries in 1879, and it wasn't until the Alameda Parkway was constructed in 1937, to provide access to Red Rocks Park, that workers discovered hundreds of dinosaur footprints. Noah would be sixty-nine. It was possible he could return and be part of that discovery.

"Why are the bones the same color as rocks?"

"You can answer that one. Think about it."

He tapped his pencil against his journal, studying the picture he had copied from her notes. It was a large vertebra drawn in bas relief on a flat slab of sandstone. "Because they *are* rocks."

"Go on," she said.

He tapped his pencil faster, as if he was playing his drum, as he focused on something beyond the window. "A fossilized object is just a rock model"—he stopped tapping, his eyes wide—"of an ancient object."

"That's excellent, Noah. Now let me add something else. Fossils come in many colors, depending on the surrounding rock matrix."

"What's that?"

"Your next lesson," she said. "See how exciting that was to figure it out on your own instead of asking someone for the answer?" She lightly knocked on his head. "It's up there now. It'll never go away."

"That's where Ma is. And," he lowered his head, then slowly lifted his eyes to her. "I guess that's where you'll be someday, too."

She hugged him again. "Oh, Noah. You know how to break a girl's heart and you're only ten. God only knows what will happen when you're fifteen."

He sniffed and returned to his journal and she took a rest break.

"If Dr. Lakes has been working on the hogback for a year and a half, do you know where he found fossils?"

She flipped back a few more pages. "Here's a picture of the hogback with Xs marking the fourteen quarries where he's found fossils. Only four of these have yielded significant discoveries. He found the first fossils here." She pointed to a spot half way up the slope, on the northern side of the gap, through which Bear Creek crossed the hogback.

"I love Dr. Lakes' description of the hogback." She ran her finger along the ridge. "He said, 'A mighty ocean wave capped with a crest of rugged sandstone for six hundred feet. And from the crest, looking toward Denver, the prairie undulates like the waves of the sea.'"

Noah examined the sketch. "I've never seen the ocean. Pa has been to California and Virginia. He's seen both oceans, but I haven't. When I grow up, I'm going to Scotland. I'll see the ocean then."

"That'll be exciting"

He returned to his sketching, trying to copy hers in every detail.

"But Amber… How did Dr. Lakes know what he found? How did he know the bones were from a dinosaur?"

"He didn't. He sent fossils to Dr. Marsh who coined the name *Stegosaurus*. He thought the bones were from a turtle."

Noah laughed. "A turtle?"

"A giant prehistoric turtle."

"When did he realize he made a mistake?"

Amber leaned over and whispered, "He doesn't know yet, but I know the truth."

"How do you know?"

She put her finger to her lips. "It's a secret. You can't tell anybody."

Ripley stood and did a doggy stretch.

"Ripley's probably bored. Why don't you take her for a walk to the next car and back?"

"Yes, ma'am." He tucked his pencil into the loop attached to the journal, closed it, and stowed it away in a canvas sack.

"What do you have in your sack?" Rick asked.

"Books," Noah said. "When I don't have anything else to do, I read. Pa always carries books with him, too. He reads a lot."

"I do, too. Maybe I'll read one of your books on the way back to Denver." The tension around Rick's eyes had slipped away, and it seemed the dark place had released him again, after taking only a short detour this time.

"Have you read *Alice's Adventures in Wonderland*?"

"I've heard the story many times, but I've never read the book."

"It's in my sack, if you want to read it."

As soon as he was out of ear shot, Amber put her feet up, leaned back on the sofa, and asked Rick, "If I go home now can I come back?"

"Now? Right now?"

"No, tonight maybe. Kenzie and David can come and go, but

can I?"

"They don't have any special powers. At least, not that I know of. The whole family used the ruby, sapphire, and emerald brooches to go back to 1881, so I don't know why you couldn't go home and come back. Did you ask Kenzie?"

Amber put her hand on her chest. Her heart was beating faster, and each breath was a struggle. "She said she didn't know."

Rick scrubbed the back of his neck, contemplatively. "If you're thinking about going home, it's because you're feeling worse. Your breathing is shallow, and you're constantly stopping to catch your breath. You can't even take deep breaths, can you?"

"Sometimes."

"And you don't have an appetite either."

"I do, too."

He stared stubbornly at her. "Amber, you move food around a plate to make it look like you're eating. You filled your breakfast plate yesterday and only ate part of a biscuit. You pushed the eggs around the flower pattern. You made a pretty design, but that didn't do your stomach any good. But it's not your appetite that concerns me. It's your lungs."

She poured spring water from Noah's canteen into a tin cup and took a long drink. She offered to refill Rick's cup, but he declined with a polite wave of his hand.

"I'll wait for the steward to bring coffee," he said. "But here's my suggestion for today. Let's go back to Denver."

"No. I can ride in a buggy. I can't…" She paused to give the lump in her throat time to settle and her breathing to catch up. "I can't give up yet. This would be like you meeting Doc Holliday or Bat Masterson. I can't miss it."

He folded the last newspaper and tossed it on the stack of the papers he'd read. "Here's the deal. When we get to Morrison, I'll take you up to the Swiss Cottage and get you a room. Noah and I will go search for Dr. Lakes. If we find him, we'll bring him back to talk to you."

"What will you tell him?"

"That a geologist and amateur paleontologist would like to engage him for an afternoon's discussion on fossils."

"Don't tell him I'm a woman."

"I wouldn't dare." Rick's intensity had moved from eyes to voice.

She glanced at her lapel watch to see if a visit could coincide with lunch. "Tell him I'll buy him lunch, but I still don't think he'll give up an afternoon to talk to a visitor. You never know, though."

"How much do you think Dr. Marsh is paying him to dig for fossils?"

"About a hundred dollars a month."

"I'll offer him that much to come talk to you."

She closed her eyes and focused on the shallow flow of her breath. "He'd probably come for that."

"Does that mean you're not going to make any site visits?"

"The locations of Dr. Lakes quarries have been lost to history. He described the excavations and the bones in considerable detail, but the precise locations were never recorded." Her heart was working so hard to help her breathe. She hoped she wasn't putting too much stress on it.

"I want to know where they are," she continued. "He left a sketch of the ridge in 1879 after most of the excavating was completed, but it's sparsely labeled, not to scale, and lacks reference points. I'll ask him to identify where they are and any geological markers. If he only identifies last year's sites, that'll be more than what history has now."

"You still haven't answered my question," Rick said with only an ounce of his previous patience.

She handed him her journal. "On the last page is a list of sites and a sketch of the ridge. Those are the places I want to visit. Tear it out and take it with you. Go to those places and take pictures. I'll be satisfied with that. Then I'll be ready to go home."

"Home? Or back to Denver."

Tears streaked down her cheeks. "Home."

41

1878 Morrison, Colorado—Amber

WHEN THE TRAIN arrived in Morrison, Amber exited their private car with Rick's assistance and carefully stepped into the station yard. There was no platform, just gravel, and it was now skimmed with mud. The roar of the Bear River racketed behind the station. Yesterday, she'd been able to disembark under her own power.

But not today. She was sick, and she well knew it.

Despite the sun, the temperature was several degrees cooler than in Denver, evidenced by the sprinkling of snow on both sides of the rail bed. Although the scent of pine was heavy in the air, she was more concerned about breathing than what she breathed in. She only had to survive a few more hours, and then she could go home and get a pill that would magically make her better.

Rick found a backless bench in the sun, yet out of the wind, and left her there while he and Noah jogged across South Park Avenue to the Spotswood Stage Coach House and Livery to hire a carriage. Bundled up in her bear coat, she was quite warm. While Ripley sniffed the ground around her, she closed her eyes and let the sun beat down on her face.

Jingling harnesses and a warning bark from Ripley had her opening her eyes. She laughed. She'd never seen Rick so out of place. The hired carriage was not a hansom four-in-hand but a buckboard with an actual two-by-four nailed across the top of the wagon to provide seating for the driver and one passenger. No springs. The heel of his boot was cocked against the edge of the wagon.

He tipped back his hat. "Howdy, ma'am. Need a ride?"

She walked toward the wagon, weighted down by the thick coat and layers of clothing. "I thank you, sir, for your kind offer. My escort abandoned me for the silver mines." She stopped to take a few breaths. "I'll be needin' a lift up to the Swiss Cottage. Are ya familiar with the hotel? It's back up a ways." Not only did she need a lift, she needed an oxygen tank.

He scratched his whiskered chin. "I believe I can find it." He jumped down and swooped her up into his arms. She lacked the energy to protest. "But if I can't find my way 'round, I'm sure you'll lead me where ya want me to go."

She didn't have the energy to react to the teasing double entendre, either. He wore a grim look—different from his black mood look—when he set her on the seat. She didn't have the energy to analyze it. He quickly gathered up Ripley and put her in the back with Noah.

Surreal was the only way she could describe the buckboard ride across Bear Creek. It seemed like a scene from *Little House on the Prairie*, with Pa driving the buckboard down South Park Avenue to Spring Street.

The Swiss Cottage, a three-story structure constructed of large blocks of red and white rusticated sandstone, stood atop a stepstool-like rise at the base of an imposing hill. An expansive porch supported by white columns framed the grand hotel and from its porch, Amber could see the hogback and the red rock formations. The widow's walk would provide an even more expansive view, but she doubted she could get up there.

On the hotel's second-story veranda, several couples lingered at the rail, staring in the direction of the red rocks. And on the ground-floor veranda, the gliders of the occupied rocking chairs squeaked as they rocked to and fro.

Rick lifted her from the buckboard. At the porch steps, the

owner had pounded into the dirt a neatly lettered wooden placard that read: REMOVE SPURS & CLEAN BOOTS. Amber was instantly reminded of Hughes Cabin and the beginning of her adventure. It seemed like months ago now instead of only two weeks.

They skirted the rocking chairs and entered the grand hotel, built for Governor John Evans by George Morrison in 1874. That tidbit of historical information was on another placard next to the front door.

Inside, the lobby showed subtle signs of refined taste. The heavy but well-appointed sofas and chairs were accented with rich rugs, vases, expensive lighting fixtures, and recognizable paintings by George Caleb Bingham, a famous nineteenth-century Western artist.

While Rick arranged for a room, she and Noah sat on a settee in the lobby and looked out the large windows overlooking the red rocks, that would evolve into the ten thousand–seat open-air Red Rock Amphitheatre. She'd seen dozens of performances there, but her parents had seen the greats—The Beatles in 1964, Jimi Hendrix in 1968, and later, the likes of John Denver, Sonny & Cher, Carole King, U2, The Grateful Dead, and so many others.

God, she missed her parents. She hadn't seen them in almost two months and a century and a half. Every so often, Amber got slammed with the fear that she'd never see them again.

"This place is quite a resort to be out in the middle of nowhere," Rick said.

She looked up, coming out of her reverie that had placed her safely at home under her mom's watchful eye. "They don't think they're in the middle of nowhere. They think they're in God's country."

"Then God's country has a mineral spring, ballroom, tennis court, stable, and an eighteen-hole golf course."

"A golf course?"

"That's what the advertisement says, but when I asked the clerk, he said it was only on paper."

"Looks like the governor hopes to develop tourism in the area. But false advertisements aren't good for business. It's just as well,

I'm not up for eighteen holes today. What about you, Noah?" Amber asked.

"No, ma'am. I have a full calendar, thank you."

Amber snickered because that was all she had the energy for. "Did they have any vacancies?"

"Out of forty-two rooms... No, but I offered to pay an outrageous fee to rent a room until dinnertime. The clerk bumped a couple from Colorado Springs." Rick handed her the key. "You have a large room on the second floor with access to the deck walk. I hope you can make it up the steps because they don't have an elevator."

"I'm not an invalid. I can walk."

The climb upstairs was not an easy one-foot-in-front-of-the-other endeavor. In fact, she couldn't make it past the first landing. Breathing became so difficult she had to stop and rest. Rick's patience seemed limitless, but the look she'd seen on his face when he set her in the buckboard, she was now able to identify as fear. And that exacerbated her own.

"Let's go home, Amber. You don't have to do this."

"Just a few more hours," she pleaded. "I've come this far, I have to see it through."

"Then I'll ask the front desk to send up the doctor."

"What can he do? There's no magic pill. I need a pulmonologist and cardiologist. Please, just give me a few more hours. Help me, Rick. I need my dream to come true."

"At the expense of your life? Is it really worth it?" He didn't wait for her to answer. Instead, he picked her up. "Come on, sweetheart, I'll help you." It was one of the smoothest moves she'd ever seen, and Clark Gable couldn't have done it any better.

When they reached the room, Noah took the key and opened the door. The breathtaking view would have stolen her breath if she'd had any to steal. Rick set her gently on a reclining sofa and turned it toward the window overlooking the hogback. Ripley jumped up on the end and put her head in Amber's lap, guarding her. She didn't know how Ripley knew something was terribly wrong, but she did.

"I'll have a lunch tray sent up," Rick said. "Try to eat something."

"I will."

"And don't go out on the walk. I'd hate for you to faint with nobody there to catch you."

"I'm not prone to fainting, and I promise not to leave this spot." She pointed toward her rucksack. "Will you give me my journal?"

Noah handed it to her. "I better stay here with you. Rick can go find Dr. Lakes."

She put the sack aside and cupped his cheek. "No, sweetie. You go with him. You know the things I want to see. And if you find Dr. Lakes, and he won't come to town, you know what to ask him."

Noah shook his head. "No, I don't."

"Yes, you do. Ask him the questions you would ask me. Be my eyes, Noah. Be my heart and voice. Share our passion with him."

He hugged her, and his tears wet the side of her face. "I don't want to leave you. What if something bad happens while we're gone and you're all alone?" He looked at her with an odd expression, and she couldn't fathom the meaning.

She put her hand to her chest, wishing she could push air into her lungs. "Nothing will happen. I want you to enjoy the hogback for both of us."

He walked away, head down, shoulders slumped. What was wrong with him? He should be excited, not worried. Then it dawned on her. "Noah," she said. "Come here." She took his hand and squeezed it. "I'm not sick like your mom was." She stopped to breathe and then continued. "Nothing's going to happen to me. I'll be right here when you return, and then we'll take the train back to Denver."

And then what? She would have to tell him goodbye.

His face went through a series of emotions, none of which relieved her worry for him, and then he seemed to relax. "Maybe you'll feel like having dinner in the fancy restaurant downstairs before we leave."

"That sounds like a lovely idea. On your way out, why don't you make a reservation."

Rick kissed her forehead, scratching her with his whiskers. "If anything happens to you while we're gone"—He gave her a wicked grin that usually did the trick in boosting her spirits—"I swear I'll never volunteer to be your bodyguard again."

"I hope I'll never need a bodyguard again, but I'll behave myself, so you won't turn down the job."

Noah called to his dog, "Come on, Ripley." Ripley glanced up, whined, then nestled her head on Amber's lap.

Rick petted the dog. "Looks like you want to stay and guard your mistress. Okay, but don't let her leave the room." Then to Amber he said, "I'll lock the door, but that means you'll have to get up to let in the room service attendant."

"I can handle that."

She worked hard to appear untroubled. Acting was not her forte, and Rick had learned to read her well. He knelt so they were face to face. "I don't like this at all. I promised David I wouldn't leave you."

"You have to go. This is the only chance I'll have…" She stopped for a breath. "You have to take it for me."

He butted his head with hers. "I love you, sweetheart, like I love my sister. When you meet her, you'll see how difficult she can be to love. Don't take any risks. We'll be back in an hour or two."

If Rick teared up, she'd call off the whole thing and get right back on the train. But he smiled. "Remember, you have no way to communicate with me. If it's an emergency and you have to go home, go."

"I won't go without you, and the stone doesn't seem to work anyway."

She gave them a toodle-oo wave, and as soon as the door closed, she cried. This was one of the biggest days in her life and some stupid bug was keeping her from enjoying it. On top of her breathing issues, she'd shed more tears in the last few days than she had in her entire life. If she were ten years older, she'd buy into a pre-menopausal diagnosis. Since she was compiling a list of specialists to see upon her return, she might as well add an OB/GYN.

She dozed off and woke when Ripley barked. "What is it, girl?" She petted her head. "What's the matter?" A knock on the door produced another bark. "That's just room service." Then she noticed the lunch tray on the table that she hadn't touched, and vaguely remembered opening the door for room service then immediately falling back to sleep. They must be coming for the tray. She pushed to her feet and Ripley trotted behind her. "I'm coming."

She unlocked and partially opened the door. Ripley growled at the two men standing there. They definitely weren't hotel employees. She tried to slam the door, but one of the men put his boot in the way. He pushed his way in, forcing her to step aside.

Ripley growled again.

One of the two men, a rangy-looking man wearing a sheepskin coat drew a Colt .45 from a gun belt and pointed it at Ripley. "Shut her up, or I will."

"Shh, Ripley. What do you want?" She backed away from the door. "I don't have any money or anything of value." She had the brooch, but she would guard that with her life. She wobbled and leaned against the wall. "I have to sit down." Her heart raced. Perspiration broke out on her forehead, above her lip, and her limbs shivered. She should be afraid of the men, but she was more worried about her next breath than whether they intended to steal her last one.

The man without the gun had a tidy Van Dyke beard, a great mane of… She stopped cataloging personal details when she realized she had seen him at the train station shipping crates to Yale.

Bluntly he asked, "What's wrong with you?"

"I don't know." She collapsed on the sofa, her head swimming. What time was it? Rick said they would be back in an hour or two. If he came in now, the situation would escalate. She had to find out what the men wanted and get rid of them. She glanced at her lapel watch. It was almost one o'clock. There was still time.

"Come here, Ripley." She held her by the scruff of her neck, and she sat obediently at her side but growled low in her throat. "What do you want?" Her patina of bravery was thinner than she wanted to admit.

"I'm Leonard Hendrix." He pointed to the man guarding the door. "My associate." Hendrix sat in a chair opposite her.

Then she remembered she'd seen both men in Leadville. "You walked out on my performance at the Tabor Opera House. I'm sorry you didn't enjoy it. I hope you got a refund."

There was a look of surprise on Hendrix's face. "You had a standing room only crowd. I'm surprised you noticed."

"How could I not. You were the only patrons leaving."

"We found out what we needed to know. No point sticking around. You see"—He flicked an imaginary piece of lint from his coat sleeve—"we believe you're in the employ of Dr. Cope and are here to sabotage Dr. Marsh's project." He looked hard, angry, at her, as if he thought she was too sick to listen. "You've been spreading drawings of unknown creatures along with rumors and innuendo. We're here to see that you desist slandering our employer."

"I know all about Cope's and Marsh's hatred for each other, and the lengths they're willing to go to discredit each other's work." She stopped to breathe and after a long pause continued, "I'm not here to interfere. I'm strictly an observer."

The man pulled a piece of paper from his pocket and held it in front of her. "This is your work, correct?" His tone made it clear he didn't expect her to deny it. It was the sketch she had drawn for Noah her first night in Leadville.

"Where'd you get that?"

"Doesn't matter. What I want to know, what Dr. Marsh wants to know, is where it came from."

She reached for the drawing. "I drew it from memory. It's mine."

He folded it and returned it to his pocket. "We talked to Judge Adams in Leadville. He said you told him that you attended Smith College, then studied geology under Dr. Marsh at the Peabody Museum of Natural History at Yale—unofficially. Dr. Marsh said a woman has never studied under him and that you're a fraud."

"That's not nice," she said. "If that's what he thinks…" She stopped to take a few breaths before continuing, "then why does he care about my sketch?"

"He believes you're working for Dr. Cope and spreading falsehoods to discredit his work."

"I'm not here to interfere with their work. They're both…" She pursed her lips and took several shallow breaths. "They're both outstanding geologists and paleontologists. I'd like to see them work together. I believe they can accomplish more together than separately."

"That wasn't your position last night at the Robinson residence." Hendrix removed a small notebook from his inside jacket pocket and flipped to the last page. "I believe your comment was, 'Aren't you more interested in dinosaurs and prehistoric life because of their intense rivalry and hatred for each other?' That sounds to me like you were encouraging the dissension between them."

"Gossip travels faster in Denver than the news does by telegraph…" She put her hand to her throat and closed her eyes for a moment. Then continued, "I want the doctors to work together so it won't take them years to realize the *Stegosaurus* isn't a gigantic prehistoric turtle."

"If it's not, what is it?"

"A Jurassic dinosaur, and that's all I can say."

"Where's your proof?"

She pointed in the direction of the hogback. "Everything Marsh and Cope need to understand about the *Stegosaurus* is out there. They just need to work together to figure it out. If they do, they'll come to an understanding about the dermal plates, too." She had to stop talking. Every word made the next breath that much harder to claim.

Her chest pains were more intense. She turned to straighten out on the settee to see if that would ease her breathing. When she switched positions, her journal fell to the floor.

Hendrix made a hard, scraping noise as he pushed forward to pick it up. "What's this?"

She made a move to stand but she couldn't. "Give it to me. You can't have that."

He thumbed through several pages. No one's eyes ever went wider in recognition. He knew what he had, and he was mentally calculating how much money he could extort from Marsh for the treasure trove of information. Hendrix's Adam's apple bobbed with an involuntary gulp. He croaked, "Where'd you get this?"

"I'll tell you, if you give it back."

He seemed shocked, amused. "This is better than I expected." He stood and walked toward the door.

Amber pushed to her feet, wobbled. Her journal contained sketches and descriptions of every dinosaur found in Colorado. Marsh would consider the book to be the Holy Grail of paleontology. "It's mine. You can't have it."

The man guarding the door opened it. She tried to scream, but her voice was only a whimper. "Wait. She stumbled, grabbed the wall for support. "Give me my journal."

Growling, Ripley jumped up on Hendrix and bit into his arm, shaking him like a toy, forcing him to drop the journal. He screamed and kicked Ripley. The gunman brought his gun down on Ripley's skull, and she dropped to the floor, her head bleeding.

It all happened too fast.

Hendrix snatched up the journal and both men hurried from the room. "We've got to get this to Mudge in Cañon City." The door slammed behind them.

The room swirled around her, the light dimmed. She reached out, almost blindly, for something to support her—the wall, a chair, anything—nothing. She dropped to her knees, crawled to Ripley, and held her head in her lap.

She dug at her blouse to reach her brooch. "I have something more valuable," she cried, breathy to the point of hyperventilating. "Don't take my journal."

Oh Christ she couldn't breathe. Her lips were open, but no air would draw into her fear-frozen lungs. The harder she tried, the more scared she became. Her nails clawed at her throat, at her collar, seeking just a little room to breathe. She was going to suffocate. She closed her eyes, holding Ripley in her lap. Her hand stayed on her chest, feeling the slow beat of her heart beneath her spread fingers.

"Don't die, Ripley. Noah can't lose us both."

42

1878 Morrison, Colorado—Rick

RICK ENTERED THE stable at the Spotswood Stage Coach House and Livery to return the buckboard and rent two horses for a short ride up the hogback. A section of the barn had been partitioned into an office. A battered wooden desk faced the entrance, a swivel chair positioned to see the comings and goings of horses, mules, wagons, and men. Pieces of tack lay tossed in the corners and hung on walls. Nearly motionless dust motes hung in the air.

He paid in advance for the rentals and while waiting for his change, asked the owner, "Do you know Dr. Lakes, the geologist?"

The four legs of Mr. Spotswood's swivel chair splayed out from a central stanchion. He used his boot to push against one of the legs until it tilted back far enough that gravity threatened to upend him. Rick stood close by, prepared to pick him up off the floor.

"Sure do," he said. "Lakes has been coming to town since early last year. Didn't think much of him wandering around the hills until he pulled out wheelbarrows of those big bones. The entire town got excited then."

"Do you know where he's working? My…son has read about him. It'll make me out to be a hero if I can find Dr. Lakes today." Rick brushed a knuckle across the bridge of his nose, afraid the hundred lies he'd told in the last two weeks had morphed his nose into one similar to Cyrano de Bergerac.

Mr. Spotswood shot a glance out the window toward the corral where Noah was waiting with the rental horses. "I've got a boy about his age. Dr. Lakes was here a few days ago. He needed a wagon to carry some crates to the train." Spotswood tugged on his chin thoughtfully. "If I recall correctly, he said he'd be working a couple of miles from town about midway up the hogback."

"We'll look there," Rick said. "Appreciate your help."

Noah was standing between an Appaloosa and a piebald, picking stray burrs from the Appaloosa's forelock. When he saw Rick walking toward him, he asked, "What'd you find out? Is Dr. Lakes nearby?"

Rick jerked a thumb over his shoulder. "About two miles up Hogback Road."

"That's good news. Are we ready to leave now?"

"The sooner we go, the sooner we can get back for Amber."

"Which horse do you want?"

Rick made a gesture to indicate it didn't matter, so Noah swung into the Appaloosa's saddle and spurred his horse out of the stable yard. Rick freed the piebald's reins from the hitching post, put his foot in the stirrup, and heaved himself into the saddle. He wasn't the best equestrian in the family of wannabe horsemen, but he could hold his own. The piebald didn't seem to mind a new rider and promptly pointed his nose toward the Appaloosa several yards ahead.

Rick spurred the piebald to catch up with Noah. "We'll ride along Hogback Road to see if we can find him. If we don't, we'll ride to the end where Amber marked the Dakota Ridge Trail on her sketch. We'll check that out, then circle back."

"Let's ride fast," Noah suggested.

"Be careful, Noah. If you fall again, you might end up with a broken bone or worse." It was bad enough that the under-fifteen-year-olds in the family could outride Rick, he didn't want to be shown up by another one.

Luckily for him, the piebald showed puppy-like devotion and

understood verbal communication. He was a perfect horse for an inexperienced rider and responded not only to bit and spurs but seemed to sense Rick's mood as well. His body was tense with worry about Amber. Not just her illness, though that was his biggest concern, but he didn't know what she was going to do about Daniel and Noah. If she went home without them, her heart would remain broken for a long time.

After twenty minutes or so, Noah reined in and glanced behind him.

"Why do you keep looking back?" Rick asked. "Do you think someone's following us?"

"I was just checking the view," Noah said.

Rick used the break to remove a cigar from a slim silver case he'd purchased in Leadville. He struck a match against his thigh and waved it in front of the tip. "I'm glad Ripley wanted to stay with Amber." After a few gentle puffs, the cigar started glowing cherry red. "This would have been a long walk for her."

"I know, but I still miss her."

Rick rolled the cigar between his fingers. "I was worried about leaving Amber there alone, but knowing Ripley's with her—"

"She won't let anything happen to Amber."

Rick watched the hot cigar smoke as if he could divine hidden meaning in the way the plume curled as it rose into the cooler air. "You know, I had a dog like Ripley once. She was a good companion for me and my brothers."

"Do you have one now?"

"Yep. I still have all three of my brothers."

Noah cackled. "I know you have a brother, but I didn't know you had three. I meant do you have a dog."

"We share one with other family members. His name is Tater Tot, and he's a Standard Poodle. Do you know what they look like?"

Noah shook his head.

"He has a medium-sized frame with a rounded skull, a long head, dark oval eyes, close-hanging ears, springy step, and a curly coat, and is one of the smartest dogs around."

Noah touched the horse with his heels and brought his wandering mount back on the trail, and he and Rick rode side by side. "I bet he's not as smart as Ripley."

"Are you kidding? Nobody is as smart as Ripley," Rick said.

About two miles outside of town, they spotted a handful of men working about two hundred feet above the Bear Creek. "Do you think that's Dr. Lakes?" Noah asked.

"We're in the right spot. Let's leave the horses here, walk up the hill, and ask."

They hobbled their horses in an area sheltered in a copse of scraggly firs. Noah grabbed his knapsack and canteen and they hiked up the sloping cliff through scrub brush and rocks.

"Amber couldn't have hiked up here," Noah said.

Rick looked up, following the cries of hawks rearing their young in inaccessible holes on the side of the cliff. There was something about the starkness that reminded him of Afghanistan. He became instantly alarmed that he had no sidearm. He considered returning to the horses to retrieve a gun from his saddlebag, but he didn't want to hike down, hike back up, and then hike back down again if Lakes wasn't on site.

"Look, Rick." Noah pointed ahead. "See the brick-red marls and shales and variegated limestone? Those are the best lime quarries. At least that's what a note in Amber's journal said. I don't really understand it all, but she does. That's where they're digging."

"Did Amber sketch a picture of Lakes in her journal?"

"No, but he's from England, so he'll have an accent."

They approached the group of diggers working in a trench about thirty feet long, fifteen feet deep, and ten feet wide. "We're looking for Dr. Lakes. Is he here?" Rick asked.

"I'm Lakes," a man with a British accent said.

Rick extended his hand, but it was ignored by Lakes as he picked up the handles of a wheelbarrow. Rick tried to be nonchalant and made a dismissive wave. "Noah and I would like to invite you to town for lunch."

Lakes pushed the fossil-filled wheelbarrow over to another section of the dig where a member of the team was packing bones carefully into a crate.

Noah followed him. "Will you join us?"

"I have a can of oysters that'll see me through till dinner at camp."

"If you won't come with us, would you mind answering questions about geology and Jurassic era dinosaurs?"

"Sure. But talk loud."

Noah stepped up close to the doctor and shouted, "I heard you were about a mile from here when you found the first fossil. Will you tell me about it?"

"You don't need to talk that loud." Lakes lifted his hat, wiped his brow with his sleeve, and resettled the hat. "I was standing in the middle of yellow, brown, and gray sandstone like a battlement of a fortress defending the slope of the hill. We were standing at an angle about fifty to sixty degrees. Captain Beckwith over there"—Dr. Lakes pointed to a man sitting on a rock writing in a notebook—"called me over to examine what looked like a fossil or a branch of a tree compressed in a loose slab of sandstone. We'd found trunks and branches of petrified trees in the rocks capping the summit of the hogback before, so I wasn't surprised at this discovery. But the impression was too smooth to be have been left by a tree. Then I spotted the little patches of purplish hue on the ends and knew they were fragments of bone. A large bone that belonged to a gigantic animal. The question was, where was the rest of him?"

"And that was part of a *Stegosaurus*?"

"The bones found here became the holotype of *Stegosaurus armatus*. Dr. Marsh believes the remains are from an aquatic turtle-like animal."

"What do you believe?" Noah asked.

"That we found the skeleton of a monster. We boxed and shipped nearly a ton's weight of bones to Dr. Marsh at Yale. He later informed us that our discoveries were dinosaurs of a new and gigantic species. We were ecstatic."

Dr. Lakes demonstrated how to hoe the top soil, sift through it, and collect tiny bits of bone. Then after a short while, Noah's hand cramped and Rick took over note-taking responsibilities. His sketches were lousy but identifiable.

Noah and the doctor sallied out among the stratified sandstone that rose tier upon tier on the flanks of the mountain to explore caves and crevices. He told the doctor about Amber's interest in his work and how that had encouraged his own interest. He peppered the doctor with questions, and when Lakes answered one, Noah thought of six more.

Noah matured by the minute. Dr. Lakes, realizing he had an unusual student, went from a general to a more specific geology lecture. Rick was fascinated by Noah's intelligence and understanding of the subject matter. He couldn't wait to report back to Amber about her protégé.

About an hour later, Dr. Lakes announced, "It's lunch time. If you'll give me thirty minutes to wash up at camp, I'll meet you in town. You can buy me a late lunch, and we'll review today's lesson and I'll answer any more questions you have."

Noah glanced up at Rick, silently asking if that would be okay.

"We're staying at the Swiss Cottage," Rick said. "Shall we meet in the dining room at one o'clock?"

"One it is." Dr. Lakes patted Noah's shoulder. "You're a good student. I look forward to meeting your Miss Amber."

Noah seemed humbled by the doctor's praise.

They walked down the slope together and parted ways where the horses had been hobbled. Rick and Noah mounted up, reined around, and trotted down the road. As they neared Morrison, Noah said, "I hope with all that talk of rocks, I'll have something new to tell Amber."

Rick laughed. "I just thought a rock was a rock. I was proud of you, Noah. You sure did surprise Dr. Lakes. He thought he'd answer one question and get back to work, but you changed his mind quickly. He wanted to teach you everything he knew. He was impressed."

"He was easy to talk to. Amber is, too, but she holds back. Like she's afraid to tell me things. I thought it was because she didn't think I'd understand. But that's not it. Maybe now since Dr. Lakes trusts me with information, she'll share more of what she knows."

"I thought she shared a lot with you."

"You can see it in her eyes that's she's holding back. Pa does that when I ask about Ma. He wants to tell me, but it hurts him."

They arrived back in Morrison and rode straight to the hotel. Rick would return the horses before they caught the afternoon train to Denver. "We've barely got time to wash up before lunch. The train to Denver leaves at two-thirty."

"I can't wait to tell Amber. Do you think she'll feel well enough to join us?"

"If she's rested, maybe."

When they walked through the lobby, Rick was stopped by a desk clerk with an oversize-handlebar mustache and fuzzy hair. He wasn't the same clerk who checked them in.

"Mr. O'Grady. A moment, please. Room service delivered the luncheon tray but was unable to reclaim the dirty dishes. Miss Kelly didn't answer the door."

"How many times did you try?"

"Only once."

Rick pursed his lips tightly, thinking. Could she have gone outside? "Did you try using your master key to get into the room?"

"When she didn't answer the door, we tried but something was blocking it, and we couldn't get in."

Rick became immediately alarmed. "Did you go around and look in the window?"

"No. That would have been inappropriate."

"If anything has happened to her, I'm holding you responsible."

Rick never should have left her, regardless of the pressure she put on him. Living her dream was a dumb reason and he couldn't believe he fell for it. This screw-up only magnified the canopy of guilt that hung over him like a mushroom cloud full of sad memories, mistakes, and bad decisions. Since his gut was already a raw nerve with edges of jagged glass shredding him in two, he might as well dump a few broken pieces on top of the clerk.

"Management will hear about your incompetence."

There was a small almost imperceptible wince in the clerk's eyes. "Forgive me, Mr. O'Grady." His voice was soft now, almost a plea, and one side of his mustache drooped. "Is there anything I can do to make up for this oversight?"

Noah stepped between the clerk and Rick. "We're meeting Dr. Lakes in the dining room in a few minutes. Would you please make a reservation for four?" Noah then took Rick's hand and pulled him toward the steps. "We don't have time to argue with that annoying little man."

Rick looked down at the precocious pre-teen. "You're not the same kid who came to Denver on the stagecoach the other day. What'd you do with that Noah Grant?"

"Since I met Amber, I've grown up. She doesn't talk to me like I'm a child. And Pa and I have talked about things lately, too. Adult stuff you talk about in the parlor. It makes me feel older, more responsible."

"I like the changes. Come on. Let's go check on Amber and find out what's blocking the door."

"Maybe she put a chair there so nobody could come in and bother her while she was napping."

They hurried up the stairs. When Rick inserted the key to unlock the door, it found it already unlocked. He tried to push it open, but whatever had been blocking the door before was still there.

"Amber." She didn't answer, and Ripley didn't bark. Rick's heart was in his throat. He tried to squeeze his head between the door and the frame but there wasn't enough room. "Noah, see if you can tell why the door won't open."

He stepped aside to give Noah room to try. Rick caught the faintest quiver of fear in him, but Noah squared his narrow shoulders despite it and squeezed his head through the opening.

"What do you see?" Rick's own fear ratcheted up several more notches.

"Amber's on the floor."

An image of Amber huddled on the floor plastered itself at the forefront of Rick's brain.

"So is Ripley."

Rick's mouth dried up and panic grabbed a foothold in a pocket of fear.

"Ripley's head is bleeding. She's not moving." Noah's voice was oddly thick like someone with a plugged nose.

Cold sweat streamed between Rick's shoulder blades.

"Amber's not moving. Ripley's blocking the door."

Almost incapacitating fear had control of Rick now.

Noah withdrew his head, his face as white as a freshly laundered shirt. "I'll go around and come through the window."

Rick had to punch himself in the chest to restart his heart. He wasn't in a war zone. Mortars weren't going off around him. Gun fire wasn't being sprayed in all directions. "Stay here." If either of them was dead, he needed to know first and find a way to prepare Noah before he entered the room.

Rick dropped his saddlebags, ran down to the second-floor lobby, and pushed through the door to the balcony. Amber was in the corner room. He ran along the widow's walk until he reached the last window. He looked in. "Amber." She was lying on the floor with Ripley's head on her leg. He jerked up the window and jumped through.

Noah's head was still between the door and the frame, watching what was happening, tears streaming down his cheeks. Rick dashed across the room. Amber was gasping, grabbing her throat. Her face was the color of the lace on her blouse. Her eyes were barely open, and her lips were bluish.

His voice shaking, he said to Noah, "We've got to get her to the hospital."

"What about Ripley?"

The knot lodged further in Rick's throat as he put his hand on Ripley's chest. She was still warm and breathing. "Looks like she got wacked on the head. Go around and climb through the window.

He pushed damp hair off Amber's forehead. "What happened to

you, sweetheart?"

"They took my journal. Can't breathe."

"Who did?"

"Men. Take me home."

Noah plowed in through the window and ran to Amber's side. "What's wrong?"

"She can't breathe. She needs oxygen," Rick said. "Check on Ripley. See how deep the cut is."

Noah checked Ripley's head. "The cut doesn't look deep. Her eyes are open a little bit, but she's not moving. What's wrong with her?"

"She's probably got a concussion."

"Take me home, Rick." The words were barely audible.

"We'll have to take Noah and Ripley with us."

"You can bring them back."

He didn't have time to think about the consequences of kidnapping Daniel's son. Amber had to get to a hospital and Ripley needed emergency care, too.

"Take the brooch. It's burning my skin." She fidgeted with the top button of her blouse. Her blueish tipped fingers looked even bluer against the white of the fabric.

"I'll get it." Rick unbuttoned her blouse until he could reach the brooch pinned beneath her chemise.

She shivered when he brushed her breast with the back of his fingers. "Cold."

"Sorry."

With the brooch in hand, he crossed the room to the roll top desk that teemed with paper-stuffed cubbyholes—marketing pamphlets, stationery, envelopes. Even though she hadn't asked and didn't know how extraordinary the time with Dr. Lakes had been, she would want him to leave a note and repay him for his time. He took thirty seconds to address an envelope to Dr. Lakes and write a note thanking him for spending time with Noah. Before sealing the envelope, he pulled out all the cash he had in his pockets and included the bills with the thank-you letter. He left the envelope on the desk with instructions to deliver it to Dr. Lakes in the dining room.

Noah's brow furrowed. "Rick, are they going to be all right?"

"I believe so." A great claw of fear gripped his stomach and tightened it hard, but he remained focused on what he had to do. "Gather up our gear and put everything in a pile next to Amber and Ripley."

Noah brought in Rick's saddlebags and added his own knapsack, Amber's bag, coat, and shoes to the pile of gear. "What now?"

"Now? You must trust me. You need to be brave. Braver than you've ever been in your life. The only way Amber and Ripley are going to get well is to go to the hospital. This is what I want you to do, and you must do exactly what I tell you. Lay down next to Ripley and hold her as tightly as you can."

The hairs on the back of Rick's neck stood on end as he thought about leaving. Where should they go? Amber disappeared from Hughes Cabin. They couldn't go there. It was too far from medical care. If he focused on a Denver hospital, they could end up anywhere at any time. If he focused on the University of Kentucky Medical Center, they would be all alone in Lexington. Was that the best choice? He racked his brain, and then he knew.

"Noah, this is going to sound crazy, but I want you to say, 'Take us to Charlotte Mallory. Take us to Charlotte Mallory.' Say that over and over, either out loud or in your head."

"Who is she?"

"My cousin. She's a doctor. Now snuggle with Ripley and Amber, and I'm going to snuggle on top of you, so we'll be one tight group. You'll smell something yucky and the room will start to spin. It won't hurt you. Just keep saying Charlotte's name."

"I thought we were going to a hospital."

"We are, but it's far away. Don't be scared. I'll be with you." Rick opened the brooch, straddled Amber and wrapped his body around her, Noah, and Ripley. "Soon everything will be all right."

He kissed Amber's forehead. "Stay with me, sweetheart."

Within a few minutes of entering the hotel room, he was repeating the ancient words: *"Chan ann le tìm no àite a bhios sinn a' tomhais a' gaol ach 's ann le neart anama."*

Dustoff outbound…

43

1878 Pueblo, Colorado—Olivia

A CHANGE IN the tempo of the hoofbeats alerted Olivia that the carriage was slowing down. Shortly, it came to a stop. There was a slight racket from above, then a dip and rise as the driver jumped down from the box. A loud crunch of hasty footsteps on gravel preceded the door creaking open.

The South Park & Pacific Railroad Nathrop Station was a nondescript stone building with a surrounding platform. The station's gravel drive led to a single dusty red road, crowded on both sides by scrub brush. Looking westward beyond the brush was a to-die-for view of the Rockies. Her clients would pay a premium to buy a house with a view like that. Heck, so would she.

Connor disembarked but stood there, straightening his worsted waistcoat as he slowly scanned the outskirts of Denver. In the last several days, she'd seen him assume that cop-like posture often, or maybe it was more noticeable now that she was tuned in to the way he moved, full of physical grace and strength, yet determined and fully aware. There was no multitasking for him. He was singularly focused.

As she climbed down the folding step with Connor holding her gloved hand, she felt like an actress playing a role in a Victorian-era movie. She glanced up, half-expecting to see camera and boom operators, lighting technicians, and a director telling her where to go and what to say. But there was no one there. This was the real deal.

She untied the ribbon around her parasol and opened it, not because she needed protection from the morning sun, but because it was so dang cute. She stopped and took a closer look at the depot platform. No one was standing around waiting for a train.

"I think we're really early. I envisioned Union Station in LoDo. If you don't arrive early, you'll never make it to your train on time."

"I've seen Union Station, but what's LoDo?" Then he snapped his fingers. "Oh, I remember. Lower downtown, the mile-high hood, the cutesy So-Ho. You told me. I just can't think straight when I'm around you."

She dipped the parasol slightly and glanced at him coyly. "I'd hate to think I was so spellbound by my client, I forgot to describe one of the charming aspects of the city."

"You didn't forget anything."

She laced her arm around Connor's elbow and the fringed tips of her open parasol brushed against his hat. He caught the tumbling topper before it hit the dirt and tossed it back onto his head.

"Wow. That's impressive. Can you roll it down your arm, too?"

He tilted his head, let the hat roll down his arm into his hand, flipped his wrist backward, and tossed the hat. It landed squarely on his head.

She had a flash-forward moment and could easily see Connor teaching the move to their son, and she smiled. "How'd you learn to do that?"

He ran his fingers along the brim of the hat and winked, as a finishing touch. "We all took dance lessons and watched old movies with Mom. We had a contest to see who could pull off the hat trick first."

"Who won?"

"Rick. That's his signature move when he wants to impress a woman. He even has the gestures down so well, he can pantomime the trick."

"I'm impressed with *your* moves." She gazed into his eyes, letting them linger there until she had to break contact and step away, wishing she had a fan instead of a parasol, to whisk away the heat rising in her face.

"You're blushing, my love."

At his words of endearment, her step faltered. He caught her arm and tugged her closer, and whispered, his breath warm against her cheek. "I do love you, Olivia. And I have for the longest time."

She looked up at him, licking her bottom lip. "I want to kiss you, but we'd probably make the front page of the *Denver Times* for our scandalous behavior."

He gripped his hand above hers on the shaft of the parasol. Then he tilted the cover to block their heads from the view of those in the station who might be looking in their direction.

"Tell them to take the picture now."

He kissed her, and she clung to him. Her arm went around his neck, prolonging the kiss. When sanity returned, she pulled away from him, breathless and somewhat dizzy.

"You know how to make a moment memorable."

He laughed and released his grip on the parasol. "You gotta do something else when the hat trick doesn't work."

She looped her arm with his again. "The hat trick worked." She had thought it would be wonderful to get a love letter like the one Daniel wrote Amber, but Connor's hat trick fit him perfectly. It showed the depth of the love he had for his mother, the fun competitive nature of the O'Grady boys, and how much he wanted to please her. Olivia didn't need a love letter.

He squeezed her hand as if he could read her thoughts and threaded himself between her and a stack of crates and baggage at the corner of the platform. "During our ranch hunting expeditions, we saw the entire city, but I haven't seen anything since we've been here that resembles Denver of the future, except the mountains."

"I know. It really makes me appreciate the old sections of the city to see how much they've changed. I'll be able to give clients a better feel for Denver's early days now that I've seen it, experienced it." She bit the corner of her lip. "I would have lost out on so much if I hadn't come here with you. It scares me to think how close I came to…"

He faced her and thumbed away a single tear hanging on her eyelashes. "It's all behind us now."

"I know, but it still—"

He placed his finger across her lips. "Let's get through today. Tonight, we can have dinner with Amber and Rick, and maybe Daniel will return with us. We'll have a Champagne celebration. How's that?"

"Wonderful."

He opened the door to the station and held it while she closed her parasol and swept through, her skirt sweeping around her ankles. She reclaimed his arm. "You know, I looked forward to every one of your visits. I spent days planning what I would wear, where I would take you for lunch, whether the weather report would require a change to my carefully planned schedule."

He shook his head tsking. "And you never went out with me."

"You never asked," she teased.

"I did ask, but you turned me down. After that, you never gave me a signal that you'd accept. Some guys like to crash and burn, but not me."

"I didn't want to screw up a good thing. Not the commission. I wasn't worried about that. I was worried about us. I didn't want *us* to be over." The heat rose in her cheeks again, but she was rescued from embarrassment when a young man came out from behind the windowed ticket office, waving an envelope.

"Mr. O'Grady. Mr. Connor O'Grady."

Connor walked toward him, a single finger raised in acknowledgment. "Here. I'm O'Grady."

"Telegram for you, sir."

Connor plucked a coin from the pocket of his waistcoat and flipped it to the young man. It arced and caught the morning light, glinting through its downward spiral. An easy catch for the young man who rolled the coin across his knuckles as he returned to the ticket office.

Olivia smiled. "It must be a guy thing, rolling hats and coins and balls?"

"It's part of our DNA." Connor unfolded the piece of paper. "It's from Daniel. He wants us to disembark in Pueblo. He and General Palmer are on their way there from Cañon City."

"Pueblo, huh?"

She stepped over to the window and gazed out at the mountains. She brushed her hand along the windowsill, as if checking for dust, while considering the timeline of events in the Royal Gorge War. She remained quiet, gathering what she knew, trying to pin down her uneasiness about going to Pueblo. There was a standoff there involving Bat Masterson and Doc Holliday, but she didn't know the exact date. She and Amber had talked briefly about the gorge war while getting ready for the day, but they weren't concerned about the standoff at the roundhouse since the plan was to go to Cañon City and not Pueblo.

"What are you thinking?" Connor asked.

She gave the windowsill one more brisk brush with her fingers, turned, and said quietly, "There's a gun battle at the roundhouse in Pueblo, but I don't know when. Two men were killed. I can hear my dad telling the story, but exactly when it happens," she said with a shrug, "is a blur."

He ran his hand up her back softly, and although he wasn't touching her skin, every inch of her quivered. "I won't put you in harm's way. We won't go."

"No, we have to go. I want to meet the general. I just wish I was better informed."

"You know more than anyone else. It all happened over a hundred years ago. The exact date has probably been lost to history. You know the places, players, and events. Once you get there, you might be able to piece it together based on who's in town."

The young man who had delivered the telegram returned. "Mr. O'Grady, your car is ready to board."

Olivia looked for a clock but didn't see one. "Is the train ready to leave? It's early."

"No, ma'am. Your car will hook up to the train when it's close to departure time. If you'll come with me, I'll take you there now."

Olivia looked at Connor, expecting an explanation.

Giving her a wicked grin, he said, "This is our first date. I wanted to make it memorable."

"You mean *more* memorable."

They'd been on an emotional roller coaster for days. Now that they'd cleared the air, apologized, and been forgiven they could finally enjoy each other. Besides being a handsome, sexy guy who made her laugh, he was dependable and caring, and one heck of a kisser. She ran her finger along her bottom lip, still sensitive from making out in his room last night.

He tucked her gloved hand under his arm again, and they departed the station behind the young messenger. Directly ahead, sitting on a short track by itself, was a two-story carriage with a gleaming shell of mahogany, brass, and spotless glass.

"What is that?" she asked.

"A private car. I wanted time alone with you."

Olivia raised the hem of her skirts to avoid the muck in the rail yard. "Amber will be so jealous. I wish I had a camera to take pictures."

"Rick and I booked transportation at the same time. Amber won't be disappointed."

"The O'Grady men certainly know how to please women."

"Pops was a good teacher."

Olivia mounted the steps to the canopied open platform. "We can make a whistle-stop and campaign from here."

"Are you running for something?" he teased.

"Not this year, but I'd like to run for a local office one day—school board, municipal office, something."

"Why stop there? What's wrong with a Congressional or Senate seat?"

"One step at a time." She walked into the drawing room-style Pullman car. "Wow. This is spectacular." She dropped her parasol, unclasped her cloak, slung it over the back of a chair, removed her gloves, and unpinned her hat.

First impression of the car, it was gorgeous. Second impression, it was expensive. Third impression, she was in love with the man who rented it to please her.

"I want to explore every inch, but first I want to do this…"

She dropped his hat on the chair with her belongings and kissed him, and he kissed her back. The tender touch of his lips had heat dancing all over her—belly and breast, neck and face, fingers and toes. His tongue was soon inside her mouth giving, taking, tasting. And she clung to him, threading her hands into his thick hair. The hypnotizing scent of him—apple cider and leather and fresh air—was as arousing as his hands caressing her. The softness of his lips against her temples, the butterfly touch of his tongue, and the pressure of his hands on the curve of her hips had her melting in his arms.

A knock on the door forced them apart. A steward dressed in a white shirt and black vest entered. He bowed far enough to reveal a bald spot on the crown of his head. "I'm Chester, Mr. O'Grady. I'll be with you until you return to Denver. Is there anything I can get you and the missus from the kitchen? Even though your carriage isn't connected to the train, I can bring over whatever you'd like."

Connor lifted his brow. "Olivia?"

She let his question hang in the air for a moment. She knew exactly what she would like, but Connor wasn't on the menu. "Maybe coffee, fruit, rolls or biscuits. I don't want to spoil lunch. I assume we'll eat in Pueblo with Daniel."

"Probably not until mid-afternoon," Connor said. "Get whatever you want."

"That's enough for now."

"I'll have the same," Connor said.

Before leaving with their order, the steward picked up her cloak and Connor's hat and hung them on a row of pegs near the door.

"I think I'll explore while we wait on room service. If we pick up where we were interrupted, I might not be fully clothed the next time Chester barges in."

"I'll lock the door."

"He'll only come back again." She picked up a copy of *The Denver Times* and handed it to him. "Why don't you check out the local news while I play Realtor."

"Take your time." After unbuckling the heavy leather belt at his waist, he coiled the cartridge belt around his holster and set the gun rig on the opposite chair. Then he snapped open the paper.

She made mental notes and checked off items as she walked through the car: new carpet, polished furniture, velvet drapes over tasseled shades, mahogany paneled walls and ceiling, crystal chandelier, green velvet wallpaper, matching settee and deep cushioned chairs, and green-shaded lamps. It was market ready. If she had the listing, and planned an open house, she would dress just as she was now. How fun would that be?

At the opposite end of the car, a washroom gleamed with porcelain and polished brass. Directly across from the washroom was a small door that opened to reveal an elegant wrought-iron staircase. "I'm going upstairs," she said.

The paper snapped again. "Call me if you need me. I'll be right there."

Upstairs, she found a hallway with two doors. The first door opened into a room with a double bed, wardrobe, night table, and a large window to look out at the stars at night. She opened her mouth to call Connor but closed it. If he came up, there would be no stopping them. One kiss and the clothes would come off. At that point, the train could go non-stop to Chicago. The second room had a single bed, a night table, and a wardrobe. She closed the door. That room wouldn't be used on this trip.

She returned to the lower level, and Connor's head came up alertly, the newspaper crinkling in his hands. "What'd you find?"

"Oh, just two rooms…" Then she smiled. "But we'll only need one."

He tossed the paper aside, stood, and bracketed her hips with his strong hands before claiming her mouth in a kiss so deeply passionate, so uniquely him, that she wanted to stay in his arms for the rest of her life. "I have so much to make up for," he said against her lips.

It felt so good, so right to be in his arms. "It's all behind us now."

They sat on the settee, close together, and she gazed out at the mountains, a majestic sight she never took for granted. "Beautiful."

"Yes, *you* are."

She turned and looked at him, and she could hardly breathe or hear his words, from having him so close. The one coherent thought that surfaced was making love with him.

"I hate to break the mood with business, but have you given any thought to what you're going to tell General Palmer?"

The thought of work, or the purpose for this trip, ruined the mood. "Here we are alone, and you want to talk business. You're more romantic than that."

"I am, but other than quick kisses, I'm limited to what I can do right now. My mind, however, is upstairs in that big bed. Although the small bed will work for what I have in mind."

"How'd you know what was upstairs?"

"Because I asked for a car with certain"—he winked—"accoutrements."

She blushed. "Okay. You're right. It's safer to talk about General Palmer. In answer to your question, yes, I have notes. Some I'll put away for a later conversation, if there is one. Some I'll discard because it'll be too complicated to explain my opinions. But he's not interested in whether my legal advice has any merit. He only wants to report back to his board members that he met me."

Connor seemed amused. "I heard you last night. Your legal advice and insights were timely and intuitively articulated. Why would he not want to hear from you?"

"Because he's a general and doesn't intend to accept business advice from a woman. In 1878, it's rare for women to be educated, and opportunities for upper working-class women are limited to positions as a governess or a lady's companion. A female lawyer is a rarity."

"You're selling yourself short. I was there, remember? Those men engaged with a lawyer who could answer their questions succinctly. They forgot you were a woman. And I forgot you were a real estate agent."

She bristled, hearing echoes of her parents' complaints when she decided to quit the firm. "What's wrong with being a Realtor? It makes me happy."

"Olivia, I've been hanging out with you for almost a year, I have never seen you as engaged as you were last night. I don't know the real reason you left the law firm—"

"I was bored. Nothing challenged me. I wanted to be out traveling, making deals, so I left."

Chester knocked, and Connor waved him in. "We'll be connecting you to the train shortly, and we should be leaving on time." He set the table with a white tablecloth, china, and silver, put the serving dishes on a sideboard. After hanging up Connor's jacket, Chester quietly slipped away.

Olivia and Connor moved to the dining table and while enjoying brunch their carriage hooked up to the train, and they departed on time. While the eastern part of Colorado passed by in a blur of blue skies and mountain ranges, their conversation moved easily through their lives as teenagers, college years, and Connor's military service.

Sipping his coffee, Connor asked, "Given that we're close to our destination, give me some background. What kind of place is Pueblo? What can we expect?"

"I've only brought a couple of clients down here and my knowledge has several holes, but here's my spiel: The city sprung up after coal and iron were found in the surrounding lands. Pueblo grew into the west's largest steel-milling town, thanks in large part to Santa Fe Railroad's completion of its line from Kansas. The Arkansas River cuts through the center of town, but due to flooding, the boundaries have changed over the last century and a half. It's also one of the sunniest places in the United States. It has more sunshine than San Diego and Honolulu."

"Are you trying to sell me a house here?"

"No, but it's a nice place to live. Winters can be cold and snowy, but the snow typically melts the next day and you might be able to play golf in short sleeves within forty-eight hours."

"I don't play golf."

"You can run, bike, or have a picnic."

He finished his biscuit and wiped his hands on the cloth napkin. "Thanks for the sales pitch, but let's get back to the standoff. Where's the roundhouse located? Do citizens live nearby?"

"Pueblo was established in the early 1870s. General Palmer created a new town on the south side of the Arkansas River and named it South Pueblo. That's where he built Rio Grande's depot and roundhouse. The pictures I've seen show it set apart from the residential section."

"Is it really a round building?"

"Really. The complex redirects trains onto connecting lines. Originally, steam engines only traveled forward, so they built roundhouses to service trains and turn them in the right direction for the return trip. I don't know how big the original roundhouse is, but it held about sixty men at the time of the standoff."

"Got it. Large round building. When we arrive in Pueblo, I want this car parked as far away as possible."

"I don't think the standoff is going to happen today."

"I'm not taking any chances. We're going back to Denver tonight. We'll see General Palmer, have lunch with Daniel if he's available, and get back on this train." Connor smiled. "And enjoy our ride home."

The train whistle blasted, and the train slowed to a stop. "Sounds like we've arrived." She stared out the opposite window. He came up behind her and kissed her neck. "Okay. You sold me. Let's look for a house while we're here."

She looked up at him. "Why get a house when we could get a car like this and travel around the country?"

"God, I love a woman with a plan."

She laid her hand on his chest and for the first time realized he was wearing a vest underneath his shirt. "Is that a bulletproof vest?"

"A requirement for traveling. We don't have many rules or guidelines but wearing this is one of them."

The whistle blew again, and they began to move backward. The car bucked and rattled as it decoupled from the rest of the train. "I guess we'll be without service while we're here," she said. "No internet."

Connor kissed her again. "I wouldn't do that to you. Chester will get anything we want. As soon as you're ready, we'll go find your general."

"Give me five minutes to freshen up."

After using the small bathroom, she primped in front of a gilded mirror hanging on the wall and repinned her hat with its waves of feathers. Connor was holding her cloak when she came out of the bathroom and placed it around her shoulders. She collected her purse with its decorative pleats that echoed those of her skirt and collected her parasol.

"Do you have your notes?" Connor asked.

She thumped the side of her head. "It's all up here." She tugged on her gloves, tweaking them to line up the pearl buttons. "I'm ready."

"You have always been fascinating to watch, but dressed as you are, I'm enthralled. I can't figure out where to start undressing you, or do I just flip up your skirts and take you on the sofa."

"Ha. Don't even think of it. I'm not interested in a quickie the first time around."

He crossed his arms, cocked his head, smiling. "I wasn't thinking about a quickie. I was thinking about an appetizer."

"Thanks for that mental image. I'm going into an important meeting, and you're leaving my mind rattled." She raised an eyebrow. "I'd like that very much, by the way."

He opened the door, smiling. "Let's go find Daniel."

44

1878 Pueblo, Colorado—Olivia

CONNOR AND OLIVIA walked out onto the car's platform and glanced around. She groaned. Their private car was parked at least twenty yards from the depot and even further from the roundhouse. They'd have to plod across the rutted yard and iron rails and dodge scattered clumps of dried and steaming manure.

Her dainty shoes would take a beating.

Connor drummed his fingers on her hand, obviously sensing her distress. "Do you want me to carry you?"

"No, I'll just step lightly. I refuse to go into a meeting with General Palmer with crap on my shoes."

With her head down against the wind, she hoisted her hem a couple of inches and stepped nimbly off the car's platform. Connor, with a firm hold on her arm, guided her through the train yard to the depot, avoiding mud puddles and the rest of the yucky stuff she preferred not to identify.

"Look at all the men with rifles," she said.

"The standoff must be sooner rather than later," Connor said. "We'll get this meeting over with and get the hell out of here."

"Maybe we should warn Daniel. Two men are killed during the standoff. I don't know how many were injured."

"You don't have to warn him." Connor's face telegraphed his concern. "It's obvious something is about to go down."

By the time they reached the depot, an anxious dread moved through her and the hairs on her arms and the back of her neck stood on end. "Daniel told us to come here. He must not have thought the standoff was imminent."

Connor touched a finger to her jaw, lifting her face to look into her eyes. "When I see dozens of men with Winchester rifles, I assume the worse. Promise me, if I tell you to do something, you'll do it immediately without objecting or asking why. And if you can't make that promise, we're getting right back on that private car and hooking up to the next train out of here, regardless of where it's headed. Got it?"

He was more than concerned, more than alarmed, and his body seemed to vibrate with tension that rolled off him and rippled over her. She gave him a simple two-finger salute. "Got it."

"Let's get inside."

The Pueblo train station was constructed of adobe instead of stone, but otherwise looked identical to the depot in Denver. Benches edged the scarred floor, and men ringed the potbellied stove, warming their hands and backs, rifles strategically placed for easy access. The floorboards around the unpolished brass spittoons were damp. The air was bad, stale with the taint of coal, tobacco smoke, and unwashed bodies. If she got a listing for this building, she'd sell it, but it would immediately be razed. A new depot with shiny spittoons and big windows to enjoy the view of Pikes Peak, which was currently marred by a circular two-spouted water tank looming in the foreground, would be built in its place.

Connor pulled his pocket watch from his waistcoat, clicked it open. "It's almost one o'clock. Let's find someone, preferably without a rifle, to ask where we can find the general."

They walked out the opposite side of the building. A fading blast of a locomotive's exhaust echoed over the wind's low grumbling rush. Nearby, a guard with heavy-lidded eyes belied his intimidating pose. A rifle rested across his arms, and two revolvers in a cross-draw configuration were strapped to his hips.

Olivia was curious about the guard. Did he have an allegiance to one railroad over the other, or was guard duty just a paid gig? Emboldened by her successful venture across the train yard without destroying her shoes, she marched over to him and asked politely, "Sir, who's paying you this week?"

The guard's eyes opened wide and his overgrown eyebrows—black and tangled—like his scrawny mustache reared at the sight of her. "Santa Fe, ma'am."

Connor gripped her arm, but she wasn't moving until she got answers. "Who paid you last week?"

When the guard adjusted the rifle in his arms, Connor pulled her back and angled his body, putting himself between the guard and Olivia. "Rio Grande. Santa Fe hired me away."

"Who's got more men here, you think?" she asked, looking around Connor.

"I'm guessing Santa Fe. But I ain't been out asking men who they work for either."

Connor escorted her in the opposite direction of the guard and shot her a look that probably made most people take cover. "What the hell was that for? That's not a toy in his hands." His razor-sharp tone of voice matched the anger glinting in his eyes.

She blurted out, "He was trying to be polite to a pretty lady. He wasn't looking for trouble."

"Every man in this yard is looking and waiting for trouble."

"That man was half asleep on his feet."

Connor let go of the vise grip he had on her arm. "You have *I am crazy* plainly stamped across your features. I have a mind to take you back to the car while I go look for the general."

"Don't be a bully. I had a reason for asking. I wanted to know where his loyalties were. It's not to either railroad. It's a job to him, and he's working for the company that pays more. All these men work for Santa Fe. If the Rio Grande offered more, they'd turn their jerseys inside out and play defense."

Connor scanned the platform and the tracks beyond, his forehead furrowed. "Let's get out of here. I don't like being in enemy territory."

She glanced back at the depot entrance. "I want to ask that guard if he knows where the general is."

"No." Connor's tone was low and forceful. "Let's go to town, look for Daniel. These men work for Santa Fe. I don't have a horse in this race, but you do. My job is to protect you, and you're making it difficult."

She lifted her chin. "If you won't let me ask, you do it. He worked for the general three days ago. He'll know where he is."

In a steely voice she barely recognized, he said, "Don't move one damn inch." He approached the guard. "Do you know where General Palmer is? We've got an appointment in five minutes."

The guard nodded with his chin. "That's his private car down there on the siding. Pulled up about an hour ago."

Connor turned to look where the guard was pointing. "We want to go over there. Is that a problem?"

"Might be. Reckon I'll need to take ya so nobody uses ya for target practice."

Connor signaled to Olivia, and when she approached, he tucked her hand more firmly into the crook of his arm. There would be no breaking away from him to chat up another guard. Connor pointed. "This man has volunteered to escort us to the general's train over there."

She glanced in the direction he indicated, and quickly scanned the yard. Crossing this side of the depot would be as difficult as the other. Her shoes had survived one crossing. If she was careful, they could survive another. Her persnickety attention to her wardrobe was just part of who she was, regardless of the century.

She opened her parasol, hoisted her hem, and stepped carefully off the platform. The distance to the train was doubled by her constant backtracking to avoid the mud, but surprisingly their escort didn't grow impatient. Connor, on the other hand, huffed. Every part of him seemed to fume. She realized too late that her demand to backtrack left them out in the open, a perfect target for an anxious guard.

They reached their destination, and their escort mounted the steps to the rear of the train. "Stay put." He rapped loudly on the coach's door.

The knock was answered immediately. The door swung open on a burly, dark-haired, dark-eyed figure dressed in black trousers and vest. "A man here wants to see the general, Mr. DeRemer."

"A man? Supposed to be a woman."

"There's a woman, too."

DeRemer came out onto the platform and stared down at Connor and Olivia. "Are you Miss Kelly?"

Olivia looked up at him, mentally rifling through her Royal Gorge file, trying to place his name. "Yes, I am. And this is my…" What? Boyfriend? Bodyguard? Future lover? She settled on a nondescript term, saying, "My companion, Connor O'Grady."

DeRemer held open the door. "Come in. The general's expecting you."

Connor lay a detaining hand on her sleeve. "Wait." He entered the train, glanced around, and then stepped aside so she could come in.

She folded her parasol, thanked their escort, and mounted the steps. The warmth of the train's interior matched the warmth of DeRemer's smile, but the sentiment didn't seem to reach his eyes.

Glancing around, she found the richness and quiet taste of the interior impressive. She would have been more impressed, though, if she'd seen the general's coach first instead of the one Connor rented for her. That was the nuanced world of the real estate business. Once you find the perfect property, settling for anything less is almost impossible.

"Your name is familiar to me," she said to DeRemer. "But I can't place it. What do you do for the railroad?"

"I'm an engineer. If you'll follow me, I'll take you to the general."

She moved swiftly through the narrow passageway, or as swiftly as her skirts allowed, holding tightly to the brass rail. "Now I remember who you are. You're an engineer but you're also a man who's never courted notoriety. You deserve recognition for the hundreds of miles of railroad you've built in Colorado."

DeRemer seemed amused. "I'm surprised you've heard of me. But thank you." He knocked on a paneled door in the middle of a narrow hallway.

A commanding voice said, "Come in."

DeRemer turned the knob and gestured for Olivia and Connor to enter. Despite the size of the room, the ornate paneled walls and elegant rosewood desk gave the office a closed-in feeling. Delicately etched chimneys atop coal oil lamps threw back shadows that mingled with the haze of cigar smoke, further darkening the room and giving it an additional claustrophobic effect. She sidestepped DeRemer and, holding up her overskirts, proceeded into the general's domain.

The general looked at her and instantly removed his glasses. The puzzlement on his face lasted only an instant before giving way to the sudden gathering of wrinkles at the corners of his eyes. Because of the crinkling in his skin, she assumed a smile crouched beneath the waves of his bushy mustache. He came out from behind the desk, extending his hand, his gaze sliding over her body in a manner she found unwarranted and irritating.

"Miss Kelly," he said, almost as a question.

"Yes, sir," she said.

"I received several reports about you this morning. All of them intriguing."

"And I've heard extraordinary stories about you." She turned to Connor. "This is my companion, Mr. O'Grady."

The general extended his hand to Connor. "Major Grant has spoken highly of you and your brother. He hopes to make Pinkerton men of you. I'm always looking for good men as well. What unit did you fight in?"

"Fight? Oh, in the war?" Connor said. Olivia froze, waiting for him to dodge the question. He didn't. "I was part of the Irish Brigade, sir."

"Were you at First Manassas?"

"Yes, sir, but I'd rather talk about the railroad."

Olivia tried not to stare at Connor, imagining a vivid family story she hoped he would share with her.

The general gave a hearty laugh as he gestured to a cluster of chairs on a green-patterned Wilton carpet surrounded by an inlaid wood floor. "Please, sit." It wasn't an invitation, but a command.

She undid the clasp of her cloak.

"Allow me." Connor's voice at her ear, as he lifted the cloak from her shoulders, was both warm and intimate. He hung it on a peg behind the door. Then he waited attentively while she adjusted her skirts and sat in the offered chair, the bulky train of the dress flattening. The leather seemed to sigh beneath her, but she couldn't allow herself the luxury of sighing with it. The general was a distinguished and intelligent former soldier and she had to stay alert.

He returned to his chair. The spectacles he had pulled off upon standing he now tapped idly on a notepad set askew on the desktop, as if wondering how to broach the subject they were there to discuss.

"You would suppose," he began, setting the glasses aside, "that reasonable men could find a solution to the problems facing us. Yet there's been nothing reasonable about it."

"You would have thought reasonable men could have stopped a horrible war," she said.

He arched an eyebrow. "Many tried. Many refused to listen." He glanced at a cavalry saber hanging on the wall. Then after a moment, he shook off what must have been a grim vision.

"You didn't come here today to talk about the war. But like the war, we have a problem without a solution. It doesn't help either side that the courts contradict themselves. And now we're forced to hire gangs of cutthroats to protect our rights. Rio Grande's investors are bleeding money and want to lease the tracks to Santa Fe, hoping that will be a solution." He tilted back in his chair and fiddled with one side of his mustache.

She leaned forward but kept her gloved hands crossed in her lap. "General, if you lease the tracks, part of the consideration has to be that you control the freight rates south of Denver. If you don't,

Santa Fe can and probably will raise rates to Denver from Pueblo, Colorado Springs, and Cañon City, and they'll divert additional traffic eastward over its own line. You'll lose money and any benefits leasing the tracks might give you. Once shippers undercut you, your income will fall below what you need to pay interest on your bonds, and you'll be thrown into the hands of a receiver."

"You don't paint a pretty picture, Miss Kelly." He dropped the chair's legs to the floor and the gravity of the situation seemed to pour into his face.

"I'm not an artist, sir, but I know war is never pretty, and that's exactly what's going on here. You're fighting on two fronts: in the gorge and in the courtroom."

"How'd you come to be so familiar with this situation?"

She was prepared for the question. "I've read every article I could find. I've studied the law in this case, and I've conferred with other lawyers. It's my opinion that the Supreme Court will grant you the primary right to build through the gorge."

"Your opinion? I have lawyers who differ. In your opinion then, what will the court base its ruling on?" he asked.

"That the Circuit Court for the District of Colorado erred in not recognizing that an 1872 Act of Congress granted you the right to use the entire fifty-mile stretch through the gorge. Further, it's my opinion, after studying the court's calendar, that the ruling will come down any day now."

The general nodded soberly, moving his head up and down to the rhythm of the ticking pendulum in the clock atop a corner bookcase. It was filled with leather-bound books, but she was too far away to read the titles.

"You are a canny woman. The company's board members advised me of your expertise, but I was wary. I believed you had simply bewitched them."

"So you wanted to hear directly from the source. I understand that, but the most important advice I can give you is this: If you lease your track, hoping to stop the bleeding, you'll spend thousands of dollars in legal fees later trying to get out of it. You'll eventually get so tired of fighting that you'll settle out of court. If you hold out now, you'll come out better in the long run. Surely, sir, you can keep from inking on the dotted line a few more days."

"How many?"

"A week, ten days. But in the meantime, as you well know, Santa Fe is laying track in the gorge. When the court hands down a favorable ruling, you'll have to pay Santa Fe for the track they've already put down. Let them lay all the track they want. It will put you that much closer to completing the line to Leadville."

"Pay them? Pshaw. If the company had full coffers we wouldn't consider this step. How much are you suggesting?"

"For the track Santa Fe's laid in the gorge, grading, materials on hand, interest, it could be a million and a half."

The general gasped, pushed to his feet, and leaned over the desk, knocking over a standing leather photocase. He supported his weight on two fists. "That's outrageous."

Olivia refused to be cowed. She jumped up, leaned forward, and supported her weight on her fists, mirroring him. "Look into the future, General. This line could provide passenger and freight service for a century. Whatever you're bleeding now, you'll make back a hundredfold."

"Why should I believe you?"

She waited for him to sit down before she moved, but then realized the general was too polite to reclaim his chair while she remained standing. She adjusted her skirts and sat on the edge of her chair. From the corner of her eye, she caught a slight twitch of Connor's lips.

"There's no reason I can think of. I'm just an educated woman with opinions, but I hope the issues I've raised will give you food for thought, and that you'll discuss them with your board members. There's only one way to win this war, sir, and that's through the courts."

He made a noncommittal head wag. "You're spouting only assumptions and suppositions, nothing a scout could verify. My attorneys don't have your confidence. Why is that?"

"I guess they don't have a crystal ball."

A knock on the door drew their attention. "Come in," the general said.

Daniel entered the room and Connor stood. After acknowledging the general, Daniel took Olivia's proffered hand and bowed over it before shaking hands with Connor.

"I'm sorry I was detained. Did ye have any trouble?"

"No, we came right here," Olivia said.

The general sat back, fingers interlaced across his waistcoat. There was an expectant air about him that she found unnerving. "Any news, Major?"

"It's quiet right now, sir."

"Good. Miss Kelly just told me the Rio Grande would ultimately win this war because her crystal ball told her. What do you think of that?"

The look Connor had given her earlier paled in comparison to the one Daniel gave her now. Connor saw it, too, and immediately stepped between Daniel and Olivia. Once again, playing the role of protector. But what was he protecting her from? Daniel looked angry, but he wouldn't physically hurt her. Her sister wouldn't have fallen for a violent man. And Noah was not an abused child. He had such a gentle and loving spirit.

Then what was the source of Daniel's anger? The unknown? Lies? Lack of trust? Whoa, she could identify with that. If he was suspicious of Amber, he would also be suspicious of Olivia. She and her sister could divine the future and that had to be scary as hell to an alpha male who had to be in control of his world.

"Ye'll have to evaluate her scrying against the recommendations of yer attorneys, board members, and bondholders," Daniel said. "Ultimately, ye'll have to make decisions based on what's best for the long-term health of the railroad, not on prognostications."

The general sat forward and adjusted the lamp's wick, adding additional light to his desk. "Excellent advice, Major." He hooked his reading glasses over his ears, withdrew a piece of paper from one of a dozen pigeon holes on the side of the desk's writing surface, and inked the steel nip of his pen. "That'll be all."

Olivia bristled. *What? That'll be all? Excellent advice, Major.*

The general might as well have slapped her. He didn't even have the guts to look her in the eye. She glared, hoping he'd raise his head. If he'd paid a retainer for her legal advice she would have thrown the money back in his face. Never in her life had she been summarily dismissed. She couldn't speak around her mounting anger. Instead, she tugged at her gloves, making a show of her impatience to quit his company.

Connor lifted her cloak from the peg and folded it over his arm. Once the door closed behind them, he placed it around her shoulders, hissing in her ear. "Don't say a word until we get back to the train."

Her anger had grown to the size of a fist in her throat. Not even a scream could get past the blockade. Daniel's rhetoric abilities and relentless honesty aside, his comment confirmed what she suspected. Whatever she and Amber had said to him that he couldn't understand or fit within the limitations of his world scared him, but he was courageous enough to face that fear, and a showdown was coming.

But the general… There was no excusing his behavior. He was simply rude. She and Connor had come to Pueblo at his request and he could at least… What? He did listen to her. He asked questions. He seemed engaged. That really was more than she'd expected.

She marched out, holding her umbrella in a stranglehold, thankful her long skirts masked her unsteady gait. Get over it. She'd had rude clients before, and she'd have others. She swept back small twists of hair that escaped from the pins and took a deep breath to settle her umbrage. By the time they crossed the rutted yard in front of the depot, her pique had played out—almost. She and Connor could now get back on the train for a delightful return trip to Denver.

Daniel's horse was hitched at the tie rail. He yanked the reins and held them in his hand. "I'm staying at the St. James Hotel at Fifth and Santa Fe. It overlooks the town square. I have an appointment with R.F. Weitbrec. He's the onsite commander of the hired army, which includes the Pinkertons. Whatever is going to happen here, he'll be at the forefront of the action."

"Do you think there'll be violence?" she asked.

"What do ye think?"

"Do you want my opinion, or was that a rhetorical question?"

Daniel ignored her. "There's a dining room at the hotel. If ye'd like to join me for a late lunch, I could meet ye there in thirty minutes."

Connor glanced at her, one eyebrow slightly raised. He was leaving the decision to her.

"Thank you for the invitation. We'd like to join you," Olivia said, imagining a crescendo of additional questions she might have to sidestep and dance around. "We'll hire a hack and be right along."

Daniel swung up on the horse, reined the black Morgan around, and put two fingers to the edge of his hat. Then he touched the horse with his heels and galloped off, straight up, shoulders back. She'd never seen a Union officer before, and now she'd seen two—the general and Daniel.

And two was one too many. "You saw the look Daniel gave me, right?"

"In Palmer's office. Yeah, I did. I almost punched him in the face. What'd you do to piss him off?"

"He seemed fine when he came in, but at soon as the general mentioned a crystal ball you could see the anger rise in his face. He's struggling with what he doesn't understand. It scares him."

"Hell, it'd scare me, too, if two beautiful women—"

"Three. Don't forget Kenzie."

"Three beautiful women came into my life and challenged my beliefs and one of my core values—"

"Would that be honesty?" Olivia asked.

Connor nodded. "I believe the stones were created for the benefit of mankind, to force the owners to exhibit selflessness. But it also forces us to go against the grain of our core value—honesty. It's a juxtaposition. Daniel sees the goodness in us, but he knows innately that we're lying. It's like a pink, lacey T-shirt with a motocross emblem. They just don't go together."

She laughed. "Thanks for that visual."

He gave her a smoldering look. "If you want something to visualize, visualize yourself naked in my arms."

"I have." She took a deep breath and blew it out slowly, hoping to cool the sudden heat in her lower body. "And I can't wait to replace it with the real thing."

He grinned. "Consider yourself kissed, woman."

She pressed two fingers against her lips and puckered. "Thanks."

"Okay, let's switch gears, if we can. No more prognosticating. Let's have a quiet lunch with Daniel, unless he hasn't cooled off," Connor said. "Then we'll head back to Denver. This town is heating up. I don't want to be here, and I definitely don't want you here."

"And if Amber is finished at Morrison, we can go home tonight. What do you think of that?"

Connor signaled a hack driver and it squeaked to a stop in front of them. "It's a great idea. Your parents are due home, and it's time I met them."

He helped her up into a two-passenger carriage. "You'll love them, and they'll love you," she said.

He shook his head. "I don't know. I'm just an ex-cop from New York City. I might not be the kind of guy they want for their daughter."

"Once they get past your accent, they'll love you as much as I do."

He removed his hat, lowered his face to hers, and tenderly lifted her chin with the tip of his finger. His hot breath fanned her cheek, and goose bumps peppered her arms in anticipation. When his lips found hers—a touch at first, molding lips against lips—a burst of unbridled hunger drove her to distraction. His tongue slid deep within her mouth for a few blissful seconds. Then, she became aware of where they were, and she pulled away.

"We keep getting to this point and circumstances force us apart."

He laughed, and the sound was deep and rich and sensual. "This is the last time."

A few minutes later, they were driving down Santa Fe Street toward the center of town, where armed men lined both sides of the street.

"One hour," he said, his face creased with concern, "and we're out of here."

"One hour might be sixty minutes too long. Those men are preparing to storm the Bastille."

45

The Present, Richmond, Virginia—Rick

WHEN THE FOG lifted, Rick was lying in damp grass with Amber, Noah, and Ripley. Glancing around, he took in their surroundings. They were in a grassy area at the edge of a full parking lot next to the entrance of the VCU Medical Center Department of Emergency Medicine. Sirens blasted, along with the sounds of heavy traffic. The weather was balmy, and shades of yellow leaves predominated in the landscaping.

He made some assumptions. They were in Virginia on a weekday in late fall, probably mid-morning.

"Where are we?" Amber asked.

"If VCU stands for Virginia Commonwealth University," Rick said, "then we're in Richmond."

"How's Ripley?"

Rick checked on the dog. "She's listless and appears unaware. I'll get her medical attention as soon as I take care of you." He pulled his phone from his pocket and turned it on. "I'll call Charlotte and give her a heads-up that we're coming in. She'll cut through red tape that could slow us down once we get inside."

Noah looked around, his eyes wide, his breathing erratic. Rick hugged him. "Hang in there, buddy. I'll explain everything in a minute."

When his phone came on, the first thing he noticed was the date.

The second thing was the time. Same date and within one or two minutes of his departure from the farm with Kenzie and David. He'd be sure to include that piece of information in his After Action Report. He hadn't written an AAR since... He shook his head, needing to forget that Charlie Foxtrot that almost got him killed.

He scrolled through his contacts until he found Charlotte's number. He'd never phoned her before, so his name wouldn't show up with his phone number. She might not answer an unknown caller.

It rang twice, and a woman's voice said, "Dr. Mallory."

Rick blew out a tense breath. "Charlotte, this is Rick O'Grady. I have an emergency and need your help. I just arrived back from 1878. I'm inside your wire—"

"You're where?" she asked.

"Sorry. Military term. We're on hospital property. A grassy area near the Emergency Department parking lot. I have a thirty-two-year-old skinny white woman with severe breathing complications, a frightened ten-year-old boy, and a dog with a head injury."

"Stay put. I'll be right there. I'll call Braham to help with the dog."

"Tango Mike." Rick disconnected, wondering why he was reverting to military slang. "Charlotte's coming out. Help is on its way, sweetheart."

"Where are we?" The tremor in Noah's voice said he was fighting back tears.

Rick hugged him again. "I'd sugarcoat this for you, if I could. But we don't have time. We're in Richmond, Virginia, in the twenty-first century. This is a temporary stop for you. I'll get you back to your pa as soon as we get help for Amber and Ripley. Okay?"

"Did...did we fall down a rabbit hole?"

"Like Alice? Probably seems like it. If your stomach is doing flips of fear that's normal. But you're not in danger. There's a lot going on that you don't understand, but no one is going to hurt you. You're not going to be stranded. There are people here who will walk across hot coals for you." Rick pulled a business card from his phone case. "Put this in your pocket. It has all my contact information. You'll always be able to reach me if we get separated."

Noah grabbed Rick's hand, held it tightly, and in a panicked voice asked, "Aren't we staying together?"

"I'm not leaving you, buddy. This is for an emergency. Hold on to it."

Noah relaxed his grip and studied the card. "You're a director?"

"Yep, but it's only a fancy title. No big deal." Rick had a flashback to being in the hospital when he returned from Afghanistan. A mental health professional had handed him a card with contact information and told him to call when he was ready to talk. He never lost the card. He never made the call either.

Two minutes, forty seconds later, three people in scrubs pushed a gurney out of the ED and hurried across the parking lot toward them. Rick had never seen Charlotte in scrubs and a white doctor's coat, and at first, he didn't recognize her.

"Let's get her on the gurney," Charlotte said.

The two attendants bent to pick Amber up off the grass, but Rick wouldn't let them. "I'll do it." He laid her gently on the stretcher then tenderly cupped her cheek. He wanted her to know she was in good hands.

To Charlotte he said, "Her name is Amber Kelly. She's from Denver. She's complained of breathing problems for the last ten days and believed she was suffering from altitude sickness."

"From the way y'all are dressed, it looks like you've been involved in a nineteenth-century reenactment," Charlotte said, in a wink-wink sort of way. "We have reenactors show up in the ED all the time."

He glanced down at his trousers, vest, and jacket, and almost crossed himself in grateful thanks that his gun wasn't strapped to his hip. "Right. That's what we were doing."

"I didn't know there was one going on right now," one of the attendants said.

"Must have been a small one," Charlotte said, offering cover for Rick.

"Probably weren't a hundred people there." Rick never thought he'd have to lie about the adventure once he came home. Was there no end to it?

"Breathing…worse today," Amber said. "Couldn't wear my corset."

"That was a wise decision." Charlotte nodded to the two attendants. "Take her on in. I'll be right behind you." The attendants, one pushing from the end of the gurney and the other at Amber's side, headed back across the parking lot.

"We'll take it from here," Charlotte said.

"I need to go, too. David told me not to leave her. I did for a couple of hours, and this happened."

Charlotte gave him a clear-eyed look and spoke directly to him so there was no misunderstanding. "I don't know what's wrong with her yet, and I don't know what happened earlier, but—"

"Two men entered her room and stole her journal while I was gone," Rick interrupted. "It must have been hell trying to breathe when she was so scared."

With the knot lodging in his throat, he wondered about his own next breath. After David got hold of him, it wouldn't matter. Hell, not only David, but Pops, too. His father could give a tongue lashing worse than any sergeant Rick ever met in the Marines. And he'd deserve every bit of the punishment.

The attendants reached the ED entrance and disappeared inside the hospital.

"There's nothing you can do for her right now," Charlotte said. "We need to do a workup first." She knelt in front of Noah, gently rubbed Ripley's belly with one hand and laid the other on top of Noah's. "What's your name?"

"Ripley." Noah's fingers, clamped tightly on his sharp-boned kneecap, visibly relaxed beneath her touch.

"That's a lovely name," Charlotte said, "So, Ripley, what's your friend's name?"

Noah gave her a shy smile. "I knew you weren't asking about Ripley. I was just being funny. Amber laughs when I do that."

Charlotte smiled in return. "You're quite the jokester. Are you going to tell me your name?"

"Noah Grant, and I'm not from here." He nodded toward Ripley. "Neither is she."

"You know what? My husband isn't from here and neither is my nephew."

Rick tousled Noah's hair. "Did you reach Braham?"

"He'll be here shortly." She smiled. "My son Lincoln and my nephew are about your age. They'll be here in a few minutes." Charlotte stood, still smiling warmly at Noah. "The boys were going to soccer practice but they're coming here instead. Braham will take Ripley to the vet and Lincoln and Patrick will take care of Noah. As soon as things are settled here, go to the ED waiting room. I'll come out as soon as I have news."

"Don't keep me waiting long. I have your number if you do." As soon as the words were spoken, he wished he could reel back the demand and the impatient undertone, but it was too late.

Charlotte's expression sobered, and she said simply, "Amber is my chief concern." And with that, she turned and jogged after her patient.

Rick sat on the ground with Noah and Ripley. His relief, if there was any, evaporated. Today was just a Groundhog Day. No matter what he did to try to change it, another bad day was coming. Amber was seriously ill. Pleasing her instead of protecting her had been a mistake and ignoring his responsibility had created this mess.

"I don't think that lady in the funny clothes understood what I meant when I said I'm not from here."

Noah's musing interrupted Rick's consternation. "She knew exactly what you meant. Her husband fought in the Civil War. In 1869, he came to this time. And her nephew, Patrick, arrived last year from New York City in 1909."

Noah visibly swallowed hard. "Oh, then I guess she did understand. Does that mean there are other people like me, like them?"

"I don't know the answer to that. We'll have to ask David."

Noah smacked his forehead in a comical exaggeration. "David

and Kenzie are from here, too?"

"And Connor and Olivia."

"Does my pa know where you're from?" Noah's musical voice trilled up the scale an octave or more.

"No," Rick grumbled, "and he won't like it at all."

"Why not?" Noah's voice descended to the lower register faster than it had ascended to the upper register. Why Rick was thinking in musical terms was as confusing to him as why he was using military slang.

And then he knew.

Hospitals reminded him of his musically talented mother and her death, and military terms reminded him of his own weeks of painful recuperation. He just didn't want to be here.

"Why not, Rick?" Noah repeated the question.

Rick watched a black Suburban pull into the parking lot. He should have asked Charlotte what kind of vehicle Braham was driving. The Suburban moved slowly through the lot toward the grassy edge. It had to be Braham.

Noah elbowed Rick, waiting for an answer. "Oh, sorry. It'll complicate his life."

The Suburban pulled to a stop in front of them. "Hey, man. Ye looking for a ride?" Braham swung open the driver's door and two boys climbed out of the back.

The boys rushed over to Rick and squeezed him in a clamshell hug. "You've been on an adventure." Lincoln tugged on Rick's jacket sleeve. "Your jacket smells like peat. Where'd you go?"

"Hunting dinosaur bones in 1878 Colorado, and I brought Noah back with me. Can you guys help him out?"

"Sure." The boys released Rick, plopped down on the grass with Noah and Ripley, and introduced themselves.

After Braham and Rick gave each other a quick guy-hug and slap on the back, Braham stepped over to the dog and looked at the cut on her head. "What happened to her?"

"She must have been hit on the head and might have a concussion. Will you take her to a vet? I need to go see about Amber."

"She's the injured woman ye brought back?"

"Yep. She can't breathe. Charlotte said she'd let me know after they did a workup on her."

Braham picked up Ripley, carried her to the Suburban, and laid her on the back seat. When she whimpered, Braham hitched his hip on the edge of the seat and gently rubbed her belly. "If Amber's from the past, she'll find the hospital a scary place."

"She's a lawyer in Denver. Have you heard Connor mention Olivia Kelly, the Realtor he's been working with to find Elliott a ranch in Colorado?"

"Ye mean the woman Connor's in love with? Aye, David mentioned her recently. Is Amber related?"

"She's Olivia's sister. She found an amber brooch. David, Kenzie, and I went back to help her. Same story. Different players."

"I don't get it. Kenzie and David said they'd never travel again. What's up with that?" Braham asked.

"It was personal for Kenzie. Trey Kelly was Amber and Olivia's first cousin."

"The soldier who saved Kenzie's life?"

Rick nodded.

"Ah. Makes sense now. So, was this yer adventure?"

"Mine? No. Not mine. The hero of this story is Noah's dad. He's a Pinkerton agent Amber met in Leadville."

"A Pinkerton, huh? What's his name? I knew most of the agents a decade earlier. Unless they died, most of them are probably still working."

"Daniel Grant."

"Crap," Braham said. "What does he look like? How old is he?"

"Looks like David, sounds like him, too. Few years younger."

"That description fits a Pinkerton I knew. He was on Lincoln's detail when the president was assassinated."

"He told me he was there the night Lincoln was shot." Rick nodded toward Noah. "That's his son."

Braham turned and looked at the three boys sitting in the grass. "How'd ye end up with him?"

"We were in Denver. Amber wanted to spend the day in Morrison hunting dinosaur bones and Noah asked to go with us. We took the train and spent a few hours there. Then the day turned into a Charlie Foxtrot."

"A what?"

The situation shadowed Rick's concentration, and he automatically used what was familiar—military slang. "Sorry. It's a clusterfuck."

"Ye gotta take the lad back."

"He won't leave without his dog."

"The lad's got to be scared to death." Braham walked over to Noah, knelt, and extended his hand. "I'm Braham McCabe. I was a major in the Union Army on special assignment to President Lincoln. I knew lots of Pinkertons, including yer pa. He's a good man."

Noah shook Braham's hand. "Mighty proud to meet you, Major McCabe. My pa's still a Pinkerton man, but he doesn't like to talk about what happened to the president."

"I know, lad. I don't either. We all failed Mr. Lincoln that night." Braham stood and tapped Lincoln on the back. "I'm going to take Ripley to the vet. Ye boys going with me?"

Noah glanced at the car, turned his eyes toward the hospital, then back to the car, his loyalties obviously pulled in two different directions.

Patrick sensed Noah's divided loyalties and said, "Lincoln and I can stay here with Noah while you take Ripley to the vet. Is that okay, Uncle Braham? I know what it feels like to just get here. It's scary. And Noah doesn't want to leave his mom."

Rick watched Noah to see if he was going to correct Patrick's belief that Amber was his mom. But Noah let it slide. He did, though, shyly glance at Rick, which put him in an awkward place. He was now Noah's designated guardian. He had to protect him, and if he failed Noah as badly as he had failed Amber, then God help them all.

"Ye know yer boundaries in the hospital, Lincoln. Send yer mom a text and let her know ye're staying here. If ye go to her office, ye know—"

"Not to read any patient files. We know, Dad."

"Do ye have money to go to the cafeteria?"

Lincoln held out his hand and Braham handed over a few bills. "Don't load Noah up with sugary foods. It'll make him sick. Bland food. Maybe a hamburger and fruit. No pizza. No Mexican. No Chinese."

"We got it," Lincoln said. "Patrick knows what to do and what to eat."

"And we won't flirt with the nurses," Patrick said.

Braham folded his arms and glared down at his nephew. "What do ye know about flirting with nurses?"

"Come on, Uncle Braham. We're old enough to know stuff like that." Patrick slapped Lincoln's arm. "Let's get out of here before your dad changes his mind."

Lincoln grabbed Noah's arm. "Let's race to the door."

"We should FaceTime James Cullen," Patrick said. "He'll want to know about Noah."

"No. Wait." Rick funneled his fingers through his hair. "Lincoln, you can't tell JC. Elliott, Kenzie, and David are flying to Denver late this afternoon. They're planning to go back to 1878 with Connor and Amber's sister. There are reasons why they have to go. We can't stop their trip. If they know we're here, they won't go back, and that could screw everything up."

"Elliott's going?" Braham asked.

"No. He plans to meet up with Meredith in Reno."

"James Cullen will be pissed when he finds out," Patrick said. "We've taken a blood oath to tell each other everything."

"Hey, wait a minute," Lincoln said. "This is like the Amy-Effect?"

Rick wasn't sure what he was talking about. "Explain, please."

"When Amy came home from 1909 before Patrick and the others," Lincoln said, "she couldn't contact them for months until after they were supposed to return. Remember? Uncle Jack didn't think

Amy loved him because she didn't call. It got really screwy."

"This is a similar situation," Rick said. "So let's keep it to ourselves for now."

"What am I going to tell my parents?" Patrick asked. "And what if James Cullen calls us? He'll know we're hiding something."

"Tell him ye're out of school today, that ye have plans with a friend, and ye'll call him later. That's not a lie. As for your parents, Patrick, I'll talk to them. Jack and Amy will understand," Braham said.

Rick put his head in his hands. It gave him a headache thinking how convoluted it was. Why couldn't it be a simple mission—there and back?

Because brooch adventures were never simple.

"We'll keep Noah a secret for now," Lincoln said. "Come on, let's go." The boys crossed the parking lot, two in soccer uniforms and the other wearing nineteenth-century trousers and jacket. Noah glanced back briefly. After Rick waved to him, he ran off with the others.

"He'll be acclimated within an hour, and no one will ever know he's from the nineteenth century," Braham said.

"Getting that acclimated will make it harder for him to return home," Rick said.

"That's not today's problem. Amber and Ripley are. Let me get the dog to the vet. If ye want to clean up, I keep a change of clothes in Charlotte's office. She has a bathroom with a shower. The jeans might be a little big around the waist." Braham slapped his stomach. "I'm not as thin as ye are, but they won't fall off. At least ye can put on clothes that don't smell"—Braham scrunched his face, sniffing—"like peat." He reached into the back seat and grabbed the boys' soccer bags. "There are clean clothes in here if Noah wants to clean up."

"Thanks. I'll take you up on the offer. Noah and I visited a dinosaur dig this afternoon. The dust there was almost as bad as the moon dust in Afghanistan."

"Is that like sand?"

"Heavy construction vehicles rip up the earth around combat outposts. When the dust dries it turns into the consistency of flour. You can't get rid of it. I feel like I spent a day in an outpost."

"Ye smell like it too. Clean up before ye go back to see Amber. I'll send Lincoln a text. They'll meet ye at the door."

"Will you take our gear? I've got a couple of guns in my saddlebags. I better not try to go inside the hospital with them."

They loaded Amber's belongings, Noah's bag, and Rick's saddlebags into the front seat of the Suburban. "Thanks for doing this."

Braham checked the time. "I'll be back in about an hour."

Rick watched Braham drive away before he made his way to the Emergency Department. The boys were waiting there for him, and he handed over the soccer bags.

"We'll take you to Mom's office, then we're going to the cafeteria," Lincoln said.

The bathroom was complete with the necessary amenities, and the office included a pullout sofa if he wanted to take a nap. Braham's jeans were only slightly loose, but the long-sleeve polo shirt fit perfectly. He folded his dirty clothes and stowed them in a shopping bag he found folded up on the window ledge. He'd pick the bag up later.

Feeling refreshed from a quick shower, he returned to the ED waiting room just in time to meet the boys coming back from the cafeteria. The kid who returned with Lincoln and Patrick, dressed in jeans and a T-shirt, wasn't the same one who'd left with them. Noah had a cell phone, clicking with his thumbs like he'd been using one his entire life. Braham was right. Noah was acclimating within an hour. But Rick knew he'd be proven right, too. How could you live here with all the advantages then choose to go back? Kit and Cullen Montgomery kept saying they were returning to 1881, but they'd been here two years now and had yet to set a date for their return.

Noah would not go quietly into the night. Rick couldn't think about Noah's return until he knew Amber's prognosis. He closed his eyes and tried to rest.

"Rick. Rick. Wake up."

Startled, he jerked away from the hand shaking his shoulder.

"Sorry to wake you," Charlotte said. "Come with me. I'll give you an update."

He jumped to his feet, groggy and slightly confused.

"Where are you going, Rick?" Noah asked.

"Oh, hi, Noah. Ah, with Charlotte. I'll be right back." He shook his head, trying to snap his brain cells back into organized thoughts as he shambled behind her into a small consulting room.

Charlotte closed the door and didn't let a beat pass between the click of the bolt in the doorknob's strike plate and her announcement. "Amber is really sick. Her pulseOx is 67."

"That's low, isn't it?"

"Yes, but she got better when we put her on oxygen and she is resting comfortably now. There's fluid in her lungs. That's a big part of why she's short of breath. She's also got a big heart murmur."

Rick dropped into the closest chair, unable to speak from the shock of it.

Charlotte sat beside him. "It sounds like significant mitral valve disease. The nurses started IVs, and we're getting a chest X-ray and labs. I've called radiology to get a cardiac ultrasound. They should be on their way."

"This is my fault. I should have insisted she come back earlier."

"One or two days isn't significant. The disease has been progressing for some time. I've called in our best cardiologist. We should have a better handle on what's going on within the hour."

"Is she going to be okay?"

"We're doing everything we can. If anything changes, I'll let you know right away." Charlotte walked over to the door to leave.

He pushed to his feet and threw his arms up. "That's it. That's all you've got. That's all you're going to tell me? That's crap, Charlotte. You've got to give me more. Amber's scared to death of hospitals and doctors. She needs me. I need to go see her."

Charlotte grasped the door handle. "That's all I can tell you until the cardiologist does his workup."

"Please, let me see her. Just five minutes. Two minutes. One minute."

"Not yet. There are a lot of people going in and out of her room. Until we get a handle on her problem, you need to let us work on her. Does she have any family? They should be notified."

"Why? Is she going to get worse?" He couldn't even find the words to form the question—*Is she going to die?*

"We're doing all we can, but she might need surgery. I'll know more after the cardiologist evaluates her. But if you know her family, you should call them."

"Her parents are in London, and her sister is still in the past."

"Can you reach her parents?"

"Probably, but they're not going to understand why Olivia isn't here."

"Olivia Kelly? Is she the woman Connor's been interested in?"

"Yep."

"Do the best you can. I've got to go. Oh, Braham said Ripley has a mild concussion and she's staying for a few days at the vet hospital. He also said we can expect a full recovery. Now, have you had anything to eat?"

Rick shook his head, unable to think about food or anything else but Amber's health.

"There's an upscale American café about a mile away. Braham likes to eat there. Get a decent meal, Rick. It's going to be a long night. I've got to go."

"I'm not leaving. When Braham gets here, we can eat in the cafeteria."

Charlotte left him there in that small room with its plastic furniture and antiseptic smells. He couldn't remember ever being so alone. His brothers would be with him now, if he could only call them. He leaned his head against the wall, listening to the squeak of wheels, a female announcer on the cable news channel, the ping of an elevator door, and canned music. He hated it all. He hadn't signed up for this, but *this*—the damn brooches—had seduced him with hopes of living out a Western fantasy.

He had to see it through, no matter what it cost him.

Moving like a zombie, he walked back to the waiting room with its tables covered with soda cans, snack food wrappers, unfinished cups of stale coffee, and year-old magazines. It smelled like vomit and pee, sweat and booze breath, perfume and stale tobacco on people's clothing. He hated hospitals. Maybe he could get Pops to come out here. He'd come on the QT, but his father was involved in the winery evacuation. God, that seemed so long ago. But it was recent enough that the fires were still smoldering—according to the reporters on the TV that never shut up.

Braham was huddled with the boys, updating them on Ripley's condition. They saw Rick coming and Noah jumped up out of his chair, his smile dropping to the floor in fear. He chewed his bottom lip before he asked, "How is she?"

"She's breathing easier. We can't see her yet, but she's feeling much better. We'll know more in about an hour." That seemed to satisfy Noah, and he returned to his seat between Lincoln and Patrick, two iPads and an iPhone.

Rick sat down next to Braham and said in a low voice, "She's seriously ill."

Braham dragged his hands down his face. "I'm sorry to hear that. What about her family? They should know what's going on."

"Her parents have been on an African safari. They're in London now. And her sister is still in the past. I can't think about them yet. I'll wait for the cardiologist's report and then decide. If Amber needs open-heart surgery, I'll get her parents here and Olivia, too."

"Come on. Let's go downstairs or we can go out. But ye need to eat."

"I'm not leaving. I don't want to miss the next report."

"Then let's go downstairs," Braham said. "Hey, boys. We're going to get something to eat. Ye staying or going?"

"We'll go," Lincoln said. "Will you buy us ice cream?"

"Yeah, but don't tell yer mothers."

After hamburgers and ice cream they all returned to their plastic chairs to wait on Charlotte's next report. It didn't take long. Braham and Rick followed her into the same consulting room as before and she closed the door.

"The cardiologist has seen her. The good news is that we think we know what's going on. I watched the ultrasound with the cardiologist while it was being done and it's pretty clear that my initial impression was right. She has severe mitral valve disease."

Rick's gut gripped him, and he gagged.

Braham put a hand on Rick's shoulder. "Ye okay, buddy? Ye need a trashcan?"

"Give me a minute."

Charlotte left and returned with a cup of water.

After a few seconds, the hamburger, fries, and ice cream settled back in Rick's stomach. He sipped from the cup of water.

"If you need something—"

He waved her off. "I'm fine now. Go on."

"The oxygen therapy and medicine we've given her are keeping her comfortable. From talking to her, it sounds like she has a history of untreated strep throats. This sudden onset of bad mitral valve disease coupled with that history leads us to believe she has rheumatic heart disease."

"That's curable, right?"

Charlotte leaned forward in her chair, rested her forearms on her thighs. "It's rare to see an adult with this situation, but it does happen."

"So what are you going to do? Give her medicine?"

"She needs to have her mitral valve replaced. I suspect the cardiac surgeons will want to do the surgery in the morning."

"Open-heart surgery?" Rick clenched and unclenched his fists. "Amber is only thirty-two. You can't be right about this." *It's not true. It's not true.* If he kept repeating it to himself, maybe Charlotte would settle on another diagnosis. "Go back and look again. It's got to be something else."

A knock on the door brought Charlotte to her feet. She opened it to find two doctors, their names stamped above the pockets of their white coats. Charlotte made the introductions of the two surgeons: Drs. Wilkes and Scully.

Dr. Scully said, "I've reviewed the ultrasound, examined Miss Kelly, and talked to the other doctors about their findings. I agree, she has significant mitral valve disease, probably from rheumatic fever. I recommended to Miss Kelly that we replace her mitral valve with an artificial valve tomorrow. She agreed but only if her parents and sister can be here. She said you'd make that happen, Mr. O'Grady."

Time seemed to slow as emotional numbness took hold. He was unable to absorb all the information he'd been given. Even if he was Houdini, how could he possibly make it happen?

"As you know," Dr. Scully said, "this is a serious surgery, but we do it a lot. She's an otherwise healthy woman and should tolerate surgery well. It should take us two to four hours to replace the valve. After that, she'll be in the hospital for at least a week, including one to three days in ICU. Recovery is anywhere from four to eight weeks."

"Two to four hours," Rick mumbled. "A week in the hospital. At least four weeks in recovery." It was a handful of information to absorb. If he was finding it difficult, how was Amber handling it all alone? "When can I see her?"

"She's feeling better now, and has asked to see you and Noah, I believe," Dr. Wilkes said. "You can go back for a few minutes."

Rick stood on shaky legs. "How long has she had this condition?"

"This could have started several years ago when she had her first strep throat infection that wasn't treated with antibiotics," Dr. Scully said. "Since she hasn't seen a doctor in years, the rheumatic heart disease has gotten progressively worse. Did it happen overnight? No. Did it happen last week? No. If you had brought her in last month, I'd be telling you the same thing, but she'd have been in better condition for surgery."

"Are you saying if she'd had an antibiotic for a strep infection years ago she wouldn't be in this condition today?"

"This used to be the most common cause of mitral regurgitation in the United States but has significantly declined due to early treatment of strep infection." The doctor reached for the door handle. "If there aren't any other questions—"

Rick leaned against the wall for support. "Noah and I can see her now, but can I stay in her room tonight?"

"She'll be in the cardiac care unit until surgery. You can visit her during special visiting hours. I don't believe they have moved her to the unit yet. You can visit her here in the ED for a few minutes. Anything else?"

Rick looked at Braham and then Charlotte. "I guess not," he said in a flat voice.

"I'll see you before surgery tomorrow morning," Dr. Scully said.

The surgeons left, leaving Rick with Braham and Charlotte in the claustrophobic consulting room. "Amber said if she could have one day hunting fossils, she'd go home, go to the doctor, and get a magic pill. If she'd only taken those pills…"

Charlotte touched his arm. The warmth of her fingers reminded him that he wasn't alone, but it didn't ease the restrictive band tightening around his chest. He thought back to what he could have done differently that would have eased Amber's suffering.

Covering for her on stage when her shortness of breath interfered with her ability to sing, had been his first mistake. He'd had so much fun performing that he allowed her to continue even though she was struggling to breathe.

Going to Denver had been his second mistake. He'd wanted to extend his own western adventure so much that he agreed to take her, knowing she was sick.

Escorting her to Morrison had been his third. When Amber begged to have her dream come true, he wanted to make that happen because he cared for her. He let his emotions get in the way of doing his job—protecting her.

Charlotte gave his arm a little shake, pulling him back to the present. "We all make decisions about our health care," she said. "Sometimes we get it right. Sometimes we don't. How many things are you not doing since you were released from Walter Reed?"

"This isn't about me, Charlotte."

"I know it isn't. My point is that you shouldn't get mad at Amber for what she didn't do while you are—"

Rick slammed his fist into his palm. "I'm not mad at her. I'm mad at myself because I wasn't strong enough to do my job and tell her no." He headed toward the door. "Noah and I will visit her then check into a hotel."

"We have plenty of room for you, Noah, and Amber's family when they arrive. Don't give it another thought," Charlotte said.

"And I've got whisky and cigars," Braham said. "We'll sit out by the river and ye can tell me everything about yer trip to 1878."

"Thanks…" Rick squeezed his eyes shut, pressed his fingers against the bridge of his nose, desperately trying to control his emotions, but his legs still shook. He was too damn scared.

Braham gave him a hug. "We're family. Now ye and Noah go see her and tell her she's got a pile of people wishing her well."

"Give me a minute," Rick said, signaling to Braham and Charlotte to leave him alone. It took him a few minutes to regain his composure and settle his restless mind. When he had himself together again, he left the consulting room to find Noah.

"Come on, buddy. We can see Amber now."

Charlotte met them at the door leading to the ED patient rooms. "Noah, Amber is hooked up to a lot of equipment. It's scary looking, but it's there to make her feel better."

Noah took Charlotte's hand with an almost desperate grasp. "Will you come with me? You know… In case I have questions that Rick can't answer."

Rick glanced at Charlotte, nodding. It was okay with him. He'd probably have questions, too.

She led the way into Amber's room and Rick smiled when he saw her. She wore a nasal cannula, and he could hear oxygen blowing from it into her nostrils. Her lips were no longer blueish. There were IV poles on both sides of the bed with IV bags hanging off the poles, IVs in both arms. A vital-signs monitor near the head of the bed beeped with each heartbeat. A blood pressure cuff rode her upper right arm. She appeared more comfortable, but she was shivering.

"Can we get heated blankets?" Rick asked.

"Sure," Charlotte said.

Rick kissed Amber's forehead, then took her hand and kissed each finger. "How're you feeling, sweetheart?"

"Much better. It doesn't hurt to breathe now."

Noah stepped up to the bed, staring at all the equipment. With the tip of his finger, he lightly touched the IV bags, tubes, and cords, his head flinching back slightly. "What is all this?"

"Modern medicine," she said.

"Are you scared?" he asked.

"A little." She smiled. "The doctors are going to fix me up, but there's something I need to talk to you about. We shouldn't have brought you here, but it was an emergency. Rick needs to take you back to your dad."

Noah shook his head. "I won't go."

"You have to, Noah. Your dad has to be worried sick about you."

"Lincoln said my dad is dead."

"No," Rick said. "Lincoln shouldn't have said that. When you go back, he'll be there for you."

"I'm not leaving until Amber's better. You can't make me."

Charlotte came back with a heated blanket and spread it out over Amber.

Rick gave her a *Please help me* look.

"Come with me, Noah," Charlotte said. "I want to talk to Lincoln and Patrick about what y'all can do tonight. And I bet Braham will take you by the vet's office, so you can visit Ripley. Would you like that?"

"Yes ma'am." He kissed Amber's cheek. "Can I come back tomorrow?"

"We'll talk about it later, Noah," Rick said.

"Have fun with the boys," Amber said.

"I've never had friends like them before. They're smart, but they don't know much about dinosaurs. I'm teaching them all I know."

"Good for you," Amber said. "Later you can tell me about your meeting with Dr. Lakes."

Charlotte made a last check of Amber's connections and monitor readings, then took Noah out of the room.

"Will you take him home, please, and bring Olivia back in time for surgery? The thought of Daniel believing he's lost his son just breaks my heart."

"I'll have to leave this afternoon. Noah won't want to go knowing you and Ripley are so sick."

"Then bring Daniel here."

Rick was about to explain how difficult that would be, but then he noticed the uptick on the heart rate monitor. He was upsetting her, and he couldn't do that. "I'll work it out, and I'll get your parents here, too."

"Give me your phone," she said. "I want you to have contact information for my parents and my assistant." He gave her the phone, and she punched in names, email addresses, and phone numbers.

A nurse came to the door and told Rick they were ready to transport Amber to the CCU. "I wish I could stay with you, but they won't let me."

"You have to go get Daniel and Olivia. Charlotte told me she'd be close by, so I won't be alone."

Tears pushed to his eyes. Leaving her was the hardest thing he'd ever done. "Take care, sweetheart. I'll be back soon." This time he gently kissed her lips. "Rest easy."

46

1878 Pueblo, Colorado—Daniel

Horses crammed, flank to flank, along the hitching rail in front of the square, three-story brick St. James Hotel. Daniel rode past the crowded rail and dismounted next door at the haberdashery. He racked his mount then set a gentle hand on Rambler's withers as he surveyed the crowded street.

The equine flesh was warm and comforting to the touch and seemed to seep into crevices of his soul that longed for peace and comfort. The kind of peace that would come from having Amber at his side and a mother for Noah.

Until recently, he hadn't realized how important that was to his son.

Until recently, he hadn't realized how important it was to have a loving woman in his life again, either.

Hell, until recently he'd been so entangled with the business of the railroad that he'd been blind to the needs of father and son.

And that had to end.

The clang of a distant train engine, the hiss and roar of the continuously moving water of the nearby Arkansas River, the drunken curses of out-of-work miners mixed into a discordant sound that filled the crevices and pushed away thoughts of peace and comfort, of Amber and Noah, of a different kind of life.

The horse snorted, swished his tail, and Daniel jerked himself from the mental brink. He snapped out of it, as he'd long ago trained himself to do. And once again found himself on a rutted thoroughfare in Pueblo, Colorado. And tomorrow, or whenever this assignment ended, would find him on another rutted thoroughfare in Somewhere Else, Colorado or Kansas or Utah or…

Subdued, he gave the Morgan one last pat before moving on.

Dressed in his recognizable Pinkerton dark duster and pearl-buttoned vest, he ambled toward the hotel entrance. The boards creaked beneath his boots as he made his way through a smoky huddle of construction crewmen released from laying track around Cañon City and men laid off from the mines. Both groups hung around town drinking and gambling and picking up work to feed both habits. For a bottle and a rifle, they'd fight for anyone. And today, the owners of the Rio Grande hired them to fight for their cause. Hired Daniel and his men, too. If there was going to be a fight, he hoped to God it wouldn't be a bloodbath.

A man, looking for trouble and knowing where to find it, leaned against the wall near the hotel entrance. His sheepskin coat hung open, thumbs hooked in a shell-belt that sagged about his scrawny waist. He smelled of blood, piss, and a hard ride. Daniel paused before the hotel door and was reaching for the knob when he spotted the man's glance swing his way and come sharply alive. Daniel let his hand fall alongside his Colt, and he turned slightly to face him. The move was understood.

Come off cock, you son of a bitch.

The man acknowledged him with a sweep of his eyes, then lazily pushed out from the brick wall and ambled down the plank walk, disappearing in the crowd of men. Daniel's heart was beating hard enough to be heard at the haberdashery, had anyone been listening. He hadn't drawn down on a man in a couple of years and hoped to hell he never would again.

The nondescript exterior of the hotel hid a lavish interior with a heavily masculine décor that reminded Daniel of gentlemen's clubs in San Francisco and Chicago. But it was the lobby bustling with armed men that reminded him of the hotels in Washington, DC, during the war. He quickly pushed that reminder aside.

Eyeing the distinctive envelope used by the telegraph office stuffed into his room's designated mailbox, he approached the reception desk. One of the hotel's overly ambitious clerks spotted him and claimed the message, having it in hand before Daniel could ask.

"It just came in, Major." There was something in the young clerk who sported a determined line of peach fuzz, exerting itself to become a mustache, that reminded Daniel of what Noah would look like in a few years.

Daniel set his hat on the desk. "Thanks." He ripped open the telegram and while reading the message, the clerk gave his hat a quick pass with a hat brush.

I have a business opportunity in San Francisco and must depart immediately. The house and staff remain at your disposal. Regards, Alec.

Daniel flapped the envelope against his palm. *Bastard.* Alec had invited Noah for a visit and after a few days intended to abandon him. Daniel had hoped his father-in-law would show interest in his grandson, but it wasn't to be. Thank God, he'd convinced Amber to stay awhile. The lad would be devastated if everyone abandoned him.

"Major Grant."

Daniel looked up to see Mr. Weitbrec, Rio Grande's treasurer, smoothing his painter's brush mustache as he crossed the lobby at a brisk pace. Daniel flipped the eager clerk a coin before sliding the telegram into his pocket. He'd have to consider what this meant for Noah, but first he had to finish the job for the railroad.

"Your hat, sir," the clerk said. "Next time, I'll be glad to give your boots a quick brush, too." The clerk didn't dally but moved quickly to address the needs of his next customer. Daniel wouldn't be a bit surprised to find the young man in an assistant manager's position before he had enough hair on his face to shave.

Daniel extended his hand. "Mr. Weitbrec. Looks like ye've

pulled a contingent of men off yer work crews and added a few ruffians to the mix. Hope they have a heart for what's coming."

Weitbrec shook hands then gave Daniel a perfunctory slap on the back. "As long as Santa Fe doesn't offer them more money, they'll fight for the Rio Grande." He pointed toward Daniel's pocket. "I saw you received a telegram. Is the agency sending more men?"

"I'm expecting a response from the Denver office today." Daniel patted his pocket. "This was from my father-in-law."

"How is Alec? I heard he might be traveling soon. Any news on that front?"

Weitbrec and Alec were not only business associates, but personal friends. Was he already aware of his father-in-law's business opportunity in San Francisco? Regardless, Daniel didn't intend to discuss Alec's business unless instructed to do so. Instead, he remained on safe ground, saying only, "My son's visiting his grandfather, and Alec hired a tutor for him."

"I heard Noah was visiting." Weitbrec's face, so expressive in its weathered lines, seemed closed up in worry, and the unseen burden bent his shoulders. "Let's eat in the dining room. I sense an escalation of the situation here in Pueblo, and we might not get dinner tonight."

The head waiter escorted the two men to a table—one of the last available—in the shadow of sunlight beaming in from two west-facing windows. The table was set with a white linen tablecloth, polished silverware, china, napkins folded into fans and set in crystal goblets, and menus set square for viewing. A half-dozen waiters in white jackets moved about with silver coffee pots, ready to pour. Catering to heavy gamblers with an appreciation for the finer things, along with the reputation of being the largest gambling establishment west of the Mississippi, kept the hotel in business.

Daniel wouldn't have registered at the hotel or eaten in the dining room if he'd been footing the bill, but he was working for the Rio Grande and his tab was covered for the duration of the assignment. It wasn't that he didn't enjoy the lifestyle, he did, but it was an extravagance reserved for dinner jackets, not spurs and a Colt strapped to his hip.

The waiter picked up Daniel's coat that he'd slung over the back of his chair. "I'll hang this up for you, sir."

Daniel acknowledged the waiter's offer and added, "I'll just have coffee." His china cup chattered against its saucer as he moved it to the near side of the table, making it easier for the waiter to reach.

Weitbrec removed his hat, patting his hair as if checking to be sure it was still there, then he perused the menu. "Lunch is on the company. You should eat."

"I have two guests joining me for a late lunch before they leave town."

"I hope they're going to Denver. The line to Cañon City is closed. Santa Fe doesn't want more Rio Grande men rushing here to defend our property."

"Miss Kelly and her companion came down this morning from Denver to meet with the general."

Weitbrec set his menu aside. "Is she the woman who was at Alec's dinner party last night?"

"She and her sister Amber."

"I heard from Colonel Greenwood, Colonel Dodge, Mr. Hunt, and Mr. Lambord this morning. The Kelly sisters made quite an impression on the board members."

"I came home late and didn't hear the discussion about the railroad, but I had mentioned Miss Amber Kelly to the general yesterday. He extended an invitation to meet with her today. Although her sister Miss Olivia Kelly came in her stead."

Weitbrec tapped his glass with a silver knife and a waiter instantly appeared at his elbow. "I'll have the oyster soup and baked pickerel." The waiter filled Weitbrec's cup and refreshed Daniel's. "What was the general's reaction to Miss Kelly?"

"General Palmer dismissed her as easily as he would have dismissed an aide-de-camp."

Weitbrec poured a generous amount of cream into his coffee, and after stirring, the dark liquid faded to a wheat-colored brown.

"Which tells me the general was impressed, but because she's a woman, he didn't want to admit it."

The waiter returned with the soup. "We're expecting two additional diners," Weitbrec said. "Hold the baked pickerel until you bring out the rest of the orders." He spooned his soup away from him, allowing dribbles to fall back into the bowl, then he ate from the side of the spoon. "I want to meet Miss Kelly if she's still in town. What's she like?"

"Beautiful, charming, intelligent, and I must warn ye, a suffragette."

Weitbrec had been leaning forward, over the table. He now settled back, wiping his mouth with the napkin, and looked directly at Daniel. "You know, they're not all intolerable."

Daniel laughed. "Interestingly, neither sister tries to force their beliefs on others. They unapologetically assume everyone already shares them. They believe they have a right to a seat in the conference room or in the gentlemen's smoking room, whichever one is applicable."

Now it was Weitbrec's turn to laugh. "Sounds like you might have a personal interest in one of the ladies. Are your days as a widower coming to an end, Major?"

"Perhaps, but it's too soon to know for certain."

"Alec and I both agree it's time Noah had a mother. Now, as for your scouting report. I read it quickly, but not thoroughly. Tell me what I need to know."

Daniel drank his coffee, sans dollop of cream or cube of sugar. "It's rumored that Sheriff Masterson and sixty well-armed Kansans are barricaded inside the roundhouse. But my scouts put Holliday and Masterson in Cañon City, and Ben Thompson with about forty men in the roundhouse."

"Which do you believe?"

"My scouts."

"Do you think Thompson can be paid to walk away?" Weitbrec asked.

"Having the Supreme Court's ruling, plus a satchel of cash might persuade him."

"The company's lawyers believe the ruling should be issued today or tomorrow. Since it'll take weeks to trickle down to the district level, our attorneys have a complaint ready to file in the Fourth Judicial District. We're confident Judge Bowen will issue a writ of injunction. We have sheriffs, backed up by deputies, lined up in every county where we have track. They'll serve the writs and reclaim all property Santa Fe has confiscated." Weitbrec finished his soup and pushed the bowl away. "How smoothly do you think it will go here in Pueblo?"

"That depends on Ben Thompson."

In Daniel's peripheral vision, he glimpsed Olivia and Connor and raised a finger, signaling to Connor who was scanning the room. Connor spoke to Olivia, and a smile tugged a dimple into one cheek. What had Connor said to elicit such a reaction in her? It was a look Daniel had seen on Amber's face last night when she fell asleep in his arms, and all he had done was stroke her cheek.

"My guests have arrived," Daniel said. "Miss Kelly is escorted by Mr. O'Grady. I'm trying to recruit him and his brother. The Pinkerton Agency needs men like them."

"The Rio Grande is always looking for qualified men. I might try to hire them first."

"Ye can try."

Daniel and Weitbrec stood and introductions were made. Connor lifted Olivia's cloak from her shoulders and gently brushed her neck with his fingertips. The erotic touch didn't go unnoticed by Daniel and sent a wave of longing through him. The waiter removed the cloak, parasol, and the gentlemen's hats to a small room near the entrance where coats and hats were kept. When he returned, he served coffee and took their lunch orders.

Weitbrec cradled his coffee cup, watching Olivia closely. "Major Grant mentioned your meeting with General Palmer. I'm treasurer of the Rio Grande so you won't be divulging a confidence by relaying details of the meeting."

Olivia glanced at Daniel, and he tipped his hand to her in a go-ahead gesture.

"I advised him against signing a lease that didn't grant the company full control over freight rates. It's my belief that once a lease is signed, Santa Fe will raise rates to Denver from Pueblo, Colorado Springs, and Cañon City, and will divert additional traffic eastward over its own line. You'll lose money and any benefits leasing the tracks might give you. Once shippers undercut you, your income will fall below what you need to pay interest on your bonds, and the assets will be thrown into the hands of a receiver."

Weitbrec's jaw dropped and then he laughed. "What'd the general say to that?"

She patted her lips delicately with a napkin. "He said I didn't paint a pretty picture. I told him I wasn't an artist, but I knew about war." She stopped and studied Weitbrec for a moment. "Speaking of which, I heard you were captured at Fairfax Court House with Brigadier General Stoughton and taken to Libby Prison. That was an atrocious place. That building should be torn down, every nail melted, and a monument created to honor the men who were imprisoned there."

Weitbrec mused, "Men find it necessary to retell their war stories, this battle and that, where they were when Lee and Grant met at Appomattox, where they were when Lincoln was assassinated. I prefer to talk about today and tomorrow instead."

Daniel had never heard Weitbrec wax ruefully over the war, and he was surprised the treasurer reflected on it now. Even when men didn't talk about the war, you could see in their eyes that they remembered. The war was always with those who survived—like an invisible shadow that quavered below the surface, a reminder of the horror, a tangle of longing, guilt, and overwhelming loss. If Daniel never talked about it again, never thought about it again, he could live with that.

"Then we shall talk about today." She sipped her coffee and refolded her hands in her lap. "I told the general, in my opinion, the Supreme Court will grant you the primary right to build through the gorge. If you're stuck in a lease, then you'll spend thousands of dollars in legal fees trying to get out of it."

Weitbrec twirled his mustache. "I expect the ruling any day now, but if it doesn't come, the board of directors will push for the lease."

"I'm sorry I couldn't persuade them. They'll be making a mistake." She glanced at Daniel. "And before you ask, I don't own a crystal ball. The future can't be seen, it can only be speculated about based on present information."

Weitbrec chortled. "I was going to ask if you had one."

The waiter delivered their luncheon plates, and after he stepped away, Weitbrec asked, "While you're speculating, do you have any insight as to what'll happen when we assert our rights and try to reclaim our property here in Pueblo?"

Olivia set down her fork and looked directly at Weitbrec. "Masterson and his sixty hardcases from Dodge are hoping to cow your men. They might have a well-defended position, but they can't see they're outnumbered. Why not go to the state armory and borrow the Mountain Howitzer? Roll that thing right up to those mammoth gates and threaten to blow the place up."

Daniel jerked as if smacked with a whip, and his gaze bounced from Olivia to Weitbrec. His men had stopped by the armory earlier, and there had been no mention of a cannon, and Masterson wasn't even in town. Daniel smoothed his short beard, thinking of the consequences if Masterson was in town and had possession of such a weapon.

"Masterson and Holliday are in Cañon City," he said.

She raised her brow, her back rigid. If he hadn't been watching her so closely, he wouldn't have seen her assuredness fade a little, or the moue of doubt. "Are you sure?"

Connor shifted slightly in his chair, toward Olivia, in a protective sort of way, but otherwise showed no emotion.

Weitbrec glared at Daniel, an awful light growing behind his eyes. The message was clear: *Confirm the scouting report.*

"If ye'll excuse me." Daniel pushed back from the table, the scrape of his chair echoing through the dining room as he rose, nodded to his luncheon guests and sailed out.

The Pinkertons had commandeered the gentlemen's smoking room, much to the chagrin of the management, and set up a command post for Weitbrec. One of his agents stood at the door to keep non-essential personnel out of the room.

"Major Grant," the agent said. "Have you heard anything from the Denver office? Are they sending more agents?"

"Don't know yet." Daniel pulled the man aside. "Take another agent with ye. Find Sheriff Price and Deputy Desmond. Go to the state armory. If they have a cannon, borrow it. Also ask anyone who's recently been in Cañon City if they've seen Sheriff Masterson. If he's in Colorado, I want to know where."

"I personally inspected the armory an hour ago. There's no ordnance on the property." The agent then nodded toward a sheriff's deputy sitting nearby reading a newspaper. "Hey, John. Didn't you just come in from Cañon City?"

John put the paper aside and walked over. "Wish I'd never gone. Got caught in a poker game last night with Sheriff Masterson. Lost my watch. Almost lost my horse."

"Is he still there?" Daniel asked.

"Saw him at breakfast. He's got a big game tonight. He's not going anywhere."

"If ye hear any different, let me know immediately." Daniel left the room and walked down a quiet corridor away from the lobby to gather his thoughts. What exactly had Olivia said about the sheriff: *Masterson and his sixty hardcases from Dodge are hoping to cow your men.* Why would she have said that if the sheriff was playing poker in Cañon City?

Then there was the matter of the ordnance. She had specifically mentioned a Mountain Howitzer, not a cannon. Why the specificity if the damn thing didn't even exist? He reached the end of the corridor where a small window with heavy dark curtains pulled back an arm's width shed a ray of afternoon light into the doorless hall. But it did nothing to shed light on the mystery perplexing him. The tangle of his thinking might never unknot itself.

Did Olivia work for Santa Fe? Was she sent to infiltrate Rio

Grande's headquarters and spread false information about the size and preparedness of Santa Fe's forces? Was it her assignment to cow Rio Grande, not Masterson's?

Daniel scratched his head and continued to mull over the bits and pieces, hoping his thoughts would settle into a discernible rhythm. He had met female spies during the war, but Olivia wasn't a spy, only ill-informed. If she worked for Santa Fe, she would have encouraged the general to sign the lease, not the reverse.

He made a U-turn and retraced his steps. The Kelly sisters were a mystery. His job was to advise and assist Weitbrec, but what could he say about Olivia's recommendations? That she had been given an advanced plan that was altered prior to execution and her crystal ball failed to advise her?

His life had been out of kilter since he first met Amber in Leadville. It was as if at the end of each day a cup was emptied only to be refilled overnight, which emptied again, much like the cycle of an hour-glass where the level of sand drops, the glass is turned, and the level drops once again, never revealing its truth.

He clenched his teeth against his rising frustration.

After one last steadied march to the end of the corridor and back, Daniel returned to the dining room. He looked at Olivia, and her large hazel-brown eyes, identical to Amber's, sparkled in the light gleaming in through the window.

So much damn light, but so little illumination.

He reclaimed his seat, aslant from the table, crossed his legs, folded his hands on his knee, and tapped his top fingers against his bottom hand. He let tension build in the moment before he said, "Sheriff Masterson is in Cañon City playing poker. And no one has stolen or borrowed"—he lifted his brow—"the cannon because…" He let the word hang in the air for a beat before adding, "one doesn't exist." The tone of his pronouncements came across cold, pointed, dangerous, just as he'd intended.

Her hands jumped a bit, sending her cup splashing. She looked down at the spilled coffee on the tablecloth, then glanced up at him, eyes no longer sparkling, as if he were a disembodied spirit that had crept out of the shadow world of dreams and threatened her with his ghostly appearance.

She attempted a smile, but it quickly faded. "You've been misinformed. He's here." Confusion replaced the smile, followed by a wary cautiousness.

"What made ye believe there was a cannon at the armory?"

Rather than answer right away, she sipped her coffee, letting her own uncomfortable silence stretch between them. Finally, she softened the sharpness of his question with a smile and said, "Colorado has only been a state for two years. It needed a well-armed militia. I made an assumption."

Abruptly, Weitbrec pushed back from the table. "If you'll excuse me, I have a meeting with my staff."

Daniel stood, too, intending to leave with Weitbrec to join the meeting.

Connor extended his hand to both Weitbrec and Daniel. "Good luck to both of you."

After Weitbrec departed, Daniel said, "I'd like to have a man like ye covering my back. If ye're interested in joining the Pinkertons, I can deputize ye right now."

"That's tempting," Connor said glancing at Olivia, "but I already have a full-time job, and we need to return to Denver."

"If ye change yer mind…" What could Daniel say? What could he offer Connor and Rick that would keep them in Colorado, that would keep Amber and Olivia here, too? Nothing. "As soon as the situation is resolved here, I'll return to Denver. I hope ye will still be in town."

"We can stay in Pueblo until this evening, but then we have to return to Denver. Amber has to go home to see our family doctor. She's not well, Daniel."

"I have encouraged her to see Alec's physician, but she refuses. I'll send a wire and ask him to stop by the house later today. Maybe she'll agree."

"I wish she wasn't so set against the medical profession, but she's feeling bad enough right now, she might relent," Olivia said.

"Then I'll send a wire. Now, if ye're staying, ye're welcome to use my second-floor suite. It has a view of the street." Daniel wanted to keep her in town for now and assign one of his agents to watch her. He didn't believe she was a spy, but the circumstances were suspicious enough to keep him alert to any possibility. And their sudden arrival with the McBains still had him racking his brain.

"That might be safer than going back to our private car parked at the depot." Olivia glanced at Connor, then said to Daniel, "Excuse us a minute."

She came up out of the chair with a lift of her slight square shoulders and pulled Connor aside. They spoke privately. She glanced at Daniel then she returned her gaze to Connor. They were speaking quietly enough that he couldn't hear a word they said. They weren't arguing, but Olivia was asserting a position. Connor finally nodded, sighed deeply, and she mouthed *Thank you.*

They stepped back over to the table. "Deputize me," Connor said.

Disbelief rolled over Daniel and he gave Connor a level stare. "Are ye sure?"

Connor looked away, deep in thought. The gas-fed flame inside the wall sconce's glass lampshade hissed and flared and highlighted the stress lines at the sides of his mouth. "If I don't go with you, Olivia will."

The waiter returned with their belongings from the cloak room. "Put the charge on my account," Daniel said.

"Mr. Weitbrec has already taken care of the bill," the waiter said.

"I need to stop at the desk and claim the room key. I'll meet ye at the staircase."

They parted at the entrance to the dining room and Daniel returned to the reception desk where a different hotel employee, one with a longhorn mustache, was arguing with a man wearing a Van Dyke beard.

"I hurried out of Morrison to get to Cañon City." The man's face reddened, and his voice rose in pitch. "Now the railroad has delayed all departures. I'm stuck here until morning and I need a room."

When Daniel heard Morrison mentioned, he leaned over the counter to eavesdrop on the discussion. Noah and Amber were there, and if trouble had found its way to Morrison, too, he needed to know.

"I'm sorry you've been inconvenienced, Mr. Hendrix. Pueblo is thronged constantly with miners and gamblers. The city's hotels are overflowing, and many of our visitors are forced to seek accommodations in private homes. Here at the St. James, we have no rooms available. You'll have to check other establishments," the clerk said.

"I refuse to stay in one of those fleabag hovels. I'll pay twice the room rate."

"The St. James is fully booked," the clerk insisted.

"Excuse me," Daniel said.

The man glared at Daniel with a face full of thunder. "Can't you see I'm talking to the clerk? You'll have to wait your turn."

The man had eyes cold as a winter sky. If Daniel had his druthers, he'd haul the man's ass off to jail just for irritating the hardworking clerk. Daniel made a point of turning so the man could see the tin star winking on his vest.

Hendrix stepped aside with growing unease. "If the Pinkertons are in town, then this mess should be cleared up and service restored within a few hours. Don't let me interfere with your business, sir."

"Would ye hand me my room key?" Daniel asked.

"Certainly, Major." The desk clerk removed a key with a leather fob from the keyboard. "Is there anything else?"

Daniel was about to advise the clerk that Olivia would, in his absence, be spending the afternoon in his room resting, but decided against it. It could easily be misconstrued, and he didn't want to tarnish her reputation. Then he almost groaned, remembering in whose bed he'd spent most of last night.

Daniel lightly tossed the key in his hand, wondering if he should mention the rude traveler to Connor, but decided against that, too. There was no indication of trouble in Morrison, only an inconvenienced traveler, and alarming Connor was unnecessary.

Connor and Olivia were waiting by the newel post at the bottom of the staircase. She was gazing up at Connor, and although he was glancing down at her, he was watching the comings and goings in the lobby. It was a talent developed through years of training and surveilling criminals. There was more to the O'Grady brothers than they wanted Daniel to know.

He pitched the numbered key to Connor. "The room is on the second floor, front corner. I'll be in the men's smoking room, which is now Weitbrec's command center. After Olivia is settled, meet me there and we'll take care of business. Welcome to the Pinkertons." Daniel slowly walked away, but stopped and watched them, imagining Amber looking at him with the same adoring eyes; imagining her with an outstretched hand beckoning him to share her bed; imagining her with his bairn at her breast.

"Pops, JL, and my brothers will never believe this," he overheard Connor say.

"I'm not sure I do either, but it's the right thing to do. Amber will be pleased to know you're working with Daniel and watching his back."

"But who's going to watch mine?"

She patted his chest, and her mouth, usually so quick to smile, curved downward. "Mr. Vest, I guess."

Who is Mr. Vest?

Daniel puzzled through that one as he watched Connor escort her up to the second-floor landing. Jealousy stabbed him through and through, sharper than any saber could. If he couldn't keep the green stab at bay, it would easily develop into a mortal wound.

"Major Grant."

A voice calling his name disquieted his enviousness, and he turned to see the young dispatcher from the Rio Grande telegraph office. He held out his hand to accept the envelope.

"It's for Mr. Weitbrec." He leaned in toward Daniel and whispered. "It's the telegram he's been expecting."

"I'll see that he gets it." Daniel tipped the young man then opened the envelope. As was the practice with all Rio Grande and

Santa Fe communications—since they were connected into the same telegraphic system and shared wires—messages were written in code. Daniel quickly deciphered the message to confirm what he'd been told.

Court ruled in Denver & Rio Grande's favor. Sheriffs serving writ.

Daniel marched into the command center, the telegram clenched in his hand.

And so it begins…

47

The Present, Richmond, Virginia—Rick

An hour after leaving the hospital, Rick and Braham walked along the James River on a path that wound its way through Mallory Plantation. The estate, settled in 1613, held the distinction of being Virginia's first plantation.

The homeplace, built in the early 1800s, was home to Charlotte's brother Jack, his bride-to-be, and their adopted son Patrick. Charlotte and Braham lived on the grounds, too, but in a separate residence Braham designed and had built when he married Charlotte. It was a Greek Revival-style mansion with a quarter mile avenue of twenty-eight live oaks leading up to an estate house with gleaming hardwood floors, shimmering chandeliers, and twenty-five rooms. Its magnificence and allure represented a bygone era.

As he and Braham strolled along the James River, Braham handed Rick a frosted glass tube. "Have ye ever smoked a Gurkha Black Dragon?"

Rick studied the tube. "Nope. But I've heard of your constant quest for the perfect cigar. Is this your Rolls-Royce?"

Braham gave him an appraising look. "This week, it is." Braham peeled back the tab on the waxed end of the glass tube, opened it, extracted the cigar, and held it to his nose for a moment.

Matching Braham's step-by-step dance, Rick opened his case and sniffed, sighing sweetly. "Rolls-Royce, huh? We should be celebrat ing something."

Braham struck a wooden match with his thumb nail, a trick Rick had tried dozens of times but failed to match Braham's finesse. Braham rotated the cigar while he toasted it in the flame then put it in his mouth and drew on it, keeping the cigar just above the flame as he drew and twisted to get the entire foot lit. He easily slid into a rhythm of puff turn, puff turn until it was evenly lit. It was like watching an orchestra director—a true aficionado. To Braham, smoking a cigar was an art form.

"This is a special edition, rare, ultra-premium, possibly the hardest to find Gurkha," Braham said between puffs with pleasure in his voice. "The blend is made of an aged Connecticut broadleaf binder with a delicate five-year Cameroon binder and five-year Dominican tobaccos in the filler. The flavor, ye'll notice, is complex and ranges from a strong buttery toast flavor in the first third, complemented by a lightly sour peppery finish. The sour finish will fade in the second third and be replaced with a sweet honey finish." Sounding like an ad for the company, he continued, "The peppery finish will increase dramatically toward the end of the smoke." He puffed again. "That was my review of the first one I smoked. I've had a dozen since, and my opinion hasn't changed. So I bought the company."

"I hope you get a good return on your investment." Rick lit his and drew a short draw, then removed the cigar from his mouth and studied it, blowing out puffs, as if the luxury cigar held all the answers. "There is no crisis a good cigar can't cure."

"That's what they say. So what are ye going to do about yers?"

"Sounds like the preliminaries are over, and it's time to get down to the purpose of this smoking stroll. Okay, this is what I'm planning to do. I'm going to close my eyes and think of nothing but smoking this," Rick mused.

"That'll give ye a forty-five-minute reprieve. Then what?"

"I guess a thousand-dollar cigar entitles you to bug the hell out of me and spoil my pleasure."

Braham's lips twitched, begging to pour into a smile. "Eleven hundred and fifty."

Shaking his head at Braham's extravagance that extended to wine, whisky, cigars, and Thoroughbreds, Rick puffed, sending the rich tobacco's scent into the air between them. "I'm going back to get Daniel and Olivia, so they'll be here for Amber's surgery."

"Plans for Noah are up in the air." The lilt at the end of Braham's statement meant he was really asking a question.

"Noah would be traumatized if he had to leave Amber and his dog. I can't do that to him. I don't know what or how I'm going to tell Daniel."

"Noah can send his dad a video message like the one ye and Amber sent her sister."

"Daniel won't understand, and he'll probably just shoot me."

Braham parked the cigar in the corner of his mouth. "I know a way to make it easier for him."

Rick found Braham's sudden buoyant mood disconcerting and gave him a sideways glance, as if looking at him head-on would fail to protect him from incoming fire. He finally gave Braham a so-spill-it gesture.

"Charlotte won't like this idea, but it's the right thing to do. I'm going with ye."

"You can't do that. You'd be stepping back into your former life. You know people. They know you."

Braham nodded, and they continued walking, keeping their thoughts to themselves while enjoying their Gurkhas. A slight breeze kicked up, enough to make the tops of the trees sound like they were whispering secrets. Whirls of wind touched down in the piles of gold and red leaves and they flitted around in upward spirals.

"Daniel was sent to Cañon City to work for General Palmer. You know him, don't you?"

"The general and I share the dubious honor of having been prisoners of Castle Thunder. He got out during a prisoner exchange. I got out the night Richmond burned." Braham shivered. "The only good thing to come out of that war, at least for me, was meeting Charlotte."

"It must have been horrendous. I've heard David talk about what happened, but I have a feeling he just skimmed the surface."

"What's Palmer doing in Cañon City?"

"His railroad, the Denver & Rio Grande, is in a war with the Atchison, Topeka and Santa Fe over a right-of-way to lay track through the ten-mile-long Royal Gorge canyon. The case is tied up in the Supreme Court. Olivia was invited to meet with the general to talk about the case. From what I understand, the general's railroad is losing a pile of money, so they're considering leasing its track to Santa Fe."

"I thought she was a real estate agent."

"She's a lawyer, too. She knows that if Santa Fe leases Rio Grande's track, Santa Fe will manipulate freight rates south of Denver in favor of shippers from Kansas City. The Rio Grande will ultimately lose more money. It's a bad deal and will string the litigation out several years. Olivia is hoping to talk the general out of signing a lease."

"If it's a legal war going on in Cañon City, why send Pinkertons?"

"To protect Rio Grande's crews from sabotage. Both sides have hired armed guards. Now rifles and pistols accompany picks and shovels. And," Rick paused, "I have to tell you…Bat Masterson and Doc Holliday work for Santa Fe."

The look on Braham's face said a serious question hovered in the air between them. "Ye're telling me"—He balanced his cigar between two fingers—"we're walking into a war with infamous gunslingers."

Rick tilted his head in a yes-and-no gesture. "If it's any relief, and if reports can be believed, only a couple of people get killed."

"I'm relieved." The tone in Braham's voice said he wasn't at all relieved and was probably trying to figure out how he could rescind his offer. But instead he said, "Let's get in, get out, and leave it to the courts to do the rest. If we leave this afternoon, when will we return?"

Despite the cool air, tiny beads of sweat broke out on Rick's forehead. He didn't want to get mixed up in another war. "I don't know," he said. "But here's the thing. Amber's brooch took her into the past two weeks ago from her family's cabin near Leadville. But it returned us to the moment I left MacKlenna Farm this morning. The only difference was the person holding the stone. In theory, if we leave at three o'clock, we should return at three o'clock, or thereabouts."

"When will Olivia and Connor return?"

"When they left the ranch with Kenzie and David, they had the diamond and the amethyst. Since both of those stones return travelers to the moment they left, Connor and Olivia should return later tonight."

"But they left from Denver, right? Do they have to return there, or can they come here?"

Rick's brain froze for a moment. Trying to figure out brooch travel was more complicated than military logistics. "Why ask me? You have more experience with these goddamn stones than I do."

Braham didn't respond. Instead, he picked up a small rock, walked to the edge of the water, and threw it. It skipped twice before it sank.

"Sorry. You didn't deserve that." Rick leaned against a live oak and puffed, not saying anything for a couple of minutes while Braham skipped more rocks. Finally, he said, "I think Connor and Olivia can return here instead of Denver."

Braham threw one last stone and chomped down on the cigar. "Let's get dressed and go. The sooner we leave, the sooner we come back. I've got all the clothes I used when we went back to 1881. They're in mothballs in the attic."

"Mothballs will smell better than the dinosaur dust on my clothes, but we need money. I gave all my cash to a dinosaur hunter."

"Sounds like an appropriate use of yer funds."

"I did it for Amber. I knew it would make her happy."

Braham's face creased with suspicion. "Somebody needs to remind ye that ye're not the hero of this story."

"Save your breath. David already did."

Braham shrugged. "He's the best person to set ye straight. Listen to him."

Rick shot him an irritated glance. He'd heard dozens of family and brooch stories, but not one about David believing he was the hero of someone else's story. It sounded like a tale Rick intended to avoid. Life lessons, unless they were his own, never impressed him. Failure and mistakes were the evidence that he had tried his best and lost.

"Hold the lectures. Do you have any money we can use?"

"Several large gold nuggets and some double eagle coins. Enough to buy a railroad. Let's finish our smokes, then I'll call Charlotte and give her the bad news."

"What will she say?"

"This time, she'll say hurry back. When she's focused on a patient, not much else matters."

A bass boat sped by and distracted Rick for a moment. Beautiful boat. Great place to be. No worries except finding the bass.

"Must be hard coming in second behind sick people."

"Nah," Braham said. "When I got shot, she risked her life and reputation, and ultimately moved mountains for me. I'll never stand in the way of her doing that for other patients. Right now, Amber is her priority. If we can eliminate some of Amber's worries by getting Daniel and her sister here before surgery, Charlotte will be all over it."

Braham's phone dinged with a text message. He looked at the face then clicked to open it and read out loud: "*Amber drew a sketch of the creeps who broke into her room and stole her journal. I'll fax it to the house. She's preparing a video for Daniel.*"

"We don't have time to go back to Morrison to find them, which is a shame. Nothing would make me happier than beating the shit out of those assholes," Rick said.

Braham's phone dinged again. "Looks like we don't have to: '*When they left my room, they said they had to get the journal to Mudge in Cañon City.*' Does that make any sense to ye?"

"Whose phone is she using?"

"Charlotte's."

"Text her back and ask about Mudge."

Braham sent another text and a minute later, his phone dinged again. *"Geologist who worked for Marsh."* Another message dinged. *"Creeps believed I worked for Cope. Heard from Leadville judge that I studied under Marsh. Marsh said impossible."*

Rick curled his lip with contempt. "If I find those sons of bitches, they'll have as much trouble breathing as Amber."

"What's in her journal?" Braham asked.

"I haven't read it. She said she bought it the day she arrived in Leadville. She sketches in it and write notes and reflections."

"Did she put any information in there about the brooch?" Braham asked.

That thought scared the piss out of Rick. "I don't know. Ask her."

Braham sent the text. It took a couple of minutes before Amber responded. *"Yes."* A moment later, another text: *"And a sketch."*

Rick jerked as if smacked by a whip. "Holy shit."

48

1878 Pueblo, Colorado—Daniel

AGENCY MEN IN black dusters—Daniel, Connor, and two additional Pinkertons—accompanied Weitbrec to the Pueblo County Courthouse at 12th and Court Streets. Inside the three-story building were the offices of the sheriff and the district attorney. Both men had roles to play in Weitbrec's military-style action to retake Rio Grande's property.

"The sheriff will serve the writ on Santa Fe," Weitbrec said. "We just need a sufficient number of deputies to back him up. Enough men to intimidate Santa Fe and take the fight out them. We're going to do this right, without bloodshed."

Daniel tried unsuccessfully to curb his irritation. "My men have their orders, but if the sheriff intends to deputize a hundred drunk out-of-work miners, it could get violent quickly."

"I'll depend on you to keep order," Weitbrec said.

They steered their way through a crowd of men hanging outside the courtroom who had been called in for jury duty. Following Weitbrec, they hastened down the corridor en route to the sheriff's office. The heavy *clack-tap* of their boot heels and clink of spurs on the wood planks resounded throughout the first floor of the courthouse.

When they reached the end of the corridor, Weitbrec gestured with his thumb in the direction of the last door on the right, indicating Sheriff Price's office. Daniel took the lead. The office door was slightly ajar with a murmur of voices coming from within. He put knuckles to wood, giving the door three distinctive knocks.

"Come in," the familiar gruff voice of the sheriff ordered.

As the first to enter, Daniel scanned the room swiftly. Shelves filled with gear and books lined one wall behind a large desk overflowing with wanted posters. Three ladder-backed wooden chairs clustered on the near side of the desk. One held cigarette-smoking Deputy Desmond who stood abruptly, and his chair careened into the wall with a bang. His thin lips disappeared under his mustache in a tight scowl as he righted the chair. District Attorney Waldron was also present.

The office had one other door toward the rear, also slightly ajar, providing a slice of blackness beyond. Daniel strode over to the door and using his boot pushed it open the rest of the way. A short corridor led to an outside entrance. He closed the interior door and turned the key in the lock plate. Satisfied, Daniel nodded to both Weitbrec and Connor to enter.

Daniel then signaled one agent to remain between the courtroom and the main entrance, a hint of toughness in the agent's strong shoulders qualified him to be the first line of defense. The other agent was assigned to stand guard outside the sheriff's door.

"This should go quickly. Stay alert," Daniel said to the agent.

Since the railroad companies shared telegraph wires, Santa Fe was bound to know the writ had been issued and Rio Grande's representatives would be coming to reclaim its property. Logically, Santa Fe would send representatives to the sheriff demanding protection, and Daniel didn't want anyone intruding on their meeting.

Inside the office, he stood a few feet behind Weitbrec, close enough to protect him if the office was stormed—an unlikely event, but that was his job. Connor took a position in the back of the room, easily accessible to the door and the closed window.

Sheriff Price's chair squawked as he leaned back, brushing at his wide mustache as if removing crumbs. "You got the writ?"

Weitbrec slapped the document down on the sheriff's battle-scarred oak desk. "Serve it on the train dispatcher at South Pueblo now. The court says it's our property, our track, our rights to the canyon. It's time Santa Fe got out of Colorado."

Deputy Desmond, his blond hair sun-bleached to a near-white corn silk, stood behind Price. Cigarette smoke puffed from his nostrils in a derisive snort as he read the writ over the sheriff's shoulder. The district attorney, right butt cheek balanced on the edge of the desk, read along as well.

The sheriff put down the writ, leaned his elbows on the desk, and laced his thick fingers together. His pained face gave the impression he was praying Weitbrec would depart his office, his city, and Colorado.

The fire in the ubiquitous brass parlor stove popped and pushed heat into only a fraction of the office closest to the sheriff's desk. The rest of the room held an uneasy chill. The sheriff slowly rubbed his face, as if trying to bring life back into a countenance too weary for another round of fighting between the railroads. He rose to his feet, scraping the wooden floor with the legs of his chair, gathered up his dark duster and put it on over a once-white shirt now stained with sweat and trail dirt.

"Don't want any trouble, Mr. Weitbrec." The sheriff turned down the smoking wick of the lamp, hanging low over his desk, gathered up the writ and his Winchester, and headed toward the door, his deputy keeping in lockstep behind him.

"Do your job and we won't have any." For Weitbrec, caution was gone, replaced by iron determination to bring the situation to a resolution.

The district attorney snatched up his coat and hat. "You know, don't you, that there's a legal remedy if Santa Fe refuses to comply with the writ. The court will punish the individual served with a contempt of court charge."

Weitbrec fell into line next to the district attorney. "I don't care what the court usually does. I only care about what you intend to do."

"There'll be no shooting," the sheriff said. "Understood? I don't want to spend time in my own jail."

"You have your orders, Sheriff." Weitbrec's expression gave hints as to what lay behind his intentions. If he didn't do what the Rio Grande expected him to do, he wouldn't have a job come next election.

Daniel cracked open the door and checked to be sure there weren't any rogue Santa Fe guards present. The agent signaled with a finger that the corridor was clear. Daniel stepped out in front of the others then joined Connor at the end of the line as they all exited the building.

Outside, Daniel squinted against the bright sunlight and tipped his hat a wee bit lower. His agents' mounts were hitched at the tie rail, including the horse he had borrowed from the agent he left behind to guard Olivia. He loaned the horse to Connor, along with the agent's black duster. Daniel withdrew his rifle from the scabbard, then pulled the lever down far enough to be sure a cartridge had been chambered. Satisfied, he resettled the rifle.

The agents, simultaneously, snapped the reins loose and swung up into leather. The slow and rhythmic footfalls of their horses echoed down a wide street lined with brick-front stores and a few tree-shaded yards—although the leaves had fallen—fronting prosperous-looking frame and brick houses. From there they spurred their horses, quickening the cadence from a lope to a gallop.

Mr. Weitbrec, Sheriff Price, Deputy Desmond, District Attorney Waldron, and four Pinkertons rode out of Pueblo with their black dusters flapping. When they reached the bridge to South Pueblo, Weitbrec reined in his horse. The others followed suit. The wind blew across the rushing water, and he clutched his Stetson to keep it from taking flight.

"Listen up, men. When we reach the Union Depot Complex, we'll go directly to the office of the train dispatcher. For those of you from out of town, that's the triangular-shaped building next to the depot. Sheriff Price will escort me and District Attorney Waldron into the building. Mr. Hardy, Santa Fe's dispatcher, should be there. Sheriff Price will serve him." Weitbrec looked each man in the eye. "Any questions?" When no one responded, he added, "Major Grant and Deputy Desmond will go in armed. The rest of you will remain outside guarding the door."

Daniel glanced at Connor and gave him a silent nod. Whatever Connor had been doing the last few years, a situation like this wasn't new to him. Even facing the possibility of hostile action, there was a relative calm about him.

The men crossed the Union Avenue passenger bridge and rode four abreast toward the train dispatcher's office. The hoof strikes grew louder, and their appearance, like eight avenging archangels, cleared the avenue of wagons, carriages, and pedestrians. The citizenry knew General Palmer's showdown with Santa Fe was coming. Men and women strolling the sidewalks hurried inside buildings at the sound of the thundering hooves, and the sight of the wind-spread tails of the black dusters. As they neared the property, they slowed their horses to a walk.

"Rick should be here. He'd get into this O.K. Corral-type showdown with outlaws and railroad magnates," Connor said.

Daniel pulled his hat another degree lower to shade his eyes. "Where's the O.K. Corral?"

"Tombstone, Arizona, although I wouldn't bet on it being a real place."

Neck-reining his Morgan, Daniel rode tall and easy in the saddle, both reins in his left hand, the other hand falling naturally at his side within easy reach of his six-shooter. "Been to Tombstone. Never heard of it."

"The corral must not be real, then. Sort of like today. When the history books are written, it'll probably have Doc Holliday and Bat Masterson with a cannon and a hundred men locked inside the roundhouse."

Daniel laughed. "I doubt today will ever be written about, but if it is, I'd much rather those two be mentioned in history books than here in Pueblo."

"Funny thing about history," Connor said, "once it's written, it's hard to correct the record. And if this goes down the way I think it will, with forcible removal, false imprisonment, and bribery, no one will ever want the record to reflect what really happened."

"We're not breaking the law," Daniel said.

"Funny thing about the law, too. Those who wear badges, for the right cause, get to bend it sometimes."

"Didn't know I was partnering up with a philosopher."

"Not me. I'm a cynical, beer-drinking former New York City cop. The only philosophizing I do is arguing with my stubborn sister and her former partner."

"New York City cop?"

Connor gave him a crooked smile. "Forget it. Long story. I'll tell you one day over a good cigar and a bottle of whisky."

"Sounds like a story that'll need more than one cigar."

Daniel rode into the complex and sat there a minute putting his questions aside before swinging aground. Shadows from the roof's overhang dappled the yard in shades of black and white. Rangy little trees, no more than seedlings, stood as dubious guards before the frame and brick building. Most of the trees in the area had been cut down and reborn as buildings for the rapidly growing town. Same as other mining towns throughout Colorado. Hard to tell one boomtown from another. The trains today were eerily silent, and except for some drunken hootin' and hollerin' a few blocks away, so was the town.

His men removed their rifles from hand-tooled scabbards, and together they tramped across the grade and climbed the porch leading to the office of the train dispatcher.

Sheriff Price stood at the door. "Mr. Waldron, Deputy Desmond, Mr. Weitbrec, and Major Grant, come with me. The rest of you stay here and keep watch."

Daniel hooked his coat behind his back, granting himself easy access to his Colt, then followed the sheriff, the district attorney, and Weitbrec into the office. He and the deputy took up positions near the closed door. A cold sweat slicked Daniel's neck that had nothing to do with the still air of the dispatcher's office and everything to do with Weitbrec's intentions.

With a sudden scraping of chairs, the men in the room, all attired in green eye-shades and leather cuffs at their wrists, bounded to their feet.

"Mr. Hardy," Sheriff Price said, "as you are an official of the Atchison, Topeka & Santa Fe Railroad, I'm serving you with this writ. You are to vacate the Rio Grande's property immediately or be arrested."

Mr. Hardy, a short man even in wedge-heeled boots, took the paper and read it. His face, anchored with a bushy black beard cut spade fashion, was pinched tight. He waved the writ in the air. "I can't honor this until I consult my superiors." He crinkled it in his hand and shoved it against Weitbrec's chest. "Come back tomorrow."

Weitbrec ripped the writ from Hardy's hand and smashed it into the opening of his vest. "You have twenty minutes. If you don't vacate the property, Sheriff Price will arrest you. Do you want to go to jail for Santa Fe?"

"Get out," Hardy said.

"You have twenty minutes. We'll be back," the sheriff said.

Weitbrec headed for the door. Daniel reached behind him, opened it, and was the last one to leave the office, never showing the occupants his back. Out on the porch, they regrouped.

"Hardy isn't going to leave voluntarily. Let's return to the hotel," Weitbrec said. "We need more men. Once we take this place, we'll move on to the roundhouse."

"The men have been gathering down the street at the Grand Central Hotel," one of Daniel's men said. "If we need deputies, that's where we should start. They're close by and ready to fight."

"If all that yelling is coming from them, then it sounds like the prefight drinking has already started," the sheriff said.

Weitbrec grabbed Deputy Desmond by the suspenders. "Take two Pinkertons with you to the Grand Central Hotel. Deputize a dozen men and get your asses back here in fifteen minutes. We're taking this place in twenty. Got it?"

Daniel huddled with his men. "We've got to keep the lid on this. Don't bring back any liquored-up recruits."

"What if they're all inebriated?" a Pinkerton asked.

Daniel let the brim of his hat intentionally hide his face, as if up close he was afraid of what his eyes might reveal. This was crazy shit, and if he and his men got out of here with no one getting shot, it would be a lucky day for the Pinkertons.

"Don't give them any damn bullets," he said.

When the men swung up into leather and galloped off, Daniel grabbed Connor's arm. "Come on. Let's go look around back." They circled the building, finding a door at the rear, windows on each side. "We've got to do this without any shooting. Any suggestions?"

"Don't post any guards at the windows or back door," Connor said. "If the men inside want to leave, let them go."

"There's no fight in Hardy. He made a show of it, but it was all bombast for his men. He won't put up any resistance. What worries me is a drunken deputized mob. If they smell blood, we'll have no control."

Weitbrec came around to the side of the building, slanting a suspicious look at Daniel. "What are you two talking about that has you glowering like a pair of thunderclouds?"

"We don't want any trouble. If we go in the front door and the men inside want to leave out the back, we'll let them go."

Weitbrec's eyes narrowed. "All I want is possession. Do it your way. But do it."

At the sound of pounding hooves, Daniel, Connor, and Weitbrec returned to the front of the depot. A dozen armed men carrying an overpowering smell of alcohol dismounted. Daniel wasn't sure any of the newly sworn could stand with their hand raised long enough to have recited the oath. The beat of his heart, throbbing along his neck, beat even faster.

"Line up," the deputy ordered, stringing his new recruits along the front of the building. "Let the men inside see they're surrounded."

The deputies, unsteady on their feet, lined up in a crooked line and pointed their weapons. The sheriff entered the building again along with Weitbrec, the district attorney, and Daniel. With the jeering deputies visible from the window, Hardy surrendered to the sheriff.

Daniel came out and walked with Connor a short distance from the building. "I was right. Hardy didn't want to fight. If that's the type of resistance we'll encounter at the roundhouse, we'll be out of here in an hour."

"This is like reality TV with actors pointing loaded weapons at innocent people."

"I don't know what reality teevee is, but alcohol and loaded guns are never a good mix. Let's get this finished."

Weitbrec came over and slapped Daniel on the shoulder. "It's time to take the depot. If it falls as easily as the dispatcher's office, this will go down without incident." He walked away to join the sheriff and district attorney in front of the depot.

"Police takedowns rarely happen without incident," Connor said.

"Weitbrec was a soldier," Daniel said. "He knows." Daniel walked away but returned immediately. "Look, I don't have a good feeling about this. Stay out of the way. I'm not taking ye back to Olivia with a bullet hole in yer gut."

Connor grabbed his arm. "I'm wearing protection. You aren't. Let me go first next time."

Daniel threw a glance at Connor's gripping hand. "Let go, agent." Connor released his hold. "Lady luck might be shining on ye, Irish, but I've a job to do. I'm ordering ye, hang back."

"You're not sidelining me to watch for bears to come galumphing down off those cliffs up there. I'm part of this."

Daniel shook his head, laughing. "Galumphing? Well, hell. Go around the back and if ye see any galumphing Santa Fe men, shoot 'em dead."

He sauntered off to join Weitbrec, the sheriff, and a dozen drunk deputies. He stopped just short of the single broad step to the porch. Mr. Brady, an agent for Santa Fe, met them at the door, hands on his hips.

"I have a writ signed by Judge Bowen, ordering you to vacate all Rio Grande property," the sheriff said.

"We're not vacating," Brady said, his jaws working methodically on a plug of tobacco. "If Judge Bowen wants to hold me in contempt, so be it."

From the side of the building came a slow drawl asking, "What are you doing here, Sheriff Price?"

Daniel spun around, his senses instantly turning toward trouble, and he silently groaned. Ben Thompson was pointing a shotgun, the barrels agleam in the sunlight. A .45 sagging along his flat thigh told Daniel he was possibly the most dangerous man he'd ever encountered. Anger written clearly across his features gave way to a calculating look. The shotgun rocked into line and now Daniel was staring into its twin bores. His mouth was dry with a salty taste. The taste of fear… But nothing happened. Thompson had a reputation as a fast gun, but he'd never killed anyone except in a fair fight. The muscles in Daniel's stomach knotted so tight they ached.

The seconds dragged on…

Finally, Thompson said, "I've been placed in charge of the company's property. I won't give it up without authorization by those in authority."

"Disburse your armed mob," Weitbrec said.

"There's no armed mob here, Mr. Weitbrec," Thompson said. "If any of these men are guilty of violating the law, you're at liberty to come in and arrest them."

Weitbrec waved his arm. "Come on, men. Let's go."

Thompson held his position. "Just you, Weitbrec, and the district attorney. No Pinkertons. No deputies."

49

1878 Pueblo, Colorado—Daniel

WEITBREC HUDDLED WITH the sheriff, the district attorney, and Daniel. "Go with Thompson," Daniel said, gun hanging at his side. "He isn't looking for trouble. Maybe ye can make a deal and bring this situation to an end before anyone gets hurt."

Weitbrec looked hard at Daniel. After a long moment, he nodded. "Come on, Waldron. Let's go." Weitbrec and the district attorney left with Thompson and entered the roundhouse.

Daniel and Connor waited with the others, counting the minutes as they ticked by at a turtle's pace. Finally, Weitbrec and Waldron returned, without the gunslinger.

"Let's go down to the hotel and organize," Weitbrec said. "I want this done right." While the men headed toward their horses, he pulled Daniel aside. "Take O'Grady with you. The bank has a black case filled with money. If we pay Thompson, he'll vacate the property, and there will be no more trouble."

"How much are ye paying him?" Daniel asked.

Weitbrec began cursing, pacing beyond them, then turned back again. "The case contains ten thousand dollars. Guard it well."

Daniel whistled. "Come on, Connor. Let's go collect the bribe."

Weitbrec grabbed Daniel's arm. "Keep this between us, Major. Bring the cash back to me at the Victoria Hotel."

Daniel pulled his arm from Weitbrec's grip.

"Good thing Masterson's not here," Connor said. "He'd never accept a bribe, and he won't like it when the story's told either." There was something in his tone, in the gravity etched on his features, that said he knew the truth and this wasn't it.

Daniel and Connor raked their horses with spurs and galloped away from the depot, away from South Pueblo, and over the bridge. If he could keep riding all the way back to Denver, he would. He was done with the Pinkertons. Done with life and death assignments. Done with men like Weitbrec and Thompson, and crooked sheriffs, and bought-off district attorneys.

Gray clouds scuttled across the sun and puffs of wind kicked up dust devils that swirled through the street. Daniel lowered his hat again to keep the dust from his eyes, and he seemed to shrivel from the outside in...

Enough. Enough. Enough.

Outside the bank, Daniel reined in his horse and tied up at the hitching rail where a half-dozen men had already racked their horses. "I'll be back."

He strode up to the teller's desk and asked for a satchel the bank was holding for Mr. Weitbrec. For the next several seconds the room's stillness hung heavy in the air, but a vast relief settled through Daniel when a man identified as the bank president walked out with a valise. "Are you Major Grant?"

Daniel nodded. "Is that Weitbrec's money?"

"You have to sign for it," the president said.

Daniel took possession of the bag, opened it, and checked the contents. "I'm not counting this."

"It's all there," the president said. "Ten thousand."

Daniel dipped a pen into an inkwell, signed his name, and included a note below his signature to indicate that he hadn't counted the money and was accepting it as-is.

The president blotted the signature then slipped the sheet of paper into a leather portfolio. "Do you need a guard to accompany you?"

Daniel shook his head. "Two Pinkertons can handle it." He left the bank, tied the valise to his rig, then stepped back into the saddle. "Let's get this done."

"I'm right behind you," Connor said.

They galloped back to South Pueblo, keeping their thoughts to themselves.

Opposite the Victoria Hotel, Daniel and Connor slid aground and looped the reins around the hitching rail. With an irritable shrug, Daniel, with Connor following, picked his way through the gathering mob and entered the hotel, removing his hat, and running his fingers through his sweaty hair.

He found Weitbrec pacing the lobby. "Are ye sure this is what ye want? Those men out there are drunk and well-armed. Somebody's going to get killed."

Weitbrec took the money bag. "If the situation gets out of control, we'll pay Thompson. He'll quit the depot property as soon as he gets paid. Now, get out there and keep those men from killing each other."

They walked away, and Daniel gave Connor a partner-style backhand across the chest. "Let's ride." Then he gave Connor an odd look. "What are ye wearing? A brick?"

"I told you I was wearing protection."

"Yeah, but I thought ye were talking about an Irish blessing or something."

"I'll show you later."

Daniel resettled his hat with careful deliberation. "Another long story."

They walked outside to find Deputy Desmond yelling at the new recruits. "Fix bayonets, men, and follow me."

"What the hell?" Connor said. "What do they think this is? A war?"

"Come on. We've got to beat them there."

Daniel led the way, riding hard down a side street, trying to get ahead of the men running the three-block distance to the depot where Sheriff Price was reportedly waiting. Daniel and Connor arrived moments before the mob, leaving their horses tied to the rail in front of the telegraph office. They ran to the depot, arriving in time to see a man in front of the pack knocked down. The solid *thwut* of fist hitting flesh was followed by yelps, and the prone man was hit repeatedly as he tried to rise.

Daniel pushed his way through the crowd. "Back. Move back." But he was rebuffed in the sweeping tide.

Connor ran into the crowd from another direction trying to steer the mob to one side of the man or the other, but he was pushed aside, and the crowd stepped on the injured man, squashing him into the dirt.

When Daniel finally reached him, the mangled, bloodied body lay seemingly lifeless.

Connor grabbed two men at the rear of the mob and ordered them at gunpoint to take the man to the doctor.

"We'll miss the showdown if we leave."

Connor noticed a newspaperman observing the scene from a distance and waved him over. "Get their names. Turn them into heroes for saving this injured man."

The writer lifted his hat briefly, his bald pate appearing and disappearing in a snap. He hurried behind the two new heroes and the victim.

The violence and blood fed the appetite of the already well-lubricated deputies. They yelled their next objective, "Let's take the telegraph office."

The mob ran toward the building. Deputy Desmond used the butt of his gun to break open the door. "Surrender now." The door was slammed shut, and the assaulting party commenced firing through the building.

When there was no return fire, Desmond ordered, "Cease firing."

Daniel and Connor ran to the back of the building as the drunken deputies stormed through the front door. A faint but sharp echo of a gunshot rode straight out on daylight and buzzed Daniel's head. A scream followed, and Daniel wheeled around.

"There," Connor said, pointing. "Man down!"

A bulky male figure loomed on the ground outside a busted window, blood seeping from a wound in his lower back.

"Man down!" Connor yelled again, grabbing a man running out of the building. "Get that wagon over there. This man needs a doctor."

The newspaper reporter stood over the victim licking the tip of his pencil before jotting in a small notebook. "This place is full of boorish brutes shooting guns, as if this is some ghastly dime novel come to life. What's this man's name? Anybody know?"

Deputy Desmond rolled the man over. "Looks like Harry Jenkins. He's from Dodge City." Desmond grabbed two deputies. "Get this man into the wagon. Take him to town."

The deputies carried Jenkins to the express wagon and dumped him unceremoniously into the bed. Then they jumped into the back of the wagon with the injured man. The driver slapped the team to a smart trot and headed toward town.

"Jesus. This is like the Keystone Cops," Connor said.

Daniel wiped his cheek with a handkerchief. "Who are they?" He folded over the blood on the handkerchief and wiped again.

"An incompetent group in pursuit of failure. Chaos on wheels. Ineffectiveness on steroids. Take your pick." Connor examined Daniel's face. "Looks like a bullet grazed your cheek. You need to get that looked at."

"Not now," Daniel said. "I'm still standing. Scratches can wait."

Weitbrec rounded the side of the depot with the black satchel snugged under his arm. "This situation has deteriorated. We have to pay Thompson now. Take the money to the back of the roundhouse. He's expecting you. Hurry before someone else gets shot."

Daniel could hardly speak around his mounting anger. "This never should have happened."

"It's on your shoulders," Weitbrec shouted, shoving Daniel in the arm. "I told you I didn't want any trouble."

Daniel stepped up close, almost nose to nose. "Ye didn't give a damn how this came down. Desmond gave guns and bayonets to drunks. What'd ye expect?" He yanked the satchel out of Weitbrec's hands and marched toward the roundhouse.

"If Weitbrec tries to blame this on the Pinkertons, I'll set his ass straight," Connor said, "and so will that newspaper man who's been tailing us since we first left the St. James."

"I never saw him," Daniel said. "I must be slipping."

"Nah, tailing is my specialty."

As they neared the roundhouse, Daniel wiped more blood from his cheek. "I guess I should get this looked at when we get back across the river."

"I got something that will work for now." Connor withdrew a paper square from his pocket, ripped part of it off, then pressed the remainder on Daniel's cheek. "There you go, buddy. If anybody notices it, just say a medic put it on you."

"Medic, huh. I guess that's the best I'm going to get."

"For right now, yeah."

They circled around to the back of the roundhouse. "Thompson. Get yer ass out here," Daniel yelled.

The door edged open. "Not likely," a disembodied voice said.

"If ye want yer money, ye'll get yer ass out here."

"If you're Major Grant, drop it by the door."

Daniel ordered Connor to stay back then yelled at Thompson, "Not until I see yer ugly face. Two men are severely injured. Probably won't make it. This is yer damn blood money. Get out here."

Thompson appeared, nostrils flaring, his thumb curled over the hammer of a horn-handled .45 against his thigh. The dark pattern of his beard plainly shadowed a broad face, and deep lines surrounded eyes and mouth. The knife-edge bridge of his nose was slightly thickened near the base by the ridge of a healed fracture.

Daniel set the bag on the unfinished wood floor. "Take the money. Get yer men out of this building now before that mob tears down that big old wooden door that ye think will protect ye. Trust me. It won't. Those men out front are crazed lions. They've smelled blood. They're coming after ye."

Thompson scooted the money bag with his foot. "Is it all

there?"

An old man with a tobacco-stained longhorn mustache snuck out the door, snatched up the bag, and ran back inside.

"Ye got all I was given."

Thompson slammed the door in his face.

Connor, standing at Daniel's back, said, "That's a fine how-do-you-do."

Daniel turned, glowering at Connor. "I told ye to stay back."

"And Olivia told me different."

Daniel stalked away. "When I give an order, I expect it to be followed. This is my command."

Connor followed him to the front of the roundhouse where a knot of men hovered near the door, their hands up, surrendering to the sheriff. With help from the inebriated deputies, the Santa Fe men were herded off the property. Interestingly, there was no sign of Thompson. Daniel considered searching the roundhouse, but he had no stomach for chasing after the gunslinger.

The newspaperman, writing in his notebook, followed behind the sheriff.

Daniel took off his hat and swiped his arm across his brow, removing a mixture of blood, sweat, and dirt. "Looks like ye were right. Somebody is writing down this story."

"I paid him. Told him I wanted the headline to be: 'Four Pinkertons and a Lady Rode into Town and Saved the Rio Grande.'"

Puzzled, Daniel faced him. "Ye did what?"

"Somebody had to set the narrative," Connor said with a hint of boyish mischief. "I don't want to read the story of what happened here and discover Masterson and Holliday led the resistance. They're not here and they're not getting credit. The Pinkertons deserve recognition."

"Olivia and Amber were the ones spreading the false story that Masterson and Holliday would be here."

The wariness that had settled in Connor's face over the last hour lifted. "They had bad intel."

Instead of looking directly at Connor, Daniel focused on the brim of his hat, which he was feeding through his fingers. "I don't understand ye, Connor. I don't understand Amber, Olivia, or Rick either, or Kenzie and David. I can't go on listening to all yer lies. We've got to part ways. I appreciate what ye did here today. But I can't skirt the truth with ye anymore. I'm done." He slammed his hat against his thigh. "I got to cut ye loose." He clapped his hat back on his head and strode away.

"Daniel, wait." Connor hurried after him. "On the trip back to Denver, Olivia and I will answer all your questions."

Daniel reached his horse and snapped the reins to untie them from the tie rail. "Ye'll just feed me more crap. I love Amber, but I can't do this anymore."

"I'm serious. We'll tell you everything. We'll open the kimono."

Daniel glared at him. "What the hell does that mean?" He swung up into the saddle and turned his horse in the direction of Pueblo. But he sat there, rubbing the back of his neck, wishing he could wipe away the desperate mixture of hope—that they would be honest with him—and fear—that they never would. Rambler pranced in excited circles.

"We'll open up, be honest. We'll tell you whatever you want to know." Connor mounted his borrowed horse. "No more side-stepping."

"Can I expect the same honesty from Olivia and Rick?"

"Yes, but after you hear it all, you'll be in the same pickle barrel you are now."

Daniel slanted a suspicious look at him. "I don't see how that's possible." He spanked the reins on Rambler's rump and rode off toward Pueblo, Connor riding after him.

When they reached the bridge, Daniel reined to a stop. "Let's take another bridge. Get away from the crowd." He spurred the horse and took a side street with a barely visible set of wheel-tracks branching off to the right.

"I vote we pick up Olivia and get the hell out of Dodge," Connor said.

"You've mentioned Tombstone and Dodge. Is that where ye've

been?"

"It's just an expression when you want to leave someplace."

"Why Dodge? Why not Kansas City or Denver?"

"What can I say? It's a piece of trivia from the dustbin of history." Connor's expression sobered. "Put it on your list of questions."

A trickle of sweat ran down Daniel's back between his shoulder blades, but he ignored it. Did he really want to know? Yes, dammit. He did. He had the grit to handle the ugly truth. Whatever it was.

Connor interrupted Daniel's reflection when he asked, "Is your assignment with the railroad over?"

"My career as a Pinkerton is over," Daniel said. "A stray bullet almost made Noah an orphan." Feeling a tightness in his chest, his gaze slid to the distant scrub-filled hills, stripped of timber. The thought of leaving his son alone scared Daniel more than his own death. "I got a telegram from Alec earlier today. He's leaving for San Francisco. He doesn't care enough for his grandson to stay with him while I'm on assignment."

Connor turned in his saddle to face Daniel, his mouth falling open. "I can't imagine a grandfather not wanting to be with a kid like Noah. What are you going to do?"

Daniel shook his head, sighing. "I don't know. I could always return to banking."

"That sounds boring."

"It is. That's why I quit and went back to the Pinkertons."

They rode in silence until they reached the St. James. As they dismounted, Daniel asked, "Ye got any whisky in that car ye rented?"

Connor looped the reins around the post and stretched his back. "I left the steward with a shopping list. The carriage should be supplied by the time we get there."

Daniel stepped up on the sidewalk and glanced around. The drunken mob had stayed on the other side of the river, leaving Pueblo's streets ringing with only the din of endless construction.

"I know it was hard to leave Olivia to go with me. I appreciate what ye did."

"If she hadn't insisted, I wouldn't have gone."

Daniel clapped Connor on the back. "Then I appreciate what Olivia did."

"I'm just relieved it's over and we can leave town."

Their flood of relief lasted until they cleared the threshold and ran smack into Rick. "What the hell are you doing here? You're supposed to be in Morrison," Connor said.

"You're supposed to be in Cañon City," Rick said.

"Where's Amber?" Connor asked.

Rick put his hands on his hips, and his gaze shifted from his brother to the floor and back again. "We have a problem. Her journal was stolen, and I'm tracking the asshole who took it." Rick reached into his pocket and pulled out a sketch. "She drew this. Have you seen him?"

Daniel looked over Rick's shoulder. He tugged the drawing out of his hand and thumped the paper with his finger. "He was here a couple of hours ago. Train service to Cañon City shut down, and he was forced to spend the night. There wasn't any room here. I don't know where he went. His name is Hendrix."

"If he's still here, we'll find him," Rick said.

"It's just a journal. I can't believe you came down for that," Connor said.

"She insisted. And I couldn't say no. Besides, there's a sketch of a family heirloom in the journal with a detailed description of how it works. There are also sketches of unknown dinosaurs."

Connor ripped off his hat and ran his hand through his hair. "Damn. We have to get it back. Where have you looked?"

"We've hit every saloon in Pueblo, and we're almost through our list of hotels," Rick said.

"We? Who's with you? David?" Connor asked.

Rick pointed over his shoulder at a man talking to the clerk at the registration desk. "Not this time."

Connor looked at the man, then shot a hot glance back at Rick. "What the hell? You've got some explaining to do."

The man turned, and Daniel came face to face with a ghost. He grabbed Connor's shoulder for support, shaking his head in denial. The man was the spitting image of Major McCabe, but that was impossible. He was dead.

Braham strode toward Daniel, extending his hand. "Good to see ye, Dan. I didn't know if ye'd recognize me. It's been a while."

Daniel clasped McCabe's hand, warm as summer sun. His own was cold as death. "Thirteen years. Ye haven't changed." Daniel released his grip on McCabe's hand and his hold on Connor's shoulder, as he slowly regained his senses. "I heard ye had a riding accident and died from the fall. So where have ye been all these years?"

"After we find Amber's journal, I'll tell ye what happened and why I disappeared."

To hear the same crap from Braham that he'd heard from the others pushed Daniel over the edge. He walked away, swallowing to dispel the thick ache in his throat.

Connor came after him. "Daniel. Wait."

Daniel pivoted. "No. Ye've yanked my chain long enough."

"But we're at the same place we were thirty minutes ago," Connor said. "Braham is a friend of ours. We're connected in an unusual way. But it's all part of the same story. Let's find Amber's journal, go back to the train, and we'll lay it all out for you."

"And after we find the journal, what will yer excuses be then?"

Connor blew out a long breath. "I won't have any. Neither will Rick, Braham, or the girls."

"Where's Amber now?"

"I assume she's in Denver."

Rick walked up and interrupted Connor's huddle with Daniel. "We're short on time. Are you going to help us, or not?"

"Where's Amber?" Daniel asked.

"She's with the doctor. That's why we're in a hurry. Are you going to help us?"

Daniel stiffened at the news, but then relaxed. He'd sent a telegram to Alec's doctor asking him to visit Amber. He must be with her now. A weight lifted from his shoulders. If finding her journal would make her happy, he had to help.

"Where have ye looked?" he asked.

Rick handed him a piece of paper. "Here's a list of all the hotels, boardinghouses, and saloons in Pueblo. We've visited more than half of them."

"What about the hotels and saloons in South Pueblo?" Connor asked.

"We've only looked on this side of the river," Rick said.

"Daniel and I will go back over there. We'll check the Grand Central Hotel, Victoria, Lindell, Topeka House, Commercial Hotel, a handful of saloons, and then meet back here."

"Where's the railroad car you rented for the day?" Rick asked.

"At Union Depot."

"Where's Olivia? Did she go back to Denver?" Rick asked.

"She stayed in Daniel's room upstairs while we settled a few matters."

Braham pointed to the side of Daniel's face. "That butterfly Band-Aid looks new. Must have been some serious settling."

"My head was in the wrong place, but others got it worse. There are hundreds of drunks running around with rifles and bayonets looking for trouble. Be careful."

Connor and Rick left the hotel ahead of Braham and Daniel, leaning into each other as they talked privately.

Out on the sidewalk, Rick said, "When we finish here, we'll pick up Olivia and meet you at the railroad car in, say…ninety minutes for a progress report? If we haven't found our guy by then, we'll start paying people to look."

Daniel opened his pocket watch. "Five o'clock?"

Braham checked the time on his watch. "We'll be there."

Connor and Daniel mounted up for another hard ride across the bridge. When they reached town and saw the streets still crowded with drunks, they proceeded cautiously.

"How long have ye known Major McCabe?"

"A few years. I met him at Montgomery Winery in Napa. I'm shocked to see him here."

"Why?"

Connor was quiet for a moment, as if deliberating where to start, and a frown creased his forehead. "It doesn't fit."

"What doesn't?"

"Something's wrong, but Rick wouldn't tell me."

Daniel turned in the saddle and leaned his hand on the horn. "He said Amber was with the doctor?"

"If something happened to her when her journal was stolen, and she needed immediate medical attention, the logical person to help her would be Braham's wife, Charlotte," Connor said.

"Why?"

"Because she's a damn good doctor. But if Rick took Amber to Charlotte…" Connor's eyes blinked rapidly, as if he couldn't believe what his mind was telling him.

"What?" Daniel asked. "Whatever yer thinking is turning yer face white."

In a shaky voice Connor said, "I think Rick took Noah and Ripley to the doctor, too."

Daniel let out a huge breath. "God, ye scared me. If Noah's with her, that's good. I trust the lad to watch over her."

Connor reined his horse around a large gopher hole. "I'm glad you feel that way. Let's find the journal, then figure out what to do next. Decisions will have to be made that won't be easy."

For Daniel there was only one action to be taken next. Go to Amber and Noah. Everything else was of little consequence.

50

1878 Pueblo, Colorado—Daniel

In South Pueblo, a rumble of unrest still hung in the air like a heavy thundercloud ready to burst open and flood the city. It would force the drunks to sober up or sink. From the blasts of honky-tonk music and raucous voices spilling out through the saloons' bat-wing doors, sobering up wasn't on anyone's mind. The tobacco juice-splattered boards were littered with broken bottles. Busted boxes filled with debris lined the alleys. It would take more than a heavy dousing to wash away the stink and filth.

The slow and rhythmic hoof falls of their horses accompanied Daniel and Connor's uncomfortable silence, each lost in their own thoughts of Amber and Olivia. What happened to one sister impacted the other and vice versa, which tied the four of them in a tightly bound circle, sort of like Dumas' *The Three Musketeers*—all for one, and one for all.

After threading their way through the clog of drivers sawing the reins of their carriages, construction workers hauling building materials, and pedestrians dodging wheels and hooves, they arrived at the Victoria Hotel. The previous crowds had disbursed, and hotel employees were sweeping rubbish from the boardwalk in front of the entrance.

Daniel reined up alongside the hotel and dismounted with a groan, bones creaking. "Let's split up and meet back here in forty-five minutes."

"Sounds like a plan. You go left. I'll go right. When we finish this side of the street, cross over and go down the other." Connor unfolded his copy of the sketch and looked hard at Hendrix's face, scowling as he did.

"Son of a bitch's face is imprinted on my brain. Hope ye find him first."

"We're tried to control the violence all afternoon. Let's not lose it now," Connor said.

"Put your badge in a more prominent place. Let everyone ye ask know ye're on official business."

Connor repinned the badge on the collar of his borrowed duster. "If Hendrix hears Pinkertons are looking for him, he'll leave town or go to ground."

"Where's he going to go? This isn't a big city, and it'll be dark soon. He won't leave now for a forty-mile trek to Cañon City. We'll find him."

Daniel left Connor in front of the Victoria Hotel and walked east, his spurs clinking on the boardwalk as he elbowed his way into one establishment after another. At the end of Union Avenue's business district, he crossed over and headed down the other side.

Each time a barkeep or desk clerk said, "I haven't seen him," Daniel's impatience grew. Twice, he was sent chasing men who looked nothing like Hendrix. Sooner or later, someone would point a finger in the man's direction just to get Daniel—the looking-for-a-fight Pinkerton agent—off the streets.

He was tired, pissed, and hungry. But most of all, he was worried about Amber. If she was under Charlotte's care, what did that mean? He had to get back to Denver to be with her. Memories of his late wife's death haunted him. She'd already delivered one healthy baby, and the midwife had no reason to believe she'd have trouble with the second. Alec had sent him a wire, telling Daniel to come home, which he did. Two days later, he had buried his beloved wife and newborn daughter. He couldn't bury another woman he loved.

By the time he met Connor in the middle of the block, he was ready to call it quits. "I can't waste more time looking for him. I'm going back to see Amber."

"I found him," Connor said. "He's sitting at a table in a saloon next to the Linton Hotel. I paid a man to keep buying him drinks until I returned. It will only take a few minutes. If Rick came here for the journal, it's important to Amber. And I don't want to disappoint her."

What Connor didn't say was that it would be important to Olivia, too.

"All right," Daniel said. "But are ye sure it's him?"

Connor's green eyes creased briefly. "Give me a break. I'm a former Marine and a decade-long New York City detective with a master's degree in criminal justice. I can identify a perp across a goddamn crowded bar."

The normally even-tempered Connor O'Grady had reached the proverbial limit. He was disheveled, sweaty—and not to put too fine a term on it—almost done in. Daniel's shoulders raised and lowered on a deep breath. The term applied to him, too.

"How do ye want to play it?"

Connor hammered a loose sidewalk board with the heel of his boot, taking his frustration out on a rusty nail. "Short of dragging him out and beating the shit out of him, I don't know. He's holding tight to a leather-tooled piece of hand luggage. The journal is probably in there."

"Noah wanted a journal like Amber's for their trip today. I took him to the store first thing this morning. He picked one out that he said resembled hers. It has a brown leather wrap cover, looped tie, with a tree design on the front."

"What size?"

"Four by five."

"We need to separate him from the valise." Connor stomped on the board one last time and it slipped back into place. "Hendrix has a look about him. Like he's holding the Holy Grail. If he's hoping for a big payoff, he won't let go of the bag until he gets his money. Not for a drink. Not for a woman. Not even at gunpoint."

"No man can resist all three. The first two are easy enough. The last one not so much," Daniel said.

"I got an idea," Connor said. "You said Hendrix was looking for a room at the St. James. Tell him you're checking out and he can have yours, but he has to go with you now. We'll take him someplace, I don't know, private, and search him. If he doesn't have the journal, then I'll beat the shit out of him." Connor unpinned the Pinkerton badge and dropped it in Daniel's pocket. "I'm tired, hungry, and I want my woman. I'm done with this nineteenth-century crap. Whatever I do going forward, I don't want it to reflect on you or the agency."

Daniel didn't completely understand what Connor meant, but he got the gist of it. Except for the two years he worked as a banker, he'd been a member of the Pinkerton Agency since he was twenty years old. He unpinned his own badge and stared at the tin, glinting in his hand. Then he shoved it into his pocket where it joined its mate.

"Whatever I do, I don't want it to reflect on the agency either. Let's get the son of a bitch."

They marched up the street with more purpose than a couple of generals about to go into battle. When they reached the saloon, they split up. Daniel went in the open front door and Connor used the side door. The cool air blowing in from the street did little to alleviate the stench of sweat, the stale smell of tobacco, and the heavy scent of whisky and beer leaking from broken bottles and soaking into the sawdust covered floorboards. Upturned tables were in the process of being righted and busted chairs tossed aside.

Daniel spotted Hendrix the moment he entered the saloon. He didn't acknowledge the man, he just kept walking. When he reached the bar, he rested his foot on the footrail. "What the hell happened here?"

The barkeep dipped a rag into a bucket of soapy water, rinsed it out, and washed another section of the sticky bar top. "The Rio Grande deputized a slew of liquored-up miners to help reclaim its property. Trashed the town and got two men killed."

Daniel removed his hat, scratched a thatch of sweat-soaked hair, then clapped it back on his head. No one was supposed to get hurt. The responsibility for the damage to the town and the loss of two lives fell on the sheriff's shoulders, Weitbrec's, and the Pinkertons. The agency had been hired to protect the Rio Grande's property and people, and to keep the lid on a volatile situation. They'd failed. He'd failed. A bad day all around. Was there ever going to be an end to it? Would he ever find the peace he so desperately wanted?

"Do you want a drink, or are you just going to watch me work?" the barkeep asked.

"Whisky. And not the cheap stuff," Daniel said.

The barkeep opened a cabinet behind the bar, and the tinkle of glass against glass followed as he moved bottles around to find a specific one. He lifted a bottle of Macallan for Daniel to see. Daniel gave him a nod. After pouring a measure of the amber-colored liquor, he slid the glass across the now-clean oak top to Daniel.

"That good enough?"

Daniel placed a one-dollar note on the bar and fingered the worn greenback before letting go of it, eyeing the barkeep closely. "Keep the bottle out." He leaned against the bar and tilted his head back to let the robust liquor slide down his throat. The first sip was to quench his thirst. It burned a clear path through his dusty throat to his stomach. The second was a restorative gulp. The third was for pleasure.

Without acknowledging Daniel, Connor walked up to the bar and ordered a drink from the same bottle, slapped down a couple of coins, then carried the glass over to a table. He righted a chair and sat with his back to the wall. Daniel watched him for a beat or two, waiting for him to point out the man he believed to be Hendrix.

The signal came—a look, a nod. Connor downed his drink, and after a minute or two, pushed to his feet, and casually left the saloon.

It was Hendrix, all right, with his recognizable Van Dyke beard. He didn't need Connor's confirmation, but after chasing the wrong guy twice, it was nice to have. Daniel ordered another drink and strode over to the table where Hendrix sat alone, observing every man who plodded into the saloon.

"Didn't I see ye at the St. James earlier? Hendrix, right?"

The man tipped back his bowler hat and looked up at Daniel. "You're the Pinkerton man. You get the trains running?" Hendrix drew circles with his wet glass on the dark wood table.

Daniel put his foot on a chair and braced his forearm on his knee, leaning forward. "Trains to Cañon City will be running tomorrow."

Hendrix's eyes darted about the dimly lit saloon, doubt plain in his expression.

"Did ye find a room?" Daniel asked.

"Still looking."

"I can tell." Daniel let his condescension hang in the air for a moment. Then, "Ye're in luck. I'm checking out of the hotel. I just came here to meet my men to let them know. If ye want the room, it's all yers. It's paid for."

Hendrix's eyes popped wide open, as if he'd been half asleep and just woke up. "Mighty kind of you."

"The only problem is, ye have to go now. I need to be in Denver early in the morning, so I'm leaving town. The hotel won't hold the room for ye. They'll just rent it to someone else and get paid double." Hendrix looked unconvinced, so Daniel added, "It's a big room. I even left a half bottle of whisky."

The hunger in Hendrix's face was palpable. He clutched the handle of the valise in his lap, as if it were a Leadville silver mine that had assayed well and was worth staking a claim on. "Can't believe they'd rent it again. That's not right. Not fair."

"Ye know," Daniel said, "there's not much in life that is fair."

Hendrix rubbed his face, rearranging the creases, as he looked about the crowded saloon. "Better not leave. Supposed to meet a man here." He broke eye contact, hawked, and spat on the floor, barely missing Daniel's boot.

Daniel itched to yank the asshole out of the chair by his scrawny neck and shake him until it broke right off. "Suit yerself. Just trying to help. Maybe yer new friend can get ye a room at the St. James."

Daniel swirled the remaining liquid in his glass before draining what was left. He glared at the tumbler as if it had betrayed him, then set it down and moved away from the table.

Hendrix shoved to his feet, the valise nestled under his arm. "Wait. I'll go. If I don't take your room, I'll be sleeping on the street."

"My horse is in front of the Victoria," Daniel said. "How'd ye get here?"

"Rented a horse. It's tied up at the rail outside."

"Mount up. I'll be right behind ye." Daniel walked off the sidewalk into the broad dirt-packed street, like so many others he'd seen in Colorado towns, a quagmire of mud when it rained or snowed and rutted and dangerous when dried. He'd walked across too many and had never seen much improvement from the other side.

"Didn't know Pinkertons were so helpful."

"I'm not a Pinkerton. I just borrowed the badge." He seized the reins and swung into the saddle and rode away, trusting Connor to be close by. He caught up with Hendrix and together they headed down Union Avenue.

"Let's go this way," Daniel said. "I've ridden across that passenger bridge so many times today, I can't fight the crowd again. It's shorter this way."

With the afternoon dipping into sunset, they took the same detour he and Connor had taken earlier in the day. The clop-clop of Daniel's horse echoed along the unusually quiet street. He slapped the reins occasionally to encourage Rambler forward. It had been a long day for his horse, too. He deserved a good brushing and a fresh bucket of oats.

"I've got to take a piss," Daniel said. "I'm going to stop at that abandoned building over there."

Hendrix grumbled. "Hurry it along. I got to get back."

As soon as Daniel reined into the empty lot, Connor rode up from another direction, whistling an old Irish sea shanty, one of the songs Rick and Amber had sung in Leadville. Connor stopped when his horse stood nose to nose with Hendrix's horse. He lifted his hat, wiped the grime from his forehead with a bandanna pulled from his coat pocket, and slapped the hat back on again.

"I thought that was you, Major. Heard you were leaving town. Sheriff wants to see you before you go."

Daniel swung down and tied the reins to a stunted pine that couldn't decide whether it was a bush or a tree. "Don't care to see the sheriff tonight. Spent too much time with him today already."

"Suit yourself. I'm just passing along the message."

Daniel turned his back to Connor and Hendrix, unbuttoned his trousers and relieved himself. After rebuttoning his pants, he sidled up next to Hendrix, who was slumping in his saddle. If he could find Amber's journal without resorting to violence, he would, but something told him the asshole wouldn't give it up easily.

Daniel reached up and jerked Hendrix out of the saddle. The man landed with a *whuff* facedown, the valise cocooned between his stomach and the ground. He rolled, carrying the bag with him, and sprang to his feet.

"What the hell are you doing?"

Daniel snatched the valise from him. Hendrix looked around as if he were seeking allies, but Connor only scowled at him, arms crossed over the pommel.

"Leave my property alone."

Connor dismounted. "We're only looking for something that belongs to a friend."

Daniel unbuckled the straps, dumped the contents on the ground, and tossed the valise aside. He stooped and pilfered through shirts and vests, a collar and cuff box, and another small wooden box with shaving gear and hairbrush. No journal.

Hendrix snatched up the valise, hugging it to his chest, and stepped back.

Daniel swept through the clothes. "It's not here." He opened the collar and cuff box, dumped the contents. Nothing. He emptied the other box and searched it, too. Nothing.

"Look inside the valise," Daniel said.

Connor made a move to grab the case from Hendrix, but he

wasn't going to give it up easily. They twisted and jerked for control, until Connor, taller and heavier, ripped it away. When he did, a Colt Derringer appeared in Hendrix's hand.

"Give it back."

Connor, ignoring Hendrix's threat, opened the valise and thumped against the stiff-leather sides. The sound of ripping cloth rent the air. "Oops," Connor said, lifting out a leather journal. "I sort of tore your fancy bag." He threw it down but held tightly to the journal.

Daniel stood and took a step forward.

"Stay where you are." Hendrix waved the gun in Daniel's direction. "Drop your guns. Both of you." When they didn't move, Hendrix cocked the Derringer. "Drop them. Now."

If Daniel could distract Hendrix, it would give Connor an opening. If Connor could distract him, Daniel would have an opening.

Daniel and Connor lifted their Colts from their holsters.

"Set 'em down," Hendrix said.

They set the guns on the ground.

"Now, kick 'em over here," Hendrix said.

They gave their guns a little shove with their boots.

"Give him the journal, Connor. It's not worth it." Getting back to Amber and Noah in one piece was more important than returning her notebook. Hendrix could have it. Sell it. Burn it. Daniel didn't care.

Connor waved it in the air like a Bible-thumping preacher. "This has all of Amber's notes for the book she's writing about dinosaurs. It took her years to create these creatures. It's all make-believe. It's original and creative. And I'm not letting Marsh have it."

Shocked warred with caution in Hendrix's face. "You're lying. The boy told his teacher in Leadville about the *Stegosaurus*. Told him the Kelly woman had more pictures. I saw 'em in that book."

Just as Daniel had his panic spooled up and put away, he stiffened. "What boy?"

"How much do you want for the book?" Connor did an eyebrow hike. "Whatever you've been offered, I'll double." He reached toward his pocket.

"What boy?" Daniel asked again.

"Leave your hands where I can see them," Hendrix said.

"I've got plenty of money. How much is Marsh paying you?" Connor asked.

There was a flash of something in Hendrix's eyes, as if he was calculating how he could benefit the most.

Running out of patience, Daniel asked a third time, "What boy?"

Hendrix gestured toward Daniel with the gun. "Your kid." Then he swept the gun back to Connor. "You don't have the kind of money Marsh has."

Daniel advanced on Hendrix, his hands curling into fists. "What does Noah have to do with this?" Hendrix swung the gun toward Daniel again, and he backed off.

"We dogged you all the way from Leadville to Denver and waited for our chance. It came today. Now, give me the journal."

"You only have one bullet." Connor's tone was both deliberate and cold. "You might get one of us but not both."

"I have more than one. I don't want to shoot either one of you, but I will." He held out his hand, wiggling his fingers. "Give me the journal."

"Can't do it," Connor said. "The sketches aren't real. Marsh will realize he's been tricked and will come after us."

Daniel calculated the steps he had to take to end the standoff without anyone getting hurt, but before he could make a move...

Connor lunged.

Hendrix pulled the trigger.

Connor went down.

"No!" Daniel yelled and braced himself, but there was no second shot, only a punch that grazed the point of his jaw, solidly jarring his senses. The second of a one-two punch was a hard right, low in the chest. The wind *whooshed* from Daniel's lungs and for a full second, he stood there shocked and paralyzed by the pain in his ribs.

Hendrix took a step back and cocked his shoulder for another swing, but Daniel blocked it, planted his boots wide and threw a punch, hitting the left side of Hendrix's jaw with the full weight of his body, causing a bone-crunching snap.

Teeth and blood spurted out.

Daniel threw another jab, breaking Hendrix's nose, then a body shot—like dry wood splintering—landed on the bottom of Hendrix's rib cage. He fell face down in the slime. In his semi-smothered breathing, he coughed a muffled sob against the stillness of the abandoned lot.

Daniel thrust his boot, pitched Hendrix onto his back, staring with disgust at the half-conscious man. He stooped over him and jerked the coat open, finding a Navy Colt revolver in a holster at Hendrix's left armpit. Anger flared anew, and he threw the weapon far out over the empty lot. "Ye goddamn son of a bitch." The gun landed with a splat.

He turned quickly to Connor, who was on the ground in a partially sitting position.

"Remind me to never to piss you off," Connor said. "You've got a mean right hook."

Daniel, his heart in his throat, patted Connor's chest. "Where are ye shot?"

"Got me dead center."

Daniel snagged one of Hendrix's shirts to staunch the bleeding but when he yanked Connor's coat open, he didn't see any blood. "Ye aren't bleeding?"

Connor made a move to stand. "You sound disappointed? Help me up."

"Are ye sure?"

"No, I'd rather sit here in the muck."

Connor picked up the journal and leaned on Daniel, who was stiff and sore, and the flexing of his muscles to help Connor made him wince at his complaining ribs.

"Damn, it hurts," Connor said.

"Where?"

Connor glanced down at his foot. "My ankle. I've got to get my boot off before it swells."

Daniel thrust out a breath and allowed himself a semblance of a smile. "Are ye telling me he shot yer ankle?"

"No, when I lunged, I tripped on a blasted rock, turned my ankle, and went down."

"Ye tripped? Ye weren't shot?"

"Yes, I was shot. Didn't you hear it?"

"But ye're not bleeding."

"That old pea-shooter wouldn't penetrate my lucky vest." Connor hobbled toward his horse. "Let's get out of here. I need to ice my ankle."

"A vest stopped the bullet?" Daniel patted his hand down Connor's chest. "It feels soft on the outside." Daniel thumped near Connor's breast bone. "But it sounds hard on the inside. What's it made of?"

"A synthetic fiber called Kevlar. And, I need a drink."

"I want to see it."

"Hell, you can have it, just get me a whisky within the next thirty seconds, and you can sleep in it for the rest of your life." Connor reached his horse, held on to the pommel, and swung up into the saddle.

Hendrix groaned, and Daniel shot a look back at the man twitching on the ground. After terrorizing Amber, he wasn't inclined to help the son of a bitch. He picked up their guns and his hat. He slapped it against his leg to shake off the mud, then settled it on his head.

"I don't like it when people mess with my friends, and I hate it when they mess with my family. Let's get out of here," Connor said.

Daniel swung up into the saddle, rubbing Rambler's neck. "I promise ye some oats, boy, just hang on a wee bit longer."

The railroad complex was two blocks away, back toward town. They rode off, leaving Hendrix still moaning on the ground. They passed the dispatcher and telegraph offices and kept riding. A well-lit carriage stood off by itself on the other side of the roundhouse. The roller blinds had been pulled down and shadowy outlines of two men and a woman were visible.

"Looks like Rick, Olivia, and Braham are already there," Connor said.

Daniel glanced around for the general's car. He must have left town before they'd marched on the dispatcher's office. Tomorrow, Daniel would write his report, turn in his badge, then call on the general. He didn't intend to burn bridges, but he would let the general know all the mistakes the railroad made today.

He and Connor dismounted at the car's rear platform and Daniel helped Connor mount the steps. "I'm going over to the dispatcher's office and arrange a hookup to take us back to Denver. Pour me a drink."

Daniel left his horse tied to the railroad car but took the borrowed horse with him. After arranging the return trip to Denver, he walked outside and whistled. A minute later, the Pinkerton agent he'd left to guard Olivia came out of the shadows.

"What'd ye find out?" Daniel asked.

"The lady never left her hotel room until two men showed up ten minutes ago and brought her here."

Daniel handed the agent the reins to the borrowed horse. "I appreciate ye watching her. I wasn't sure how it would shake out. I'll see ye back in Denver. Oh," he reached into his pocket and took out a few bills. "Yer duster has a bullet hole. Buy yerself a new one." They shook hands and Daniel walked slowly back to the carriage.

Olivia's innocence, at least as far as the railroad was concerned, had never been an issue, but she and Connor and Rick, and now Braham were hiding something big, and it was time everyone laid their cards on the table.

The fumes inside the carriage poured out to greet him—a heady mix of roast turkey, fresh rolls, lake trout, and whisky blended with a fog of cigar smoke.

Connor invited him in with a limp and a grand sweep of his arm, and Olivia, pulling off her gloves, finger by finger, welcomed him with her hazel eyes. An emotion Daniel couldn't identify nearly brought him to his knees.

From the window, Pikes Peak, its highest reaches snow-powdered in the fall moonlight, rose above the darkling lower range.

And a story began that Daniel knew in his heart would change the rest of his life.

51

1878 South Pueblo, Colorado—Daniel

DANIEL SAT FORWARD in one of the over-stuffed chairs in the sitting room of Connor's rented railroad car, watching Connor and Braham shuttle uneasy glances back and forth. But it was Olivia's barely leashed composure that concerned him most. Her eyes were filled with tears, and she was mangling a limp linen handkerchief, sniffing and dabbing at her nose. Connor's arm encircled her, holding her close, her head on his shoulder. His bootless foot was propped up on an ice-soaked towel. Rick paced the carriage, chomping down on an unlit cigar. Tension rumbled through the carriage, and Daniel was about to snap like a cut wire.

"Is Amber at Alec's house?"

"She's in the hospital resting comfortably," Braham said. "She's receiving excellent medical attention. If ye want to see her, ye can. Ye can hold her hand, talk to her, hug her, but first we have a few things to talk about." Braham handed Daniel a glass of whisky. "Let's take this slowly. There's a lot to digest."

"I don't need whisky to hear the truth. Connor said ye'd tell me everything. Start talking."

"The whisky will help what I have to tell ye go down easier." Braham nudged Daniel's hand with the glass. "Look at yer hands. They're shaking." When Daniel still refused to accept the drink, Braham gave up and set the crystal on a table next to the chair. Then he dug into a saddlebag, pulled out a cigar, and laid it next to the glass. "That's the best cigar ye'll ever smoke."

"I don't want a damn cigar. I don't want whisky. Ye're stalling and that makes me madder than hell. If my hands are shaking, it's because they want to wrap around yer neck and squeeze the truth from ye. Spill it. My hands aren't going to listen to me much longer."

Braham withdrew another cigar and ran it under his nose. "The wrapper is Connecticut, the binder is Cameroon, and filler is Dominican. It's a dark, toothy five-year-old wrapper and the mix of Cameroon and Dominican long-leaf fillers brings out a different type of flavor. Ye'll get sweet earth and maybe a wee bit of coffee off the foot."

Braham was pushing him. But why? Finally, Daniel reacted. He bounded to his feet and grabbed Braham by the lapels. "I don't give a damn about the cigar's foot. What are ye hiding. Where's my son? Where's Amber?"

Braham waited a beat before saying, "She's gone home. To the twenty-first century."

Daniel's head snapped to the side as if he'd been slugged in the jaw. Hendrix had slugged him, but this verbal punch was ten times worse. He shot hot glances to Rick, Connor, Olivia. Their expressions were identical to Braham's.

"Gone home?" Daniel ignored the rest of Braham's statement. It was incomprehensible. He let go of Braham's lapels and dropped to the chair.

She's gone home.

A cold sweat slicked his neck that had nothing to do with the still air in the carriage. It took a minute or two to pull himself together. When he could finally speak again, he asked, "Where's Noah?"

Rick pulled a chair up in front of Daniel, holding Noah's face in a shiny little black box. It was too real looking to be a photograph. Daniel recoiled at the image, and then he touched his son's face, and it moved. He jerked his hand, and yelled, "Noah. My God. Where are ye, lad? What's happened to ye?" He shoved away Rick's hand holding the shiny box. "Where's my son? What have ye done to him?"

"Hey, Pa. Don't be scared."

Daniel quivered. He looked at the box again, his muscles tightening with a strange sense of fear—an urge to protect—yet helpless to do so.

"I'm not really inside the box, Pa. This is called a video. It's a moving picture of me. I'm in Richmond, Virginia. In the twenty-first century. Amber is sick and needs an operation. Ripley got hit on the head and she has a concussion. I'm here with Lincoln. He belongs to Braham and Charlotte. He was named after the president. Lincoln and Patrick are the smartest kids I've ever met. Patrick is from 1909. He's only been here a few months, but you'd never know he came from someplace else. He knows what it's like to jump in time."

Jump in time?

Terror, unlike anything Daniel had ever experienced, even in the war, took hold and rattled him. He leaned forward and yelled at the box, "Noah. What have they done to ye?"

"Pa, I know you don't understand where I am. You're looking at my likeness and listening to my voice. Rick and Braham and Olivia and Connor know the truth. Trust them, Pa. Amber wants to see you before the doctors operate on her heart. Rick asked me if I wanted to go back with him to find you, but I couldn't leave Amber and Ripley. That's why I'm still here. If I left Amber, I'd never see her again. Just like Ma. I had to stay with Amber and Ripley. They need me."

"Noah. I need ye."

"Don't be afraid, Pa. I know it looks scary, but when you get here, you won't be scared. I promise. If I was afraid, I'd tell you. But I'm not. It's nice here. The people are nice. I don't understand most of what I see and hear, but Patrick said it won't take me long. Hurry up, Pa."

"Noah, come back, lad. Come back to me." Daniel had lost his wife and infant daughter and now he'd lost his son and Amber. A drop of blood from one of his cuts fell onto Noah's face.

"It's okay," Rick said. "I can fix it." He used a napkin and Noah's clean face appeared again.

"Noah," Daniel groaned.

Then Amber came on the little box, and Daniel jerked. She had tubes and gadgets all around her and something stuck in her nose. He touched her face. "Amber."

"Daniel…" Her voice sounded less stressed and she wasn't struggling to breathe. "I'm going to be operated on in a few hours. If you come with Rick and Braham, you'll get here in time. We can talk. I'm so sorry I lied to you, but I didn't think you'd understand. Please come. I love you."

And then she was frozen inside the little shiny box.

Daniel glanced up at the people in the room. "Ye took my lad. Now he's stuck in this little box with Amber." He got up and walked to the door. "I don't know who ye are, what kind of magic ye're using, or how I'll ever get Noah back, but I swear to God, I will."

He left the railroad car and swung up into the saddle, but he just sat there, arms crossed over the pommel. Where did he think he was going? He couldn't leave, not without knowing how to get Noah back.

Braham walked out onto the platform and held up a glass of whisky. "I thought ye might want this while ye plan what to do next. Sometimes it clears a man's thinking. Other times it hops around like hail and dulls the imagination." He lifted the glass in a mock salute. "Here's to clear thinking."

Daniel took it. "Ye can't imagine how confusing this is."

Braham chuckled. "Afraid I do. It happened to me, too."

"I doubt it."

Braham lit a cigar and puffed to get a good burn.

"Did ye bring one of those for me?" A cigar materialized, and Daniel lit it, puffing, sending the rich fragrance into the air. "How long has it been since we shared a cigar?"

"Probably when we were chasing the Confederate gold."

Rambler pricked his ears and whickered as if agreeing. "I doubt it'll ever be found."

Braham's face, perfectly at peace in the lamplight spilling from the open door, burst into a smile. "Kenzie found it."

"Kenzie is a canny woman, but if two dozen Union officers couldn't find a lead, I doubt she could."

"My wife's brother got a lead on it first. Then Kenzie deciphered the clues and identified the location. David and I dug it up. It was a group effort."

"Did ye keep it? I never heard it was found."

"We turned it over to the state of California. But I digress." Braham leaned against the railing, cigar propped between his fingers. "There's a lot to talk about before we get to the treasure hunt."

Daniel dismounted and joined Braham on the platform. "Start talking." A blue cloud of smoke quickly obscured the air between them.

"Do ye remember when I was captured by the Rebs in Richmond?"

"Shot in the gut. Yeah, I remember."

"If I survived they intended to hang me," Braham continued. "That didn't sit well with President Lincoln. He twisted the arm of a Confederate surgeon to smuggle me out of Chimborazo Hospital."

"I remember ye disappeared then showed up weeks later in Washington, miraculously healed," Daniel said.

"The Confederate surgeon..." Braham puffed on his cigar. "Her name is Charlotte Mallory. She took me to her hospital in the twenty-first century."

Daniel stared at Braham, recalling what Connor had said... *If she needed immediate medical attention, the logical person to help her would be Braham's wife Charlotte.* He stared incredulously at Braham.

"She operated on me and saved my life," Braham said. "After surgery, I recuperated at her plantation near Richmond. While I was there, I found a book about President Lincoln. It described his assassination. I knew then that I had to return and save the President's life. Charlotte was adamant that I couldn't change history. But I had to try."

"Ye knew he was going to be shot, yet ye didn't save him. After all he did for ye, and ye couldn't do it for him?"

"I was going to Ford's Theatre, but he wanted me to take a document to Secretary Seward's house. I was caught in the assassination attempt on Seward's life and arrived at the theatre too late."

"Why didn't ye tell someone? They could have stopped it."

"The president knew assassins would try to kill him. If not that night, the next. I could have told the whole damn city an attempt would be made on his life. He was an easy target, and he didn't intend to change. The Lincolns could have stayed home that night. Gone the next. Booth and his group of conspirators would have adjusted their plans. The president was determined not to hide or show any fear."

"Ye should have told him."

"I decided to stay by his side and prevent it from happening. But what we learned was that we can't change history. We can tweak it a wee bit, but we can't change major events. For me, it will always be a personal failure."

"Not saving the president is more than a personal failure."

"Ye don't have to remind me."

"So where have ye been for a decade?"

"I fell in love with Charlotte," Braham said, "but she wouldn't stay in the past and I refused to go back to the future. We separated, and I returned to California. After a couple of years, I asked a woman to marry me, but I never stopped loving Charlotte. Before I could marry, I came to my senses, cancelled the wedding, faked my death, and disappeared. I've been living in Richmond, Virginia, in the twenty-first century with her and our three children. I'm a contented man. I have my vineyards and racehorses. I write books and search for the perfect cigar."

"I'm glad ye're happy, but where are Amber and Noah, and how do I get them back?"

"Amber is in a hospital in Richmond, Virginia. She's very sick. As Noah said in his video, he didn't want to leave her and Ripley. He wanted us to come here to get ye."

Olivia walked out onto the platform, clutching Amber's journal.

"My sister needs open-heart surgery to replace a valve in her heart. She wants to see you, Daniel, before she has surgery. If I have to tie you up and kidnap you, I will. I'll do anything for her. When Kenzie and Connor told me that Amber traveled back to 1878, I didn't believe them. I said some hateful things that I regret now. Every time Amber lied to you, it ripped out pieces of her heart. You're having trouble with the truth now. What would you have done if she'd told you the truth the day you met?

"Would you have believed her if she'd told you Craig Hughes is our seven-times great-grandfather? Would you have believed her if she admitted to graduating from Yale with a degree in geology? She is the gutsiest woman I've ever met. And I need to go home. I need to see her, and I need to call our parents. It's time to go, Daniel."

All the odd words and inconsistencies he'd heard from Amber, Olivia, Kenzie, David, Rick, and Connor all spun around in his head. It didn't make sense, but if his son wasn't afraid, it couldn't be so bad.

"I'll go, but I won't live in a little box."

"Amber and Noah aren't living in a little box. That's how we communicate with each other. Like you send telegrams. We have other methods. You'll be just like you are now. Same stubborn Scot, and when you meet Elliott Fraser, you'll be in great company."

"And ye're certain I can come back with Noah and Ripley?"

The air on the platform was clouded by the haze of cigar smoke and coal oil lamps. Olivia used her hand to fan it away. "This isn't a forever decision."

Daniel flicked the cigar ash over the railing, wishing he could flick away his fears as easily. "When is Amber's surgery?"

"Without getting into time traveling technicalities, surgery is scheduled for early in the morning," Braham said.

Daniel did a few mental calculations. He'd taken the train from the East coast to the West coast and knew from personal experience getting to Virginia from Colorado in twelve hours was impossible. He clicked open his pocket watch and checked the time. "We can't get to Richmond by morning."

"The way we travel, we can," Braham said.

Daniel tucked the watch back into his waistcoat. "And Noah will get out of the box."

"He's not..." Olivia raised an eyebrow without further comment. "Never mind."

Daniel didn't really believe Noah was captured in the box, but until he understood the technology involved and how the talking images got there, it was easier for his small brain to accept.

"And Noah and I can come back?"

"As easily as Kenzie and David reappeared in Denver, you can reappear, too," Olivia said.

"In what? Days? Weeks? Months?"

"I believe ye can come back soon enough that explaining yer absence won't be difficult," Braham said.

Daniel's voice took on an edge when he asked, "How do we get there? Do ye have a magic ring like Aladdin?"

"No ring," Braham said. "Just a brooch and a few magic words."

52

The Present, Richmond, Virginia—Daniel

WHEN THE FOG lifted, Daniel's gaze darted all around. Rick and Braham stood next to him. The sun peeked through the shedding branches of a live-oak lined drive that led to a stately Southern mansion. There wasn't a loud roar of rushing water, but the distinctive smell of a river told him one ran through the property. The land held a prevailing peacefulness, and an ease, unlike anything he'd ever experienced, came over him in a healing wash.

It was as if he'd been called home.

He hugged Amber's journal to his chest, sensing her nearby. "Where are we?" His tone was soft, reverent, as if speaking any louder would make it all evaporate.

"A sweet little place on the James River." Rick closed the amber brooch and slipped it into his waistcoat pocket. "If you can't relax here, you can't relax anywhere."

"Charlotte's family has owned this land since the 1600s," Braham said. "Her brother and his family live in the homeplace on the other side of that tree line." He clapped Daniel on the shoulder. "Come on. Let's go find Noah."

They walked along the bricked drive toward the front door of the mansion. "Did her family come from Scotland?" Daniel asked. "I know several families who settled here in Virginia."

"Charlotte's ancestors were Protestant dissenters from Ulster,"

Braham said. "Michael Mallory married Lorna MacKlenna, who was James MacKlenna's great-aunt. But here's a connection you can relate to: James MacKlenna's daughter, Lindsey, married Craig Hughes."

"From Leadville?" Daniel asked. "Interesting. So Charlotte is distantly related to the Hughes family?"

"Distantly," Braham said.

Daniel followed Braham up the steps—their spurs clinking against the brick—to a wide veranda lined with pots of gold and red chrysanthemums. The earthy scent of the skinny petals created a warm welcoming embrace.

"We need to take off what we can. Our housekeeper won't be happy if we track in mud." They sat in the porch rockers and removed hats, boots, and coats.

"I'm so dirty, I need to strip completely," Rick said.

"Brush off what ye can," Braham said.

Daniel brushed the legs of his trousers. Most of the dirt was embedded in the heavy cotton and would need a few washings to get the pants clean enough to wear again. He unfastened the buckle at his waist and coiled the cartridge belt around his holster.

"I'll take yer rig and lock it up in my safe," Braham said. "Ye can have it anytime, but ye won't need it here."

"God made man, but Sam Colt made them equal until McCabe locked up everybody's guns," Rick said, lining his boots up against the wall. Then he folded his coat and left it and his hat in one of the chairs.

Daniel slapped the rig into the major's hand. "Where exactly is *here*?" He followed Rick's lead, lined up his boots, folded his coat, and left it in a chair with his hat.

Braham lined up his boots, too, but left his coat and hat where he'd slung them on the porch rail. "We're a few miles north of Richmond." He opened the screen door and gestured with his thumb for Daniel to precede him. "Let's go find yer lad."

Daniel glanced around the large foyer and up at the cupola flooding light down three stories.

Rick nudged Daniel with his elbow. "You'll have to check out the view. Braham goes up to the observation walkway to smoke cigars away from Charlotte and watch the river. In a former life, I think he was a riverboat captain."

A wrought iron and crystal chandelier hung from the top of the cupola, extending down to a point level with the second floor. It was truly a magnificent design. The cupola and upper floors were accessed by dual self-supporting staircases that spiraled upward, level after level.

"Who designed the house, the cupola, the staircases?"

Rick pointed to Braham. "He envisioned it."

"I found an architect who could interpret my vision and sketches, and a wife who tolerated my obsession."

"Yer winery and racehorses must be doing well."

"I was heavily invested in the railroad. Made a fortune in 1869 when the Union Pacific and Central Pacific Railroads met in Promontory, Utah. I sold everything I owned. Turned it into gold and buried it at MacKlenna Farm in Lexington, Kentucky. It's now locked in a vault. I sell nuggets every now and again." He pointed down a hallway. "There's a visitor's wing in that direction. Ye're welcome to stay there as long as ye want."

Daniel couldn't think about how long he'd stay. His mind was focused only on Noah and Amber. "Is Amber close by? And where is Noah?"

"In distance, yes, she's close. But with traffic it will take thirty-five minutes, maybe longer. But ye need to clean up a wee bit. Ye can't go to the hospital looking like a nineteenth-century Pinkerton agent who's been in a gunfight."

Daniel caught his reflection in the gilded-framed mirrors hanging on both sides of the foyer. He shivered at the sight of his bloodied face and filthy clothes. "Do ye have an extra pair of trousers I could borrow?"

"Trousers, shirts, underwear, socks. We're close enough in size, but as soon as we have an extra hour, we'll go shopping and pick up a few things. I work with a personal shopper who knows all of

Charlotte's preferences. I shop to please my bride. But an old pair of jeans and a soft cotton shirt are all I need."

"Are ye saying I should shop to please Charlotte?"

Braham laughed. "Charlotte has exquisite, yet subtle taste in everything from shoes to clothes to furniture for men, women, and children. If ye listen to her personal shopper's advice, ye can't go wrong. In thirty minutes, she completely outfitted Noah and even gave Rick a refresher course on what's new in men's fashion since he went off to war."

"Where is Noah?" Daniel asked for the third time, letting an edge of impatience into his tone.

"The boys were under strict orders not to leave." Braham stepped over to a small white box on the wall and pushed a button. "Lincoln, we're back. Come to the foyer and bring Noah."

Within moments, three boys tore through a doorway on the second floor and ran toward the stairs. "Is Pa here?" Noah hung over the rail to look. Seeing Daniel, he yelled, "Pa!" He ran down the steps so fast Daniel thought for sure he'd tumble, so he hurried over to catch him. But Noah navigated the spiral staircase safely and reached the bottom step without mishap, plowing right into Daniel. If his feet hadn't been well-planted, they'd both be on the floor.

"Whoa, there. Let me look at ye." His hair was slicked back on the sides and spikey on the top. He wore a shirt with short sleeves and no collar with *New York Yankees* written on the front, blue jeans, and multi-colored shoes. But it was his smile, reflecting in his bright blue eyes, that shocked Daniel more than the shirt or shoes.

"I'm glad you're here. I have so much to tell you," Noah said, squeezing Daniel around his waist. "What happened to your face?" Before Daniel could answer, Noah noticed what he held in his hand. Beaming, he said, "You got Amber's journal back." He hugged Daniel again. "Oh, Pa, she'll be so happy. Lincoln said if Dr. Marsh got hold of Amber's dinosaur pictures he'd know the future. And travelers, that's what we are now, can't change the future or it will mess up the world."

Daniel squeezed his son, rubbing up and down Noah's knobby

spine through the soft fabric of his shirt. "That's okay, lad. I understand." Did that mean he also understood Braham's conundrum about saving the president? And what would Daniel discover while he was in the twenty-first century that could mess up the future once he returned to his own time? He shivered at the thought.

A little girl with blond curls gracefully walked down the stairs, holding onto the railing. "Daddy, the boys won't play with me. I told them they had to because I didn't have a play date today."

When she reached the bottom step, Braham tucked Daniel's rig under one arm and picked her up with the other. "Lincoln knows the rules. Nobody gets left out."

"I reminded him, but he said they were playing games that I didn't know how to play, and I should go play with Amelia Rose. But Daddy, Amelia Rose is a baby and I'm older. Can the twins come play?"

"David and Kenzie will probably be here late tonight so ye can play with the twins tomorrow."

The little girl scrunched her face and peered over her father's shoulder at Daniel. "I'm Kitherina, and if you didn't have a beard, you'd look like Noah. I like Noah. He's sweet."

"I'm Major Grant. I'm Noah's pa. And I'm happy to make yer acquaintance. How old are ye?"

"I'm five. How old are you?"

A knife-edged pain gutted Daniel and he clutched his belly reflexively. If his daughter Heather had survived, she'd be five, too. "I'm older than—" He spoke through the lump in his throat. "I'm older than that, ma'am. And ye're the prettiest five-year-old I've ever seen."

Kitherina touched his cheek. "You have a cut here, here, and here. And a big tear right here," she said, pressing gently beneath his eye. "You need to see Dr. Mallory ASAP. That means as soon as possible so she can fix your boo-boos." She looked at him closely. "Did a bullet graze your face? The Band-Aid doesn't cover the entire wound. Looks like a picture I saw on Mommy's desk. We're not supposed to look at the papers on her desk because of…because of…hippo." She shrugged like a turtle sneaking back into its shell and put her finger to her lips. Then she whispered, "Don't tell Mommy."

Then she continued, as if she'd been given a lifetime allotment of words and was determined to use them all in one conversation. "Mommy fixes bullet wounds. She's the best around. Lincoln said she even fixed Daddy's bullet wound. Guns are dangerous." She gave her daddy a disapproving glance. "You better lock that gun in the safe. You know guns aren't allowed in the house."

Kitherina took a breath and smiled at her daddy, who was watching attentively. "I'm going to be a surgeon, equestrian, and vintner when I grow up. Noah wants to be a scientist. Lincoln wants to be president, and Patrick wants to be an explorer and a writer."

Then she stopped and sighed dramatically before adding, "But don't get me started on Robbie and Henry. They change their minds like the wind. First, they're here…" She tossed her hands about, socking her pa in the head. "Then they're over there. They can't make up their minds. But that's okay, because Lincoln says their daddy is the problem solver, so he can fix the twins' problems, too."

Daniel took the breath Kitherina failed to take. "I'm sure ye'll make an excellent surgeon or vintner, whatever ye want to be."

Her eyebrows drew in over her eyes. "Phew. You and Daddy smell." She wrinkled her nose. "Uncle Rick smells, too. Have you been on a 'venture? Whirling back and forth?" She waved her hands all around her head again, wiggling her fingers, shaking her blond curls. "Ventures always make you smell bad."

"Lincoln and Patrick said it's the peat in the fog that smells," Noah said, watching Kitherina with the same intensity he'd watched Amber on stage in Leadville.

Kitherina's pout receded and her brow cleared. "I have to go. Nanny Sue is walking with Amelia Rose in the garden. I need to smell something sweet." She pushed against Braham to climb down, giving him a quick peck on his mouth.

"It's listening time now. You have to do that after you talk, and I've talked way too much. Daddy lets me ramble on, and then I have to be quiet and read Shakespeare. 'Out, damned spot! Out, I say!—One, two. Why, then, 'tis time to do 't. Hell is murky!—Fie, my lord, fie!'" She took a breath. "Sometimes," she sighed, "I wonder if it's worth it to talk so much. Goodbye." She ran off, and the patter of her little feet was followed by a slamming door.

Daniel stood there benumbed by grief and overwhelmed by the precocious child. And he shook, like the tremors of a distant quake had set upon him. Noah squeezed his hand. "I always wondered, Pa, what Heather would be like if she'd lived. Now I know. Don't you think she'd be like wee Kit? That's what Lincoln and Patrick call her. Like you used to call Heather, wee Heather."

Daniel hugged his son fiercely, afraid to let him go, and feeling once again the small bones of his arms and shoulders and back—his flesh and blood. If not for Amber, his son would have been taken from him, too.

"It's okay, Pa. Ma and Heather are together forever. Just like us."

Braham squeezed Daniel's shoulder. "I'm sorry for yer loss."

The shock passed, and Daniel blew out a breath. If he'd learned anything over the years, it was how to sequester his emotions. After President Lincoln died, he was told, "Carry on, soldier." After Lorna and wee Heather died, he was told, "Carry on, Daniel." After his partner at the agency died, he was told, "Carry on, Agent Grant."

He was tired of carrying on. He just wanted a wee bit of peace and quiet.

One of the other two boys, who strongly resembled Braham, stuck out his hand. "I'm Lincoln McCabe, sir, and this is my cousin, Patrick Mallory."

Patrick thrust out his hand. "I came here from 1909. It's different but once you get used to it, you'll never want to return."

"I must apologize for my sister," Lincoln said. "She gets like that when no one pays attention to her. It all stores up and has to bubble out."

"Ye mean explode," Braham said, laughing.

"Does she really read Shakespeare?" Daniel asked.

"She's been reading since she was two. Shakespeare is required reading, but she reads a special children's edition," Lincoln said. "We also read Plato, Aristotle, and all the Greek philosophers. We're home schooled, but we play sports, go to scout meetings, cultural events, and other activities for socialization."

"We don't study and socialize all the time," Patrick said. "We spend time outdoors camping, hunting, and horseback riding, learning how to live off the land. When Uncle Braham first explained my curriculum, I wasn't happy about the riding and camping part. You see, I was living on the streets of New York City. I'd done enough camping out and hunting for food. But Uncle Braham teaches us how to use our brains along with our skills to accomplish tasks. If I went back to the city in 1909, I'd have the skills to not only survive but thrive."

"If Noah stays here," Lincoln said, "it will be the same for him. But my dad will add archaeology and paleontology to our curriculum. I've already Googled paleontology digs and found one in Utah. We can go there one weekend after Amber recovers from surgery."

Daniel glanced at Braham. There was not only pride in his face, but an expression of deep love. It was as if he was molding these children to live and adapt anywhere at any time.

"Come with me, Pa," Noah said. "I'll take you to my room and show you how to shower and where to pee and stuff. You don't have to go outside or even use a chamber pot."

Braham laughed. "Ye might want to shave. Or the hospital will do it for ye. Ye're going to need a few stitches."

Noah cocked his head. "I've never seen Pa without his beard."

Braham scratched his chin. "When I shaved mine off after the war, it took a while to get used to it. I'll bring clothes to yer room. And Noah, there should be shaving gear in the bathroom drawers. Help yer dad find what he needs. I'll have a snack sent up."

Daniel had a sudden fear of shaving. What if he discovered his beard had been covering an ugly face? Lorna had said he was handsome, but that was years ago, and only one woman's opinion. What if Amber was repulsed? Maybe he shouldn't shave at all.

He followed Noah upstairs. "How many days have ye been here, lad?"

"Only a few hours, but Patrick, Lincoln, and I have been together constantly talking and stuff. I don't understand half of what they tell me or show me, but I'm catching on a little bit at a time. This place is like a castle. And wait until you see the iPad. The world is at your fingertips, Pa. Whatever you want to know, you ask Siri, and she tells you."

Noah turned into a bedroom that was larger than two bedrooms in Alec's house in Denver. "Whose room is this? Braham's?"

"It's mine for now. Lincoln said I'd probably want to move to the visitor's wing to be close to you. Come on, the bathroom is in here. It's sort of like Mrs. Garland's washroom, but fancier."

Daniel entered a room with mirrors and towels and odd gadgets. Noah opened a glass door and turned on water.

"Take off your clothes and stand under here. There's soap for your body and special liquid soap for your hair. The water is hot, and it lasts forever. Come on, get in." Noah tugged at Daniel's vest. "Get these old clothes off. You won't need them now. Throw them in that basket in the corner. That's for dirty clothes."

"I'll need them back to wear home," Daniel said.

"Home?" Something akin to panic stole the color from Noah's face. "I don't want to think about leaving right now, Pa. Can we talk about it later?"

"Sure, lad, but…"

"Not now, please."

Seeing how distressed the idea made Noah, Daniel put it aside as he stripped down to his skin and entered the glass enclosure. When he stepped under the hot water, he gasped. It was one of the most luxurious sensations he'd ever experienced, but he didn't want to take all the water and deprive Braham and Rick of a quick wash. "How do ye turn it off?"

"You haven't been in long enough."

"Braham and Rick will want to use this room."

"No, Pa. This is just for us. They have their own rooms and there's enough hot water for everyone."

Daniel didn't understand how that was possible, or how many pots were heating on a stove to refill the tank. At Noah's urging, Daniel stayed in the glass box and allowed the water and soap to wash away the mud and dirt until it all slithered down the drain in the floor.

"Turn the handle to the right when you're done," Noah said.

Daniel turned off the water and stepped out onto a thick, soft mat. Noah handed him a warm towel that smelled like a rose garden.

"Pa."

Daniel rubbed his body dry and wrapped the thick cloth around his middle. "What's on yer mind, lad?"

"Amber. I think about her all the time."

"I do, too, Noah."

"She's really sick. Lincoln showed me a report on the iPad about her surgery. They're going to cut her chest open and replace a piece of her heart. Lincoln said doctors do this surgery all the time."

"Lincoln sounds like a smart lad."

"He is, Pa. I like him. Patrick, too." Noah's brows furrowed, and despair clouded his eyes, and along with the slouch in his body signaled how worried he was. "I don't want Amber to die."

Daniel hugged his son, the small muscles of his shoulders shuddering beneath his hands. Noah smelled fresh and clean, like cedar wood and apple, and the fabric of his shirt was cottony soft. Not since Noah was a bairn had Daniel thought of his son as fragile, but he did now. Everything about Noah had changed—the way he smelled, the feel of his clothes, the style of his hair, everything—except his heart.

"Do you love her, Pa? Do you love her enough to marry her? Because I want Amber to be my ma."

"Aye, I do…love her." Daniel's voice cracked. He tried to swallow but his throat was dry. If he broke down now, so would Noah. He squeezed him tightly, then released him, looked him in the eye. "Nothing would make me happier than to marry her, but right now," he paused to gain control of his emotions, "all that matters is getting Amber well. Later, we'll talk about our future."

Noah looked at him, his smile fading. "I want to stay here with Amber and Lincoln and Patrick. But if you want to go back, I'll go with you, but I'll never forget the people here."

"How'd I get so lucky to have a son like ye?"

"I don't know. But I'm lucky to have a pa like you."

Noah opened the cabinets below the counter and dug through the drawers. He held up what looked like a razor and a can that read shaving cream. Between the two of them, they figured out how to dispense the cream. But by the time they learned how to direct the stream of foam, it was all over the counter, the mirror, and Daniel. Although he was terrified to see himself without his beard, he did the best shaving job he could around the paper square on his cheek and the cuts and abrasions on his chin.

When he finished shaving, Noah just stared at him in the mirror. "Pa. You look like me."

Relieved that he wasn't ugly, Daniel laughed and chucked his son under the chin. "Since I'm older, I suppose ye look like me."

"If Amber didn't already love you, she would now. You're handsome."

"Love has more to do with who ye are inside than how ye look outside."

Noah flicked at his hair spikes. "In the twenty-first century, folks spend a lot of time making themselves look special, but I've seen their hearts. The McCabes, McBains, O'Gradys, and the Kellys are all good people."

Braham yelled from the other side of the door. "I left a pair of jeans and polo shirt on the bed. If they don't fit, I'll find others."

Noah fiddled with his hair once more before leaving the bathroom.

Was it possible to adapt that quickly? Daniel thought back to the war years, and how he had adapted to living in a tent, going days without a bath, and killing the enemy. Yes, humans adapted quickly to changing environments, or they died.

When Daniel came out of the bathroom, Noah was holding up a pair of short blue pants. "What are those? They won't fit me. They don't look like they'd fit ye either."

"Lincoln calls them briefs. The white shirt is an undershirt. Put these on first. They'll feel tight, but I kind of like them now."

Daniel put on the undergarments, then shoved his legs into blue pants. They resembled the riveted-for-strength blue denim work pants sold in Hughes Store. He'd never worn them, but the ones he'd seen miners wear weren't this fitted.

The white short-sleeve shirt smelled fresh and clean like the towel and fit tight against the muscles of his chest and arms. The green cotton long-sleeve shirt fit over the smaller white one. The clothes were tight and constricting and he wondered if women's corsets felt as confining.

"Are ye sure these garments are supposed to look like this?"

"I saw lots of men in the hospital. And they were dressed like you are now."

Catching a glimpse of himself in the mirror over the dresser, Daniel didn't know what to think. But if that's what men wore, he could do it for a while.

They sat at a small table in front of a window that overlooked the river. "Beautiful view," Daniel said, snacking on a bite of apple. "Have ye walked around outside?"

Noah finished a glass of juice. "We've gone down to the river, over to the stables, and through the vineyards." He bit into an apple. "The property goes on and on. You'll love it, Pa."

When they finished their snack, they returned to the foyer where Braham was waiting. "Good God. I thought Lincoln and I looked alike, but ye two got us beat. Amber will like the clean-face look."

Daniel rubbed his chin. "Haven't seen this skin since I was twenty."

"Except for the cuts and scratches, ye look respectable."

"Where are Lincoln and Patrick?" Noah asked.

"They're catching up on their lessons while ye're gone so they won't have to do them later. I already brought the car around front. If ye're ready, let's go."

"Now, Pa. We're going to ride in a car. It's like a carriage, but without horses, and it goes fast. It's scary at first, but Braham is a good driver. So put your seatbelt on, sit back, and enjoy the view."

Daniel had no idea what Noah was talking about, but when he climbed into a black, shiny conveyance with doors and windows, smelling of rich leather, he was even less sure of what was about to happen. He only hoped it didn't twist him about like the fog. His stomach had yet to recover.

When Braham pulled away from the front of the house, Daniel grabbed the door and yelled, "Slow down!"

From the back seat, Noah patted his shoulder. "Relax, Pa. It's safe. You're wearing a seatbelt just like me. You're not going to get hurt. Close your eyes. That helps."

"I remember my first car ride," Braham said, laughing. "My fingernails clawed the leather. Scared the crap out of me. I got over it, and even taught myself to drive while Charlotte was away at the hospital. When she refused to help me return to the past, I drove to Lexington, Kentucky, knowing I would find help there, all in my attempt to save the president."

Daniel stared at Braham. "Ye learned to drive this conveyance so ye could save Lincoln?"

"That was my plan."

"I'm sorry I accused ye of not trying to save him. This would have taken a great deal of courage. I couldn't have done it."

"Aye, ye could. We learned during the war to do whatever we had to do."

Daniel watched the landscape fly by, but when Braham passed other conveyances, Daniel closed his eyes. At intersections, red and green lights directed traffic and he thought that was a clever idea. Green light, go. Red light, stop. The yellow light, however, was a wee bit confusing.

"There's the hospital, Pa."

Noah pointed to a large stone and glass structure. Daniel had seen buildings as large or larger in Europe, but what surprised him was that the hospital had little character or artistic flare. It struck him as sterile.

"If it's not visiting hours," Noah said, "we'll have to wait before we can see Amber."

"I'm so nervous, I'm sweating like a pig. I'll have to get back in that glass waterfall and take another rinse."

"You put stuff on under your armpits, Pa. You won't stink. Around here they don't like people to smell. That's what Lincoln said."

"If Lincoln said so, it must be true," Daniel said.

Braham stopped the conveyance and they all got out. Noah took Daniel's hand. "When I came through the fog with Rick, Amber, and Ripley, we landed over there in the grass. Charlotte came out and took Amber inside. Braham showed up a few minutes later, and he took Ripley to a dog doctor. Rick and I went with Lincoln and Patrick to Charlotte's office. She has a bathroom there. I took a bath and put these clothes on."

"Come on," Braham said. "Charlotte's waiting for us."

They followed Braham into the hospital. A woman dressed in green pants and shirt and a white coat was the first person Daniel saw. "I know ye," he said.

The woman scratched the side of her face, studying him. "Did I sew you up during the war?"

Daniel nodded. "K Street Barracks Post Hospital."

"Gunshot?" she asked.

He rubbed his side. "I don't know which hurt more. Getting shot or ye digging the bullet out."

"Sorry I hurt you, but I'm glad to know you're okay. What happened to your face?"

Daniel pointed to his cheek. "Bullet." Then he pointed to his chin. "Fist."

"I'm going to have those cuts looked at first. You can't visit Amber with open wounds." Charlotte put her arm around Noah's shoulder. "But you can go see her and tell her your dad will be up in a little while. Rick is with her now."

"Yes, ma'am," he said. "Bye, Pa."

"I'll be in the waiting room," Braham said.

Daniel went through another set of doors with Charlotte, and after she conferred with women in two different offices, she took him behind a curtain and instructed him to lie down on a bed with wheels. The room was like the one Amber had been in during the talking picture. He closed his eyes, and tried not to listen to the clangs, beeps, and voices in the ceiling. But he couldn't ignore the strong astringent smells that made him scrunch his nose. It made no sense to him why, in this century, cloths to dry your body smelled like flower gardens but rooms smelled like cheap whisky.

Charlotte snapped on tight, white gloves and peeled the bandage from his face. "You need a stitch or two to cut down on the scarring."

"I don't care about a scar." He tried to sit up, but she pressed on his chest.

"Amber will. I'm doing this for her." Then Charlotte leaned closer and whispered, "If the sights and sounds get scary, close your eyes and think of something pleasant. Braham went through this and so did our cousin Cullen. Relax. It'll be fine."

After Charlotte finished sewing him up, she escorted him out to the corridor near the door where they'd entered the hospital. He had bandages on his cheek and chin.

"Visiting hours are over," she said, "but I can get you in to see Amber for a few minutes."

"I should have seen her first."

"They wouldn't have let you in the unit. Amber is having major surgery, and they don't want your germs."

"What are those?"

"Nasty little buggers you can't see but can kill people."

When they didn't find Braham in the waiting room, they climbed two flights of stairs and arrived in a corridor with double doors and a banner sign: CORONARY CARE UNIT. "This unit delivers high-intensity care to heart patients. You can only stay a few minutes, so let those minutes count."

"Where's Braham?"

"Probably in my office writing, checking his stock portfolio, or designing another curriculum for the children. He has a team of experts he brings in regularly to introduce new topics or teach an advance-level course. His focus is history and the classics. Math, foreign languages, and science are taught by tutors."

"I saw the boys have little black boxes like the one Rick had with moving pictures."

"Those are iPhones. They use them to communicate with people who aren't in the room."

Rick and Noah came through the door. "She's smiling, Pa. I told her you shaved."

"What'd she say?"

Noah blushed.

Daniel's heart fled to his throat. "What'd she say, lad?"

"That she'd love you even if you looked like a *Stegosaurus*."

Daniel smiled.

"Noah, wait here with Rick," Charlotte said. "Your dad will only be a few minutes."

Daniel was about to tousle his son's hair but remembered how particular he'd become in just a few hours in this strange new time and place.

Rick slapped Daniel on the back. "Don't upset my girl."

Daniel didn't take offense at Rick's comment. From the beginning, he'd noticed how protective Rick was of Amber. And he had no doubt that Rick would try to beat the crap out of him if Daniel ever hurt her. He smiled to himself. There was some satisfaction in knowing that Amber had never been intimate with Rick, so he could call Amber his girl all he wanted. Daniel knew in his heart, she belonged to him.

Charlotte escorted Daniel down a corridor lined with curtains. He had to bring his emotions under control. What was he afraid of? That she was so sick, he might lose her, too.

Charlotte stopped in front of a curtain. "Here you go. Are you ready?"

He nodded.

"I'll be back in a few minutes."

She pushed the curtain and a glass door aside, and his heart nearly stopped. Amber sat propped up in bed. Her long hair curled over her shoulder. A smile was curving her lips. Her cheeks had more color than he'd seen in her face before. There were beeping machines to her right and left. The room felt cool on his skin. He stepped to the side of the bed and gripped the railing, just taking her in.

"Noah warned me that you'd shaved." She cocked her head, looking at him closely. "Your eyes, nose, and cheeks are the same. It's just around your mouth and chin that you look different. You have a strong square chin, and you're more handsome without your beard."

He was silently pleased that she liked the way he looked. He rested his forearms on the railing and leaned forward. "I want to kiss ye."

She smiled. "I'd like that."

There was a slight quaver in her voice and he didn't know if it was because of her illness or him. He lifted her chin, and his mouth came down on hers slowly and tentatively at first, then deeper. The kiss moved like a warm light from the center of his heart. He caressed her lips with his tongue as he threaded his hands under her hair to cradle her head.

"What happened to your face?"

"Hmm. What?" he asked, nibbling at her lips.

"What happened to your face?"

"A few deputies got carried away."

"I'm so sorry I lied to you. I wanted to tell you the truth."

Daniel didn't want to hear apologies. He wanted to kiss her. Hold her. Love her. Keep her safe. "I don't care what happened or why. I only care about ye and doing whatever we have to do to get ye well again. I love ye, Amber."

She gazed into his eyes. "You'll be here after surgery. You're not going to take Noah and leave."

"No, I'm not." He kissed her again, letting his lips linger above hers. "I love ye."

"You've only known me two weeks."

"Two days. Two hours. Two minutes. I fell in love with ye the moment I glanced up and saw the look in yer eyes after ye saved Noah's life."

The sound of a throat clear had them turning toward the doorway. Daniel straightened like the caught lover he was.

"Visitation is over." A different woman dressed in green pants and shirt stood at the curtain, smiling at him. "Miss Kelly needs her rest."

He didn't want to leave. He wanted to hold Amber the way he'd held her the night before. "If ye need a reminder of how much I love ye, how much I need ye, read this." He pulled an envelope from his pants' pocket. "It's the note I wrote this morning. I found it in yer journal. I'll write a longer one tonight." He kissed her again, letting her absorb the impact of his words. "I don't think they'll let me come back, but I'll be here in the morning."

"I love you, Daniel."

He kissed her again. "Sleep well tonight, lass. Tomorrow will be the first day of our new life together."

He stole one more kiss before he walked away from her. The long walk to the door that would take him back to Noah reminded him of leaving the cemetery following Lorna's funeral, and he was filled with utter terror. As he neared the door, he stopped and pressed his forehead against the cool wall, and he tried to calm his breathing. If he lost Amber, it would end his life. He would continue to go through the motions, but there would only be a shell of a man left behind.

A warm hand pressed against his back. "She'll do fine," Charlotte said. "I know you're scared, but you have to have faith and trust in her medical team."

"I don't know if I can find that faith."

"Noah has faith, and if he sees that you don't, his faith will fade, and he'll have doubts. Amber will see his doubts and yours. She can't go into this surgery without believing she'll have a complete recovery."

"Do ye believe she will?"

Charlotte gently turned Daniel's head to face her. "I believe she will. If I had doubts, you would know it."

Daniel hugged her. He could feel everything about her, her soft breasts pressing against his chest and the hard, defining muscles of her back and arms. The juxtaposition of softness against strength was the epitome of a healer.

And he had absolutely faith in Charlotte Mallory.

"I have faith in ye, and because of that, I will have no doubts."

She kissed his cheek. "You remind me so much of Braham. I will enjoy getting to know you. Get some rest. Tomorrow will be a long day of waiting."

She walked the rest of the way to the door of the unit with him. Braham and Noah were waiting on the other side. Braham went to her and enveloped her in his arms. "How are ye, lass?"

"I'm holding up."

"Can ye leave?"

"I'll wait for Connor and Olivia. They're supposed to be here around eleven, right?"

"That's what Rick said."

"I'll take a nap upstairs. I don't have any surgeries tomorrow. So," she smiled. "After Amber's surgery, I'll come home for a few hours to spend time with you and the kids. Pencil me in."

He kissed her squarely on the mouth. "Consider it done."

"What are you going to do now?" she asked.

"Take Daniel and Noah back to the house, get something to eat, and pick up the horse trailer. Connor and Olivia are bringing Daniel's horse, so we'll need to transport him back to the plantation."

"Why didn't you bring the horse with you?"

"We didn't know for sure where we'd all land, so we figured Olivia should have the horse. Just in case."

"That was thoughtful." She kissed Braham again. "Hug the kids good night for me. When you come back, bring Olivia a change of clothes. I'm sure she'll want to see Amber. I'll try to sneak her in for a few minutes." She glanced at Daniel. "You're dead on your feet. You need to rest. But if you want to come back later to see her, you can."

"I've gone longer without sleep."

"I'm sure you have," Charlotte said, "but Olivia and Amber's parents will be here soon, and I'm sure you'll want to make a good impression."

He hadn't thought about Amber's parents. My God. What would he say to them? Should he ask Mr. Kelly for permission to court his daughter? He pinched the skin of his throat, thinking of the many liberties he'd taken with Amber. Her father would surely know.

As if Charlotte had been reading his mind, she said, "I hear the Kellys are lovely people. And you have to remember, Amber is a twenty-first century woman. Whatever you two have done, it won't concern Mr. Kelly. Go home and eat something." Then to Braham she said, "Let him read a few issues of *Cosmopolitan* and *Men's Health*."

"Ye want him to learn twenty-first century mores by reading pop culture?"

"How did you learn?"

Braham laughed. "Yer brother Jack told me everything I needed to know."

Charlotte threw up her hands. "Pick your poison." She pushed the door open and returned to the CCU, chuckling.

53

The Present, Richmond, Virginia—Olivia

WHEN THE FOG cleared, Olivia and Connor found themselves on the edge of a well-lit parking lot in front of a large hospital. The evening was cool, but not cold, and the nearby vehicular traffic was moderate for a city the size of Richmond at this hour of the night.

"I assume we are in Richmond?" Olivia's grip on Connor's arm relaxed.

"If VCU means Virginia Commonwealth University then we're exactly where we want to be. Braham should be here with the horse trailer. Let's go over there and stand under the light pole so he can see us." As soon as they stepped under the light, a truck's headlights dimmed, brightened, and dimmed again.

"Looks like our ride," she said.

A black Suburban pulling a horse trailer nudged up alongside them. The driver's window rolled down. "Heard a horse was stranded at the VCU Medical Center. I'm always looking for good horseflesh."

Connor and Braham did a knuckle bump. "What's the latest on Amber?" Olivia asked.

Braham put the vehicle into park, stepped out, and hugged her. "There's no change, and she's chomping at the bit to see ye."

Connor removed his coat, jacket, cravat, and hat and tossed the items into the back of the vehicle. "How's Daniel handling the twenty-first century?"

"It helps that Noah has acclimated so easily, but Daniel is so worried about Amber he can't think about much else." Braham patted Rambler's withers, and the horse rolled a dark eye toward him. "Ye don't like standing in a concrete parking lot in the middle of the night, do ye? Ye're ready to be turned out."

Rambler answered with a turn of his ear, a stomp, and a whicker.

Braham unsaddled him and put the saddle on a rack inside the trailer. "Did ye have any trouble after we left ye?"

"You talking to me or the horse?" Connor asked.

"Unless Rambler's sire is Mister Ed, I'm talking to ye."

"Other than the gouges Olivia dug into my arm during the trip, it was uneventful."

Olivia looked at her fingernails. "I was going to say I didn't do that, but it looks like I broke a nail."

"Oh God, the world has come to an end. Would you believe we had to reschedule an appointment to see a ranch once because Olivia needed a nail repair?"

She shifted her gaze from her broken nail to Connor. "That's not true at all. You had an emergency call from Elliott and I had to entertain myself for an hour. So I got my nails done."

Braham grabbed two bottles of water from a camping cooler inside the trailer and handed them to Olivia and Connor. "How long have ye two known each other?"

"About a year," Connor said.

"Ten months," Olivia said over him.

Braham led the horse into the trailer and pointed him toward a bucket of oats. "Olivia, Charlotte thought ye might want to change. I raided her closet. There's a bag on the front seat with yoga pants, sports bra, tank top, and a jacket. If ye want to come in here and change, I'm sure Rambler won't mind."

"How thoughtful. I don't want to go inside the hospital dressed like this." She grabbed the bag but couldn't hold it and her skirts at the same time and dropped the bag.

Connor picked it up. "Let me help."

She gathered up her petticoats, layered skirts, and cloak and climbed into the trailer as Braham climbed out. "It took two of us this morning to get me into this dress. I can't get out of it by myself."

Connor followed her in. "I love it when a woman begs me to take off her clothes."

She moved into the shadows, so she couldn't be seen from the parking lot and turned her back to Connor. After he unhooked and unbuttoned her, she shooed him away. "I can take it from here." He left, and she shimmied out of all the layers and into the yoga pants and sports bra, sighing in relief to be free of the corset. She folded the skirts and undergarments and placed the clothes on an empty shelf.

"Is it okay if I leave everything folded up in here? I'll pick them up tomorrow and have them cleaned. Somebody might want to wear them one day, but not me. My time traveling days are over."

"I'll take care of it. We have a local cleaner who specializes in reenactment clothes," Braham said.

When Olivia exited the trailer, Connor had his cell phone to his ear. "As soon as I check in with David, we'll go see Amber. Will we have any trouble getting in?"

"I'll let Charlotte know ye're here. She'll meet ye at the Emergency Department entrance and take ye upstairs."

Olivia took a big gulp of water. Her stomach was cramping, a sure sign of dehydration. She hadn't had much to drink, other than alcohol and coffee, in the last twenty-four hours. Now she was paying for it.

"Have you been in to see Amber?" Olivia asked.

Braham grabbed his phone from the front seat console and sent a text message. "Visitation is restricted. I didn't want to take time away from Rick, Daniel, and Noah. They've all said her spirits are good and that she's comfortable."

After four rings, Connor disconnected. "David and Kenzie must not be back yet." Within thirty seconds his phone rang. "O'Grady."

"Where are ye?" David asked.

"We just got back," Connor said. "Are you at the ranch?"

"Kenzie and I are just now walking up the steps. But ye're not here unless ye're coming in through the front door."

Olivia moved to stand next to Connor and he encircled her with his arm. "Olivia and I are standing in the parking lot of the VCU Medical Center with Braham."

"Why?" David's one-word question held a surprising edge of steel.

Connor tensed against her. It was a convoluted story to tell, but why Connor was stressed over explaining what happened to David didn't make sense.

"Rick had to make a split-second medical decision. He's heard of Charlotte's *sang-froid* in situations like this. Right or wrong, he brought Amber here."

Ah. Now Olivia understood. Connor had to defend his younger brother's decision. It would have been easier on everyone, logistically speaking, if he'd returned Amber to Denver, but Olivia wasn't going to second-guess Rick's decisive action.

"What's wrong with her?"

Connor put the phone on the hood of the Suburban, leaned over it, resting his weight on his forearms. Olivia put her hand on his back, feeling the muscles tighten.

"Amber has mitral valve disease and needs to have the valve replaced. She's scheduled for open-heart surgery in the morning."

A door slammed, probably the one leading from the porch to the kitchen at her parents' house. She could picture David and Kenzie walking in, looking around for JL and Elliott, heading to the bar for a drink.

"How could Amber be so sick, and we didn't know it?" David asked. "It sounds like the mission went to shit fast. What happened?"

"We knew she was ill, but she was downplaying it. We just didn't know how serious it was, and she did her best to hide her symptoms," Connor said. "She was determined to go to Morrison today.

There was no talking her out of it."

"Connor." There was an even nastier edge to Kenzie's voice. "Your story doesn't add up. If Rick came back earlier with Amber, and you and Olivia just now returned, how did you know about Amber's condition and scheduled surgery in Virginia?"

Connor took a deep breath. "Rick, Amber, and Noah were in Morrison. When Amber collapsed, Rick had no choice but to bring Noah and Ripley to the present with them."

"Okay. Got that. But the dots still aren't connecting. Spill it."

"Noah refused to return home, so Braham went back with Rick to get Daniel, and they came here this afternoon."

"Are you telling me that Rick arrived in Richmond, returned to Denver, and arrived back in Richmond before the four of us even left the ranch? Why didn't he call? It would have saved us all a trip." The nasty edge in Kenzie's voice changed to pissed-as-hell.

"Rick wasn't sure what would happen if you, David, Olivia, and I didn't go back. The kids called it the Amy-Effect. So, Braham blacked out all communications."

David came back on the phone. "I'm not prepared to say that was the right decision, but I'm not ruling it out until I analyze it. What happened when Braham and Rick went to Denver?"

"They didn't go to Denver. They thought they were going to Cañon City, which was where Olivia and I were supposed to be for the meeting with General Palmer, but we all ended up in Pueblo."

"There's still dots missing. But I don't want to take more time right now. I've got to get the helicopter ready and notify the captain we're flying out of Denver tonight. We'll leave here within thirty minutes. Kenzie will want to stop in Lexington to pick up the kids, and I'm sure James Cullen will want to come, too. We probably won't get there until daybreak. What time is surgery?"

"First thing. Maybe seven-ish," Connor said.

"As soon as ye get a break, call back. We'll be on the plane in about an hour. I want a complete report."

"I'll give you one then," Connor said, "but you've got to cover me with Elliott and JL. I can't deal with them right now."

"I can handle Elliott, but ye're on yer own with JL."

"Thanks," Connor said.

Olivia tapped him on the shoulder. "Tell them not to worry about locking up the house or turning off the landing pad lights. I'll send the farm manager a text."

"Did you hear that?" Connor asked.

"Got it." David ended the call.

Olivia used Connor's phone to send the farm manager a text with instructions. "Why will JL be mad at you?"

"Because Rick and I didn't tell her what was going on." Connor emptied his water bottle and took a sip from hers. "After they figure out the time line, they'll be fine with it, but until then, JL will be pissed as hell."

Braham cleared his throat. "I hate to interrupt this little interlude, but it's going on midnight. If ye want to see Amber, ye need to go." Braham checked his watch. "Charlotte will meet ye at the ED entrance in about thirty seconds. Ye can only stay a couple of minutes. We'll wait here for ye."

"I'll go and introduce you." Connor took her hand and they jogged over to meet Charlotte at the door. He kissed Charlotte's cheek. "Olivia Kelly, Charlotte Mallory." Then he kissed Olivia on the mouth. "I'll be waiting right here. Take as much time as they'll give you."

Olivia and Charlotte headed off down the corridor. "Thanks for the yoga outfit. It looks quite smashing, don't you think?" Olivia asked.

"From personal experience, I figured you'd want to change. I'm surprised Braham found a jacket and pants to match."

"He's very thoughtful," Olivia said.

They headed up a flight of stairs. "Amber has been anxiously waiting for you to get here."

"I'm sorry it took so long."

"I think she's more anxious about calling your parents. I hope you'll take that worry off her shoulders. She doesn't need it right now."

"Is it still the plan for Rick to call them with details of their flight as soon as I notify them of Amber's condition?" Olivia asked.

"That hasn't changed."

Charlotte headed up another flight of stairs and Olivia followed. "Connor mentioned his sister JL would go ballistic after she learned about the comings and goings today, but Elizabeth Kelly will have her beat all to hell. Mom will be so distraught she'll probably fly here under her own steam. I need to warn you, she's a force to be reckoned with."

"She sounds like my brother's late mother."

"Oh, you're halves, not wholes?"

Charlotte gave her a crestfallen look. "We have the same parents, but the brooches screwed up the way we were raised. It's a story for another day."

"I've heard"—Amber made air quotes—"'It's a long story,' 'It's a for-later story,' 'It's a complicated story,' so many times that I'm wondering if anything with this extended family is ever simple, easy, or uncomplicated."

Charlotte directed inquiring eyes at Olivia. "If you're looking for simple and uncomplicated, you'll have to look elsewhere. Tomorrow, most of the family will be here. The O'Gradys are a handful, but add in the McCabes, McBains, Frasers, and Montgomerys, and you'll be overwhelmed."

"Do you have any advice?"

"Stay focused on what's important—Amber's health."

"Oh, one more thing. Who do I talk to about money? The private plane is expensive. Dad will reimburse whoever paid for that. And we have excellent insurance. Is Amber in a private room?"

Charlotte turned and placed her hands squarely on Olivia's shoulders. "Honey, Amber is very ill. She's in a critical care unit. The surgery she's having tomorrow is not a tonsillectomy."

Olivia's eyes filled with tears. "I know. I just can't think..." She stopped, sniffed, swiped at her nose, then continued. "I can't think about how serious this is, or the possibility of losing her. If she sees I'm worried, she'll worry, too. And she's already as scared as she can be. I'd rather believe she's having her tonsils removed than knowing a doctor will be holding her heart in his hands. Please don't shatter my illusions just yet. I have to get through the next few minutes without breaking down."

A warm smile softened Charlotte's concerned expression, and her blue eyes glinted. "I should have known Connor wouldn't fall in love with a woman more concerned with her clothes and a private room than the seriousness of her sister's condition."

Olivia wiped her eyes with her fingers. "I'm dyslexic, and Amber has covered for me since we were kids. I couldn't have made it through law school without her help. I love her to the moon and back and would give her anything I have. She can shop at the Olivia store and take my blood, my marrow, my organs—whatever she needs."

Charlotte dug into the pocket of her white coat and pulled out a package of tissues. Olivia took one and wiped her eyes, and Charlotte used one to wipe her nose. "We need to pull it together before we go in to see Amber. We don't want to upset her."

Olivia jammed her clammy hands into her armpits and hugged herself. "Why can't it be me in that bed?"

Charlotte rubbed Olivia's back. "If you were in there, she'd be asking the same question."

"I wouldn't want her to be as worried about me as I am about her. But I don't want her to go through surgery either."

"That's the only way she's going to get well. You have to be encouraging when you go in to see her. Are you ready?"

Olivia closed her eyes and took a few deep breaths to calm herself. It didn't help much, but at this point, nothing would. She sensed a warm hand on her cheek and opened her eyes to find Charlotte watching her. Both of her hands were in the pockets of her white coat. Olivia cupped her face where the touch had been, and she knew instantly her granny was there with her.

It is in our darkest hours, Olivia, that we find our courage. Be a light for Amber to find hers.

Okay, Granny. Stay with me, and I can do this.

Feeling a warm pressure on her shoulder, as if she were gently pushed forward, Olivia said, "I'm ready. Let's go."

Charlotte opened the door to the CCU. They weren't ten feet inside the unit when they were approached by a nurse.

"Your patient said she was ready to get this over with, so she could have sex with her handsome boyfriend. I swear, I think she's the first heart patient I've ever had who's going into surgery dizzy with love."

"Thank you, June," Charlotte said. "That's good to hear. This is her sister, Olivia. She just arrived in Richmond and wants to see Amber for a minute."

"Go on in, honey," the nurse said, "but don't stay too long. She's got a big date tomorrow."

Charlotte directed her into Amber's room. Olivia stood at the foot of the bed and watched her sister sleep, surrounded by machines and IVs. Her legs trembled, and she gripped the stainless-steel railing as if it were a life raft, and if she let go, she would be separated from Amber forever. It took her a moment to work up the courage to kiss Amber's forehead.

Amber opened her eyes. "You're here. Did you meet General Palmer?"

Olivia held Amber's hand. "I did, and I'll tell you all about it later."

"Have you seen Daniel?"

"We just arrived. Braham said he went home to sleep."

Amber smiled. "He went home to write me another letter." She reached under the covers and pulled out the one Olivia had seen earlier that day. Amber folded it carefully and pushed it gingerly into Olivia's hand. "Take care of this for me. I don't want anything to happen to it. And if I get another one, take care of that one, too. Promise me."

"I promise."

"If I don't make it through surgery—"

Be the light for Amber...

"You're going to sail through this. Just like you've always aced everything. You and Daniel have so much to do."

"If I don't, Olivia, put the letter in my hand before the casket is sealed."

"There won't be any—"

"Promise me."

Olivia spoke through the lump in her throat. "I promise, but I don't want to hear any more talk like that."

"I'm so scared," Amber said. "Do you remember when you found me in the mine, playing with rocks?"

"Yes, you were just sitting there."

"I was playing with rocks because I was too scared to look for a way out. I counted rocks and waited. You've always been stronger and braver than me."

"You're wrong. You're the one who climbs up on that big rock and yells at the sky."

"I cry all the way up there, I'm so scared."

Olivia slanted a suspicious look at Amber. "I don't believe that."

"Okay, it's not true, but it could be," Amber's old grin appeared, with a hint of the mischievousness that had always glinted in her eyes. "Since I'm in this bed and you're not, you have to call Mom and Dad."

"I don't have a phone."

Amber struggled to raise herself, but Charlotte applied gentle pressure to her arm to keep her down. "I don't either, but you have to do it. I can't talk to them. They'll blame me for not going to the doctor. And I don't want to listen to that."

"They're not going to blame you. They'll be worried sick."

"And Mom will start crying." Amber sniffed. "Save me from them, Olivia. Or take the coward's way out and ask Rick to call them. He'll do it." Tears straggled down her face.

Olivia used the edge of the bedsheet to wipe Amber's tears. "I wouldn't put that burden on him. He doesn't deserve it. You know he's in love with you, don't you?"

"He's not. We're just good friends. And he knows how I feel about Daniel."

Charlotte shook her head slightly, signaling Olivia to back off.

Olivia picked up Amber's thick hair and started braiding it from her neck down. "I'll call them and explain what's happened and the arrangements that have been made for them." When Olivia reached the end of the braid, she looked around for something to use to wrap the bottom. She found a twist tie on the bedside table that was probably left behind when the trash bags were emptied and used it to secure the ends.

Amber chewed on her pinky nail. She looked up at Charlotte. "Can Olivia use your phone? Let's just call them right now. If Mom acts up, take the call out of here. Deal."

Charlotte handed her phone to Olivia. "I think your mother would like to hear Amber's voice, if just for a moment. But don't let her upset Amber."

"Whose phone should I call? Mom's? Dad's?"

"Mom's. Although Dad will probably answer it," Amber said.

Olivia dialed her mother's phone. After three rings, her dad answered. "Matthew Kelly. Who is this?"

"Hi, Dad. It's Olivia."

"What's wrong, sweetie?"

"I'm here with Amber. We're both in love with these great guys, and we can't wait for you to meet them."

"That's great. Your mom and I can't wait to hear all about them. We'll be home in two days. Can you bring them over for dinner? I'll grill steaks?"

Amber rolled her hand, gesturing Olivia to speed it up. "Here's the thing, Dad. There's a private plane waiting for you at Heathrow, and you need to go there now."

"What aren't you telling me, Olivia?" he asked.

"All the arrangements have been made for a plane to fly you and Mom to Richmond, Virginia. A car service will be there waiting when you deplane. It will bring you to the VCU Medical Center."

"What for?" His voice was raspy, neither deep nor high, just rough.

"Amber has to have surgery in the morning and we want you to be here."

"Let me talk to her."

Olivia put the call on speaker.

"Hi, Dad," Amber said.

"If you're in the hospital, sweetie, something is seriously wrong. What happened?"

"I've had several cases of strep throat that were never treated, and I got rheumatic heart disease. The disease damaged my mitral valve, and I have to have it replaced tomorrow."

After a few beats of silence, Olivia thought the call had dropped. "Dad, are you still there?"

"What's the doctor's name? I need to make some calls. Why are you in Virginia and not Denver?"

Amber muted the phone. "I can't deal with him. You'll have to explain it all."

"Dad, a friend of ours, Rick O'Grady, is going to call you with details about the flight. Amber has a fantastic medical team. It's led by Dr. Charlotte Mallory, renowned surgeon."

"What kind of surgeon?"

"She's a general surgeon. She's not doing the surgery. Rick O'Grady will call you in a few minutes. Or maybe his brother Connor. Connor is the love of my life, Dad, so don't you dare be mean to him."

"Olivia."

She nearly cried at the sound of her mother's voice. "Hi, Mom."

"From what I overheard, Amber is about to have open-heart surgery and you're both in love. Is that the gist of it?"

Amber mouthed, "Noah."

Olivia scrunched her face. "Amber's boyfriend is a widower with a ten-year-old son. You'll love him. His name is Noah."

"I'm sure I will," her mother said. "Can this Rick person explain all the details you're leaving out?"

Olivia did a maybe-maybe-not flip of her head. "Some, but the rest you'll have to hear from Elliott Fraser."

"Who's he?"

"Google him, along with Kenzie Wallis-Manning…McBain."

There was a slight gasp on her mother's end of the phone, and Olivia mentally kicked herself for not starting the conversation with the connection to Trey. It would have eased both of her parents' concerns. "Trey's friend?"

"One and the same," Olivia said.

"Is there anyone else I should Google?"

"Braham McCabe, David McBain, Meredith Montgomery."

"Jack Mallory," Amber said.

"And Jack Mallory."

"The *New York Times* best-selling author? I heard he's marrying that beautiful ESPN baseball analyst in a big, fancy wedding on his plantation."

"Reading about them will keep you busy during the flight, Mom. Oh, I forgot someone else. Chris Dalton."

"From the Golden State Warriors? He's going to be there, too?"

"No, but you might meet Chris' son, Austin O'Grady. He's Connor's nephew."

"It already sounds confusing."

"Oh, trust me, it is. You might also want to study Lindsey MacKlenna Hughes' family tree."

"Why?"

"Elliott will explain."

"Olivia, this is all sounding mysterious. It wouldn't have anything to do with that old MacKlenna brooch lore your great-grandmother Hughes used to talk about, would it?"

"Ah, crap, Mom. You know about the brooch?"

"The amber brooch in the loom? Yes, I've known about it since I was a little girl. I was warned never to touch it until I was ready to find the love of my life."

"You never told us?"

"Told you what, dear? That there was an old Scottish brooch buried in the loom? A brooch that would take you to your soul mate? I didn't believe it. I found my soul mate in law school."

There was a strange blending of exhaustion in Olivia's soul. She ignored the leap of her pulse, the knot in her stomach, the fear surrounding her, and the heavy dose of frustration at her mother and granny because they had never shared the brooch lore with her and Amber. How much easier would the last several days have been if they'd been told the truth?

"We'll see you in a few hours, Mom. Have a safe flight," Olivia said.

"Olivia," her mom said. "Kiss Amber for me."

Olivia kissed Amber's cheek. "Done. And back atcha. Goodbye, Mom." Olivia disconnected the call.

"I can't believe she knew about the brooch," Amber said.

"But she didn't believe the family stories."

Amber took Daniel's letter back and held it against her breasts. "The brooch led me to my soul mate."

Charlotte twirled the wedding band on her ring finger. "And to mine."

Olivia handed Charlotte back her phone. "I don't think it led me to mine, but it opened my eyes and heart into believing the man in my life was truly the love of my life."

54

The Present, Richmond, Virginia—Amber

Four days later, Amber was sitting up in her hospital bed eating small portions of salmon and asparagus that Daniel had prepared. When he'd asked for recipes, she'd given them to him, assuming Charlotte's cook would prepare the dishes.

Amber was wrong.

"I can't believe you made this without help." She wiped her mouth and pushed away the tray table. "It was delicious. Thank you."

Daniel's eyes gleamed. "I told Charlotte I wanted to do something special for ye. She said since ye were a foodie—she had to explain what that meant—that ye'd like a meal that didn't come from the hospital kitchen. I don't blame ye. It's terrible food."

"Noah and I watched YouTube videos about how to use the appliances, but we did it by ourselves. Pretty good, huh? I think we might have a budding chef in him. He asked for more recipes. He wants to create a meal all by himself next time."

"Both of you have caught on so quickly to twenty-first century technology." She snagged Daniel's arm and tugged him down for a kiss. First, she kissed his cheek. "That's for the sous chef." Then she kissed Daniel, and the effects of the tender touch of their mouths tingled her lips. "That's for the executive chef, and I'm so impressed."

Elizabeth Kelly strode into the room, wearing yoga pants and a T-shirt from a half-marathon she'd run in September. "What are you impressed about?"

Connor and Olivia came in behind her, holding hands. "Who's impressed?" Olivia asked.

"I'm impressed with Daniel's salmon dinner. It was delicious."

Daniel stood and pushed the recliner aside to make room for Elizabeth at the side of the bed, and he shifted his gaze to the activity outside the window. Amber watched him do that every hour or so, as if to be sure nothing had changed, and he hadn't been transported to yet another realm of the universe.

The streets beyond the hospital, the adjacent buildings, and the shapes, colors, and sizes of the vehicles filling the parking lot amazed him. He would describe what he saw and pepper her with questions on a variety of topics. But mostly, he stared out the window to find in the layout of the streets the Richmond he knew in 1865.

She grew more and more in love with him each moment they spent together. He seduced her with his compassion and thoughtfulness. Whenever he touched her, he did so with gentleness and strength, charm and steely patience, and she marveled at how powerfully she was drawn to him.

And he to her…

Elizabeth Kelly kissed her daughter. "How are you feeling?"

"As long as I don't laugh, cough, or get up, I'm fine."

Daniel turned away from the window. "She walked down to the nurses' station and back about an hour ago. Later, we're scheduled to try the loop around the floor."

"You can do the loop," Amber said. "Or you can push me in a wheelchair."

He leaned against the windowsill and crossed his arms. "Ye have to walk to get yer strength back so we can take Noah to visit yer dinosaurs in Washington."

"We're not going to see dinosaurs today," Connor said. "We're going to drink beer at a pub down the street. David, Braham, and

Jack are waiting in the car. Grab your jacket and let's go."

Daniel looked at Connor. "A pub? To drink beer? Like a saloon?" He turned his gaze to Amber. "Do ye mind?"

"Not at all, and I think you'll be safe enough with those guys."

Olivia eyed Connor suspiciously. "Are you taking him to a campus bar?"

He grinned and tugged her in for a hug. "It's the only one close by."

"Right," Olivia said. "Just remember, you guys are twice the age of those coeds."

He kissed her. "I'm just kidding. It's a sports bar with pool tables. Braham wants to teach Daniel how to play eight-ball. We'll be back in a couple of hours."

Daniel reached into his pocket and pulled out his pocket watch and a handful of coins. "I haven't learned yer money yet. Do I have enough for beers?"

Amber gawked. "Are you kidding me? Let me see those." She flipped through a couple dozen coins. "I can't be sure, but this Shield Nickel might be worth three thousand dollars. And you've got a dozen Liberty Head Double Eagles." She looked up at Daniel. "What else did you bring with you?"

"A few books. Do ye need something to read?"

"Like…"

"Noah has *The Three Musketeers* and *Alice's Adventures in Wonderland*. I have"—he glanced up, tapping his fingers on the windowsill—"*Moby-Dick, A Key to Uncle Tom's Cabin, Life in the Woods, The Mysterious Key,* and *Anna Karenina.*"

Amber shook her head and returned the coins to him. "Would you please give those to Braham, along with all the books, and ask him to put them in his safe."

"Should I give him my Denver & Rio Grande Railroad stocks and bonds, too?"

"The actual certificates?" she asked.

He nodded. "I had them with me to talk to General Palmer about selling them, but we never had time."

"Please do. They might be very valuable." Amber trembled. Daniel could liquidate his coins, books, stocks, and bonds and have a revenue stream he could invest. If he had his own money, he wouldn't feel like he was living off Braham's charity. "Do you have anything else?"

"Only a copy of a speech and a few letters that have sentimental value. Nothing like the coins."

"Who wrote them?" Elizabeth asked.

"The speech was written by President Lincoln at Gettysburg, and I have a few letters from General Grant written after Appomattox. I've carried them in my Bible for years."

"Daniel," Amber asked slowly. "Are you saying you have a handwritten copy of Lincoln's address at Gettysburg?"

"I have one he wrote in pencil. It may have been only the first draft. I also have a Bible he gave me that he used in the second inauguration."

She stared with disbelief. "Braham needs to lock everything up immediately. Is there anything else?"

"This won't win me any honor points, but I took the quilt off Lincoln's death bed. After everyone left, I saw it and thought I'd have it cleaned, but I couldn't wash away the blood he shed for the country. It's been wrapped up in my bedroll since he died."

Elizabeth passed her iPhone to Amber. "Read this."

"According to this article Mom found there's a standing ten-million-dollar reward for the original Gettysburg Address penciled in Lincoln's hand."

Daniel's eyes snapped into focus, as if he'd been only half awake before and hadn't fully understood the significance of what he had in his possession. "Ten million dollars for an old piece of paper?"

"It's not just any piece of paper." Amber continued to read, "The quilt from his death bed and the second inaugural Bible are relics that have never surfaced." She glanced up at Daniel. "With your Lincoln relics, stocks and bonds, coins, and first-edition classics, you could have a twenty- to thirty-million-dollar collection. If it's all sold at auction, you could get more."

His face turned white and he curled his hands around the edge of the windowsill. "Millions? Are ye sure?"

"It depends on what you have, and we'll only know that after the experts examine it all."

"How will you explain where this treasure came from?" Elizabeth asked.

Connor laughed. "Are you kidding? Braham, Kenzie, and Jack Mallory found the Confederate gold. A few Lincoln relics, coins, and books discovered by those two treasure hunters wouldn't cause much of a stir." He clapped Daniel on the shoulder. "Just so you know. You're buying drinks this afternoon."

"Oh, Connor, wait. Before you go, did Rick leave?" Amber said. "He said he would call, but he didn't, and now he's not answering his cell."

"He's flying commercial, so you'll have to wait until he lands in California. We were on a conference call with Meredith until he had to turn his phone off."

"What'd she say?"

"She was finally allowed back on the winery property. The vineyards survived but none of the structures. For the next few months, it's all hands on deck. I'll be splitting my time between Denver and Napa," Connor said.

"JL won't go, will she?" Olivia asked.

"Meredith sent a company-wide email advising all employees and board members that anyone with a health issue was banned from the property for at least six months."

"I don't have a health issue," Elizabeth said. "I can go. Meredith will need someone to handle contracts and insurance companies. That's right up my alley."

"That's nice, Mom, but I'm sure Kenzie has it under control," Amber said.

"We were talking about the fire this morning at breakfast. Kenzie said she couldn't go there because the soot created a health issue for her. She didn't elaborate, and I didn't ask."

"Why is it an issue for her and not everyone else?" As soon as

Amber asked the question, she slapped her hand over her mouth.

"It looks like you already know the answer," Elizabeth said.

Amber mimed zippering her lips.

Elizabeth gave her that all-knowing mother look. But when Amber noticed Daniel's pink cheeks, she started laughing, which hurt her chest. Daniel grabbed her heart pillow off the bedside table, and she clutched it for sternal support.

When the giggles passed, she asked, "Where's Kenzie now and where's Dad?"

"Kenzie is in Braham's office working and your father is the guest lecturer today for the kids. When we left the house, he had James Cullen, Emily, Lincoln, Patrick, and Noah gathered around a table looking at maps. He's teaching a unit on the ecology and conservation of the animals and plants of Africa."

"And the kids are interested?" Olivia asked.

"Except for the twins, Robbie and Henry. They were there for the first part of the lecture but got side-tracked when Matt started talking about the wildlife. They wondered what kind of rifle they'd need to shoot an elephant."

Amber hugged her pillow again. "Please don't make me laugh. Did they really ask that? What'd Dad say?"

"He let David answer," Elizabeth said. "A wise decision."

"I've got to hear this. What'd David say?" Connor asked.

"David told the twins to use a Holland and Holland .700 Nitro Express double rifle, which is designed for fast shooting on extremely large game animals like rhinos and elephants. He then went on to say, if they didn't hit the target in two shots they would be eaten or trampled by their prey. And he said, if they shot an elephant they'd have to eat the entire animal all by themselves because they knew the rule."

"Which is?" Amber asked.

Elizabeth laughed. "You never shoot anything you don't intend to eat."

Amber hugged her pillow tighter, trying not to laugh.

"What'd the twins say to that?" Olivia asked.

"They said they couldn't eat an elephant and they'd rather play with wee Kit than listen to a boring lecture on plants and inedible animals. So, they left."

"What'd the big kids think of Dad's class?" Olivia asked.

"James Cullen was in contact with a travel agent checking dates for a time they could all go to Africa for a field study. Then Noah found an article on the dinosaur renaissance in South Africa."

Amber yawned, and her eyelids started to drift closed. The company had exhausted her, and she needed to take a nap while Daniel was gone. "South Africa has a really long paleontological history. They were collecting dinosaurs there in the 1840s."

"If they want to take a trip, I'm sure Matt will go with them. I've never seen him so excited about anything as he was today planning his lecture. This perfectly aligns with his interests and expertise."

"You all can jabber away, but we're going to drink beer and play pool," Connor said. "Before we go back to the plantation, we're picking Ripley up from the vet. She's recovered enough to go home."

"I'm sure Noah will be thrilled," Amber said. "Give Ripley a hug from me."

"Take your time playing pool." Olivia held up a bottle of blue nail polish. "I'm going to paint Amber's toenails."

Daniel studied the bottle in Olivia's hand. "So that's how they got to be blue."

"We've been painting each other's toes since we were teenagers," Amber said.

Connor slapped Daniel on the shoulder. "Let's go. You already know more than you need to."

But Daniel just stood there with a nervous lift of his square shoulders, looking uneasy over parting with her.

"What's the matter?" As soon as Amber asked, she knew. Daniel was adapting well to the twenty-first century, but he was still uncomfortable with public displays of affection. He never left her, even to go refill the water pitcher, without kissing her goodbye. With a room full of people, especially her mother, he was conflicted.

"Mom turn around, so Daniel can kiss me."

Elizabeth spun. "Daniel and Connor have such nice manners. It's so refreshing."

Daniel kissed Amber. "I won't be gone long."

"I'm going to take a nap. Have fun with the boys."

Connor kissed Olivia, and the door closed behind both men.

Olivia sat down on the foot of the bed. "So how is it? Does it hurt much today?"

"It's tolerable, but Daniel has been amazing. Whatever I need, want, wish for. He's there."

"I couldn't be happier with both of your men," Elizabeth said. "Now, what about weddings? June is such a nice month."

"Daniel and I aren't talking about that yet. We're focused on my health right now. We don't even know where we're going to live."

"You'll come back to Denver."

"Not right away, Mom. Noah is so attached to the boys, and Daniel depends on Braham. Neither of them wants to leave here."

Elizabeth fell silent, and her face tensed. Then, as if remembering something, she seemed to relax. "Where do you want to live?"

"Wherever they are. Wherever they can be happy. We'll see."

"I guess this means you're leaving the firm, too."

Amber hugged her heart pillow, knowing how difficult this would be for her mom to accept, and wishing she could make it easier for her. "I was going to tell you I wanted out before all of this happened."

Elizabeth fingered wisps of hair at Amber's temple. "Your father and I had long talks about both of you while we were away. All we've ever wanted was for you to be happy. You have our blessing to work remotely or leave completely. Whatever you want to do."

"Why don't you focus on Noah, Mom. He's going to be your first grandson. He'll love having you for his granny. And if you're hoping for a wedding soon, you'll have to look to Olivia and Connor."

Elizabeth's eyes glistened as she smiled, deepening the lines in the corners of her eyes and lips. "Noah and I already have an outing planned for tomorrow."

Amber yawned again. "Where are you going?"

"We're doing the Civil War tour, starting at the American Civil War Museum. He's putting the itinerary together. I told him he could invite the others, but he wanted it to be just us, and Matt if he wants to go, too. He's so precious." She took a deep breath, blew it out, then once she was composed, asked Olivia, "What are your wedding plans?"

"Good grief, you guys, we're not even engaged. Next week we're going back to Denver. Connor will be splitting his time between California and Colorado for the next few months and I'll fly out to meet him when I can."

"But this is definitely a for-sure thing."

"It's for sure," Olivia said.

Elizabeth's cell phone rang. She looked at the face. "I don't recognize the number."

"Take the call, Mom," Amber said.

She pushed accept. "Elizabeth Kelly."

"This is Meredith Montgomery."

Elizabeth put the call on speaker.

"Hi Meredith, I was just talking about you."

"I know. Connor told me. He said you offered to help. And I need all I can get. I know you're tied up with Amber right now, but when do you think you could come to Napa? I need a full-time attorney who specializes in contracts and insurance claims. You don't have to be on-site, but I do need daily access."

"How much of your inventory did you lose?" Elizabeth asked.

"Everything bottled or in barrels is in the cave with our records, antiques, and paintings. Ninety percent of our crop was in. The fruit left on the vine will have some smoke taint. That's all a loss, and all our fermenting wines were left open to the smoke-tainted air. That's all a loss, too. I'm going to be working with the architects and contractors, and I need someone to work with the insurance companies, settling claims, and rewriting our contracts. I've read everything I could find about you and talked to several of your clients. I know you did something similar for a large conglomerate in Kansas that lost its entire operation to a fire. You saved it from bankruptcy."

"We're expensive," Elizabeth said. "If Connor just told you, how could you have talked to our clients?"

"I've been on the phone for several days. I was going to call you even before you volunteered, but I was waiting until Amber was feeling better."

"Let me talk to Matt this evening, and I'll call you back."

"Fantastic," Meredith said. "Give Amber a hug and tell her I can't wait to meet her and Daniel and Noah. Kenzie has told me everything."

Elizabeth disconnected the call. "That's interesting."

"Connor said she's highly successful and one of the nicest and most thoughtful women he's ever met. He's crazy about her, but she's a control freak," Olivia said.

Elizabeth laughed. "Sounds like a few women I know." She kissed Amber's cheek. "You're tired. You need to rest. I'm going back to the plantation to do some research on the winery and Meredith Montgomery. If you need me to bring up anything tonight, call."

"Bye, Mom," Amber said.

Elizabeth left and Amber just looked at her sister. "I'm so tired."

"I know you are. Close your eyes. I'm going to paint your toe-nails." She pulled the sheet back, exposing Amber's feet. "What happened to your polish?"

"The nurses took it off before surgery."

"Well, I'm putting it back on." She put the toe separators on both feet, used an emery board to file each nail down a bit, and polished her toes. "While you're falling asleep, tell me about Daniel. How's it going?"

"I'm head over heels in love and I know you are, too. I never thought I'd feel this way. I didn't want to tell Mom, but I think we'll stay here. Charlotte said she'd sell us a few acres to build a house and a building to use for Amber's Kitchen, and there would be room for a garden. We're just tossing ideas around, but we might do a joint venture that combines my meals with Braham's boutique wines."

"That's so exciting. What will Daniel do?"

"After discovering he's a multi-millionaire, he doesn't have to do anything, but he will. His biggest challenge right now is adjusting to the twenty-first century and catching up on the history of the world."

"Dad will help with that." Olivia closed the bottle of nail polish and dropped it into her purse. "Okay, all done. And don't you dare let the nurses take it off again."

"Does that statement have a hidden message?"

"Yes. No more emergency surgeries."

"You know, sooner or later, I'll have to have a new valve."

"I don't know why you didn't get a titanium one?"

Amber yawned. "Because I didn't want to take blood thinners for the rest of my life."

"I probably wouldn't want to either." Olivia picked up a magazine from the tray table and waved it back and forth over Amber's toes. "I was watching Noah at breakfast and you couldn't tell from the way he interacted with the other kids that he'd only been in the twenty-first century a few days. He's an amazing little guy, just like his dad."

"I can't wait until I'm released, and Daniel and I have time alone. What about you and Connor?"

Olivia waved the magazine over Amber's toes again. "We're waiting."

"For what? You've known him for almost a year. Every time I see you together you've got your hands all over each other. So what are you waiting for?"

Olivia wiggled her ring finger. "He said he's planning something special. That's all he'd say."

Amber carefully scooted over. "Get your butt over here, lie down with me, and let's talk about our boys."

As Olivia removed her shoes and climbed into bed next to Amber she sang, *"Country boy, ain't got no shoes/Country boy, ain't got no blues…"*

Amber joined her in a duet, singing quietly, *"Well, you work all day/While you're wanting to play/In the sun and the sand…"* Then she tired out, without having the energy to even hum along, but she was thankful she could breathe easily. Her stamina would return. It had to. She had big plans.

"I had a long talk with Dad about the Royal Gorge War," Olivia said. "It was weird because I knew the story we heard as kids, and I knew the real story from being there. The current story, the story Dad knows, is a combination of the two. And get this. Masterson is back in the story. Go figure. I don't know how that happened."

"He must have had a great marketing team, or a great biographer."

"Connor even paid a newspaperman to write the real story. I guess he discovered he could sell more papers if he fabricated one," Olivia said.

"Or else he got a book deal. Is Dad going to search the newspaper archives?"

"He's determined to write the real story, instead of one filled with lies."

"He needs to talk to Rick. He's planning to write an article on Chief Ouray. Since Rick was in Pueblo for part of the day, they could help each other. I know Dad has always been interested in the chief's story."

"Rick is such a nice guy, Amber."

"While Daniel went out for dinner with Braham last night, Rick and I had a long talk and cried our eyes out. We had made a pledge to hook up when you and Connor married if we weren't in love with someone else. Well, I rescinded my pledge." Amber unbraided her hair and combed through the ends with her fingers. "It was so sad. I love Rick to pieces, but I could never be in love with him. He's a friend for life."

"I'm glad you had a long talk. Connor and I were worried about him."

"He promised me when he got to California he'd start going to therapy. He's got a few issues to deal with. But whatever he needs, I'll always be there for him."

"I think Rick was the only major player in this story who didn't get lied to," Olivia said.

"I hadn't thought of that, but I think you're right. There were so many lies told and lies of omission."

"Great-Granny, Granny Hughes, and Mom kept the brooch a secret all these years. History lied about what happened in Pueblo. Connor lied to me. You lied to Daniel. I lied to the general."

"I lied to a judge," Amber said. "That's worse."

Olivia groaned. "You're right. Lying to a judge tops the list."

"Daniel knew I was lying from the moment he met me." Amber shivered. "If my toes are dry, will you cover my feet?"

Olivia removed the toe separators and tossed the blanket over Amber's freshly painted toes. "Even though you lied to Daniel, he still fell in love with you."

"How could he resist my charm?"

Olivia cuddled up next to Amber. "He couldn't. No one can."

"That creep who stole my journal wasn't impressed."

"Maybe not, but your gallant knight beat the crap out of him."

Amber pushed the head-down-button on the controller and flattened the bed. "Daniel didn't have to do that."

"Yeah, he did. Daniel thought the jerk shot Connor."

"That's different. Then he deserved what he got."

"A broken jaw, nose, and ribs."

"Ouch. After having my ribs sawn in two, I know how painful broken ribs are." Just thinking about her ribs made them hurt. Amber hugged her heart pillow tighter. "Do you think you'll ever go on another adventure?"

"I can't handle the sexism and I'm not the adventurous type. This was Connor's third trip, and he said he's had enough."

"I'd go again," Amber said. "But not for a while. If I start Amber's Kitchen, I'll be too busy. But you know who would go?"

"Mom and Dad?"

"Yep. They've been all over the world and still have the explorer bug. A time traveling adventure is right in their lane."

"Wouldn't you rather be snuggling with Daniel right now instead of me?"

"Yes, but I can't hold him without crying or gasping in pain, so I'll have to wait, but man oh man, it'll be worth it. He's so tender, and when he kisses me, I just melt."

"Has he seen Steggy?"

"My tattoo? Yes. I was getting out of bed this morning to go to the bathroom. The covers were tangled, and I flashed him wearing this hospital gown. I thought he was going to faint. He wanted a better view, but I told him he'd have to wait. He got on the iPad and Googled tattoos. Then he found out from Noah that David, Kenzie, Braham, Connor, and Rick all have one."

"Connor does? Hmm," Olivia said.

"Yep, but I didn't ask what or where. You'll have to discover that on your own."

"Does Daniel want one now?"

"You know," Amber said, "I have a feeling if he doesn't have one when he comes back from playing pool and drinking beer, he'll get one soon enough."

"What do you think he'll get?"

"A tat that represents his past life, so he won't forget where he came from. That's my guess. But I could be wrong." Amber yawned again. "If I don't wake up when you leave, I'll see you tomorrow. And thanks for doing my toes." She rested her head on Olivia's shoulder. "I love you, sis, to the moon and back."

"Back atcha, sweetie."

55

Four Weeks Later, MacKlenna Farm, Lexington, Kentucky—Elliott

ELLIOTT ROLLED OVER in bed and placed his hands over his eyes, pressing down on the lids to block out the light from the bedside lamp. The boys had slammed one too many doors, and he was awake now. His skin still had the lingering coolness of drying sweat. Maybe a shower would ease him back down into slumber.

No, he doubted that would happen. He'd been keyed up all day, and even after a couple hours alone with his bride, he was still hyped up.

After four weeks in Napa, Meredith had finally come home. The separation had been hell on them. She stirred now, and he pulled her close, snuggling against her shoulder, nose to warm skin.

"That was a nice respite, but now I'm wide awake," he whispered in her ear.

"Shh. Go back to sleep," she said.

He moved away, and the sheets hissed, as he slid out from underneath them. Slowly, he crossed the room of their master suite and climbed into the shower, hoping the hot water would send him off to dreamland again.

A few minutes later, he sat on the edge of the bed, close to her, towel drying his hair. "What did Rick say about the contractors?"

"You're not going to let me sleep, are you?"

She reached over and trailed one finger down his spine, resting her hand on the skin of his back as he stretched and flexed. He slipped his hand under the covers and ran his fingers up her leg and stopped at the juncture of her thighs, and there, he teased her until she squirmed. There was a quick intake of breath, held for a moment in deliberation, then released in surrender.

"I miss real face-to-face time with ye. Talk to me and then we'll…" He winked, and she smiled with that smile that made him feel like he was the only man on earth.

"Hmm. Everything is on schedule. They're going to start construction of the Welcome Center on Monday. Oh, don't stop. That's nice. Now come back to bed. I've talked enough." Her chest rose and fell in a long sigh.

"What about yer house?" He leaned over and kissed her, and she lifted her throat as his mouth left hers and proceeded along the line of her neck.

"The architect and I have a meeting scheduled next week. I need a mediator, and I'd like you to be there. But since you can't come to Napa, we can meet in San Francisco or even fly to the new ranch."

"I need to go to Colorado next week. Let's meet there since Kit and Cullen are already there and I need your help with them."

"They're yer relatives. If ye can't handle them—"

"Kit's your goddaughter and she learned stubbornness from you."

"So, ye want to put me in the middle again. Have ye forgotten what happened last time? Kit ended up with a broken leg, and I had a stroke."

"I remember, but I think we can do this calmly and find a compromise. Kit and Cullen want a house like the original one. I want a house like the villa I grew up in. We need a mediator."

"If mediating is up to me, Cullen is out of luck. I'll give ye whatever ye want."

"I want you."

Her warm voice wrapped him in a blanket hotter than any quilt could. He gathered her to him. "Ye've already had me."

Her gaze strayed to the crumpled sheets, the hollow where he had lain next to her and he kissed her. First on the forehead then again, more lingering, on the mouth. She patted the bed. "But I want you again."

"God, woman. Ye're insatiable. After seventeen years together, ye're still my wanton bride."

"Let your body go to fat, lose your teeth and hair, and we'll see how wanton I am."

"So ye're saying I turn ye on?"

"You're a handsome, sexy man in his late sixties, and yes, you turn me on. And your bride doesn't like spending so much time apart. It's not good for us."

"There's a solution for that, my dear. Spend more time at MacKlenna Farm and empower Rick to make decisions."

"He's doing a fantastic job. I'm lucky to have him. And Elizabeth, my God, she's the Energizer Bunny. Kenzie is a top-rated attorney. So is Elizabeth, but she has twice the experience, especially negotiating with insurance companies, which I've learned, you can never have enough—"

"Sex?"

"Well, yeah, but I was referring to insurance."

This was why he loved her so much. Her sassy humor, the easy dialogue, the potent attraction? "Do ye think Elizabeth would ever join us full-time? They are brooch owners."

"Speaking of which, where is the amber brooch?"

"In the box in the desk. Rick gave it to me the day of Amber's surgery."

"Good. Elizabeth asked about it. Her granny had described it to her, but Elizabeth had never seen it."

"Is that how Amber got her name?" Elliott asked.

Meredith laughed. "When Elizabeth found herself pregnant a few weeks after she delivered Olivia, she recalled the soul mate legend, and decided the babies would be soul mates, raised as twins. After hearing stories of how close they are, I believe it. They're inseparable. Daniel and Connor will have their hands full. But speaking of Rick—

"Were we speaking of Rick?"

"Yes." She gathered her dark hair, taming it for a bun at her nape, and using a clip from the nightstand, clipped it there. "I worry about him. He fell in love with Amber. It's like the David—Charlotte—Braham triangle all over again."

"David had a long talk with him, and Pops said Rick had started therapy and was doing much better handling his black moods." Elliott gathered Meredith closer as if by molding her body to his they could shut out the rest of the family with all its complications and heartaches. He kissed her then, not deeply, but lightly and as a sort of affirmation.

"Where'd Connor and Olivia and Daniel and Amber decide to go for their big double-date vacation?"

"After the clan's Thanksgiving next weekend at the plantation, if Amber is up for it, and Charlotte lets her, they're flying to Scotland for two blissful weeks at the castle."

Meredith pretended to ponder, rubbing her chin. "That's interesting. Why there?"

"Daniel and Connor said they wanted to treat the sisters like princesses. So they're spending two weeks in the Highlands."

"Be sure to tell the guys about the sleigh in the barn. Taking me out on Christmas Day was the most romantic thing you've ever done."

"I remember ye asking me, 'Does everything with ye always come back around to sex?'"

"And you answered, 'I am in the breeding business.' And now it seems our roles have reversed."

He kissed the tip of her nose. "It was a slick move, wasn't it? If the boys take the Kelly girls out for a sleigh ride through the Highlands, we'll be planning a huge engagement and house warming party at the Colorado ranch when they come home."

"I hope so. Elizabeth and Matt hope so, too. Having the Kellys around is a godsend. I love Elizabeth, and the timing couldn't be more perfect. Kenzie couldn't continue working the hours she was working. Now she can really cut back and take it easy through this pregnancy."

"What are they going to do about their law firm?"

"Since the girls don't want to practice law, I think they'll sell it. Matt wants to be a full-time grandfather and professor. The kids adore him. They're planning trips all over the world. I heard whispers the other day about a trip back to the late 1700s, so the kids could meet America's Founding Fathers. I shiver to think of it."

His arms slipped to her waist, rested loosely there. "I'll have to sign up for that trip."

"You, Matt, and five kids. Sounds like a disaster waiting to happen."

"Maybe not." Elliott kissed her nose, and the centuries-old floorboards creaked as he got up, tossed the towel on the bathroom floor, and moved about the room gathering pants and T-shirt.

Meredith rolled her eyes at the pile of towels she could see from her side of the bed. "I saw the call from Sotheby's on your call log. I assume you talked to someone about Daniel's property. What'd they say?"

"I had a few questions about valuations. I didn't talk specifics since the treasure hasn't been found yet. We're waiting on David to put all the ducks in a row. The first two steps have been completed. Olivia deeded her house to Amber, and Amber assumed Olivia's contract for the renovations. Before work begins, David will bury the documents, quilt, stock and bond certificates, books, coins, and relics in a Civil War cartridge crate in the basement."

"How's he going to make it look like it's been there for a hundred and fifty years?"

"When I talked to him this afternoon, he was reviewing videos and photographs of the Confederate gold and antiquities he and Braham uncovered in California. He's writing a computer program using all the data he can find on Colorado's weather dating back to the late 1800s. Then he plans to create a cave-like environment in the basement using nineteenth-century technology to control humidity and temperature."

"What about water runoff and pest control?"

"He's factoring that in, too."

Meredith lifted her brow. "So when specialists evaluate the condition of the items, they'll be in awe of the owner's forethought to protect the documents and books for posterity's sake. I don't buy it."

"That's just one or two of the moves in this chess game he's creating. He'll figure it out. He always does."

"Does David have a plan for establishing provenance?"

"Daniel's identity is baked in. There's a historical record of him dating back to 1862 as a Pinkerton agent and a member of President Lincoln's security detail. He's mentioned in the Denver newspaper as the surviving spouse of Lorna Robinson, daughter of Denver banker Alec Robinson. And a few years later, he appears in several articles about the Royal Gorge War when he worked as a Pinkerton agent for the Rio Grande Railroad. That puts him in and around Denver in the 1870s."

"Impressive. I guess all the ducks are lining up. Hope David stays on his ulcer medicine, so he can get this done."

"He's taking it religiously," Elliott said.

"Good. So once Sotheby's gets the items, their specialists will photograph, catalogue the property, and schedule an auction."

"Wham, bam, here's yer check, ma'am. That about sums it up." Elliott sat on her side of the bed and bent to draw up his khakis.

"Where are you going?"

"I heard the older boys heading into the bedroom about thirty minutes ago. I wanted to give them time to fall asleep before I went in to say good night."

"Don't you think they're getting a little old for the ritual?"

The thin, intervening quilt that separated them slithered down to her lap, and his fingers traced the contours of one breast. "Did ye ever get too old for this?"

"Never," she said.

He kissed her, and she scooted closer, settling her head on his chest. "Do not move. I'll be right back."

She rubbed her cheek against the ridge of muscle overlaying his ribs. "Are you really going to leave me like this?"

"Exactly like this." He enjoyed the surprised look on her face.

She shrugged and picked up her phone. "Okay. I'll send some texts while you're gone."

Like a tire running over a spike strip, she punctured his ego. *Whish!* When he glanced back at her, a coy smile said all he needed to know. She'd be ready with open arms when he returned.

He left the bedroom and strolled down the hallway. None of the other adults were sleeping in the mansion tonight, which was probably why all the kids had congregated in James Cullen's room for a sleepover. With Kenzie pregnant again and more weddings to come, he'd have to build a lodge at the farm to house all the kids, which wasn't a bad idea. They enjoyed the lodge at the winery, and now that it was gone, a replacement was needed. Why not put one in Lexington, too? He'd talk to David about it tomorrow.

Elliott tiptoed into the bedroom, sniffing the air. He used to smell popcorn and baby soap. Now the room smelled like dirty gym socks and unisex hair products.

The room was divided tonight with the boys sleeping close to their idol, University of Kentucky basketball standout and power forward Austin O'Grady; and the girls sleeping close to theirs, UK pre-med student Isabella Ricci.

As Elliott threaded his way around the sleeping bags, turning this way and that, listening to their snickering, he counted heads: Amelia Rose, Laurie Wallis, Kitherina, Robbie, Henry, Noah, Patrick, Lincoln, Emily, James Cullen, Isabella, and Austin.

What a crew. How many years had it been since he first stood over Kit's crib and blessed her precious head? Forty years, maybe more. With her comings and goings from one century to another, he couldn't keep up with it.

With all the children accounted for, he stood at the door, smiling. "Good night, lads and lassies. May God hold each of ye in the palm of His hand."

Sighing, Elliott retraced his steps, only to find Meredith putting on a pair of jeans. "What are ye doing out of bed?"

"Kevin just texted. He and JL are on their way to the hospital. Your grandson will be here before breakfast."

Elliott closed his eyes. "Lord, I hope Yer palm has room for one more wee lad."

THE END

ABOUT THE AUTHOR

Katherine graduated from Rowan University in New Jersey, where she earned a BA in Psychology with a minor in Criminal Justice. Following college, she returned to Central Kentucky, where she worked as a real estate and tax paralegal.

Katherine is a marathoner and lives in Lexington, Kentucky. When she's not running or writing romance, she's enjoying her five grandchildren: Charlotte Lyle, Lincoln Thomas, James Cullen, Henry Patrick, and Meredith Lyle, and a dog named Ripley.

Please stop by and visit Katherine on her social media sites or drop her an email. She loves to hear from readers.

Website
www.katherinellogan.com

Facebook
facebook.com/katherine.l.logan

Twitter
twitter.com/KathyLLogan

I'm A Runner (Runner's World Magazine Interview)
www.runnersworld.com/celebrity-runners/im-a-runner-katherine-lowry-logan

Email:
KatherineLLogan@gmail.com

Family trees are available on Katherine's website
www.katherinellogan.com/books/the-celtic-brooch-family-trees

* * *

THE CELTIC BROOCH SERIES

THE RUBY BROOCH (Book 1)
Kitherina MacKlenna and Cullen Montgomery's love story

THE LAST MACKLENNA (Book 2 – not a time travel story)
Meredith Montgomery and Elliott Fraser's love story

THE SAPPHIRE BROOCH (Book 3)
Charlotte Mallory and Braham McCabe's love story

THE EMERALD BROOCH (Book 4)
Kenzie Wallis-Manning and David McBain's love story

THE BROKEN BROOCH (Book 5 – not a time travel story)
JL O'Grady and Kevin Allen's love story

THE THREE BROOCHES (Book 6)
A reunion with Kit and Cullen Montgomery

THE DIAMOND BROOCH (Book 7)
Jack Mallory and Amy Spalding's love story

Many More Brooch Books to Come!

If you would like to receive notification of future releases
Sign up today at KatherineLowryLogan.com or
Send an email to KatherineLLogan@gmail.com and put "Sequel" in the subject line

* * *

Thank you for reading THE AMBER BROOCH.
I hope you enjoyed reading this story as much as I enjoyed writing it.
Reviews help other readers find books.
I appreciate all reviews, whether positive or negative.

AUTHOR NOTES

Leadville, Colorado (leadville.com): The day I drove down from Denver to visit Leadville was the weekend of the Leadville Trail 100 MTB. This is the race of all races. One hundred miles across the high-altitude, extreme terrain of the Colorado Rockies. In 2017, it took the winner six hours and fifteen minutes to complete the race. It was fun being in the city with all the bikers. Olivia claims she snuck in under the sub-twelve-hour cut-off by only ten minutes. I'd still be pedaling. If you visit Colorado, be sure to go to Leadville—a small city with a big history.

The Bones War (www.ucmp.berkeley.edu/history/marsh.html): The war between Dr. Marsh and Dr. Cope is well-documented. They constantly sabotaged each other's sites and publications. If you have an interest in dinosaurs, I highly recommend visits to Dinosaur Ridge (www.dinoridge.org) and the Denver Museum of Nature & Science (www.dmns.org). And if you would like to immerse yourself in dinosaurs, check out: Dino 101: Dinosaur Paleobiology (www.coursera.org/learn/dino101).

Rheumatic Heart Disease "RHD" (www.world-heart-federation.org/programmes/rheumatic-heart-disease): RHD is the most commonly acquired heart disease in young people under the age of 25. It most often begins in childhood as strep throat and can progress to serious heart damage that kills or debilitates adolescents and young adults. The disease has been virtually eliminated in Europe and North America, but remains common in Africa, the Middle East, Central and South Asia, the South Pacific, and impoverished pockets of developed nations.

The Royal Gorge War (cozine.com/2011-january/the-%E2%80%9Cwar%E2%80%9D-for-the-royal-gorge): I read several accounts of the Royal Gorge War in books, blog posts, and newspaper articles and there was one thing they all had in common—Bat Masterson. After talking at length with Larry Green, a Royal Gorge War expert, and reviewing a summary of his thirty years of research, I decided to write The Amber Brooch as close as I could to his findings. Although for the sake of the story, my plot took a few liberties. If Bat Masterson was in Pueblo or Canon City on June 11, 1879, the day Rio Grande took the roundhouse, it's likely he was at the gambling tables and was not part of Santa Fe's armed militia.

By November 1878 the Rio Grande had run out of money and signed a lease with Santa Fe which gave them the use of the rail lines and all equipment, including the rolling stock. This lease was signed six months before the battle of the roundhouse—and almost from the first day Rio Grande claimed foul and plotted to find a way to break it.

The Royal Gorge War officially came to an end on March 27, 1880 with the signing of the Treaty of Boston, and the payment of $1,800,000 by the Rio Grande to Santa Fe. By August 1883, financial difficulties led to a shake up among the Rio Grande board of directors, and General Palmer resigned as president.

Creative Liberties: I opted to take some creative liberties with the battle of the roundhouse so it would coincide with Dr. Lakes' (morrisonhistory.wordpress.com/2017/03/24/a-tuesday-in-late-march) appearance in Morrison, I had to adjust both the dates of the lease and the battle. All the events occurred, but in a different order. The true events of the day may never be completely known or understood. I'm sure no one wanted to admit to any criminal activities.

I would especially like to thank the following:

- Dr. Ken Muse (Medical Consultant) and Annette Glahn (Story Consultant and early reader): Without their ongoing assistance, suggestions, and advice this story could not have been written.
- Beta Readers: Patty Chapa, Robin Epstein, Mary L. Johnston, Marjorie Lague, Rebecca Partington, Rosanna Phelan, Nancy Porter, Paula Retelsdorf
- Larry Green: Consultant on the Royal Gorge War
- Kevin Rucker: Consultant on 19th century Denver (Metropolitan State University of Denver, history professor (msudenver.edu/history/facultyandstaff) and LoDo Historic Walking Tour Guide (www.lodo.org/itineraries-and-tours/historic-lodo-walking-tours)
- John Retelsdorf: Pinkerton Agency research
- Robin Epstein: Music research on sea shanties
- Cover art by Damonza and Interior design by BB eBooks
- Staff at Dinosaur Ridge (www.dinoridge.org), Morrison, Colorado
- Staff at the Denver Museum of Nature & Science (www.dmns.org)
- Sarah Chrisman (www.thisvictorianlife.com): Consultant on Victorian life
- Jeffco Open Space (www.jeffco.us/open-space): Provided information on the Dakota Ridge Trail
- Mick Major, owner of EVOO Marketplace (evoomarketplace.com) located in the Wells Fargo Building (www.denverite.com/oldest-buildings-denver-matter-37635) in Denver
- Anne's Healing Hands (anneshealinghands.com): Anne Tsamas CMA, LMT, Lexington, Kentucky

Printed in Poland
by Amazon Fulfillment
Poland Sp. z o.o., Wrocław